Christopher Priest is t
two collections of shor
the 1995 James Tait Black Memorial Prize for Best Novel
and the World Fantasy Award, and was shortlisted for the
Arthur C. Clarke Award. His novel *The Glamour* won the
1988 Kurd Lasswitz Best Novel Award.

Christopher Priest lives in Hastings with his wife and twin
children.

THE SPACE MACHINE
&
A DREAM OF WESSEX
Omnibus 1

Christopher
PRIEST

EARTHLIGHT

LONDON · SYDNEY · NEW YORK · TOKYO · SINGAPORE · TORONTO

www.earthlight.co.uk

First published in this omnibus editon in Great Britain by Earthlight, 1999
An imprint of Simon & Schuster UK Ltd
A Viacom Company

Simon & Schuster UK Ltd
Africa House
64-78 Kingsway
London
WC2B 6AH

Simon & Schuster Australia
Sydney

A CIP catalogue record for this book is available from the British Library.

ISBN 0-671-03389-1

1 3 5 7 9 10 8 6 4 2

Printed and bound in Great Britain by Caledonian International Book
Manufacturing, Glasgow

CONTENTS

THE SPACE MACHINE

TO

H. G. WELLS

CONTENTS

Chapter One
THE LADY COMMERCIAL

In the April of 1893 I was staying in the course of my business at the Devonshire Arms in Skipton, Yorkshire. I was then twenty-three years of age, and enjoying a modest and not unsuccessful career as commercial representative of the firm of Josiah Westerman & Sons, Purveyors of Leather Fancy Goods. Not much will be said in this narrative of my employment, for even at that time it was not my major preoccupation, but it was instrumental, in its inglorious fashion, in precipitating the chain of events which are the major purpose of my story.

The Devonshire was a low, grey-brick commercial hotel, threaded with draughty and ill-lit corridors, drab with ageing paint and dark-stained panelling. The only congenial place in the hotel was the commercials' lounge, for although it was small and burdened with furniture—the over-stuffed easy chairs were placed so close together it was scarcely possible to walk between them—the room was warm in winter and had the advantage of gas-mantle lighting, whereas the only sources of illumination in the bedrooms were dim and smoky oil-lamps.

During the evenings there was little for a resident commercial to do but stay within the confines of the lounge and converse with his colleagues. For me, the hour between the completion of dinner and nine p.m. was the one that made me the most impatient, for by long-observed tacit agreement no one would smoke between those times, and it was the accepted period for conversation. At nine, though, the pipes and cigars would appear, the air would slowly turn a suffocating blue, heads would lean back on the antimacassars and eyes would close. Then, unobtrusively, I would perhaps read for a while, or write a letter or two.

On the evening of which I am particularly thinking I had been for a short stroll after dinner, and had returned to the hotel before nine. I made a brief visit to my room to don my smoking-jacket, then went to the ground floor and entered the commercials' lounge.

Three men were already there, and although it was still only seven minutes before nine I noticed that Hughes, a representative from a Birmingham machine-tool manufacturer, had started his pipe.

I nodded to the others, and went to a chair in the furthest corner of the room.

At nine-fifteen, Dykes came into the lounge. Dykes was a young man of about my own age, and although I had affected no interest in him it was his wont to address me in some confidence.

He came directly to my corner and sat opposite me. I pulled down the top leaf over the letter I had been drafting.

"Will you smoke, Turnbull?" he said to me, offering his cigarette case.

"No thank you." I had smoked a pipe for a while, but had desisted for more than a year.

He took a cigarette for himself, and made a display of lighting it. Like me, Dykes was a commercial representative, and often declared I was too conservative in my outlook. I was usually entertained by his outgoing manner, in the way one may enjoy the excesses of others.

"I hear there's a lady commercial in tonight," he said casually now, but leaning towards me slightly to add emphasis to his words. "What do you make of that, Turnbull?"

"You surprise me," I admitted. "Are you sure of that?"

"I came in late this evening," he said, lowering his voice. "Happened to glance at the register. Miss A. Fitzgibbon of Surrey. Interesting, wouldn't you say?"

Somewhat aloof, as I saw myself to be, from the day-to-day concerns of my fellow commercials, I was nevertheless interested by what he said. One cannot help but become aware of the lore of one's own occupation, and it had long been rumoured that women were now being employed as representatives. I had never before met one myself, but it seemed logical that sales of certain requisites—shall we say of a toilette or boudoir nature—might be better negotiated by women. Certainly, some of the stores I called at employed women buyers, so there was no precedent barring their entry into the sales aspect of a transaction.

I glanced over my shoulder, although I knew that she could not have entered the lounge unnoticed.

"I haven't seen her," I said.

"No, and we're not likely to! Do you think that Mrs Anson would allow a young lady of gentle breeding into a commercial lounge?"

"So you have seen the lady?" I said.

Dykes shook his head. "She dined with Mrs Anson in the coffee-room. I saw a tray being taken there."

I said, for my interest was persisting: "Do you suppose that what is said about lady commercials has any substance?"

"Undoubtedly!" said Dykes at once. "No profession for a gentlewoman."

"But you said that this Miss Fitzgibbon was a gentle—"

"A euphemism, dear chap." He leaned back in his easy chair, and drew pleasurably on his cigarette.

I usually found Dykes an amusing companion, for his ready abandonment of social niceties often meant that he would regale me with bawdy anecdotes. These I would listen to in envious silence, as most of my time was passed in enforced solitude. Many commercials were bachelors—perhaps by nature—and the life of constant movement from one town to another led to an inability to make permanent ties. Thus, when word that some firms now employed ladies as their representatives was rumoured, the smoking-rooms and commercial lounges of hotels all over the country had been sibilant with salacious speculation. Dykes himself had been a source of much information on the subject, but as time passed it became clear that there was to be no substantial change to our way of life. Indeed, this was the very first occasion on which I had even been aware that a lady commercial was staying in the same hotel as myself.

"You know, Turnbull, I fancy I shall introduce myself to Miss Fitzgibbon before the evening is out."

"But what will you say? Surely you would require an introduction?"

"That will be simple to arrange. I shall merely go to the door of Mrs Anson's sitting-room, knock boldly, and invite Miss Fitzgibbon to take a short stroll with me before turning in."

"I—" My sentence was cut short, for I had suddenly realized that Dykes could not be in earnest. He knew the proprietress of this hotel as well as I, and we both understood what kind of reception such a move could expect. Miss Fitzgibbon might well be an Emancipationist, but Mrs Anson was still firmly rooted in the 1860s.

"Why should I describe my strategy to you?" Dykes said. "We shall both be here until the weekend; I shall tell you then how I have fared."

I said: "Could you not somehow discover which firm she represents? Then you could contrive a chance meeting with her during the day."

Dykes smiled at me mysteriously.

"Maybe you and I think alike, Turnbull. I have already obtained that information. Would you care to place a small wager with me, the winner being the man who first speaks to the lady?"

I felt my face reddening. "I do not bet, Dykes. Anyway, it would be foolish for me to compete with you, since you have an advantage."

"Then I shall tell you what I know. She is not a commercial at all, but an amanuensis. She works for no firm, but is in the personal employ of an inventor. Or so my informant tells me."

"An inventor?" I said, disbelieving. "You cannot be serious!"

"That is what I have been told," Dykes said. "Sir William Reynolds by name, and a man of great eminence. I know nothing of that, nor care, for my interests lie with his assistant."

I sat with my writing-tablet on my knees, quite taken aback by this unexpected information. In truth I had no interest in Dykes's nefarious designs, for I tried at all times to conduct myself with propriety, but the name of Sir William Reynolds was a different matter.

I stared at Dykes thoughtfully while he finished his cigarette, then stood up.

"I think I shall retire," I said.

"But it's still early. Let us have a glass of wine together, on my account." He reached over and pressed the electrical bell-push. "I want to see you place that wager with me."

"Thank you but no, Dykes. I have this letter to finish, if you will excuse me. Perhaps tomorrow evening . . .?"

I nodded to him, then worked my way towards the door. As I reached the corridor outside, Mrs Anson approached the lounge door.

"Good evening, Mr Turnbull."

"Good night, Mrs Anson."

By the bottom of the staircase I noticed that the door to the sitting-room was ajar, but there was no sign of the lady guest.

Once in my room, I lighted the lamps and sat on the edge of my bed, trying to order my thoughts.

ii

The mention of Sir William's name had a startling effect on me, for he was at that time one of the most famous scientists in England. Moreover, I had a great personal interest in matters indirectly concerned with Sir William, and the casual information Dykes had imparted was of the greatest interest to me.

In the 1880s and 1890s there was a sudden upsurge in scientific developments, and for those with an interest in such matters it was an enthralling period. We were on the verge of the Twentieth Century, and the prospect of going into a new era surrounded by scientific wonders was stimulating the best minds in the world. It seemed that almost every week produced a new device which promised to alter our mode of existence: electric omnibuses, horseless carriages, the kinematograph, the American talking machines . . . all these were very much on my mind.

Of these, it was the horseless carriage which had most caught my imagination. About a year before I had been fortunate enough to be given a ride on one of the marvellous devices, and since then had felt that in spite of the attendant noise and inconvenience such machines held great potential for the future.

It was as a direct result of this experience that I had involved myself—in however small a way—with this burgeoning development. Having noticed a newspaper article about American motorists, I had persuaded the proprietor of the firm that employed me, Mr Westerman himself, to introduce a new line to his range of goods. This was an instrument which I had named the Visibility Protection Mask. It was made of leather and glass, and was held in place over the eyes by means of straps, thus protecting them from flying grit, insects, and so forth.

Mr Westerman, it should be added, was not himself wholly convinced of the desirability of such a Mask. Indeed, he had manufactured only three sample models, and I had been given the commission to offer them to our regular customers, on the understanding that only after I had obtained firm orders would the Mask be made a permanent part of the Westerman range.

I treasured my idea, and I was still proud of my initiative, but I had been carrying my Masks in my samples-case for six months, and so far I had awakened not the slightest interest of any customer. It seemed that other people were not so convinced as I of the future of the horseless carriage.

Sir William Reynolds, though, was a different matter. He was already one of the most famous motorists in the country. His record speed of just over seventeen miles an hour, established on the run between Richmond and Hyde Park Corner, was as yet unbeaten by any other.

If I could interest him in my Mask, then surely others would follow!

In this way it became imperative that I introduce myself to Miss Fitzgibbon. That night, though, as I lay fretfully in my hotel bed, I could have had no conception of how deeply my Visibility Protection Mask was to change my life.

iii

All during the following day, I was preoccupied with the problem of how to approach Miss Fitzgibbon. Although I made my rounds to the stores in the district I could not concentrate, and returned early to the Devonshire Arms.

As Dykes had said the evening before, it was most difficult to contrive a meeting with a member of the opposite sex in this hotel. There were no social courtesies open to me, and so I should have to approach Miss Fitzgibbon directly. I could, of course, ask Mrs Anson to introduce me to her, but I felt in all sincerity that her presence at the interview would be an impediment.

Further distracting me during the day had been my curiosity about Miss Fitzgibbon herself. Mrs Anson's protective behaviour seemed to indicate that she must be quite young, and indeed her style as a single woman was further evidence of this. If this were so, my task was greater, for surely she would mistake any advance I made towards her for one of the kind Dykes had been planning?

As the reception-desk was not attended, I took the opportunity to look surreptitiously at the register of guests. Dykes's information had not been misleading, for the last entry was in a neat, clear handwriting: *Miss A. Fitzgibbon, Reynolds House, Richmond Hill, Surrey.*

I looked into the commercial lounge before going up to my room. Dykes was there, standing in front of the fireplace reading *The Times.*

I proposed that we dine together, and afterwards take a stroll down to one of the public-houses in the town.

"What a splendid notion!" he said. "Are you celebrating a success?"

"Not quite. I'm thinking more of the future."

"Good strategy, Turnbull. Shall we dine at six?"

This we did, and soon after dinner we were ensconced in the snug bar of a public-house called The King's Head. When we were settled with two glasses of porter, and Dykes had started a cigar, I broached the subject uppermost on my mind.

"Are you wishing I'd made a wager with you last night?" I said.

"What do you mean?"

"Surely you understand."

"Ah!" said Dykes. "The lady commercial!"

"Yes. I was wondering if I would owe you five shillings now, had I entered a bet with you."

"No such luck, old chap. The mysterious lady was closeted with Mrs Anson until I retired, and I saw no sign of her this morning. She is a prize which Mrs Anson guards jealously."

"Do you suppose she is a personal friend?"

"I think not. She is registered as a guest."

"Of course," I said.

"You've changed your tune since last night. I thought you had no interest in the lady."

I said quickly: "I was just enquiring. You seemed bent on introducing yourself to her, and I wanted to know how you had fared."

"Let me put it this way, Turnbull. I considered the circumstances, and judged that my talents were best spent in London. I can see no way of making the lady's acquaintance without involving Mrs Anson. In other words, dear chap, I am saving my energies for the weekend."

I smiled to myself as Dykes launched into an account of his latest conquest, because although I had learned no more about the young lady I had at least established that I would not be in a misleading and embarrassing competitive situation.

I listened to Dykes until a quarter to nine, then suggested we return to the hotel, explaining that I had a letter to write. We parted company in the hall; Dykes walked into the commercial lounge, and I went upstairs to my room. The door to the sitting-room was closed, and beyond it I could hear the sound of Mrs Anson's voice.

Chapter Two
A CONVERSATION IN THE NIGHT

i

The staff of the Devonshire Arms were in the habit—presumably at Mrs Anson's instruction—of sprinkling the shades of the oil-lamps with *eau de cologne*. This had the effect of infusing a cloying perfume through the first floor of the hotel, one so persistent that even now I cannot smell *cologne* without being reminded of the place.

On this evening, though, I thought I detected a different fragrance as I climbed the stairs. It was drier, less sickly, more redolent of herbs than Mrs Anson's perfumes ... but then I could smell it no more, and I went on into my room and closed the door.

I lit the two oil-lamps in my room, then tidied my appearance in front of the mirror. I knew I had alcohol on my breath, so I brushed my teeth, then sucked a peppermint lozenge. I shaved, combed my hair and moustache, and put on a clean shirt.

When this was done I placed an easy chair beside the door, and moved a table towards it. On this I placed one of the lamps, and blew out the other. As an afterthought I took one of Mrs Anson's bath-towels, and folded it over the arm of the chair. Then I was ready.

I sat down, and opened a novel.

More than an hour passed, during which although I sat with the book on my knee, I read not one word. I could hear the gentle murmur of conversation drifting up from the downstairs rooms, but all else was still.

At last I heard a light tread on the stairs, and at once I was ready. I put aside the book, and draped the bath-towel over my arm. I waited until the footsteps had passed my door, and then I let myself out.

In the dim light of the corridor I saw a female figure, and as she heard me she turned. It was a chambermaid, carrying a hot water bottle in a dark-red cover.

"Good evening, sir," she said, making a small sullen curtsey in my direction, then continued on her way.

I went across the corridor into the bath-room, closed the door, counted to one hundred slowly, and then returned to my room.

Once more I waited, this time in considerably greater agitation than before.

Within a few minutes I heard another tread on the stairs, this time rather heavier. Again I waited until the footsteps had passed before emerging. It was Hughes, on his way to his room. We nodded to each other as I opened the door of the bath-room.

When I returned to my own room I was growing angry with myself for having to resort to such elaborate preparations and minor deceptions. But I was determined to go through with this in the way I had planned.

On the third occasion I heard footsteps I recognized Dykes's tread, as he bounded up taking two steps at a time. I was thankful not to have to go through the charade with the bath-towel.

Another half-hour passed and I was beginning to despair, wondering if I had miscalculated. After all, Miss Fitzgibbon might well be staying in Mrs Anson's private quarters; I had no reason to suppose that she would have been allocated a room on this floor. At length, though, I was in luck. I heard a soft tread on the staircase, and this time when I looked down the corridor I saw the retreating back of a tall young woman. I tossed the towel back into my room, snatched up my samples-case, closed the door quietly and followed her.

If she was aware that I was behind her, she showed no sign of it. She walked to the very end of the corridor, to where a small staircase led upwards. She turned, and climbed the steps.

I hastened to the end of the corridor, and as I reached the

bottom of the steps I saw that she was on the point of inserting a key into the door. She looked down at me.

"Excuse me, ma'am," I said. "Allow me to introduce myself. I am Turnbull, Edward Turnbull."

As she regarded me I felt immensely foolish, peering up at her from the bottom of the steps. She said nothing, but nodded slightly at me.

"Do I have the pleasure of addressing Miss Fitzgibbon?" I went on. "Miss A. Fitzgibbon?"

"That is I," she said, in a pleasant, well modulated voice.

"Miss Fitzgibbon, I know you will think this an extraordinary request, but I have something here I think will be of interest to you. I wondered if I might show it to you?"

For a moment she said nothing, but continued to stare down at me. Then she said: "What is it, Mr Turnbull?"

I glanced along the corridor, fearing that at any moment another of the guests would appear.

I said: "Miss Fitzgibbon, may I come up to you?"

"No, you may not. I shall come down."

She had a large leather hand-bag, and she placed this on the tiny landing beside her door. Then, raising her skirt slightly, she came slowly down the steps towards me.

When she stood before me in the corridor, I said: "I will not detain you for more than a few moments. It was most fortunate that you should be staying in this hotel."

While I spoke I had crouched down on the floor, and was fumbling with the catch of my samples-case. The lid came open, and I took out one of the Visibility Protection Masks. I stood up, holding it in my hand, and noticed that Miss Fitzgibbon was regarding me curiously. There was something about her forthright gaze that was most disconcerting.

She said: "What do you have there, Mr Turnbull?"

"I call it the Visibility Protection Mask," I said. She made no reply, so I went on in some confusion: "You see, it is suited for passengers as well as the driver, and can be removed at a moment's notice."

At this, the young lady stepped back from me, and seemed to be about to ascend the steps once more.

"Please wait!" I said. "I am not explaining very well."

"Indeed you are not. What is it you have in your hand, and why should it be of such interest to me that you accost me in an hotel corridor?"

Her expression was so cold and formal I did not know how to phrase my words. "Miss Fitzgibbon, I understand that you are in the employ of Sir William Reynolds?"

She nodded to confirm this, so at once I stuttered out an account of how I felt sure he would be interested in my Mask.

"But you have still not told me what it is."

"It keeps grit out of one's eyes when motoring," I said, and on a sudden impulse I raised the Mask to my eyes, and held it in place with my hands. At this the young lady laughed abruptly, but I felt that it was not an unkind laughter.

"They are motoring goggles!" she said. "Why did you not say?"

"You have seen them before?" I said in surprise.

"They are common in America."

"Then Sir William already possesses some?" I said.

"No . . . but he probably feels he does not need them."

I crouched down again, hunting through my samples-case.

"There is a ladies' model," I said, searching anxiously through the various products that I kept in my case. At last I found the smaller variety that Mr Westerman's factory had produced, and stood up, holding it out to her. In my haste I inadvertently knocked my case, and a pile of photograph albums, wallets and writing-cases spilled on the floor. "You may try this on, Miss Fitzgibbon. It's made of the best kid."

As I looked again at the young lady, I thought for a moment that her laughter was continuing, but she held her face perfectly seriously.

"I'm not sure that I need—"

"I assure you that it is comfortable to wear."

My earnestness at last won through, for she took the leather goggles from me.

"There's an adjustable strap," I said. "Please try it on."

I bent down once more, and thrust my spilled samples back

into the case. As I did so, I glanced down the corridor again.

When I stood up, Miss Fitzgibbon had raised the Mask to her forehead, and was trying to connect the strap. The large, flowered hat that she was wearing made this exceptionally difficult. If I had felt foolish at the beginning of this interview, then it was nothing to what I now felt. My impulsive nature and awkwardness of manner had led me to a situation of the most embarrassing kind. Miss Fitzgibbon was clearly trying to humour me, and as she fumbled with the clasp I wished I had the strength to snatch the goggles away from her and run shamefacedly to my room. Instead, I stood lamely before her, watching her efforts with the strap. She was wearing a patient smile.

"It appears to have become caught in my hair, Mr Turnbull." ·

She tugged at the strap, but frowned as the hairs were pulled. I wanted to help her in some way, but I was too nervous of her.

She tugged again at the strap, but the metal clasp was tangled in the strands of hair.

At the far end of the corridor I heard the sound of voices, and the creak of the wooden staircase. Miss Fitzgibbon heard the sounds too, for she also looked that way.

"What am I to do?" she said softly. "I cannot be found with this in my hair."

She pulled again, but winced.

"May I help?" I said, reaching forward.

A shadow appeared on the wall by the top of the staircase, thrown by the lamps in the hallway.

"We will be discovered at any moment!" said Miss Fitzgibbon, the goggles swinging beside her face. "We had better step into my room for a few minutes."

The voices were coming closer.

"Your room?" I said in astonishment. "Do you not want a chaperone? After all—"

"Whom would you propose to chaperone me?" said Miss Fitzgibbon. "Mrs Anson?"

Raising her skirt again, she hurried up the steps towards the door. After hesitating another second or two I took up my samples-case, holding the lid down with my hand, and followed. I waited while the young lady unlocked the door, and a moment later we were inside.

ii

The room was larger than mine, and more comfortable. There were two gas-mantles against the wall, and when Miss Fitzgibbon turned them up the room was filled with a bright, warm radiance. A coal fire burned in the grate, and the windows were richly curtained with long, velvet drapes. In one corner there was a large French bedstead, with the covers turned down. Most of the space, however, was given over to furniture which would not have looked out of place in the average parlour, with a *chaise longue*, two easy chairs, several rugs, an immense dresser, a bookcase and a small table.

I stood nervously by the door, while Miss Fitzgibbon went to a mirror and untangled the goggles from her hair. She placed these on the table.

When she had removed her hat, she said: "Please sit down, Mr Turnbull."

I looked at the goggles. "I think I should leave now."

Miss Fitzgibbon was silent, listening to the sound of the voices as they passed the bottom of the stairs.

"Perhaps it would be as well if you stayed a little longer," she said. "It would not do for you to be seen leaving my room at this late hour."

I laughed politely with her, but I must confess to being considerably taken aback by such a remark.

I sat down in one of the easy chairs beside the table and Miss Fitzgibbon went to the fireplace and poked the coals so that they flared up more brightly.

"Please excuse me for a moment," she said. As she passed me I sensed that she had about her a trace of the herbal fragrance I had noticed earlier. She went through an inner door, and closed it.

I sat silently, cursing my impulsive nature. I was sorely embarrassed by this incident, for Miss Fitzgibbon clearly had no need for, nor interest in, my motoring Mask. The notion that she would persuade Sir William to experiment with my goggles was even more unlikely. I had annoyed and compromised her, for if Mrs Anson, or indeed anyone else in the hotel, should discover that I had been alone in her room at night, then the young lady's reputation would be permanently marked.

When Miss Fitzgibbon returned, some ten minutes later, I heard the sound of a cistern hissing in the next room, and surmised that it must be a private bath-room. This seemed to be so, for Miss Fitzgibbon had apparently renewed her *maquillage*, and her hair was arranged differently, so that the tight bun she had been wearing had been loosened to allow some strands of her hair to fall about her shoulders. As she moved past me to sit in the other chair I noticed that the herbal fragrance was more noticeable.

She sat down, and leaned back with a sigh. Her behaviour towards me was entirely without ceremony.

"Well, Mr Turnbull," she said. "I find I owe you an apology. I'm sorry I was stuffy to you outside."

"It is I who should apologize," I said at once. "I—"

"It was a natural reaction, I'm afraid," she went on, as if she had not heard me. "I've just spent the last four hours with Mrs Anson, and she seems never to be at a loss for words."

"I felt sure you were a friend of hers," I said.

"She has appointed herself my guardian and mentor. I accept a lot of advice from her." Miss Fitzgibbon stood up again, and went to the dresser and produced two glasses. "I know you drink, Mr Turnbull, for I have smelled your breath. Would you care for a glass of brandy?"

"Thank you, yes," I said, swallowing hard.

She poured some brandy from a metal flask which she took from her hand-bag, and placed the two glasses on the table between us. "Like you, Mr Turnbull, I sometimes find the need for fortification."

She sat down again. We raised glasses, and sipped the drink.

"You have lapsed into silence," she said. "I hope I have not alarmed you."

I stared at her helplessly, wishing that I had never set out on this naïve enterprise.

"Do you come to Skipton frequently?" she said.

"About two or three times a year. Miss Fitzgibbon, I think I should bid you good-night. It is not proper for me to be here with you alone."

"But I still haven't discovered why you were so eager to show me your goggles."

"I felt you might influence Sir William to consider trying them."

She nodded her understanding. "And you are a goggles salesman?"

"No, Miss Fitzgibbon. You see, the firm I am employed by is a manufacturer of . . ."

My voice had tailed away, for I had heard in the same instant the sound that now clearly distracted Miss Fitzgibbon. We had both heard, just beyond the door, a creaking of floorboards.

Miss Fitzgibbon raised a finger to her lips, and we sat in anguished silence. A few moments later there was a sharp and peremptory rapping on the door!

iii

"Miss Fitzgibbon!" It was Mrs Anson's voice.

I stared desperately at my new friend.

"What shall we do?" I whispered. "If I am found here at this hour. . . ."

"Keep quiet . . . leave it to me."

From outside, again: "Miss Fitzgibbon!"

She moved quickly to the far side of the room, and stood beside the bed.

"What is it, Mrs Anson?" she called, in a faint, tired-seeming voice.

There was a short silence. Then: "Has the maid brought a hot water bottle to your room?"

"Yes, thank you. I am already abed."

"With the lamps still alight, Miss Fitzgibbon?"

The young lady pointed desperately at the door, and waved her hands at me. I understood immediately, and moved quickly to one side so that I could not be seen through the keyhole.

"I am doing a little reading, Mrs Anson. Good night to you."

There was another silence from beyond the door, during which I felt I must surely shout aloud to break the tension!

"I thought I heard the sound of a man's voice," said Mrs Anson.

"I am quite alone," said Miss Fitzgibbon. I saw that her face was flushing red, although whether it was from embarrassment or anger I could not tell.

"I don't think I am mistaken."

"Please wait a moment," said Miss Fitzgibbon.

She crept over to me, and raised her mouth until it was beside my ear.

"I shall have to let her in," she whispered. "I know what to do. Please turn your back."

"What?" I said in astonishment.

"Turn your back . . . *please!*"

I stared at her in anguish for a moment longer, then did as she said. I heard her move away from me towards the wardrobe, and then there came the sound of her pulling at the clasps and buttons of her gown. I closed my eyes firmly, covering them with my hand. The enormity of my situation was without parallel.

I heard the wardrobe door close, and then felt the touch of a hand on my arm. I looked: Miss Fitzgibbon was standing beside me, a long striped flannel dressing-gown covering her. She had taken the pins from her hair so that it fell loosely about her face.

"Take these," she whispered, thrusting the two brandy-glasses into my hands. "Wait inside the bath-room."

"Miss Fitzgibbon, I really must insist!" said Mrs Anson.

I stumbled towards the bath-room door. As I did so I glanced back and saw Miss Fitzgibbon throwing back the covers of the bed and crumpling the linen and bolster. She took my samples-case, and thrust it under the *chaise longue*. I went inside the bath-room and closed the door. In the dark I leaned back against the door frame, and felt my hands trembling.

The outer door was opened.

"Mrs Anson, what is it you want?"

I heard Mrs Anson march into the room. I could imagine her glaring suspiciously about, and I waited for the moment of her irruption into the bath-room.

"Miss Fitzgibbon, it is very late. Why are you not yet asleep?"

"I am doing some reading. Had you not knocked when you did, I dare say I should be asleep at this moment."

"I distinctly heard a male voice."

"But you can see . . . I am alone. Could it not have been from the next room?"

"It came from in here."

"Were you listening at the door?"

"Of course not! I was passing down the lower corridor on the way to my own room."

"Then you could easily have been mistaken. I too have heard voices."

The tone of Mrs Anson's words changed suddenly. "My dear Amelia, I am concerned only for your well-being. You do not know these commercial men as well as I. You are young and innocent, and I am responsible for your safety."

"I'm twenty-two years of age, Mrs Anson and *I* am responsible for my safety. Now please leave me, as I wish to go to sleep."

Again, Mrs Anson's tone changed. "How do I know you're not deceiving me?"

"Look around, Mrs Anson!" Miss Fitzgibbon came to the bath-room door, and threw it open. It banged against my shoulder, but served to conceal me behind it. "Look everywhere! Would you care to inspect my wardrobe? Or would you prefer to peer under my bed?"

"There is no need for unpleasantness, Miss Fitzgibbon. I am quite prepared to take your word."

"Then kindly leave me in peace, as I have had a long day at work, and I wish to go to sleep."

There was a short silence. Then Mrs Anson said: "Very well, Amelia. Good night to you."

"Good night, Mrs Anson."

I heard the woman walk from the room, and down the stairs outside. There was a much longer silence, and then I heard the outer door close.

Miss Fitzgibbon came to the bath-room, and leaned weakly against the door-post.

"She's gone," she said.

iv

Miss Fitzgibbon took one of the glasses from me, and swallowed the brandy.

"Would you like some more?" she said softly.

"Yes, please."

The flask was now nearly empty, but we shared what remained.

I looked at Miss Fitzgibbon's face, pale in the gaslight, and wondered if I looked as ashen.

"I must leave at once, of course," I said.

She shook her head. "You would be seen. Mrs Anson wouldn't dare come to the room again, but she will not go straight to bed."

"Then what can I do?"

"We'll have to wait. I should think if you leave in about an hour's time she will no longer be around."

"We are behaving as if we are guilty," I said. "Why can I not go now, and tell Mrs Anson the truth of the matter?"

"Because we have already resorted to deception, and she has seen me in my nightwear."

"Yes, of course."

"I shall have to turn off the gaslights, as if I have gone to bed. There is a small oil-lamp, and we can sit by that." She indicated a folding dressing-screen. "If you would move that in front of the door, Mr Turnbull, it will mask the light and help subdue our voices."

"I'll move it at once," I said.

Miss Fitzgibbon put another lump of coal on the fire, lit the oil-lamp, and turned off the gas-mantles.

I helped her move the two easy chairs towards the fireplace, then placed the lamp on the mantelpiece.

"Do you mind waiting a while?" she asked me.

"I should prefer to leave," I said uncomfortably, "but I think you are right. I should not care to face Mrs Anson at this moment."

"Then please try to be less agitated."

I said: "Miss Fitzgibbon, I should feel much more relaxed if you would put on your clothes again."

"But beneath this gown I am wearing my underclothing."

"Even so."

I went into the bath-room for a few minutes, and when I returned she had replaced her dress. Her hair was still loose, though, which I found pleasing, for I felt her face was better suited when framed in this way.

As I sat down, she said to me: "Can I ask one more favour of you, without further shocking you?"

"What is that?"

"I will be more at ease during the next hour if you would stop addressing me by my surname. My name is Amelia."

"I know," I said. "I heard Mrs Anson. I am Edward."

"You are so formal, Edward."

"I can't help it," I said. "It is what I am used to."

The tension had left me, and I felt very tired. Judging by the way Miss Fitzgibbon—or Amelia—was sitting, she felt the same. The abandonment of formal address was a similar relaxation, as if Mrs Anson's abrupt intrusion had swept aside the normal courtesies. We had suffered, and survived, a potential catastrophe and it had drawn us together.

"Do you think that Mrs Anson suspected I was here, Amelia?" I said.

She glanced shrewdly at me. "No, she knew you were here."

"Then I have compromised you!"

"It is I who have compromised you. The deception was of my own invention."

I said: "You're very candid. I don't think I have ever met anyone like you."

"Well, in spite of your stuffiness, Edward, I don't think I've ever met anyone quite like you before."

v

Now that the worst was over, and the rest could be dealt with in good time, I found that I was able to enjoy the intimacy of the situation. Our two chairs were close together in warmth and semi-darkness, the brandy was glowing within, and the light from the oil-lamp laid subtle and pleasing highlights on Amelia's features. All this made me reflective in a way that had nothing whatsoever to do with the circumstances that had brought us together. She seemed to me to be a person of wonderful beauty and presence of mind, and the thought of leaving her when my hour's wait was over was too unwelcome to contemplate.

At first it was I who led the conversation, talking a little of myself. I explained how my parents had emigrated to America soon after I had left school, and that since then I had lived alone while working for Mr Westerman.

"You never felt any desire to go with your parents to America?" Amelia said.

"I was very tempted. They write to me frequently, and America seems to be an exciting country. But I felt that I scarcely knew England, and that I should like to live my own life here for a while, before joining them."

"And do you know England any better now?"

"Hardly," I said. "Although I spend my weeks outside London, I spend most of my time in hotels like this."

With this, I enquired politely of her own background.

She told me that her parents were dead—there had been a sinking at sea while she was still a child—and that since then she had been under the legal guardianship of Sir William. He and her father had been friends since their own schooldays, and in her father's will this wish had been expressed.

"So you also live at Reynolds House?" I said. "It is not merely employment?"

"I am paid a small wage for my work, but Sir William has made a suite of rooms in one of the wings available to me."

"I should greatly like to meet Sir William," I said, fervently.

"So that he may try your goggles in your presence?" Amelia said.

"I am regretting that I brought them to you."

"And I am glad you did. You have inadvertently enlivened my evening. I was beginning to suspect that Mrs Anson was the only person in this hotel, so tight was her hold on me. Anyway, I'm sure Sir William will consider purchasing your goggles, even though he does not drive his horseless carriage these days."

I looked at her in surprise. "But I understood Sir William was a keen motorist. Why has he lost interest?"

"He is a scientist, Edward. His invention is prolific, and he is constantly turning to new devices."

In this way we conversed for a long time, and the longer we spoke the more relaxed I became. Our subjects were inconsequential for the most part, dwelling on our past lives and experiences. I soon learnt that Amelia was much better travelled than me, having accompanied Sir William on some of his overseas journeys. She told me of her visit to New York, and to Dresden and Leipzig, and I was greatly interested.

At last the fire burned down, and we had drunk the last of the brandy.

I said, regretfully: "Amelia, do you think I should now return to my room?"

For a moment her expression did not change, but then she smiled briefly and to my surprise laid her hand gently on my arm.

"Only if you wish to," she said.

"Then I think I shall stay a few minutes longer."

Immediately I said this I regretted it. In spite of her friendly gesture I felt that we had spoken enough of the matters that interested us, and that further delay was only an admission of the considerable degree of distraction her nearness to me was causing. I had no idea how long it was since Mrs Anson had left us—and to take out my watch would have been unpardonable—but I felt sure that it must be much more than the hour we had agreed. Further delay was improper.

Amelia had not removed her hand from my arm.

"We must speak again, Edward," she said. "Let us meet in London one evening; perhaps you would invite me to join you for dinner. Then, without having to hush our voices, we can talk to our hearts' content."

I said: "When are you returning to Surrey?"

"I think it will be tomorrow afternoon."

"I shall be in town during the day. Will you join me for luncheon? There is a small inn on the Ilkley road. . . ."

"Yes, Edward. I shall enjoy that."

"Now I had better return." I took my watch from my pocket, and saw that an hour and a half had elapsed since Mrs Anson's intrusion. "I'm very sorry to have talked for so long."

Amelia said nothing, but simply shook her head slowly.

I took my samples-case, and walked quietly to the door. Amelia stood up too, and blew out the oil-lamp.

"I'll help you with the screen," she said.

The only illumination in the room was from the dying embers of the fire. I saw Amelia silhouetted against the glow as she came towards me. Together we shifted the folding screen to one side, then I turned the handle of the door. All was still and silent beyond. Suddenly, in that great quietness I wondered how well the screen had muffled our voices, and whether in fact our innocent liaison had been overheard by more than one other person.

I turned back to her.

"Good night, Miss Fitzgibbon," I said.

Her hand touched my arm again, and I felt a warmth of

breath on my cheek. Her lips touched me for a fraction of a second.

"Good night, Mr Turnbull." Her fingers tightened on my arm, then she moved back and her door closed silently.

vi

My room and bed were cold, and I could not sleep. I lay awake all night, my thoughts circling endlessly around subjects that could not be further removed from my immediate surroundings. In the morning, surprisingly alert in spite of my sleeplessness, I was first down to the breakfast-room, and as I sat at my usual table the head waiter approached me.

"Mrs Anson's compliments, sir," he said. "Would you kindly attend to this directly you have finished breakfast?"

I opened the slim brown envelope and found that it contained my account. When I left the breakfast-room I discovered that my luggage had been packed, and was ready for me in the entrance hall. The head waiter took my money, and conducted me to the door. None of the other guests had seen me leave; there had been no sign of Mrs Anson. I stood in the sharp cool of the morning air, still stunned by the abruptness of my enforced departure.

After a while I carried my bags to the station and deposited them at the luggage office. I stayed in the vicinity of the hotel all day, but saw no sign of Amelia. At midday I went to the inn on the Ilkley road, but she did not appear. As evening drew on I went back to the station, and caught the last train of the day to London.

Chapter Three
THE HOUSE ON RICHMOND HILL

i

During the week following my premature return to Skipton, I was away on business in Nottingham. Here I applied myself to my work to such a degree that I adequately made up for the poor sales I had achieved in Skipton. By the Saturday evening, when I returned to my lodgings near Regent's Park, the incident had receded to a regrettable memory. To say this is not wholly accurate, however, for in spite of the consequences, meeting Amelia had been an uplifting experience. I felt I should not hope to see her again, but I did feel the need to apologize.

As I should have known it would, though, the next move came from Amelia, for waiting for me on that Saturday evening was a letter postmarked in Richmond.

The main part of the letter was type-written, and simply stated that Sir William had been told of the motoring aid I had demonstrated, and that he had expressed a desire to meet me. Accordingly, I was invited to the house on Sunday, 21st May, when Sir William would be glad to speak to me over afternoon tea. It was signed: "A. Fitzgibbon".

Underneath this main message, Amelia had added a hand-written postscript:

> Sir William is usually busy in his laboratory during most of the daylight hours, so would you care to arrive at about 2.00 p.m.? As the weather is now so much finer I thought you and I might enjoy bicycling through Richmond Park.
> Amelia

I did not take long to make up my mind. Indeed, within

minutes I had written my acceptance, and posted it within the hour. I was very glad to be invited to tea.

ii

On the appointed day I left Richmond Station, and walked slowly through the town. Most of the shops were closed, but there was much traffic—mostly phaetons and broughams, carrying families on Sunday outings—and the pavements were crowded with pedestrians. I strolled along with everyone else, feeling smart and fashionable in the new clothes I had bought the day before. To celebrate the occasion I had even indulged myself in the extravagance of a new straw boater, and this I wore at a jaunty angle, reflecting the carefree mood I was in. The only reminder of my normal way of life was the samples-case I carried. This I had emptied of everything except the three pairs of goggles. Even the unwonted lightness of the case, though, emphasized the special nature of this visit.

I was far too early, of course, having left my lodgings soon after breakfast. I was determined not to be late, and so had over-estimated the amount of time it would take me to reach here. I had enjoyed a leisurely walk through London to Waterloo Station, the train journey had taken only twenty minutes or so, and here I was, enjoying the mild air and warm sunshine of a May morning.

In the centre of the little town I passed the church as the congregation was leaving, walking out into the sunlight, the gentlemen calm and formal in their suits, the ladies gay in bright clothes and carrying sunshades. I walked on until I reached Richmond Bridge, and here I stepped out over the Thames, looking down at the boats plying between the wooded banks.

It was all such a contrast from the bustle and smells of London; much as I liked to live in the metropolis, the ever-present press of people, the racket of the traffic and the dampening grey of the industrial pall that drifted over the rooftops all made for an unconscionable pressure on one's mind. It was reassuring to find a place like this, such a short journey from the centre of London, that enjoyed an elegance that too often I found easy to forget still existed.

I continued my stroll along one of the riverside walks, then turned round and headed back into the town. Here I found a restaurant open, and ordered myself a substantial lunch. With this finished, I returned to the station, having previously forgotten to find out the times of the trains returning to London in the evening.

At last it was time to set out for Richmond Hill, and I walked back through the town, following The Quadrant until I came to the junction with the road which led down to Richmond Bridge. Here I followed a smaller road which forked to the left, climbing the Hill. All along my left-hand side there were buildings; at first, near the bottom of the Hill, the houses were terraced, with one or two shops. At the end of the terrace there was a public house—The Queen Victoria, as I recall—and beyond this the style and class of house changed noticeably.

Several were set a long way back from the road, almost invisible behind the thickly growing trees. To my right there was parkland and more trees, and as I climbed higher I saw the sweeping curve of the Thames through the meadows by Twickenham. It was a most beautiful and peaceful place.

At the top of the Hill the road became a pitted cart-track, leading through Richmond Gate into the Park itself, and the pavement ceased to exist altogether. At this point there was a narrower track, leading more directly up the slope of the Hill, and I walked this way. Shortly along this track I saw a gateway with *Reynolds House* carved into the sandstone posts, and I knew I had come to the right place.

The driveway was short, but described a sharp S, so that the house was not visible from the gate. I followed the drive, remarking to myself on the way in which the trees and shrubbery had been allowed to grow unhindered. In several places the growths were so wild that the drive was barely wide enough to allow passage of a carriage.

In a moment the house came into sight, and I was at once impressed by its size. The main part of the house seemed, to my

untrained eye, to be about one hundred years old, but two large
and more modern wings had been added at each end, and a part
of the courtyard so produced had been roofed over with a
wooden-framed glass structure, rather like a greenhouse.

In the immediate vicinity of the house the shrubbery had
been cut back, and a well-kept lawn lay to one side of the house,
stretching round to the far side.

I saw that the main entrance was partially concealed behind
a part of the glasshouse—at first glance I had not noticed
it—and walked in that direction. There seemed to be no one
about; the house and grounds were silent, and there was no
movement at any of the windows.

As I walked past the windows of the conservatory-like extension, there was a sudden scream of metal upon metal, accompanied by a blaze of yellow light. For an instant I saw the
shape of a man, hunched forward, and silhouetted by a blaze of
sparks. Then the grinding ceased, and again all became dim
within.

I pressed the electrical bell-push by the door, and after a few
moments the door was opened by a plump, middle-aged woman
in a black dress and white apron. I removed my hat.

"I should like to see Miss Fitzgibbon," I said, as I stepped
into the hall. "I believe I am expected."

"Do you have a card, sir?"

I was about to produce my regular business-card, supplied
by Mr Westerman, but then recalled that this was more of a
personal visit. "No, but if you would say it is Mr Edward
Turnbull."

"Will you wait?"

She showed me into a reception-room, and closed the doors
behind me.

I must have walked a little too energetically up the Hill, for I
found that I was hot and flushed, and my face was damp with
perspiration. I mopped my face with my kerchief as quickly as
possible, then, to calm myself, I glanced around the room,
hoping that an appraisal of its furniture would gain me an
insight into Sir William's tastes. In fact, the room was ill-
furnished to the point of bareness. A small octagonal table

stood before the fireplace, and beside it were two faded easy chairs, but these, apart from the curtains and a threadbare carpet, were all that were there.

Presently, the servant returned.

"Would you please come this way, Mr Turnbull?" she said. "You may leave your case here in the hallway."

I followed her along a corridor, then turned to the left and came into a comfortable drawing-room, which opened on to the garden by way of a french window. The servant indicated that I should pass through, and as I did so I saw Amelia sitting at a white, wrought-iron table placed beneath two apple trees on the lawn.

"Mr Turnbull, ma'am," said the woman, and Amelia set aside the book she had been reading.

"Edward," she said. "You're earlier than I expected. That's wonderful . . . it's such a lovely day for a ride!"

I sat down on the opposite side of the little table. I was aware that the servant was still standing by the french window.

"Mrs Watchets, will you bring us some lemonade?" Amelia said to her, then turned to me. "You must be thirsty from your walk up the Hill. We'll have just one glass each, then set off at once."

It was delightful to be with her again, and such a pleasant surprise that she was as lovely as I had remembered her. She was wearing a most pleasing combination of white blouse and dark blue silk skirt, and on her head she had a flowered raffia bonnet. Her long auburn hair, finely brushed and held behind her ears with a clip, fell neatly down her back. She was sitting so that the sunlight fell across her face, and as the branches of the apple trees moved in the gentle breeze, their shadows seemed to stroke the skin of her face. Her profile was presented to me: she was beautiful in many ways, not least that her fine features were exquisitely framed by the style of hair. I admired the graceful way she sat, the delicacy of her fair skin, the candour of her eyes.

"I haven't brought a bicycle with me," I said. "I wasn't—"

"We have plenty here, and you may use one of those. I'm

delighted you could come today, Edward. There are so many things I have to tell you."

"I'm terribly sorry if I got you into trouble," I said, wanting to get off my chest the one matter that had been preoccupying me. "Mrs Anson was in no doubt as to my presence in your room."

"I understand you were shown the door."

"Directly after breakfast," I said. "I didn't see Mrs Anson. . . ."

At that moment Mrs Watchets reappeared, bearing a tray with a glass jug and two tumblers, and I allowed my sentence to go unfinished. While Mrs Watchets poured out the drinks, Amelia pointed out to me a rare South American shrub growing in the garden (Sir William had brought it back with him from one of his overseas journeys), and I expressed the greatest interest in it.

When we were once more alone, Amelia said: "Let us talk of those matters while we are riding. I'm sure Mrs Watchets would be as scandalized as Mrs Anson to hear of our nocturnal liaisons."

There was something about her use of the plural that sent a pleasurable, though not entirely guiltless, thrill through me.

The lemonade was delicious: ice-cold, and with a sharp hint of sourness that stimulated the palate. I finished mine with immoderate speed.

"Tell me a little of Sir William's work," I said. "You told me that he has lost interest in his horseless carriage. What is he engaged in at the moment?"

"Perhaps if you are to meet Sir William, you should ask him that yourself. But it is no secret that he has built a heavier-than-air flying machine."

I looked at her in amazement.

"You cannot be serious!" I said. "No machine can fly!"

"Birds fly; they are heavier than air."

"Yes, but they have wings."

She stared at me thoughtfully for a moment. "You had better see it for yourself, Edward. It's just beyond those trees."

"In which case," I said, "yes, let me see this impossible thing!"

We left our glasses on the table, and Amelia led me across the lawn towards a thicket of trees. We passed through these in the direction of Richmond Park—which ran right up to the boundary of the house grounds—until we came to an area which had been levelled, and the surface compacted with a hard covering. On this stood the flying machine.

It was larger than I could have imagined it would be, extending some twenty feet at its widest point. It was clearly unfinished: the framework, which was of wooden struts, was uncovered, and there appeared to be nowhere that the driver could sit. On each side of the main body there was a wing, sagging so that the tip touched the ground. The overall appearance was similar to that of a dragonfly at rest, although it had none of the beauty of that insect.

We walked over to it, and I ran my fingers along the surface of the nearer wing. There seemed to be several wooden formers under the fabric, which itself had the texture of silk. It was stretched very tightly, so that drumming one's fingers on the fabric produced a hollow sound.

"How does it work?" I said.

Amelia went over to the main body of the machine.

"The motor was fixed in this position," she said, indicating four struts more substantial than the others. "Then this system of pulleys carried the cables which raised and lowered the wings."

She pointed out the hinges which allowed the wings to flap up and down, and I found by lifting one that the motion was very smooth and strong.

"Sir William should have continued with this!" I said. "Surely to fly would be a wonderful thing!"

"He became disillusioned with it," Amelia said. "He was discontented with the design. One evening he told me that he needed the time to reconsider his theory of flight, because this machine simply imitates unsuccessfully the movements of a bird. He said that it needed a thorough reappraisal. Also, the reciprocating engine he was using was too heavy for the machine, and not powerful enough."

"I should have thought that a man of Sir William's genius could have modified the motor," I said.

"Oh, but he did. See this." Amelia pointed out a queer assemblage, placed deep inside the structure. It seemed on first sight to be made of ivory and brass, but there was a crystalline quality to it that somehow deceived the eye, so that within its winking, multifaceted depths it was not possible to see the constituent parts.

"What is this?" I said, very interested.

"A device of Sir William's own invention. It is a substance that enhances power, and it was not without effect. But as I say, he was not content with the design and has abandoned the machine altogether."

"Where is the engine now?" I said.

"In the house. He uses it to generate electricity for his laboratory."

I bent down to examine the crystalline material more closely, but even near to, it was difficult to see how it was made. I was disappointed with the flying machine, and thought it would have been fun to see it in the air.

I straightened, and saw that Amelia had stepped back a little.

I said to her: "Tell me, do you ever assist Sir William in his laboratory?"

"If I am called upon to do so."

"So you are Sir William's confidante?"

Amelia said: "If you mean that I could persuade him to purchase your goggles, then I suppose so."

I said nothing to this, for the wretched affair of the goggles was not on my mind.

We had started walking slowly back towards the house, and as we came to the lawn, Amelia said: "Shall we now go for our bicycle ride?"

"I'd like that."

We went into the house and Amelia summoned Mrs Watchets. She told her that we would be out for the rest of the afternoon, but that tea should be served as normal at four-thirty. Then we went to an outhouse where several bicycles were stacked, selected one each, and pushed them through the grounds until we reached the edge of the Park.

iii

We rested in the shade of some trees overlooking the Pen Ponds, and Amelia at last told me what had happened to her on the morning following our conversation.

"I was not called for breakfast," she said, "and being tired I overslept. At eight-thirty I was awakened by Mrs Anson bringing a breakfast-tray into the room. Then, as you might expect, I was given the benefit of Mrs Anson's views on morality . . . at her customary length."

"Was she angry with you? Did you try to explain?"

"Well, she wasn't angry, or at least she didn't reveal her anger. And I had no chance to explain. She was tight-lipped and solicitous. She knew what had happened, or she had made up her mind what had happened, and at first I thought that had I made any attempt to deny what was already a foregone conclusion it would have provoked her to a rage, so I sat and listened humbly to her advice. This was, in substance, that I was a young lady of education and breeding, and that what she referred to as 'loose living' was not for the likes of me. It was, however, very revealing in another way. I realized that she could censure the imagined actions of others, yet at the same time display a prurient and consuming curiosity about them. For all her anger, Mrs Anson was hoping for insights into what had happened."

"I suppose her curiosity was disappointed," I said.

"Not at all," said Amelia, smiling as she held a stem of grass in her hand and stripped away the outer leaves to reveal the bright-green, soft inner stalk. "I supplied her with a few illuminating details."

I found myself laughing in spite of the fact that I was at once very embarrassed and rather excited.

"I should like to hear one or two of those details," I said, boldly.

"Sir, what of my modesty?" Amelia said, fluttering her eyelashes at me in an exaggerated way, then she too laughed aloud. "With her curiosity satisfied, and with my life revealed to be on the downward path, she hastened from my room, and that was the end of that. I left the hotel as soon as I could. The delay had made me late for my appointment at the engineering works, and I wasn't able to get to our luncheon in time. I'm very sorry."

"That's all right," I said, feeling well pleased with myself, even if my scandalous reputation were a fiction.

We were sitting together against the bole of a huge tree, the bicycles leaning against another tree. A few yards away, two little boys in sailor suits were trying to make a toy yacht sail out across the Pond. Near by, their nanny watched without interest.

"Let's ride further," I said. "I'd like to see more of the Park."

I leaped up and extended my hands to help Amelia to her feet. We ran over to the bicycles and disentangled them. We mounted and turned into the breeze, heading in the general direction of Kingston-upon-Thames.

We pedalled at a leisurely rate for a few minutes, but then, just as we were approaching a slight rise in the ground, Amelia called out: "Let's race!"

I pedalled harder, but with the combination of the headwind and the gradient it was heavy going. Amelia kept abreast of me.

"Come on, you're not trying!" she shouted, and surged slightly ahead of me.

I pressed down harder on the pedals and managed to catch her up, but at once she pulled ahead again. I raised myself from the saddle, and used all my strength to try to make up the difference, but for all my efforts Amelia managed somehow to stay a few yards ahead. Suddenly, as if tired of playing with me, Amelia shot quickly forward and, bumping alarmingly over the uneven surface of the path, climbed quickly up the slope. I knew I could never keep up with her, and at once gave up the unequal struggle. I watched her ahead of me ... then realized with a shock that she was still sitting upright in the saddle, and, as far as I could see, was *free-wheeling*!

Aghast, I watched her bicycle spin over the crest of the slope, at a speed that must have been well in excess of twenty miles an hour, and then vanish from my sight.

I pedalled on peevishly, sulking a little at the way my pride had been thwarted. As I came over the crest I saw Amelia a few yards further on. She had dismounted, and her bicycle was lying on its side, the front wheel spinning. She was sitting on the grass beside it, laughing at the sight of my hot and perspiring face.

I flung my bicycle down beside hers, and sat down in a mood as near displeasure as I had ever experienced in her company.

"You cheated," I said.

"You could have done so too," she cried, still laughing at me.

I mopped my face with my kerchief. "That wasn't a race, it was a deliberate humiliation."

"Oh, Edward! Don't take it so seriously. I only wanted to show you something."

"What?" I said in a surly tone.

"My bicycle. Do you notice anything about it?"

"No." I was still not mollified.

"What about the front wheel?"

"It's still spinning," I said.

"Then stop it."

I reached out and gripped the pneumatic tyre with my hand, but snatched it away as the friction burned me. The wheel continued to spin.

"What is it?" I said, my distemper immediately forgotten.

"It is one of Sir William's devices," she said. "Your bicycle is fitted with one too."

"But how does it work? You were free-wheeling up the hill. That is against all the laws of physics."

"Look, I'll show you."

She reached over to her machine and took hold of the handle-bar. She held the right-hand grip in a certain way, and the front wheel stopped its uncanny spinning. She righted the bicycle.

"Under here." She showed me where to look, and between the rubber grip and the brake-bar I saw a tiny strip of mica. "Move this forward with your fingers, so, and—"

The bicycle started to move forward, but she raised the front wheel from the ground and it spun effortlessly in the air.

"When you wish to stop, you simply slide the strip back, and the bicycle may be ridden normally."

"And you say my machine is fitted with this?"

"Yes."

"Why did you not tell me? Then we need not have expended any effort on the ride!"

Amelia was laughing again as I hastened to my own machine and righted it. Sure enough, under the right-hand grip there was a similar piece of mica.

"I must try this at once!" I shouted, and mounted my machine. As soon as I had found my balance I slid the mica strip forward, and the bicycle moved faster.

"It works!" I cried to Amelia, waving to her in delight . . . and at that moment the front wheel hit a tuft of grass, and I was unseated.

Amelia ran over to me and helped me to my feet. My bicycle lay a few yards from me, the front wheel spinning merrily.

"What a marvellous invention!" I cried, full of enthusiasm for it. "Now we shall race in style!"

"All right," Amelia said. "First back to the Ponds!"

I retrieved my machine, and she ran back to hers. In a few moments we were both mounted, and speeding spectacularly towards the crest of the slope. This time the race was more even, and as we rolled down the long gradient towards the distant Ponds we kept abreast of each other. The wind drummed against my face, and it was not long before I felt my boater snatched away. Amelia's bonnet was blowing backwards, but stayed around her neck because of its strap.

As we came to the Ponds we speeded past the nanny and the two little boys, who stared after us in amazement. Laughing aloud, we circled around the larger of the two Ponds, then pulled back the mica strips and pedalled towards the trees at a moderate pace.

As we dismounted, I said: "What is it, Amelia? How does it work?"

I was feeling breathless, even though the actual physical energy expended had been negligible.

"It's in here," she said.

With a twisting motion she slid back the moulded rubber hand-grip, so exposing the tubular steel of the handle-bar. She held the bar so that I could see into its interior . . . and there, nestling inside, was some of the crystalline material I had seen on the flying machine.

"There is a wire which runs through the frame," Amelia said, "and that is connected to the wheel. Inside the hub is some more of that."

"What is this crystalline material?" I said. "What does it consist of?"

"That I don't know. I'm aware of some of the materials it comprises, for I have to order them, but I'm not sure how they are joined to produce the effect."

She explained that the adapted bicycle had been developed by Sir William when bicycling became popular a few years before. His idea had been to assist the weak or elderly whenever they encountered a hill.

"Do you realize that this device alone would make him a fortune?"

"Sir William does not want for money."

"No, but think of the public good it would do. A machine like this could transform the carriage industry."

Amelia was shaking her head. "You don't understand Sir William. I'm sure he has considered taking out a Patent on this, but I think he judged it better unknown. Bicycling is a sport, mostly enjoyed by the young, and it is done for fresh air and exercise. As you have seen, it requires no effort to ride a bicycle like this."

"Yes, but there would be other uses."

"Indeed, and that is why I say you do not understand Sir William, nor could you be expected to. He is a man of restless intellect, and no sooner has he developed one device than he goes on to another. The bicycles were adapted before he built his horseless cariage, and that was before his flying machine."

I said: "And he has abandoned his flying machine for a new project?"

"Yes."

"May I enquire what that is to be?"

She said: "You will be meeting Sir William shortly. Perhaps he will tell you himself."

I thought about this for a moment. "You say he is sometimes an uncommunicative man. Maybe he would not tell me."

We were once more seated close together beneath the tree.

Amelia said: "Then you may ask me about it again, Edward."

Chapter Four
SIR WILLIAM EXPOUNDS A THEORY

i

Time was passing, and soon Amelia suggested that we return to the house.

"Shall we race or ride?" I said, not especially anxious to do either, for I had been finding our rest together beneath the trees an exquisite experience. It was still sunny and warm, and there was a pleasant dusty heat rolling through the Park.

"We will ride," she said firmly. "There is no exercise in free-wheeling."

"And we may take it more slowly," I said. "Shall we do this again, Amelia? I mean, shall we bicycle together on another weekend?"

"It will not be possible every weekend," she said. "Sometimes I am called upon to work, and occasionally I have to be away."

I felt a pang of unreasoned jealousy at the idea of her travelling with Sir William.

"But when you are here, shall we bicycle then?"

"You will have to invite me," she said.

"Then I will."

When we mounted our machines we first retraced the way of our race, and retrieved my lost boater. It was undamaged, and I placed it on my head, keeping the brim well down over my eyes so as to prevent it blowing off again.

The ride back to the house was uneventful and, for the most part, conducted in silence. I was at last understanding the real reason why I had come to Richmond this afternoon; it was not at all to meet Sir William, for although I was still fascinated by what I knew of him I would have gladly exchanged the coming interview for another hour, two hours, or the entire evening in the Park with Amelia.

We entered the grounds of the house through a small gateway by Sir William's abandoned flying machine, and wheeled the bicycles back to the outhouse.

"I am going to change my clothes," Amelia said.

"You are delightful just as you are," I said.

"And you? Are you going to meet Sir William with grass all over your suit?" She reached over and plucked a stem of grass that had somehow lodged itself under the collar of my jacket.

We entered the house through the French window, and Amelia pressed a bell-push. In a moment, a manservant appeared.

'Hillyer, this is Mr Turnbull. He will be staying with us to tea and dinner. Would you help him prepare?"

"Certainly, Miss Fitzgibbon." He turned towards me. "Would you step this way, sir?"

He indicated that I should follow him, and we moved towards the corridor. From behind, Amelia called to him.

"And Hillyer?" she said. "Would you please tell Mrs Watchets that we shall be ready for tea in ten minutes, and that it is to be served in the smoking-room?"

"Yes, ma'am."

Hillyer led me through the house to the first floor, where there was a small bath-room. Inside, soap and towels were laid out, and while I washed Hillyer took away my jacket to have it brushed.

The smoking-room was on the ground floor, and it was a small, well-used room, comfortably furnished. Amelia was waiting for me; perhaps my remark about her appearance had flattered her, for she had not after all changed, but had merely put on a tiny jacket over her blouse.

Crockery had been laid on a small octagonal table, and we sat down to wait for Sir William to arrive. According to the clock on the mantelpiece it was now some minutes after four-thirty, and Amelia summoned Mrs Watchets.

"Have you sounded the tea-bell?" Amelia said.

"Yes, ma'am, but Sir William is still in his laboratory."

"Then perhaps you would remind him that he has a guest this afternoon."

Mrs Watchets left the room, but a moment or two later a door at the far end of the room opened, and a tall, well-built man came in hurriedly. He was in his shirt and waistcoat, and carried a jacket over his arm. He was trying to roll down his shirtsleeves, and as he came in he glanced in my direction. I stood up at once.

He said to Amelia: "Is tea here? I'm nearly finished!"

"Sir William, do you remember I mentioned Edward Turnbull to you?"

He looked at me again. "Turnbull? Good to meet you!" He gestured impatiently at me. "Do sit down. Amelia, help me with my cuff."

He extended his arm to her, and she reached under it to connect the cuff-link. When this was done, he rolled down his other sleeve and Amelia connected this cuff too. Then he put on his jacket and went to the mantelpiece. He selected a pipe and filled its bowl with tobacco from a jar.

I waited apprehensively; I wondered if the fact that he had been about to finish his work indicated that this was an unfortunate moment to call on him.

"What do you think of that chair, Turnbull?" he said, without turning.

"Sit right back into it," Amelia said. "Not on the edge."

I complied, and as I did so it seemed that the substance of the cushion remoulded itself beneath me to adapt to the shape of my body. The further back I leaned, the more resilient it seemed.

"That is a chair of my own design," Sir William said, turning towards us again as he applied a lighted match to the bowl of his pipe. Then he said, seemingly irrelevantly: "What exactly is your faculty?"

"My, er—?"

"Your field of research. You're a scientist, are you not?"

"Sir William," said Amelia, "Mr Turnbull is interested in motoring, if you will recall."

At that moment I remembered that my samples-case was still where I had left it when I arrived: in the hall.

Sir William looked at me again. "Motoring, eh? A good hobby for a young man. It was a passing phase with me, I'm afraid. I dismantled my carriage because its components were more useful to me in the laboratory."

"But it is a growing fashion, sir," I said. "After all, in America—"

"Yes, yes, but I am a scientist, Turnbull. Motoring is just one aspect of a whole field of new research. We are now on the brink of the Twentieth Century, and that is to be the century of science. There is no limit to what science might achieve."

As Sir William was speaking he did not look at me, but stared over my head. His fingers were fretting with the match he had blown out.

"I agree that it is a subject of great interest to many people, sir," I said.

"Yes, but I think it is in the wrong way. The popular thought is to make what we already have work better. The talk is of faster railway-trains, larger ships. My belief is that all these will be obsolete soon. By the end of the Twentieth Century, Turnbull, man will travel as freely about the planets of the Solar System as he now drives about London. We will know the peoples of Mars and Venus as well as we now know the French and Germans. I dare say we will even travel further . . . out to the stars of the Universe!"

At that moment Mrs Watchets came into the room bearing a silver tray loaded with teapot, milk-jug and a sugar-bowl. I was glad of the intrusion, for I found the combination of Sir William's startling ideas and his nervous manner almost more than I could bear. He too was glad to be interrupted, I think, for as the servant set the tray on the table, and began to pour the tea for us, Sir William stepped back and stood by the end of the mantel. He was relighting his pipe, and as he did so I was able to look at him for the first time without the distraction of his manner.

He was, as I have said, a tall and large man, but what was most striking about him was his head. This was high and broad, the face pale and with grey eyes. His hair was thinning at the temples, but on the crown it grew thickly and wildly, exaggerating the size of his head, and he wore a bushy beard which itself made more marked the pallor of his skin.

I wished I had found him more at his ease, for in the few moments he had been in the room he had destroyed the pleasant sense of well-being that had developed while I was with Amelia, and now I was as nervous as he.

A sudden inspiration came to me, that he himself might be a man not used to meeting strangers, that he was better accustomed to long hours of solitary work. My own occupation involved meeting many strangers, and it was a part of my job to be able to mix well, and so, paradoxical as it might sound, I suddenly realized that here I could take the lead.

As Mrs Watchets left the room, I said to him: "Sir, you say you are nearly finished? I hope I have not disturbed you."

The simplicity of my device had its desired effect. He went towards one of the vacant chairs and sat down, and as he replied his words were phrased more calmly.

"No, of course not," he said. "I can continue after tea. I needed a short rest in any event."

"May I enquire as to the nature of your work?"

Sir William glanced at Amelia for a moment, but her expression remained neutral.

"Has Miss Fitzgibbon told you what I am currently building?"

"She has told me a little, sir. I have seen your flying machine, for instance."

To my surprise, he laughed at that. "Do you think I am insane to meddle with such follies, Turnbull? My scientific colleagues tell me that heavier-than-air flight is impossible. What do you say?"

"It's a novel concept, sir." He made no response but continued to stare at me, so I went on hastily: "It seems to me that the problem is a lack of an adequate power-supply. The design is sound."

"No, no, the design is wrong too. I was going about it the

wrong way. Already I have made machine flight obsolete, and before I even tested that contraption you saw!"

He drank some of his tea quickly, then, astounding me with his speed, jerked out of his chair and moved across the room to a dresser. Opening a drawer he brought forth a thin package, and handed it to me.

"Have a look at those, Turnbull. Tell me what you think."

I opened the package and inside found that there were seven photographic portraits. The first one was a head and shoulders picture of a boy, the second was a slightly older boy, the third was that of a youth, the fourth that of a very young man, and so on.

"Are they all of the same person?" I said, having recognized a recurring facial similarity.

"Yes," said Sir William. "The subject is a cousin of mine, and by chance he has sat for photographic portraits at regular intervals. Now then, Turnbull, do you notice anything about the *quality* of the portraits? No! How can I expect you to anticipate me? They are cross-sections of the Fourth Dimension!"

As I frowned, Amelia said: "Sir William, this is probably a concept new to Mr Turnbull."

"No more than that of heavier-than-air flight! You have grasped that, Turnbull, why should you not grasp the Fourth Dimension?"

"Do you mean the . . . concept of . . .?" I was floundering.

"Space and Time! Exactly, Turnbull . . . Time, the great mystery!"

I glanced at Amelia for more assistance, and realized that she had been studying my face. There was a half-smile on her lips, and at once I guessed that she had heard Sir William expounding on this subject many times.

"These portraits, Turnbull, are two-dimensional representations of a three-dimensional person. Individually, they can depict his height and width, and can even offer an approximation of his *depth* . . . but they can never be more than flat, two-dimensional pieces of paper. Nor can they reveal that he has been travelling all his life through Time. Placed together, they approximate the Fourth Dimension."

He was pacing about the room now, having seized the portraits from my hands, and was waving them expansively as he spoke. He crossed to the mantel and set them up, side by side.

"Time and Space are inherently the same. I walk across this room, and I have travelled in Space a matter of a few yards . . . but at the same moment I have also moved through Time by a matter of a few seconds. Do you see what I am meaning?"

"That one motion complements the other?" I said, uncertainly.

"Exactly! And I am working now to separate the two . . . to facilitate travel through Space discrete from Time, and through Time discrete from Space. Let me show you what I mean."

Abruptly, he turned on his heel and hurried from the room. The door slammed behind him.

I was dumbfounded. I simply stared at Amelia, shaking my head.

She said: "I should have known he would be agitated. He is not always like this, Edward. He has been alone in his laboratory all day, and working like that he often becomes animated."

"Where has he gone?" I said. "Should we follow him?"

"He's returned to his laboratory. I think he will be showing you something he has made."

Exactly at that moment the door opened again and Sir William returned. He was carrying a small wooden box with great care, and he looked around for somewhere to place it.

"Help me move the table," Amelia said to me.

We carried the table bearing the tea-things to one side, and brought forward another. Sir William placed his box in the centre of it, and sat down. As quickly as it had begun, his animation seemed to have passed.

"I want you to look at this closely," he said, "but I do not want you to touch it. It is very delicate."

He opened the lid of the box. The interior was padded with a soft, velvet-like material, and resting inside was a tiny mechanism which, on first sight, I took to be the workings of a clock.

Sir William withdrew it from its case with care, and rested it on the surface of the table.

I leaned forward and peered closely at it. At once, with a start of recognition, I realized that much of it was made with that queer, crystalline substance I had seen twice before that afternoon. The resemblance to a clock was misleading, I saw now, lent to it simply by the precision with which the tiny parts had been fitted together, and some of the metals with which it had been made. Those I could recognize seemed to be some tiny rods of nickel, some highly polished pieces of brass and a cog-wheel made of shining chrome or silver. Part of it had been shaped out of a white substance which could have been ivory, and the base was made of a hard, ebony-like wood. It is difficult, though, to describe what I saw, for all about there was the quartz-like substance, deceiving the eye, presenting hundreds of tiny facets at whatever angle I viewed it from.

I stood up, and stepped back a yard or two. From there, the device once more took on the aspect of a clock-mechanism, albeit a rather extraordinary one.

"It's beautiful," I said, and saw that Amelia's gaze was also on it.

"You, young man, are one of the first people in the world to see a mechanism that will make real to us the Fourth Dimension."

"And this device will really work?" I said.

"Yes, it will. It has been adequately tetsed. This engine will, depending how I choose, travel forward or backward in Time."

Amelia said: "You could demonstrate, Sir William."

He made no answer, but instead sat back in his chair. He was staring at the strange device, a thoughtful expression on his face. He maintained this posture for five minutes, and for all the awareness he showed of Amelia and me, we might not have have existed. Once he leaned forward, and closely scrutinized the device. At this I made to say something, but Amelia signed to me and I subsided into silence. Sir William raised the device in his hand, and held it up against the daylight from the window. He reached forward to touch the silver cog-wheel, then hesitated and set down the device again. Once more he sat back in his chair and regarded his invention with great concentration.

This time he was still for nearly ten minutes, and I began to grow restless, fearing that Amelia and I were a disturbance to him.

Finally, he leaned forward and replaced the device in its case. He stood up.

"You must pardon me, Mr Turnbull," he said. "I have just been stricken with the possibility of a minor modification."

"Do you wish me to leave, sir?"

"Not at all, not at all."

He seized the wooden box, then hastened from the room. The door slammed behind him.

I glanced at Amelia and she smiled, immediately lifting the tension that had marked the last few minutes.

"Is he coming back?" I said.

"I shouldn't think so. The last time he acted like this, he locked himself in his laboratory, and no one except Mrs Watchets saw him for four days."

ii

Amelia summoned Hillyer, and the manservant went around the room, lighting the lamps. Although the sun was still up, it was now behind the trees that grew around the house, and shadows were creeping on. Mrs Watchets came in to clear away the tea-things. I realized that I had drunk only half of my cup, and swallowed the rest quickly. I was thirsty from the bicycling expedition.

I said, when we were alone: "Is he mad?"

Amelia made no answer, but appeared to be listening. She signalled that I should be silent . . . and then about five seconds later the door burst open yet again, and Sir William was there, wearing a topcoat.

"Amelia, I am going up to London. Hillyer can take me in the carriage."

"Will you be back in time for dinner?"

"No ... I shall be out all evening. I'll sleep at my club tonight." He turned to me. "Inadvertently, Turnbull, my conversation with you has generated an idea. I thank you, sir."

He rushed out of the room as abruptly as he had entered, and soon we heard the sound of his voice in the hall. A few minutes later we heard a horse and carriage on the gravelled driveway.

Amelia went to the window, and watched as the manservant drove the carriage away, then returned to her seat.

She said: "No, Sir William is not mad."

"But he behaves like a madman."

"Perhaps that is how it seems. I believe he is a genius; the two are not wholly dissimilar."

"Do you understand his theory?"

"I can grasp most of it. The fact that you didn't follow it, Edward, is no reflection on your own intellect. Sir William is himself so familiar with it that when explaining it to others he omits much of it. Also, you are a stranger to him, and he is rarely at ease unless surrounded by those he knows. He has a group of acquaintances from the Linnaean—his club in London—and they are the only people to whom I have ever heard him speak naturally and fluently."

"Then perhaps I should not have asked him."

"No, it is his obsession; had you not expressed an interest, he would have volunteered his theory. Everyone about him has to bear it. Even Mrs Watchets has heard him out twice."

"Does she understand it?"

"I think not," said Amelia, smiling.

"Then I shall not expect clarification from her. You will have to explain."

"There isn't much I can say. Sir William has built a Time Machine. It has been tested, and I have been present during some of the tests, and the results have been conclusive. He has not said so as yet, but I suspect that he is planning an expedition into futurity."

I smiled a little, and covered my mouth with my hand.

Amelia said: "Sir William is in perfect earnest."

"Yes ... but I cannot see a man of his physique entering a device so small."

"What you have seen is only a working model. He has a full-sized version." Unexpectedly, she laughed. "You don't think I meant the model he showed you?"

"Yes, I did."

When Amelia laughed she looked most beautiful, and I did not mind having misunderstood.

"But large or small, I cannot believe such a Machine is possible!" I said.

"Then you may see it for yourself. It is only a dozen yards from where you are sitting."

I jumped to my feet. "Where is it?"

"In Sir William's laboratory." Amelia seemed to have been infected with my enthusiasm, for she too had left her seat with great alacrity. "I'll show you."

iii

We left the smoking-room by the door which Sir William had used, and walked along a passage to what was clearly a newly constructed door. This led directly into the laboratory, which was, I now realized, the glass-covered annexe which had been built between the two wings of the house.

I do not know what I had been expecting the laboratory to be like, but my first impression was that it bore a considerable resemblance to the milling-shop of an engineering works I had once visited.

Along the ceiling, to one side, was a steam-lathe which, by the means of several adjustable leather straps, provided motive power to the many pieces of engineering equipment I saw ranged along a huge bench beneath it. Several of these were metal-turning lathes, and there was also a sheet-metal stamp, a presser, some acetylene welding equipment, two massive vices and any number of assorted tools scattered about. The floor was liberally spread with the shavings and fragments of metals removed in the processes, and in many parts of the laboratory were what appeared to be long-abandoned pieces of cut or turned metal.

"Sir William does much of the engineering himself," said Amelia, "but occasionally he is obliged to contract out for certain items. I was in Skipton on one of these errands when I met you."

"Where is the Time Machine?" I said.

"You are standing beside it."

I realized with a start that what I had taken at first to be another collection of discarded metals did, in fact, have a coherent scheme to it. I saw now that it bore a certain resemblance to the model he had shown me, but whereas that had had the perfection of miniaturism, this by its very size appeared to be more crude.

In fact, however, as soon as I bent to examine it I saw that every single constituent part had been turned and polished until it shone as new.

The Time Machine was some seven or eight feet in length, and four or five feet in width. At its highest point it stood about six feet from the floor, but as its construction had been strictly functional, perhaps a description in terms of overall dimension is misleading. For much of its length the Time Machine was standing only three feet high, and in the form of a skeletal metal frame.

All its working parts were visible . . . and here my description becomes vague of necessity. What I saw was a repetition *in extremis* of the mysterious substances I had earlier that day seen in Sir William's bicycles and flying machine: in other words, much of what was apparently visible was rendered invisible by the eye-deceiving crystalline substance. This encased thousands of fine wires and rods, and much as I peered at the mechanism from many different angles, I was unable to learn very much.

What was more comprehensible was the arrangement of controls.

Towards one end of the frame was a leather-covered seat,

rounded like a horse-saddle. Around this was a multiplicity of levers, rods and dials.

The main control appeared to be a large lever situated directly in front of the saddle. Attached to the top of this—incongruous in the context—was the handle-bar of a bicycle. This, I supposed, enabled the driver to grip the lever with both hands. To each side of this lever were dozens of subsidiary rods, all of which were attached at different swivelling joints, so that as the lever was moved, others would be simultaneously brought into play.

In my preoccupation I had temporarily forgotten Amelia's presence, but now she spoke, startling me a little.

"It looks substantial, does it not?" she said.

"How long has it taken Sir William to build this?" I said.

"Nearly two years. But touch it, Edward . . . see how substantial it is."

"I wouldn't dare," I said. "I would not know what I was doing."

"Hold one of these bars. It is perfectly safe."

She took my hand, and led it towards one of the brass rods which formed part of the frame. I laid my fingers gingerly on this rail . . . then immediately snatched them away, for as my fingers closed on the rod the entire Machine had visibly and audibly shuddered, like a living being.

"What is it?" I cried.

"The Time Machine is attenuated, existing as it were in the Fourth Dimension. It is real, but it does not exist in the real world as we know it. It is, you must understand, travelling through Time even as we stand here."

"But you cannot be serious . . . because if it were travelling it would not be here now!"

"On the contrary, Edward." She indicated a huge metal flywheel directly in front of the saddle, which corresponded approximately with the silver cog-wheel I had seen on Sir William's model. "It is turning. Can you see that?"

"Yes, yes I can," I said, leaning as near it as I dared. The great wheel was rotating almost imperceptibly.

"If it were not turning, the Machine would be stationary in

Time. To us, as Sir William explained, the Machine would then vanish into the past, for we ourselves are moving forward in Time."

"So the Machine must always be in operation."

While we had been there the evening had deepened, and gloom was spreading in the eerie laboratory.

Amelia stepped to one side and went to yet another infernal contraption. Attached to this was a cord wound around an external wheel, and she pulled the cord sharply. At once the device emitted a coughing, spitting sound, and as it picked up speed, light poured forth from eight incandescent globes hanging from the frame ceiling.

Amelia glanced up at a clock on the wall, which showed the time of twenty-five minutes past six.

"It will be time for dinner in half an hour," she said. "Do you think a stroll around the garden would be enjoyable before then?"

I tore my attention away from the wondrous machines Sir William had made.

The Time Machine might slowly move into futurity, but Amelia was, to my way of thinking, stationary in Time. She was not attenuated, and not at all a creature of past or future.

I said, for I was understanding that my time here in Richmond must soon be at an end: "Will you take my arm?"

She slipped her hand around my elbow, and together we walked past the Time Machine, and the noisy reciprocating engine, through a door in the far corner of the laboratory, and out into the cool evening light of the garden. Only once did I glance back, seeing the pure-white radiance of the electrical lamps shining through the glass walls of the annexe.

Chapter Five

INTO FUTURITY!

i

I had ascertained that the last train to London left Richmond at ten-thirty, and I knew that to catch it I should have to leave by ten. At eight-thirty, though, I was in no mood to think of returning to my lodgings. Furthermore, the prospect of returning to work the next day was one I greeted with the utmost despondency. This was because with the completion of dinner, which had been accompanied by a dry and intoxicating wine, and with the move from the dining-room to the semi-dark intimacy of the drawing-room, and with a glass of port inside me and another half finished, and the subtle fragrance of Amelia's perfume distracting my senses, I was subject to the most perturbing fantasies.

Amelia was no less intoxicated than I, and I fancied that she could not have mistaken the change in my manner. Until this moment I had felt awkward in her company. This was partly because I had had only the barest experience with young women, but more especially because of all young women Amelia seemed to me the most extraordinary. I had grown used to her forthright manner, and the emancipated airs she assumed, but what I had not until this moment realized was that I had, most inappropriately, fallen blindly and rashly in love with her.

In wine there is truth, and although I was able to contain my excesses, and fell short of protesting my undying amour, our conversation had touched on most remarkably personal matters.

Soon after nine-thirty, I knew I could delay no more. I had

only half an hour before I had to leave, and as I had no idea of when or how I should see her again, I felt that then was the moment to state, in no uncertain terms, that to me she was already more than just a pleasant companion.

I poured myself a liberal helping of port, and then, still uncertain of how I was to phrase my words, I reached into my waistcoat pocket and consulted my watch.

"My dear Amelia," I started to say. "I see that it is twenty-five minutes to ten, and at ten I must leave. Before that I have something I must tell you."

"But why must you leave?" she said, instantly destroying the thread of my thoughts.

"I have a train to catch."

"Oh, please don't go yet!"

"But I must return to London."

"Hillyer can take you. If you miss your train, he will take you all the way to London."

"Hillyer is already in London," I said.

She laughed, a little drunkenly. "I had forgotten. Then you must walk."

"And so I must leave at ten."

"No ... I will have Mrs Watchets prepare a room for you."

"Amelia, I cannot stay, much as I would wish to. I must work in the morning."

She leaned towards me, and I saw light dancing in her eyes. "Then I shall take you to the station myself."

"There is another carriage?" I said.

"In a manner of speaking." She stood up, and knocked over her empty glass. "Come with me, Edward, and I shall convey you to the station in Sir William's Time Machine!"

She took my hand in hers, and half-dragged me towards the door. We started to laugh; it is difficult to write of this in retrospect, for intoxication, however mild, is not a state in which one acts one's finest. For me it was the gaiety of the moment that contributed to the compliance.

I shouted to her as we ran along: "But to travel in Time will not take me to the station!"

"Yes it will!"

We reached the laboratory and went inside, closing the door behind us. The electrical lamps were still burning, and in the comparatively harsh glare our escapade took on a different aspect.

"Amelia," I said, trying to restrain her. "What are you doing?"

"I am doing what I said. We will travel to the station."

I stood before her, and took her hands in mine.

"We have both had a little too much to drink," I said. "Please don't jest with me. You cannot seriously propose to operate Sir William's Machine."

Her hands tightened on mine. "I am not as intoxicated as you believe. My manner is gay, but I am in perfect earnest."

"Then let us return to the drawing-room at once."

She turned away from me, and walked towards the Time Machine. She gripped one of the brass rails in her hands, and immediately the Machine trembled as before.

She said: "You heard what Sir William said. Time and Space are inseparable. There is no need for you to leave in the next few minutes. Although the Machine is designed to travel into futurity, it will also move across spatial distances. In short, although it will journey across thousands of years, it can also be used for a trip as prosaic as taking a friend to the station."

"You are still jesting," I said. "Nor am I convinced that the Machine will even travel in Time."

"But it has been proved."

"Not to my satisfaction it hasn't," I said.

She turned to face me, and her expression was as serious as before. "Then allow me to demonstrate it to you!"

"No, Amelia! It would be foolhardy to drive the Machine!"

"Why, Edward? I know what to do ... I have watched Sir William's tests often enough."

"But we do not know the craft is safe!"

"There would be no danger."

I simply shook my head with the agony of the moment. Amelia turned back to the Machine and reached over to one of the dials. She did something to this, then pulled back the lever with the bicycle handle-bar attached.

Instantly, the Time Machine vanished!

ii

"Look at the clock on the wall, Edward."

"What have you done with the Machine?" I said.

"Never mind that . . . what is the time by the clock?"

I stared up. "Eighteen minutes to ten."

"Very well. At exactly sixteen minutes to ten the Machine will re-appear."

"From where?" I said.

"From the past . . . or, more precisely, from now. It is presently travelling through Time, to a point two minutes in the future of its departure."

"But why has it vanished? Where is it at this moment?"

"Within the attenuated Temporal Dimension."

Amelia stepped forward to where the Machine had been, and walked through the vacancy waving her arms. She glanced up at the clock.

"Stand well back, Edward. The Machine will re-appear exactly where it was."

"Then you must come away too," I said.

I pulled her by the arm, and held her close beside me a few yards from where the Machine had been. We both watched the clock. The second hand moved slowly round . . . and at exactly four seconds after sixteen minutes to ten, the Time Machine re-appeared.

"There!" said Amelia, triumphantly. "Just as I said."

I stared dumbly at the Machine. The great fly-wheel was turning slowly as before.

Amelia took my hand again. "Edward . . . we must now mount the Machine."

"What?" I said, appalled at the idea.

"It is absolutely imperative. You see, while Sir William has been testing the Machine he has incorporated a safety-device into it, which automatically returns the Machine to its moment of departure. That is activated exactly three minutes after its arrival here, and if we are not aboard it will be lost forever in the past."

I frowned a little at this, but said: "You could switch that off, though?"

"Yes ... but I'm not going to. I wish to prove that the Machine is no folly."

"I say you are drunk."

"And I say you are too. Come on!"

Before I could stop her, Amelia had skipped over to the Machine, squeezed under the brass rail and mounted the saddle. To do this she was obliged to raise her skirt a few inches above her ankles, and I confess that I found this sight considerably more alluring than any expedition through Time could have been.

She said: "The Machine will return in under a minute, Edward. Are you to be left behind?"

I hesitated no more. I went to her side, and clambered on to the saddle behind her. At her instruction I put my arms around her waist, and pressed my chest against her back.

She said: "Look at the clock, Edward."

I stared up at it. The time was now thirteen minutes to ten. The second hand reached the minute, moved on, then reached the time of four seconds past.

It stopped moving.

Then, it began to move in reverse ... slowly at first, then faster.

"We are travelling backwards in Time," Amelia said, a little breathlessly. "Do you see the clock, Edward?"

"Yes," I said, my whole attention on it. "Yes, I do!"

The second hand moved backwards through four minutes, then began to slow down. As it approached four seconds past eighteen minutes to ten it slowed right down, then halted altogether. Presently it began to sweep forward in a normal way.

"We are back at the moment in which I pressed the lever," said Amelia. "Do you now believe that the Time Machine is no fraud?"

I still sat with my arms around her waist, and our bodies were pressed together in the most intimate way imaginable. Her hair lay gently against my face, and I could think of nothing but the nearness of her.

"Show me again," I said, dreaming of an eternity of such closeness. "Take me into futurity!"

iii

"Can you see what I am doing?" Amelia said. "These dials can be pre-set to the very second. I can choose how many hours, days or even years we can travel."

I roused myself from my passionate imaginings, and peered over her shoulder. I saw her indicating a row of small dials, which were marked with days of the week, months of the year ... and then several others which counted tens, hundreds and then thousands of years.

"Please don't set our destination too far," I said, looking at the last dial. "I still have to think of my train."

"But we will return to our moment of departure, even if we should travel a hundred years!"

"Maybe so. Let us not be rash."

"If you are nervous, Edward, we need travel only as far as tomorrow."

"No ... let us make a long trip. You have shown me the Time Machine is safe. Let us go to the next century!"

"As you wish. We can go to the one beyond, if you prefer."

"It is the Twentieth Century I am interested in ... let us first go forward ten years."

"Only ten? That hardly seems adventurous."

"We must be systematic," I said, for although I am not faint-hearted, I am not an adventurous person. "Let us go first to 1903, and then to 1913, and so on at ten-yearly intervals through the century. Perhaps we will see a few changes."

"All right. Are you ready now?"

"That I am," I said, settling my arms about her waist again. Amelia made further adjustments to the dials. I saw her select the year 1903, but the day and month dials were too low for me to see.

She said: "I have selected 22nd June. That is the first day of summer, so we shall probably find the weather clement."

She placed her hands on the lever, and then straightened. I braced myself for our departure.

Then, much to my surprise, Amelia suddenly stood up and moved away from the saddle.

"Please wait for a moment, Edward," she said.

"Where are you going?" I said, in some alarm. "The Machine will take me with it."

"Not until the lever is moved. It is just. . . . Well, if we are going such a long distance, I should like to take my hand-bag."

"Whatever for?" I said, hardly believing my ears.

Amelia looked a little embarrassed. "I don't know, Edward. It is just that I never go anywhere without my hand-bag."

"Then bring your bonnet too," I said, laughing at this most unlikely revelation of feminine foibles.

She hastened from the laboratory. I stared blankly at the dials for a moment, then, on an impulse, I too dismounted and went into the hallway to collect my boater. If an expedition it was to be, I too would travel in style!

On a further impulse I walked into the drawing-room, poured some more port into the two glasses, and carried them back to the laboratory.

Amelia had returned before me, and was already mounted on the saddle. She had placed her hand-bag on the floor of the Machine, directly in front of the saddle, and on her head she wore her bonnet.

I passed one of the port-glasses to her. "Let us toast the success of our adventure."

"And futurity," she replied.

We each drank about half what was there, then I placed the glasses on a bench to one side. I climbed on to the saddle behind Amelia.

"We are now ready," I said, making sure my boater was firmly seated on my head.

Amelia gripped the lever in both hands, and pulled it towards her.

iv

The whole Time Machine lurched, as if it had somehow fallen headlong into an abyss, and I shouted aloud with alarm, bracing myself against the coming impact.

"Hold on!" Amelia said, somewhat unnecessarily, for I would not have released her for anything.

"What is happening?" I cried.

"We are quite safe . . . it is an effect of the attenuation."

I opened my eyes, and glanced timorously about the laboratory, and saw to my astonishment that the Machine was still firmly situated on the floor. The clock on the wall was already spinning insanely forwards, and even as I watched the sun came up behind the house and was soon passing quickly overhead. Almost before I had registered its passing, darkness fell again like a black blanket thrown over the roof.

I sucked in my breath involuntarily, and discovered that in so doing I had inadvertently inhaled several of Amelia's long hairs. Even in the immense distractions of the journey I found a moment to rejoice at this furtive intimacy.

Amelia shouted to me: "Are you frightened?"

This was no time for prevarication. "Yes!" I shouted back.

"Hold tight . . . there is no danger."

Our raised voices were necessary only as an expression of our excitement; in the attenuated dimension all was silent.

The sun came up, and set again almost as quickly. The next period of darkness was shorter, and the following daylight shorter still. The Time Machine was accelerating into futurity!

In what seemed to us only a few more seconds the procession of day and night was so fast as to be virtually undetectable, and our surroundings were visible only in a grey, twilight glow.

About us, details of the laboratory became hazy, and the image of the sun became a path of light seemingly fixed in a deep-blue sky.

When I spoke to Amelia I had lost the strands of her hair from my mouth. About me was a spectacular sight, and yet for all its wonder it did not compare with the feel of this girl in my arms. Prompted no doubt by the new infusion of port into my blood I became emboldened, and I moved my face nearer and took several strands of her hair between my lips. I raised my head slightly, allowing the hair to slide sensuously across my tongue. Amelia made no response I could detect, and so I allowed the strands to fall and took a few more. Still she did not stop me. The third time I tipped my head to one side, so as not to dislodge my hat, and pressed my lips gently but very firmly on the smooth white skin of her neck.

I was allowed to linger there for no more than a second, but then she sat forward as if in sudden excitement, and said: "The Machine is slowing, Edward!"

Beyond the glass roof the sun was now moving visibly slower, and the periods of dark, between the sun's passages, were distinct, if only as the briefest flickers of darkness.

Amelia started reading off the dials before her: "We are in December, Edward! January ... January 1903. February...."

One by one the months were called, and the pauses between her words were growing longer.

Then: "This is June, Edward ... we are nearly there!"

I glanced up at the clock for confirmation of this, but I saw that the device had unaccountably stopped.

"Have we arrived?" I said.

"Not quite."

"But the clock on the wall is not moving."

Amelia looked briefly at it. "No one has wound it, that is all."

"Then you will have to tell me when we arrive."

"The wheel is slowing ... we are almost at rest ... now!"

And with that word the silence of attenuation was broken. Somewhere just outside the house there was a massive explo-

sion, and some of the panes of glass cracked. Splinters fell
down upon us.

Beyond the transparent walls I saw that it was daytime and
the sun was shining ... but there was smoke drifting past, and
we heard the crackle of burning timber.

v

There came a second explosion, but this was further away. I
felt Amelia stiffen in my arms, and she turned awkwardly in
the saddle to face me.

"What have we come to?" she said.

"I cannot say."

Some distance away somebody screamed horribly, and as if
this were a signal the scream was echoed by two other voices. A
third blast occurred, louder than either of the previous two.
More panes cracked, and splinters tinkled down to the floor.
One piece fell on to the Time Machine itself, not six inches
from my foot.

Gradually, as our ears adapted to the confusion of sounds
around us, one noise in particular stood out above all others: a
deep-throated braying, rising like a factory siren, then howling
around the upper note. It drowned temporarily the crackle of
the fires and the cries of the men. The siren note fell away, but
then it was repeated.

"Edward!" Amelia's face was snow-white, and her voice had
become a high-pitched whisper. "What is happening?"

"I cannot imagine. We must leave. Take the controls!"

"I don't know how. We must wait for the automatic
return."

"How long have we been here?"

Before she could answer there was another shattering explosion.

"Hold still," I said. "We cannot be here much longer. We
have blundered into a war."

"But the world is at peace!"

"In our time, yes."

I wondered how long we had been waiting here in this hell of 1903, and cursed again that the clock was not working. It could not be long before the automatic return took us back through the safety of attenuation to our own blissfully peaceful time.

Amelia had turned her face so that it was now buried in my shoulder, her body twisted awkwardly on the saddle. I kept my arms around her, doing what I could to calm her in that fearful bedlam.

I looked around the laboratory, seeing how strangely it had changed from the first time I had seen it: debris was everywhere, and filth and dust overlaid everything bar the Time Machine itself.

Unexpectedly, I saw a movement beyond the walls of the laboratory, and looking that way I saw that there was someone running desperately across the lawn towards the house. As the figure came nearer I saw that it was that of a woman. She came right up to the wall, pressing her face against the glass. Behind her I saw another figure, running too.

I said: "Amelia ... look!"

"What is it?"

"There!"

She turned to look at the two figures, but just as she did two things happened simultaneously. One was a shattering explosion accompanied by a gust of flame erupting across the lawn and consuming the woman ... and the other was a vertiginous lurch from the Time Machine. The silence of attenuation fell about us, the laboratory appeared whole once more, and overhead began the reverse procession of day and night.

Still turned uncomfortably towards me, Amelia burst into tears of relief, and I held her in my arms in silence.

When she had calmed, she said: "What were you seeing just before we returned?"

"Nothing," I said. "My eyes deceived me."

There was no way I could describe to her the woman I had seen. She had been like a wild animal: hair matted and in disarray, blood disfiguring her face, clothes torn so as to reveal the nakedness beneath. Nor did I know how to say what was for me the greatest horror of all.

I had recognized the woman and knew her to be Amelia, suffering her dying moments in the hellish war of 1903!

I could not say this, could not even believe what I myself had seen. But it was so: futurity was real, and that was Amelia's real destiny. In June 1903, on the 22nd day, she would be consumed by fire in the garden of Sir William's house.

The girl was cradled in my arms, and I felt her trembling still. I could not allow that destiny to be fulfilled!

So it was, without understanding the precipitate nature of my actions, that I moved to avert destiny. The Time Machine would now carry us *further* into futurity, beyond that terrible day!

vi

I was in a mad trance. I stood up abruptly and Amelia, who had been leaning against me, stared up in astonishment. Over my head, the days and nights were flickering.

There was a startling and heady rush of sensations coursing through me, caused I suppose, by the vertigo of the attenuation, but also because some instinct was preparing me for the act that followed. I stepped forward, placing my foot on the floor of the Machine in front of the saddle, and supporting myself on the brass rail, I managed to crouch down in front of Amelia.

"Edward, what are you doing?" Her voice was trembling, and she sobbed as soon as her sentence was said. I paid her no attention, peering instead at the dials which were now but a few inches from my face.

In that uncanny light of the procession of days, I saw that the Machine was speeding backwards through Time. We were now in 1902, and I saw the needle pass from August to July as I first glanced at it. The lever, centrally mounted in front of the dials, was standing almost vertically, its attached nickel rods extending forwards into the heart of the crystalline engine.

I raised myself a little, and sat on the front of the saddle, causing Amelia to move back to accommodate me.

"You must not interfere with the controls," she said, and I felt her leaning to one side to see what I was doing.

I grasped the bicycle handle in both hands, and pulled it towards me. As far as I could see, this had no effect on our journey. July slipped back to June.

Amelia's concern became more urgent.

"Edward, you must not tamper!" she said loudly.

"We must go on into futurity!" I cried, and swung the handle-bar from side to side, as one does when cornering on a bicycle.

"*No!* The Machine must be allowed to return automatically!"

For all my efforts at the controls, the reverse procession continued smoothly. Amelia was now holding my arms, trying to pull my hands away from the lever. I noticed that above each of the dials was a small metal knob, and I took one of these in my hands. I saw, by turning it, that it was possible to change the setting of the destination. Evidently, this was the way to interrupt our progress, for as soon as Amelia realized what I was doing, her efforts to restrain me became violent. She was reaching, trying to take my hand, and when this failed she took a handful of my hair and snatched it painfully back.

At this, I released the controls, but my feet kicked instinctively forwards. The heel of my right boot made contact with one of the nickel rods attached to the main lever, and in that instant there was the most appalling lurch to one side, and everything went black around us.

vii

The laboratory had vanished, the procession of day and night had ceased. We were in absolute darkness and absolute silence.

Amelia's desperate hold on me eased, and we sat numbly in awe of the event that had overtaken us. Only the headlong vertigo—which had now taken on the characteristic of a sickening swoop from one side to another—told us that our journey through Time continued.

Amelia moved closer to me, wrapping her arms around my body, and pressed her face against my neck.

The swooping was growing worse, and I turned the handle-bar to one side, hoping to correct it. All I achieved was to introduce a new motion: a most unsettling pitching movement, complicating the ever-worsening sideways swing.

"I can't stop it!" I cried. "I don't know what to do!"

"What has happened to us?"

"You made me kick the lever," I said. "I felt something break."

We both gasped aloud then, for the Machine seemed to turn right over. Light suddenly burst in upon us, emanating from one brilliant source. I closed my eyes, for the brilliance was dazzling, and tried again to work the lever to ease our sickening motion. The erratic movements of the Machine were causing the point of light to waltz crazily about us, casting black shadows confusingly over the dials.

The lever had a new feel to it. The breaking of the rod had made it looser, and as soon as I tried to let go it would sag to one side, thus precipitating more of the violent sideways manoeuvres.

"If only I can find that broken rod," I said, and reached downwards with my free hand to see if I could find the pieces. As I did so, there was another swooping to one side, and I was all but unseated. Fortunately, Amelia had not relaxed her hold on me and with her help I struggled back upright.

"Do keep still, Edward," she said, softly and reassuringly. "So long as we are inside the Machine, we are safe. No harm can come to us while we are attenuated."

"But we might collide with something!"

"We cannot . . . we will pass through it."

"But what has happened?"

She said: "Those nickel rods are there to proscribe movement through Space. By dislodging one of them, you have released the Spatial Dimension, and we are now moving rapidly away from Richmond."

I was aghast at this thought, and the dizzying effect of our passage only emphasized the terrible dangers we were facing.

"Then where will we fetch up?" I said. "Who knows where the Machine will deposit us?"

Again, Amelia spoke in a reassuring voice: "We are in no danger, Edward. I grant you the Machine is careering wildly, but only its controls have been affected. The field of attenuation is still around us, and so the engine itself is still working. Now we are moving through Space, we are likely to traverse many hundreds of miles . . . but even if we should find ourselves a thousand miles from home, the automatic return will bear us safely back to the laboratory."

"A thousand miles . . .?" I said, horrified at the velocity at which we must be travelling.

She tightened her hold on me momentarily. "I think it will not be as far as that. It seems to me we are spinning wildly in a circle."

There was some substance in this, for even as we had been talking the point of light had been circling insanely around us. I was, naturally, comforted by what she said, but the sickening lurches continued, and the sooner this adventure was brought to its end the happier I would be. With this in mind, I decided to search again for the dislodged nickel rod.

I told Amelia what I was intending to do, and she reached forward to take the main lever in her hand. Thus freed from the necessity to hold on to the lever, I bent forward and groped on the floor of the Machine, dreading that the rod had been thrown to one side by our violent motion. I fumbled around in the erratic light, and felt Amelia's hand-bag where she had placed it, on the floor in front of the saddle. Thankfully, I found the rod a moment later: it had rolled and wedged itself between the front of the saddle and Amelia's bag.

"I've found it," I said, sitting up and holding it so that she could see it. "It is not broken."

"Then how was it dislodged?"

I looked more closely at it, and saw that at each end were helical screw shapings, and that at the tip of these were markings of bright metal which revealed how the rod had been torn from its sockets. I showed this to Amelia.

"I remember Sir William saying that some of the nickel

controls had been machined incorrectly," she said. "Can you replace it?"

"I shall try."

It took several more minutes of my fumbling in the eerie light to locate both of the metal bushes from which the rod had been torn, and then it took much longer to manipulate the lever so as to bring it into a suitable position so that I could fit the rod into the bushes.

"It's still too short!" I said in some desperation. "No matter how I try, the rod is too short."

"But it must have come from there!"

I found a way of loosening the bush on the lever itself, and this helped to some measure. Now the connection could be made at each end, and with great patience I managed to screw the rod into each of the two sockets (fortunately, Sir William had engineered the screws so that one turn tightened both connections). It was held, but only tenuously so, for barely half a turn had been possible.

I sat up wearily in the saddle, and Amelia's arms went around my waist. The Time Machine was still lurching, but far less so than before, and the movement of the brilliant point of light was almost imperceptible. We sat in its harsh glare, hardly believing that I had succeeded in correcting the terrible motion.

Directly in front of me the fly-wheel continued to turn quickly, but there had been no return to the orderly procession of day and night.

"I think we are safe again," I said, but I did not feel sure.

"We must soon be coming to a halt. As soon as the Machine is at rest, we must neither of us move. It will take three minutes for the automatic return to start."

"And will we be taken back to the laboratory?" I said.

Amelia hesitated before replying, and then said: "Yes." I felt she was no more sure than I.

Quite unexpectedly, the Time Machine gave another lurch, and we both gasped. I saw that the fly-wheel was still . . . and then I realized that air was whistling past us, chilling us instantly. I knew that we were no longer attenuated, that we were

falling . . . and in great desperation I reached forward to seize
the lever—

"*Edward!*" Amelia screamed in my ear.

It was the last thing I heard, for at that instant there was a
terrible concussion, and the Machine came to a sudden halt.
Both Amelia and I were catapulted from it into the night.

viii

I was lying in absolute darkness, seeming to be entirely covered
by something leathery and wet. As I tried to stand, all I could
accomplish was a futile thrashing with my arms and legs, and I
slid further into the morass of slippery stuff. A sheet of something fell across my face, and I thrust it aside, gasping for
breath. Suddenly I was coughing, trying to suck air into my
lungs, and like a drowning man I struck instinctively upwards,
feeling I should otherwise suffocate. There was nothing on
which I could get a hold, as everything that surrounded me was
soft, slippery and moist. It was as if I had been pitched head
first into an immense bank of seaweed.

I felt myself falling, and this time allowed myself to
go, despairing. I would surely drown in this dank foliage,
for with each turn of my head my face was covered with
the repulsive stuff. I could taste it now: a flat, iron-tainted
wateriness.

Somewhere near to hand I heard a gasp.

I shouted: "Amelia!"

My voice emerged as a wheezing croak, and at once I was
coughing again.

"Edward?" Her voice was high-pitched and frightened, and
then I heard her coughing too. She could not have been more
than a few yards away from me, but I could not see her, hardly
knew in which direction she lay.

"Are you unhurt?" I called, then coughed weakly again.

"The Time Machine, Edward. We must climb aboard . . . it
will be returning. . . ."

"Where is it?"

"I am by it. I cannot reach it, but I can feel it with my foot."

I realized she was over to my left, and I struck out that way, floundering through the noisome weeds, reaching out, hoping to strike something solid.

"Where are you?" I shouted, trying to make more of my voice than the wretched wheeze which was all I had so far managed.

"I am here, Edward. Come towards my voice." She was nearer now, but her words were strangely choked, as if she too were drowning. "I've slipped ... I can't find the Time Machine ... it's somewhere here. ..."

I struck desperately through the weed, and almost at once I found her. My arm fell across her chest, and as it did so she grabbed me.

"Edward ... we must find the Machine!"

"You say it is here?"

"Somewhere ... by my legs. ..."

I crawled over her, thrashing my arms to and fro, desperately seeking the Machine. Behind me, Amelia had somehow righted herself, and she moved to my side. Face down, slithering and sliding, coughing and wheezing, trembling with the cold that was even now seeping into our bones, we conducted our desperate search well beyond the three minutes neither of us would admit was all the time we had ever had to find it.

Chapter Six
FUTURITY'S ALIEN LAND

i

Our struggles had been leading us inevitably downwards, and after a few more minutes I found solid ground beneath my feet. At once, I shouted aloud and helped Amelia to her feet. We pressed forward again, trying to maintain our balance while the vegetation tangled around our legs. We were both soaked through, and the air was freezing cold.

At last we broke free of the vegetation, and found we were on rough, pebbly soil. We walked a few yards beyond the fringe of the vegetation then sank down in exhaustion. Amelia was shaking with cold, and she made no protest when I placed my arm around her and hugged her to me for warmth.

At last, I said: "We must find cover."

I had been glancing around, hoping to see houses, but all I could see by the light of the stars was an apparent wasteland. The only visible feature was the bank of vegetation, looming perhaps a hundred feet into the air.

Amelia had made no reply, and I could feel her shivering still, so I stood up and started to remove my jacket. "Please put this about your shoulders."

"But you will freeze to death."

"You are soaked through, Amelia."

"We are both wet. We must exercise to keep warm."

"In a moment," I said, and sat down beside her once more. I kept my jacket on, but I opened it so that she was partially covered by it when I placed my arm around her shoulders. "First I must regain my breath."

Amelia pressed herself close to me, then said: "Edward, where have we landed?"

"I cannot say. We are somewhere in futurity."

"But why is it so cold? Why is it so difficult to breathe?"

I could only surmise.

"We must be very high," I said. "We are in a mountainous region."

"But the ground is flat."

"Then we must be on a plateau," I said. "The air is thin because of the altitude."

"I think I have reached the same conclusion," Amelia said. "Last summer I was mountaineering in Switzerland, and on the higher peaks we found a similar difficulty with breathing."

"But this is obviously not Switzerland."

"We will have to wait until morning to discover our whereabouts," Amelia said, decisively. "There must be people near here."

"And suppose we are in a foreign country, which does seem probable?"

"I have four languages, Edward, and can identify several others. All we need to know is the location of the nearest town, and there we will likely find a British Consul."

Through all this I had been remembering that moment of violence I had glimpsed through the windows of the laboratory.

"We have seen that there is a war in 1903," I said. "Wherever we are now, or whichever year this is, could that war still be in progress?"

"We see no sign of it. Even if a war has started, innocent travellers will be protected. There are Consuls in every major city of the world."

She seemed remarkably optimistic under the circumstances, and I was reassured. On first realizing that we had lost the Machine I had been plunged into despair. Even so, our prospects were doubtful, to say the very least, and I wondered if Amelia appreciated the full scale of our disaster. We had very little money with us, and no knowledge of the political situation, the breakdown of which had certainly caused the war of 1903. For all we knew we could be in enemy territory, and were likely to be imprisoned as soon as we were discovered.

Our immediate problem—that of surviving the rest of the night exposed to the elements—grew worse with every moment. Fortunately, there was no wind, but that was the only clemency we were being afforded. The very soil beneath us was frozen hard, and our breath was clouding about our faces.

"We must exercise," I said. "Otherwise we will contract pneumonia."

Amelia did not dissent, and we climbed to our feet. I started jogging, but I must have been weaker than I knew, for I stumbled almost at once. Amelia too was having difficulties, for in swinging her arms about her head she staggered backwards.

"I am a little light-headed," I said, gasping unexpectedly.

"And I."

"Then we must not exert ourselves."

I looked around desperately; in this Stygian gloom all that could be seen was the bank of weeds silhouetted against the starlight. It seemed to me that dank and wet as they were, they offered the only hope of shelter, and I put this to Amelia. She had no better proposal, and so with our arms around one another we returned to the vegetation. We found a clump of fronds standing about two feet high, on the very edge of the growth, and I felt experimentally with my hands. The stalks seemed to be dry, and beneath them the ground was not as hard as that on which we had been sitting.

An idea came to me, and I took one of the stalks and broke it off with my hand. At once, I felt cold fluid run over my fingers.

"The plants issue sap if they are broken," I said, holding out the stalk for Amelia to take. "If we can climb under the leaves without snapping the branches, we should remain dry."

I sat down on the soil and began to move forward, feet first. Crawling gently in this fashion I was soon beneath the vegetation, and in a dark, silent cocoon of plants. A moment later, Amelia followed, and when she was beside me we lay still.

To say that lying there under the fronds was pleasant would be utterly misleading, but it was certainly preferable to being exposed on the plain. Indeed, as the minutes passed and we made no movement I felt a little more comfortable, and realized that the confinement of our bodies was warming us a little.

I reached out to Amelia, who was lying not six inches from me, and placed my hand on her side. The fabric of her jacket was still damp, but I sensed that she too was rather warmer.

"Let us hold each other," I said. "We must not get any colder."

I placed my arm around her back, and pulled her towards me. She came willingly enough, and soon we were lying together, face to face in the dark. I moved my head and our noses touched; I pressed forward and kissed her full on the lips.

At once she pulled her face away from mine.

"Please don't take advantage of me, Edward."

"How can you accuse me of that? We must stay warm."

"Then let us do just that. I do not want you to kiss me."

"But I thought—"

"Circumstance has thrown us together. Let us not forget that we barely know each other."

I could hardly believe my ears. Amelia's friendly manner during the day had seemed an unmistakable confirmation of my own feelings, and in spite of our dreadful situation her very presence was enough to inflame my passions. I had expected her to allow me to kiss her, and after this rebuff I lay in silence, hurt and embarrassed.

A few minutes later Amelia moved again, and kissed me briefly on my forehead.

"I'm very fond of you, Edward," she said. "Is that not enough?"

"I thought . . . well, I'd been feeling that you—"

"Have I said or done anything to indicate that I felt for you more than friendship?"

"Well . . . no."

"Then please, lie still."

She placed one of her arms around me, and pressed me to her a little more tightly. We lay like that for a long time, barely moving except to ease cramped muscles, and during the rest of that long night we managed to doze for only a few short periods.

Sunrise came more suddenly than either of us had expected. One moment we had been lying in that dark, silent growth, the next there was a brilliance of light, filtering through the fronds. We moved simultaneously in response, both sensing that the day ahead was to be momentous.

We rose painfully, and walked haltingly away from the vegetation, towards the sun. It was still touching the horizon, dazzlingly white. The sky above us was a deep blue. There were no clouds.

We walked for ten yards, then turned to look back at the bank of vegetation.

Amelia, who had been holding my arm, now clutched me suddenly. I too stared in amazement, for the vegetation stretched as far as we could see to left and right of us. It stood in a line that was generally straight, but parts of it advanced and others receded. In places the weeds heaped together, forming mounds two hundred feet or more in height. This much we could have expected from our experience of it during the night, but nothing could have warned us of the profoundest surprise of all: that there was not a stem, not a leaf, not a bulbous, spreading tuber lying grotesquely across the sandy soil that was not a vivid blood-red.

ii

We stared for a long time at that wall of scarlet plant-life, lacking the vocabulary to express our reactions to it.

The higher part of the weed-bank had the appearance of being smooth and rounded, especially towards its visible crest. Here it looked like a gentle, undulating hill, although by looking in more detail at its surface we could see that what appeared to be an unbroken face was in fact made up of thousands or millions of branches.

Lower down, in the part of the growth were we had laid, its appearance was quite different. Here the newer plants were growing, presumably from seeds thrown out from the main bulk of vegetation. Both Amelia and I remarked on a horrible feeling that the wall was inexorably advancing, throwing out new shoots and piling up its mass behind.

Then, even as we looked aghast at this incredible weed-bank, we saw that the impact of the sun's rays was having an effect, for from all along the wall there came a deep-throated groaning, and a thrashing, breaking sound. One branch moved, then another ... then all along that living cliff-face branches and stems moved in a semblance of unthinking animation.

Amelia clutched my arm again, and pointed directly in front of us.

"See, Edward!" she said. "My bag is there! We must have my bag!"

I saw that about thirty feet up the wall of vegetation there was what appeared to be a broken hole in the smooth-seeming surface. As Amelia started forward towards it, I realized that that must be the place where the Time Machine had so precipitately deposited us.

A few feet away, absurd in its context, lay Amelia's handbag, caught on a stem.

I hurried forward and caught up with Amelia, just as she was preparing to push through the nearest plants, her skirt raised almost to her knees.

"You can't go in there," I said. "The plants are coming to life!"

As I spoke to her a long, creeper-like plant snaked silently towards us, and a seed-pod exploded with a report like a pistol. A cloud of dust-like seeds drifted away from the plant.

"Edward, it is imperative that I have my bag!"

"You can't go up there to get it!"

"I must."

"You will have to manage without your powders and creams."

She glared angrily at me for a moment. "There is more in it than face-powder. Money ... and my brandy-flask. Many things."

She plunged desperately into the vegetation, but as she did so a branch creaked into apparent life, and raised itself up. It caught the hem of her skirt, tore the fabric and spun her round. She fell, screaming.

I hurried to her, and helped her away from the plants. "Stay here . . . I'll go."

Without further hesitation I plunged into that forest of groaning, moving stems, and scrambled towards where I had last seen her bag. It was not too difficult at first; I quickly learned which stems would, and which would not, bear my weight. As the height of the plants grew to a point where they were above my head I started to climb, slipping several times as the branch I gripped broke in my hand and released a flood of sap. All around me the plants were moving; growing and waving like the arms of a cheering crowd. Glancing up, I saw Amelia's hand-bag on one such stem, dangling some twenty feet above my head. I had managed to climb only three or four feet towards it. There was nothing here that would bear my weight.

There came a crashing noise a few yards to my right, and I ducked, imagining in my horror that some major trunk was moving into life . . . but then I saw that it had been Amelia's bag, slipping from its perch.

Thankfully, I abandoned my futile attempt to climb, and thrust myself through the waving lower stems. The noise of this riotous growth was now considerable, and when another seed-pod exploded by my ear I was temporarily deafened by it. My only thought now was to retrieve Amelia's bag and get away from this nightmare vegetation. Not caring where I placed my feet, nor how many stems I broke and how much I drenched myself, I pushed wildly through the stalks, seized the bag and headed at once for the edge of the growth.

Amelia was sitting on the ground, and I threw the bag down beside her. Unreasonably, I felt angry with her, although I knew it was simply a reaction to my terror.

As she thanked me for collecting the bag, I turned away from her and stared at the wall of scarlet vegetation. It was visibly much more disordered than before, with branches and stems swinging out from every place. In the soil at the very edge of the growth I saw new, pink seedlings appearing. The plants *were* advancing on us, slowly but relentlessly. I watched the process for a few minutes more, seeing how sap from the adult plants dripped down on the soil, crudely irrigating the new shoots.

When I turned back to Amelia she was wiping her face and hands with a piece of flannel she had taken from her bag. Beside her on the ground was her flask. She held this out to me.

"Would you like some brandy, Edward?"

"Thank you."

The liquor flowed over my tongue, immediately warming me. I took only one small mouthful, sensing that we should have to make last what we had.

With the rising of the sun, we both felt the benefit of its heat. We were evidently in an equatorial region, for the sun was rising steeply, and its rays were warm.

"Edward, come here."

I squatted on the ground in front of Amelia. She looked remarkably fresh, but then I realized that in addition to having had a cursory wash with her dampened face-flannel, she had brushed her hair. Her clothes, though, were in a dreadful state: the sleeve of her jacket had been torn, and there was a long rent in her skirt where the plant had swung her round. There were dirty pink streaks and stains all over her clothes. Glancing down at myself, I saw that my new suit had become equally spoiled.

"Would you like to clean yourself?" she said, offering me the flannel.

I took it from her, and wiped my face and hands.

"How do you come to have this with you?" I said, marvelling at the unexpected pleasure of washing myself.

"I have travelled a lot," she said. "One grows accustomed to anticipating any contingency."

She showed me that she had a traveller's tidy, containing as well as the face-flannel, a square of soap, a toothbrush, a mirror, a pair of folding nail-scissors and a comb.

I ran my hand over my chin, thinking I should soon need a shave, but that was one contingency she seemed not to have anticipated.

I borrowed her comb to straighten my hair, and then allowed her to tidy my moustache.

"There," she said, giving it a final twirl. "Now we are fit to re-enter civilization. But first, we must have some breakfast to sustain us."

She dipped into her bag and produced a large bar of Menier's chocolate.

"May I ask what else you have concealed in there?" I said.

"Nothing that will be of use to us. Now, we will have to ration this, for it is the only food I have. We shall have two squares each now, and a little more as we need it."

We munched the chocolate hungrily, then followed it with another mouthful of brandy.

Amelia closed her bag, and we stood up.

"We will walk in that direction," she said, pointing parallel to the wall of vegetation.

"Why that way?" I said, curious at her apparent resolution.

"Because the sun rose over there," she pointed across the desert, "and so the weed-bank must run from north to south. We have seen how cold it can be at night, therefore we can do no better than move southwards."

It was unassailable logic. We had walked several yards before an argument occurred to me.

"You assume we are still in the northern hemisphere," I said.

"Of course. For your information, Edward, I have already deduced where we have landed. It is so high and cold that this can only be Tibet."

"Then we are walking towards the Himalayas," I said.

"We will deal with that problem when we encounter it."

iii

We found that walking across this terrain was not easy. Although our surroundings became quite pleasant as the sun rose higher, and there was a distinct spring in our step, lent, we assumed, by the clean cold air and the altitude, we discovered that we tired readily and were forced to make frequent halts.

For about three hours we maintained a steady pace, by walking and resting at regular periods, and we took it in turns to carry the bag. I felt invigorated by the exercise, but Amelia did not find it easy; her breathing became laboured and she complained frequently of dizziness.

What we both found dispiriting was that the landscape had not changed from the moment we set out. With minor variations in size, the wall of vegetation ran in an unbroken line across the desert.

As the sun moved higher its radiant heat increased, and our clothes were soon completely dry. Unprotected as we were (Amelia's bonnet had no brim, and I had lost my straw hat in the weeds) we soon began to suffer the first effects of sunburn, and we both complained of an unpleasant tingling on the skin of our faces.

A further effect of the hotter sunshine was yet another change in the activity of the weeds. The unsettling life-like movement lasted for about an hour after sunrise, but now such movements were rare; instead, we could see that the seedlings were growing at a prodigious pace, and sap trickled down constantly from the higher shoots.

One matter had been troubling me ever since our accident, and as we walked along I felt I should bring it up.

I said: "Amelia, I do accept full responsibility for our predicament."

"What do you mean?"

"I should not have interfered with the Time Machine. It was a reckless thing to do."

"You are no more to blame than I. Please don't speak of it any more."

"But we may now be in danger of our lives."

"We shall have to face that together," she said. "Life will be intolerable if you continue blaming yourself. It was I ... who first tampered with the Machine. Our main concern ... now should be to return to. . . ."

I looked sharply at Amelia, and saw that her face had gone pale and her eyes were half closed. A moment later she staggered slightly, looked at me helplessly, then stumbled and fell full-length on the sandy soil, I rushed to her.

"Amelia!" I cried in alarm, but she did not move. I took her hand and felt for her pulse: it was faint, and irregular.

I had been carrying the bag, and I fumbled with the catch and threw it open. I searched frantically through the bag, knowing that what I sought would be somewhere there. After a moment I found it: a tiny bottle of smelling-salts. I unscrewed the top, and waved it under her nose.

The response was immediate. Amelia coughed violently, and tried to move away. I placed my arms around her shoulders, and helped her into a sitting position. She continued to cough, and her eyes were streaming with tears. Remembering something I had once seen I bent her over, gently pushing her head down towards her knees.

After five minutes she straightened and looked at me. Her face was still pale, and her eyes were watery.

"We have walked too long without food," she said. "I came over dizzy, and—"

"It must be the altitude," I said. "We will find some way down from this plateau as soon as possible."

I delved into her bag, and found the chocolate. We had still eaten only a fraction of what we had, so I broke off two more squares and gave them to her.

"No, Edward."

"Eat it," I said. "You are weaker than I am."

"We have just had some. We must make it last."

She took the broken-off squares and the rest of the chocolate, and put them firmly back inside the bag.

"What I should really like," she said, "is a glass of water. I'm very thirsty indeed."

"Do you suppose the sap of the plants is drinkable?"

"If we do not find any water, we will have to try it in the end."

I said: "When we were first thrown into the weeds I swallowed some of the sap. It was not unlike water, but rather bitter."

After a few more minutes Amelia stood up, a little unsteadily I thought, and declared that she was fit to continue. I made her take another sip of brandy before moving on.

But then, although we walked much more slowly, Amelia stumbled again. This time she did not lose consciousness, but said she felt as if she was about to be sick. We rested for a full thirty minutes, while the sun moved to its zenith.

"Please, Amelia, eat some more chocolate. I'm sure that all you are suffering from is lack of sustenance."

"I'm no more hungry than you," she said. "It is not that."

"Then what is it?"

"I cannot tell you."

"You do know what is the matter?"

She nodded.

"Then please tell me, and I can do something to help."

"You could do nothing, Edward. I shall be all right."

I knelt on the sand before her, and placed my hands on her shoulders. "Amelia, we do not know how much further we have to walk. We cannot go on if you are ill."

"I am not ill."

"It looks very much like it to me."

"I am uncomfortable, but not ill."

"Then please do something about it," I said, my concern changing abruptly to irritation.

She was silent for a moment, but then, with my assistance, climbed to her feet. "Wait here, Edward. I shall not be long."

She took her bag, and walked slowly towards the weed-bank. She stepped carefully through the lower plants, and headed towards a growth of higher stalks. When she reached these she turned round and looked in my direction, then crouched down and moved behind them.

I turned my back, assuming she would prefer her privacy.

Several minutes passed, and she did not emerge. I waited for a quarter of an hour, then began to get worried. There had been an absolute silence since she had disappeared ... but even in my growing sense of alarm I felt I should wait and respect her privacy.

I had just consulted my watch, and discovered that more than twenty minutes had passed, when I heard her voice.

"Edward ...?"

Without further delay I ran in her direction, racing through the scarlet vegetation towards where I had last seen her. I was tormented by the vision of some momentous disaster that had befallen her, but nothing could have prepared me for what I saw.

I came to a sudden halt, and immediately averted my gaze: Amelia had removed her skirt and blouse, and was standing in her underwear!

She held her skirt protectively over her body, and was looking at me with an expression of cowed embarrassment.

"Edward, I cannot get them off. . . . Please help me. . . ."

"What are you doing?" I cried in astonishment.

"It is my stays that are too tight ... I can hardly breathe. But I cannot unlace them." She sobbed more loudly, then went on: "I did not want you to know, but I have not been alone since yesterday. They are so tight ... please help me ..."

I cannot deny that I found her pathetic expression amusing, but I covered my smile and moved round behind her.

I said: "What do I do?"

"There are two laces ... they should be tied at the bottom with a bow, but I've accidentally knotted them."

I looked more closely, and saw what she had done. I worked at the knot with my fingernails, and loosened it without difficulty.

"There," I said, turning away. "It is free."

"Please undo it, Edward. I can't reach it myself."

The agonies I had been suppressing came abruptly to the surface. "Amelia, you cannot ask me to undress you!"

"I just want these laces undone," she said. "That is all."

Reluctantly I went back to her and started the laborious process of slipping the laces through the eyelets. When the task was half-completed, and part of the restraining garment was loose, I saw just how tight it had been on her body. The laces slipped out of the last two eyelets, and the corset came free. Amelia pulled it away from her, and tossed it casually to the ground. She turned towards me.

"I can't thank you enough, Edward. I think I should have died if I'd kept it on a moment longer."

Had it not been she who had turned towards me, I should have felt my presence most improper, for she had allowed the skirt to fall away and I could see that her chemise was manufactured of the lightest material, and that her bosom was most prominent I stepped towards her, feeling that I might make the affectionate gesture of a hug, but she moved backwards at once, and brought up the skirt to conceal herself again.

"You may leave me now," she said. "I can manage to dress on my own."

iv

When, a few minutes later, Amelia emerged from the weeds, she was fully dressed and carrying the corset between the handles of her bag.

I said: "Are you not going to discard that? It is manifestly uncomfortable to wear."

"Only for long periods," she said, looking very abashed. "I shall leave it off for the rest of the day, and wear it again tomorrow."

"I shall look forward to helping you," I said, sincerely.

"There is no need for that. By tomorrow we will be back in civilization, and I will hire a servant."

Since she was still flushed, and I was not a little excited, I felt it appropriate to say: "If my opinion is at all valuable to you I can assure you that your figure is just as trim without it."

"That is not to the point. Shall we continue on our way?"

She stepped away from me, and I followed.

All this had been a temporary distraction from our plight, for soon the sun had moved far enough towards the west for the weed-bank to start throwing a shadow. Whenever we walked through this we felt immediately much colder.

After another half an hour's walking I was just about to propose a rest, when Amelia suddenly halted and looked towards a shallow depression in the ground. She walked briskly towards it.

I followed her, and she said: "We shall have to bivouac again. I think we should prepare now."

"I agree in principle. But I feel we should walk as far as possible."

"No, this place is ideal. We shall stay the night here."

"In the open?"

"There is no need for that. We have time to prepare a camp-site before nightfall." She was regarding the depression with a calculating manner. "When I was in Switzerland I was shown how to build emergency shelters. We will need to make this hole rather deeper, and build up the sides. If you would do that, I will cut some of the fronds."

We argued for a few minutes—I felt we should take advantage of the daylight and press on—but Amelia had made up her mind. In the end, she removed her jacket and walked over to the weed-bank, while I crouched down and, with my hands, started to scoop out the sandy soil.

It took approximately two hours to construct a camp-site to our mutual satisfaction. By this time I had removed most of the larger pebbles from the depression, and Amelia had broken off a huge pile of the leafiest, fern-like branches. These we had laid in the depression, making a bonfire-like mound of leaves, into the base of which we proposed to insinuate ourselves.

The sun was now almost out of sight beyond the weed-bank, and we were both feeling cold.

"I think we have done all we can," Amelia said.

"Then shall we shelter inside?" I had now seen the wisdom of Amelia's wish for early preparation. Had we walked further we could never have made such elaborate precautions against the cold.

"Are you thirsty?"

"I'm all right," I said, but I was lying. My throat had been parched all day.

"But you have taken no liquid."

"I can survive the night."

Amelia indicated one of the long, creeper-like stalks that she had also brought to our bivouac. She broke off a piece and held it out to me. "Drink the sap, Edward. It is perfectly safe."

"It could be poisonous."

"No, I tried it earlier while I was removing my stays. It is quite invigorating, and I have suffered no ill-effects."

I placed the end of the stalk to my lips and sucked tentatively. At once my mouth was filled with cold liquid, and I swallowed it quickly. After the first mouthful, the flavour did not seem so unpleasant.

I said: "It reminds me of an iron-tonic I had as a child."

Amelia smiled. "So you too were given Parrish's Food. I wondered if you would notice the similarity."

"I was usually given a spoonful of honey, to take away the taste."

"This time you will have to manage without."

I said, boldly: "Maybe not."

Amelia looked sharply at me, and I saw the faint return of her earlier blush. I threw aside the creeper, then assisted Amelia as she climbed before me into our shelter for the night.

Chapter Seven
THE AWAKENING OF AWARENESS

i

We lay still, side by side, for a long time. Although Amelia had selected those plants she judged to be the driest of sap, we discovered that they were seeping beneath us. In addition, the slightest movement allowed the air to drift in from outside. I dozed for a while, but I cannot speak for Amelia.

Then, awakened by the insidious cold which was attacking my feet and legs, I felt Amelia stiffen beside me.

She said: "Edward, are we to die out here?"

"I think not," I said at once, for during the day the possibility had often occurred to me, and I had been trying to think of some reassurance to offer her. "We cannot have much further to travel."

"But we are going to starve!"

"We still have the chocolate," I said, "and as you yourself have observed, the sap of these weeds is nutritious."

This at least was true; my body hungered for solid food, but since taking the sap I had felt somewhat stronger.

"I fear we will die of exposure. I cannot live in this cold much longer."

I knew she was trembling, and as she spoke I heard her teeth chattering. Our bivouac was not all we had hoped.

"Please allow me," I said, and without waiting for her dissent I moved towards her and slid my arm beneath her head and shoulders. The rebuff of the night before was still a painful memory, so I was pleased when she came willingly, resting her head on my shoulder and placing an arm across my chest. I raised my knees a few inches so that she could slide her legs beneath mine. In doing this we dislodged some of our covering foliage, and it took several more seconds to redistribute them.

We lay still again, trying to recapture that comparative warmth we had had until we moved. Several more minutes passed in silence, and our closer contact began to bear fruit in that I felt a little warmer.

"Are you asleep, Edward?" Her voice was very soft.

"No," I said.

"I'm still cold. Do you think we should quickly cut some more leaves?"

"I think we should stay still. Warmth will come."

"Hold me tighter."

What followed that apparently simple remark I could never have imagined, even in my most improper fancies. Spontaneously, I brought my other hand across and hugged her to me; in the same moment Amelia too placed her arms fully about me, and we discovered we were embracing each other with an intimacy that made me throw aside caution.

Her face was pressed directly against the side of mine, and I felt it moving sensuously to and fro. I responded in kind, fully aware that the love and passion I had been suppressing were growing in me at an uncontrollable rate. In the back of my mind I sensed a sudden despair, knowing that later I would regret this abandonment, but I thrust it aside for my emotions were clamouring for expression. Her neck was by my mouth, and without any attempt at subterfuge I pressed my lips to it and kissed her firmly and with great feeling. Her response was to hold me yet tighter, and uncaring of how we dislodged our shelter we rolled passionately from one side to another.

Then at last I pulled myself away, and Amelia turned her face and pressed her lips against mine. I was now lying almost completely atop her, and my weight was on her. We broke apart eventually, and I held my face half an inch from hers.

I simply said, with all the sincerity of absolute truth: "I love you, Amelia."

She made no answer other than to press my face to hers once more, and we kissed as if we had never stopped. She was everything that could ever exist for me, and for that period at least the extraordinary nature of our immediate surroundings ceased to matter. I wanted simply that we should continue kissing forever. Indeed, by the very nature of her response, I assumed that Amelia was in accord. Her hand was behind my head, her fingers spread through my hair, and she was pressing me to her as we kissed.

Then she suddenly snatched her hand away, wrenched her face from mine, and she cried out aloud.

The tension drained away, and my body slumped. I fell forward across her, my face once more buried in the hollow of her shoulder. We lay immobile for many minutes, my breathing irregular and painful, my breath hot in the confined space. Amelia was crying, and I felt her tears trickle down her cheek and against the side of my face.

ii

I moved only once more, to ease a cramp in my left arm, and then I lay still again, most of my weight on Amelia.

For a long time my mind was blank; all desire to justify my actions to myself had drained as quickly as the physical passion. Drained also were the self-recriminations. I lay still, aware only of a slight bruising around my mouth, the residual flavour of Amelia's kiss and the strands of her hair which brushed my forehead.

She sobbed quietly for a few minutes more, but then became quiet. A few minutes later her breathing became regular, and I judged she had fallen asleep. Soon, I too could feel the fatigue of the day clouding my mind, and in due course I fell asleep.

I do not know how long I slept, but some time later I realized I was awake, yet still in the same position on top of Amelia. Our earlier problem of warmth was banished, for my whole body glowed with heat. I had slept in spite of the awkward angle in which I was lying, and now my back was badly cramped. I wanted to move, to rest from this position, and in addition I could feel the stiff collar of my shirt cutting into my neck and at the front the brass stud was biting into my throat, but I did not want to rouse Amelia. I decided to lie still, and hope to fall asleep again.

I found that my spirits were high, and this in spite of all that had happened. Considered objectively our chances of survival seemed slim; Amelia had also realized this. Unless we were to reach civilization within the next twenty-four hours it was likely we would perish out here on this plateau.

However, I could not forget that glimpse I had had of Amelia's future destiny.

I knew that if Amelia were to be living in Richmond in the year 1903 she would be killed in the conflagration about the house. I had not been rational at the time, but my irresponsible tampering with the Time Machine had been an instinctive response to this. That accident had precipitated our current predicament, but I was in no way sorry.

Wherever on Earth we were, and in whatever year, I had decided what we were to do. From now I would make it my business to see that Amelia would never return to England until that day had passed!

I had already declared my love for her, and she had seemed to respond; it would be no greater step to avow my love as being eternal, and propose marriage. Whether she would accept I could not say, but I was determined to be resolute and patient. As my wife, she would be subject to my will. Of course, she was clearly of gentle birth, and my own origins were more humble, but I argued to myself that this had not so far been allowed to affect our behaviour to one another; she was an emancipationist, and if our love were true it would not be marred by—

"Are you awake, Edward?"

Her voice was close by my ear.

"Yes. Did I wake you?"

"No . . . I've been awake for some time. I heard your breathing change."

"Is it daylight yet?" I said.

"I don't think so."

"I think I should move," I said. "My weight must be crushing you."

Her arms, which were still around my back, tightened momentarily.

"Please stay as you are," she said.

"I do not wish to seem to be taking advantage of you."

"It is I who is taking the advantage. You are an excellent substitute for blankets."

I lifted myself slightly away from her, so that my face was directly above hers. Around us, the leaves rustled in the darkness.

I said: "Amelia, I have something to say to you. I am passionately in love with you."

Once again her arms tightened their hold, pulling me down so that my face was alongside hers.

"Dear Edward," she said, hugging me affectionately.

"Do you have nothing else to say?"

"Only . . . only that I'm sorry for what happened."

"Do you not love me too?"

"I'm not sure, Edward."

"Will you marry me?"

I felt her head move: it was shaking from side to side, but beyond this she made no answer.

"Amelia?"

She maintained her silence, and I waited anxiously. She was now quite immobile, her arms resting across my back but exerting no pressure of any kind.

I said: "I cannot conceive of life without you, Amelia. I have known you for such a short time, and yet it is as if I have been with you all my life."

"That is how I feel," she said, but her voice was almost inaudible, and her tone was lifeless.

"Then please marry me. When we reach civilization we will find a British Consul or a missionary church, and we may marry at once."

"We should not talk of these things."

I said, for my spirits were low: "Are you refusing me?"

"Please, Edward. . . ."

"Are you already engaged to another?"

"No, and I am not refusing you. I say we must not talk of

this because of the uncertainty of our prospects. We do not even know in which country we are. And until then. . . ."

Her voice tailed away, sounding as uncertain as her argument.

"But tomorrow," I went on, "we will find where we are, and will you then present another excuse? I'm asking only one thing: do you love me as much as I love you?"

"I don't know, Edward."

"I love you dearly. Can you say that to me?"

Unexpectedly, her head turned and for a moment her lips pressed gently against my cheek. Then she said: "I am unusually fond of you, Edward dear."

I had to be content with that. I raised my head, and brought my lips down to hers. They touched for a second, but then she turned her head away.

"We were foolish before," she said. "Let us not make the same mistake. We have been forced to pass a night together, and neither of us should take advantage of the other."

"If that is how you see it."

"My dear, we must not assume that we will not be discovered. For all we know, this might be someone's private estate."

"You have not suggested that before."

"No, but we may not be as alone as we think."

"I doubt if anyone will investigate a mound of leaves!" I said.

She laughed then, and hugged me. "We must sleep. We may have another long walk ahead of us."

"Are you still comfortable in this position?"

"Yes. And you?"

I said: "My collar is hurting me. Would you consider it improper if I were to remove my tie?"

"You are always so formal! Let me do it for you . . . it must be choking you."

I raised myself away from her, and with deft fingers she loosened the knot and released both front and back studs. When this was done I lowered myself, and felt her arms closing about my back. I pressed the side of my face to hers, kissed her once on the lobe of her ear, and then we lay still, waiting for sleep to return.

iii

We were awakened not by the rising sun, as our covering leaves effectively filtered the light to an almost imperceptible maroon glow, but by the creaking and groaning of the near-by weed-bank. Amelia and I lay in each other's arms for a few minutes before rising, as if sensing that the warmth and intimacy of the overnight tryst should be savoured. Then at last we kicked and pushed the scarlet leaves aside, and emerged into the brilliant daylight and hard radiant heat. We stretched elaborately, each of us stiff from the enforced stillness of the night.

Our morning toilet was brief, our breakfast briefer. We wiped our faces with Amelia's flannel, and combed our hair. We each took two squares of chocolate, and followed them with a draught of sap. Then we collected our few belongings, and prepared to continue on our way. I noticed that Amelia still carried her corset between the handles of her bag.

"Shall we not leave that behind?" I said, thinking how pleasant it would be if she were never to wear it again.

"And these?" she said, producing my collar and tie from the hand-bag. "Shall we leave these behind too?"

"Of course not," I said. "I must wear them when we find civilization."

"Then we are agreed."

"The difference is," I said, "that I do not need a servant. Nor have I ever had one."

"If your intentions for me are sincere, Edward, you must prepare yourself for the prospect of hiring staff."

Amelia's tone was as non-committal as ever, but the unmistakable reference to my proposal had the effect of quickening my heart. I took the bag from her, and held her hand in mine. She glanced at me once, and I thought I saw a trace of a smile, but then we were walking and we each kept our gaze directed ahead. The weed-bank was in the full throes of its seeming animation, and we stayed at a wary distance from it.

Knowing that most of our walking must be done before midday, we maintained a good pace, walking and resting at regular periods. As before, we found that the altitude made breathing difficult, and so we talked very little while we were walking.

During one of our rests, though, I brought up a subject which had been occupying me.

"In which year do you suppose we are?" I said.

"I have no idea. It depends on the degree to which you tampered with the controls."

"I didn't know what I was doing. I altered the monthly pre-setting dial, and it was then during the summer months of 1902. But I did not move the lever before I broke the nickel rod, and so I am wondering whether the automatic return was not interrupted, and we are now in 1893."

Amelia considered this for several moments, but then said: "I think not. The crucial act was the breaking of that rod. It would have interrupted the automatic return, and extended the original journey. At the end of that, the automatic return would come into operation again, as we found when we lost the Machine. On the other hand, your changing of the monthly dial might have had an effect. By how much did you alter it?"

I thought about this with great concentration. "I turned it several months forward."

"I still cannot say for certain. It seems to me that we are in one of three possible times. Either we returned to 1893, as you suggest, and are dislocated by several thousand miles, or the accident has left us in 1902, at the date showing on the dials when the rod was broken . . . or we have travelled forward those few months, and are now at, say, the end of 1902 or the beginning of 1903. In any event, one matter is certain: we have been propelled a considerable distance from Richmond."

None of these postulations was welcome, for any one of them meant that the disastrous day in June 1903 still lay ahead. I did not wish to dwell on the consequences of this, so I raised another topic that had been troubling me.

"If we were now to return to England," I said, "is it likely that we could meet ourselves?"

Amelia did not answer my question directly. She said: "What do you mean, *if* we were to return to England? Surely we will arrange that as soon as possible?"

"Yes, of course," I said, hastily, regretting that I had phrased my question in that way. "So it is not a rhetorical question: are we soon to meet ourselves?"

Amelia frowned.

"I don't think it is possible," she said at length. "We have travelled in Time just as positively as we have travelled in Space, and if my own belief is correct, we have left the world of 1893 as far behind as we seem to have left Richmond. There is at this moment neither Amelia Fitzgibbon nor Edward Turnbull in England."

"Then what," I said, having anticipated this answer, "will Sir William have made of our disappearance?"

Amelia smiled unexpectedly. "I'm sure I do not know. Nor am I sure that he will even notice my absence until several days have passed. He is a man of great preoccupations. When he realizes I have gone, I suppose he will contact the police and I will be listed as a Missing Person. That much at least he will see as his responsibility."

"But you talk of this with such coldness. Surely Sir William will be most concerned at your disappearance?"

"I am merely speaking the facts as I see them. I know that he was preparing his Time Machine for a journey of exploration, and had we not pre-empted him he would have been the first man to travel into futurity. When he returns to his laboratory he will find the Machine apparently untouched—for it would have returned directly from here—and he will continue with his plans without regard for the household."

I said: "Do you think that if Sir William were to suspect the cause of your disappearance he might use the Machine to try to find us?"

Amelia shook her head at once. "You assume two things.

First, that he would realize that we had tampered with the Machine, and second, that even if so he would know where to search for us. The first is almost impossible to suspect, for to all appearances the Machine will appear untouched, and the second is unthinkable, as the Machine has no record of its journeys when the automatic return has been in operation."

"So we must make our own way back."

At this, Amelia came a little closer and grasped my hand.

"Yes, my dear," she said.

iv

The sun was past its zenith, and already the weed-bank was throwing a shadow, and we walked stoically on. Then, just as I was feeling we should stop for another rest, I caught Amelia's elbow and pointed forward.

"Look, Amelia!" I shouted. "There . . . on the horizon!"

Directly in front of us was the most welcome sight either of us could have imagined. Something metallic and polished was ahead of us, for the sun's rays were being reflected off into our eyes. The steadiness of the dazzle was such that we knew it could not be coming from a natural feature, such as a sea or a lake. It was man-made, and our first sight of civilization.

We started towards it, but in a moment the glare vanished.

"What has happened?" Amelia said. "Did we imagine it?"

"Whatever it was, it has moved," I said. "But it was no illusion."

We walked as quickly as we could, but we were still suffering the effects of altitude and were forced to maintain our usual steady pace.

Within two or three minutes we saw the reflected light again, and knew we had not been mistaken. At last sense prevailed and we took a short rest, eating the remainder of our chocolate and drinking as much of the sap as we could stomach. Thus fortified, we continued towards the intermittent light, knowing that at last our long walk was nearly over.

After another hour we were close enough to see the source of the reflection, although by then the sun had moved further across the sky and it had been some time since we had seen the dazzle. There was a metal tower built in the desert, and it was the roof of this that had been catching the sunshine. In this rarefied atmosphere distances were deceptive, and although we had been able to see the tower for some time, it wasn't until we were almost on it that we were able to estimate its size. By then we were close enough to see that it was not alone, and that some distance beyond it were several more.

The overall height of the nearest tower was about sixty feet. In appearance, the nearest analogy I can draw is that of a huge, elongated pin, for the tower consisted of a thin central pillar, surmounted by a circular enclosed platform. This description is itself misleading, for there was not one central pillar, but three. These were built very closely together, though, and ran parallel to each other up to the platform they supported, so it was only as we walked beneath the tower that Amelia and I noticed this. These three pillars were firmly buried in the soil but staring up at them I noticed that the platform was capable of being raised or lowered, for the pillars were jointed in several places and made of telescopic tubes.

The platform at the top was perhaps ten feet in diameter, and about seven feet high. On one side there was what seemed to be a large oval window, but this was made of dark glass and it was impossible to see beyond it from where we stood. Beneath the platform was a mechanical mounting, rather like gimbals, and it was this that enabled the platform to rotate slowly to and fro, thus causing the sun's reflection to flash at us earlier. The platform was moving from side to side now, but apart from this there was no sign of anyone about.

"Hallo up there!" I called, then after a few seconds repeated the call. Either they could not hear me, or my voice was weaker than I had realized, but there was no reply from the occupants.

While I had been examining the tower, Amelia had moved past me and was staring towards the weed-bank. We had walked diagonally away from the vegetation to visit the tower, but now I saw that the bank here was even further away than I would have expected, and much lower. What was more, working at the base of it were many people.

Amelia turned towards me, and I could see the joy in her expression.

"Edward, we're safe!" she cried, and came towards me and we embraced warmly.

Safety indeed it was, for this was clear evidence of the habitation we had been seeking for so long. I was all for going over to the people at once, but Amelia delayed.

"We must make ourselves presentable," she said, and fumbled inside her bag. She passed me my collar and tie, and while I put these on she sat down and fussed with her face. After this she tried to dab off some of the worst weed-stains from her clothes, using her face-flannel, and then combed her hair. I was in dire need of a shave, but there was nothing that could be done about that.

Apart from our general untidiness, there was another matter that was troubling us both. Our long hours exposed to the hot sunshine had left their mark, in the fact that we were both suffering from sunburn. Amelia's face had gone a bright pink—and she told me mine was no better—and although she had applied some cold-cream from a pot in her bag, she said she was suffering considerably.

When we were ready, she said: "I will take your arm. We do not know who these people are, so it would be wise not to give the wrong impression. If we behave with confidence, we will be treated correctly."

"And what about that?" I said, indicating her corset, all too evident between the handles of her bag. "Now is the time to discard it. If we wish to appear as if we have been enjoying an afternoon stroll, that will make it clear we have not."

Amelia frowned, evidently undecided. At last she picked it and placed it on the soil, so that it leaned against one of the pillars of the tower.

"I'll leave it here for the moment," she said. "I can soon find it again when we have spoken to the people."

She came back to me, took my arm and together we walked

sedately towards the nearest of the people. Once again the clear air had deceived our eyes, and we soon saw that the weeds were farther away than we had imagined. I glanced back just once, and saw that the platform at the top of the tower was still rotating to and fro.

Walking towards the people—none of whom had yet noticed us—I saw something that rather alarmed me. As I wasn't sure I said something about it to Amelia, but as we came closer there was no mistaking it: most of the people—and there were both men and women—were almost completely unclothed.

I stopped at once, and turned away.

"I had better go forward alone," I said. "Please wait here."

Amelia, who had turned with me, for I had grasped her arm, stared over her shoulder at the people.

"I am not as coy as you," she said. "From what are you trying to protect me?"

"They are not decent," I said, very embarrassed. "I will speak to them on my own."

"For Heaven's sake, Edward!" Amelia cried in exasperation. "We are about to starve to death, and you smother me with modesty!"

She let go of my arm, and strode off alone. I followed immediately, my face burning with my embarrassment. Amelia headed directly for the nearest group: about two dozen men and women who were hacking at the scarlet weeds with long-bladed knives.

"You!" she cried, venting her anger with me on the nearest man. "Do you speak English?"

The man turned sharply and faced her. For an instant he looked at her in surprise—and in that moment I saw that he was very tall, that his skin was burned a reddish colour, and that he was wearing nothing more than a stained loincloth—and then prostrated himself before her. In the same instant, the other people around him dropped their knives and threw themselves face down on the ground.

Amelia glanced at me, and I saw that the imperious manner

had gone as quickly as it had been assumed. She looked frightened, and I went and stood by her side.

"What's the matter?" she said to me in a whisper. "What have I done?"

I said: "You probably scared the wits out of them."

"Excuse me," Amelia said to the people, in a much gentler voice. "Does any one of you speak English? We are very hungry, and need shelter for the night."

There was no response.

"Try another language," I said.

"*Excusez-moi, parlez-vous français?*" Amelia said. There was still no response, so she added: "*¿Habla usted Español?*" She tried German, and then Italian. "It's no good," she said to me in the end. "They don't understand."

I went over to the man whom Amelia had first addressed, and squatted down beside him. He raised his face and looked at me, and his eyes seemed haunted with terror.

"Stand up," I said, accompanying the words with suitable hand-gestures. "Come on, old chap . . . on your feet."

I put out a hand to assist him, and he stared back at me. After a moment he climbed slowly to his feet and stood before me, his head hanging.

"We aren't going to hurt you," I said, putting as much sympathy into my words as possible, but they had no effect on him. "What are you doing here?"

With this I looked at the weed-bank in a significant way. His response was immediate: he turned to the others, shouted something incomprehensible at them, then reached down and snatched up his knife.

At this I took a step back, thinking that we were about to be attacked, but I could not have been more wrong. The other people clambered up quickly, took their knives and continued with the work we had interrupted, hacking and slashing at the vegetation like men possessed.

Amelia said quietly: "Edward, these are just peasants. They have mistaken us for overseers."

"Then we must find out who their real supervisors are!"

We stood and watched the peasants for a minute or so longer.

The men were cutting the larger stems, and chopping them into more manageable lengths of about twelve feet. The women worked behind them, stripping the main stems of branches, and separating fruit or seed-pods as they found them. The stems were then thrown to one side, the leaves or fruit to another. With every slash of the knife quantities of sap issued forth, and trickled from the plants already cut. The area of soil directly in front of the weed-bank was flooded with the spilled sap, and the peasants were working in mud up to twelve inches deep.

Amelia and I walked on, carefully maintaining a distance from the peasants and walking on soil that was dry. Here we saw that the spilled sap was not wasted; as it oozed down from where the peasants were working it eventually trickled into a wooden trough that had been placed in the soil, and flowed along in a relatively liquid state, accumulating all the way.

"Did you recognize the language?" I said.

"They spoke too quickly. A guttural tongue. Perhaps it was Russian."

"But not Tibetan," I said, and Amelia frowned at me.

"I based that guess on the nature of the terrain, and our evident altitude," she said. "I think it is pointless continuing to speculate about our location until we find someone in authority."

As we moved along the weed-bank we came across more and more of the peasants, all of whom seemed to be working without supervison. Their conditions of work were atrocious, as in the more crowded areas the spilled sap created large swamps, and some of the poor wretches were standing in muddy liquid above their waists. As Amelia observed, and I could not help but agree, there was much room for reform here.

We walked for about half a mile until we reached a point where the wooden trough came to a confluence with three others, which flowed from different parts of the weed-bank. Here the sap was ducted into a large pool, from which it was pumped by several women using a crude, hand-operated device into a subsidiary system of irrigation channels. From where we were standing we could see that these flowed alongside and through a large area of cultivated land. On the far side of this stood two more of the metal towers.

Further along we saw that the peasants were cutting the weed on the slant, so that as we had been walking parallel to their workings we eventually found what it was that lay beyond the bank of weeds. It was a water-course, some three hundred yards wide. Its natural width was only exposed by the cropping of weeds, for when we looked to the north, in the direction from which we had walked, we saw that the weeds so choked the waterway that in places it was entirely blocked. The total width of the weed-bank was nearly a mile, and as the opposite side of the waterway was similarly overgrown, and with another crowd of peasants cutting back the weed, we realized that if they intended to clear the entire length of the waterway by hacking manually through the weeds then the peasants were confronted with a task that would take them many generations to accomplish.

Amelia and I walked beside the water, soon leaving the peasants behind. The ground was uneven and pitted, presumably because of the roots of the weeds which had once grown here, and the water was dark-coloured and undisturbed by ripples. Whether it was a river or a canal was difficult to say; the water was flowing, but so slowly that the movement was barely perceptible, and the banks were irregular. This seemed to indicate that it was a natural watercourse, but its very straightness belied this assumption.

We passed another metal tower, which had been built at the edge of the water, and although we were now some way from where the peasants were cutting back the weed there was still much activity about us. We saw carts carrying the cut weed being manhandled along, and several times we came across groups of peasants walking towards the weed-bank. In the fields to our left were many more people tilling the crops.

Both Amelia and I were tempted to go across to the fields and beg for something to eat—for surely food must be there in abundance—but our first experience with the peasants had made us wary. We reasoned that some kind of community, even be it just a village, could not be far away. Indeed, ahead of us we had already seen two large buildings, and we were walking faster, sensing that there lay our salvation.

v

We entered the nearer of the two buildings, and immediately discovered that it was a kind of warehouse, for most of its contents were huge bales of the cut weed, neatly sorted into types. Amelia and I walked through the ground area of the building, still seeking someone to whom we could talk, but the only people there were more of the peasants. As all their fellows had done, these men and women ignored us, bending over their tasks.

We left this building by the way we had entered: a huge metal door, which was presently held open by an arrangement of pulleys and chains. Outside, we headed for the second building, which was about fifty yards from the first. Between the two stood another of the metal towers.

We were passing beneath this tower when Amelia took my hand in hers, and said: "Edward, listen."

There was a distant sound, one attenuated by the thin air, and for a moment we could not locate its source. Then Amelia stepped away from me, towards where there was a long metal rail, raised about three feet from the ground. As we walked towards it, the sound could be identified as a queer grating and whining sound, and looking down the rail towards the south we saw that coming along it was a kind of conveyance.

Amelia said: "Edward, could that be a railway train?"

"On just one rail?" I said. "And without a locomotive?"

However, as the conveyance slowed down it became clear that a railway train was exactly what it was. There were nine coaches in all, and without much noise it came to a halt with its front end just beyond where we had been standing. We stared in amazement at this sight, for it looked to all appearances as if the carriages of a normal train had broken away from their engine. But it was not this alone that startled us. The carriages seemed to be unpainted, and were left in their unfinished metal; rust showed in several places. Furthermore, the carriages themselves were not built in the way one would expect, but were tubular. Of the nine carriages, only two—the front and the rear—bore any conceivable resemblance to the sort of trains on which Amelia and I regularly travelled in England. That is to say that these had doors and a few windows, and as the train halted we saw several passengers descending. The seven central carriages, though, were like totally enclosed metal tubes, and without any apparent door or window.

I noticed that a man was stepping down from the front of the train, and seeing that there were windows placed in the very front of the carriage I guessed that it was from there he drove the train. I pointed this out to Amelia, and we watched him with great interest.

That he was not of the peasant stock was evident, for his whole manner was assured and confident, and he was neatly dressed in a plain grey outfit. This comprised an unadorned tunic or shirt, and a pair of trousers. In this he seemed no differently dressed from the passengers, who were clustering around the seven central carriages. All these people were similar in appearance to the peasants, for they were of the reddish skin coloration, and very tall. The driver went to the second carriage and turned a large metal handle on its side. As he did this, we saw that on each of the seven enclosed carriages large doors were moving slowly upwards, like metal blinds. The men who had left the train clustered expectantly around these doors.

Within a few seconds, there was a scene of considerable confusion.

We saw that the seven enclosed carriages had been packed to capacity with men and women of peasant stock, and as the doors were wound open these stumbled or clambered on the ground, spilling out all around the train.

The men in charge moved amongst the peasants, brandishing what had seemed to us on first sight to be short canes or sticks, but which now appeared to have a vicious and peremptory function. Some kind of electrical accumulator was evidently within the sticks, for as the men used them to herd the peasants into ranks, any unfortunate soul who was so much as brushed by the stick received a nasty electrical shock, accompanied by a brilliant flash of green light and a loud hissing sound. The hapless recipients of these shocks invariably fell to the ground, clutching the part of the anatomy that had been afflicted, only to be dragged to their feet again by their fellows.

Needless to say, the wielders of these devilish instruments had little difficulty in bringing order to the crowd.

"We must bring a stop to this at once!" Amelia said. "They are treating them no better than slaves!"

I think she was all for marching forward and confronting the men in charge, but I laid my hand on her arm to restrain her.

"We must see what is happening," I said. "Wait a while ... this is not the moment to interfere."

The confusion persisted for a few minutes more, while the peasants were force-marched towards the building we had not yet visited. Then I noticed that the doors of the enclosed carriages were being wound down into place again, and that the man who had driven the train was moving towards the far end.

I said: "Quickly, Amelia, let us board this train. It is about to leave."

"But this is the end of the line."

"Precisely. Don't you see? It is now going to go in the opposite direction."

We hesitated no more, but walked quickly across to the train and climbed into the passenger compartment that had been at the front. None of the men with the electrical whips paid the least bit of attention to us, and no sooner were we inside than the train moved slowly forward.

I had expected the motion to be unbalanced—for with only one rail I could not see that it would be otherwise—but once moving the train had a remarkably smooth passage. There was not even the noise of wheels, but simply a gentle whirring noise from beneath the carriage. What we were most appreciative of in those first few seconds, though, was the fact that the carriage was heated. It had been growing cold outside, for it was not long to sunset.

The seating arrangements inside were not too dissimilar

THE AWAKENING OF AWARENESS   117

from what we were accustomed to at home, although there were no compartments and no corridor. The inside of the carriage was open, so that it was possible to move about from one part to another, and the seats themselves were metal and uncushioned. Amelia and I took seats by one of the windows, looking out across the waterway. We were alone in the carriage.

During the entire journey, which took about half an hour, the scenery beyond the windows did not much change. The railway followed the bank of the waterway for most of the distance, and we saw that in places the banks had been reinforced with brick cladding, thus tending to confirm my early suspicion that the waterway was in fact a large canal. We saw a few small boats plying along it, and in several places there were bridges across it. Every few hundred yards the train would pass another of the metal towers.

The train stopped just once before reaching its destination. On our side of the train it looked as if we had halted at a place no larger than where we had boarded, but through the windows on the other side of the carriage we could see a huge industrial area, with great chimneys issuing copious clouds of smoke, and furnaces setting up an orange glow in the dark sky. The moon was already out, and the thick smoke drifted over its face.

While we were waiting for the train to re-start, and several peasants were being herded aboard, Amelia opened the door briefly and looked up the line, in the direction in which we were heading.

"Look, Edward," she said. "We are coming to a city."

I leaned outside too, and saw in the light of the setting sun that a mile or two further on there were many large buildings, clustered together untidily. Like Amelia, I was relieved at this sight, for the all-apparent barbarities of life in the countryside had repelled me. Life in any city, however foreign, is by its nature familiar to other city-dwellers, and there we knew we would find the responsible authorities we were seeking. Whatever this country, and however repressive their local laws, we as travellers would receive favoured treatment, and as soon as Amelia and I had come to agreement (which was itself a matter I had still to resolve) we would be bound, by sea or rail, for England. Instinctively, I patted my breast pocket to make sure my wallet was still there. If we were to return immediately to England what little money we had with us—we had established earlier in the day that we had two pounds fifteen shillings and sixpence between us—would have to be used as a surety of our good faith with the Consul.

Such reassuring thoughts were in my mind as the train moved steadily towards the city. The sun had now set, and the night was upon us.

"See, Edward, the evening star is bright."

Amelia pointed to it, huge and blue-white, a few degrees above the place of the sun's setting. Next to it, looking small, and in quarter-phase, was the moon.

I stared at the evening star, remembering Sir William's words about the planets which made up our solar system. There was one such, lonely and beautiful, impossibly distant and unattainable.

Then Amelia gasped, and I felt my heart tighten in the same moment.

"Edward," she said. "There are *two* moons visible!"

The mysteries of this place could no longer be ignored. Amelia and I stared at each other in horror, understanding at long last what had become of us. I thought of the riotous growth of scarlet weed, the thinness of the atmosphere, the freezing cold, the unfiltered heat of the sun, the lightness in our tread, the deep-blue sky, the red-bodied people, the very alienness of all that surrounded us. Now, seeing the two moons, and seeing the evening star, there was a final mystery, one which placed an intolerable burden on our ability to support our dearest belief, that we were still on our home world. Sir William's Machine had taken us to futurity, but it had also borne us unwittingly through the dimension of Space. A Time Machine it might be, but also a Space Machine, for now both Amelia and I accepted the frightful knowledge that in some incredible way we had been brought to another world, one where our own planet was the herald of night. I stared down at the canal, seeing the brilliant point of light that was Earth reflecting from the water, and knew only desperation and a terrible fear. For we had been transported through Space to Mars, the planet of war.

Chapter Eight
THE CITY OF GRIEF

i

I moved across to sit next to Amelia, and she took my hand.

"We should have realized," she said, whispering. "Both of us knew we could no longer be on Earth, but neither of us would admit it."

"We could not have known. It is beyond all experience."

"So is the notion of travel through Time, and yet we readily accepted that."

The train lurched slightly, and we felt it begin to slow. I looked past Amelia's profile, across the arid desert towards that brilliant light in the sky.

"How can we be sure that that is Earth?" I said. "After all, neither of us has ever—"

"Don't you know, Edward? Can't you feel it inside you? Doesn't everything else about this place seem foreign and hostile? Is there not something that speaks to us instinctively when we look at that light? It is a sight of home, and we both feel it."

"But what are we to do?" The train braked again as I spoke, and looking through the windows on the opposite side of the carriage I saw that we were stopping inside a large, darkened train-shed. On our side of the train a wall came between us and our view of the sky and its ominous reminders.

Amelia said: "We will have no option in the matter. It is not so much what we do, as what is to be done with us."

"Are you saying that we are in danger?"

"Possibly . . . as soon as it is realized that we are not of this world. After all, what would be likely to happen to a man who came to Earth from another world?"

"I have no idea," I said.

"Therefore we can have no idea what is in store for us. We shall have to hope for the best, and trust that in spite of their primitive society we will be well treated. I should not care to spend the rest of my days like an animal."

"Nor I. But is that likely, or even feasible?"

"We have seen how the slaves are treated. If we were taken for two of those wretches, then we could well be put to work."

"But we have already been taken for two of the overseers," I reminded her. "Some accident of clothing, or something about our appearance, has compounded in our favour."

"We still need to be careful. There is no telling what we shall find here."

In spite of the resolution in our words, we were in no condition to take charge of our fate, for in addition to the multitude of questions that surrounded our prospects, we were both dishevelled, tired and hungry from our ordeal in the desert. I knew that Amelia could feel no better than I, and I was exhausted. Both of us were slurring our words, and in spite of our attempts to articulate our feelings, the realization of where we had been deposited by the Time Machine had been the final blow to our morale.

Outside, I could hear the slaves being herded from the train, and the distinctive crackle of the electrical whips was an unpleasant reminder of our precarious position.

"The train will be moving off soon," I said, pushing Amelia gently into an upright position. "We have come to a city, and we must look for shelter there."

"I don't want to go."

"We will have to."

I went to the far side of the carriage, and opened the nearest door. I took a quick glance along the length of the train; evidently the slaves were being taken from the opposite side of the train for here there was no movement, bar one man sauntering slowly away from me. I went back to Amelia, who was still sitting passively.

"In a few minutes the train will be going back to where we

came from," I said. "Do you wish to spend another night in the desert?"

"Of course not. I'm just a little nervous at the thought of entering the city."

I said: "We must eat some food, Amelia, and find somewhere safe and warm to sleep. The very fact that this is a city is to our advantage: it must be large enough for us to go unnoticed. We have already survived a great ordeal, and I do not think we need fear anything further. Tomorrow we will try to establish what rights we have."

Amelia shook her head lethargically, but to my relief she then rose wearily to her feet and followed me from the carriage. I gave her my hand to help her to the ground, and she took it. Her grasp was without pressure.

ii

The sound of the whips echoed from the other side of the train as we hurried towards where a glow of light emanated from behind a protruding corner. There was no sign of the man I had seen earlier.

As we came round the corner we saw ahead of us a tall doorway, set well back into the brick wall and painted white. Over the top was a sign, illuminated in some manner from behind, and bearing a legend in a style of printing that was totally incomprehensible to me. It was this sign that drew our attention, rather than the door itself, for this was our first sight of Martian written language.

After we had stared at this for a few seconds — the lettering was black on a white background, but here the superficial similarity with Earth scripts came to an end—I led Amelia forward, anxious to find warmth and food. It was bitterly cold in the train-shed, for it was open to the night air.

There was no handle on the door, and for a moment I wondered if there would be some alien mechanism that would defy us. I pushed experimentally, and discovered that one side of the door moved slightly.

I must have been weak from our sojourn in the wilds, for beyond this I was incapable of shifting it. Amelia helped me, and in a moment we found that we could push the door open far enough for us to pass through, but as soon as we released it the heavy device swung back and closed with a slam. We had come into a short corridor, no longer than five or six yards, at the end of which was another door. The corridor was completely featureless, with the exception of one electrical incandescent lamp fixed to the ceiling. We went to the second door and pushed it open, feeling a similar weight. This door also closed quickly behind us.

Amelia said: "My ears feel as though they are blocked."

"Mine too," I said. "I think the pressure of air is greater here."

We were in a second corridor, identical to the first. Amelia remembered something she had been taught when she was in Switzerland, and showed me how to relieve the pressure in my ears by holding my nose and blowing gently.

As we passed through the third door there was another increase in the density of the air.

"I feel I can breathe at last," I said, wondering how we had survived for so long in the thin air outside.

"We must not over-exert ourselves," Amelia said. "I feel a little dizzy already."

Even though we were anxious to continue on our way we waited in the corridor for a few minutes longer. Like Amelia, I was feeling light-headed in the richer air, and this sensation was sharpened by a barely detectable hint of ozone. My fingertips were tingling as my blood was renewed with this fresh supply of oxygen, and this coupled with the fact of the lighter Martian gravity—which, while we had been in the desert, we had attributed to some effect of high altitude—lent a spurious feeling of great energy. Spurious it surely was, for I knew we must both be near the end of the tether; Amelia's shoulders were stooped, and her eyes were still half-closed.

I placed my arm around Amelia's shoulders.

"Come along," I said. "We do not have much further to go."

"I am still a little frightened."

"There is nothing that can threaten us," I said, but in truth I shared her fears. Neither of us was in any position to understand the full implications of our predicament. Deep inside, I was feeling the first tremblings of an instinctive dread of the alien, the strange, the exotic.

We stepped slowly forward, pushed our way through the next door, and at last found ourselves looking out across a part of the Martian city.

iii

Outside the door through which we had come a street ran from left to right, and directly opposite us were two buildings. These, at first sight, loomed large and black, so used were we to the barrenness of the desert, but on a second examination we saw that they were scarcely bigger than the grander private houses of our own cities. Each one stood alone, and was intricately ornamented with moulded plaster on the outside walls; the doors were large, and there were few windows. If this lends to such buildings an aura of grace or elegance, then it should be added that both of the two buildings we then saw were in a state of advanced decay. One, indeed, had one wall partially collapsed, and a door hung open on a hinge. In the interiors we could see much rubble and litter, and it was clear that neither had been occupied for many years. The walls still standing were cracked and crumbling, and there was no visible sign that a roof still stood.

I glanced up and saw that the city was open to the sky, for I could make out the stars overhead. Curiously, though, the air was as dense here as it had been inside the corridors, and the temperature was much warmer than we had experienced in the desert.

The street we were in was lighted: at intervals along each side were several more of the towers we had seen, and now we realized a part, at least, of their function, for on the polished roof of each tower was a powerful light which swept to and fro as the platform rotated slowly. These constantly sweeping beams had a strangely sinister aspect, and they were far removed from the warm, placid gaslights to which we were both accustomed, but the very fact that the Martians illuminated their streets at night was a reassuringly human detail.

"Which way shall we go?" Amelia said.

"We must find the centre of the city," I said. "Clearly this is a quarter that has fallen into disuse. I suggest we strike directly away from this rail-terminus until we meet some of the people."

"The people? You mean . . . Martians?"

"Of course," I said, taking her hand in mine with a show of confidence. "We have already accosted several without knowing who they were. They seem very like us, so we have nothing to fear from them."

Without waiting for a reply I pulled her forward, and we walked briskly along the street towards the right. When we came to the corner we turned with it, and found we were in a similar, though rather longer, street. Along each side of this were more buildings, styled as ornately as the first we had seen, but with sufficient subtle variations in architecture to avoid obvious repetition of shape. Here too the buildings were in decay, and we had no means of knowing for what purposes they had once been used. The ruination apart, this was not a thoroughfare which would have disgraced one of the spa-towns of England.

We walked for about ten minutes without seeing any other pedestrians, although as we passed one street-junction we briefly saw, at some distance down the intersecting road, a powered conveyance moving swiftly across our view. It had appeared too quickly for us to see it in any detail, and we were left with an impression of considerable speed and incontinent noise.

Then as we approached a cluster of buildings from which several lights issued, Amelia suddenly pointed along a smaller street to our right.

"See, Edward," she said softly. "There are people by that building."

Along that street too were lighted buildings, and from one of them, as she had indicated, several people had just walked. I turned that way instantly, but Amelia held back.

"Let's not go that way," she said. "We don't know—"

"Are you prepared to starve?" I cried, although my bravura was a façade. "We must see how these people live, so that we may eat and sleep."

"Do you not think we should be more circumspect? It would be foolhardy to walk into a situation we could not escape from."

"We are in such a situation now," I said, then deliberately made my voice more persuasive. "We are in desperate trouble, Amelia dear. Maybe you are right to think it would be foolish to walk straight up to these people, but I know no other way."

Amelia said nothing for a moment, but she stood close by my side, her hand limp in mine. I wondered if she were about to faint once more, for she seemed to be swaying slightly, but after a while she looked up at me. As she did so, the sweeping beam from one of the towers fell full across her face, and I saw how tired and ill she looked.

She said: "Of course you are right, Edward. I did not think we should survive in the desert. We must of course mingle with these Martian people, for we cannot return to that."

I squeezed her hand to comfort her, and then we walked slowly towards the building where we had seen the people. As we approached, more appeared through the main doorway and headed up the street away from us. One man even glanced in our direction as two of the light-beams swept across us, so that he must have seen us clearly, but he showed no visible reaction and walked on with the others.

Amelia and I came to a halt in front of the doorway, and for a few seconds I stared down the street at the Martians. They all walked with a curious, easy loping motion; doubtless this was a product of the low gravity conditions, and doubtless a gait that Amelia and I would perfect as soon as we grew more accustomed to the conditions here.

"Do we go inside?" Amelia said.

"I can think of no other course," I said, and led the way up the three low steps in front of the door. Another group of Martian people was coming out in the opposite direction, and they passed without appearing to notice us. Their faces were indistinct in the half-light, but close to we saw just how tall they were. They were all at least six inches taller than I.

Light from within was spilling down the passage beyond the door, and as we passed through we came into a huge, brightly lit room, one so large that it seemed it must occupy the whole of the building.

We stopped just inside the door, standing warily, waiting for our eyes to adjust to the brilliance.

All was at first confusing, for what furniture was there was in haphazard order, and consisted, for the most part, of what seemed to be tubular scaffolding. From this were suspended by ropes what I can best describe as hammocks: large sheets of thick fabric or rubber, hanging some two feet from the ground. On these, and standing around them, were several dozen of the Martian people.

With the exception of the peasant-slaves—whom we surmised to be of the lowest social order—these were the first Martians we had seen closely. These were the city-dwellers, the same as those men we had seen wielding the electrical whips. These were the people who ordered this society, elected its leaders, made its laws. These were from now to be our peers, and in spite of our tiredness and mental preoccupations Amelia and I regarded them with considerable interest.

iv

I have already noted that the average Martian is a tall being; what is also most noticeable, and of emphatic importance, is that the Martians are undeniably human, or human-like.

To speak of the average Martian is as misleading as to speak of the average human on Earth, for even in those first few seconds as we regarded the occupants of the building, Amelia and I noticed that there were many superficial differences. We saw some who were taller than most, some shorter; there were thinner Martians and fatter ones; there were some with great manes of hair, others were bald or balding; the predominant skin-tone was a reddish tint, but this was more evident in some than in others.

With this in mind, then, let me say that the average adult Martian male could be roughly described thus:

He would be of the order of some six feet six inches tall, with black or brown head-hair. (We saw no red-heads, and no blonds.) He would weigh, if he were to step on scales an Earth, some two hundred pounds. His chest would be broad, and apparently well-muscled. He would have facial hair, with thin eyebrows and wispy beard; some of the males we saw were clean-shaven, but this was uncommon. His eyes would be large, uncannily pale in coloration, and set wide apart in his face. His nose would be flat and broad, and his mouth would be generously fleshed.

At first sight the Martian face is a disturbing one for it seems brutal and devoid of emotion; as we later mingled with these people, however, both Amelia and I were able to detect facial nuances, even though we were never sure how to interpret them.

(My description here is of a city-Martian. The slave people were of the same racial stock, but due to the privations they suffered, most of the slaves we saw were comparatively thin and puny.)

The Martian female—for women there were in that room, and children too—is, like her Earthly counterpart, slightly the physical inferior of the male. Even so, almost every Martian female we saw was taller than Amelia, who is, as has already been said, taller than the average Earth woman. There is no woman on Mars who could ever be considered to be a beauty by Earth standards, nor, I suspect, would that concept have any meaning on Mars. At no time did we ever sense that Martian females were appreciated for their physical charms, and indeed we often had reason to believe that, as with some animals on Earth, the rôles on Mars were reversed in this respect.

The children we saw were, almost without exception, charming to us in the way any youngster has charm. Their faces were round and eager, not yet rendered unpleasant by the broadness and flatness so evident in the adults. Their behaviour, like that of Earth children, was on the whole riotous and mischievous, but they never appeared to anger the adults, whose attitude was indulgent and solicitous to them. It often seemed to us that the children were the sole source of happiness on this world, for the only time we saw the adults laughing was in the company of children.

This brings me to an aspect of Martian life which did not at first strike us, but which in later times became increasingly obvious. That is to say that I cannot imagine a race of beings more universally lugubrious, downcast or plainly miserable than the Martians.

The aura of despondency was present in the room as Amelia and I first entered it, and it was probably this which was our eventual saving. The typical Martian I have described would be obsessed with his internal miseries to the virtual exclusion of all other factors. To no other reason can I attribute the fact that Amelia and I were able to move so freely about the city without attracting attention. Even in those first few moments, as we stood in anticipation of the first cry of alarm or excitement at our appearance, few Martians so much as glanced in our direction. I cannot imagine the arrival of a Martian in an Earth city eliciting the same indifference.

Perhaps allied to this overall depression was the fact that the room was almost silent. One or two of the Martians spoke quietly, but most stood or sat about glumly. A few children ran while their parents watched, but this was the only movement. The voices we heard were weird: soprano and mellifluous. Obviously we could not understand the words or even the tenor of the conversations—although the words were accompanied by intricate hand-signals—but the sight of these large and ugly people speaking in what seemed to us to be falsetto was most disconcerting.

Amelia and I waited by the door, unsure of everything. I looked at Amelia, and suddenly the sight of her face—tired, dirty, but so lovely—was a welcome reminder of all that was familiar to me. She looked back at me, the strain of the last two days still revealing itself in her expression, but she smiled and entwined her fingers through mine once more.

"They're just ordinary people, Edward."

"Are you still frightened?" I said.

"I'm not sure . . . they seem harmless."

"If they can live in this city, then so can we. What we must do is see how they conduct their everyday lives, and follow their example. They seem not to recognize us as strangers."

Just then a group of the Martians moved away from the hammocks and walked in their strange, loping gait towards us. At once I led Amelia back through the door, and returned to the street with its ever-sweeping lights. We crossed to the further side, then turned back to watch what the Martians were doing.

In a moment the group appeared, and without looking once in our direction they set off down the way we had seen the others go earlier. We waited for half a minute, then followed them at a distance.

v

As soon as we returned to the street we realized that it had been warmer inside, and this was cause for further reassurance. I had been fearing that the native Martians lived habitually in coldness, but the inside of the building had been heated to an acceptable level. I was not sure that I wished to sleep in a communal dormitory—and wished such conditions even less for Amelia—but even if we did not care for it, we knew at least that we could tonight sleep warmly and comfortably.

It turned out that there was not far to walk. The Martians ahead of us crossed a street-junction, joined another, much larger, group walking from a different direction, then turned into the next building they came to. This was larger than many of the buildings we had so far seen, and from what we could see of it in the fitful illumination of the tower lights it appeared to be plainer in architectural style. There was light showing from the windows, and as we came nearer we could hear much noise from within.

Amelia made an exaggerated sniffing noise.

"I smell food," she said. "And I hear clattering of dishes."

I said: "And I detect wishful thinking."

However, our mood was now much lighter, and feeble though such an exchange might be it was an indication that Amelia was sharing my feeling of renewed hope.

We did not hesitate as we approached the building, so emboldened had we been by our visit to the other building, and walked confidently through the main door into a vast, brightly lit hall.

It was clear at once that this was not another dormitory, for almost the entire floor-space was given over to long tables set in parallel rows. Each of these was crowded with Martian people apparently in the middle of a banquet. The tables were liberally spread with dishes of food, the air was laden with a steamy, greasy smell, and the walls echoed to the sound of the Martians' voices. At the far end was what we assumed was the kitchen, for here about a dozen of the slave-Martians were toiling with metal plates and huge dishfuls of food, which were set out along a raised platform by the entrance to the kitchen.

The group of Martians we had been following had walked to this platform, and were helping themselves to food.

I said: "Our problem is solved, Amelia. Here is ample food for the taking."

"Assuming we may eat it in safety."

"Do you mean it could be poisonous?"

"How are we to know? We are not Martian, and our digestive systems might be quite different."

"I don't intend to starve while I decide," I said. "And anyway we are being watched."

This was the case, for although we had been able to stand unnoticed in the dormitory building, our evident hesitation was attracting attention. I took Amelia by the elbow and propelled her towards the platform.

My hunger had been such, earlier in the day, that I had thought I could have eaten anything. In the hours between, however, the gnawing hunger had passed to be replaced by a sensation of nausea, and the compulsion to eat was now much less than I would have anticipated. Furthermore, as we approached the platform it was clear that although there was food in abundance, there was little that looked at all appetizing, and I was stricken with a most unexpected fastidiousness. Most of the food was liquid or semi-liquid, and was laid out in tureens or bowls. The scarlet weed was obviously the staple diet of these people, in spite of the several fields of green-crop we had seen, for many of the stew-like dishes contained large quantities of the red stems and leaves. There were, though, one or two plates of what could be meat (although it was very undercooked), and to one side there was something which, but for the fact we had seen no cattle, we could have taken for cheese. In addition, there were several glass jugs containing vividly coloured liquids, which were poured over the food as sauces by the Martians.

"Take small quantities of as many different kinds as possible," Amelia said softly. "Then if any of it is dangerous, the effect will be minimized."

The plates were large, and made of a dull metallic substance, and we each took a generous amount of food. Once or twice I sniffed what I was taking, but this was unedifying, to say the least.

Carrying our plates, we went towards one of the tables at the side, away from the main group of Martians.

There was a small number of the people at one end of the table we selected, but we passed them by and sat at the other end. The seats were long low benches, one on each side. Amelia and I sat next to each other, not at all at ease in this strange place, even though the Martians continued to pay no attention to us now we had moved away from the door.

We each took a little of the food: it was not pleasant, but it was still quite hot and was certainly better than an empty stomach.

After a moment, Amelia said in a low voice: "Edward, we cannot live like this for ever. We have simply been lucky so far."

"Don't let us discuss it. We are both exhausted. We'll find

somewhere to sleep tonight, and in the morning we will make plans."

"Plans to do what? Spend a lifetime in hiding?"

We ate our way stoically through the food, being reminded continually of that bitter taste we had first experienced in the desert. The meat was no better; it had a texture similar to some cuts of beef, but was sweet and bland in flavour. Even the 'cheese', which we left until the end, was acidic.

On the whole our attention was distracted away from the food by the events about us.

I have already described the Martians' habitual expression as being one of great lugubriousness, and in spite of the amount of conversation there was no levity. On our table, a Martian woman leaned forward and rested her wide forehead on her arms, and we could see tears trickling from her eyes. A little later, on the far side of the hall, a Martian man jumped abruptly back from his seat and strode around the room, waving his long arms and declaiming in his queer, high-pitched voice. He came to a wall and leant against it, banging his fists and shouting. This at last attracted the attention of his fellows, and several hurried to him and stood about, apparently trying to soothe him, but he was disconsolate.

Within a few seconds of this incident there was set up, as if the misery were contagious, such a general caterwauling that Amelia was impelled to say to me: "Do you suppose it is possible that here the responses are different? I mean, when they appear to be crying, are they actually laughing?"

"I'm not sure," I said, cautiously watching the weeping Martian. He continued his outburst a little longer, then turned away from his friends and hurried from the hall with his hands covering his face. The others waited until he had vanished through the door, then returned to their own seats, looking morose.

We noticed that most of the Martians were taking large quantities of drink from glass jugs set on every table. As this was transparent we had assumed that it was water, but when I tasted some it was instantly clear that this was not so. Although it was refreshing to drink it was strongly alcoholic, to such an extent that within a few seconds of swallowing it I felt pleasantly dizzy.

I poured some for Amelia, but she only sipped at hers.

"It is very strong," she said. "We must not lose our wits."

I had already poured myself a second draught, but she restrained me from drinking it. I suppose she was wise to do this, because as we watched the Martians it was plain that most of them were fast becoming inebriated. They were being noisier and more careless in their manners than before. We even heard laughter, although it sounded shrill and hysterical. Large quantities of the alcoholic beverage were being drunk, and kitchen-slaves brought out several more jugs of it. A bench fell backwards to the floor, tipping its sitters into a sprawling heap, and two of the young male kitchen-slaves were captured by a group of female Martians who then hemmed them into a corner; what followed we could not see in the confusion. More slaves came out of the kitchen, and most of these were young females. To our astonishment, not only were they completely unclothed but they mingled freely with their masters, embracing and enticing them.

"I think it is time we left," I said to Amelia.

She stared at the developing situation for a few moments longer before replying. Then she said: "Very well. This is grossly distasteful."

We went towards the door, not pausing to look back. Another bench and a table were overturned, accompanied by a crash of breaking glasses and shouts from the Martian people. The maudlin atmosphere had been entirely banished.

Then, as we reached the door, a sound came echoing through the hall, chilling us and forcing us to look back. It was a harsh and discordant screeching sound, apparently emanating from one distant corner of the hall, but with sufficient volume to drown every other sound.

Its effect on the Martians was dramatic: all movement ceased, and the people present looked wildly from one to the other. In the silence that followed this brutal and sudden intrusion, we heard the sound of renewed sobbing.

I said: "Come on, Amelia."

So we hurried from the building, sobered by the incident, not understanding but more than a little frightened.

There were now even fewer people about than before, but the tower lights swept across the streets as if to pick out those who wandered in the night when all others were engaged inside.

I led Amelia away from that area of the city where the Martians gathered, and back towards the part we had first walked through, where fewer lights showed. Appearances, though, were deceptive, for the fact that a building showed no light and emitted no noise did not mean it was deserted. We walked for about half a mile, and then tried the door of a darkened building. Inside, lights were shining and we saw that another feast had taken place. We saw . . . but it is not correct that I should here record what we saw. Amelia had no more wish than I to witness such depravity, and we hastened away, still not able to reconcile this world with the one we had left.

When we next tried a building I went forward alone . . . but the place was empty and dirty, and whatever had been its contents had been thoroughly destroyed by fire. The next building we explored was another dormitory-hall, well occupied by Martians. Without causing disturbance, we went away.

So it went, as we moved from one building to the next, seeking an unoccupied dormitory-hall; so long did we search that we began to think that there was none we could find. But then at last we were in luck, and came to a hall where hammocks hung unoccupied, and we went inside and slept.

Chapter Nine

EXPLORATIONS

i

During the weeks that followed, Amelia and I explored the Martian city as thoroughly as possible. We were hindered by the fact that we had perforce to go everywhere on foot, but we saw as much as we could and were soon able to make reasonable estimates as to its size, how many people it contained, where the major buildings were situated, and so forth. At the same time we tried to make what we could of the people of Mars, and how they lived; to be honest, however, we did not find much satisfaction on this score.

After two nights in the first dormitory we found, we moved to a second building, much nearer to the centre of the city and more conveniently sited by a dining-hall. This too was unoccupied, but its previous users had left many possessions behind them, and we were able to live in some comfort. The hammocks would have been unbearably hard on Earth—for the fabric of which they were made was coarse and unyielding—but in the light Martian gravity they were perfectly adequate. For bedding we used large, pillow-like sacks filled with a soft compound, which were similar to the quilts used in some European countries.

We also found clothing that had been abandoned by the previous occupants, and we wore the drab garments over our own clothes. Naturally enough they were rather large for us, but the loose fit over our clothes made our bodies appear larger, and so we were able to pass more readily as Martians.

Amelia tied her hair back in a tight bun—approximating the style favoured by the Martian women—and I allowed my new beard to grow; every few days Amelia trimmed it with her nail-scissors to give it the wispy appearance of the Martians'.

At the time all this seemed to us a matter of priority; we were very aware that we looked different from the Martians. To this extent, our two days' sojourn in the desert had been to our unwitting advantage: our sunburned faces, uncomfortable as they were, were a credible approximation of the Martians' skin-hue. As the days passed, and our complexions began to fade, we returned one day to the desert beyond the city, and a few hours in that bitter radiant heat restored the colour temporarily.

But this is taking my narrative ahead of itself, for to convey how we survived in that city I must first describe the place itself.

ii

Within a few days of our arrival, Amelia had dubbed our new home Desolation City, for reasons which should already be clear.

Desolation City was situated at the junction of two canals. One of these, the one by whose banks we had first landed, ran directly from north to south. The second approached from the north-west, and after the junction—where there was a complicated arrangements of locks—continued to the south-east. The city had been built in the obtuse angle formed by the two canals, and along its southern and western edges were several docking accesses to the waterways.

As near as we could estimate it the city covered about twelve square miles, but a comparison on this basis with Earth cities is misleading, for Desolation City was almost exactly circular. Moreover, the Martians had lighted on the ingenious notion of entirely separating the industrial life of the city from the residential, for the buildings were designed for the everyday needs of the people, while the manufacturing work was carried out in the industrial areas beyond the city's periphery.

There were two such industrial concentrations: the large one we had seen from the train, which lay to the north, and a smaller one built beside the canal to the south-east.

In terms of resident population, Desolation City was very small indeed, and it was this aspect which had most prompted Amelia to give it its unprepossessing name.

That the city had been built to accommodate many thousands of people was quite obvious, for buildings there were many and open spaces there were few; that only a fraction of the city was presently occupied was equally apparent, and large areas were laid to waste. In these parts many of the buildings were derelict, and the streets were littered with masonry and rusting girders.

We discovered that only the occupied parts of the city were lighted at night, for as we explored the city by day we frequently found areas of decay where none of the towers was present. We never ventured into these regions at night, for quite apart from being dark and threatening in their loneliness, such areas were patrolled by fast-moving vehicles which drove through the streets with a banshee howling and an ever-probing beam of light.

This sinister policing of the city was the first indication that the Martian people had inflicted on themselves a régime of Draconian suppression.

We often speculated as to the causes of the under-population. At first we surmised that the shortage of manpower was only apparent, created by the quite prodigious amount of effort poured into the industrial processes. By day we could see the industrial areas beyond the city's perimeter, belching dense smoke from hundreds of chimneys, and by night we saw the same areas brightly lit as the work continued; thus it was that we assumed most of the city's people were at work, labouring around the clock through work-shifts. However, as we grew more used to living in the city, we saw that not many of the ruling-class Martians ever left its confines, and that therefore most of the industrial workers would be of the slave class.

I have mentioned that the city was circular in shape. We discovered this by accident and over a period of several days, and were able to confirm it later by ascending one of the taller buildings in the city.

Our first realization came as follows. On our second or third full day in Desolation City, Amelia and I were walking northwards through the city, intending to see if we could cross the mile or so of desert between us and the larger of the two industrial concentrations.

We came to a street which led directly northwards, seeming to open eventually on to the desert. This was in one of the populated areas of the city, and watch-towers abounded. I noticed, as we approached, that the tower nearest to the desert had stopped rotating to and fro, and I pointed this out to Amelia. We considered for a few moments whether or not to continue, but Amelia said she saw no harm.

However, as we passed the tower it was quite obvious that the man or men inside were rotating the observation-platform to watch us, and the dark, oval window at the front mutely followed our progress past it. No action was taken against us, so we continued, but with a distinct feeling of apprehension.

So taken were we with this silent monitoring that we fetched up unexpectedly and shockingly against the true perimeter of the city; this took the form of an invisible, or nearly invisible, wall, stretching from one side of the roadway to the other. Naturally enough, we thought at first that the substance was glass, but this could not be the case. Nor was it, indeed, any other form of material that we knew. Our best notion was that it was some kind of energetic field, induced by electrical means. It was, though, completely inert, and under the gaze of the watch-tower we made a few rudimentary attempts to fathom it. All we could feel was the impermeable, invisible barrier, cold to the touch.

Chastened, we walked back the way we had come.

On a later occasion, we walked through one of the empty quarters of the city, and found that there too the wall existed. Before long we had established that the wall extended all around the city, crossing not just streets but behind buildings too.

Later, from the aspect of the roof, we saw that few if any of the buildings lay beyond this circle.

It was Amelia who first posited a solution, linking this phenomenon with the undoubted one that air-density and over-all temperature in the city were higher than outside. She suggested that the invisible barrier was not merely a wall, but in fact a hemisphere which covered the entire city. Beneath this, she said, air-pressure could be maintained at an acceptable level, and the effect of the sun through it would be closely akin to that of a glasshouse.

iii

Desolation City was not, however, a prison. To leave it was as easy as it had been for us to enter it initially. On our journeys of exploration we came across several places where it was possible merely to walk through some specially maintained fault in the wall and enter the rarefied atmosphere of the desert.

One such fault was the series of doors and corridors at the railway terminus; there were similar ones at the wharves built by the canals, and some of these were immense structures by which imported materials could be taken into the city. Several of the major streets, which ran towards the industrial areas, had transit buildings through which people could pass freely.

What was most interesting of all, though, was that the vehicles of the city were able to pass directly through the wall without either hesitation or detectable leakage of the pressurized atmosphere. We saw this occur many times.

I must now turn the attention of this narrative towards the nature of these vehicles, for among the many marvels Amelia and I saw on Mars these numbered among the most amazing.

The fundamental difference lay in the fact that, unlike Earth engineers, the Martian inventors had dispensed with the wheel entirely. Having seen the efficiency of the Martians' vehicles I was, indeed, forced to wonder how far Earthly developments in this field had been retarded by the obsession with the wheel! Furthermore, the only wheeled vehicles we saw on Mars were the crude hand-carts used by the slaves; an indication of how lowly the Martians considered such methods!

The first Martian vehicle we saw (not counting the train in which we had arrived, although we assumed that this too was without wheels) was the one which had raced through the streets that first dismal night in Desolation City. The second we saw was during the morning of the next day; that too was moving at such a lick that we were left with a confused impression of speed and noise. Later, however, we saw one moving more slowly, and later still we saw several at rest.

To say that Martian vehicles *walked* would be inaccurate, although I can think of no closer verb. Beneath the main body (which, according to its use, was designed in a fashion more or less conventional to us) were rows of long or short metal *legs*, the length being determined by the kind of use to which the vehicle was put. These legs were mounted in groups of three, connected by a transmission device to the main body, and powered from within by some hidden power source.

The motion of these legs was at once curiously life-like and rigidly mechanical: at any one time only one of the three legs of each mounting would be in contact with the ground. In motion, the legs would ripple with a quasi-peristaltic motion, the two raised legs reaching forward to take the load, the third one lifting and reaching forward in its turn.

The largest vehicle we saw at close quarters was a goods-haulage machine, with two parallel rows of sixteen groups of these legs. The smallest machines, which were used to police the city, had two rows of three groups.

Each leg, on close examination, turned out to be made of several dozen finely-machined disks, balanced on top of each other like a pile of pennies, and yet activated in some way by an electrical current. As each of the legs was encased in a transparent integument, it was possible to see the device in operation, but how each movement was controlled was beyond us. In any event, the efficiency of these machines was in no doubt: we frequently saw the policing-vehicles driving through the streets at a velocity well in excess of anything a horse-drawn vehicle could attain.

iv

Perhaps even more puzzling to us than the design of these vehicles was the men who drove them.

That men were inside them was apparent, for on many occasions we saw ordinary Martians speaking to the driver or other occupants, with spoken replies coming through a metal grille set in the side of the machine. What was also quite clear was that the drivers were in positions of extraordinary authority, for when addressed by them the Martians in the street adopted a cowed or respectful manner, and spoke in subdued tones. However, at no time did we see the drivers, for all the vehicles were totally enclosed—at least, the driver's compartment was enclosed—with only a piece of the black glass set at the front, behind which the driver presumably stood or sat. As these windows were similar to those we saw on every watch-tower, we presumed that they were operated by the same group of people.

Nor were all the vehicles as prosaic as maybe I have made them appear.

Confronted, as we were, with a multitude of strange sights, Amelia and I were constantly trying to find Earthly parallels for what we saw. It is likely, therefore, that many of the assumptions we made at this time were incorrect. It was relatively safe to assume that the vehicles we thought of as drays were just that, for we saw them performing similar tasks to those we knew on Earth. There was no way, though, of finding an Earthly equivalent for some of the machines.

One such was a device used by the Martians in conjunction with their watch-towers.

Directly outside the dormitory building we settled in, and visible to us from our hammocks, was one of the watch-towers. After we had been in occupation for about eight days, Amelia pointed out that there appeared to be something wrong with it, for its observation platform had ceased to rotate to and fro. That night we saw that its light was not on.

The very next day one of the vehicles came to a halt beside

the tower, and there took place a repair operation I can only describe as fantastic.

The vehicle in question was of a type we had occasionally seen about the city: a long, low machine which, above its drive-leg platform, was an apparent mass of glittering tubing, heaped in disorder. As the legged vehicle halted beside the watch-tower, this confusion of metal reared itself up, to reveal that it possessed five of the peristaltic legs, the remainder of the appendages being a score or more of tentacular arms.

It stepped down from the platform of the vehicle, the jointed arms clanging and ringing, then walked the short distance to the base of the tower with a movement remarkably like that of a spider. We both looked for some clue as to how the thing was being driven, but it seemed that either the monstrous machine had an intelligence of its own, or else it was controlled in some incredible way by the driver of the vehicle, for there was plainly no one anywhere near it. As it reached the base of the tower, one of its tentacles was brought into contact with a raised metal plate on one of the pillars, and in a moment we saw that the observation platform was lowering. Apparently it could lower itself only so far, for when the platform was about twenty feet from the ground the tentacular device seized the tower's legs in its horrid embrace, and began to climb slowly upwards, like a spider climbing a strand of its web.

When it reached the observation-platform it settled itself in position by clinging on with its legs, and then with several tentacles reached through a number of tiny ports, apparently searching for the parts of the mechanism which had failed.

Amelia and I watched the whole operation, unnoticed inside the building. From the arrival of the legged vehicle to its eventual departure, only twelve minutes elapsed, and by the time the iron monster had returned to its place on the rear of the vehicle, the observation-platform had been raised to its erst-while height, and was rotating to and fro in its usual way.

v

So far, I have not had much to say about our day-to-day survival in this desolate city, nor, for the moment, will I. Our
internal preoccupations were many and great, and, in several
ways, more important than what we were seeing about us.
Before turning to this, though, I must first establish the context. We are all creatures of our environment, and in dis-
turbingly subtle ways Amelia and I were becoming a little
Martian in our outlook. The desolation about us was reaching
our souls.

vi

As we moved about the city one question remained ever un-
answered. That is to say: how did the ordinary Martian occupy
his time?

We now understood something of the social ramifications of
Mars. This was in effect that the lowest social stratum was the
slave-people, who were forced to do all the manual and de-
meaning tasks necessary to any civilized society. Then came
the Martians of the city, who had powers of supervision over
the slaves. Above these were the men who drove the legged
vehicles and, presumably, operated the other mechanical
devices we saw.

It was the city-dwelling Martians in whom we were most
interested, for it was among them that we lived. However, not
all of these were occupied. For instance, it took relatively few
of them to supervise the slaves (we often saw just one or two
men able to control several hundred slaves, armed with only the
electrical whips), and although the vehicles were many in
number, there were always plenty of people in the city, apparently idle.

On our perambulations Amelia and I saw much evidence
that time hung heavy on these people. The nightly carousing
was obviously a result of two factors: partly a way of appeasing

the endless grief, and partly a way of expressing boredom. We frequently saw people squabbling, and there were several fights, although these were dissipated instantly at the sight of one of the vehicles. Many of the women appeared to be pregnant; another indication that there was not much to occupy either the minds or the energies of the people. At the height of the day, when the sun was overhead (we had come to the conclusion that the city must be built almost exactly on the Martian equator), the pavements of the streets were littered with the bodies of men and women relaxing in the warmth.

One possibility that would account for the apparent idleness was that some of them were employed in the near-by industrial area, and that the Martians we saw about the city were enjoying some leave.

As we were both curious to see the industrial areas and discover, if we could, what was the nature of all the furious activity that took place, one day, about fifteen days after our arrival, Amelia and I determined to leave the city and explore the smaller of the two complexes. We had already observed that a road ran to it, and that although the majority of the traffic was the haulage type of vehicle, several people—both city-dweller and slave—were to be seen walking along it. We decided, therefore, that we would not attract unwanted attention by going there ourselves.

We left the city by a system of pressurized corridors, and emerged into the open. At once our lungs were labouring in the sparse atmosphere, and we both remarked on the extreme climate: the thin coldness of the air and the harsh radiance of the sun.

We walked slowly, knowing from experience how exercise debilitated us in this climate, and so after half an hour we had not covered much more than about a quarter of the distance to the industrial site. Already, though, we could smell something of the smoke and fumes released from the factories although none of the clangour we associated with such works was audible.

During a pause for rest, Amelia laid her hand on my arm and pointed towards the south.

"What is that, Edward?" she said.

I looked in the direction she had indicated.

We had been walking almost due south-east towards the industrial site, parallel to the canal, but on the far side of the water, well away from the factories, was what appeared at first sight to be an immense pipeline. It did not, however, appear to be connected to anything, and indeed we could see an open end to it.

The continuation of the pipe was invisible to us, lying as it did beyond the industrial buildings. Such an apparatus would not normally have attracted our attention, but what was remarkable was the fact of the intense activity around the open end. The pipe lay perhaps two miles from where we stood, but in the clear air we could see distinctly that hundreds of workers were swarming about the place.

We had agreed to rest for fifteen minutes, so unaccustomed were we to the thin air, and as we moved on afterwards we could not help but glance frequently in that direction.

"Could it be some kind of irrigation duct?" I said after a while, having noticed that the pipe ran from east to west between the two diverging canals.

"With a bore of that diameter?"

I had to admit that this explanation was unlikely, because we could see how the pipe dwarfed those men nearest to it. A reasonable estimate of the internal diameter of the pipe would be about twenty feet, and in addition the metal of the tube was some eight or nine feet thick.

We agreed to take a closer look at the strange construction, and so left the road, striking due south across the broken rock and sand of the desert. There were no bridges across the canal here, so the bank was as far as we could proceed, but it was close enough to allow us an uninterrupted view.

The overall length of the pipe turned out to be approximately one mile. From this closer position we could see the further end, which was overhanging a small lake. This had apparently been artificially dug, for its banks were straight and reinforced, and the water undermined at least half of the length of the pipe.

At the very edge of the lake, two large buildings had been constructed side by side, with the pipe running between them.

We sat down by the edge of the canal to watch what was happening.

At the moment many of the men at the nearer end of the pipe were concentrating on extracting from it a huge vehicle which had emerged from the interior. This was being guided out of the pipe, and down a ramp to the desert floor. Some difficulty seemed to have arisen, for more men were being force-marched across to help.

Half an hour later the vehicle had been successfully extricated, and was moved some distance to one side. Meanwhile, the men who had been working by the end of the pipe were dispersing.

A few more minutes passed, and then I suddenly pointed.

"Look, Amelia!" I said. "It is moving!"

The end of the pipe nearer to us was being lifted from the ground. At the same moment the further end was sinking slowly into the lake. The buildings at the edge of the lake were the instruments of this motion, for not only were they the pivot by which the pipe turned, but we also heard a great clattering and roaring from engines inside the buildings, and green smoke poured from several vents.

The raising of the pipe was the work of only a minute or so, because for all its size it moved smoothly and with precision.

When the pipe had been lifted to an angle of about forty-five degrees from horizontal, the clattering of the engines died away and the last traces of the green smoke drifted to one side. The time was near midday, and the sun was overhead.

In this new configuration the pipe had taken on the unmistakable appearance of a vast cannon, raised towards the sky!

The waters of the lake became still, the men who had been working had taken refuge in a series of buildings low on the ground. Not realizing what was about to happen, Amelia and I stayed where we were.

The first indication that the cannon was being fired was an

eruption of white water boiling up to the surface of the lake. A moment later we felt a deep trembling in the very soil on which we sat, and before us the waters of the canal broke into a million tiny wavelets.

I reached over to Amelia, threw my arms around her shoulders and pushed her sideways to the ground. She fell awkwardly, but I flung myself over her, covering her face with my shoulder and wrapping my arms about her head. We could feel the concussions in the ground, as if an earthquake were about to strike, and then a noise came, like the deepest growlings in the heart of a thundercloud.

The violence of this event grew rapidly to a peak, and then it ended as abruptly as it had begun. In the same instant we heard a protracted, shrieking explosion, howling and screaming like a thousand whistles blown simultaneously in one's ear. This noise started at its highest frequency, dying away rapidly.

As the racket was stilled, we sat up and looked across the canal towards the cannon.

Of the projectile—if any there had been—there was no sign, but belching from the muzzle of the cannon was one of the largest clouds of vapour I have ever seen in my life. It was brilliant white, and it spread out in an almost spherical cloud above the muzzle, being constantly replenished by the quantities still pouring from the barrel. In less than a minute the vapour had occluded the sun, and at once we felt much colder. The shadow lay across most of the land we could see from our vantage point, and being almost directly beneath the cloud as we were, we had no way of estimating its depth. That this was considerable was evidenced by the darkness of its shadow.

We stood up. Already, the cannon was being lowered once more, and the engines in the pivotal buildings were roaring. The slaves and their supervisors were emerging from their shelters.

We turned back towards the city, and walked as quickly as we could towards its relative comforts. In the moment the sun had been shaded the apparent temperature around us had fallen to well below freezing point. We were not much surprised, therefore, when a few minutes later we saw the first snowflakes falling about us, and as time passed the light fall became a dense and blinding blizzard.

We looked up just once, and saw that the cloud from which the snow fell—the very cloud of vapour which had issued from the cannon!—now covered almost the entire sky.

We almost missed the entrance to the city, so deep was the snow when we reached it. Here too we saw for the first time the dome-shape of the invisible shield that protected the city, for snow lay thickly on it.

A few hours later there was another concussion, and later another. In all there were twelve, repeated at intervals of about five or six hours. The sun, when its rays could penetrate the clouds, quickly melted the snow on the city's dome, but for the most part those days were dark and frightening ones in Desolation City, and we were not alone in thinking it.

vii

So much for some of the mysteries we saw in the Martian city. In describing them I have of necessity had to portray Amelia and myself as curious, objective tourists, craning our necks in wonder as any traveller in a foreign land will do. However, although we were much exercised by what we saw, this seeming objectivity was far from the case, for we were alarmed by our predicament.

There was one matter of which we rarely spoke, except obliquely; this was not because we did not think of it, but because we both knew that if the subject were raised then there was nothing hopeful that could be said. This was the manifest impossibility that we should ever be able to return to Earth.

It was, though, at the centre of our very thoughts and actions, for we knew we could not exist like this for ever, but to plan the rest of our lives in Desolation City would be a tacit acceptance of our fate.

The nearest either of us came to confronting our problem directly was on the day we first saw how advanced was the Martians' science.

Thinking that in a society as modern as this we should have no difficulty in laying our hands on the necessary materials, I said to Amelia: "We must find somewhere we can set aside as a laboratory."

She looked at me quizzically.

"Are you proposing to embark on a scientific career?" she said.

"I'm thinking we must try to build another Time Machine."

"Do you have any notion of how the Machine worked?"

I shook my head. "I had hoped that you, as Sir William's assistant, would know."

"My dear," Amelia said, and for a moment she took my hand affectionately in hers, "I would have as little idea as you."

There we had let it rest. It had been an extreme hope of mine until then, but I knew Amelia well enough to appreciate that her reply meant more than the words themselves. I realized she had already considered the idea herself, and had come to the conclusion that there was no chance that we could duplicate Sir William's work.

So, without further discussion of our prospects, we existed from day to day, each of us knowing that a return to Earth was impossible. One day we should have to confront our situation, but until then we were simply putting off the moment.

If we did not have peace of mind, then the physical needs of our bodies were adequately met.

Our two-day sojourn in the desert had not apparently caused lasting harm, although I had contracted a mild head-cold at some time. Neither of us kept down that first meal we ate, and during the night that followed we were both unpleasantly ill. Since then we had been taking the food in smaller quantities. There were three of the dining halls within walking distance of our dormitory, and we alternated between them.

As I have already mentioned, we slept in a dormitory to ourselves. The hammocks were large enough for two people, so, remembering what had passed between us earlier, I suggested a little wistfully to Amelia that we would be warmer if we shared a hammock.

"We are no longer in the desert, Edward," was her reply, and from then we slept separately.

I felt a little hurt at her response, because although my designs on her were still modest and proper I had good cause to believe that we were less than strangers. But I was prepared to abide by her wishes.

During the days our behaviour together was friendly and intimate. She would often take my hand or my arm as we walked, and at night we would kiss chastely before I turned my back to allow her to undress. At such times my desires were neither modest nor proper, and often I was tempted most inappropriately to ask her again to marry me. Inappropriate it was, for where on Mars would we find a church? This too was a matter I had to put aside until we could accept our fate.

On the whole, thoughts of home predominated. For my own part I spent considerable time thinking about my parents, and the fact that I would not see them again. Trivialities occupied me too. One such was the irresistible certainty that I had left my lamp burning in my room at Mrs Tait's. I had been in such high spirits that Sunday morning I departed for Richmond that I did not recall having extinguished the flame before I left. With irritating conviction I remembered having lit it when I got out of bed ... but had I left it burning? It was no consolation to reason with myself that now, eight or nine years later, the matter was of no consequence. But still the uncertainty nagged at me, and would not leave me.

Amelia too seemed preoccupied, although she kept her thoughts to herself. She made an effort not to appear introspective, and affected a bright and lively interest in what we saw in the city, but there were long periods in which we were both silent, and this was itself significant. An indication of the degree to which she was distracted was that she sometimes talked in her sleep; much of this was incoherent, but occasionally she spoke my name, and sometimes Sir William's. Once I found a way of asking tactfully about her dreams, but she said she had no memory of them.

viii

Within a few days of our arrival in the city, Amelia set herself the task of learning the Martian language. She had always had, she said, a facility with languages, and in spite of the fact that she had no access to either a dictionary or a grammar she was optimistic. There were, she said, basic situations she could identify, and by listening to the words spoken at the time she could establish a rudimentary vocabulary. This would be of great use to us, for we were both severely limited by the muteness imposed upon us.

Her first task was to essay an interpretation of the written language, in the form of what few signs we had seen posted about the city.

These were few in number. There were some signs at each of the city's entrances, and one or two of the legged vehicles had words inscribed upon them. Here Amelia encountered her first difficulty, because as far as she could discern no sign was ever repeated. Furthermore, there appeared to be a great number of scripts in use, and she was incapable of establishing even one or two letters of the Martian alphabet.

When she turned her attention to the spoken word her problems multiplied.

The major difficulty here was an apparent multitude of voice-tones. Quite apart from the fact that the Martians' vocal chords pitched their voices higher than would have been natural on Earth (and both Amelia and I tried in private to reproduce the sound, with comical effects), there was an apparently endless subtlety of tone variations.

Sometimes a Martian voice we heard was hard, with what we on Earth would call a sneer lending an unpleasant edge to it; another would seem musical and soft by comparison. Some Martians would speak with a complex sibilance, others with protracted vowel-sounds and pronounced plosives.

Further complicating everything was the fact that all Martians appeared to accompany their conversation with elaborate hand and head movements, and additionally would address some Martians with one voice-tone, and others in a different way.

Also, the slave-Martians appeared to have a dialect all of their own.

After several days of trying, Amelia came to the sad conclusion that the complexity of the language (or languages) was beyond her. Even so, until our last days together in Desolation City she was trying to identify individual sounds, and I was very admiring of her diligence.

There was, though, one vocal sound whose meaning was unmistakable. It was a sound common to all races on Earth, and had the same meaning on Mars. That was the scream of terror, and we were to hear much of that eventually.

ix

We had been in Desolation City for fourteen days when the epidemic struck. At first we were unaware that anything was amiss, although we noticed some early effects without realizing the cause. Specifically, this was that one evening there seemed to be far fewer Martians present in the dining hall, but so accustomed were we to odd things on this world that neither of us attributed to it anything untoward.

The day following was the one on which we witnessed the firing of the snow-cannon (for such was what we came to call it) and so our interests lay elsewhere. But by the end of those days when snow fell more or less without let over the city, there was no mistaking that something was seriously wrong. We saw several Martians dead or unconscious in the streets, a visit to one of the dormitories was confirmation enough that many of the people were ill, and even the activities of the vehicles reflected a change, for there were fewer of them about and one or two were clearly being used as ambulances.

Needless to say, as the full realization came to us, Amelia and I stayed away from the populated areas of the city. Fortunately, neither of us displayed any symptoms; the stuffiness as a result of my head-cold stayed with me rather longer than it might have done at home, but that was all.

Amelia's latent nursing instincts came to the surface, and her conscience told her she should go to help the sick, but it would have been grossly unwise to do so. We tried to cut ourselves off from the anguish, and hoped the disease would soon pass.

It seemed that the plague was not virulent. Many people had contracted it, and by the evidence of the number of bodies we saw being transported in one of the legged vehicles we knew that many had died. But after five days we noticed that life was beginning to return to normal. If anything, there was more misery about than ever before—for once we felt the Martians had good cause—and there were, regrettably, even fewer people in the underpopulated city, but the vehicles returned to their policing and haulage, and we saw no more dead in the streets.

But then, just as we were sensing the return to normal, there came the night of the green explosions.

Chapter Ten
A TERRIBLE INVASION

i

I was awakened by the first concussion, but in my sleepy state I presumed that the snow-cannon had been fired once more. During those nights of its firing we had grown accustomed to the tremors and distant explosions. The bang that woke me, though, was different.

"Edward?"

"I'm awake," I said. "Was that the cannon again?"

"No, it was different. And there was a flash. It lighted the whole room."

I stayed silent, for I had long since learned the futility of speculating about what we saw in this place. A few minutes passed, and the city was unmoving.

"It was nothing," I said. "Let's go back to sleep."

"Listen."

Some distance away, across the sleeping city, a policing-vehicle was driving quickly, its banshee siren howling. A moment later a second one started up, and passed within a few streets of where we lay.

Just then the room was lit for an instant with the most vivid and lurid flash of green. In its light I saw Amelia sitting up in her hammock, clutching her quilt around her. A second or two later we heard a tremendous explosion, somewhere beyond the city's limits.

Amelia climbed with the usual difficulty from the hammock, and walked to the nearest window.

"Can you see anything?"

"I think there's a fire," she said. "It's difficult to tell. There is something burning with a green light."

I started to move from my hammock, for I wished to see this, but Amelia stopped me.

"Please don't come to the window," she said. "I am un-clothed."

"Then please put something on, for I wish to see what is happening."

She turned and hurried towards where she placed her clothes at night, and as she did so the room was once more filled with brilliant green light. For a moment I caught an inadvertent glimpse of her, but managed to look away in time to spare her embarrassment. Two seconds later there was another loud ex-plosion; this was either much closer or much larger, for the ground shook with the force of it.

Amelia said: "I have my chemise on, Edward. You may come to the window with me now."

I normally slept wearing a pair of the Martian trouser-gar-ments, and so climbed hastily from the hammock and joined her at the window. As she had said, there was an area of green light visible away towards the east. It was neither large nor bright, but it had an intensity about the centre of the glow that would indicate a fire. It was dimming as we watched it, but then came another explosion just beside it and I pulled Amelia away from the window. The blast effect was this time the greatest yet, and we began to grow frightened.

Amelia stood up to look through the window again, but I placed my arm around her shoulder and pulled her forcibly away.

Outside, there was the sound of more sirens, and then another flash of green light followed by a concussion.

"Go back to the hammocks, Amelia," I said. "At least on those we will be shielded from the blast through the floor."

To my surprise Amelia did not demur, but walked quickly towards the nearest hammock and climbed on. I took one more look in the direction of the explosions, staring past the watch-tower that stood outside our building and seeing the ever-spreading diffusion of green fire. Even as I looked there was another brilliant flare of green light, followed by the con-cussion, and so I hurried over to the hammocks.

Amelia was sitting up in the one I normally used.

"I think tonight I should like you to be with me," she said, and her voice was trembling. I too felt a little shaken, for the force of those explosions was considerable, and although they were a good distance away were certainly greater than anything in my experience.

I could just make out her shape in the darkened room. I had been holding the edge of the hammock in my hand, and now Amelia reached forward and touched me. At that moment there was yet another flash, one far brighter than any of the others. This time the shock-wave, when it came, shook the very foundations of the building. With this, I threw aside my inhibitions, climbed on to the hammock, and wriggled under the quilt beside Amelia. At once her arms went around me, and for a moment I was able to forget about the mysterious explosions outside.

These continued, however, at irregular intervals for the best part of two hours, and as if they were provoked by the explosions the sound of the Martians' vehicle sirens doubled and redoubled as one after another hurtled through the streets.

So the night passed, with neither of us sleeping. My attention was divided, partly between the unseen events outside and the precious closeness of Amelia beside me. I so loved her, and even such a temporary intimacy was without parallel to me.

At long last dawn came, and the sound of the sirens faded. The sun had been up for an hour before the last one was heard, but after that all was silent, and Amelia and I climbed from the hammock and dressed.

I walked to the window, and stared towards the east . . . but there was no sign of the source of the explosions, beyond a faint smudge of smoke drifting across the horizon. I was about to turn back and report this to Amelia when I noticed that the watch-tower outside our building had vanished during the night. Looking further along the street I saw that all the others, which were now such a familiar part of the city, had also gone.

ii

After the bedlam of the night the city was unnaturally quiet, and so it was with quite understandable misgivings that we left the dormitory to investigate. If the atmosphere in the city had been in the past one of dreadful anticipation, then this stillness was like the approach of expected death. Desolation City was never a noisy place, but now it was empty and silent. We saw evidence of the night's activity in the streets, in the form of heavy marks in the road-surface where one of the vehicles had taken a corner too fast, and outside one of the dormitory halls was a pile of spilled and abandoned vegetables.

Rendered uneasy by what we saw, I said to Amelia: "Do you think we should be out? Would we not be safer inside?"

"But we must discover what is going on."

"Not at risk to ourselves."

"My dear, we have nowhere to hide on this world," she said.

We came at last to the building where we had once ascended to see the extent of the city. We agreed to climb to the roof, and survey the situation from there.

From the top the view told us little more than we already knew, for there was no sign of movement anywhere in the city. Then Amelia pointed to the east.

"So that is where the watch-towers have been taken!" she said.

Beyond the city's protective dome we could just make out a cluster of the tall objects. If those were the towers then that would certainly account for their disappearance from the city. It was impossible to see how many were out there, but at a reasonable estimate it was certainly a hundred or more. They had been lined up in a defensive formation, placed between the city and where we had seen the explosions in the night.

"Edward, do you suppose there is a war going on here?"

"I think there must be. Certainly there has not been a happy atmosphere in the city."

"But we have seen no soldiers."

"Maybe we are to see some for the first time."

I was in the lowest of spirits, sensing that at last we were going to be forced into accepting our plight. I saw at that moment no alternative to the prospect of becoming embroiled forever in Martian life. If a war it was for this city, then two aliens such as ourselves would soon be discovered. If we stayed in hiding we would doubtless be found, and, if so, would be taken for spies or infiltrators. We must, very soon, declare ourselves to those in authority and become as one with the inhabitants here.

Seeing no better vantage point available to us, we agreed to stay where we were until the situation became clearer. Neither of us had any wish to explore further; death and destruction were in the winds.

We did not have long to wait ... for even as we first saw the line of watch-towers defending the city the invasion, unbeknown to us, had already begun. What happened out there beyond the city's dome must be a matter of conjecture, but having seen the aftermath I can say with some certainty that the first line of defence was a troop of Martians armed only with hand-weapons. These wretched men were soon overwhelmed, and those not killed fled to the temporary safety of the city. This much was happening even as we walked through the streets to our present vantage point.

The next development was twofold.

In the first place, we at last saw signs of movement; these were the fleeing defenders, returning to the city. Secondly, the watch-towers were attacked. This was over in a matter of minutes. The antagonists were armed with some kind of heat thrower which, when turned on the towers, almost immediately rendered them molten. We saw the destruction as bursts of flame, as one tower after another was struck with this heat, and exploded violently.

If by this description I seem to imply that the towers were defenceless, then I must add that this was not so. When, somewhat later, I saw the wreckage of the battle, I realized that a spirited, if ultimately ineffectual, defence had been put up, for several of the attackers' vehicles had been destroyed.

Amelia's hand crept into mine, and I squeezed it reassuringly. I was placing secret faith in the city's dome, hoping that the marauders would have no way of penetrating it.

We heard screams. There were more of the people about the streets now, both city-Martians and slaves, running with the strange, loping gait, looking frantically about, intent on finding safety in the maze of city streets.

Suddenly, flame exploded about one of the buildings by the perimeter of the city, and screams could distantly be heard. Another building burst into flames, and then another.

We heard a new sound: a deep-throated siren, rising and falling, quite unlike the noises we had grown accustomed to in the city.

I said: "They have penetrated the dome."

"What shall we do?" Amelia's voice was calm, but I felt that she was forcing herself not to panic. I could feel her hand trembling in mine, and our palms were damp with perspiration.

"We must stay here," I said. "We are as safe here as anywhere."

Down in the streets more Martians had appeared, some running out from the buildings where they had been hiding. I saw that some of the people fleeing from the battle had been wounded, and one man was being carried by two of his fellows, his legs dragging.

One of the policing-vehicles appeared, moving quickly through the streets towards the battle. It slowed as it passed some of the Martians, and I heard the driver's voice, apparently ordering them to return to the fight. The people took no notice and continued their confused retreat, and the vehicle drove away. More sirens could be heard, and soon several more legged vehicles hurried past our building towards the fray. In the meantime, more buildings on the edge of the city had been fired.

I heard an explosion to the south of us, and I looked that way. I saw that flames and smoke were rising there, and realized that another force of invaders had broken through!

The plight of the city seemed desperate, for nowhere could I see a concerted defence, and there was certainly no resistance on the new front.

There came a grinding, roaring sound from the east, and another blast of that alien siren, immediately followed by a second. The Martians in the street near our building screamed terribly, their voices more high-pitched than ever.

Then at last we saw one of the marauders.

It was a large, ironclad vehicle, the rows of articulate legs concealed by metal plating at each side. Mounted high on its rear was a grey metal gun-barrel, some six or eight feet in length, which by the pivotal device on which it was mounted was able to point in any direction the driver of the vehicle chose. As soon as we saw the invading vehicle, this cannon rotated and a building to one side burst abruptly into flame. There was a terrible noise, like sheets of metal torn asunder.

The marauding vehicle was quite close to us, not more than two hundred yards away and in clear view. It showed no sign of halting, and as it passed a road junction it released another bolt of infernal energy, and one of the dining halls where we had often eaten exploded into flame.

"Edward! There!"

Amelia pointed down the intersecting street, along which we now saw five of the city's policing-vehicles approaching. I saw that they had been equipped with smaller versions of the invaders' heat-cannons, and as soon as they had a clear line of sight the two leading vehicles fired.

The effect was instantaneous: with a deafening explosion the invading vehicle blew apart, showering debris in all directions. I just had time to see that one of the attacking city-vehicles was blown backwards by the blast before the shock-wave hit the building we were on. Fortunately, Amelia and I were already crouching low, otherwise we should certainly have been knocked off our feet. Part of the parapet was blown inwards, narrowly missing me, and part of the roof behind us collapsed. For a few seconds the only sound we could hear was the crash of metal debris as it fell across the streets and buildings.

The four undamaged policing-vehicles continued on without hesitation, skirted around their damaged colleague and drove over the shattered remains of the enemy. A few seconds later they were lost to sight as they headed rapidly towards the scene of the main invasion.

We had only a few moments' respite.

With the sinister combination of clanking metal legs and ear-piercing sirens, four more of the marauders were coming into the centre of the city from the southern penetration. They moved with frightening speed, blasting occasionally at previously undamaged buildings. The smoke pouring out of the fired buildings was now swirling about our heads, and it was often difficult either to see or breathe.

We looked round desperately to see if any defenders were in the vicinity, but there was none. Scores of Martians still ran wildly in the streets.

Three of the marauders roared past our building, and disappeared into the smoke-filled streets to the north. The last, though, slowed as it came to the wreckage of its ally, and halted before the tangled metal. It waited there for a minute, then came slowly down the street towards us.

In a moment it stopped directly beneath our vantage point. Amelia and I stared down tremulously.

I said suddenly: "Oh my God, Amelia! *Don't look!!*"

It was too late. She too had seen the incredible sight that had caught my attention. For a few seconds it was as if all the confusion of this invasion had stilled, while we stared numbly at the enemy machine.

It had clearly been specially designed and built for operations such as this. As I have said, there was mounted on its rear the destruction-dealing heat projector, and stowed just in front of this was a much larger version of the metallic spider-machine we had seen repairing the watch-tower, crouching with its uncanny mechanical life momentarily stilled.

At the front of the vehicle was the position where the driver of the craft was situated; this was shielded in front, behind and to each side with iron armour. The top, though, was open, and Amelia and I were looking straight down into it.

What we saw inside the vehicle was not a man, let that be abundantly clear from the outset. That it was organic and not mechanical was equally apparent, for it pulsed and rippled with repellent life. Its colour was a dull grey-green, and its glistening main body was bloated and roughly globular, some five feet in diameter. From our position we could see few details, bar a light-coloured patch on the back of the body, roughly comparable to the blow-hole on the head of a whale. But we could also see its tentacles. . . . These lay in a grotesque formation at the front of the body, writhing and slithering in a most revolting fashion. Later I was to see that there numbered sixteen of these evil extensions, but in that first moment of appalled fascination it seemed that the whole cab was filled with these creeping, winding abominations.

I turned away from the sight, and glanced at Amelia.

She had gone deathly pale, and her eyes were closing. I placed my arm about her shoulders, and she shuddered instinctively, as if it had been that disgusting monster-creature, and not I, that had touched her.

"In the name of all that is good," she said. "What have we come to?"

I said nothing, a deep nausea stifling all words and thoughts. I simply looked down again at the loathsome sight, and registered that in those few seconds the monster-creature had levelled its heat-cannon into the heart of the building on which we crouched.

A second later there was a massive explosion, and smoke and flame leapt about us!

iii

In great terror, for in the impact more of the roof had fallen away behind us, we climbed unsteadily to our feet and headed blindly for the staircase by which we had ascended. Smoke was pouring densely from the heart of the building, and the heat was intense.

Amelia clutched my arm as more of the fabric collapsed beneath us, and a curtain of flame and sparks flared fifty feet above our heads.

The stairs were built of the same rock as the walls of the building, and still seemed sound, even as gusts of heat were billowing up them.

I wrapped my arm over my nose and mouth, and closing my eyes to slits I plunged down, dragging Amelia behind me. Two-thirds of the way to the bottom, part of the staircase had fallen away and we had to slow our flight, reaching hesitantly for footholds on the jagged parts of the slabs remaining. Here it was that the conflagration did its worst: we could not breathe, could not see, could not feel anything but the searing heat of the inferno below us. Miraculously, we found the rest of the steps undamaged, and thrust ourselves down again . . . at last emerging into the street, choking and weeping.

Amelia sank to the ground, just as several Martians rushed past us, screaming and shouting in their shrill, soprano voices.

"We must run, Amelia!" I shouted over the roar and confusion around us.

Gamely, she staggered to her feet. Holding my arm with one hand, and still clutching her hand-bag with the other, she followed me as we set off in the direction taken by the Martians.

We had gone but a few yards before we came to the corner of the blazing building.

Amelia screamed, and snatched at my arm: the invading vehicle had driven up behind us, hitherto concealed by the smoke. Thought of the repulsive occupant was alone enough to spur us on, and we half-fell, half-ran around the corner . . . to find a second vehicle blocking our way! It seemed to loom over us, fifteen or twenty feet high.

The Martians who had run before us were there; some were cowering on the ground, others were milling frantically about, searching for an escape.

On the back of the monstrous vehicle the glittering, spider-like machine was rearing up on its metal legs, its long articulate arms already reaching out like slow-moving whip-cord.

"*Run!*" I shouted at Amelia. "For God's sake, we must escape!"

Amelia made no response, but her clutch on my arm loosened, the hand-bag slipped from her fingers, and in a moment she fell to the ground in a dead faint. I crouched over her, trying to revive her.

Just once I looked up, and saw the dreadful arachnoid lurching through the crowd of Martians, its legs clanking, its metal tentacles swinging wildly about. Many of the Martians had fallen to the ground beneath it, writhing in agony.

I leaned forward over Amelia's crumpled figure, and bent over her protectively. She had rolled on to her back, and her face stared vacantly upwards. I placed my head beside hers, tried to cover her body with mine.

Then one of the metal tentacles lashed against me, wrapping itself around my throat, and the most hideous bolt of electrical energy coursed through me. My body contorted in agony, and I was hurled to one side away from Amelia!

As I fell to the ground I felt the tentacle snatching away from me, ripping open part of the flesh of my neck.

I lay supine, head lolling to one side, my limbs completely paralysed.

The machine advanced, stunning and crippling with its arms. I saw one wrap itself around Amelia's waist, and the jolt of electricity broke through her faint and I saw her face convulsing. She screamed, horribly and pitiably.

I saw now that the foul machine had picked up many of those Martians it had stunned, and was carrying them in rolls of its glittering tentacles, some still conscious and struggling, others inert.

The machine was returning to its parent vehicle. I could just see the control-cab from where I was lying, and to my ultimate horror I suddenly saw the face of one of the abominable beings who had initiated this invasion, staring at us through an opening in the armour. It was a broad, wicked face, devoid of any sign of good. Two large pale eyes stared expressionlessly across the carnage it was wreaking. They were unblinking eyes, merciless eyes.

The spider-machine had remounted the vehicle, dragging in its tentacles behind it. The Martians it had seized were wrapped in folds of jointed, tubular metal, imprisoned in this heaving cage. Amelia was among them, pinned down by three of the tentacles, held without care so that her body was twisted painfully. She was still conscious, and staring at me.

I was totally unable to respond as I saw her mouth open, and then her voice echoed shrilly across the few yards of space that separated us. She screamed my name, again and again.

I lay still, the blood pumping from the wound in my throat, and in a moment I saw the invading vehicle move away, driving with its unnatural gait through the broken masonry and swirling smoke of the devastated city.

Chapter Eleven
A VOYAGE ACROSS THE SKY

i

I do not know for how long I was paralysed, although it must have been several hours. I cannot remember much of the experience, for it was one of immense physical agony and mental torment, compounded by an impotence of such grossness that to dwell for even a moment on Amelia's likely fate was sufficient to send my thoughts into a maëlstrom of anger and futility.

Only one memory remains clear and undimmed, and that is of a piece of wreckage that happened to lie directly within my view. I did not notice it at first, so wild and blinding were my thoughts, but later it seemed to occupy the whole of my vision. Lying in the centre of the tangle of broken metal was the body of one of the noisome monster-creatures. It had been crushed in the explosion that had wrecked the vehicle, and the part of it I could see revealed an ugly mass of contusions and blood. I could also see two or three of its tentacles, curled in death.

In spite of my mute loathing and revulsion, I was satisfied to realize that beings so powerful and ruthless were themselves mortal.

At length I felt the first sensations returning to my body; I felt them first in my fingers, and then in my toes. Later, my arms and legs began to hurt, and I knew that control over my muscles was being restored. I tried moving my head, and although I was taken with dizziness I found I could raise it from the ground.

As soon as I could move my arm, I placed my hand against my neck and explored the extent of my throat-wound. I could feel a long and ugly cut, but the blood had stopped flowing and

I knew the wound must be superficial, otherwise I should have died within seconds.

After several minutes of trying I managed to lift myself into a sitting position, and then at last I found I could stand. Painfully, I looked about me.

I was the only living thing in that street. On the ground about me were several Martians; I did not examine them all, but those I did were certainly dead. Across by the other side of the street was the damaged vehicle, and its hateful occupant. And a few yards from where I stood, poignantly abandoned, was Amelia's hand-bag.

I walked over to it with heavy heart, and picked it up. I glanced inside, feeling as if I were invading her privacy, but the bag contained the only material possessions we had had, and it was important to know if they were still there. Nothing appeared to have been moved, and I closed the bag quickly. There were too many things inside it that reminded me of Amelia.

The body of the monster creature was still dominating my thoughts, in spite of my dread and loathing. Almost against my own will I walked across to the wreck, carrying Amelia's bag in my hand.

I stopped a few feet away from the hideous corpse, fascinated by the grisly sight.

I stepped back, not having learnt anything, but still there was something uncannily familiar about it that detained me. I diverted my attention from the dead being to the wreck that contained it. I had assumed that the vehicle had been one of those that had invaded the city. But then, looking anew, I remembered the policing-vehicle that had been blasted in the explosion, and realized that this must be it!

With that sudden awareness, the awful implications of the anonymous and faceless drivers of those city vehicles came to me . . . and I stepped back from the wreck in horror and amazement, more frightened than I had ever been in my life.

ii

A few minutes later, as I walked in a dazed fashion through the streets, a vehicle suddenly appeared in front of me. The driver must have seen me, for the vehicle halted at once. I saw that it was one of the city haulage-vehicles, and that standing in the back were between twenty and thirty Martian humans.

I stared at the control-cab, trying not to imagine the being that was behind the black oval window. A voice rasped out through the metal grille.

I stood quite still, panicking inside. I had no idea what to do, no idea what was expected of me.

The voice came again, sounding to my ready ear angry and peremptory.

I realized that several of the men in the back of the vehicle were leaning over towards me, extending their arms. I took this to mean that I was expected to join them, and so I walked over to them, and without further ado was helped aboard.

As soon as I and my bag were in the open rear compartment, the vehicle moved off.

My bloodied appearance ensured that I was the centre of attention as soon as I had boarded. Several of the Martians spoke directly to me, clearly awaiting some kind of reply. For a moment I was in a renewed state of panic, thinking that at last I should have to reveal my alien origins. . . .

But then a most fortunate inspiration came to me. I opened my mouth, made a gagging noise, and pointed at the heinous wound in my neck. The Martians spoke again, but I simply looked blank and continued to gag at them, hoping thereby to convince them that I had been stricken dumb.

For a few more seconds the unwanted attention continued, but then they seemed to lose interest in me. More survivors had been seen, and the vehicle had halted. Soon, three more men and a woman were being helped aboard. They had apparently not suffered at the hands of the invaders, for they were uninjured.

The vehicle moved off again, prowling the streets and oc-

casionally letting forth an unpleasant braying sound through its
metal grille. It was reassuring to be in the company of these
Martian humans, but I could never quite put from my mind the
grotesque presence of the monster-creature in the control-
cab.

The slow journey around the city continued for another two
hours, and gradually more survivors were picked up. From time
to time we saw other vehicles engaged in the same operation,
and I presumed from this that the invasion was over.

I found a corner at the back of the compartment, and sat
down, cradling Amelia's bag in my arms.

I was wondering if what we had seen was, after all, a full-
scale invasion. With the marauders departed, and the city
smoking and damaged, it seemed more likely that what we had
witnessed was more in the nature of a skirmish, or a reprisal
mission. I recalled the firing of the snow-cannon, and wondered
if those shells had been aimed at the cities of the enemy. If so,
then Amelia and I had blundered into a fracas in which we had
no part, and of which Amelia at least had become an unwitting
victim.

I thrust this thought aside: it was unbearable to think of her
at the mercy of these monster-creatures.

Somewhat later another thought occurred to me, one which
gave me several unpleasant minutes. Could it be, I wondered,
that I had been mistaken about the departure of the enemy?
Was this truck being driven by one of the conquerors?

I pondered this for some time, but then remembered the
dead monster I had seen. That was apparently of this city, and
furthermore the humans I was with did not show the same
symptoms of fear as I had seen during the fighting. Could it be
that *every* city on Mars was managed by the vile monster-
creatures?

There was hardly any time to consider this, for soon the
compartment was filled, and the vehicle set off at a steady pace
towards the edge of the city. We were deposited outside a large
building, and directed inside. Here, slaves had prepared a meal,
and with the others I ate what was put before me. Afterwards,
we were taken to one of the undamaged dormitory buildings

and allocated hammock-space. I spent that night lying in a cramped position with four Martian males on one hammock.

iii

There followed a long period of time (one so painful to me that I can barely bring myself to record it here), during which I was assigned to a labour-team set to repair the damaged streets and buildings. There was much to do, and, with the reduced population, no apparent end to the time I would be forced to work in this way.

There was never the least possibility of escape. We were guarded by the monster-creatures every moment of every day, and the apparent freedoms of the city, which had allowed Amelia and I to explore it so thoroughly, were long gone. Now only a minute area of the city was occupied, and this was policed not only by the vehicles, but also overseen by the watch-towers not damaged in the raid. These were occupied by the monsters, who were apparently capable of staying immobile in their perches for hours at a time.

Large number of slaves had been drafted in to the city, and the worst and heaviest tasks were given to them. Even so, much of the work I had to do was onerous.

I was glad in one way that the work was demanding, for it helped me not to dwell too long on Amelia's plight. I found myself wishing that she were dead, for I could not contemplate the horrible perversions the obscene creatures would put her to if she remained alive in their captivity. But at the same time, I could not for one moment allow myself to think she was dead. I wanted her alive, for she was my own *raison d'être*. She was always in my thoughts, however distracting the events around me, and at nights I would lie awake, tormenting myself with guilt and self-acrimony. I wanted and loved her so, that scarcely a night passed when I did not sob in my hammock.

It was no consolation that the misery of the Martians was an equal to mine, nor that at last I was understanding the causes of their eternal grief.

iv

I soon lost count of the days, but it could not have been less
than six of Earth's months before there came a dramatic change
in my circumstances. One day, without prior warning, I was
force-marched with about a dozen men and women away from
the city. A monster-vehicle followed us.

I thought at first we were being taken to one of the industrial
sites, but shortly after leaving the protective dome we headed
south, and crossed the canal by one of the bridges. Ahead of us
I saw the barrel of the snow-cannon looming up.

It appeared to have escaped undamaged in the raid—or else
had been efficiently repaired—for there was an activity about
the muzzle equal to the amount Amelia and I had seen that first
time. At sight of this my heart sank, for I did not relish the
thought of having to work in the thin, outer atmosphere; I was
not the only one breathing laboriously as we marched, but I felt
the native Martians would be better suited to working in the
open. The weight of Amelia's hand-bag—which I took with me
everywhere—was a further encumbrance.

We marched as far as the centre of the activity: close to the
muzzle itself. By this time I was on the point of collapse, so
difficult was it to breathe. As we came to a halt I discovered I
was not alone in my agony, for everyone sat weakly on the
ground. I joined them, trying to force my heart to still its
furious beating.

So occupied was I with my discomforts that I had neglected
to take stock of the events around me. I was aware of the great,
black muzzle twenty yards from me, and the fact that we had
halted by a crowd of slaves, but that was all.

There were two city-Martians standing to one side, and they
were regarding us with some interest. Once I realized this, I
looked back at them and saw that in certain respects they were
different from other men I had seen here. They seemed very
poised, for one thing, and they wore clothes that were different
from those worn by everyone else. These were black garments,
cut in almost military style.

Apparently my looking back at them had drawn attention to myself, for a moment later the two Martians walked over to me and said something. Playing my rôle as a mute, I stared back at them. Their patience was thin: one reached down to me and pulled me to my feet. I was pushed to one side, where three male slaves were already standing apart. The two city-Martians then went to where the rest of the slaves were standing, selected a young girl, and brought her over to join us.

I was uneasily aware that I and the four slaves had become the focus of some interest. Several of the Martians were staring at us, but as the two men in black came over to us they turned away, leaving us to whatever plight was in store.

An order was issued, and the slaves turned obediently away. I followed at once, still anxious not to seem different. We were herded towards what appeared at first sight to be an immense vehicle. As we approached, however, I saw that it consisted in fact of two objects, temporarily joined together.

Both parts were cylindrical in shape. The longer of the two was really the most bizarre machine I had seen during my time on Mars. It was about sixty feet in length, and, apart from its overall conformation to a cylindrical diameter of about twenty feet, was not regularly shaped. Along its base were many groups of the mechanical legs, but on the whole its exterior was smooth. At several places around its outer skin were perforations, and I could see water dribbling from some of these. At the far end of the machine a long, flexible pipe led away. This ran right across the desert, at least as far as the canal, and was looped and coiled in several places.

The smaller of the two objects is simpler to describe, in that its shape was readily identifiable. So familiar was this shape that my heart began to beat wildly once more: this was the projectile that would be fired from the cannon!

It was itself cylindrical for most of its length, but with a curving, pointed nose. The resemblance to an artillery-shell was startling . . . but there was never on Earth any shell of this size! From one end to another it must have been at least fifty feet long, and with a diameter of about twenty feet. The outer surface was finely machined so that it shone and dazzled in the bright sunlight. The smoothness of the surface was broken only in one place, and this was on the flat, rear end of the projectile. Here were four extrusions, and as we walked closer I saw that they were four of the heat-cannons we had seen the monster-creatures using. The four were placed symmetrically: one at the centre, the other three in an equilateral triangle about it.

The two Martians led us past this to where a hatchway had been opened, near the nose of the projectile. At this I hesitated, for it had suddenly become clear that we were to go inside. The slaves had hesitated too, and the Martians raised their whips in a menacing fashion. Before another move could be made, one of the slaves was touched across the shoulders. He howled with pain, and fell to the ground.

Two of the other slaves immediately bent to pick up the stricken man, and then, without further delay, we hurried up the sloping metal ramp into the projectile.

v

So it was that I began my voyage across the skies of Mars.

There were seven human beings aboard that craft: myself and the four slaves, and the two black-suited city-Martians who were in control.

The projectile itself was divided into three parts. At the very front of the craft was the small compartment where the two drivers stood during the flight. Immediately behind this, and separated from it by a metal partition, was a second compartment, and it was into this that I and the slaves were ushered. At the back of this compartment was a solid metal wall, entirely dividing this part of the craft from the main hold. It was there that the detestable monster-creatures and their deadly machines were carried. All this I discovered by a means I shall presently explain, but first I must describe the compartment in which I was placed.

I had by chance been the last to enter the craft, and so I found myself nearest to the partition. The two men in charge were shouting instructions to more men outside, and this lasted for several minutes, allowing me to take stock of where we were.

The interior of our compartment was almost bare. The walls were of unpainted metal, and because of the shape of the craft the floor where we stood curved up to become the ceiling too. Suspended from top to bottom, if my meaning is understood, were five tubes of what seemed to be a transparent fabric. Standing against the wall which separated this compartment from the main hold was what I at first took to be a large cupboard or cubicle, with two doors closed across it. I noticed that the slaves huddled away from it, and not knowing what it was for I too kept my distance.

The forward area was small and rather cramped, but what most overwhelmed me was the array of scientific equipment it contained. There was little here that I could comprehend, but there was one instrument whose function was immediately self-evident.

This was a large glass panel, placed directly in front of where the two drivers would stand. It was illuminated in some wise from behind, so that displays were projected on to it, not unlike several magic lanterns being operated at once. These displays revealed a number of views, and my attention was drawn to them.

The largest of the pictures showed the view directly forward of the projectile; that is to say, at the moment I first saw it the picture was entirely occupied by the machine presently connected to the nose of the projectile. Then there were views of what was happening to each side of the projectile, and behind. Another showed the very compartment in which I stood, and I could see my own figure standing by the partition. I waved my hand to myself for several moments, enjoying the novelty. The last showed what I presumed was the interior of the main hold of the craft, but here the image was dark and it was not possible to make out details.

Less interesting than this panel were the other instruments, the largest of which were clustered before two more of the flexible, transparent tubes which ran from top to bottom of the compartment.

At last the men at the hatch finished their instructions, and they stepped back. One of them wound a wheeled handle, and the hatch door was slowly brought up until it was flush with the rest of the hull. As it did so, our one source of daylight was sealed, and artificial lighting came on. Neither of the two men paid any attention to us, but moved across to the controls.

I looked at the slaves with me inside the compartment. The girl and one of the men were squatting on the floor, while a third spoke reassuringly to the man who had been struck with the whip. This last was in a bad way: he was trembling uncontrollably, and had lost the use of his facial muscles so that his eyes were slack, and saliva trickled from his mouth.

Returning my gaze to the displays I saw that with the turning on of the artificial lights, the main hold of the craft could now be seen. Here, in conditions which looked intolerably cramped, were the monster-creatures. I counted five of them, and each had already installed itself in a larger version of the transparent fabric tubes that I had already seen. Seeing these ghastly beings thus suspended was no less horrific for being slightly comical.

Looking at the other panels I saw that there was still considerable activity around the projectile. There seemed to be several hundred people outside, mostly slaves, and they were engaged in hauling away various pieces of heavy equipment which stood around the muzzle of the cannon.

Many minutes passed, with no apparent movement in the craft. The two men at the controls were busy checking their instruments. Then, unexpectedly, the whole projectile lurched, and looking at the various panels I saw that we were moving slowly backwards. Another panel showed the view at the rear of the craft: we were being propelled slowly up the ramp towards the muzzle of the cannon.

vi

The legged vehicle attached to the nose of the craft appeared to be in control of this operation. As the shell itself was pushed into the mouth of the barrel I noticed two things more or less simultaneously. The first was that the temperature inside the craft immediately lowered, as if the metal of the barrel were somehow artificially cooled, and thus sucking the warmth from the projectile; the second was that on the forward-looking panel I saw great fountains of water spraying from the controlling vehicle. The collar from which the spray was shot was rotating about the main body of the vehicle, for the spray was circling. This much I saw as we entered the barrel, but after a few seconds we had been advanced so far that the controlling vehicle itself entered the barrel and so blocked the daylight.

Now, although there were a few electrical lights implanted in the walls of the cannon, very little could be seen on the panels. Faintly, though, beyond the metal hull of the projectile, I could hear the hiss of the water spraying about us.

The temperature inside the projectile continued to fall. Soon it seemed as cold as it had been that first night Amelia and I had spent in the desert, and had I not been long accustomed to this frozen and hostile world I should have thought I would surely die of frostbite. My teeth were beginning to chatter when I heard a sound I had learned to dread: the harsh grating of the monster-creatures' voices, coming from a grille in the control cabin. Soon after this, I saw one of the men in charge pull a lever, and in a moment a draught of warmer air flowed through the compartment.

So our long passage down the barrel of the cannon continued. After the first moments, when the men in control were working furiously, there was not much for anyone to do but wait until the operation was completed. I passed the time by watching the monster-creatures in the hold: the one nearest me on the display-panel seemed to be staring directly at me with its cold, expressionless eyes.

The end of the operation, when it came, was without ceremony. We simply came to the deepest recess of the barrel—where there had already been placed a solid core of ice, blocking our way—and waited while the vehicle in control finished its water-spraying operation. Looking at the rearward display-panel I saw that the projectile had come to rest only inches from the core of ice.

From this moment, the remainder of the operation passed smoothly and quickly. The controlling vehicle separated from the projectile, and retreated quickly away up the barrel. Without the load of the craft the vehicle travelled much faster, and within a matter of minutes it had cleared the end of the barrel.

On the forward display-panel I could see up the entire length of the barrel, to a tiny point of daylight at the very end. The barrel between us and the daylight had been coated with a thick layer of ice.

vii

Once more came the sound of the monster-creatures' voices from the grille, and the four slaves I was with leapt to obey. They hastened towards the flexible tubes, helping the wounded man to his own. I saw that in the control cabin the other two men were climbing into the tubes that stood before the controls, and I realized that I too must obey.

Glancing round, I saw that one of the transparent tubes was placed in such a position that view of the control cabin could be maintained, but that one of the men slaves was already climbing into it. Not wishing to lose my advantageous view of the proceedings, I caught the man by his shoulder and waved my arms angrily. Without hesitation the slave cowered away from me, and moved to another tube.

I picked up Amelia's bag and climbed into the tube through a fold in the fabric, wondering what I was in for. When I was inside the fabric hung loosely about me like a curtain. Air was ducted through it from above, so in spite of the feeling of total enclosure it was not unbearable.

My view was rather more restricted, but I could still see three of the displays: the ones facing fore and aft of the projectile, and one of those facing to the side. This last, of course, was presently black, for it showed nothing but the wall of the barrel.

Quite unexpectedly there came a deep vibration in the projectile, and at the same moment I felt myself being tipped backwards. I tried to step back to maintain balance, but I was totally enclosed by the transparent fabric. Indeed, I was now understanding part of the function of this transparent tube, for as the muzzle of the cannon was being raised, the tube was tightening around me and so supporting me. The further the cannon barrel was raised the tighter the tube wrapped itself about me, to the point that as the tilting came to an end I was totally incapable of any movement at all. I was now lying with most of my weight supported by the tube, for although my feet were still touching the floor, the cannon had been raised until we were about forty-five degrees from horizontal.

No sooner had we come to rest than I saw a blaze of light shine out on the rearward-facing panel, and there was a tremendous jolt. A great and ineluctable pressure bore down on me, and the transparent tube tightened still more. Even so, the thrust of acceleration pressed against me as if with an immense hand.

After the first jolt there was no discernible sensation of motion apart from this pressure, for the ice had been laid with great precision and polished like a mirror. Looking at the rearward display I saw only darkness, stabbed with four beams of white light; ahead, the point of daylight visible at the muzzle was approaching. At first its apparent approach was almost undetectable, but within a few seconds it was rushing towards us with ever-increasing velocity.

Then we were out of the barrel, and in the same instant the pressure of acceleration was gone, and bright pictures flooded to the three displays I could see.

In the rearward panel I could see for a few seconds a receding view of the cannon, a huge cloud of steam pouring from the muzzle; on the side panel I caught erratic glimpses of land and sky whirling about; on the forward display I could see only the deep blue of the sky.

Thinking that at last it would be safe to leave the protection of the fabric I tried to step out, but discovered that I was still firmly held. There was a terrible vertiginous sensation spinning my head, as if I were falling from a great height, and at last I experienced in full the terrors of helpless confinement; I was truly trapped in this projectile, incapable of movement, tumbling through the sky.

I closed my eyes and took a deep breath. The air ducted through the tube was cool, and it reassured me to know that I was not intended to die here.

I took another deep breath, then a third, forcing myself to be calm.

At length I opened my eyes. Nothing inside the projectile had changed, as far as I could see. The scenes on the three displays were uniform: each showed the blue of the sky, but on the rearward one I could see a number of objects floating behind our craft. I wondered for a while as to what these could be, but then identified them as the four heat-projectors which had been played on the ice inside the cannon. I presumed by the fact of their being discarded that they had no further function.

That the craft was turning slowly on its axis became apparent a few seconds later, when the sideways panel unexpectedly revealed the horizon of the land, swinging up and across the picture. Soon the entire display was filled with a high view of land, but we were at such an altitude that it was almost impossible to see details. We were passing over what looked like a dry, mountainous region, but a major war had obviously taken place at some time as the ground was pock-marked with huge craters. Later, the craft rolled further so that the sky returned to fill the display.

From the forward display I learned that the craft must now have levelled off, for the horizon could be seen here. I presumed that this meant we were now in level flight, although the axial spin continued, evidenced by the fact that the forward horizon was spinning confusingly. The men controlling the craft must have had some way of correcting this, for I heard a series of hissing noises and gradually the horizon steadied.

I had thought that once we were in flight there would be no more shocks in store, so I was very alarmed a few minutes later when there was a loud explosion and a brilliant green light flooded across all the panels I could see. The flash was momentary, but another followed seconds later. Having seen those green flashes in the hours before the invasion I thought at first we must be under attack, but between each explosion the atmosphere inside the craft remained calm.

The frequency of these green explosions increased, until there was one almost every second, deafening me. Then they ceased for a while, and I saw that the projectile's trajectory had been drastically lowered. For an instant I saw in the forward panel the image of a vast city on the ground before us, then there was another burst of green fire burning continually outside the craft, and all became obscured by the blaze. In the noise of the roaring, explosive light I felt the transparent fabric tightening around me ... and my last impression was of an almost intolerable deceleration, followed by a tremendous crash.

Chapter Twelve
WHAT I SAW INSIDE THE CRAFT

i

The panels had gone black, the fabric tubes had relaxed, and all was silent. The floor was tilted sharply forward, and so I fell from the supporting folds and collapsed against the partition, hardly daring to believe that once more the projectile was on solid ground. Beside me, the four slaves also fell or stepped from their tubes, and we all crouched together, trembling a little after the shocks of the flight.

We were not left alone for long. From beyond the partition I heard the sound of voices, and in a moment one of the men appeared; he too looked shaken, but he was on his feet and carrying his whip.

To my anger and surprise he raised this devilish instrument, and shouted imprecations at us in his soprano voice. Naturally, I could not understand, but the effect on the slaves was immediate. One of the men-slaves clambered to his feet and shouted back, but he was struck with the whip and fell to the floor.

Again the man in charge shouted at us. He pointed first at the slave who had been whipped as we entered the projectile, then at the man he had just stunned, then at the third male slave, then at the girl and finally at me. He shouted once more, pointed at each of us in turn, then fell silent.

As if to reinforce his authority, the villainous voice of one of the monster-creatures came braying through the grille, echoing in the tiny metal compartment.

The slave who had been pointed at first was lying nervelessly on the floor, where he had fallen from his protective tube, and the girl and the other slave bent to help him to his feet. He was still conscious, but like the other man he appeared to have lost all use of his muscles. I went forward to help them with him, but they ignored me.

Now their attention was directed towards the protruding cubicle I had noticed earlier. The doors had remained closed throughout the flight, and I had assumed that the cubicle contained some equipment. That this was not so was instantly revealed when the girl pulled the doors open.

Because of the tilting of the craft the doors swung right open, and I was able to see what was inside. The entire space was no larger than that of a cupboard, with just enough room for a man to stand within it. Attached to the metal bulkhead were five clamps, like manacles, but made with a fiendish precision that lent to them a distinctly surgical air.

The male slave was pushed awkwardly to the entrance to this cubicle, his head lolling and his legs slack. However, some awareness must have been filtering through his befuddled mind, for as soon as he saw where he was about to be put he set up as much resistance as he could muster; he was, though, no match for the other two, and after about a minute's struggle they managed to get him upright into the cubicle.

As soon as the relevant part of his body was in contact, the manacles closed of their own accord. His two arms were held first, then his legs, and finally his neck. A low moaning noise came from his mouth, and he moved his head desperately, trying to escape. The girl moved quickly to close the doors on him, and at once his feeble cries could scarcely be heard.

I looked in appalled silence at the others. They stared at the floor, avoiding everyone else's gaze. I noticed that the man in charge still stood by the partition, his whip ready for further use.

Five anguished minutes passed, then with a shocking suddenness the doors of the cubicle fell open and the man collapsed across the floor.

I bent down to examine him, as he had fallen near my feet. He was certainly unconscious, probably dead. Where the manacles had held him were rows of punctures, about one-eighth of an inch in diameter. A trace of blood flowed from each one, on his limbs and his neck. There was not much blood oozing, for his body was as white as snow; it was as if every drop of blood had been sucked away.

Even as I was examining this unfortunate, the second stunned man was being dragged towards the cubicle. His resistance was less, for the electrical shock had been administered more recently, and within a few seconds his body had been manacled in place. The doors were closed.

One of the most shocking aspects of all this was the uncomplaining acceptance by the slaves of their lot. The two remaining slaves, the man and the girl, stood passively, waiting for the wretch in the cubicle to be bled dry. I could not believe that such barbarities would be tolerated, and yet so strong was the régime of the monster-creatures that even this atrocity was implemented by the city-Martians.

I looked away from the man with the whip, hoping he would lose interest in me. When, a few moments later, the man in the cubicle was released and fell inertly across the floor, I followed the lead of the other two and calmly moved his body out of the way to make access again to the cubicle.

The remaining male slave went of his own accord to the cubicle, the manacles closed around him, and I shut the doors quickly.

The man with the whip stared at the girl and me for a few seconds longer, then, evidently satisfied that we were capable of continuing unsupervised, returned unexpectedly to the control cabin.

Sensing a minuscule chance of escape, I glanced at the girl; she seemed uninterested and had sat down with her back to the partition. Free for a moment to act and think independently, I looked desperately around the compartment. As far as I could see there was no way out except by the hatchway beyond the partition. I looked at the curving ceiling and floor, but these were unbroken except for the fittings of the flexible tubes.

I went quietly to the partition, and peered around it at the two Martians in charge. They had their backs towards me, attending to some matter at the controls of the craft. I looked at the wheel-device which opened and closed the hatch; it would be impossible for me to open it without their hearing me.

Behind me, the cubicle door burst open and the male slave fell out, his bloodless arm falling across the girl. At the sound of this, the two Martians at the controls turned round, and I ducked out of sight. The girl was looking at me, and for a moment I was mortified by the expression of stark fear which contorted her features. Then, without a sound, she stepped into the cubicle, and I was alone with the three bodies of the slaves.

I closed the doors of the cubicle without glancing inside, then went to a part of the compartment where no bodies lay, and was violently sick.

ii

I could no longer stay in that hellish compartment with its sights and odours of death; blindly, I struggled over the heaped bodies and hurled myself around the partition, determined to do to death the two Martian humans who were the instruments of the torturous slaughter.

I had never in all my life been taken with such a blinding and all-consuming rage and nausea. In my hatred I threw myself across the control cabin and landed a huge blow with my arm on the back of the neck of the Martian nearer to me. He crumpled immediately, his forehead smiting a jagged edge of the instrumentation.

His electrical whip fell to the floor beside him, and I snatched it up.

The other Martian was already seated on the floor, and in the two or three seconds my first attack had taken had time only to turn his face towards me. I swung the whip viciously, catching him across his collar-bone, and at once he jerked and fell sideways. Coldly and deliberately I stood over him, pressing the end of the whip against his temple. He jerked spasmically for a few seconds, then was still. I turned my attention to the other

Martian, who was now lying semi-conscious on the floor, blood pouring from the wound in his head. He too I treated with the whip, then at last I threw aside the terrible weapon, and turned away. I was taken with dizziness, and in a moment I passed out. My last memory was of hearing the sound of the slave-girl's body as it fell into the compartment behind me.

Chapter Thirteen
A MIGHTY BATTLE

i

My faint must have turned naturally to sleep, for the next few hours are unremembered.

When at last I awoke my mind was tranquil, and for several minutes I had no memory of the hideous events I had witnessed. As soon as I sat up, though, I was confronted with the bodies of the two city-Martians, and everything returned in vivid detail.

I consulted my watch. I had kept this wound, as I had discovered that the length of a Martian day was almost the same as that on Earth, and although a knowledge of the exact hour was unnecessary on Mars, it was a useful guide to elapsed time. Now I saw that I had been aboard the projectile for more than twelve hours. Every minute I stayed within its confines was reminder of what I had seen and done, so I crossed directly to the hatch and attempted to open it. I had seen it being closed, so I assumed that a simple reversal of the action would be sufficient. This was not so; after moving an inch or two the mechanism jammed. I wasted several minutes trying, before I abandoned the effort.

I looked around the cabin, sensing for the first time that I might well be trapped here. It was a terrifying thought and I began to panic, pacing up and down in the confined space, my mind anguished.

At last sense filtered through, and I set myself to a meticulous and systematic examination of the cabin.

First, I examined the controls, hoping that there might be some way I could set the display-panels working, so that I could see where the craft had landed. With no success here (the impact of landing appeared to have broken the workings), I turned my attention to the flying controls themselves.

Although at first sight there seemed to be an amazing confusion of levers and wheels, I soon noticed that certain instruments were placed inside one of the transparent pressure-tubes. It was in these that the two Martians had passed the flight, and so it was logical that they would have had to be able to control the trajectory from within.

I parted the fabric with my hands (now that the flight was over it was quite limp), and inspected these instruments.

They were solidly built—presumably to withstand the various pressures of the firing and final impact—and simple in design. A kind of podium had been built on the floor of the cabin, and it was on this that they were mounted. Although there were certain needle-dials whose function I could not even guess, the two major controls were metal levers. One of these bore a remarkable resemblance to the lever on Sir William's Time Machine: it was mounted pivotally and could be moved fore or aft, or to either side. I touched it experimentally, and moved it away from me. At once, there was a noise in another part of the hull, and the craft trembled slightly.

The other lever was surmounted by a piece of some bright-green substance. This had only one apparent movement—downwards—and at the same moment I laid my hand on it there was a tremendous explosion outside the hull, and I was thrown from my feet by a sudden, sharp movement of the entire craft.

As I clambered to my feet again I realized that I had discovered the device that triggered the green flashes which had controlled our landing.

Understanding at last that the projectile was still functioning, if momentarily at rest, I decided that it would be safer if I were instead to concentrate on escaping.

I returned to the hatch and renewed my efforts to turn the wheel. Much to my surprise it was freer, and the hatch itself actually shifted a few inches before jamming again. As it did so a quantity of gravel and dry soil poured through the crack. This was rather perplexing, until I realized that in the impact of our landing a large part of the craft, and most certainly the nose, would have been buried in the ground.

I considered this with some care, then closed the hatch thoughtfully. I returned to the controls, then, bracing myself, I depressed the green-tipped lever.

A few seconds later, slightly deafened and certainly unsteady on my feet, I returned to the hatch. It was still jammed, but there was more play than before.

It took four more attempts before the hatch opened far enough to admit a minor avalanche of soil and pebbles, and daylight showed above. I hesitated only long enough to pick up Amelia's hand-bag, then squeezed my way through the aperture to freedom.

ii

After a long climb through loose soil, using the solid bulk of the hull to support myself, I reached the top of the wall of dirt.

I saw that the projectile had on landing created for itself a vast pit, in which it now rested. On every side of it had been thrown up large mounds of soil, and acrid green smoke —produced presumably as a result of my efforts—drifted about. I had no way of telling how deeply the projectile had been buried on its first impact, although I guessed I had shifted it from its original position during my escape.

I walked around to the rear end of the projectile, which was clear of the ground and overhanging unbroken soil. The monster-creatures had thrown open the huge hatch, which was the rear wall of the projectile, and the main hold—which I now saw as taking up most of the volume of the craft—was empty both of beings and their devices. The bottom lip was only a foot or two above the ground, so it was easy to enter the hold. I went inside.

It was the work of a few moments to walk through the cavernous hold and inspect the traces of the monsters' presence, and yet it was nearly an hour before I finally emerged from the craft.

I found that my earlier count had been accurate: that there was space for five of the monsters in the hold. There had also been several of the vehicles aboard, for I saw many bulkheads and clamps built into the metal hull by which they had been restrained.

In the deepest part of the hold, against the wall which separated it from the forward section, I came across a large canopy, the shape and volume of which indicated unerringly that it was for the use of the monsters. With some trepidation I peered inside . . . then recoiled away.

Here was the mechanism which operated the blood-sucking cubicle in the slaves' compartment, for I saw an arrangement of blades and pipettes, joined by transparent tubes to a large glass reservoir still containing much blood.

By this device did these vampiric monsters take the lives of humans!

I went to the opened end of the hold, and cleared my lungs of the stench. I was utterly appalled by what I had found, and my whole body was trembling with revulsion.

A little later I returned to the interior of the craft. I went to examine the various pieces of equipment the monsters had left behind them, and in doing this I made a discovery that made my elaborate escape seem unnecessary. I found that the hull of the projectile was actually of double thickness, and that leading from the main hold was a network of narrow passages which traversed most of the length of the craft. By clambering through these I came eventually, through a trap-door in the floor that I had not previously noticed, into the control-cabin.

The bodies of the two Martian humans were enough reminder of what I had seen aboard the projectile, so without further delay I returned through the passages to the main hold. I was about to jump down to the floor of the desert when it occurred to me that in this dangerous world it would be as well to be armed, and so I searched the hold for something that might serve as a weapon. There was not much to choose from, for the monsters had taken all movable pieces with them . . .

but then I remembered the blades in the blood-letting canopy.

I filled my lungs with fresh air, then hurried to the canopy. There I found that the blades were held in place by a simple sheath, and so I selected one of about nine inches in length. I unscrewed it, wiped it clean on the fabric of one of the pressure-tubes, and placed it inside Amelia's hand-bag.

Then at last I hurried from the craft, and went out into the desert.

iii

I looked about me, wondering which way I should travel to find shelter. I knew I was somewhere near another city, for I had seen it on the display as we landed, but where it was I did not know.

I glanced first at the sun, and saw that it was near meridian. At first this confused me, for the projectile had been launched at the height of the day and I had slept for only a few hours, but then I realized just how far the craft must have travelled. It had been launched in a westerly direction, so I must now be on the other side of the planet during the same day!

However, what was important was that there were still several hours to nightfall.

I walked away from the projectile towards an outcropping of rock some five hundred yards away. This was the highest point I could see, and I judged that from its peak I should be able to survey the whole region.

I was not being mindful of my surroundings: I kept my eyes directed towards the ground in front of me. I was not elated at my escape, and indeed there was a great gloom in me; a familiar emotion, for I had lived with it since that day in Desolation City when Amelia had been snatched away from me. Nothing had served to remind me of her. It was simply that now I was freed of my immediate concerns, my thoughts returned inevitably to her.

Thus it was that I was halfway to the rocks before I noticed what was going on around me.

I saw that many more projectiles had landed. There were a dozen within my view, and to one side I could see three of the legged ground vehicles standing together. Of the monsters themselves, or the humans who had brought them here, there was no sign, although I knew that most of the monsters were probably already seated inside the armoured housings of their vehicles.

My lonely presence attracted no attention as I trudged across the reddish sand. The monsters cared little for the affairs of humans, and I cared nothing for theirs. My only hope was to locate the city, and so I continued on my way to the rocks.

Here I paused for a moment, staring around. The texture of the rocks was brittle, and as I placed my weight on a low ledge, tiny chips of the alluvial rock fell away.

I climbed carefully, balancing my weight with Amelia's bag.

When I was about twenty feet above the desert floor I came to a broad shelf across the face of the rocks, and I rested for a few seconds.

I looked out across the desert, seeing the ugly craters made by the projectiles as they landed, and seeing the blunt, open ends of the projectiles themselves. I stared as far I could see in all directions, but there was no sign of the city. I picked up the bag again, and started to work my way around the face of the rocks, climbing all the way.

The outcrop was larger than I had first supposed, and it took me several minutes to reach the other side. Here the rocks were more broken, and my hold was precarious.

I came around a large rocky protuberance, feeling my way along a narrow ledge. As I cleared the obstacle, I stopped in amazement.

Directly in front of me—and, coincidentally, blocking my view across the desert—was the platform of one of the watch-towers!

I was so surprised to see one here that I felt no sense of danger. The thing was still; the black, oval window was on the further side, so even if there were a monster-creature inside I would not be noticed.

I looked across the rock-face in the direction I had been

climbing towards, and saw that here there was a deep cleft. I leaned forward, supporting myself with my hand, and glanced down; I was now about fifty feet above the desert floor, and it was a sheer drop. My only way down was by the way I had come. I hesitated, debating what to do.

I felt certain that there was one of the monster-creatures inside the platform of the tower, but why it was standing here in the shelter of the rocks I could not say. I remembered the towers in the city: during normal times the towers seemed to be left to work mechanically. I wondered if this were one such. Certainly, the fact that its platform was immobile lent weight to the notion that the platform was unoccupied. Furthermore, by its very presence it was denying me the purpose of my climb. I needed to locate the city, and from where I was forced to stand by nature of the rocks' configuration, my view was blocked by the tower.

Looking again at the platform of the tower I wondered if this obstacle might be turned to my advantage.

I had never before been quite as close to one as this, and the details of its construction became of great interest to me. Around the base of the platform itself was a shelf or ledge some twenty-four inches in depth; a man could stand in comfort on it, and indeed in greater safety than in my present position on the rocks. Above this shelf was the body of the platform itself: a broad, shallow cylinder with a sloping roof, some seven feet high at the back, and about ten feet high at the front. The roof itself was domed slightly, and around part of its circumference was a rail about three feet high. On the rear wall were three metal rungs, which presumably assisted entry to and exit from the platform itself, for set into a part of the roof directly above them was a large hatch, which was presently closed.

Without further delay I gripped the rungs and hauled myself up to the roof, swinging Amelia's bag before me. I stood up and stepped gingerly towards the rail, gripping it with my free hand. Now at last my view across the desert was uninterrupted.

The sight I saw was one which no man before me had ever beheld.

I have already described how much of the Martian terrain is flat and desert-like; that there are also mountainous regions was evidenced by my view from the projectile in flight. What I did not until that moment realize was that, in certain parts of the desert, single mountains—of a height and breadth with no Earthly parallel—thrust themselves out of the plain, standing alone.

One such stood before me.

Now, lest my words should mislead, I must immediately modify my description, for my very first impression of this mountain was that its scale was quite insignificant. Indeed, my attention was drawn first to the city I had been seeking, which lay some five miles from where I stood. This I saw through the crystal-clear Martian air, and registered that it was built on a scale that vastly exceeded that of Desolation City.

Only when I had established the direction in which I should have to travel, and the distance I would have to cover to reach it, did I look beyond the city towards the mountains against whose lower slopes it had been built.

At first sight this mountain appeared to be the beginnings of a rounded plateau region; instead of the upper surface being sharply defined, however, the heights were vague and unclear. As my senses adapted, I realized that this lack of definition was caused by my looking along the very surface of the mountain's slope. So large was the mountain, in fact, that the major part of it lay beyond the horizon, so that the thrust of its height was competing with the planet's curvature! In the far distance I could just make out what must have been the mountain's peak: white and conical, with vapour drifting from the volcanic crater.

This summit seemed to be no more than a few thousand feet high; taking into account the fact of the planet's curvature, I dare say that a more accurate estimate of the height would be at least ten or fifteen *miles* above ground level! Such physical scale was almost beyond the comprehension of a man from Earth, and it was many minutes before I could accept what I saw.

I was preparing to climb back to the rocks, and start my

descent to the ground, when I noticed a movement some distance to my left.

I saw that it was one of the legged vehicles, moving slowly across the desert in the direction of the city. It was not alone; in fact, there were several dozen of these vehicles, presumably brought in the many projectiles which lay scattered across the desert.

What was more, there were scores of the watch-towers, some standing about the vehicles, others sheltering, like the one on which I was perched, beside one or another outcropping of rock, of which there were several between here and the city.

I had long realized that the flight in which I had taken part was a military mission, retaliating against the invasion of Desolation City. I had further assumed that the target would be a minor foe, for I had seen the might of those invaders and did not think that vengeance would be sought directly against them. But this was not the case. The city against which the vehicles were ranged was immense, and when I looked towards it I could just make out the extent to which the place was defended. The outer limits of the city, for example, seemed forested with watch-towers, lining the perimeter so thickly in places that it was as if a stockade had been erected. Moreover, the ground was swarming with fighting-vehicles, and I could see orderly patterns of them, like black metal soldiers on parade.

Against this was the pitiful attacking force on whose side accident had placed me. I counted sixty of the legged ground vehicles, and about fifty of the watch-towers.

I was so fascinated by this spectacle of a coming battle that I forgot for a moment where I was standing. Indeed, I was speculating about just what kind of rôle the watch-towers would play, neglecting the fact that if I did not move I should surely find out! My best estimate was that the legged vehicles would move forward to attack the city, while the watch-towers would stand defence over the projectiles.

At first this seemed to be the case. The legged vehicles moved slowly and steadily towards the city, and those watch-towers unprotected by the rocks began to raise their platforms to the full height of sixty feet.

I decided that it was time I left my vantage point, and turned round to look back at the rocks, still gripping the rail in my hand.

Then something happened I could never have anticipated. I heard a slight noise to my right, and I looked round in surprise. There, emerging from behind the bluff wall of the rocks, came a watch-tower.

It was *walking*: the three metal shafts that were the legs of the tower were striding eerily beneath the platform!

The tower on which I stood suddenly lurched, and we fell forward. All around, the other watch-towers withdrew their legs from the gravelly soil, and strode forward in the wake of the ground-vehicles.

It was too late to jump to safety on the rock-face: already it was twenty yards away. I gripped the rail for all I was worth, as the walking watch-tower bore me out into battle!

iv

It was no good recriminating with myself for my lack of fore-sight; the incredible machine was already moving at about twenty miles an hour, and accelerating all the while. The air roared past my ears, and my hair flew. My eyes were streaming.

The watch-tower that had been beside mine at the rocks was a few yards ahead of us, but we were keeping pace. Because of this I was able to see how the contraption managed its ungainly gait. I saw that it was no less than a larger version of the tripodal legs that powered the ground-vehicles, but the effect here was quite startling in its total alienness. When driving forward at speed there were never more than two legs in contact with the ground at any moment, and that only for a fleeting instant. The weight was transferred constantly from one leg to the next in turn, while the other two swung up and forwards. To effect this the platform at the top was tilted slightly to the right, but the very smoothness of the motion indicated that there was a kind of transmission mounting below the platform that absorbed the minor irregularities of the ground. I felt far from secure on my precarious perch, but for the moment a firm grip on the rail was enough to ensure that I would not be easily pitched to the ground.

In the heat of the moment I cursed myself for not having realized that these towers themselves must be mobile. It was true that I had never before seen one in motion, but none of my speculations about their use had made any kind of consistent sense.

We were still increasing our speed, moving in a wide formation towards the enemy city.

In the van was a line of the vehicles. They were flanked on each side by four of the towers. Behind them, spread out in a second rank about half a mile long, were ten more of the ground-vehicles. The rest, including the tower on which I stood, holding on for dear life, followed in open formation behind. Already we were moving at such a speed that the legs were throwing up a cloud of sand and grit, and the wake from the leading vehicles was stinging my face. My own machine ran smoothly on, the engine humming powerfully.

Within about a minute we were travelling as fast as any steam-train could go, and here the speed stayed constant. There was no longer any question of escaping from this frightful situation; it was all I could do to stay upright and not be dislodged.

My downfall was nearly precipitated when, without warning, a metal flap opened beneath my legs! I hauled myself to one side away from it, thankful that the motion of the machine was steady, and watched incredulously as there unfolded from the aperture an immense metal contraption, extended on telescopic rods. As it brushed within a few inches of my face I saw to my horror that the object mounted was the barrel of one of the heat-cannons. It raised itself higher, until it was protruding above the roof of the tower by some eight feet or more.

Ahead of us I saw that the other towers had also extended their cannons, and we plunged on across the desert, headlong in this most bizarre of cavalry-charges!

I was now almost blinded by the sand being thrown up by the leading vehicles, so for the next minute or two I was unable to see more than the two hurtling towers immediately ahead of my own. The leading vehicles must have wheeled to left and right suddenly, for without warning there came a break in the cloud of grit and I was able to see directly ahead.

We had been flung, by the diversion of the leading vehicles, into the front-line of the battle!

Ahead of me now I could see the machines of the defending city coming across the desert to meet us. And what machines they were! There were few of the ground-vehicles, but the defenders strode confidently towards us on their towers. I could hardly believe what I saw. These battle-machines easily dwarfed those of my side, rising at least one hundred feet into the air.

The nearest to us were now less than half a mile away, and coming nearer with every second.

I stared in amazement at these Titans striding towards us with such effortless ease. The assemblage at the top of the three legs was no unadorned platform, but a complicated engine of tremendous size. Its walls were littered with devices of inconceivable function, and where on the smaller watch-towers was the black oval window, was a series of multi-faceted ports, winking and glittering in the sunlight. Dangling articulate arms, like those of the spiderlike handling-machines, swung menacingly as the battle-machines advanced, and at each joint of the incredible legs, bright-green flashes emanated with every movement.

They were now almost upon us! One of the towers that ran to the right of mine let fly with its heat-cannon, but ineffectually. An instant later more towers on my side fired at these mammoth defenders. There were several hits, evidenced by brilliant patches of fire that glowed momentarily against the upper platform of the enemy, but none of the battle-machines fell. They came on towards us, holding their fire but weaving from side to side, their slender metal legs stepping gracefully and nimbly over the rocky soil.

I realized that my whole body was tingling, and there was a

crackling noise above my head. I glanced up, and saw a queer
radiance about the muzzle of the heat-cannon, and saw that it
must be firing at the defenders. In the instant it took me to so
glance up, the defending battle-machines had passed our lines,
still holding their fire, and the watch-tower on which I stood
turned sharply to the right.

Now began a sequence of attacking manoeuvres and evasive
tactics that had me simultaneously in fear for my life and
aghast with the fiendish brilliance of these machines.

I have compared our running attack to that of a cavalry-
charge, but I soon saw that this had merely been the preamble
to the battle proper. The tripodal legs did more than facilitate a
fast forwards motion; in close combat they allowed a man-
oeuvrability unequalled by anything I had ever seen.

My tower, no less than any other, was in the thick of the
fighting. As one with the others, the driver of my watch-tower
wheeled his machine from side to side, spinning the platform,
ducking, flailing the metal legs, balancing, charging.

All the while, the heat-cannon unleashed its deadly energy,
and in that mêlée of whirling, pirouetting towers the beams
seared through the air, striking home, flaring constantly against
the armoured sides of the upper platforms. And now the defenders were no longer holding their fire; the battle-machines
danced through the confusion, letting fly their deadly bolts with
horrifying accuracy.

It was an unequal conflict. Not only were the towers of my
side dwarfed by the hundred-feet high defenders, but out-
numbered too. For every one of the towers on my side there
seemed to be four of the giants, and already their beams of
destructive heat were having a telling effect. One by one the
smaller towers were struck from above; some exploded violently, others simply toppled to the ground, making ever more
hazardous the upthrown soil on which the battle was pitched.
Now it was that I became frightened for my own life, realizing
that if the fortunes of the battle continued, it was only a matter
of seconds before I was struck down.

I was, therefore, greatly relieved when the tower on which I
stood abruptly wheeled round and hastened from the centre of

the fighting. In all the confusion I had been able to do no more than maintain my hold, but as soon as we were away from the immediate dangers I discovered that I was shaking with fear.

I had no time to recover my poise. Instead of retreating fully, the tower hurried around the fringes of the battle, and joined two others which had similarly separated themselves. Without a pause we rejoined the fight, following what was clearly a pre-arranged tactical plan.

Marching as a phalanx we advanced towards the nearest of the colossal defenders. As one, our three cannons fired, the beams concentrating on the upper part of the glittering engine. Almost at once there came a minor explosion, and the battle-machine whirled uncontrollably round and crashed to the ground in a thrashing of metal limbs.

So excited was I by this demonstration of intelligent tactics that I found myself cheering aloud!

However, this battle would not be won by destroying one defender, a fact well understood by the monstrous drivers of these watch-towers. The three of us hurtled on into the fighting, heading towards our second intended victim.

Once again we were attacking from the rear, and as the heat-beams came into play the second defender was disposed of as spectacularly and efficiently as the first.

Such fortune could not last for ever. Scarcely had the second battle-machine fallen to the ground than a third stood before us. This one did not have its attention diverted by the ineffectual sniping of the other attackers—for there were few left in the fray—and as we plunged towards it the barrel of its heat-cannon was turned full on us.

What happened next was over in seconds, and yet I can recall the incident in detail, as if it had unfolded over a matter of minutes. I have said that we charged as a phalanx of three; I was mounted on the tower which was to the right and on the outside of the group. The battle-machine's heat-beam fell full across the tower in the centre, and this exploded at once. So great was the blast that only the fact that I was thrown against the telescopic mount of the cannon saved me from being dashed to the ground. My tower was damaged by the blast, a fact which became instantly clear as it lurched and staggered wildly, and as I clung to the telescopic mount I awaited our crashing to the desert floor as an already established matter of fact.

The third of the attacking towers, though, was as yet undamaged, and it marched on towards its taller antagonist, the heat-cannon playing its beam without effect across the armoured face of the defender. It was a last, desperate attack, and the monstrous creature which drove the tower must have expected its own annihilation at any moment. Although the defender responded with its own heat-cannon, the watch-tower went on unheeding, and flung itself suicidally against the very legs of the other. As they made contact there was a massive discharge of electrical energy, and both machines fell sideways to the ground, their legs still working wildly.

As this happened I was fighting for my own survival, clutching the telescopic rods of the cannon-mount as the damaged tower staggered away from the battle.

The first shock of damage had passed, and the driver—brilliant and evil—had managed to regain a semblance of control. The wildness of the tower's career was corrected, and with some unevenness of gait, which would have been enough to throw me to the ground had I not had a firm purchase on the mounting, it limped away from the fracas.

Within a minute, the battle—which still continued—was half a mile behind us, and some of the tension which had gripped me began to drain away. Only then did I realize that but for the faint humming of the engines, and the intermittent clangour of crashing machines, the entire engagement had been conducted in a deadly silence.

· v

I did not know how badly damaged the ambulant tower had been, but there was an unprecedented grinding noise whenever one of the three legs bore the weight. This could not be the only damage, though, for I could tell that the motive power was failing. We had left the battle at a considerable velocity, having gained momentum during the charge, but now we were moving much slower. I had no real measure of speed, but the grinding of the damaged leg came at less frequent intervals and the air no longer roared past my ears.

The original charge across the desert had taken me much nearer to the city, a fact for which I had been thankful, but now we were heading away from it, towards one of the banks of red weed.

My immediate concern was how I could leave my perch on the tower. It seemed to me that the monster-creature which sat at the controls might well attempt a repair of his tower, and would leave the platform to do so. If that was to happen, I had no desire to be anywhere near at the time. There was, though, no chance for me to escape until the tower halted.

I became aware of a pressure in my left hand, and looking down at it for the first time since the tower had lurched into battle I found that I was still holding Amelia's hand-bag. How it had not been dropped in the excitement of the fighting I did not know, but some instinct had made me retain it. I changed my position cautiously, taking the bag into my other hand. I had suddenly remembered the blade I had placed inside it, and I took it out, thinking that at last I might need it.

The tower had virtually halted now, and was walking slowly through an area of irrigated land where green crops grew. Not two hundred yards away I could see the scarlet weed-bank, and working at its base, hacking at the stems and releasing the sap, were the slaves.

There were many more than any group I had seen in Desolation City, and the wretched people were working in the slimy soil as far along the weed-bank as I could see in either direction. Our arrival had not gone unnoticed, for I saw many of the people look in our direction before turning back hurriedly to their work.

The damaged leg was making a terrible noise, setting up a metallic screech whenever it took the weight, and I knew we could not travel much further. At last the tower came to a halt, the three legs splayed out beneath us.

I leaned over the edge of the platform roof, trying to see if it would be possible to shin down one of the legs to the ground.

Now the excitement of the battle was past, I found my thoughts were more pragmatic. I had, for a time, been aroused by the thrill of the fighting, even to the extent of admiring the plucky way the smaller force had thrown itself against the far superior defenders. But on Mars there was no element of goodness in the monster-creatures; I had no place in this war between monsters, and the fact that chance had placed me on one of two warring sides should not have beguiled me into spurious sympathies. The creature which had driven this tower into battle had earned my respect for its valour, but as I stood on the roof of the platform, planning my escape, its essential cowardice and beastliness were suddenly revealed.

I heard again the crackling noise above my head, and I realized the heat-cannon was being fired.

At first I thought that one of the defending battle-machines must have followed us, but then I saw where the deadly beam was being directed. Far away, over to the right, flame and smoke were leaping up from the weed-bank!

I saw several slaves caught by the full force of the beam, and they fell, lifeless, to the muddy ground.

The monster was not content with this atrocity, for then it started to swing the cannon to the side, sweeping the beam along the weed-bank.

The flames burst and leapt, as if spontaneously, as the invisible beam touched on vegetation and slave alike. Where the malign heat fell on the spilled sap, gouts of steam exploded outwards. I could see the slaves struggling to escape as they heard the screams of those afflicted, but in the swampy mire in which they had to work it was difficult for them to scramble away in time. Many of them threw themselves prostrate in the mud, but others were killed instantly.

This unspeakable deed had been continuing for no more than two or three seconds before I took a part in ending it.

Ever since I had understood the full monstrosity of the power these beings held, a part of my self had been overwhelmed with hatred and loathing of the monsters. I did not need to debate the rights or wrongs of this: the monster with its damaged tower, taking its unpardonable spite on the helpless humans below, with cold deliberation and serene malice.

I took a deep breath, then turned away from the awful sight. Fighting down the revulsion within me, I reached for the handle of the metal door built into the sloping roof of the tower. I turned it in vain; it seemed to be jammed.

I glanced back over my shoulder. The heat-beam was still creeping along the weed-bank, wreaking its hideous carnage . . . but now some of the slaves nearest to the vindictive tower had seen me, for one or two of them were waving helplessly as they struggled through the swamp to avoid the beam.

The handle was one I had not seen or used on Mars before, but I knew that it could not be a sophisticated lock, for the monster itself, with its clumsy tentacles, must be capable of using it. Then, on an inspiration, I turned it the other way, the way that on Earth would normally close a lock.

Instantly, the handle turned and the door sprung open.

Filling most of the interior of the platform was the body of the monster; like a sickening bladder, the grey-green sac bulged and pulsed, shining moistly as if with perspiration.

In utter loathing I swung my long blade down, bringing it smartly against the very centre of the back. The blade sunk in, but as I withdrew it for a second plunge I saw that it had not penetrated the sponge-like consistency of the creature's flesh. I stabbed again, but with as little effect.

However, the creature had felt the blows even if it had not been harmed by them. A vile screech was emitted from the beak-like mouth at its front, and before I could evade it one of the tentacles slithered quickly towards me and wrapped itself about my chest.

Taken unawares, I stumbled down into the interior of the platform, pulled forward by the tentacle, and was dragged between the metal wall and the nauseous body itself!

My knife-arm was not constricted, and so in desperation I hacked again and again at the serpentine tentacle. Beside me the monster was braying hoarsely, in fear or in pain. At last, my knife was beginning to tell, for the pressure of the tentacle

eased as I drew blood. A second tentacle slinked towards me,
and just in time I slashed the first one away, causing blood to
pump from the wound. As the second tentacle wound itself
about my knife-arm, I panicked momentarily, before transfer-
ring the blade to my other hand. Now I knew the vulnerable
place on the tentacle, it took only seconds to hack it away.

My exertions, and the drag of the tentacles, had taken me to
the very front of the platform, so that I was before the face of
the monster itself!

Here it was as if the whole interior was alive with the tentacles, for ten or a dozen were wrapping themselves around me.
I cannot record how appalling was that touch! The tentacles
themselves were weak, but the combined effect of several,
stroking and clutching me, was as if I had fallen headlong into a
nest of constrictors. Before me, the beak-like mouth opened and
closed, shrieking in pain or anger; once the beak closed around
my leg, but there was no strength in it and it was not able even
to rip the cloth.

Above all were the eyes: those large, expressionless eyes,
watching my every action.

I was now in trouble, for both my arms were pinned, and
although I still held the knife I could not use it. Instead, I
kicked at the soft face before me, aiming at the roots of the
tentacles, the shrilling mouth, the saucer eyes . . . anything that
came within range. Then at last my knife-arm came free, and I
slashed wildly at any part of the filthy body that presented
itself.

This was the turning-point in the squalid affair, for from then
on I knew I could win. The front of the creature's body was
firm to the touch, and therefore vulnerable to the knife. Every
blow I landed now drew forth blood, and soon the platform was
a bedlam of gore, severed tentacles and the frightful screams of
the dying monster.

At last I drove the blade straight in between the creature's
eyes, and with one last fading scream it finally expired.

The tentacles relaxed and sagged to the floor, the beak-
mouth fell open, from within the corpse there came a long
eructation of noxious vapours and the great lidless eyes stared

bleakly and lifelessly through the darkened oval window at the
front of the platform.

I glanced through this window just once, and saw dimly that
the massacre had been brought to a timely end. The weed-bank
no longer shot forth flame, although steam and smoke still
drifted from various places, and the surviving slaves were dragging themselves from the mire.

vi

With a shudder I flung aside the bloodied knife, and hauled
myself past the sagging corpse to the door. I struggled through
with some difficulty for my hands were slick with blood and
ichor. At last I pulled myself back to the roof, breathing in the
thin air with relief, now that I was away from the rank odours
of the monster. The hand-bag was where I had left it on the
roof.

I picked it up, and, because I should need free use of my
hands, looped one of the long handles over my neck.

For a moment I stared down at the ground. For as far as I
could see in every direction those slaves that had survived the
massacre had abandoned their toils and were wading through
the mud towards the tower. Some had already reached dry
land, and were running across to me, waving their long spindly
arms and calling out in their high, reedy voices.

The leg nearest me seemed to be the straightest of the three,
bent in only one place. With the greatest difficulty I eased
myself over the protruding shelf, and managed to grip the
metal limb with my knees. Then I released my hold on the
platform, and placed my hands around the rough metal of
the leg. Much blood had spilled from the platform, and although it was drying quickly in the sunshine it made the metal
perilously slippery. With great caution at first, then with more
confidence as I grew accustomed to it, I shinned down the leg
towards the ground, the hand-bag swinging ludicrously across
my chest.

As I reached the ground and turned, I saw that a huge crowd

of the slaves had watched my descent and were waiting to greet me. I took the bag from around my neck, and stepped towards them. At once they moved back nervously, and I heard their voices twittering in alarm. Glancing down at myself I saw that my clothes and skin were soaked with the blood of the monster, and in the few minutes I had been in the sunlight the radiant heat had dried the mess and an unpleasant smell was exuding.

The slaves regarded me in silence.

Then I saw that one slave in particular was struggling through the crowd towards me, pushing the others aside in her haste. I saw that she was shorter than the rest, and fairer of skin. Although she was caked in the mud of the weed-bank, and raggedly dressed, I saw that her eyes were blue, and bright with tears, and her hair tumbled around her shoulders.

Amelia, my lovely Amelia, rushed forward and embraced me with such violence that I was nearly toppled from my feet!

"Edward!" she shouted deliriously, covering my face with kisses. "Oh, Edward! How brave you were!"

I was overcome with such excitement and emotion that I could hardly speak. Then at last I managed a sentence, choking it out through my tears of joy.

"I've still got your bag," I said.

It was all I could think to say.

Chapter Fourteen
IN THE SLAVE-CAMP

i

Amelia was safe, and I was safe! Life was to be lived again! We disregarded everything and everyone around us; ignored the malodorous condition we were both in; forgot the encircling, curious Martian slaves. The mysteries and dangers of this world were of no consequence, for we were together again!

We stood in each other's arms for many minutes, saying nothing. We wept a little, and we held each other so tight that I thought we might never separate but become fused in one single organism of undistilled joy.

We could not, of course, stand like that forever, and the interruption was approaching even as we embraced. Soon we could not ignore the warning voices of the slaves around us, and we pulled reluctantly apart, still holding each other's hand.

Glancing towards the distant city I saw that one of the huge battle-machines was striding across the desert towards us.

Amelia looked about the slaves.

"Edwina?" she called. "Are you there?"

In a moment a young, female Martian stepped forward. She was no more than a child, roughly equivalent to about twelve Earth years old.

She said (or at least it sounded as if she said): "Yes, Amelia?"

"Tell the others to go back to work quickly. We will return to the camp."

The little girl turned to the other slaves, made some intricate hand and head signs (accompanied by a few of the high, sibilant words), and within seconds the crowd was dispersing.

"Come along, Edward," said Amelia. "The thing in that machine will want to know how the monster was killed."

I followed her as she strode towards a long, dark building set near the weed-bank. After a moment, one of the city-Martians appeared and fell in beside us. He was carrying one of the electrical whips.

Amelia noticed the askance expression with which I registered this.

"Don't worry, Edward," she said. "He won't hurt us."

"Are you sure?"

In answer, Amelia held out her hand and the Martian passed her the whip. She took it carefully, held it out for me to see, then returned it.

"We are no longer in Desolation City. I have established a new social order for the slaves."

"So it would appear," I said. "Who is Edwina?"

"One of the children. She is naturally adept at languages—most young Martians are—and so I have taught her the rudiments of English."

I was going to ask more, but the ferocious pace Amelia was setting in this thin air was making me breathless.

We came to the building, and at the doorway I paused to stare back. The battle-machine had stopped by the crippled tower on which I had ridden, and was examining it.

There were four short corridors into the building, and inside I was relieved to find that it was pressurized. The city-Martian walked away and left us, while I found myself coughing uncontrollably after the exertions of our walk. When I had recovered I embraced Amelia once more, still unable to believe the good fortune that had reunited us. She returned my embraces no less warmly, but after a moment drew away.

"My dear, we are both filthy. We can wash here."

"I should very much like a change of clothes," I said.

"There is no chance of that," Amelia said. "You will have to wash your clothes as you wash yourself."

She led me to an area of the building where there was an arrangement of overhead pipes. At the turn of a tap, a shower of liquid—which was not water, but probably a diluted solution of the sap—issued forth. Amelia explained that all the slaves used these baths after work, then she went away to use another in private.

Although the flow of liquid was cold I drenched myself luxuriously, taking off my clothes and wringing them to free them of the last vestiges of the foul fluids they had absorbed.

When I considered neither I nor my clothes could be any further cleansed, I turned off the flow and squeezed my clothes, trying to dry them. I pulled on my trousers, but the cloth was dank and heavy and felt most uncomfortable. Dressed like this I went in search of Amelia.

There was a large metal grille set in one of the walls just beyond the bathing area. Amelia stood before it, holding out her ragged garment to dry it. At once I turned away.

"Bring your clothes here, Edward," she said.

"When you have finished," I said, trying not to reveal by the sound of my voice that I had noticed she was completely unclad.

She placed her garment on the floor, and walked over and stood facing me.

"Edward, we are no longer in England," she said. "You will contract pneumonia if you wear damp clothes."

"They will dry in time."

"In this climate you will be seriously ill before then. It takes only a few minutes to dry them this way."

She went past me into the bathing area, and came back with the remainder of my clothes.

"I will dry my trousers later," I said.

"You will dry them now," she replied.

I stood in consternation for a moment, then reluctantly removed my trousers. Holding them before me, in such a way that I was still covered, I allowed the draught of warmth to blow over them. We stood a little apart, and although I was determined not to gaze immodestly at Amelia, the very presence of the girl who meant so much to me, and with whom I had suffered so much, made it impossible not to glance her way several times. She was so beautiful, and, unclad as she was, she bore herself with grace and propriety, rendering innocent a situation which would have scandalized the most forward-looking of our neighbours on Earth. My inhibitions waned, and after a few minutes I could contain my impulses no more.

I dropped the garment I was holding, went quickly to her, then took her in my arms and we kissed passionately for a minute or more.

ii

We were virtually alone in the building. It was still two hours before sunset, and the slaves would not return before then. When our clothes had dried, and we had put them on again, Amelia took me around the building to show me how the slaves were housed. Their conditions were primitive and without convenience: the hammocks were hard and cramped, what food there was had to be eaten raw, and nowhere was there any possibility of privacy.

"And you have been living like this?" I said.

"At first," Amelia said. "But then I discovered I was someone rather important. Let me show you where I sleep."

She led me to one corner of the communal sleeping-quarters. Here the hammocks were arranged no differently, or so it appeared, but when Amelia tugged on a rope attached to an overhead pulley, several of the hammocks were lifted up to form an ingenious screen.

"During the days we leave these down, in case a new overseer is sent to inspect us, but when I wish to be private ... I have a boudoir all of my own!"

She led me into her boudoir, and once again, sensing that foreign eyes could not light upon us, I kissed Amelia with passion. I knew now what I had been hungering for during that dire period of loneliness!

"You seem to have made yourself at home," I said at length. Amelia had sprawled across her hammock, while I sat down on a step that ran across part of the floor.

"One has to make the best of what one finds."

I said: "Amelia, tell me what happened after you were taken by that machine.'

"I was brought here."

"Is that all? It cannot have been as simple as that!"

"I should not wish to experience it again," she said. "But what about you? How is it that after all this time you appear from within a watch-tower?"

"I should prefer to hear your story first."

So we exchanged the news of each other that we both so eagerly sought. The prime concern was that neither of us was the worse for our adventures, and we had each satisfied the other as to that. Amelia spoke first, describing the journey across land to this slave-camp.

She kept her account brief and seemed to omit much detail. Whether this was to spare me the more unpleasant aspects, or because she did not wish to remind herself of them, I do not know. The journey had taken many days, most of it inside covered vehicles. There was no sanitation, and food was supplied only once a day. During the journey Amelia had seen, as I had seen aboard the projectile, how the monsters themselves took food. Finally, in a wretched state, she and the other survivors of the journey—some three hundred people in all, for the spiderlike machines had been busy that day in Desolation City—had been brought to this weed-bank, and under supervision of Martians from the near-by city had been put to work on the red weed.

I assumed at this point that Amelia had finished her story, for I then launched into a detailed account of my own adventures. I felt I had much to tell her, and spared few details. When I came to describe the use of the killing-cubicle aboard the projectile I felt no need to expurgate my account, for she too had seen the device in operation. However, as I described what I had seen, she paled a little.

"Please do not dwell on this," she said.

"But is it not familiar to you?"

"Of course it is. But you need not colour your account with such relish. The barbaric instrument you describe is everywhere used. There is one in this building."

That revelation took me by surprise, and I regretted having mentioned it. Amelia told me that each evening six or more of the slaves were sacrificed to the cubicle.

"But this is outrageous!" I said.

"Why do you think the oppressed people of this world are so few in number?" Amelia cried. "It is because the very best of the people are drained of life to keep the monsters alive!"

"I shall not mention it again," I said, and passed on to relate the rest of my story.

I described how I escaped from the projectile, then the battle I had witnessed, and finally, with not inconsiderable pride, I described how I had tackled and slain the monster in the tower.

At this Amelia seemed pleased, and so once more I garnished my narrative with adjectives. This time my authentic details were not disapproved of, and indeed as I described how the creature had finally expired she clapped her hands together and laughed.

"You must tell your story again tonight," she said. "My people will be very encouraged."

I said: "*Your* people?"

"My dear, you must understand that I do not survive here by good fortune. I have discovered that I am their promised leader, the one who in folklore is said to deliver them from oppression."

iii

A little later we were disturbed by the slaves returning from their labours, and for the moment our accounts were put aside.

As the slaves entered the building through the two main pressurizing corridors, the overseeing Martians, who apparently had quarters of their own within the building, came in with them. Several were carrying the electrical whips, but once inside they tossed them casually to one side.

I have recorded before that the habitual expression of a Martian is one of extreme despair, and these wretched slaves were no exception. Knowing what I did, and having seen the massacre that afternoon, my reaction was more sympathetic than before.

With the return of the slaves there was a period of activity, during which the dirt of the day's work was washed away, and food was brought out. It had been some time since I had eaten, and although in its uncooked state the weed was almost inedible I took as much as I could manage.

We were joined during the meal by the slave-child Amelia called Edwina. I was amazed at the apparent grasp she had of English, and, what is more, rather amused by the fact that although the girl could not manage some of the more sophisticated English consonants, Amelia had vested her with distinct echoes of her own cultured voice. (In rendering Edwina's words in this narrative I shall make no attempt to phoneticize her unique accent, but state her words in plain English; however, at first I had difficulty in understanding what she said.)

I noticed that while we ate (there were no tables here; we all squatted on the floor) the slaves kept a distance from Amelia and me. Many covert glances came our way and only Edwina, who sat with us, seemed at ease in our company.

"Surely they are used to you by now?" I said to Amelia.

"It is of you they are nervous. You too have fulfilled a legendary rôle."

At this, Edwina, who had heard and understood my question, said: "You are the pale dwarf."

I frowned at this, and looked to see if Amelia knew what she meant.

Edwina went on: "Our wise men tell of the pale dwarf who walks from the battle-machine."

"I see," I said, and nodded to her with a polite smile.

Somewhat later, when Edwina was no longer within hearing, I said: "If you are the messiah to these people, why do you have to work at the weed-bank?"

"It is not my choice. Most of the overseers are used to me now, but if any new ones came from the city I might be singled out if I were not with the others. Also, it is said in the myths that the one who leads the people will be one of them. In other words, a slave."

"I think I should hear these myths," I said.

"Edwina will recite them for you."

I said: "You talk about the overseers. How is it that no one seems to fear them now?"

"Because I have persuaded them that all humans have a common enemy. I am more than playing a rôle, Edward. I am convinced that there must be a revolution. The monsters rule the people by dividing them: they have set one group of humans against the other. The slaves fear the overseers because it seems the overseers have the authority of the monsters behind them. The city-Martians are content to support the system, for they enjoy certain privileges. But as you and I have seen, this is merely an expedient to the monsters. Human blood is their only demand, and the slave-system is a means to an end. All I have done here is to persuade the overseers—who also know the folk-lore—that the monsters are an enemy common to all."

While we were talking, the slave people were carrying away the remains of the meal, but suddenly all activities were halted by an outburst of sound: the most horrible, high-pitched siren, echoing around the inside of the hall.

Amelia had gone very pale, and she turned away and walked into her private area. I followed her inside, and found her in tears.

"That call," I said. "Does it mean what I think?"

"They have come for their food," Amelia said, and her sobs were renewed.

iv

I will not recount the ghastliness of the scene that followed, but it should be said that the slaves had devised a system of lots, and the six hapless losers went to the killing-cubicle in silence.

Amelia explained that she had not expected the monsters to visit the slave-camps tonight. There were many dead scattered about the weed-bank, and she had hoped that the monsters would have drained these bodies for their nightly repast.

v

Edwina came to see Amelia and me.

"We would like to hear the adventures of the pale dwarf," she said to Amelia. "It would make us happy."

"Does she mean I have to address them?" I said. "I should not know what to say. And how would they understand me?"

"It is expected of you. Your arrival was spectacular, and they want to hear it in your own words. Edwina will interpret for you."

"Have you done this?"

She nodded. "I was told about this ritual when I was teaching Edwina to speak English. When she had mastered enough vocabulary, we rehearsed a little speech and from that day I was accepted as their leader. You will not be fully acknowledged by them until you have done it too."

I said: "But how much should I tell them? Have you told them we are from Earth?"

"I felt they would not understand, and so I have not. Earth is mentioned in their legends—they call it the 'warm world'—but only as a celestial body. So I have not revealed my origins. Incidentally, Edward, I think it is time you and I recognized that we shall never again see Earth. There is no means of return. Since I have been here I have been reconciled to that. We are both Martians now."

I pondered this in silence. It was not a notion I cared for, but I understood what Amelia meant. While we clung to a false hope we should never settle.

Finally, I said: "Then I will tell them how I flew in the projectile, how I mounted the watch-tower and how I disposed of the monster."

"I think, Edward, that as you are fulfilling a mythic prophecy, you should find a stronger verb than 'dispose'."

"Would Edwina understand?"

"If you accompany your words with the appropriate actions."

"But they have already seen me leave the tower covered in blood!"

"It is the telling of the tale that is important. Just repeat to them what you told me."

Edwina was looking as happy as any Martian I had ever seen.

"We will hear the adventures now?" she said.

"I suppose so," I said. We stood up and followed Edwina into the main part of the hall. Several of the hammocks had been moved away, and all the slaves were sitting on the floor. As we appeared they climbed to their feet, and started to jump up and down. It was a rather comical action—and one not wholly re-assuring—but Amelia whispered to me that this was their sign of enthusiasm.

I noticed that there were about half a dozen of the city-Martians present, standing at the back of the hall. They were clearly not yet at one with the slaves, but at least the sense of intimidation we had seen in Desolation City was absent.

Amelia quietened the crowd by raising her hand and spreading her fingers. When they were silent, she said: "My people. Today we saw the killing of one of the tyrants by this man. He is here now to describe his adventures in his own words."

As she spoke, Edwina translated simultaneously by uttering a few syllables, and accompanying them with elaborate hand-signs. As they both finished, the slaves jumped up and down again, emitting a high-pitched whining noise. It was most disconcerting, and appeared to have no end.

Amelia whispered to me: "Raise your hand."

I was regretting having agreed to this, but I raised my hand and to my surprise silence fell at once. I regarded these queer folk—these tall, hot-coloured alien beings amongst whom fate had cast our lot, and with whom our future now lay—and tried to find the words with which to begin. The silence persisted, and with some diffidence I described how I had been put aboard the projectile. Immediately, Edwina accompanied my words with her weird interpretation.

I began hesitantly, not sure of how much I should say. The audience remained silent. As I warmed to my story, and found opportunities for description, Edwina's interpretation became more florid, and thus encouraged I indulged myself in a little exaggeration.

My description of the battle became a clashing of metallic giants, a pandemonium of hideous screams and a veritable storm of blazing heat-beams. At this, I saw that several of the slaves had risen, and were jumping up and down enthusiastically. As I came to the point in the story where I realized that the monster was turning its heat-beam on to the people, the whole audience was on its feet and Edwina was signing most dramatically.

Perhaps in this telling rather more tentacles were hacked away than there had been in actuality, and perhaps it seemed more difficult to kill the beast than had been my experience, but I felt obliged to remain true to the spirit of the occasion rather than satisfy the demands of scrupulous authenticity.

I finished my story to a splendid cheer from the audience, and a most remarkable display of leaping. I glanced at Amelia to see her reaction, but before we had a chance to speak we were both mobbed by the crowd. The Martians surrounded us, jostling and thumping us gently, in what I interpreted as further enthusiasms. We were being propelled steadily and firmly towards Amelia's private quarters, and as we came to where the hammocks had been slung to form the partition, the noise reached its climax. After a little more genial pummelling, we were thrust together through the partition.

At once, the noise outside subsided.

I was still buoyed up by the reception I had been given, and swept Amelia into my arms. She was as excited as I, and responded to my kisses with great warmth and affection.

As our kissing became prolonged I found rising in me those natural desires I had had to suppress for so long, and so, reluctantly, I turned my face away from hers and loosened my hold, expecting her to draw away. Instead, she held me tightly, pressing her face into the hollow of my neck.

Beyond the partition I could hear the slaves. They seemed to be singing now, a high, tuneless crooning noise. It was very restful and strangely pleasant.

"What do we do next?" I said after several minutes had passed.

Amelia did not reply at once.

Then she held me more tightly, and said: "Do you need to be told, Edward?"

I felt myself blushing.

"I meant, is there any more ceremonial we must observe?" I said.

"Only what is expected of us in legend. On the night the pale dwarf descends from the tower. . . ." She whispered the rest in my ear.

She could not see my face, so I clenched my eyes tightly closed, almost breathless with excitement!

"Amelia, we cannot. We are not married."

It was my last concession to the conventions that had ruled my life.

"We are Martians now," Amelia said. "We do not observe marriage."

And so, as the Martian slaves sang in their high, melancholy voices beyond the hanging partition, we abandoned all that remained within us of our Englishness and Earthliness, and became, through that night, committed to our new rôles and lives as leaders of the oppressed Martian peoples.

Chapter Fifteen
A REVOLUTION IS PLANNED

i

From the moment of our waking the following morning, Amelia and I were treated with deference and humility. Even so, the legends that were now directing our lives seemed quite emphatic that we were to work with the others on the weed-bank, and so much of our day was spent in cold mud up to our knees. Edwina worked with us, and although there was something about her bland stare that made me uneasy, she was undoubtedly useful to us.

Neither Amelia nor I did much actual weed-cutting. As soon as we were established at the bank we received many different visitors: some of them slaves, others overseers, all of them evidently anxious to meet those who would lead the revolt. Hearing what was said—translated earnestly, if not always entirely comprehensibly, by Edwina—I realized that Amelia's talk of revolution had not been made lightly. Several of the overseers had come from the city itself, and we learnt that there elaborate plans were being made to overthrow the monsters.

It was an enthralling day, realizing that we might at last have provided the stimulus to these people to take revenge on their abhorrent masters. Indeed, Amelia reminded our visitors many times of my heroic deed the day before. The phrase was repeated often: *the monsters are mortal.*

However, mortal or not, the monsters were still in evidence, and presented a constant threat. Often during the day the weed-bank was patrolled by one of the immense tripodal battle-machines, and at those times all revolutionary activities were suspended while we attended to the cutting.

During one period when we were left alone, I asked Amelia why the weed-cutting continued if the revolution was so far advanced. She explained that the vast majority of the slaves were employed in this work, and that if it was stopped before the revolution was under way the monsters would instantly realize something was afoot. In any event, the main benefactors were the humans themselves, as the weed was the staple diet.

And the blood-letting? I asked her. Could that not then be stopped?

She replied that refusal to give any more blood was the only sure way the humans had of conquering the monsters, and there had been frequent attempts to disobey the most dreaded injunction on this world. On those occasions, the monsters' reprisals had been summary and widespread. In the most recent incident, which had occurred some sixty days before, over one thousand slaves had been massacred. The terror of the monsters was constant, and even while the insurgency was planned, the daily sacrifices had to be made.

In the city, though, the established order was in imminent danger of being overthrown. Slaves and city-people were uniting at last, and throughout the city there were organized cells of volunteers; men and women who, when the command was given, would attack specified targets. It was the battle-machines which presented the greatest threat: unless several heat-cannons could be commandeered by the humans, there could be no defence against them.

I said: "Should we not be in the city? If you are controlling the revolution, surely it should be done from there?"

"Of course. I was intending to visit the city again tomorrow. You will see for yourself just how advanced we are."

Then more visitors arrived: this time, a delegation of overseers who worked in one of the industrial areas. They told us, through Edwina, that small acts of sabotage were already taking place, and output had been temporarily halved.

So the day passed, and by the time we returned to the building I was exhausted and exhilarated. I had had no conception of the good use to which Amelia had put her time with the slaves. There was an air of vibrancy and purpose ... and great urgency. Several times I heard her exhorting the Martains to bring forward their preparations, so that the revolution itself might begin a little earlier.

After we had washed and eaten, Amelia and I returned to what were now our shared quarters. Once in there, and alone with her, I asked her why there was such need for urgency. After all, I argued, surely the revolution would be more assured of success if it was prepared more carefully?

"It is a question of timing, Edward," she said. "We must attack when the monsters are unprepared and weak. This is such a time."

"But they are at the height of their power!" I said in surprise. "You cannot be blind to that."

"My dear," said Amelia, "if we do not strike against the monsters within the next few days, then the cause of humanity on this world will be lost forever."

"I cannot see why. The monsters have held their sway until now. Why should they be any less prepared for an uprising?"

This was the answer that Amelia gave me, gleaned from the legends of the Martians amongst whom she had been living for so long:

ii

Mars is a world much older than Earth, and the ancient Martians had achieved a stable scientific civilization many thousands of years ago. Like Earth, Mars had had its empires and wars, and like Earthmen the Martians were ambitious and forward-looking. Unfortunately, Mars is unlike Earth in one crucial way, which is to say that it is physically much smaller. As a consequence, the two substances essential to intelligent human life—air and water—were gradually leaking away into space, in such a way that the ancient Martians knew that their existence could not be expected to survive for more than another thousand of their years.

There was no conceivable method that the Martians had at their command to combat the insidious dying of their planet.

Unable to solve the problem directly, the ancient Martians essayed an indirect solution. Their plan was to breed a new race—using human cells selected from the brains of the ancient scientists themselves—which would have no other function than to contain a vast intellect. In time, and Amelia said that it must have taken many hundreds of years, the first monster-creatures were evolved.

The first successful monsters were completely dependent on mankind, for they were incapable of movement, could survive only by being given transfusions of blood from domestic animals, and were subject to the slightest infection. They had, however, been given the means to reproduce themselves, and as the generations of monster-creatures proceeded, so the beings developed more resistance and an ability to move, albeit with great difficulty. Once the beings were relatively independent, they were set the task of confronting the problem which threatened all existence on Mars.

What those ancient scientists could not have foreseen was that as well as being of immense intellect, the monster-creatures were wholly ruthless, and once set to this task would allow no impediment to their science. The very interests of mankind, for which they were ultimately working, were of necessity subordinated to the pursuit of a solution! In this way, mankind on Mars eventually became enslaved to the creatures.

As the centuries passed the demands for blood increased, until the inferior blood of animals was not enough; so began the terrible blood-letting that we had witnessed.

In the initial stages of their work the monster-creatures, for all their ruthlessness, had not been entirely evil, and had indeed brought much good to the world. They had conceived and supervised the digging of the canals that irrigated the dry equatorial regions, and, to prevent as much water as possible from evaporating into space, they had developed plants of high water-content which could be grown as a staple crop alongside the canals.

In addition, they had devised a highly efficient heat-source which was used to provide power for the cities (and which, latterly, had been adapted to become the heat-cannon), as well as the domes of electrical force which contained the atmosphere around the cities.

As time passed, however, some of the monster-creatures had despaired of finding a solution to the central problem. Others of their kind disagreed that the task was insurmountable, and maintained that however much the rôle of humans may have changed, their primary task was to continue.

After centuries of squabbling, the monster-creatures had started fighting amongst themselves, and the skirmishes continued until today. The wars were worsening, for now the humans themselves were an issue: as their numbers were being steadily depleted, so the monsters were becoming concerned about shortages of their own food.

The situation had resolved into two groups: the monsters who controlled this city—which was the largest on Mars—and who had convinced themselves that no solution to the eventual death of Mars was possible, and those of the other three cities—of which Desolation City was one—who were prepared to continue the quest. From the humans' viewpoint, neither side had anything to commend it, for the slavery would continue whatever the outcome.

But at the present moment the monster-creatures of this city were vulnerable. They were preparing a migration to another planet, and in their preoccupation with this the rule of slavery was the weakest the Martian humans could remember. The migration was due to start within a few days, and as many of the monster-creatures would remain on Mars, the revolution must take place during the migration itself if it was to have any chance of success.

iii

As Amelia finished her account I found that my hands had started to tremble, and even in the customary coldness of the building I found that my face and hands were damp with perspiration. For many moments I could not say anything, as I tried to find a way of expressing the turbulence of my emotions.

In the end my words were plain.

I said: "Amelia, do you have any notion which planet it is these beings are intending to colonize?"

She gestured impatiently.

"What does it matter?" she said. "While they are occupied with this, they are vulnerable to attack. If we miss this chance, we may never have another."

I suddenly saw an aspect of Amelia I had not seen before. She, in her own way, had become a little ruthless. Then I thought again, and realized she seemed ruthless only because our own acceptance of our fate had destroyed her sense of perspective.

It was with love, then, that I said: "Amelia . . . are you now wholly Martian? Or do you fear what might happen if these monsters were to invade Earth?"

The perspective returned to her with the same shock as I myself had experienced. Her face became ashen and her eyes suddenly filled with tears. She gasped, and her fingers went to her lips. Abruptly, she pushed past me, went through the partition and ran across the main hall. As she reached the further wall, she covered her face with her hands and her shoulders shook as she wept.

iv

We passed a restless night, and in the morning set off, as planned, for the city.

Three Martians travelled with us: one was Edwina, for we still required an interpreter, and the other two were city-Martians, each brandishing an electrical whip. We had said nothing of our conversation to any of the Martians, and our plan was still ostensibly to visit several of the insurgents' cells in the city.

In fact, I was much preoccupied with my own thoughts, and I knew Amelia was suffering a torment of conflicting loyalties.

Our silence as the train moved steadily towards the city must have intrigued the Martians, because normally we both had much to say. Occasionally, Edwina would point out landmarks to us, but I at least could not summon much interest.

Before we had left the slave-camp, I had managed a few more words with Amelia in private.

"We must get back to Earth," I said. "If these monsters land there is no telling what damage they might cause."

"But what could we do to stop that?"

"You agree, though, that we must find a way to Earth?"

"Yes, of course. But how?"

"If they are travelling by projectile," I had said, "then we must somehow stow away. The journey will not take more than a day or two, and we could survive that long. Once we are on Earth we can alert the authorities."

For a makeshift plan this was good enough, and Amelia had agreed with it in principle. Her main doubts, though, were elsewhere.

"Edward, I cannot just abandon these people now. I have encouraged them to revolt, and now I propose to leave them at the crucial moment."

"I could leave you here with them," I had said, with deliberate coldness.

"Oh no." She had taken my hand then. "My loyalties are with Earth. It is simply that I have a responsibility here for what I have started."

"Isn't that at the centre of your dilemma?" I said. "You have *started* the revolution. You have been the necessary catalyst for the people. But it is their fight for freedom, not yours. In any event, you cannot direct an entire revolution alone, with an alien race you barely understand, in a language you do not speak. If the preparations are being made, and you have not yet seen most of them, already you have become little more than a figurehead."

"I suppose so."

She was still absorbed in thought, though, as we sat in the train, and I knew it was a decision she would have to make for herself.

The two Martian overseers were pointing proudly towards one of the industrial sites the train was passing. There seemed to be little activity here, for no smoke came from any of the chimneys. There were several of the battle-machines standing about, and we saw many legged vehicles. Edwina explained that it was here that sabotage had already been committed. There had been no reprisals, for the various acts had been made to appear accidental.

For my part, I had been taken by an enthralling notion, and was presently considering every aspect of it.

The revolution that meant so much to Amelia was of less concern to me, for it had been conceived and planned in my absence. I think, had I not heard of the monsters' planned migration from Mars, that I too would have thrown myself into the cause and fought for it, and risked my life for it. But in all the weeks and months I had been on Mars, I had never lost an inner ache: the feeling of isolation, the sense of homesickness. I wanted desperately to return to my own world, or that part of it I knew as home.

I had been missing London—for all its crowds and noises and rank odours—and I had been hungering for the sight of greenery. There is nothing so beautiful as the English countryside in spring, and if, in the past, I had taken it for granted, I knew that I could never do so again. This was a world of foreign colours: grey cities, rufous soil, scarlet vegetation. If there had been so much as one oak-tree, or one bumpy meadow, or one bank of wild flowers, I might at last have learned to live on Mars, but none of these existed.

That the monster-creatures had the means of reaching Earth was therefore of intense importance to me, for it provided a way back to our home.

I had proposed to Amelia that we stow away on one of their deadly projectiles, but this was a dangerous idea.

Quite apart from the fact that we might be discovered during the voyage, or that some other danger might appear, we would be arriving on Earth in the company of the most hostile and ruthless enemy mankind would have ever had to face!

We did not know the monsters' plans, but we had no reason

to suppose that their mission was one of peace. Neither Amelia
nor I had the right to participate in an invasion of Earth, however passive the part we played. Moreover, we had a bounden
duty to warn the world of the Martians' plans.

There was a solution to this, and from the moment it occurred to me the simple audacity of it made it irresistible.

I had been aboard one of the projectiles; I had seen it in
flight; I had examined its controls.

Amelia and I would *steal* one of the projectiles, and fly it
ourselves to Earth!

v

We arrived in the city without being challenged, and were led
through the streets by our Martian accomplices.

The sparseness of the population was not as evident here as
it had been in Desolation City. There were fewer empty buildings, and the obvious military strength of the monster-
creatures had averted any invasions. Another difference was
that there were factories within the city itself—as well as in
separate areas outside—for there was a smoky industrial pall that
served to heighten my feelings of homesickness for London.

We had no time to see much of the city, for we were taken
immediately to one of the dormitories. Here, in a small room at
the rear, we met one of the main cells of the revolution.

As we entered, the Martians showed their enthusiasm by
leaping up and down as before. I could not help but warm to
these poor, enslaved people, and share their excitement as the
overthrow of the monsters became ever a more realistic
proposition.

We were treated as royalty is treated in England, and I realized that Amelia and I were acting regally. Our every response was eagerly awaited, and mute as we had to be, we
smiled and nodded as one Martian after another explained to
us, through Edwina, what his assigned task was to be.

From here we were taken to another place, and more of the
same happened. It was almost exactly as I had described it to

Amelia: she had catalysed the Martians to action, and set in motion a sequance of events she could no longer control.

I was becoming tired and impatient, and as we walked to inspect a third cell, I said to Amelia: "We are not spending our time well."

"We must do as they wish. We owe them at least this."

"I would like to see more of the city. We do not even know where the snow-cannon is to be found."

In spite of the fact that we were with six Martians, each of whom was trying to speak to her through Edwina, Amelia expressed her feelings with a tired shrug.

"I cannot leave them now," she said. "Perhaps you could go alone."

"Then who would interpret for me?"

Edwina was tugging at Amelia's hand, trying to show her the building to which we were presently walking and where, presumably, the next cell was concealed. Amelia dutifully smiled and nodded.

"We had best not separate," she said. "But if you ask Edwina, she could find out what you want to know."

A few moments later we entered the building, and in the darkened basement we were greeted by some forty enthusiastic Martians.

A little later I managed to take Edwina away from Amelia long enough to convey to her what I wanted. She seemed not interested, but passed on the message to one of the city-Martians present. He left the basement soon after, while we continued the inspection of our revolutionary troops.

vi

Just as we were readying ourselves to leave for the next port of call, my emissary returned, bringing with him two young Martian men dressed in the black uniforms of the men who drove the projectiles.

At the sight of them I was a little taken aback. Of all the humans I had met here, the men trained to fly the projectiles had seemed the closest to the monster-creatures, and were therefore the ones I had least expected to be trusted now the old order was about to be overthrown. But here the two men were, admitted to one of the revolutionary nerve-centres.

Suddenly, my idea became easier to put into effect. I had intended to gain entry to the snow-cannon, while Amelia and I were disguised, and attempt to work out the controls for myself. However, if I could communicate to these two what I wanted they could show me themselves how to operate the craft, or even come with us to Earth.

I said to Edwina: "I want you to ask these two men to take me to their flying war-machine, and show me how it is operated."

She repeated my sentence to me, and when I had made sure she understood me correctly, she passed it on. One of the Martians replied.

"He wants to know where you are taking the craft," said Edwina.

"Tell them that I wish to steal it from the monsters, and take it to the warm world."

Edwina replied immediately: "Will you go alone, pale dwarf, or will Amelia go with you?"

"We will go together."

Edwina's response to this was not what I would have wished. She turned towards the revolutionaries, and embarked on a long speech, with much sibilance and waving arms. Before she had finished, about a dozen Martian men hurried towards me, took me by the arms and held me with my face pressing against the wall.

From the far side of the room, Amelia called: "What *have* you said now, Edward?"

vii

It took Amelia ten minutes to secure my release. In the meantime I suffered considerable discomfort, with both my arms twisted painfully behind my back. For all their frail appearance, the Martians were very strong.

When I was freed, Amelia and I went into a small room at the back, accompanied by two of the Martian men. In this they played unwittingly into our hands, for without Edwina they could not understand us, and it was to talk to Amelia that I wanted.

"Now please tell me what that was all about," she said.

"I have worked out a new idea for our return to Earth. I was trying to put it into effect, and the Martians misunderstood my motives."

"Then what did you say?"

I outlined for her the essence of my plan to steal a projectile in advance of the monsters' invasion.

"Could you drive such a machine?" she said when I had finished.

"I shouldn't imagine there would be any difficulty. I have examined the controls. It would be a matter of a few minutes to familiarize myself."

Amelia looked doubtful, but she said: "Even so, you have seen how the people react. They will not let me go with you. Does your plan allow for that?"

"You have already said that you will not stay here."

"Of my own free will I would not."

"Then we must somehow persuade them," I said.

The two Martians guarding us were shifting restlessly. As I had been speaking I had laid my hand on Amelia's arm, and at this they had started forward protectively.

"We had better return to the others," Amelia said. "They do not trust you as it is."

"We have resolved nothing," I said.

"At this moment we have not. But if I intervene I think we may persuade them."

I was learning at last to interpret the expressions of the Martians, and when we returned to the basement I sensed that the feeling had moved even further against me. Several people went forward to Amelia with their hands raised, and I was thrust aside. The two men who had been guarding us stayed with me, and I was forced to stand apart while Amelia was acclaimed possessively. Edwina was with her, and hasty words were exchanged for several minutes. In the uproar I could not hear what was being said.

I watched Amelia.

In the midst of the confusion she stayed placid and in control of her emotions, listening to Edwina's translations, then waiting while more voices harangued her in that foreign sibilance. It was, in spite of the tension, a wonderful moment, because in that enforced objectivity I was able to see her from a standpoint that was at once more intimate and more distanced than I cared. We had been thrust into each other's company by our adventures, and yet now we were being torn away from each other as a consequence. The fundamental alienness of these Martian people never seemed more affecting to me than at that moment.

I knew that if Amelia was prevented from flying with me in the projectile, then I would stay with her on Mars.

At last order was restored, and Amelia moved to the end of the room. With Edwina by her side she turned to face the crowd. I was still kept to one side, hemmed in by my two guards.

Amelia raised her right hand, spreading her fingers, and silence fell.

"My people, what has happened has forced me to reveal to you my origins." She was speaking slowly and softly, allowing Edwina to interpret for her. "I have not done so before, because your legends spoke of your freedom being delivered by one who was enslaved from birth. I have suffered with you and worked with you, and although you have accepted me as your leader I was not born to slavery."

There was an instant reaction to this, but Amelia went on: "Now I have learned that the race of beings which has enslaved you, and which will shortly be overthrown by your valour, is intending to spread its dominance to another world . . . the one you know as the warm world. What I have not told you before is that I am myself from the warm world, and I travelled across the sky in a craft similar to the one your masters use."

She was interrupted here by much noise from the Martians.

"Our revolution here cannot fail, for our determination is as great as our bravery. But if some of these creatures are allowed to escape to another world, who could say that they would never return at a later time? But then, the passions of revolution would be spent, and the creatures would easily enslave you once more.

"For the revolution to succeed, we must ensure that every one of the creatures is killed!

"Therefore it is essential that I return to my own world to warn my people of what is being planned here. The man you call the pale dwarf, and I, must carry this warning, and unite the people of the warm world as we have united you here to fight this menace. Then, when we are able, I will return to share with you the glories of freedom!"

I knew that Amelia had already allayed the worst of the Martians' suspicions, for several were leaping enthusiastically.

She had more to say, though: "Finally, you must no longer distrust the man you call the pale dwarf. It is his heroic deed which must become your example. He, and only he, has shown that the monsters are mortal. Let his brave act be the first blow for freedom!"

All the Martians were leaping and shrilling, and in the noise I doubted if any could hear her. But she looked at me and spoke softly, and her words carried to me as clearly as if the room were silent.

She said: "You must trust and love him, just as I trust and love him."

Then I rushed across the room towards her and took her in my arms, oblivious of the demonstrative approval of the Martians.

Chapter Sixteen
ESCAPE FROM OPPRESSION!

i

With our plan of action finally understood and approved by the Martians, Amelia and I separated for the rest of the day. She continued with her tour of the revolutionary units, while I went with the two Martians to inspect the snow-cannon and projectile. Edwina came with us, for there was much that would have to be explained.

The cannon-site was outside the main part of the city, but to reach it we did not have to cross open territory. By a clever device, the monster-creatures had extended their electrical force-screen into a tunnel shape, through which it was possible to walk in warm and breathable air. This tunnel led directly towards the mountain, and although from this level not much of the mountain could be seen, ahead of us I noticed the immense buildings of the cannon-site.

There was much traffic in this extension, both pedestrian and vehicular, and I found the activity reassuring. I had been given a suit of the black clothes, but the 'dwarf' sobriquet was a reminder of my abnormal appearance.

As the extension reached the place where the protective screen opened out again, by the entrance to the cannon-site itself, we came under the direct scrutiny of several of the monsters. These were mounted inside permanent guard-positions, and the monsters themselves sat behind faintly tinted glass screens, observing all who passed with their broad, expressionless eyes.

To pass this point we adopted a previously agreed deception. I and the two men pushed Edwina before us, as if she were being taken for some inhuman treatment. One of the Martians was holding an electrical whip, and he brandished it with great conviction.

Inside the area itself there were more monsters in evidence than I had ever seen anywhere on Mars, but once past the guard-post we were ignored. Most of the odious creatures had legged vehicles in which to move about, but I saw several who were dragging themselves slowly along the ground. This was the first time I had seen this; until now I had assumed that without their mechanical aids the monsters were helpless. Indeed, in face-to-face combat with a human a monster would be totally vulnerable, for the motion was slow and painful, four of the tentacles being used as clumsy, crab-like legs.

The presence of the monsters was not, however, the most intimidating aspect of this area.

Having noticed the cannon-site buildings while walking towards them from the city, I had registered that they were of great size, but now we were among them I realized just how enormous were the engines of science on this world. Walking between the buildings, it was as if we were ants in a city street.

My guides attempted to explain the purpose of each building as we passed it. Edwina's vocabulary was limited, and I obtained only the vaguest idea of the overall plan. As far as I could understand, the various components of the battle-machines were manufactured in the outlying factories, then brought to this place where they were assembled and primed. In one building—which must have been at least three hundred feet high—I could see through immense open doors that several of the tripodal battle-machines were in the process of being built: the one furthest from us was no more than a skeletal framework suspended from pulleys, while beneath it one of the three legs was being attached, but the battle-machine nearest us seemed to be complete, for its platform was being rotated while around it many supplementary instruments scanned and tested.

Both men and monsters worked in these mighty sheds, and to my eyes it seemed that the co-existence was unforced. There were no obvious signs of the slave-rule, and it occurred to me that perhaps not every human on Mars would welcome the revolution.

After we had passed some twenty or so of these sheds, we came to a vast stretch of open land, and I stopped dead in my tracks, speechless at what I saw.

Here were the fruits of such prodigious industry. Lined up, in one rank after another, were the projectiles. Each one was identical to the next, as if each had been turned on the same lathe by the same craftsman. Each one was machined and polished to a gleaming, golden shine; there were no extrusions to mar the cleanness of the line. Each one was nearly three hundred feet in length; sharply pointed at the nose, curving up so that the craft had a cylindrical body for most of its length, and its rear was circular, revealing the huge diameter. I had stood amazed at the size of the craft fired by the monsters of Desolation City, but they were mere playthings compared to these. I could hardly credit what I saw, but as I walked past the nearest of the projectiles I realized that it must have an overall diameter of around ninety feet!

My guides walked on unconcerned, and after a moment I followed them, craning my neck and marvelling.

I tried to estimate how many projectiles there were, but the area on which they were laid was so vast that I was not even sure I could see all the craft. Perhaps each rank had upwards of a hundred such waiting projectiles, and I passed through eight ranks of them.

Then, as we emerged from between the projectiles in the front rank, I was confronted with the most astonishing sight of all.

Here is was that the ascending slope of the volcano became pronounced, rising before us. Here it was that the monster-creatures of this hateful city had laid their snow-cannons.

There were five in all. Four of them were of the same order as the one at Desolation City, but there was no complication here with pivotal buildings and a lake to absorb the heat, for the barrels of the cannon were laid along the slope of the mountain itself! Nor was there any need for the elaborate process of inserting the projectile through the muzzle, for by a cunning arrangement of railway lines, and a stout entrance at the breech of the barrel, the projectiles could be loaded here.

But my attention was not drawn towards these pieces of ordnance, for, mighty as they were, their presence was overshadowed by the fifth snow-cannon.

Whereas the lesser snow-cannons had barrels a mile or so long, with bores of about twenty feet, this central cannon had a barrel with an external diameter well in excess of one hundred feet. As for its length . . . well, it extended further than the eye could see, running straight and true up the side of the mountain, sometimes resting on the soil, sometimes carried by huge viaducts where the slope was less pronounced, sometimes running through canyons blasted from the rock itself. At its base, the very breech was like a metal mountain of its own: a great, bulbous piece of black armour, thick enough and mighty enough to support the ferocious blast of the vaporizing ice which powered the projectiles. It loomed over everything, a stark reminder of the terrible skills and sciences these accursed monster-creatures commanded.

It was with this cannon, and with these hundreds of gleaming projectiles, that the monster-creatures plotted their invasion of Earth!

ii

A projectile had been placed already in the breech, and my guides led me up a metal companionway that attached to the bulk of the cannon like a flying buttress against the wall of a cathedral. From its dizzying height I looked down across the massed machines of the monsters, and beyond them, across the dividing strip of land to the near-by city.

The companionway ended at one of the access-points to the barrel itself, and we entered through a narrow tunnel. At once the temperature fell sharply. Interpreting for one of the men, Edwina explained that the barrel was already lined with ice, and that its entire length could be relined and frozen in just over half a day.

The tunnel led directly to a hatch into the craft itself. I suppose I had been expecting a larger version of the projectile in which I had already flown, but this was so only in its overall design.

We stepped out of the hatch into the forward control-area, and from here explored the entire craft.

As with the smaller projectiles, this one was divided into three main areas: the control section, a hold in which the slaves would be carried and the main hold in which the monsters and their terrible battle-machines were to ride. These last two compartments were linked by one of the blood-letting devices. That at least was no different, but one of the men explained that during the flight the monsters would be sedated with a sleeping-draught, and that their food requirements would be minimal.

I had no desire to dwell on this aspect of the monsters' arrangements, and so we passed on into the main hold itself.

Here I saw the full scale of the monsters' arsenal. Five of the tripodal battle-machines were stored here, their legs detached and neatly folded, the platforms collapsed to occupy as little space as possible. Also aboard were several of the small, legged vehicles, a score or more of the heat-cannons, and innumerable quantities of different substances, packaged away in dozens of huge containers. Neither I nor my guides could hazard a guess as to what these might be.

At various parts of the hold hung the tubes of transparent material which absorbed the shocks of launch and landing.

We did not stay long in this hold, but I saw enough to realize that what was here was in itself reason enough to fly to Earth. What a prize this would be for our scientists!

The control-area, in the prow of the ship, was a huge room with the overall shape of the pointed nose of the craft. The projectile had been set in the barrel in such a way that the controls were on what was presently the floor, but it was explained to me that in flight the craft would be rotated so as to produce weight. (This was a concept lost on me, and I decided that Edwina's translation was inadequate.) After the cramped quarters of the other projectile the control-area was palatial indeed, and the builders had gone to some pains to make the drivers comfortable. There was much dried food available, a tiny commode, and in one part of the wall was a shower-system, rather like the one we had used at the slave-camp. The siting of this, and the hammocks on which we would sleep, was rather puzzling, for they had been hung from the ceiling, some eighty feet above our heads.

I was told that in flight we would have no difficulty reaching them, although this was clearly something I would have to take on trust.

The controls themselves were many, and when I saw them, and thought about the bulk of the craft they directed, it was daunting to recall that until this day the most elaborate vehicle I had ever driven was a pony and trap!

The men explained everything in great detail, but I grasped little of what was said. In this, I felt Edwina's interpretations were unreliable, and even when I was confident she was conveying the meaning of their words accurately, I had difficulty with the concept described.

For example, I was shown a large glass panel—which was currently blank—and told that in flight there would be displayed upon it a picture of what was directly in front of the ship. This I could grasp, as it seemed to be common with the smaller projectile. However, there was a subtle refinement here. I was told repeatedly of a 'target', and this was talked of in conjunction with a series of metal knobs protruding from a place below the screen. Furthermore, I was told that target was applied when using the green-tipped lever which, I already knew from my earlier flight, released a blast of green fire from the nose.

I decided that much of what puzzled me now would become clear by experimentation in flight.

The explanations went on until my mind was spinning. At last I had a broad idea of what was to happen—the actual firing of the cannon, for instance, would be controlled from a building outside the ship—and further, I knew roughly how much I could manoeuvre the craft while in flight.

My guides told me that the monsters were not planning their

first launch for another four days. We should therefore have plenty of time to make our escape before the monsters were ready.

I said that I would be happy to leave as soon as possible, for now the means was open to us I had no desire to stay on Mars a moment longer than necessary.

iii

Amelia and I passed that night in one of the city dormitories. It had again been difficult for us to say much to each other, for Edwina was always in attendance, but when at last we took to a hammock we were able to talk quietly.

We lay in each other's arms; this was the one burden of our legendary rôles that I found easiest to fulfil.

"Have you inspected the craft?" Amelia said.

"Yes. I think there will be no problem. The area is crowded with monsters, but they are all occupied with their preparations."

I told her what I had seen: the number of projectiles ready to be fired at Earth, the arrangements within the craft.

"Then how many of the creatures are planning to invade?" Amelia said.

"The projectile we will be going in carries five of the brutes. I could not count the other projectiles ... certainly there were several hundred."

Amelia lay in silence for a while, but then she said: "I wonder, Edward ... if the revolution is now necessary. If this is to be the scale of the migration, then how many monsters will be left on Mars? Could the plan be for a total exodus?"

"That had crossed my mind too."

"I saw this as a moment of unpreparedness, but how ironical it would be if in a few days' time there would be no monsters left to overthrow!"

"And the adversary would be on Earth," I said. "Do you not see how urgent it is that we fly to Earth before the monsters?"

A little later, Amelia said: "The revolution is to start to-morrow."

"Could the Martians not wait?"

"No ... the firing of our craft is to be the signal for action."

"But could we not deter them? If they would only wait...."

"You have not seen all their preparations, Edward. The excitement of the people is irrepressible. I have lit a gunpowder trail, and the explosion is no more than a few hours away."

We said no more after this, but I for one could hardly sleep. I was wondering if this was indeed to be our last night on this unhappy world, or whether we should ever be free of it.

iv

We had gone to bed in a mood of worried calm, but when we awoke it was to a very different situation.

What awakened us was a sound which sent chills of fear down my spine: the howling of the monsters' sirens, and the reverberations of distant explosions. My first thought, prompted by experience, was that there had been another invasion, but then, as we jumped from the hammock and saw that the dormitory was deserted, we realized that the fighting must be between opposing forces within the city. The Martians had not waited!

A battle-machine strode past the building, and we felt the walls tremble with the vibration of its passage.

Edwina, who until this moment had been hiding beside the door, rushed over to us when she saw we were awake.

"Where are the others?" Amelia said immediately.

"They went in the night."

"Why were we not told?"

"They said you were now only wanting to fly in the machine."

"Who started this?" I said, indicating the bedlam beyond the building.

"It began in the night, when the others left."

And we had slept through this noise and confusion? It seemed hardly likely. I went to the door and peered into the street. The battle-machine had gone its way, and its armoured platform could be seen above some near-by buildings. Some distance from me I could see a column of black smoke rising, and over to my left there was a smaller fire. In the distance there was another explosion, although I could not see any smoke, and in a moment I heard two battle-machines braying in response.

I went back to Amelia.

"We had better get to the cannon-site," I said. "It might still be possible to take the projectile."

She nodded, and went to where our erstwhile friends had laid out two of the black uniforms for us. When we had put these on, and were preparing to leave, Edwina looked at us uncertainly.

"Are you coming with us?" I said, brusquely. I had been growing tired of her fluting voice and the unreliability of her translations. I wondered how much of our information had been misrepresented by her.

She said: "You would like me to come, Amelia?"

Now Amelia looked doubtful, and said to me: "What do you think?"

"Will we need her?"

"Only if we have something to say."

I considered for a few seconds. Much as I distrusted her, she was our only contact with the people here, and she had at least stayed behind when the others left.

I said: "She can come with us as far as the cannon-site."

With that, and pausing only to collect Amelia's hand-bag, we set off at once.

As we hurried across the city it became obvious that although the Martians had started their revolution, damage was as yet minor, and confined to a few areas. The streets were not empty of people, nor yet were they crowded. Several Martians gathered together in small groups, watched over by the battle-machines, and in the distance we heard many sirens. Somewhere near the centre of the city we came across evidence of more direct revolt: several of the battle-machines had been somehow overturned, and lay helplessly across the streets; these provided effective barricades, for once set on its side a tower could not by itself stand up again, and so blocked the passage of the ground vehicles.

When we came to the place where the electrical force-screen was extended towards the cannon-site, we found that the monsters and their machines were much in evidence. Several ground vehicles, and five battle-machines, stood thickly together, their heat-cannons raised.

We paused at this sight, not sure whether to go on. There were no Martian humans to be seen, although we noticed that several charred bodies had been swept roughly into a heap at the base of one of the buildings. Clearly there had been fighting here, and the monsters retained their supremacy. To approach now would bring almost certain death.

Standing there, undecided, I sensed the urgency of reaching the projectile before the trouble worsened.

"We had better wait," Amelia said.

"I think we should go on," I said quietly. "We will not be stopped wearing these uniforms."

"What about Edwina?"

"She will have to stay here."

However, in spite of my apparent resolution I was not confident. As we watched, one of the battle-machines moved off to the side, its heat-cannon pivoting menacingly. With its dangling metal arms it reached into one of the near-by buildings, apparently feeling for anyone hiding within. After a few moments it moved off again, this time striding at a faster pace.

Then Amelia said: "Over there, Edward!"

A Martian was signalling to us from one of the other buildings, waving his long arms. Casting a watchful glance at the machines, we hurried over to him and at once he and Edwina exchanged several words. I recognized him as one of the men we had met the day before.

Eventually, Edwina said: "He says that only drivers of the

flying war-machines can go further. The two who showed you yesterday are waiting for you."

Something about the way she said this aroused a faint suspicion, but for want of further evidence I could not say why.

"Are you to come with us?" said Amelia.

"No. I stay to fight."

"Then where are the others?" I said.

"At the flying war-machine."

I took Amelia to one side. "What shall we do?"

"We must go on. If the revolution causes any more trouble, we might not be able to leave."

"How do we know we are not walking into a trap?" I said.

"But who would lay it? If we cannot trust the people, then we are lost."

"That is precisely my worry," I said.

The man who had signalled to us had already disappeared into the building, and Edwina seemed to be on the point of running in after him. I looked over my shoulder at the monsters' machines, but there appeared to have been no movement.

Amelia said: "Good-bye, Edwina."

She raised her hand, spreading her fingers, then the Martian girl did the same.

"Good-bye, Amelia,' she said, then turned her back and walked through the doorway.

"That was a cool farewell," I said. "Considering you are the leader of the revolution."

"I don't understand, Edward."

"Neither do I. I think we must get to the projectile without further delay."

v

We approached the battle-machines with considerable trepidation, fearing the worst with every step. But we went unmolested, and soon we had passed beneath the high platforms and were walking up the extension towards the cannon-site.

A deep mistrust of the situation was growing in me, and I was dreading the fact that soon we should have to pass beneath the scrutiny of the monsters who guarded the entrance. My feeling of unease was increased when, a few minutes later, we heard more explosions from the city, and saw several of the battle-machines dashing about the streets with their cannons flaring.

"I wonder," I said, "if our part in the revolt is now suspected. Your young friend was remarkably reluctant to be with us."

"She does not have one of these uniforms."

"That's true," I said, but I was still not at ease.

The entrance to the cannon-site was nearly upon us, and the great sheds were looming up.

At the last moment, when we were no more than five yards from the monsters' observation-seats, we saw one of the two young Martians I'd been with the previous day. We went directly to him. There was an empty vehicle by the roadway, and we went around the back of it with him.

Once away from the sight of the monster-creatures at the gate, he launched into a most expressive foray of sibilance and expository gestures.

"What's he saying?" I said to Amelia.

"I haven't the faintest notion."

We waited until he had finished, and then he stared at us as if awaiting a response. He was about to start his tirade again, when Amelia indicated the cannon-site.

"May we go in?" she said, evidently working on the assumption that if he could speak his language to us, we could speak ours to him, but assisting him by pointing towards the site.

His reply was not understood.

"Do you think he said yes?" I said.

"There is only one way to tell."

Amelia raised her hand to him, then walked towards the entrance. I followed, and we both glanced back to see if this action provoked a negative response. He appeared to be making no move to stop us, but raised his hand in greeting, and so we walked on.

Now determined to see this through, we were past the monsters' observation panels almost before we realized it. However, a few paces further on a screech from one of the positions chilled our blood. We had been spotted.

We both halted, and at once I found I was trembling. Amelia had paled.

The screech came again, and was then repeated.

"Edward . . . we must walk on!"

"But we have been challenged!" I cried.

"We do not know what for. We can only walk on."

So, expecting at best another bestial screech, or at worst to be smitten by the heat-beam, we stepped on towards the snow-cannon.

Miraculously, there was no further challenge.

vi

We were now almost running, for our objective was in sight. We passed through the ranks of waiting projectiles, and headed for the breech of the mighty cannon. Amelia, whose first visit to the site this was, could hardly believe what she saw.

"There are so many!" she said, gasping with the exertion of hurrying up the gradient of the mountain slope.

"It is to be a full-scale invasion," I said. "We cannot allow these monsters to attack Earth."

During my visit the day before, the activities of the monsters had been confined to the area where the machines were assembled, and this store of gleaming projectiles had been left unattended. Now, though, there were the monsters and their vehicles all about. We hurried on, unchallenged.

There was no sign of any humans, although I had been told that by the time we entered the projectile our friends would be in charge of the device which fired the cannon. I hoped that word of our arrival had been passed, for I did not wish to wait too long inside the projectile itself.

The companionway was still in place, and I led Amelia up it

to the entrance to the inner chamber. Such was our haste that when one of the monster-creatures by the base of the companionway uttered a series of modulated screeches, we paid no attention to it. We were now so close to our objective, so near to the instrument of our return to Earth, that we felt nothing could bar our way.

I stood back to allow Amelia to go first, but she pointed out that it would be sensible for me to lead. This I did, heading down that dark, frigid tunnel through the breech-block, away from the wan sunlight of Mars.

The hatch of the ship was open, and this time Amelia did go in before me. She stepped down the ramp into the heart of the projectile, while I attended to closing the hatch as I'd been shown. Now we were inside, away from the noises and enigmas of the Martian civilization, I suddenly felt very calm and purposeful.

This spacious interior, quiet, dimly lit, quite empty, was another world from that city and its beleaguered peoples; this craft, product of the most ruthless intellect in the Universe, was our salvation and home.

Once it would have been in the van of a terrible invasion of Earth; now, in the safe charge of Amelia and myself, it could become our world's salvation. It was a prize of war, a war of which even now the peoples of Earth were quite unsuspecting.

I checked the hatch once more, making certain that it was quite secure, then took Amelia in my arms and kissed her lightly.

She said: "The craft is awfully big, Edward. Are you sure you know what to do?"

"Leave it to me."

For once my confidence was not assumed. Once before I had made a reckless act to avert an evil destiny, and now again I saw destiny as being in my own hands. So much depended on my skills and actions, and the responsibility of my homeworld's future lay on my shoulders. It could not be that I should fail!

I led Amelia up the sloping floor of the cabin, and showed her the pressure tubes that would support and protect us during the firing of the cannon. I judged it best that we should enter them at once, for we had no way of telling when our friends outside would fire the craft. In the confused situation, events were unpredictable.

Amelia stepped into her own tube, and I watched as the eerie substance folded itself about her.

"Can you breathe?" I said to her.

"Yes." Her voice was muffled, but quite audible. "How do I climb out of this? I feel I am imprisoned."

"You simply step forward," I said. "It will not resist unless we are under acceleration."

Inside her transparent tube Amelia smiled to show she understood, and so I moved back to my own tube. Here I squeezed past the controls which were placed within easy reach, then felt the soft fabric closing in on me. When my body was contained I allowed myself to relax, and waited for the launch to begin.

A long time passed. There was nothing to do but stare across the few feet that separated us, and watch Amelia and smile to her. We could hear each other if we spoke, but the effort was considerable.

The first hint of vibration, when it came, was so minute as to be attributable to the imagination, but it was followed a few moments later by another. Then there came a sudden jolt, and I felt the folds of fabric tightening about my body.

"We are moving, Amelia!" I shouted, but needlessly, for there was no mistaking what was happening.

After the first concussion there followed several more, of increasing severity, but after a while the motion became smooth and the acceleration steady. The fabric tube was clutching me like a giant hand, but even so I could feel the pressure of our speed against me, far greater than I had experienced on the smaller craft. Furthermore, the period of acceleration was much longer, presumably because of the immense length of the barrel. There was now a noise, the like of which was quite unprecedented: a great rushing and roaring, as the enormous craft shot through its tube of ice.

Just as the acceleration was reaching the point where I felt I could no longer stand it, even inside the protective grasp of the tube, I saw that Amelia's eyes had closed and that inside her tube she appeared to have fallen unconscious. I shouted out to her, but in the din of our firing there was no hope that she would hear me. The pressure and noise were each now intolerable, and I felt a lightness in my brain and a darkness occluding my sight. As my vision failed, and the roaring became a dull muttering in the background, the pressure abruptly ceased.

The folds of the fabric loosened, and I stumbled forward out of the tube. Amelia, similarly released, fell unconscious to the metal floor. I leant over her, slapping her cheeks gently . . . and it was not for several moments that I realized that at last we had been flung headlong into the ether of space.

Chapter Seventeen
A HOMEWARD QUEST

i

So began the voyage which, in optimism, I had expected to take but a day or two, but which in actuality took nearer sixty days, as near as we could tell. They were two long months; for short periods it was an exciting experience, at other times it became terrifying, but for most of the sixty days it was a journey of the most maddening dullness.

I will not, then, delay this narrative with an account of our daily lives, but indicate those events which most exercised us at the time.

Thinking back over the experience, I recall the flight with mixed feelings. It was not an enjoyable journey in any sense of the word, but it was not without its better sides.

One of these was that Amelia and I were alone together in an environment which provided privacy, intimacy and a certain security, even if it was not the most usual of situations. It is not germane to this narrative to describe what occurred between us—even in these modern times, I feel I should not breach the trusts which we then established—but it would be true to say that I came to know her, and she to know me, in ways and to depths I had never before suspected were possible.

Moreover, the length of the journey itself had a purgatory effect on our outlooks. We had indeed become tainted by Mars, and even I, less involved than Amelia, had felt a conflict of loyalties as we blasted away from the revolution-torn city. But, surrounded as we were by a Martian artifact, and kept alive by Martian food and Martian air, as the days passed and Earth grew nearer, the conflicts faded and we became of single purpose once more. The invasion the monsters schemed was all too real; if we could not help avert such an invasion then we could never again call ourselves human.

But already my synopsis of this incredible journey through space is once more taking my narrative ahead of its natural order.

I have mentioned that certain incidents during the voyage were exciting or terrifying, and the first of these occurred shortly after we were released from the pressure-tubes, and found ourselves in command of a space ironclad.

ii

When I had revived Amelia from her faint, and ensured that neither she nor I had suffered any ill-effects during the rigours of the blast, I went first to the controls to see where we were headed. Such was the ferocity of our firing that I was sure we were about to hurtle into Earth at any moment!

I turned the knob that illuminated the main panel—as my guides had shown me—but to my disappointment nothing could be seen except for a few faint points of light. These, I later realized, were stars. After experimenting for several minutes, and achieving no more than marginally increasing the brilliance of the picture, I turned my attention to one of the smaller panels. This displayed the view behind the craft.

Here the picture was more satisfactory, for it showed a view of the world we had just left. So close to Mars were we still that it filled the entire panel: a chiaroscuro of light and shadow, mottled yellows and reds and browns. When my eyes adjusted to the scale of what I was seeing I found I could pick out certain features of the landscape, the most prominent of which was the immense volcano, standing out from the deserts like a malignant carbuncle. Bulging around its summit was a gigantic white cloud; at first I took this to be the volcano's own discharge, but later I thought that this must be the cloud of water-vapour that had thrust us on our way.

The city we had left was invisible—it lay presumably beneath the spreading white cloud—and there were few features I could definitely identify. The canals were clearly visible, or at least they became visible by virtue of the banks of weed that proliferated alongside them.

I stared at the view for some time, realizing that for all the force of our departure we had neither travelled very far nor were now moving with much velocity. Indeed, the only apparent movement was the image of the land itself, which was rotating slowly in the panel.

While I was watching this, Amelia called out to me: "Edward, shall we have some food?"

I turned away from the panel, and said: "Yes, I'm hun . . ."

I did not complete my sentence, for Amelia was nowhere in sight.

"I'm down here, Edward."

I stared down the sloping floor of the compartment, but there was no sign of her. Then I heard her laughing, and looked up in the direction of the sound. Amelia was there . . . upside-down on the ceiling!

"What are you doing?" I shouted, aghast. "You'll fall and hurt yourself!"

"Don't be silly. It's perfectly safe. Come down here and you'll see for yourself."

To demonstrate, she executed a little jump . . . and landed, feet first, on the ceiling.

"I cannot go down if you are above me," I said pedantically.

"It is you who is above me," she said. Then, surprising me, she walked across the ceiling, down the curving wall, and was soon by my side. "Come with me, and I'll show you."

She took my hand, and I went with her. I trod carefully at first, bracing myself against falling, but the gradient did not increase, and after a few moments I glanced back at my controls and saw to my surprise that they now seemed to be against the wall. We walked on, soon coming to the place where the food had been stored, and where Amelia had been. Now when I looked back at the controls they appeared to be on the ceiling above us.

During the course of our voyage, we grew used to this effect created by the spinning of the ship about its axis, but it was a novel experience. Until this moment we had taken it for granted, so accustomed were we to the lightness of the Martian gravity, and the craft was being rotated so as to simulate this.

(Later in the voyage, I found a way of increasing the rate of spin, with the intention of readying our bodies for the greater weight of Earth.)

For the first few days this phenomenon was a considerable novelty to us. The shape of the compartment itself lent peculiar effects. As one moved further up the sloping floor (or ceiling) towards the nose of the craft, so one approached the central axis of the ship and apparent gravity was less. Amelia and I often passed the time by exercising in this strange ambience: by going to the apex of the compartment and kicking oneself away, one could float across much of the space before drifting gently to the floor.

Still, those first two hours after the firing of the cannon were placid enough, and we ate a little of the Martian food, blissfully unaware of what was in store for us.

iii

When I returned to the controls, the view in the rearward-facing panel showed that the horizon of Mars had appeared. This was the first direct evidence I had that the planet was receding from us ... or, to be more accurate, that we were receding from it. The forward panel still showed its uninformative display of stars. I had, naturally enough, expected to see our homeworld looming before us. My guides on Mars had informed me that the firing of the cannon would direct the craft towards Earth, but that I should not be able to see it for some time, so there was no immediate concern.

It did seem strange to me, though, that Earth should not be directly ahead of us.

I decided that as there would be neither night nor day on the craft, we should have to establish a ship time. My watch was still working, and I took it out. As near as I could estimate it, the snow-cannon had been fired at the height of the Martian day, and that we had been in flight for about two hours. Accordingly, I set my watch at two o'clock, and thenceforward my watch became the ship's chronometer.

With this done, and with Amelia content to investigate what provisions had been made for our sojourn in the craft, I decided to explore the rest of the ship.

So it was that I discovered we were not alone. . . .

I was moving along one of the passages that ran through the double hull when I passed the hatchway that led to the compartment designed to hold the slaves. I afforded it the merest glance, but then stopped in horror! The hatch had been crudely sealed from the outside, welded closed so that the door was unopenable, either from within or without. I pressed my ear to it, and listened.

I could hear nothing: if anyone was inside they were very still. There was the faintest sound of movement, but this could well have come from Amelia's activities in the forward compartment.

I stood by that hatch for many minutes, full of forebodings and indecision. I had no evidence that anyone was within . . . but why should that hatch have been sealed, when only the day before I and the others had passed freely through it?

Could it be that this projectile carried a cargo of human food . . . ?

If so, just *what* was in the main hold . . . ?

Stricken with an awful presentiment, I hastened to the hatch that led to the hold where the monsters' machines had been stowed. This too had been welded, and I stood before it, my heart thudding. Unlike the other hatch, this was equipped with a sliding metal plate, of the sort that is installed in the doors of prison-cells.

I moved it to one side, a fraction of an inch at a time, terrified of making a noise and so drawing attention to myself.

At last it had been opened sufficiently for me to place my eye against it, and I did this, peering into the dimly lit interior.

My worst fears were instantly confirmed: there, not a dozen feet from the hatch, was the oblate body of one of the monsters. It lay before one of the protective tubes, evidently having been released from it after the launch.

I jumped back at once, fearful of being noticed. In the confined space of the passage I waved my arms in despair, cursing silently, dreading the significance of this discovery.

Eventually, I summoned enough courage to return to my peephole, and looked again at the monster that was there.

It was lying so that it presented one side of its body and most of its nasty face towards me. It had not noticed me, and indeed it had not moved an inch since I had first looked. Then I recalled what my guides had said . . . that the monsters took a sleeping-draught for the duration of the flight.

This monster's tentacles were folded, and although its eyes were open the flaccid white lids drooped over the pale eyeballs. In sleep it lost none of its beastliness, yet it was now vulnerable. I did not have the steel of rage in me that I had had before, but I knew that were the door not unopenable I would once again have been able to slay the being.

Reassured that I would not rouse the brute, I slid the plate right open, and looked along as much of the length of the hold I could. There were three other monsters in view, each one similarly unconscious. There was probably the fifth somewhere in the hold, but there was so much equipment lying about that I could not see it.

So we had not after all stolen the projectile. The craft we commanded was leading the monsters' invasion of Earth!

Was *this* what the Martians had been trying to tell us before we left? Was *this* what Edwina had been keeping back from us?

iv

I decided to say nothing of this to Amelia, remembering her loyalties to the Martian people. If she knew the monsters were aboard, she would realize that they had brought their food with them, and it would become her major preoccupation. I did not care for the knowledge myself—it was unpleasant to realize that beyond the metal wall at the rear of our compartment were imprisoned several men and women who, when needed, would sacrifice themselves to the monsters—but it would not divert my attention from the major tasks.

So, although Amelia remarked on my pallor when I returned, I said nothing of what I had seen. I slept uneasily that night, and once when I wakened I fancied I could hear a low crooning coming from the next compartment.

The following day, our second in space, an event occurred that made it difficult to keep my discovery to myself. On the day after that, and in subsequent days, there were further incidents that made it impossible.

It happened like this:

I had been experimenting with the panel that displayed the view before the ship, trying to understand the device whose nearest translation had been target. I had found that certain knobs could cause an illuminated grid-pattern to be projected over the picture. This was certainly in accord with target, for at the centre of the grid was a circle containing two crossed lines. However, beyond this I had not learned anything.

I turned my attention to the rearward panel.

In this, the view of Mars had changed somewhat while we slept. The reddish planet was now sufficiently far away for most of it to be seen as a disk in the panel, though still, because of the spinning of our craft, appearing to revolve. We were on the sunward side of the planet—which was itself reassuring, since Earth lies to the sunward of Mars—and the visible area was roughly the shape that one sees on Earth a day or two before a full moon. The planet was turning on its own axis, of course, and during the morning I had seen the great protruberance of the volcano appear.

Then, just as my watch declared the time to be nearly midday, an enormous white cloud appeared near the summit of the volcano.

I called Amelia to the controls, and showed her what I had seen.

She stared at it in silence for several minutes, then said softly: "Edward, I think a second projectile has been launched."

I nodded dumbly, for she had only confirmed my own fears.

All that afternoon we watched the rearward panel, and saw the cloud drifting slowly across the face of the world. Of the projectile itself we could see no sign, but both of us knew we were no longer alone in space.

On the third day, a third projectile was fired, and Amelia said: "We are part of an invasion of Earth."

"No," I said, grimly lying to her. "I believe we will have twenty-four hours in which to alert the authorities on Earth."

But on the fourth day another projectile was hurled into space behind us, and like each of the three before it, the moment of firing was almost exactly at midday.

Amelia said, with unassailable logic: "They are conforming to a regular pattern, and our craft was the first piece in that pattern. Edward, I maintain that we are a part of the invasion."

It was then that my secret could no longer be maintained. I took her into the passages that ran the length of the ship, and showed her what I had seen through the sliding metal panel. The monsters had not moved, still slumbering peacefully while their flight to Earth continued. Amelia took her turn at the hole in silence.

"When we arrive on Earth," she said, "we will be obliged to act quickly. We must escape from the projectile at the earliest possible moment."

"Unless we can destroy them before we land," I said.

"Is there any way?"

"I have been trying to think. There is no way we can enter the hold." I showed her how the hatch had been fused. "We could possibly devise some way of cutting off their supply of air."

"Or introducing to it some poison."

I seized on this solution eagerly, for since I had made my discovery my fears had been growing about what these creatures could do on Earth. It was unimaginable that they could be allowed to do their Devil's work! I had no idea how the air was circulated through the ship, but as my command of the controls was increasing so was my confidence, and I felt that this should not be impossible to solve.

I had said nothing to Amelia of the slaves in their compartment—for I was by now convinced that there were many aboard—but I had done her an injustice when anticipating her reaction.

That evening, Amelia said: "Where are the Martian slaves, Edward?"

Her question was so forthright that I did not know what to say.

"Are they in the compartment behind ours?" she went on.

"Yes," I said. "But it has been sealed."

"So there is no possibility of releasing them?"

"None that I know of," I said.

We were both silent after this exchange, because the awfulness of the wretches' prospects was unthinkable. Some time later, when I was on my own, I went to their hatch and tried again to see if it could be opened, but it was hopeless. As far as I can recall, neither Amelia nor I ever referred directly to the slaves again. For this, I at least was grateful.

v

On the fifth day of our voyage a fifth projectile was fired. By this time, Mars was distant on our rearwards panel, but we had little difficulty in seeing the cloud of white vapour.

On the sixth day I discovered a control attached to the screens which could enhance and enlarge the images. When midday came around we were able to see, in relatively clear detail, the firing of the sixth cylinder.

Four more days passed and on each of them the mighty snow-cannon was fired, but on the eleventh day the volcano passed across the visible portion of Mars, and no white cloud appeared. We watched until the volcano had passed beyond the terminator, but as far as we could tell no projectile was fired that day.

Nor was there on the day following. Indeed, after the tenth projectile no more were fired at all. Remembering those hundreds of gleaming craft lying at the base of the mountain, we could not believe that the monsters would call off their plans with so comparatively few missiles *en route* for the target. This did seem to be the case, though, for as the days passed we never abandoned our watch of the red planet but not once again did we see any sign of the cannon being fired.

Of course, we occupied much time in speculating as to why this should be so.

I advanced the theory that this was the monsters' plan: that an advance guard of ten projectiles would invade and occupy an area of Earth, for after all they would have an armoury of at least fifty battle-machines with which to do this. For this reason I felt our watch should be maintained, arguing that more projectiles would soon be following.

Amelia was of a different mind. She saw the surcease in terms of a victory for the Martian humans' revolution, that the people had broken through the monsters' defences and taken control.

In either event we had no way of verifying anything other than what we saw. The migration had effectively finished with ten projectiles, at least for the time being.

By this time we were many days into our voyage, and Mars itself was a small, glowing body many millions of miles behind us. Our focus of interest was moving from this, for now, in the forwards panel, we could see our homeworld looming towards us: a tiny crescent of light, so indescribably lovely and still.

vi

As the weeks passed I became more at home with the controls, feeling that I understood the function of most. I had even come to understand the device the Martians had called the target, and had realized that it was possibly the most important of all the controls.

I had learned to use this when viewing Earth through the forwards panel. It had been Amelia who had first pointed out our world: a clearly defined brilliance near the edge of the panel. Of course, we were both much affected by the sight, and the knowledge that every day carried us thousands of miles nearer to it was a source of steadily growing excitement. But as one day followed another, the image of our world slipped nearer and nearer to the edge of the display, until we realized that it could not be long before it vanished from our sight altogether. I adjusted the controls of the panel equipment to no avail.

Then, in desperation, Amelia suggested that I should turn on the illuminated grid that was projected across the panel. As I did this I saw that a second, more ghostly grid lay behind it. Unlike the main one, this had its central circle fixed on the image of our world. It was most uncanny ... as if the device had a mind of its own.

At the same moment as the second grid appeared, several lights flashed on beneath the image. We could not understand their meaning, naturally enough, but the fact that my action had produced a response was significant in itself.

Amelia said: "I think it means we must steer the craft."

"But it was aimed accurately from Mars."

"Even so ... it seems to me that we are no longer flying towards Earth."

We argued a little longer, but at last I could no longer avoid the fact that the time had come for me to demonstrate my prowess as a driver. With Amelia's encouragement I settled myself before the main driving lever, gripped it in both my hands, and moved it experimentally to one side.

Several things happened at once.

The first was that a great noise and vibration echoed through the projectile. Another was that both Amelia and I were thrown to one side. And in addition everything in our compartment that was not secured flew willy-nilly about our heads.

When we had recovered ourselves we discovered that my action had had an undesired effect. That is to say, Earth had disappeared from the panel altogether! Determined to right this at once, I moved the lever in the opposite direction, having first ensured that we were both braced. This time, the ship moved sharply the other way, and although there was much noise and rattling of our possessions, I succeeded in returning Earth to our sight.

It took several more adjustments to the controls before I managed to place the image of Earth in the small central circle of the main grid. As I did this, the display of lights went out, and I felt that our craft was now set firmly on an Earthbound course.

In fact, I discovered that the projectile was wont to drift constantly from its path, and every day I had to make more corrections.

By this process of trials and error, I understood at last how the system of grids was intended to be used. The main, brighter grid indicated the actual destination of the craft, while the less brilliant, moving grid showed the intended destination. As this was always locked on the image of Earth, we were never in doubt as to the monsters' plans.

Such moments of diversion, however, were the exception rather than the rule. Our days in the craft were dull and repetitive, and we soon adopted routines. We slept for as many hours as possible, and dawdled over our meals. We would take exercise by walking about the circumference of the hull, and when it came to attending to the controls would divert more energy and time than was actually necessary. Sometimes we became fractious, and then we would separate and stay at different parts of the compartment.

During one of these periods I returned to the problem of how to deal with the unwelcome occupants of the main hold.

Interfering with the monsters' air-supply seemed to be the logical way of killing them, and in lieu of any substance which I knew to be poisonous to them, suffocation was the obvious expedient. With this in mind I spent the best part of one day exploring the various machines which were built into the hull.

I discovered much about the operation of the craft—for example, I found the location of the quasi-photographic instruments which delivered the pictures to our viewing panels, and I learnt that the craft's directional changes were effected by means of steam expelled from a central heat-source, and ducted through the outer hull by means of an intricate system of pipes—but came no nearer to finding a solution. As far as I could tell, the air inside the craft was circulated from one unit, and that it served all parts of the ship simultaneously. In other words, to suffocate the monsters we should have to suffocate too.

vii

The nearer we came to Earth the more we were obliged to make corrections to our course. Twice or three times a day I would consult the forwards panel, and adjust the controls to bring the two grids once more into alignment. Earth was now large and clear in the picture, and Amelia and I would stand before it, watching our homeworld in silence. It glowed a brilliant blue and white, unspeakably beautiful. Sometimes we could see the moon beside it, showing, like Earth, as a slender and delicate crescent.

This was a sight which should have brought joy to our hearts, but whenever I stood at Amelia's side and stared at this vision of celestial loveliness, I felt a tremendous sadness inside me. And whenever I operated the controls to bring us more accurately towards our destination, I felt stirrings of guilt and shame.

At first I could not understand this, and said nothing to Amelia. But as the days passed, and our world sped ever nearer, I identified my misgivings, and at last was able to speak of them to Amelia. Then it was that I found she too had been experiencing the same.

I said: "In a day or two we shall be landing on Earth. I am minded to aim the craft towards the deepest ocean, and be done with it."

"If you did, I would not try to stop you," she said.

"We cannot inflict these creatures on our world," I went on. "We cannot shoulder that responsibility. If just one man or woman should die by these creatures' machinations, then neither you nor I could ever face ourselves again."

Amelia said: "But if we could escape the craft quickly enough to alert the authorities. . . ."

"That is a chance we cannot take. We do not know our way out of this ship, and if the monsters are out before us then we would be too late. My dearest, we have to face up to the fact that you and I must be prepared to sacrifice ourselves."

While we had been talking, I had turned on the control that produced the two grids across the panel. The secondary grid, showing our intended destination, lay over northern Europe. We could not see the precise place, for this part of the globe was obscured by white cloud. In England the day would be grey; perhaps it was raining.

"Is there nothing we can do?" Amelia said.

I stared gloomily at the screen. "Our actions are proscribed. As we have replaced the men who would have crewed this ship, we can only do what they would have done. That is to say, to bring the craft manually to the place already selected by the monsters. If we follow the plan, we bring the craft down in the centre of the grid. Our only choice is whether or not we do that. I can allow the craft to pass by Earth entirely, or I can head the craft to a place where its occupants can do no damage."

"You spoke of landing us in an ocean. Were you serious?"

"It is one course open to us," I said. "Although you and I would surely die, we would effectively prevent the monsters from escaping."

"I don't want to die," Amelia said, holding me tightly.

"Nor I. But do we have the right to inflict these monsters on our people?"

It was an agonizing subject, and neither of us knew the answers to the questions we raised. We stared at the image of our world for a few more minutes, then went to take a meal. Later, we were drawn again to the panels, over-awed by the responsibilities that had been thrust upon us.

On Earth, the clouds had moved away to the east, and we saw the shape of the British Isles lying in the blue seas. The central circle of the grid lay directly over England.

Amelia said, her voice strained: "Edward, we have the greatest army on Earth. Can we not trust them to deal with this menace?"

"They would be taken unawares. The responsibility is ours, Amelia, and we must not avoid it. I am prepared to die to save my world. Can I ask the same of you?"

It was a moment charged with emotion, and I found myself trembling.

Then Amelia glanced at the rearward panel, which, though dark, was an insistent reminder of the nine projectiles that followed us.

"Would false heroics save the world from those too?" she said.

viii

So it was that I continued to correct our course, and brought the main grid to bear on the green islands we loved so dearly.

We were about to go to sleep that night when a noise I had hoped never to hear again emanated from a metal grille in the bulkhead: it was the braying, screeching call of the monsters. One has often heard the idiom that one's blood runs cold; in that moment I understood the truth of the cliché.

I left the hammock directly, and hurried through the passages to the sealed door of the monsters' hold.

As soon as I slid back the metal plate I saw that the accursed beings were conscious. There were two directly in front of me, crawling awkwardly on their tentacles. I was satisfied to see that in the increased gravity (I had long since changed the spin of the ship in an attempt to approximate the gravity of Earth) their movements were more ponderous and ungainly. That was a hopeful sign, when all else seemed bleak, for with any luck they would find their extra weight on Earth a considerable disadvantage.

Amelia had followed me, and when I moved back from the door she too peered through the tiny window. I saw her shudder, and then she drew back.

"Is there nothing we can do to destroy them?" she said.

I looked at her, my expression perhaps revealing the unhappiness I felt.

"I think not," I said.

When we returned to our compartment we discovered that one or more of the monsters was still trying to communicate with us. The braying echoed through the metal room.

"What do you think it is saying?" Amelia said.

"How can we tell?"

"But suppose we are to obey its instructions?"

"We have nothing to fear from them," I said. "They can reach us no more than we can reach them."

Even so, the hideous screeching was unpleasant to hear, and when it eventually stopped some fifteen minutes later we were both relieved. We returned to the hammock, and a few minutes later we were asleep.

We were awakened some time later—a glance at my watch revealed that we had slept for about four and a half hours—by a renewed outburst of the monsters' screeching.

We lay still, hoping that it would eventually stop again, but after five minutes neither of us could bear it. I left the hammock and went to the controls.

Earth loomed large in the forwards panel. I checked the positioning of the grid system, and noticed at once that something was amiss. While we had slept our course had wandered yet again: although the fainter grid was still firmly over the British Isles, the main grid had wandered far over to the east, revealing that we were now destined to land somewhere in the Baltic Sea.

I called Amelia over, and showed her this.

"Can you correct it?" she said.

"I think so.'

Meanwhile, the braying of the monsters continued.

We braced ourselves as usual, and I swung the lever to correct the course. I achieved a minor correction, but for all my efforts I saw we were going to miss our target by hundreds of miles. Even as we watched I noticed that the brighter grid was drifting slowly towards the east.

Then Amelia pointed out that a green light was glowing, one that had never before shone. It was beside the one control I had not so far touched: the lever which I knew released the blast of green fire from the nose.

Instinctively, I understood that our journey was approaching its end, and unthinkingly I applied pressure to the lever.

The projectile's response to this action was so violent and sudden that we were both catapulted forward from the controls. Amelia landed awkwardly, and I sprawled helplessly across her. Meanwhile our few possessions, and the pieces of food we had left about the compartment, were sent flying in all directions.

I was relatively unhurt by the accident, but Amelia had caught her head against a protruding piece of metal, and blood flowed freely down her face. She was barely conscious, and in obvious agony, and I bent anxiously over her.

She was holding her head in her hands, but she reached towards me and pushed me weakly away.

"I . . . I'm all right, Edward," she said. "Please . . . I feel a little sick. Leave me. It is not serious . . ."

"Dearest, let me see what has happened!" I cried.

Both her eyes were closed, and she had gone awfully pale, but she repeated that she was not badly hurt.

"You must attend to driving this craft," she said.

I hesitated for a few more seconds, but she pushed me away again, and so I returned to the controls. I was certain that I had not lost consciousness for even a moment, but it now seemed that our destination was much nearer. However, the centre of the main grid had moved so that it lay somewhere in the North Sea, indicating that the green fire had altered our course drastically. The eastwards drift, however, continued.

I went back to Amelia, and helped her to her feet. She had recovered her poise slightly, but blood continued to flow.

"My bag," she said. "There is a towel inside it."

I looked around but could see her bag nowhere. It had evi-

dently been thrown by the first concussion, and now lay somewhere in the compartment. Out of the corner of my eye I saw
the green light still glowing, and a certainty that the grid was
moving relentlessly on towards the east made me feel I should
be at the controls.

"I'll find it," Amelia said. She held the sleeve of her black
uniform over the wound, trying to staunch the blood. Her
movements were clumsy, and she was not articulating
clearly.

I stared at her in worried desperation for a moment, then
realized what we must do.

"No," I said firmly. "I'll find it for you. You must get into
the pressure-tube, otherwise you will be killed. We will be
landing at any moment!"

I took her by the arm and propelled her gently to the flexible
tube, which had hung unused for much of the flight. I took off
the tunic of my uniform, and gave it to her as a temporary
bandage. She held it to her face, and as she went into the tube
the fabric closed about her. I entered my own, and laid my
hand on the extended controls inside. As I did so, I felt the
fabric tightening about my body. I glanced at Amelia to ensure
that she was firmly held, then applied pressure to the green
lever.

Watching the panel through the folds of fabric I saw the
image become entirely obscured by a blaze of green, I allowed
the fire to blast for several seconds, then released the lever.

The image in the panel cleared, and I saw that the grid had
moved back to the west once again. It now lay directly across
England, and we were dead on course.

However, the eastwards drift continued, and as I watched
the two grids moved out of alignment. The shape of the British
Isles was almost obscured by the night terminator, and I knew
that in England some people would be seeing a sunset, little
realizing what was to descend into their midst during the
night.

While we were both still safe inside the pressure-tubes I
decided to fire the engine again, and so over-compensate for the
continual drifting. This time I allowed the green flame to burn

for fifteen seconds, and when I looked again at the panel I saw
that I had succeeded in shifting the centre of the bright grid to
a point in the Atlantic several hundred miles to the west of
Land's End.

Time for this kind of visual confirmation was short: in a few
minutes Britain would have disappeared beyond the night terminator.

I released myseif from the tube, and went to see Amelia.

"How do you feel?" I said.

She made to step forward from the constraint of the tube,
but I held her back.

"I'll find your bag. Are you any better?"

She nodded, and I saw that the bleeding had virtually
ceased. She looked a dreadful sight, for her hair had matted
over the wound and there were smears of blood all over her face
and chest.

I hastened about the compartment in search of the bag. I
found it at last—it had lodged directly above the controls—and
took it to her. Amelia reached through the tube and fumbled
inside the bag until she found several pieces of white linen,
folded neatly together.

While she pressed one of the pieces of the absorbent material
to her wound, and dabbed off most of the blood, I wondered
why she had never mentioned the existence of these towels
before.

"I shall be all right now, Edward," she said indistinctly from
within. "It is just a cut. You must concentrate on landing this
hateful machine."

I stared at her for a few seconds, seeing that she was crying. I
realized that our journey was ending none too soon and that
she, no less than I, could think of no happier moment than that
in which we left this compartment.

I returned to my pressure-tube, and laid my hand on the
lever.

ix

As the British Isles were now invisible in the night portion of the world, I had no other guide than the two grids. So long as I kept them in alignment then I knew that I was on course. This was not as simple as it may sound, for the degree of drift was increasing with every minute. The process was complicated by the fact that whenever I turned on the engine, the panel was deluged in green light, effectively blinding me. Only when I turned off the engine could I see what my last measure had achieved.

I established a routine of trial and error: first I would examine the panel to see how much drift had occurred, then fire the braking engine for a period. When I turned off the engine, I would look again at the panel and make a further estimate of the drift. Sometimes I would have estimated accurately, but usually I had either over- or under-compensated.

Each time I fired the engine it was for a longer period, and so I fell into a system whereby I counted slowly under my breath. Soon each blast—which I discovered could be made more or less intense by the degree of pressure on the lever—was lasting for a count of one hundred and more. The mental torment was tremendous, for the concentration it demanded was total; additionally, each time the engine was fired the physical pressures on us were almost intolerable. Around us, the temperature inside the compartment was rising. The air ducted down through the tubes remained cool, but I could feel the fabric itself becoming hot.

In the few brief moments between the firings of the engine, when the constraint of the tubes relaxed a little, Amelia and I managed to exchange a few words. She told me that the blood had stopped flowing, but that she had a vile headache and felt faint and sick.

Then at last the drifting of the two grids became so rapid that I dared not slacken my attention at all. The instant I turned off the engines the grids bounced apart, and I pressed the lever down and held it in place.

Now given its full throat, the braking engine set up a noise of such immensity that I felt the projectile itself must certainly break into pieces. The entire craft shuddered and rattled, and where my feet touched the metal floor I could feel an intolerable heat. Around us, the pressure-tubes gripped so tightly we could hardly breathe. I could not move even the tiniest muscle, and had no notion of how Amelia was faring. I could feel the tremendous power of the engine as if it were a solid object against which we were ramming, for even in spite of the restraining tubes, I felt myself being pushed forward against the braking. So, in this bedlam of noise and heat and pressure, the projectile blazed across the night sky of England like a green comet.

The end of our voyage, when it came, was abrupt and violent. There was an almighty explosion outside the craft, accompanied by a stunning impact and concussion. Then, in the sudden silence that immediately followed, we fell forward from the relaxing pressure-tubes, into the blistering heat of the compartment.

We had arrived on Earth, but we were indeed in a sorry state.

Chapter Eighteen
INSIDE THE PIT

i

We lay unconscious in the compartment for nine hours, oblivious, for the most part, of the terrible disorder our landing had thrown us into. Perhaps while we lay in this coma of exhaustion we were spared the worst effects of the experience, but what we endured was unpleasant enough.

The craft had not landed at an angle best suited to our convenience; because of the craft's axial spin the actual position in relation to the ground had been a matter of chance, and that chance had left both the pressure-tubes and our hammock suspended on what now became the walls. Moreover, the craft had collided with the ground at a sharp angle, so that the force of gravity tumbled us into the nose of the projectile.

That gravity itself felt immense. My attempts to approximate Earth's gravity by spinning the craft more quickly had been too conservative by far. After several months on Mars, and in the projectile, our normal weights felt intolerable.

As I have described, Amelia injured herself shortly before we started our landing, and this new fall had reopened the wound, and blood poured from her face more profusely than before. In addition, I had hit my head as we fell from the pressure-tubes.

Finally, and most unbearable of all, the interior of the craft was overwhelmingly hot and humid. Perhaps it had been the exhaust of the green fire that slowed our flight, or the friction of the Earth's atmosphere, or most probably a combination of the two, but the metal of the hull and the air it contained, and everything within were heated to an insupportable level.

This was the degree of disorder in which we lay unconscious, and this was the kind of squalor to which I awoke.

ii

My first action was to turn to Amelia, who lay in a huddle across me. The bleeding from her injury had stopped of its own accord, but she was in a dreadful state; her face, hair and clothes were sticky with congealing blood. So still was she, and so quiet her breathing, that at first I was convinced she had died, and only when in a panic I shook her by the shoulders and slapped her face did she rouse.

We were lying in a shallow pool of water, which had gathered on the floor under the spray from a fractured pipe. This pool was very warm, for it had taken heat from the metal hull of the projectile, but the spray was as yet cool. I found Amelia's bag, and took from it two of her towels. These I soaked in the spray, and washed her face and hands, dabbing gently at the open wound. As far as I could see, there was no fracture of her cranium, but the flesh of her forehead, just below her hairline, was torn and bruised.

She said nothing while I washed her, and seemed not to be in pain. She flinched only when I cleaned the wound.

"I must get you to a more comfortable position," I said, gently.

She simply took my hand, and squeezed it affectionately.

"Can you talk?" I said.

She nodded, then said: "Edward, I love you.'

I kissed her, and she held me fondly against her. In spite of our dire circumstances I felt as if I had been relieved of a great weight; the tensions of the flight had dissipated.

"Do you feel well enough to move?" I said.

"I think so. I am a little unsteady."

"I will support you," I said.

I stood up first, feeling giddy, but I was able to balance myself by holding on to a part of the broken controls which now overhung us, and by extending a hand I helped Amelia to her feet. She was more shaken than I, so I put one arm around her waist. We moved further up the sloping floor of the projectile to a place where, although the gradient was steeper, at least there was somewhere dry and smooth to sit.

It was then that I took out my watch, and discovered that nine hours had passed since we crash-landed. What had the monsters done in the time we lay unconscious?!

iii

Feeling very sorry for ourselves, we sat and rested for several more minutes, but I was obsessed by a sense of urgency. We could not delay leaving the projectile any longer than absolutely necessary. For all we knew, the monsters might even now be marching from their hold and launching their invasion.

Immediate concerns were still to be considered, though. One was the enervating heat in which we were sitting. The very floor on which we rested was almost hotter than we could bear, and all around us the metal plates radiated suffocating warmth. The air was moist and sticky, and every breath we took seemed devoid of oxygen. Much of the food that had spilled was slowly rotting, and the stench was sickening.

I had already loosened my clothes, but as the heat showed no sign of abating it seemed wise to undress. Once Amelia had recovered her wits I suggested this, then helped her off with the black uniform. Underneath she still wore the ragged garment I had seen her in at the slave-camp. It was unrecognizable as the crisp white chemise it had once been.

I was better off, for beneath my uniform I still wore my combination underwear which, in spite of my various adventures, was not at all unpresentable.

After some consideration we agreed it would be better if I explored the present situation alone. We had no idea how active were the monsters, assuming that they had not been killed by the concussion, and that it would be safer if I were by myself. So, having made absolutely sure that Amelia was comfortable, I let myself out of the compartment and set about the climb through the passages that ran through the hull.

It will be recalled that the projectile was very long: it was certainly not much less than three hundred feet from stem to stern. During our flight through space, movement about the craft had been relatively simple, because the axial rotation provided one with an artificial floor. Now, however, the craft had buried itself in the soil of Earth, and seemed to be standing on its nose, so that I was forced to climb at a very steep angle. In the heat, which was, if anything, greater in this part of the hull, the only advantage I had was that I knew my way about.

In due course I came to the hatch that led into the slaves' compartment. Here I paused to listen, but all was silent within. I climbed on after catching my breath, and eventually arrived at the hatch to the main hold.

I slid open the metal plate with some trepidation, knowing that the monsters were certainly awake and alert, but my caution was in vain. There was no sign of the beasts within my view, but I knew they were present for I could hear the sound of their horrid, braying voices. Indeed, this noise was quite remarkable in its intensity, and I gathered that much was being discussed between the nauseous beings.

At last I moved on, climbing beyond the door to the very stern of the craft itself. Here I had hoped to find some way by which Amelia and I might leave the ship surreptitiously. (I knew that if all else failed I could operate the green blast in the way I had done in the smaller projectile, and so shift it from its landing-place, but it was crucial that the monsters should not suspect that we were not their regular crew.)

Unfortunately, my way was barred. This was the very end of the craft: the massive hatch by which the monsters themselves would exit. The fact that it was still closed was in itself hopeful: if we could not leave by this way, then at least the monsters too were confined within.

Here I rested again, before making my descent. For a few moments I speculated about where I had landed the craft. If we had fallen in the centre of a city the violence of our landing would certainly have caused untold damage; this again would be a matter for chance, and here chance would be on our side. Much of England is sparsely built upon, and it was more than likely we would have found open countryside. I could do no more than hope; I had enough on my conscience.

I could still hear the monsters beyond the inner hull wall, addressing each other in their disagreeable braying voices, and occasionally I could hear the sinister sound of metal being moved. In moments of silence, though, I fancied I could hear other noises, emanating from beyond the hull.

Our spectacular arrival would almost certainly have brought crowds to the projectile, and as I stood precariously just inside the main rear hatch, my fevered imagination summoned the notion that just a few yards from where I was there would be scores, perhaps hundreds, of people clustered about.

It was a poignant thought, for of all things I hungered to be reunited with my own kind.

A little later, when I thought more calmly, I realized that any crowd that might have gathered would be in dire danger from these monsters. How much more grimly optimistic it was to think that the monsters would emerge to a ring of rifle-barrels!

Even so, as I waited there I felt sure I could hear human voices outside the projectile, and I almost wept to think of them there.

At long last, realizing that there was nothing to be done for the moment, I went back the way I had come and returned to Amelia.

iv

A long time passed, in which there seemed to be no movement either by the monsters within the ship, or by the men whom I now presumed were outside. Every two or three hours I would ascend again through the passages, but the hatch remained firmly closed.

The conditions inside our compartment continued to deteriorate, although there was a slight drop in the temperature. The lights were still on, and air was circulating, but the food was decomposing quickly and the smell was abominable. Furthermore, water was still pouring in from the fractured pipe, and the lower parts of the compartment were deeply flooded.

We stayed quiet, not knowing if the monsters could hear us, and dreading the consequences if they should. However, they seemed busied about their own menacing affairs, for there was no decline in their noise whenever I listened by their hatch.

Hungry, tired, hot and frightened, we huddled together on the metal floor of the projectile, waiting for a chance to escape.

We must have dozed for a while, for I awoke suddenly with a sense that there was a different quality to our surroundings. I glanced at my watch—which in lieu of a pocket in my combinations I had attached by its chain to a buttonhole—and saw that nearly twenty hours had elapsed since our arrival.

I woke Amelia, whose head rested on my shoulder.

"What is it?" she said.

"What can you smell?"

She sniffed exaggeratedly, wrinkling her nose.

"Something is burning," I said.

"Yes," Amelia said, then cried it aloud: "Yes! I can smell wood-smoke!"

We were overcome with excitement and emotion, for no more homely smell could be imagined.

"The hatch," I said urgently. "It's open at last!"

Amelia was already on her feet. "Come on, Edward! Before it's too late!"

I took her hand-bag, and led her up the sloping floor to the passage. I allowed her to go first, reasoning that I would then be below her if she fell. We climbed slowly, weakened by our ordeal . . . but we were climbing for the last time, out of the hell of the Martian projectile, towards our freedom.

v

Sensing danger, we stopped a few yards short of the end of the passage, and stared up at the sky.

It was a deep blue; it was not at all like the Martian sky, but a cool and tranquil blue, the sort that one rejoices to see at the end of a hot summer's day. There were wisps of cirrus cloud, high and peaceful, still touched with the red of sunset. Lower down, though, thick clouds of smoke rolled by, heady with the smell of burning vegetation.

"Shall we go on?" Amelia said, whispering.

"I feel uneasy," I said. "I had expected there would be many people about. It's too quiet."

Then, belying my words, there was a resounding clatter of metal, and I saw a brilliant flash of green.

"Are the monsters out already?" said Amelia.

"I shall have to look. Stay here, and don't make a sound."

"You aren't leaving me?" There was an edge to her voice, making her words sound tense and brittle.

"I'm just going to the end," I said. "We must see what is happening."

"Be careful, Edward. Don't be noticed."

I passed her the hand-bag, then crawled on up. I was in a turmoil of sensations, some of them internal ones, like fright and trepidation, but others were external. I knew that I was breathing the air of Earth, smelling the soil of England.

At last I came to the lip, and lay low against the metal floor. I pulled myself forward until just my eyes peered out into the evening light. There, in the vast pit thrown up by our violent landing, I saw a sight that filled me with dread and terror.

Immediately beneath the circular end of the projectile was the discarded hatch. This was a huge disk of metal, some eighty feet in diameter. It had once been the very bulkhead which had withstood the blast of our launch, but now, unscrewed from within, and dropped to the sandy floor, it lay, its use finished.

Beyond it, the Martian monsters had already started their work of assembling their devilish machinery.

All five of the brutes were out of the craft, and they worked in a frenzy of activity. Two of them were painstakingly attaching a leg to one of the battle-machines, which squatted a short distance from where I lay. I saw that it was not yet ready for use, for its other two legs were telescoped so that the platform was no more than a few feet from the ground. Two other monsters worked beside the platform, but each of these was inside a small legged vehicle, with mechanical arms supporting the bulk of the tripod while shorter extensions hammered at the metal plates. With every blow there was a bright flash of green light, and an eerie smoke, yellow and green combined, drifted away on the breeze.

The fifth monster was taking no part in this activity.

It squatted on the flat surface of the discarded hatch, just a few feet from me. Here a heat-cannon had been mounted in a metal structure so that its barrel pointed directly upwards. Above the support was a long, telescopic mounting, at the top of which was a parabolic mirror some two feet in diameter. This was presently being rotated by the monster, which pressed one of its bland, saucer-like eyes to a sighting instrument. Even as I watched, the monster jerked spasmically in hatred, and a pale, deathly beam—clearly visible in Earth's denser air—swept out over the rim of the pit.

In the distance I heard a confusion of shouts, and heard the crackle of burning timber and vegetation.

I ducked down for a few seconds, unable to participate in even this passive way; I felt that by inaction I became a party to slaughter.

That this was not the first time the beam had been used was amply evidenced, for when I looked again across the pit I noticed that along one edge were the charred bodies of several people. I did not know why the people had been by the pit when the monsters struck, but it seemed certain that now the monsters were keeping further intruders away while the machines were assembled.

The parabolic mirror continued to rotate above the rim of the pit, but while I watched the heat-beam was not used again.

I turned my attention to the monsters themselves. I saw, with horror, that the increased gravity of Earth had wrought gross distortions to their appearance. I have already noted how soft were the bodies of these execrable beings; with the increased pressure on them, the bladder-like bodies became distended and flattened. The one nearest to me seemed to have grown by about fifty percent, which is to say it was now six or seven feet long. Its tentacles were no longer, but they too were being flattened by the pressure and seemed more than ever snake-like. The face too had altered. Although the eyes—always the most prominent feature—remained unmarked, the beak-like mouth had developed a noticeable V-shape, and the creatures' breathing was more laboured. A viscous saliva dribbled continually from their mouths.

I had never been able to see these monsters with feelings less than loathing, and seeing them in this new aspect I could hardly control myself. I allowed myself to slip back from my vantage-point, and lay trembling for several minutes.

When I had recovered my composure, I crawled back to where Amelia was waiting, and in a hoarse whisper managed to relate what I had seen.

"I must see for myself," Amelia said, preparing to make her own way to the end of the passage.

"No," I said, holding her arm. "It's too dangerous. If you were seen—"

"Then the same will happen to me that would have happened to you." Amelia freed herself from me, and climbed slowly up the steep passageway. I watched in agonized silence as she reached the end, and peered out into the pit.

She was there for several minutes, but at last she returned safely. Her face was pale.

She said: "Edward, once they have assembled that machine there will be no stopping them."

"They have four more waiting to be assembled," I said.

"We must somehow alert the authorities."

"But we cannot move from here! You have seen the slaughter in the pit. Once we show ourselves we will be as good as dead."

"We have to do something."

I thought for a few minutes. Obviously, the police and Army could not be unaware that the arrival of this projectile presented a terrible threat. What we needed to do now was not alert the authorities, but to apprise them of the *extent* of the threat. They could have no notion that another nine projectiles were flying towards Earth at this very moment.

I was trying to stay calm. I could not see that the Army

would be helpless against these monsters. Any mortal being that could die by the knife could be disposed of as easily with bullets or shells. The heat-beam was a terrifying and deadly weapon, but it did not make the Martians invulnerable. Further weighing against the invaders was the fact of our Earthly gravity. The battle-machines were all-powerful in the light gravity and thin air of Mars; would they be so agile or dangerous here on Earth?

A little later I crawled again to the end of the passage, hoping that under the cover of darkness Amelia and I would be able to slip away.

Night had indeed fallen, and any moonlight there might have been was obscured by the thick clouds of smoke that drifted from the burning heath, but the Martians worked on through the night, with great floodlamps surrounding the machines. The first battle-machine was evidently completed, for it stood, on its telescoped legs, at the far end of the pit. Meanwhile, the components of a second were being taken from the hold.

I stayed at the vantage-point for a long time, and after a while Amelia joined me. The Martian monsters did not so much as look our way even once, and so we were able to watch their preparations undisturbed.

The monsters paused in their work only once. That was when, in the darkest part of the night, and exactly twenty-four hours after our own arrival, a second projectile roared overhead in a blaze of brilliant green. It landed with a shattering explosion no more than two miles away.

At this, Amelia took my hand, and I held her head against my chest while she sobbed quietly.

vi

For the rest of that night and for most of the next day we were forced to stay in hiding inside the projectile. Sometimes we dozed, sometimes we crawled to the end of the passage to see if escape was possible, but for most of the time we crouched silently and fearfully in an uncomfortable corner of the passage.

It was unpleasant to realize that events were already beyond our control. We had been reduced to spectators, privy to the war-preparations of an implacable enemy. Moreover, we were much exercised by the knowledge that we sat in some corner of England, surrounded by familiar sights, people, language and customs, and yet were obliged by circumstances to huddle inside an artifact alien to our world.

Some time after midday, the first sign that the military forces were responding came in the form of distant sounds of artillery. The shells exploded a mile or two away, and we understood at once what must be happening. Clearly, the Army was shelling the second projectile before its grisly occupants could escape.

The Martians we were watching responded to this challenge at once. At the first sounds of the explosions, one of the monsters went to the battle-machine first assembled and climbed into it.

The machine set off at once, its legs groaning under the strain of the extra gravity and emitting several flashes of green from the joints. I noticed that the platform was not raised to its full height, but crawled along just above the ground like an iron tortoise.

We knew that if the second pit was being shelled then ours would be too, and so Amelia and I returned to the deeper recesses of the projectile, hoping that the hull would be strong enough to withstand explosions. The distant shelling continued for about half an hour, but eventually halted.

There followed a long period of silence, and we judged it safe to return to the end of the passage to see what the Martians were now doing.

Their frenzied activity continued. The battle-machine that had left the pit had not returned, but of the remaining four, three were standing by ready for use, and the last was being assembled. We watched this for about an hour, and just as we were about to return to our hiding-place to take a rest, there came a flurry of explosions all about the pit. It was our turn to be shelled!

Once again the Martians responded instantly. Three of the monstrous brutes hurried to the completed battle-machines—their bodies were already adapting to the stresses of our world!—and mounted the platforms. The fourth, sitting inside one of the assembly vehicles, continued stoically with its work on the last battle-machine.

Meanwhile, the shells continued to fall with varying degrees of accuracy; none fell directly into the pit, but some were close enough to send grit and sand flying about.

With their Martian drivers aboard, the three battle-machines came dramatically to life. With appalling speed the platforms were raised to their full one hundred feet height, the legs struck out up the sides of the pit, and wheeling around, the deadly devices went their separate ways, the heat-cannons already raised for action. In less than thirty seconds of the first shells exploding around us, the three battle-machines had gone: one towards the south, one to the north-west, and the last in the direction of the second projectile.

The last Martian monster worked hurriedly on its own tripod; this creature alone now stood between us and freedom.

A shell exploded nearby: the closest yet. The blast scorched our faces, and we fell back into the passage.

When I could again summon enough courage to look out I saw that the Martian continued its work, untroubled by the shelling. It was certainly the behaviour of a soldier under fire; it knew that it risked death but was prepared to confront it, while it readied its own counterattack.

The shelling lasted for ten minutes and in all that time no hits were scored. Then, with great suddenness, the firing halted and we guessed that the Martians had silenced the emplacement.

In the uncanny silence that followed, the Martian continued its work. At last it was finished. The hideous creature climbed into its platform, extended the legs to their full height, then turned the craft southwards and was soon lost to sight.

Without further delay we took the opportunity so presented to us. I jumped down to the sandly soil, landing awkwardly and heavily, then held out my arms to catch Amelia as she jumped.

We looked neither to right nor left, but scrambled up the loose soil of the pit walls, and hurried away in the direction no machine had so far travelled: towards the north. It was a hot, sultry evening, with dark banks of cloud building up in the west. A storm was brewing, but that was not the reason no bird sang, no animal moved. The heath was dead: it was blackened with fire, littered with the wreckage of vehicles and the corpses of both horse and man.

Chapter Nineteen
HOW WE FELL IN WITH
THE PHILOSOPHER

i

On Mars I had dreamed of greenery and wild flowers; here on the blighted heath we saw only charred and smouldering grasses, with blackness spreading in every direction. On Mars I had hungered for the sights and sounds of my fellow Earthmen; here there was no one, only the corpses of those unfortunates who had fallen foul of the heat-beam. On Mars I had gasped in the tenuous atmosphere, yearning for the sweet air of Earth; here the odour of fire and death dried our throats and choked our lungs.

Mars was desolation and war, and just as Amelia and I had been touched by it when there, so Earth now felt the first tendrils of the Martian canker.

ii

Behind us, to the south, there was a small town on a hill, and already the battle-machines had attacked it. A huge pall of smoke hung over the town, adding to the piling storm-clouds above, and through the still evening air we could hear the sounds of explosions and screams.

To the west we saw the brazen cowl of one of the machines, turning from side to side as its great engine bore it striding through distant, burning trees. Thunder rumbled, and there was no sign of the Army.

We hastened away, but we were both weak from our ordeal

inside the projectile, we had had nothing to eat, and had hardly slept, for two days. Consequently our progress was slow in spite of the urgency of our escape. I stumbled twice, and we were both afflicted with painful stitches in our sides.

Blindly we ran, dreading that the Martians would see us and deal to us the summary execution they had dealt to others. But it was not mere instinct for self-preservation that urged us on our way; although we did not wish to die, we both realized that only we knew the full scale of the threat that was before the world.

At last we came to the edge of the common, and the ground fell down to where a small brook ran through trees. The top branches had been blackened by the sweep of the beam, but below was moist grass and a flower or two.

Sobbing with fear and exhaustion, we fell by the water and scooped up handfuls and drank noisily and deeply. To our palates long jaded by the bitter, metallic waters of Mars, this stream was pure indeed!

While we had been running frantically across the common, the evening had turned to night, speeded by the storm-clouds that were gathering. Now the rumbles of thunder were louder and came more often, and sheet-lightning flickered. It could not be long before the storm broke about us. We should be moving on as soon as possible: our vague plan to alert the authorities was all we lived for, even though we knew that there could be few people who did not realize that some mighty destructive force had erupted on to the land.

We lay low by the stream for about ten minutes. I placed my arm around Amelia's shoulders, and held her to me protectively, but we did not speak. I think we were both too overawed by the immensity of the damage to find words to express our feelings. This was England, the country we loved, and this was what we had brought to it!

When we stood up we saw that the fires caused by the Martians were burning still, and to the west we saw new flames. Where were the defences of our people? The first projectile had landed nearly two days ago; surely by now the whole area would be ringed by guns?

We did not have long to wait for an answer to that, and for a few hours it afforded us a certain reassurance.

iii

The storm broke a few moments after we left our temporary refuge. Quite suddenly we were deluged with rain, of an intensity that took us completely by surprise. Within seconds we were both drenched to the skin.

I was all for taking shelter until the cloudburst had passed, but Amelia let go of my hand, and danced away from me. I saw her lit by the distant flames, the glow of red touching her. The rain was plastering her long hair about her face, and the bedraggled chemise clung wetly to her skin. She held up her palms to the downpour, and swept back the hair from her face. Her mouth was open, and I heard her laughing aloud. Then she turned about, stamping and splashing in the puddles; she took my hand, and whirled me gaily. In a moment I caught the joyous, sensuous mood from her, and together in that dark countryside we sang and laughed hysterically, totally abandoning ourselves to the thrill of the rain.

The cloudburst eased, and as the thunder and lightning intensified we sobered. I kissed Amelia fondly and briefly, and we walked on with our arms about each other.

A few minutes later we crossed a road, but there was no traffic of any kind, and shortly after this we approached more woodland. Behind us, now two miles or more away, we could see the town burning on the hill, the flames not doused by the rain.

Just as we walked beneath the first of the trees, Amelia suddenly pointed to the right. There, lined up under the cover of the woodland, was a small artillery battery, the barrels of the ordnance poking out through the camouflage of bushes and shrubs.

We had been noticed by the soldiers at the same moment—for the lightning still flickered with disconcerting brilliance—and an officer dressed in a long cape, gleaming in the rain, came over to us.

I went to him immediately. I could not see his face in the darkness, for his cap was pulled well down against the rain. Two gunners stood a short distance behind him, sparing us little attention, for they were staring back the way we had come.

"Are you in command here?" I said.

"Yes, sir. Have you come from Woking?"

"Is that the town on the hill?"

He confirmed this. "Nasty business there I believe, sir. A lot of civilian casualties."

"Do you know what you are up against?" I said.

"I've heard the rumours."

"It is no ordinary enemy," I said, raising my voice a little. "You must destroy their pit immediately."

"I have my orders, sir," the officer said, and just at that moment there was a brilliant flash of lightning, repeated three times, and I saw his face for the first time. He was a man in his mid-twenties, and the clean, regular lines of his face were so unexpectedly *human* that for a moment I was dumbfounded. In that same illuminating flash he must have seen Amelia and me too, and noticed our untidy state. He went on: "The men have heard rumours that these are men from Mars."

"Not men," Amelia said, stepping forward. "Evil, destructive monsters."

"Have you seen them, sir?" the officer said to me.

"I have more than seen them!" I cried over the rumbling of thunder. "We came with them from Mars!"

The officer turned away at once, and signed to the two gunners. They came over directly.

"These two civilians," he said. "See them to the Chertsey Road, and report back."

"You must listen to me!" I cried to the officer. "These monsters must be killed at the first opportunity!"

"My orders are quite explicit, sir," the officer said, preparing to turn away. "The Cardigan is the finest regiment of horse-artillery in the British Army, a fact which even you, in your present deranged state, must admit."

I stepped forward angrily, but I was caught by one of the

soldiers. I struggled, and shouted: "We are not deranged! You must shell their pit at once!"

The officer looked at me sympathetically for a moment or two—evidently assuming that I had seen my house and property destroyed, and was thus temporarily demented—then turned away and splashed across the muddy ground towards a row of tents.

The gunner holding me said: "C'mon, sir. Ain't no place for civvies."

I saw that the other soldier was holding Amelia by the arm, and I shouted at him to leave her go. This he did, so I took her arm myself and allowed the soldiers to lead us past the horse-lines—where the poor animals bucked and whinnied, their coats slick with rain—and into the heart of the wood. We walked for several minutes, during which we learned that the detachment had ridden down from Aldershot Barracks that afternoon, but no more information, then came to a road.

Here the soldiers pointed the way to Chertsey, then headed back to their emplacement.

I said to Amelia: "They can have no idea of what they are facing."

She was more philosophical than I. "But they are alert to the danger, Edward. We cannot tell them what to do. The Martians will be contained on the common."

"There are eight more projectiles to land!" I said.

"Then they will have to deal with them one by one." She took my hand affectionately, and we started to walk up the road towards Chertsey. "I think we must be careful how we tell people of our adventures."

I took this as a mild rebuke, so I said defensively: "The time was wrong. He thought I was mad."

"Then we must be more calm."

I said: "There is already word about that the projectiles are from Mars. How could they have known?"

"I do not know. But I am sure of one thing, and it is a matter of importance to us both. We know where we are, Edward. We have landed in Surrey."

"I wish I had thrown us into the sea."

"If we are going to Chertsey," Amelia said, not at all affected by my pessimism, "then we are not a dozen miles from Sir William's house in Richmond!"

iv

As we entered Chertsey it was clear that the town had been evacuated. The first sign we saw of this was as we passed the station, and noticed that the metal gates had been drawn across the passenger entrance. Beyond them, a chalked sign declared that the train service had been suspended until further notice.

Further on into the town, walking through unlighted roads, we saw not a single lamp in any of the houses, nor anyone about the streets. We walked as far as the River Thames, but all we could see here were several boats and dinghies bobbing at their moorings.

The thunderstorm had passed, although it continued to rain, and we were both chilled through.

"We must find somewhere to rest," I said. "We are both done for."

Amelia nodded wearily, and held a little tighter to my arm. I was glad for her sake that there was no one about to see us: our abrupt return to civilization served to remind me that Amelia, in her torn and wet chemise, was as good as unclothed, and I was little better dressed.

Amelia made an instant decision. "We must break into one of the houses. We cannot sleep in the open."

"But the Martians. . . ."

"We can leave those to the Army. My dearest, we must rest."

There were several houses backing on to the river, but as we moved from one to the other we realized that the evacuation must have been orderly and without panic, for each was securely shuttered and locked.

At last we came to a house, in a road only a short distance from the river, where a window came free as I pushed at it. I climbed inside at once, then went through and opened the door for Amelia. She came in, shivering, and I warmed her with my own body.

"Take off your chemise," I said. "I will find you some clothes."

I left her sitting in the scullery, for the range had been alight during the day, and there it was still warm. I went through the rooms upstairs, but found to my dismay that all the clothes-cupboards had been emptied, even in the servants' quarters. However, I did find several blankets and towels, and took them downstairs. Here I stripped off my combinations, and placed them with Amelia's tattered chemise over the bar at the front of the range. While I had been upstairs I had discovered that the water in the tank was still hot, and while we huddled in our blankets beside the range I told Amelia she might have a bath.

Her response to this news was of such innocent and uninhibited delight that I did not add that there was probably only enough hot water for one.

While I had searched for clothes, Amelia had not herself been idle. She had discovered some food in the pantry, and although it was all cold it tasted wonderful. I think I shall never forget that first meal we ate after our return: salted beef, cheese, tomatoes and a lettuce taken from the garden. We were even able to drink some wine with it, for the house had a modest cellar.

We dared not light any of the lamps for the houses around us were darkened, and if any of the Martians should happen by they would immediately see us. Even so, I searched the house for some kind of newspaper or magazine, hoping to learn from it what had been known of the projectiles before the Martians broke free of the pit. However, the house had been effectively cleared of all but what we found around us, and we remained unenlightened on this score.

At last Amelia said she would take her bath, and a little later I heard the sound of the water being run. Then she returned.

She said: "We are accustomed to sharing most things, Edward, and I think you are as dirty as I."

And so it was that while we lay together in the steaming water, genuinely relaxing for the first time since our escape, we saw the green glare of the third projectile as it fell to the ground several miles to the south.

v

So exhausted were we that in the morning we slept on far beyond any reasonable hour; it was, considering the emergency, an undesirable thing to do, but our encounter with the artillery the evening before had reassured us, and our fatigued bodies craved for rest. Indeed, when I awoke my first thoughts were not at all of the Martians. I had, the evening before, set my watch by the clock in the drawing-room, and as soon as I was awake I looked at it, and discovered that it was a quarter to eleven. Amelia was still asleep beside me, and as I gently touched her to awaken her I was smitten with the first feelings of unease about the casual way we were behaving together. It had been as a natural result of our confinement together on Mars that we had started acting as man and wife, and much as it was of great pleasure to me—and, I knew, to Amelia too—the very familiarity of our surroundings, the pleasant villa in the quiet riverside town, reminded me that we were now back in our own society. Soon we would reach a place where the awful impact of the Martians was not yet felt, and then it would be incumbent upon us to observe the social customs of our country. What had passed between us before we fell asleep became improper in our present surroundings.

Beyond the house the countryside was silent. I heard birds singing, and on the river the noise of the boats knocking together at their moorings ... but there were no wheels, no footsteps, no hooves clattering on the metalled roads.

"Amelia," I said softly. "We must be on our way if we wish to reach Richmond."

She awoke then, and for a few seconds we embraced fondly.

She said: "Edward ... what is that noise?"

We lay still, and then I too heard what had attracted her attention. It was akin to a large weight being dragged ... we heard bushes and trees rustling, gravel being ground, and above all a grating of metal upon metal.

For an instant I froze in terror, then broke free of the paralysis and bounded out of bed. I rushed across the room, and threw open the curtains incautiously. As the sunlight burst in I saw that directly outside our window was one of the jointed metal legs of a battle-machine! As I stared at it in horror, there was a gusting of green smoke at the joints, and the elevated engine propelled it on beyond the house.

Amelia had seen it too, and she sat up in the bed, clutching the sheets about her body.

I hurried back to her, appalled by the amount of time we had wasted. "We must leave at once."

"With *that* outside the house?" Amelia said. "Where has it gone?"

She scrambled out of the bed, and together we went quietly across the top floor of the house to a room on the other side. This was a child's bedroom, for the floor was littered with toys. Peering through the half-drawn curtains, we looked across in the direction of the river.

There were three battle-machines in sight. Their platforms were not raised to their full height, nor were their heat-cannons visible. Instead, what seemed to be an immense metal net had been attached to the rear of each platform, and into these nets were being placed the inert bodies of human beings who had been electrocuted by the dangling, metal tentacles. In the net of the battle-machine nearest us there were already seven or eight people, lying in a tangled heap where they had been dropped.

As we stared in dismay at the sight, we saw the metal tentacles of one of the more distant machines insinuate itself into a house ... and after about thirty seconds withdrew, clutching the unconscious body of a little girl.

Amelia covered her face with her hands, and turned away.

I stayed at the window for another ten minutes, immobilized by the fear of being noticed, and by the equal horror of what I was witnessing. Soon, a fourth machine appeared, and that too bore its share of human spoils. Behind me, Amelia lay on the child's bed, sobbing quietly.

"Where is the Army?" I said softly, repeating the words again and again. It was unthinkable that these atrocities should go unchallenged. Had the battery we had seen the night before allowed the monsters to pass undamaged? Or had a brief engagement already been fought, out of which the monsters had emerged unscathed?

Fortunately for Amelia and myself, the Martians' foraging expedition seemed to be at its end, for the battle-machines stood about, their drivers in apparent consultation. At length, one of the legged ground vehicles appeared, and in a short space of time the unconscious bodies were transferred to this.

Sensing that there was to be a new development, I asked Amelia to go downstairs and collect our clothes. This she did, returning almost at once. As soon as I had put on mine, I left Amelia on guard at the window, then went from one room to the next, looking to see if there were any more of the battle-machines in the vicinity. There was only one other in sight, and that was about a mile away, to the south-east.

I heard Amelia calling me, and I hurried back to her. She pointed wordlessly: the four battle-machines were turning away from us, striding slowly towards the west. Their platforms were still low, their heat-cannons as yet unraised.

"This is our chance," I said. "We can take a boat and head for Richmond."

"But is it safe?"

"No safer than at any other time. It's a chance we must take. We will keep a constant watch, and at the first sign of the Martians we'll take refuge by the bank."

Amelia looked doubtful, but put forward no other objection.

There was a trace of conformity still within us, in spite of the terrible anarchy around us, and we did not leave the house until Amelia had penned a brief note to the owner, apologizing for breaking in and promising to pay in due course for the food we had consumed.

vi

The storms of the day before had passed, and the morning was sunny, hot and still. We wasted no time in getting down to the riverside, and walked out on one of the wooden jetties to where several rowing-boats were moored. I selected what seemed to me to be a solid boat, and yet one not too heavy. I helped Amelia into it, then climbed in after her and cast off at once.

There was no sign of any of the battle-machines, but even so I rowed close to the northern bank, for here weeping willows grew beside the river and their branches overhung in many places.

We had been rowing for no more than two minutes when to our alarm there came a burst of artillery-fire from close at hand. At once I stopped rowing, and looked all about.

"Get down, Amelia!" I shouted, for I had seen over the roofs of Chertsey the four battle-machines returning. Now the glittering Titans were at their full height, and their heat-cannons were raised. The shells of the artillery exploded in the air about them, but no damage was inflicted that I could see.

Amelia had thrown herself forward across the planks at the bottom of the boat, and she crawled towards where I was sitting. She held on to my legs, clutching me as if this alone would turn the Martians away. We watched as the battle-machines abruptly altered their course, and headed towards the artillery emplacement on the northern bank opposite Chertsey. The speed of the machines was prodigious. As they reached the river's edge they did not hesitate, but plunged in, throwing up an immense spray. All the time their heat-beams were flashing forward, and in a moment we heard no more firing from our men.

In the same instant, Amelia pointed towards the east. Here, near where Weybridge was situated, the fifth battle-machine —the one I had seen earlier from the house—was charging at full spate towards the river. It had attracted the attentions of more artillery placed by Shepperton, and as it charged its gleaming platform was surrounded with fireballs from the exploding shells. None of these hit home, though, and we saw the Martian's heat-cannon swinging from side to side. The beam fell across Weybridge, and instantly sections of the town burst into flame. Weybridge itself, though, was not the machine's chosen target, for it too continued until it reached the river, and waded in at a furious speed.

Then came a moment of short-lived triumph for the Army. One of the artillery shells found its target, and with a shocking violence the platform exploded into fragments. With scarcely a pause, and as if possessed of a life of its own, the battle-machine staggered on, careening and swaying. After a few seconds it collided with the tower of a church near Shepperton, and fell back into the river. As the heat-cannon made contact with the water its furnace exploded, sending up an enormous cloud of spray and steam.

All this had taken place in less than a minute, the very speed at which the Martians were capable of making war being a decisive factor in their supremacy.

Before we had time to recover our senses, the four battle-machines which had silenced the Chertsey battery went to aid their fallen comrade. The first we knew of this was when we heard a great hissing and splashing, and glancing upstream we saw the four mighty machines racing through the water towards us. We had no time to think of hiding or escaping; indeed, so stricken with terror were we that the Martians were on us before we could react. To our own good luck, the monsters had no thought or time for us, for they were engaged in a greater war. Almost before they were beyond us, the heat-cannons were spraying their deadly beams, and once more the deep, staccato voice of the artillery by Shepperton spoke its ineffectual reply.

Then came a sight I have no wish ever to witness again. The deliberation and malice of the Martian invaders was never re-alized in a more conclusive fashion.

One machine went towards the artillery at Shepperton, and, ignoring the shells which burst about its head, calmly silenced the guns with a long sweep of its beam. Another, standing beside it, set about the systematic destruction of Shepperton itself. The other two battle-machines, standing in the confusion of islands where the Wey meets the Thames, dealt death upon Weybridge. Without compunction, both man and his effects were blasted and razed, and across the green Surrey meadows we heard one detonation after another, and the clamour of voices raised in the terror that precedes a violent death.

When the Martians had finished their evil work the land became silent again . . . but there was no stillness about. Weybridge burned, and Shepperton burned. Steam from the river mingled with smoke from the towns, joining in a great column that poured into the cloudless sky.

The Martians, unchallenged once more, folded away their cannons, and congregated at the bend of the river where the first battle-machine had fallen. As the platforms rotated to and fro, the bright sunlight reflected from the burnished cowls.

vii

During all this Amelia and I had been so taken with the events about us that we failed to notice that our boat continued to drift with the stream. Amelia still crouched at the bottom of the boat, but I had shipped my oars and sat on the wooden seat.

I looked at Amelia, and with my voice reflecting in its hoarseness the terror I felt, I said: "If this is a measure of their power, the Martians will conquer the world!"

"We cannot sit by and allow that to happen."

"What do you propose we do?"

"We must get to Richmond,' she said. "Sir William will be better placed to know."

"Then we must row on," I said.

In my terrible confusion I had overlooked the fact that four battle-machines stood between us and Richmond at that very moment, and so I took the oars and placed them in the water again. I took just one stroke, when behind me I heard a tremendous splashing of water, and Amelia screamed.

"They're coming this way!"

I released the oars at once, and they slipped into the water.

"Lie still!" I cried to Amelia. Putting my own words into effect, I threw myself backwards, lying at an awkward and painful angle across the wooden seat. Behind me I heard the tumultuous splashing of the battle-machines as they hurtled up-river. We were now drifting almost in the centre of the stream, and so lay directly in their path!

The four were advancing abreast of one another, and lying as I was I could see them upside-down. The wreckage of the battle-machine struck by the shell had been retrieved by the others, and now, carried between them, was being taken back the way they had come. I saw for an instant the torn and blasted metal that had been the platform, and saw too that there was gore and blood about much of it. I derived no satisfaction from the death of one monster-creature, for what was this to the spiteful destruction of two towns and the murder of countless people?

If the monsters had chosen to slay us then we would have had no chance of survival, yet once again we were spared by their preoccupations. Their victory over the two hapless towns was emphatic, and such stray survivors as ourselves were of no consequence. They closed on us with breathtaking speed, almost obscured by the clouds of spray thrown up by their churning legs. One of these sliced into the water not three yards from our little boat, and we were instantly deluged. The boat rocked and yawed, taking in water in such copious quantities that I felt we must surely sink.

Then, in a few seconds, the tripods were gone, leaving us waterlogged and unsteady on the troubled river.

viii

It took us several minutes of paddling to retrieve our oars, and to bale out the water to make the boat manoeuvrable again. By then the Martian battle-machines had vanished towards the south, presumably heading for their pit on the common by Woking.

Considerably shaken by the prolonged incident I set myself to rowing, and in a few minutes we were passing the blasted remains of Weybridge.

If survivors there were, we saw none about. A ferry had been plying as the Martians struck, and we saw its upturned and blackened hull awash in the river. On the towpath lay scores, perhaps hundreds, of charred bodies of those who had suffered directly under the heat-beam. The town itself was well ablaze, with few if any buildings left untouched by the murderous attack. It was like a scene from a nightmare, for when a town burns in silence, unattended, it is no less than a funeral pyre.

There were many bodies in the water, presumably of those people who had thought that there lay refuge. Here the Martians, with their magnificent and wicked cunning, had turned their heat-beams on the river itself, so raising its temperature to that of boiling. As we rowed through, the water was still steaming and bubbling, and when Amelia tested it with her hand she snatched it away. Many of the bodies which floated here revealed by the brilliant redness of their skins that the people had been, quite literally, boiled to death. Fortunately for our sensibilities, the steam had the effect of obscuring our surroundings, and so, as we passed through the carnage, we were spared the sight of much of it.

It was with considerable relief that we turned the bend in the river, but our agonies were not at an end, for now we could see what damage had been inflicted on Shepperton. At Amelia's urging I rowed more quickly, and in a few minutes I had taken us beyond the worst.

Once we had turned another bend I slackened off a little, for I was rapidly tiring. We were both in a terrible state as a result of what we had seen, and so I pulled into the bank. We climbed to the shore and sat down in a heady state of shock. What passed between us then I will not relate, but our agonizing was much coloured by our acceptance of complicity in this devastation.

By the time we had recovered our wits, two hours had passed, and our resolve to play a more active rôle in fighting these monsters had hardened. So it was with renewed sense of urgency that we returned to the boat. Sir William Reynolds, if he were not already engaged in the problem, would be able to propose some more subtle solution than the Army had so far devised.

By now there was only the occasional piece of floating wreckage to remind us of what we had seen, but the memories were clear enough. From the moment of the Martians' onslaught we had seen no one alive, and even now the only apparent movement was the smoke.

The rest had restored my strength, and I returned to the rowing with great vigour, taking long, easy strokes.

In spite of everything we had experienced, the day was all that I had hungered for while on Mars. The breeze was soft, and the sun was warm. The green trees and grasses of the banks were a joy to the eye, and we saw and heard many birds and insects. All this, and the pleasant regularity of my rowing, served to order my thoughts.

Would the Martians, now they had demonstrated their supremacy, be satisfied to consolidate their position? If so, how much time would this give our military forces to essay new tactics? Indeed, what was the strength of our forces? Apart from the three artillery batteries we had seen and heard, the Army was nowhere evident.

Beyond this, I felt that we needed to adjust to our actual circumstances. In some ways, Amelia and I had been living still to the routines we had established inside the projectile, which is to say that our lives were patterned by the dominance of the Martians. Now, though, we were in our own land, one where places had names we could recognize, and where there were days and weeks by which one ordered one's life. We had established whereabouts in England we had landed, and we could see that England was enjoying a summer of splendid weather, even if other climates were foreboding, but we did not know which day of the week this was, nor even in which month we were.

It was on such matters, admittedly rather trivial, that I was dwelling as I brought our boat around the bend in the river that lies just above the bridge at Walton-on-Thames. Here it was that we saw the first living person that day: a young man, wearing a dark jacket. He sat in the reeds by the edge of the water, staring despondently across the river.

I pointed him out to Amelia, and at once altered course and headed towards him.

As we came closer I could see that he was a man of the cloth. He seemed very youthful, for his figure was slight and his head was topped with a mass of flaxen curls. Then we saw that lying on the ground beside him was the body of another man. He was more stoutly built, and his body—which from the waist up was naked—was covered with the filth of the river.

Still dwelling on my rather trivial thoughts of the moments before, I called out to the curate as soon as we were within hailing distance.

"Sir," I shouted, "what day is this?"

The curate stared back at us, then stood up unsteadily. I could see he had been severely shocked by his experiences for his hands were never still, fretting with the torn front of his jacket. His gaze was vacant and uncertain as he answered me.

"It is the Day of Judgement, my children."

Amelia had been staring at the man lying beside the curate, and she asked: "Father, is that man alive?"

No answer was forthcoming, for the curate had turned distractedly away from us. He made as if to move off, but then turned back and looked down at us.

"Do you need any help, Father?" Amelia said.

"Who can offer help when it is God's wrath vented upon us?"

"Edward . . . row in to the shore."

I said: "But what can we do to help?"

Nevertheless, I plied the oars and in a moment we had scrambled ashore. The curate watched as we knelt beside the prostrate man. We saw at once that he was not dead, nor even unconscious, but was turning restlessly as if in a delirium.

"Water . . . have you any water?" he said, his lips parched. I saw that his skin had a slightly reddened cast to it, as if he too had been caught when the Martians boiled the river.

"Have you not given him any water?" I said to the curate.

"He keeps asking for it, but we are beside a river of blood."

I glanced at Amelia, and saw by her expression that my own opinion of the poor, distracted curate was confirmed.

"Amelia," I said quietly, "see if you can find something to bring water in."

I returned my attention to the delirious man, and in desperation I slapped him lightly about his face. This seemed to break through the delirium for he sat up at once, shaking his head.

Amelia had found a bottle by the river's edge, and she brought this and gave it to the man. He raised it thankfully to his lips, and drank deeply. I noticed that he was now in command of his senses, and he was looking shrewdly at the young curate.

The curate saw how we were helping the man, and this seemed to disconcert him. He gazed across the meadows in the direction of the distant, shattered tower of Shepperton Church.

He said: "What does it mean? All our work is undone! It is the vengeance of God, for he hath taken away the children. The burning smoke goeth up for ever. . . ."

With this cryptic incantation, he strode off determinedly through the long grass, and was soon out of our sight.

The man coughed a few times, and said: "I cannot thank you enough. I thought I must surely die."

"Was the curate your companion?" I said.

He shook his head weakly. "I have never before laid eyes on him."

"Are you well enough to move?" said Amelia.

"I believe so. I am not hurt, but I have had a narrow escape."

"Were you in Weybridge?" I said.

"I was in the thick of it. Those Martians have no mercy, no compunction—"

"How do you know they are from Mars?" I said, greatly interested by this, as I had been at hearing of the soldiers' rumours.

"It is well known. The firing of their projectiles was observed in many telescopes. Indeed, I was fortunate to observe one such myself, in the instrument at Ottershaw."

"You are an astronomer?" said Amelia.

"That I am not, but I am acquainted with many scientists. My own calling is a more philosophical nature." He paused then, and glanced down at himself, and was at once overcome with embarrassment. "My dear lady," he said to Amelia, "I must apologize for my state of undress."

"We are no better garbed ourselves," she replied, with considerable accuracy.

"You too have come from the thick of the fighting?"

"In a sense," I said. "Sir, I hope you will join us. We have a boat, and we are headed for Richmond. There I think we may find safety."

"Thank you," said the man. "But I must go my own way. I was trying to make for Leatherhead, for that is where I have left my wife."

I thought quickly, trying to visualize the geography of the land. Leatherhead was many miles to the south of us.

The man went on: "You see, I am a resident of Woking, and before the Martians attacked I managed to take my wife to safety. Since then, because I was obliged to return to Woking, I have been trying to join her. But I have found, to my cost, that the land between here and Leatherhead is overrun with the brutes."

"Then as your wife is safe," Amelia said, "would it not be wise to fall in with us until the Army deals with this menace?"

The man was clearly tempted, for we were not many miles distant from Richmond. He hesitated for a few seconds more, then nodded.

"If you are rowing, you will need an extra pair of arms," he said. "I shall be happy to oblige. But first, because I am in such a state of untidiness, I should like to wash myself."

He went down to the water's edge, and with his hands washed off much of the traces of the smoke and grime which so disfigured him. Then, when he had swept back his hair, he held out his hand and assisted Amelia as she climbed back into the boat.

Chapter Twenty
ROWING DOWN THE RIVER

i

That our new friend was a man of gentle manners was affirmed the moment we entered the boat. He would not hear of my rowing until he had served a turn at the oars, and insisted that I sit with Amelia in the rear of the boat.

"We must have our wits about us," he said, "in case those devils return. We will take turns at the oars, and all keep our eyes open."

I had been feeling for some time that the Martians' apparent inactivity must be temporary, and it was reassuring to know that my suspicions were shared. This could only be a lull in their campaign, and as such we must take the maximum advantage of it.

In accordance with our plan I kept a careful watch for sight of the tripods (although all seemed presently quiet), but Amelia's attention was elsewhere. Indeed, she was staring at our new friend with quite improper attention.

At length she said: "Sir, may I enquire if you have ever visited Reynolds House in Richmond?"

The gentleman looked at her in manifest surprise, but immediately said: "I have indeed, but not for many years."

"Then you would know Sir William Reynolds?"

"We were never the closest of friends, for I fear he was not one for intimate friendships, but we were members of the same club in St James's and were occasionally wont to exchange confidences."

Amelia was frowning in concentration. "I believe we have met before."

Our friend paused with the oars clear of the water.

"By Jove!" he cried. "Are you not Sir William's former amanuensis?"

"Yes, I am. And you, sir, I think your name is Mr Wells."

"That is my name," he said gravely. "And if I am not mistaken, I do believe you are Miss Fitzgibbon."

Amelia instantly confirmed this. "What a remarkable coincidence!"

Mr Wells politely asked me my name, and I introduced myself. I reached over to shake his hand, and he leaned forward over the oars.

"Pleased to meet you, Turnbull," he said.

Just then the sunlight fell on his face in such a way that his eyes revealed themselves to be a startling blue; in his tired and worried face they shone like optimistic beacons, and I felt myself warming to him.

Amelia was still animated in her excitement.

"It is to Reynolds House that we are going now," she said. "We feel Sir William is one of the few men who can confront this menace."

Mr Wells frowned, and returned to his rowing.

After a moment, he said: "I take it you have not seen Sir William for some time?"

Amelia glanced at me, and I knew she was uncertain how to reply.

I said for her: "Not since May of 1893, sir."

"That is the last time I, or anyone else, saw him. Surely if you were in his employ, you know about this?"

Amelia said: "I ceased to work for him in that May. Are you saying that he subsequently died?"

I knew that this last was a wild guess, but Mr Wells promptly corrected it.

"I think Sir William is not dead," he said. "He went into futurity on that infernal Time Machine of his, and although he returned once he has not been seen since his second journey."

"You know this for certain?" Amelia said.

"I was honoured to be the author of his memoirs," said Mr Wells, "for he dictated them to me himself."

ii

As we rowed along, Mr Wells told us what was known of Sir William's fate. At the same time it was interesting to realize that some of our earlier surmises had not been inaccurate.

It seemed that after the Time Machine had deposited us so abruptly in the weed-bank, it had returned unscathed to Richmond. Mr Wells could not have known of our mishap, of course, but his account of Sir William's subsequent experiments made no mention of the fact that the Machine had been missing for even a short period.

Sir William, according to Mr Wells, had been more adventurous than even we had been, taking the Time Machine into a far-distant future. Here Sir William had seen many strange sights (Mr Wells promised to let us have a copy of his account, for he said the story would take too long to recount at the moment), and although he had returned to tell his tale, he had later departed a second time for futurity. On that occasion he had never returned.

Imagining that Sir William had suffered a similar mishap with the Machine as us, I said: "The Time Machine came back empty, sir?"

"Neither the Machine nor Sir William have been seen again."

"Then there is no way we can reach him?"

"Not without a second Time Machine," said Mr Wells.

By now we were passing Walton-on-Thames, and there was much activity within the town. We saw several fire-engines rattling along the riverside road in the direction of Weybridge, the horses' hooves throwing up white dust-clouds. An orderly, but hurried, evacuation was taking place, with many hundreds of people walking or riding along the road towards London. The river itself was congested, with several boats ferrying people across to the Sunbury side, and we were obliged to steer carefully between them. Along the northern bank we saw much evidence of military activity, with scores of soldiers marching towards the west. In the meadows to the east of Halliford we saw more artillery being readied.

This distraction brought to an end our conversation about Sir William, and by the time we had passed Walton we sat in silence. Mr Wells was seeming to tire at the oars, so I changed places with him.

Once more occupied with the regular physical task of rowing, I found my thoughts returning to the orderly procession they had enjoyed shortly before we met Mr Wells and the curate.

Until this moment I had not tried to understand why we were so determined to reach Sir William's house. Mr Wells's mention of the Time Machine, though, had focused my thoughts directly on the reason: in some instinctive way it had occurred to me that the Machine itself might be used against Martians. It was, after all, the instrument by which we had first reached Mars, and its weird movements through the attenuated dimensions of Space and Time were certainly unequalled by anything the Martians commanded.

However, if the Time Machine were no longer available, then any such idea had to be abandoned. We were pressing on to Richmond, though, for Sir William's house, lying in its secluded position just behind the ridge of the Hill, would be a safer sanctuary than most from the Martians.

Facing Amelia as I was, I noticed that she too seemed lost in thought, and I wondered if she had been coming to the same conclusion.

At last, not wishing to ignore Mr Wells, I said: "Sir, do you know what preparations the Army is making?"

"Only what we have seen today. They were taken quite unawares. Even from the early moments of the invasion, no one in authority was prepared to take the situation seriously."

"You speak as if you are critical."

"I am," said Mr Wells. "The fact that the Martians were sending an invasion-fleet has been known for several weeks. As I told you, the firing of their projectiles was observed by many scientists. Any number of warnings was issued, both in scientific papers and in the popular press, yet even when the first cylinder landed the authorities were slow to move."

Amelia said: "You mean that the warnings were not taken seriously?"

"They were dismissed as sensation-mongering, even after there had been several deaths. The first cylinder landed not a mile from my house. It came down at about midnight on the 19th. I myself visited it during the morning, along with a crowd of others, and although it was clear from the outset that something was inside, the press would not publish more than a few inches about it. This I can attest to myself, because in addition to my literary activities I occasionally contribute scientific pieces to the press, and the papers are noted for their caution with all scientific matters. Even yesterday, they were treating this incursion with levity. As for the Army . . . they did not turn out until nearly twenty-four hours after the arrival of the projectile, and by then the monsters were out and well established."

"In the Army's defence," I said, still feeling that it had been incumbent upon myself to alert the authorities, "such an invasion is unprecedented."

"Maybe so," Mr Wells said. "But the second cylinder had landed before a single shot was fired by our side. How many more landings are needed before the threat is understood?"

"I think they are alert to the danger now," I said, nodding towards yet another artillery emplacement on the banks of the river. One of the gunners was hailing us, but I rowed on without answering. It was now well into the afternoon, and there were about four more hours until sunset.

Amelia said: "You say that you visited the pit. Did you see the adversary?"

"That I did," said Mr Wells, and I noticed then that his hands were trembling. "Those monsters are unspeakable!"

I suddenly realized that Amelia was about to talk of our adventures on Mars, so I frowned at her, warning her to silence. For the moment at least, I felt we should not reveal our rôle in the invasion.

Instead, I said to Mr Wells: "You are clearly shaken by your experiences."

"I have been face to face with Death. Twice I have escaped

with my life, but only by the greatest good fortune." He shook
his head. "These Martians will go on and conquer the world.
They are indestructible."

"They are mortal, sir," I said. "They can be killed as easily
as other vermin."

"That has not been the experience so far. By what evidence
do you say that?"

I thought of the screams of the dying monster inside the
platform, and the ghastly eructation of gases. And then, remembering the warning I had signalled to Amelia only a few
seconds before, I said: "There was one killed at Weybridge."

"A chance artillery shell. We cannot depend on chance to rid
the world of this menace."

iii

Mr Wells took the oars again when we reached Hampton
Court, as I was tiring. We were now only a short distance from
Richmond, but here the river swings to the south, before turning a second time to flow northwards, and so we still had a
considerable distance before us. For a while we debated
whether to abandon the boat and complete our journey on foot,
but we could see that the roads were crowded with the traffic of
those escaping towards London. On the river we had our way
almost to ourselves. The afternoon was warm and tranquil, the
sky a radiant blue.

Here, by Hampton Court Palace, we saw a curious sight. We
were now a sufficient distance from the effects of the Martians'
destruction for the immediate dangers to seem diminished, yet
still near enough for evacuations to be taking place. As a consequence, there was a conflict of moods. The local people, from
Thames Ditton, Molesey and Surbiton, were abandoning their
houses, and under the guidance of the overworked police and
fire-brigades, were leaving for London.

However, the Palace grounds are a favourite resort for excur-
sionist Londoners, and on this fine summer's afternoon the riverside paths were well thronged with people enjoying the

sunshine. They could not be unaware of the noise and bustle around them, but they seemed determined not to let such activities affect their picnics.

Thames Ditton Station, which is on the south bank opposite the Palace, was crowded, and people were queuing up along the pavement outside, waiting for a chance to board a train. Even so, each train that arrived from London brought with it a few more late-afternoon excursionists.

How many of those blazered young men, or those young ladies with silken parasols, were ever to see their homes again? Perhaps to them, in their unguarded innocence, we three in our rowing-boat presented a strange sight: Amelia and I, still wearing our much begrimed underwear, and Mr Wells, naked but for his trousers. I think the day was unusual enough for our appearance to pass unremarked upon.

iv

It was as we were rowing towards Kingston-upon-Thames that we first heard the artillery, and at once we were on our guard. Mr Wells rowed more vigorously, and Amelia and I turned in our seats, looking westwards for a first sight of the deadly tripods.

For the moment there was no sign of them, but the distant artillery muttered endlessly. Once I saw a heliograph flickering on the hills beyond Esher, and ahead of us we saw a signal-rocket burst bright red at the peak of its smoky trail, but in our immediate vicinity, at least, the guns remained silent.

At Kingston we changed hands once more, and I braced myself for the final effort towards Richmond. We were all restless, eager for this long journey to be over. As Mr Wells settled himself in the prow of the boat, he remarked on the unseemly noise of the evacuees crossing Kingston Bridge. There were no excursionists to be seen here; I think that at last the danger had been brought home to everyone.

A few minutes after we left Kingston, Amelia pointed ahead.

"Richmond Park, Edward! We're nearly there."

I glanced briefly over my shoulder, and saw the splendid rise of ground. It was not unexpected that there, on the crest of the hill and black against the sky, I saw the protruding muzzles of the artillery.

The Martians were expected, and this time they would meet their match.

Reassured, I rowed on, trying to ignore the tiredness in my arms and back.

A mile north of Kingston, the Thames, in its meandering way, swings to the north-west, and so the rise of Richmond Park moved further away to our right. Now, temporarily, we were moving towards the Martians once more, and as if this were significant, we heard a renewed volley from the distant artillery. This was echoed a few moments later by the guns laid in Bushy Park, and then too we heard the first shots from Richmond Park. All three of us craned our necks, but there was still no sign of the Martians. It was most unnerving to know that they were in our vicinity, yet invisible to us.

We passed Twickenham, and saw no signs of evacuation; perhaps the town had been emptied already, or else the people were lying low, hoping the Martians would not come their way.

Then, heading directly east again as the river turned towards Richmond, Amelia shouted that she had seen some smoke. We looked to the south-west, and saw, rising from the direction of Molesey, a column of black smoke. The artillery was speaking continuously. The Martians, moving quickly through the Surrey countryside, were difficult targets, and the towns they approached were laid helplessly before them.

Smoke rose from Kingston, and from Surbiton, and from Esher. Then, too, from Twickenham ... and at last we could see one of the Martian marauders. It was stalking quickly through the streets of Twickenham, not one mile from where we presently were. We could see its heat-beam, swinging indiscriminately, and we could see the ineffectual air-burst of the artillery-shells, never exploding less than a hundred feet from the predatory engine.

A second Martian tripod appeared, this one striking north-

wards towards Hounslow. Then a third: away to the south of
burning Kingston.

"Edward, dear . . . hurry! They are almost upon us!"

"I am doing my best!" I cried, wondering if we should now
head for the bank.

Mr Wells clambered towards me from the prow, and placed
himself on the seat beside me. He took the right-hand oar from
me, and in a moment we had established a fast rhythm.

Fortunately, the Martians seemed to be paying no attention
to the river for the moment. The towns were their main objec-
tives, and the lines of artillery. In the repeated explosions near
at hand, I realized that the deeper sounds of the more distant
batteries had long been silenced.

Then came what was perhaps the most disturbing noise of
all. The Martian driving the tripod by Kingston uttered a note
. . . and it drifted towards us, distorted by the breeze. The Martian in Twickenham took it up, and soon we heard others from
various directions. Here on Earth the note was deeper in
timbre, and seemed more prolonged . . . but there could be no
mistaking the sinister braying siren of the Martians calling for
food.

v

At last the tree-lined slope of Richmond Hill was before us,
and as we rowed frantically around the bend past the green
meadows we saw the white, wooden building of Messum's boat-
house. I remembered the day I had called on Sir William, and
how I had strolled along the riverside walk past the boat-house
. . . but then there had been promenading crowds. Now we were
apparently alone, all but for the rampaging battle-machines
and the answering artillery.

I pointed out the jetty to Mr Wells, and we rowed energetically towards it. At long last we heard the scraping of the
wooden hull against the hard stone, and without further ceremony I held out my hand to help Amelia ashore. I waited until
Mr Wells had stepped down, and then I too followed. Behind

us, the little boat bobbed away, drifting with the current of the river.

Both Mr Wells and I were exhausted from our long ordeal, but even so were prepared for the last part of our effort: the climb up the side of the Hill towards Sir William's house. Accordingly, we hastened away from the jetty, but Amelia held back. As soon as we realized she was not following, we turned and waited for her.

Amelia had not been at her most talkative for the last hour, but now said: "Mr Wells, you told us earlier that you went to the Martians' pit in Woking. What day was that?"

"It was the Friday morning," Mr Wells said.

Looking across the river towards Twickenham I saw that the brazen cowl of the nearest battle-machine was turned our way. Artillery shells burst around it.

I said, with great anxiety: "Amelia . . . we can talk later! We must get under cover!"

"Edward, this is important!" Then to Mr Wells: "And that was the 19th, you say?"

"No, the Thursday was the 19th. It came down at about midnight."

"And today we have seen excursionists . . . so this is Sunday. . . . Mr Wells, this is 1903, is it not?"

He looked a little puzzled, but confirmed this.

Amelia turned to me, and seized my hand.

"Edward! Today is the 22nd! This is the day in 1903 to which we came! The Time Machine will be in the laboratory!"

With that she turned abruptly away from me, and ran quickly up through the trees.

At once I ran after her, shouting to her to come back!

vi

Amelia, rested and agile, scrambled without difficulty up the side of the Hill; I was more tired, and although I used every remaining scrap of energy I could do no more than maintain my distance behind her. Below us, by the river, I heard the sound of the Martian's braying siren, answered at once by another. Somewhere behind us, Mr Wells followed. Ahead of me, from a point on the ridge, I heard the sound of a man's voice shouting an order . . . and then there came the detonation of the artillery-pieces mounted on the Hill. Smoke poured down from them through the trees. More shots followed, from positions all along the ridge. The noise was deafening, and the acrid cordite fumes burned in my throat.

Ahead of me, showing through the trees, I could see the towers of Reynolds House.

"Amelia!" I shouted again over the noise. "My dearest, come back! It is not safe!"

"The Time Machine! We can find the Time Machine!"

I could see her ahead of me, brushing without regard for herself through the tangle of bushes and undergrowth towards the house.

"No!" I screamed after her, in utter desperation. *"Amelia!"*

Through the multitude of intervening events, across the seeming years and the millions of miles . . . a stark memory of our first journey to 1903.

I remembered the artillery shots, the smoke, the alien sirens, the woman running across the lawn, the face at the window, and then the consuming fire . . .

Destiny!

I hurled myself after her, and saw her reach the edge of the overgrown lawn.

Amelia started to run across to the glass wall of the laboratory: a lithe, distant figure, already beyond any help, already doomed by the destiny I had not after all averted. . . .

As I also reached the lawn, too breathless to shout again, I saw her come to the glass and stop by it, pressing her face against the panes.

I stumbled across the lawn . . . and then I was behind her, and near enough to see beyond her, into the dim interior of the laboratory.

There, set beside one of the many benches, was placed a

crude mechanical device, and upon it sat two youthful figures.

One was a young man, a straw boater set at a jaunty angle on his head . . . and the other was a pretty girl holding herself to him.

The young man was staring at us, his eyes wide with surprise.

I reached out my hand to take Amelia, just as the young man within raised his own, as if to ward off the horror of what he too was seeing.

Behind us there was a scream from the Martian's siren, and the brazen cowl of the battle-machine appeared over the trees. I threw myself against Amelia, and dashed her to the ground. In the same instant the heat-beam was turned upon us, and a line of fire raced across the lawn and struck the house.

Chapter Twenty-One
UNDER SIEGE

i

I had intended to throw myself across Amelia, so protecting her with my own body, but in my haste I succeeded only in throwing us both to the ground. The explosion that followed therefore afflicted us both to an equal degree. There was one mighty blast, which hurled us bodily across the garden, and this was followed by a series of smaller explosions of varying severity. We tumbled helplessly through the long grass, and when at last we stopped there was a rain of burning timber and broken masonry, crashing to the soil about us.

In the interval that followed I heard the braying of the Martian as it turned away from us, its hatred satisfied.

Then, although we heard further concussions in the near distance, it was as if a stillness had fallen. There was a moment when I could hear an animal squealing in pain, but a revolver fired and even that stopped.

Amelia lay in the grass about ten feet from me, and as soon as I had recovered my senses I crawled hastily towards her. There was a sudden pain in my back, and at once I realized my combinations were on fire. I rolled over, and although the burning pain increased momentarily, I succeeded in extinguishing the smouldering fabric. I hurried over to Amelia, and saw that her clothes too had been ignited. I beat out the tiny flames with my hands, and at once I heard her moan.

"Is that you, Edward . . .?" she said indistinctly.

"Are you hurt?"

She shook her head, and as I tried to turn her over she

climbed painfully to her feet of her own accord. She stood before me, looking very groggy.

"By Jove! That was close!"

It was Mr Wells. He came towards us from the bushes at the side of the lawn, apparently unharmed but, like us, shocked at the ferocity of the attack.

"Miss Fitzgibbon, are you injured?" he said solicitously.

"I think not." She shook her head sharply. "I have become a little deaf."

"That is the blast," I said, for my own ears were buzzing. Just then we heard shouting beside the house, and we all turned in that direction.

A group of soldiers had appeared, all looking rather dazed. An officer was trying to organize them, and after a few moments of confusion they stepped forward to the blazing house and attempted to beat out the flames with sacking.

"We had better help them," I said to Mr Wells, and at once we set off across the lawn.

As we came around the corner of the building we met a scene of great destruction. Here the Army had mounted one of its artillery-pieces, and it was clearly at this that the Martian had fired. Its aim had been deadly accurate, for there remained just twisted and melted metal scattered about a large crater. There was almost nothing recognizable of the gun, bar one of its huge spoked wheels, which now lay about fifty yards to one side.

Further back, several horses had been tethered by one of the outhouses in the garden, and we were distressed to see that some of these had been killed; the remainder had been efficiently quieted by their handlers, who had placed blinds over their heads.

We went directly to the subaltern in charge.

"May we offer our help?" Mr Wells said.

"Is this your house, sir?"

Amelia answered. "No, I live here."

"But the house is empty."

"We have been abroad." She glanced at the soldiers beating ineffectually at the flames. "There is a garden hose in that shed."

At once the officer ordered two of the men to find the hose, and in a few moments it had been brought out and connected to a standing tap against the side of the house. Fortunately, the pressure was high and a jet of water issued at once.

We stood well back, seeing that the men had evidently been trained well, and that the firefighting was conducted intelligently and efficiently. The jet of water was played on the more ferocious concentrations of fire, while the other men continued to beat with the sacking.

The officer supervised the effort with a minimum of orders, and when he stepped back as the flames were brought under control, I went over to him.

"Have you lost any men?" I said.

"Fortunately, sir, no. We had been ordered to move back just before the attack, and so were able to take cover in time." He indicated several deep trenches dug across the lawn; they crossed the place where (so long ago!) I had sipped iced lemonade with Amelia. "If we'd been manning the piece. . . ."

I nodded. "Were you billeted here?"

"Yes, sir. We've caused no damage, I think you'll find. Just as soon as we've retrieved our equipment, we will have to withdraw."

I understood that saving the house itself was not their main concern. It was lucky indeed that they needed to save their own possessions, otherwise we should have had great difficulty dousing the fire on our own.

Within a quarter of an hour the flames were out; it was the servants' wing which had been hit, and two of the rooms on the ground floor were uninhabitable, and the six gunners who had been billeted there lost all their equipment. On the floor above, the major damage was caused by smoke and the explosion.

Of the rest of the house, the rooms on the side furthest from the exploding gun were least damaged: Sir William's former smoking-room, for instance, had not even one broken window. Throughout the rest of the house there was a varying amount of damage, mostly breakages caused by the explosion, and every pane of glass in the walls of the laboratory had been shattered. In the grounds there was a certain amount of grass and shrubbery on fire, but the gunners soon dealt with this.

Once the fire had been put out, the artillerymen took what they had retrieved of their equipment, loaded up an ammunition truck, and prepared to withdraw. Through all this we could hear the sounds of the battle continuing in the distance, and the subaltern told us he was anxious to join his unit in Richmond. He apologized for the damage caused when his gun had been destroyed, and we thanked him for his help in extinguishing the fire ... then the troop of men rode away, down the Hill towards the town.

ii

Mr Wells said that he was going to see where the Martians now were, and stepped out across the lawn towards the edge of the ridge. I followed Amelia into the house, and when we were inside I took her in my arms and held her tightly, her face nestling against the side of mine.

For several minutes we said nothing, but then at last she held back a little, and we looked lovingly into each other's eyes. That momentary vision of our past selves had been a salutary shock; Amelia, with her face bruised and scarred, and her chemise torn and scorched, bore almost no resemblance to the rather prim and elegantly clad young woman I had glimpsed on the Time Machine. And I knew, by the way in which she was looking at me, that a similar transformation had come over my appearance.

She said: "When we were on the Time Machine you saw the Martian. You knew all along."

"I only saw you," I said. "I thought I saw you dying."

"Is that why you took the Machine?"

"I don't know. I was desperate ... I loved you even then..."

She held me again, and her lips pressed briefly against my neck.

I heard her say, in words so soft they were almost inaudible: "I understand now, Edward."

iii

Mr Wells brought the sombre news that he had counted six of the monstrous tripods in the valley below, and that the fighting continued.

"They are all over the place," he said, "and as far as I could see there's almost no resistance from our men. There are three machines within a mile of this house, but they are staying in the valley. I think we shall be safe if we lie low here for a while."

"What are the Martians doing?" I said.

"The heat-beam is still in use. It seemed as if the whole Thames Valley is on fire. There is smoke everywhere, and it is of amazing intensity. The whole of Twickenham has vanished under a mountain of smoke. Black, thick smoke, like tar, but not rising. It is shaped like an immense dome."

"It will be dispersed by the wind," Amelia said.

"The wind is up," said Mr Wells, "but the smoke stays above the town. I cannot account for it."

It seemed to be a minor enigma, and so we paid little attention to it; it was enough to know that the Martians were still hostile and about.

All three of us were faint from hunger, and the preparation of a meal became a necessity. It was clear that Sir William's house had not been occupied for years, and so we held out no hope of finding any food in the pantry. We did discover that the artillerymen had left some of their rations behind—some tins of meat and a little stale bread—but it was hardly enough for one meal.

Mr Wells and I agreed to visit the houses nearest to us, and see if we could borrow some food from there. Amelia decided to stay behind; she wanted to explore the house and see how much of it would be habitable.

Mr Wells and I were away for an hour. During this time we discovered that we were alone on Richmond Hill. The other inhabitants had presumably been evacuated when the soldiers arrived, and it was evident that their departure had been hasty. Few of the houses were locked, and in most we found considerable quantities of food. By the time we were ready to return, we had with us a sackful of food—consisting of a good variety of meats, vegetables and fruit—which should certainly be enough to sustain us for many days. In addition we found several bottles of wine, and a pipe and some tobacco for Mr Wells.

Before returning to the house, Mr Wells suggested that we once more survey the valley; it was suspiciously quiet below, to a degree that was making us most uneasy.

We left the sack inside the house we had last visited, and went forward cautiously to the edge of the ridge. There, concealing ourselves amongst the trees, we were afforded an uninterrupted view to north and west. To our left we could see up the Thames Valley at least as far as Windsor Castle, and before us we could see the villages of Chiswick and Brentford. Immediately below us was Richmond itself.

The sun was setting: a deep-orange ball of fire touching the horizon. Silhouetted against it was one of the Martian battle-machines. It was not moving now, and even from this distance of three miles or so we could see that the metal-mesh net at the back of the platform had been filled with bodies.

The black kopje of smoke still obscured Twickenham; another lay heavily over Hounslow. Richmond appeared still, although several buildings were on fire.

I said: "They cannot be stopped. They will rule the entire world."

Mr Wells was silent, although his breathing was irregular and heavy. Glancing at his face I saw that his bright-blue eyes were moist. Then he said: "You opine that they are mortal, Turnbull, but we must now accept that we cannot resist them."

At that moment, as if defying his words, a solitary gun placed on the riverside walk by Richmond Bridge fired a shot. Moments later the shell burst in the air several hundred feet away from the distant battle-machine.

The Martian's response was instant. It whirled round and strode in our direction, causing Mr Wells and me to step back into the trees. We saw the Martian extend a broad tube from its platform, and a few seconds later something was fired from this. A large cylinder flew through the air, tumbling erratically and reflecting the orange brilliance of the sun. It described a high arc, and fell crashing somewhere into the streets of Richmond town. Moments later there was an incontinent release of blackness, and within sixty seconds Richmond had vanished under another of the mysterious static domes of black smoke.

The gun by the river, lost in the blackness, did not speak again.

We waited and watched until the sun went down, but heard no more shots fired by the Army. The Martians, arrogant in their total victory, went about their macabre business of seeking out the human survivors, and placing such unfortunates in their swelling nets.

Much sobered, Mr Wells and I retrieved our sack of food and returned to Reynolds House.

We were greeted by an Amelia transformed.

"Edward!" she called as soon as we walked through the broken door of the house. "Edward, my clothes are still here!"

And dancing into our sight came a girl of the most extraordinary beauty. She wore a pale-yellow dress and buttoned boots; her hair was brushed and shaped about her face; the wound which had so disfigured her was concealed by the artistic application of *maquillage*. And, as she seized my hand gaily, and exclaimed happily over the amount of food we had gathered, I sensed once more that gentle fragrance of perfume, redolent of herbs.

For no reason I could understand, I turned away from her and found myself weeping.

iv

The house had evidently been closed after Sir William's final departure on the Time Machine, for although everything was intact and in its place (excepting those items damaged or destroyed in the explosion and fire), the furniture had been covered with dust-sheets, and valuable articles had been locked away in cupboards. Mr Wells and I visited Sir William's dressing-room, and there found sufficient clothing to dress ourselves decently.

A little later, smelling slightly of moth-balls, we went through the house while Amelia prepared a meal. We discovered that the servants had confined their cleaning to the domestic areas of the house, for the laboratory was as cluttered with pieces of engineering machinery as before. Everything here was filthy dirty, though, and much littered with broken glass. The reciprocating engine which generated electricity was in its place, although we dared not turn it on for fear of attracting the Martians' attention.

We ate our meal in a ground-floor room furthest away from the valley, and sat by candlelight with the curtains closed. All was silent outside the house, but none of us could feel at ease knowing that at any moment the Martians might come by.

Afterwards, with our stomachs satisfactorily filled and our minds pleasantly relaxed by a bottle of wine, we talked again of the totalness of the Martians' victory.

"Their aim is quite clearly to take London," said Mr Wells. "If they do not do so during this night, then there can be nothing to stop them in the morning."

"But if they control London, they would control the whole country!" I said.

"That is what I fear. Of course, by now the threat is understood, and I dare say that even as we speak the garrisons in the north are travelling down. Whether they would fare any better than the unfortunates we saw in action today is a matter for conjecture. But the British Army is not slow to learn by its errors, so maybe we shall see some victories. What we do not know, of course, is what these monsters seek to gain."

"They wish to enslave us," I said. "They cannot survive unless they drink human blood."

Mr Wells glanced at me sharply. "Why do you say that, Turnbull?"

I was dumbfounded. We had all seen the gathering of the

people by the Martians, but only Amelia and I, with our privy knowledge, could know what was to happen to them.

Amelia said: "I think we must tell Mr Wells what we know, Edward."

"Do you have a specialist knowledge of these monsters?" said Mr Wells.

"We were . . . in the pit at Woking," I said.

"I too was there, but I saw no blood-drinking. This is an astonishing revelation, and, if I may say so, more than a little sensational. I take it you are speaking with authority?"

"The authority of experience," said Amelia. "We have been to Mars, Mr Wells, although I cannot expect you to believe us."

Much to my surprise, our new friend did not seem at all perturbed by this announcement.

"I have long suspected that the other planets of our Solar System can support life," he said. "It does not seem improbable to me that one day we shall visit those worlds. When we have conquered the drag of gravity we shall travel to the moon as easily as we can now travel to Birmingham." He stared intently at us both. "Yet you say you have already been to Mars?"

I nodded. "We were experimenting with Sir William's Time Machine, and we set the controls incorrectly."

"But as I understood it, Sir William intended to travel in Time only."

In a few words, Amelia explained how I had loosened the nickel rod which until then prevented movement through the Spatial Dimension. From this, the rest of our story followed naturally, and for the next hour we recounted most of our adventures. At last we came to the description of how we had returned to Earth.

Mr Wells was silent for a long time. He had helped himself to some brandy which we had found in the smoking-room, and for many minutes he cradled this in his hands.

Then at last he said: "If you are not inventing every word of this, all I can say is that it is a most extraordinary tale."

"We are not proud of what we have done," I said.

Mr Wells waved his hand dismissively. 'You should not

blame yourselves inordinately. Others would have done as you have, and although there has been much loss of life and damage to property, you could not have anticipated the power of these creatures."

He asked us several questions about our story, and we answered them as accurately as we could.

At length, he said: "It seems to me that your experience is itself the most useful weapon we have against these creatures. In any war, one's tactics are best planned by anticipating the enemy. Why we have not been able to contain this menace is because their motives have been so uncertain. We three are now custodians of intelligence. If we cannot assist the authorities, we must take some action of our own."

"I had been thinking along those lines myself," I said. "Our first intention was to contact Sir William, for it had occurred to me that the Time Machine itself would be a powerful weapon against these beings."

"In what way could it be used?"

"No creature, however powerful or ruthless, can defend itself against an invisible foe."

Mr Wells nodded his understanding, but said: "Unfortunately, we find neither Sir William nor his Machine."

"I know, sir," I said glumly.

It was getting late, and soon we discontinued our conversation, for we were all exhausted. The silence beyond the house was still absolute, but we felt we could not sleep easy in uncertainty. With this in mind, we crept out of the house before preparing for bed, and walked softly across the lawn to the edge of the ridge.

We looked down across the Thames Valley and saw the burning desolation below. In every direction, and as far as we could see, the night land was sparked with the glow of burning buildings. The sky above us was clear, and the stars shone brightly.

Amelia took my hand and said: "It is like Mars, Edward. They are turning our world into theirs."

"We cannot let them go on with this," I said. "We must find a way to fight them."

Just then, Mr Wells pointed towards the west, and we all saw a brilliant green point of light. It grew brighter as we watched it, and within a few seconds we had all recognized it as a fourth projectile. It became blindingly bright, and for a terrible moment we were convinced it was coming directly towards us, but then at last it abruptly lost height. It fell with a dazzling explosion of green light some three miles to the south-west of us, and seconds later we heard the blast of its landing.

Slowly, the green glare faded, until all was dark once more.

Mr Wells said: "There are six more of those projectiles to come."

"There is no hope for us," said Amelia.

"We must never lose hope."

I said: "We are impotent against these monsters."

"We must build a second Time Machine," said Mr Wells.

"But that would be impossible," Amelia said. "Only Sir William knows how to construct the device."

"He explained the principle to me in detail," said Mr Wells.

"To you, and to many others, but only in the most vague terms. Even I, who sometimes worked with him in the laboratory, have only a general understanding of its mechanism."

"Then we can succeed!" said Mr Wells. "You have helped to build the Machine, and I have helped design it."

We both looked at him curiously then. The flames from below lent an eerie cast to his features.

"You helped design the Time Machine?" I said, incredulously.

"In a sense, for he often showed me his blueprints and I made several suggestions which he incorporated. If the drawings are still available, it would not take me long to familiarize myself with them. I expect the drawings are still in his safe in the laboratory."

Amelia said: "That is where he always kept them."

"Then we could not get at them!" I cried. "Sir William is no longer here!"

"We will blast the safe open, if we need to," Mr Wells said, apparently determined to carry through his brave claim.

"There is no need for that," said Amelia. "I have some spare keys in my suite."

Suddenly, Mr Wells extended his hand to me, and I took it uncertainly, not sure what our compact was to be. He placed his other hand on my shoulder and gripped it warmly.

"Turnbull," he said, gravely. "You and I, and Miss Fitzgibbon too, will combine to defeat this enemy. We will become the unsuspected and invisible foe. We will fight this threat to all that is decent by descending on it and destroying it in a way it could never have anticipated. Tomorrow we shall set to and build a new Time Machine, and with it we will go out and stop this unstoppable menace!"

And then, with the excitement of having formed a positive plan, we complimented ourselves, and laughed aloud, and shouted defiance across the blighted valley. The night was silent, and the air was tainted with smoke and death, but revenge is the most satisfactory of human impulses, and as we returned to the house we were most uncommonly expectant of an immediate victory.

Chapter Twenty-Two
THE SPACE MACHINE

i

M$_R$ Wells and I each took one of the guest-rooms that night, while Amelia slept in her private suite (it was the first time for weeks that I had slept alone, and I tossed restlessly for hours), and in the morning we came down to breakfast still exercised by the zeal of vengeance.

Breakfast itself was a considerable luxury for Amelia and myself, for we were able to cook bacon and eggs on a ring in the kitchen (we judged it ill-advised to light the range).

Afterwards, we went directly to the laboratory and opened Sir William's safe. There, rolled untidily together, were the drawings he had made of his Time Machine.

We found a clear space on one of the benches and spread them out. At once my spirits fell, because Sir William—for all his inventive genius—had not been the most methodical of men. There was hardly one sheet that made immediate sense, for there was a multitude of corrections, erasures and marginal sketches, and on most sheets original designs had been over-drawn with subsequent versions.

Mr Wells maintained his optimistic tone of the night before, but I sensed that some of his previous confidence was lacking.

Amelia said: "Of course, before we start work we must be sure that the necessary materials are to hand."

Looking around at the dirty chaos of the laboratory I saw that although it was well littered with many electrical components and rods and bars of metals—as well as pieces of the crystalline substance scattered almost everywhere—it would take a diligent search to establish if we had enough to construct an entire Machine.

Mr Wells had carried some of the plans to the daylight, and was examining them minutely.

"I shall need several hours," he said. "Some of this is familiar, but I cannot say for certain. . . ."

I did not wish to infect him with my faintheartedness, so in the spirit of seeming to be of help—yet ensuring I was out of the way—I offered to search the grounds for more useful components. Amelia merely nodded, for she was already busily searching the drawer of one of the benches, and Mr Wells was absorbed with the plans, so I left the laboratory and went out of the house.

I walked first to the ridge.

It was a fine summer's day, and the sun shone brightly over the ravaged countryside. Most of the fires had burnt themselves out during the night, but the inky depths of the black vapours which covered Twickenham, Hounslow and Richmond were still impenetrable. The dome-shapes had flattened considerably, and long tendrils of the black stuff were spreading through the streets which had at first escaped being smothered.

Of the Martian invaders themselves there was no sign. Only to the south-west, in Bushy Park, did I see clouds of green smoke rising, and I guessed that it was there the fourth projectile had landed.

I turned away from the scene, and walked past the house to the other side, where the grounds opened out on to Richmond Park. Here the view was uninterrupted across to Wimbledon, and but for the total absence of any people, the Park was exactly as it had been on that first day I called at Reynolds House.

When I returned to the house I immediately discovered a problem of pressing urgency, although it was not one which in any way threatened our safety. Beside the outhouse, where the gunners' horses had been tethered, I came across the corpses of the four animals that had been killed when the Martian attacked. During the summer night the flesh had started to de-

compose, and the raw wounds were crawling with flies and an
unhealthy stench filled the air.

I could not possibly move the carcasses, and burning them
was out of the question, so the only alternative was to bury
them. Fortunately, the soldiers' trenches had been dug very
recently, and there was much fresh, upturned soil about.

I found a shovel and wheelbarrow, and began the unpleasant
and lengthy chore of covering the rotting bodies. In two hours I
had completed the task, and the horses were safely buried. The
work was not without its unexpected benefit, though, for during
it I discovered that in their haste the soldiers had left behind
them several pieces of equipment in the trenches. One of these
was a rifle and many rounds of ammunition ... but more prom-
isingly, I discovered two wooden crates, inside each of which
were twenty-five hand-grenades.

With great care I carried these to the house, and stored them
safely in the woodshed. I then returned to the laboratory to see
how the other two were faring.

ii

The fifth projectile fell in Barnes that night, about three miles
to the north-east of the house. On the night following, the sixth
projectile fell on Wimbledon Common.

Every day, at frequent intervals, we would walk out to the
ridge and search for sign of the Martians. During the evening
of the day we started work on the new Machine, we saw five of
the glittering tripods marching together, heading towards
London. Their heat-cannons were sheathed, and they strode
with the confidence of the victor who has nothing to fear. These
five must have been the occupants of the Bushy Park projectile,
who were going up to join the others which even now, we assumed, were rampaging through London.

There were marked changes taking place in the Thames
Valley, and they were not ones we cared for. The clouds of
black vapour were swept away by the Martians: for one whole
day two battle-machines worked at clearing the muck, using an

immense tube which sent forth a fierce jet of steam. This soon swept away the vapour, leaving a black, muddy liquid which flowed into the river. But the river itself was slowly changing.

The Martians had brought with them seeds of the ubiquitous red weed, and were deliberately sowing them along the banks. One day we saw a dozen or so of the legged ground vehicles, scurrying along the riverside walks and throwing up clouds of tiny seeds. In no time at all the alien vegetables were growing and spreading. Compared with the Spartan conditions under which it survived on Mars, the weed must have found the rich soil and moist atmosphere of England like a well fertilized hothouse. Within a week of our return to Reynolds House, the whole length of the river visible to us was choked with the lurid weed, and soon it was spreading to the waterside meadows. On sunny mornings, the creaking of its prodigious growth was so loud that, high and set back from the river as the house was, we could hear the sinister noise when we were inside with the doors and windows closed. It was a constant background to our secret work, and while we could hear it we were always upset by it. The weed was even taking hold on the dry, wooded slopes below the house, and as it encroached the trees turned brown, although it was still the height of summer.

How long would it be before the captive humans were set to cutting back the weed?

iii

On the day after the tenth projectile landed—this, like the three that had directly preceded it, had fallen somewhere in central London—Mr Wells summoned me to the laboratory and announced that he had at last made a substantial advance.

Order had been restored in the laboratory. It had been thoroughly cleaned and tidied, and Amelia had draped huge velvet curtains over all the window-panes, so that work could continue after nightfall. Mr Wells had been in the laboratory from the moment he had left his bed, and the air was pleasantly smoked from his pipe.

"It was the circuitry of the crystals that was baffling me," he said, stretching back comfortably in one of the chairs he had brought from the smoking-room. "You see, there is something about their chemical constituency that provides a direct current of electricity. The problem has been not to produce this effect, but to harness it to produce the attenuation field. Let me show you what I mean."

He and Amelia had constructed a tiny apparatus on the bench. It consisted of a small wheel resting on a metal strip. Two tiny pieces of the crystalline substance had been attached to either side of the wheel. Mr Wells had connected various pieces of wire to the crystals, and the bare ends of these were resting on the surface of the bench.

"If I now connect together those wires I have here, you will see what happens." Mr Wells took more pieces of wire and laid them across the various bare ends. As the last contact was made we all saw clearly that the little wheel had started to rotate slowly. "You see, with this circuit the crystals provide a motive force."

"Just like the bicycles!" I said.

Mr Wells did not know what I was talking about, but Amelia nodded vigorously.

"That's right," she said. "But there are more crystals used on the bicycles, for there is a greater weight to pull."

Mr Wells disconnected the apparatus, because as the wheel turned it was tangling the wires which were connected to it.

"Now, however," he said, "if I complete the circuit in a different way. . . ." He bent closely over his work, peering first at the plans, then at the apparatus. "Watch this carefully, for I suspect we will see something dramatic."

We both stood by his shoulder, and watched as he connected first one wire then another. Soon only one remained bare.

"Now!"

Mr Wells touched the last wires together, and in that instant the whole apparatus—wheel, crystals and wires—vanished from our sight.

"It works!" I cried in delight, and Mr Wells beamed up at me.

"That is how we enter the attenuated dimension," he said. "As you know, as soon as the crystals are connected, the entire piece becomes attenuated. By connecting the device that way, I tapped the power that resides in the dimension, and my little experiment is now lost to us forever."

"Where is it, though?" I said.

"I cannot say for certain, as it was a test-piece only. It is certainly moving in Space, at a very slow speed, and will continue to do so for ever. It is of no importance to us, for the secret of travel through the attenuated dimension is how we may control it. That is my next task."

"Then how long will it be before we can build a new Machine?" I said.

"It will be several days more, I think."

"We must be quick," I said. "With every day that passes the monsters tighten their hold on our world."

"I am working as fast as I am able," Mr Wells said without rancour, and then I noticed how his eyes showed dark circles around them. He had often been working in the laboratory long after Amelia and I had taken to our beds. "We shall need a frame in which the mechanism can be carried, and one large enough to carry passengers. I believe Miss Fitzgibbon has already had an idea about this, and if you and she were to concentrate on this now, our work will end soon enough."

"But a new Machine will be possible?" I said.

"I see no reason why it should not," said Mr Wells. "Now we have no desire to travel to futurity, our Machine need not be nearly so complicated as Sir William's."

iv

Eight more days passed with agonizing slowness, but at last we saw the Space Machine taking shape.

Amelia's plan had been to use the frame of a bed as a base for the Machine, as this would provide the necessary sturdiness and space for the passengers. Accordingly, we searched the damaged servants' wing, and found an iron bedstead some five feet wide. Although it was coated with grime after the fire, it took less than an hour to clean it up. We carried it to the laboratory, and under Mr Wells's guidance began to connect to it the various pieces he produced. Much of this comprised the crystalline substance, in such quantities that it was soon clear that we would need every piece we could lay our hands on. When Mr Wells saw how quickly our reserves of the mysterious substance were being used up he expressed his doubts, but we pressed on nonetheless.

Knowing that we intended to travel in this Machine ourselves, we left enough room for somewhere to sit, and with this in mind I fitted out one end of the bedstead with cushions.

While our secret work continued in the laboratory, the Martians themselves were not idle.

Our hopes that military reinforcements would be able to deal with the incursion had been without foundation, for whenever we saw one of the battle-machines or legged vehicles in the valley below, it strode unchallenged and arrogant. The Martians were apparently consolidating their gains, for we saw much equipment being transferred from the various landing-pits in Surrey to London, and on many occasions we saw groups of captive people either being herded by or driven in one of the legged ground vehicles. The slavery had begun, and all that we had ever feared for Earth was coming to pass.

Meanwhile, the scarlet weed continued to flourish: the Thames Valley was an expanse of garish red, and scarcely a tree was left alive on the side of Richmond Hill. Already, shoots of the weeds were starting to encroach on the lawn of the house, and I made it my daily duty to cut it back. Where the lawn met the weeds was a muddy and slippery morass.

v

"I have done all I can," said Mr Wells, as we stood before the outlandish contraption that once had been a bed. "We need many more crystals, but I have used all we could find."

Nowhere in any of Sir William's drawings had there been so

much as a single clue as to the constituency of the crystals. Therefore, unable to manufacture any more, Mr Wells had had to use those that Sir William had left behind. We had emptied the laboratory, and dismantled the four adapted bicycles which still stood in the outhouse, but even so Mr Wells declared that we needed at least twice as much crystalline substance as we had. He explained that the velocity of the Machine depended on the power the crystals produced.

"We have reached the most critical moment," Mr Wells went on. "The Machine, as it stands, is simply a collection of circuitry and metal. As you know, once it is activated it must stay permanently attenuated, and so I have had to incorporate an equivalent of Sir William's temporal fly-wheel. Once the Machine is in operation, that wheel must always turn so that it is not lost to us."

He was indicating our makeshift installation, which was the wheel of the artillery piece blown off in the explosion. We had mounted this transversely on the front of the bedstead.

Mr Wells took a small, leather-bound notebook from his breast pocket, and glanced at a list of handwritten instructions he had compiled himself. He passed this to Amelia, and as she called them out one by one, he inspected various critical parts of the Space Machine's engine. At last he declared himself satisfied.

"We must now trust to our work," he said softly, returning the notebook to his pocket. Without ceremony he placed one stout piece of wire against the iron frame of the bedstead, and turned a screw to hold it in place. Even before he had finished, Amelia and I noticed that the artillery wheel was turning slowly.

We stood back, hardly daring to hope that our work had been successful.

"Turnbull, kindly place your hand against the frame."

"Will I receive an electrical shock?" I said, wondering why he did not do this himself.

"I should not think so. There is nothing to be afraid of."

I extended my hand cautiously, then, catching Amelia's eye and seeing that she was smiling a little, I reached out resolutely and grasped the metal frame. As my fingers made contact the entire contraption shuddered visibly and audibly, just as had Sir William's Time Machine; the solid iron bedstead became as lissom as a young tree.

Amelia stretched out her hand, and then so did Mr Wells. We laughed aloud.

"You've done it, Mr Wells!" I said. "We have built a Space Machine!"

"Yes, but we have not tested it yet. We must see if it can be safely driven."

"Then let us do it at once!"

vi

Mr Wells mounted the Space Machine, and, sitting comfortably on the cushions, braced himself against the controls. By working a combination of levers he managed to shift the Machine first forwards and backwards, then to each side. Finally, he took the unwieldy Machine and drove it all around the laboratory.

None of this was seen by Amelia and myself. We have only Mr Wells's word that he tested the Machine this way . . . for as soon as he touched the levers he and the Machine instantly became invisible, reappearing only when the Machine was turned off.

"You cannot hear me when I speak to you?" he said, after his tour of the laboratory.

"We can neither hear nor see you," said Amelia. "Did you call to us?"

"Once or twice," Mr Wells said, smiling. "Turnbull, how does your foot feel?"

"My foot, sir?"

"I regret I inadvertently passed through it on my journey. You would not pull it out of the way when I called to you."

I flexed my toes inside the boots I had borrowed from Sir William's dressing-room, but there seemed to be nothing wrong.

"Come, Turnbull, we must try this further. Miss Fitzgibbon, would you kindly ascend to the next floor? We shall try to follow you in the Machine. Perhaps if you would wait inside the bedroom I am using . . .?"

Amelia nodded, then left the laboratory. In a moment we heard her running up the stairs.

"Step aboard, Mr Turnbull. Now we shall see what this Machine can do!"

Almost before I had clambered on to the cushions beside Mr Wells, he had pushed one of the levers and we were moving forward. Around us, silence had fallen abruptly, and the distant clamouring of the weed-banks was absent.

"Let us see if we can fly," said Mr Wells. His voice sounded flat and deep against the attenuated quiet. He tugged a second lever and at once we lifted smartly towards the ceiling. I raised my hands to ward off the blow . . . but as we reached the wood and jagged glass of the laboratory roof we passed right through! For a moment I had the queer experience of finding just my head out in the open, but then the bulk of the Space Machine had thrust me through, and it was as if we were hovering in the air above the conservatory-like building. Mr Wells turned one of the horizontally mounted levers, and we moved at quite prodigious speed through the brick wall of the upper storey of the main house. We found ourselves hovering above a landing. Chuckling to himself, Mr Wells guided the Machine towards his guest-room, and plunged us headlong through the closed door.

Amelia was waiting within, standing by the window.

"Here we are!" I called as soon as I saw her. "It flies too!"

Amelia showed no sign of awareness.

"She cannot hear us," Mr Wells reminded me. "Now . . . I must see if I can settle us on the floor."

We were hovering some eighteen inches above the carpet, and Mr Wells made fine adjustments to his controls. Meanwhile Amelia had left the window and was looking curiously around, evidently waiting for us to materialize. I amused myself first by blowing a kiss to her, then by pulling a face, but she responded to neither.

Suddenly, Mr Wells released his levers, and we dropped with a bump to the floor. Amelia started in surprise.

"There you are!" she said. "I wondered how you would appear."

"Allow us to take you downstairs,' said Mr Wells, gallantly. "Climb aboard, my dear, and let us make a tour of the house."

So, for the next half-hour, we experimented with the Space Machine, and Mr Wells grew accustomed to making it manoeuvre exactly as he wished. Soon he could make it turn, soar, halt, as if he had been at its controls all his life. At first, Amelia and I clung nervously to the bedstead, for it seemed to turn with reckless velocity, but gradually we too saw that for all its makeshift appearance, the Space Machine was every bit as scientific as its original.

We left the house just once, and toured the garden. Here Mr Wells tried to increase our forward speed, but to our disappointment we found that for all its other qualities, the Space Machine could travel no faster than the approximate speed of a running man.

"It is the shortage of crystals," said Mr Wells, as we soared through the upper branches of a walnut tree. "If we had more of those, there would be no limit to our velocity."

"Never mind," said Amelia. "We have no use for great speed. Invisibility is our prime advantage."

I was staring out past the house to the overgrown redness of the valley. It was the constant reminder of the urgency of our efforts.

"Mr Wells," I said quietly. "We have our Space Machine. Now is the time to put it to use."

Chapter Twenty-Three
AN INVISIBLE NEMESIS

i

When we had landed the Space Machine, and I had loaded several of the hand-grenades on to it, Mr Wells was worried about the time we had left to us.

"The sun will be setting in two hours," he said. "I should not care to drive the Machine in darkness."

"But, sir, we can come to no harm in the attenuation."

"I know, but we must at some time return to the house and leave the attenuated dimension. When we do that, we must be absolutely certain there are no Martians around. How terrible it would be if we returned to the house in the night, and discovered that the Martians were waiting for us!"

"We have been here for more than two weeks," I said, "and no Martian has so much as glanced our way."

Mr Wells had to agree with this, but he said: "I think we must not lose sight of the seriousness of our task, Turnbull. Because we have been confined so long in Richmond, we have no knowledge of the extent of the Martians' success. Certainly they have subdued all the land we can see from here; in all probability they are now the lords of the entire country. For all we know, their domain might be worldwide. If we are, as we suspect, in command of the one weapon they cannot resist, we cannot afford to lose that advantage by taking unnecessary risks. We have a tremendous responsibility thrust upon us."

"Mr Wells is right, Edward," said Amelia. "Our revenge on the Martians is late, but it is all we have."

"Very well," I said. "But we must try at least one sortie today. We do not yet know if our scheme will work."

So at last we mounted the Space Machine, and sat with suppressed excitement as Mr Wells guided us away from the house, above the obscene red tangle of weeds, and out towards the heart of the Thames Valley.

As soon as we were under way, I saw some of the wisdom of the others' words. Our search for Martian targets was to be unguided, for we had no idea where the evil brutes currently were. We could search all day for just one, and in the boundless scale of the Martians' intrusion we might never find our goal.

We flew for about half an hour, circling over the river, looking this way and that for some sign of the invaders, but without success.

At last Amelia suggested a plan which presented logic and simplicity. We knew, she said, where the projectiles had fallen, and further, we knew that the Martians used the pits as their headquarters. Surely, if we were seeking the monsters, the pits would be the most sensible places to look first.

Mr Wells agreed with this, and we turned directly for the nearest of the pits. This was the one in Bushy Park, where the fourth projectile had fallen. Suddenly, as I realized we were at last on the right track, I felt my heart pounding with excitement.

The valley was a dreadful sight: the red weed was growing rampantly over almost every physical protuberance, houses included. The landscape seemed from this height to be like a huge undulating field of red grass bent double by heavy rain. In places, the weeds had actually altered the course of the river, and wherever there was low-lying ground stagnant lakes had formed.

The pit had been made in the north-eastern corner of Bushy Park, and was difficult to distinguish by virtue of the fact that it, no less than anywhere else, was heavily overgrown with weed. At last we noticed the cavernous mouth of the projectile itself, and Mr Wells brought the Space Machine down to hover a few feet from the entrance. All was dark within, and there was no sign of either the Martians or their machines.

We were about to move away, when Amelia suddenly pointed into the heart of the projectile.

"Edward, look . . . it is one of the people!"

Her move had startled me, but I looked in the direction she was indicating. Sure enough, lying a few feet inside the hold was a human figure. I thought for a moment that this must be one of the hapless victims snatched by the Martians ... but then I saw that the body was that of a very tall man, and that he was wearing a black uniform. His skin was a mottled red, and his face, which was turned towards us, was ugly and distorted.

We stared in silence at this dead Martian human. It was perhaps even more of a shock to see one of our erstwhile allies in this place than it would have been to see one of the monsters.

We explained to Mr Wells that the man was probably one of the humans coerced into driving the projectile, and he looked at the dead Martian with great interest.

"The strain of our gravity must have been too much for his heart," said Mr Wells.

"That has not upset the monsters' plans," Amelia said.

"Those beasts are without hearts," said Mr Wells, but I supposed that he was speaking figuratively.

We recalled that another cylinder had fallen near Wimbledon, and so we turned the Space Machine away from the pathetic figure of the dead Martian human, and set off eastwards at once. From Bushy Park to Wimbledon is a distance of some five miles, and so even at our maximum speed the flight took nearly an hour. During this time we were appalled to see that even parts of Richmond Park were showing signs of the red weed.

Mr Wells had been casting several glances over his shoulder to see how long there was until sunset, and was clearly still unhappy with this expedition so soon before nightfall. I resolved that if the Martian pit at Wimbledon was also empty, then it would be I who proposed an immediate return to Reynolds House. The satisfaction of taking positive action at last had excited my nerve, though, and I would be sorry not to make at least one kill before returning.

Then at last we had our chance. Amelia suddenly cried out, and pointed towards the south. There, striding slowly from the direction of Malden, came a battle-machine.

We were at that moment travelling at a height approximately equal to that of the platform, and it was an instinct we all shared that the beast inside must have seen us, so deliberately did it march in our direction.

Mr Wells uttered a few reassuring words, and raised the Space Machine to a new height and bearing, one which would take us circling around the tripodal engine.

I reached forward with shaking hands, and took hold of one of the hand-grenades.

Amelia said: "Have you ever handled one of those before, Edward?"

"No," I said. "But I know what to do."

"Please be careful."

We were less than half a mile from the Titan, and still we headed in towards it from an oblique angle.

"Where do you want me to place the Machine?" said Mr Wells, concentrating fiercely on his controls.

"Somewhat above the platform," I said. "Approach from the side, because I do not wish to pass directly in front."

"The monster cannot see us," said Amelia.

"No," I said, remembering that ferocious visage. "But we might see it."

I found myself trembling anew as we approached. The thought of what was squatting so loathsomely inside that metal edifice was enough to reawaken all the fears and angers I had suffered on Mars, but I forced myself to be calm.

"Can you maintain the Machine at a steady speed above the platform?" I asked Mr Wells.

"I'll do what I can, Turnbull."

His cautious words gave no indication of the ease with which he brought our flying bed-frame to a point almost exactly above the platform. I leaned over the side of our Space Machine, while Amelia held my free hand, and I stared down at the roof of the platform.

There were numerous apertures here—some of which were large enough for me to make out the glistening body of the monster—and the grenade lodged in any one of them would probably do what was necessary. In the end I chose a large port just beside where the heat-cannon would emerge, reasoning that somewhere near there must be the incredible furnace which produced the heat. If that were fractured, then what damage the grenade did not inflict would be completed by the subsequent explosive release of energy.

"I see my target," I shouted to Mr Wells. "I will call out as soon as I have released the grenade, and at that moment we must move away as far as possible."

Mr Wells confirmed that he understood, and so I sat up straight for a moment, and eased the restraining pin from the detonating arm. While Amelia supported me once more, I leaned over and held the grenade above the platform.

"Ready, Mr Wells . . .?" I called. "*Now!*"

At the selfsame instant that I let go the grenade, Mr Wells took the Space Machine in a fast climbing arc away from the battle-machine. I stared back, anxious to see the effect of my attack.

A few seconds later, there was an explosion below and slightly behind the Martian tripod.

I stared in amazement. The grenade had fallen *through* the metal bulk of the platform and exploded harmlessly!

I said: "I didn't expect that to happen. . . ."

"My dear," said Amelia. "I think the grenade was still attenuated."

Below us, the Martian strode on, oblivious of the deadly attack it had just survived.

ii

I was seething with disappointment as we returned safely to the house. By then the sun had set, and a long, glowing evening lay across the transformed valley. As the other two went to their rooms to dress for dinner, I paced to and fro in the laboratory, determined that our vengeance should not be snatched away from us.

I ate with the others, but kept my silence throughout the meal. Amelia and Mr Wells, sensing my distemper, talked a little of the success of our building the Space Machine, but the abortive attack was carefully avoided.

Later, Amelia said she was going to the kitchen to bake some bread, and so Mr Wells and I repaired to the smoking-room. With the curtains carefully drawn, and sitting by the light of one candle only, we talked of general matters until Mr Wells considered it safe to discuss other tactics.

"The difficulty is twofold," he said. "Clearly, we must not be attenuated when we place the explosive, otherwise the grenade has no effect, and yet we must be attenuated during the explosion, otherwise we shall be affected by the blast."

"But if we turn off the Space Machine, the Martian will observe us," I said.

"That is why I say it will be difficult. We have both seen how fast those brutes react to any threat."

"We could land the Space Machine on the roof of the tripod itself."

Mr Wells shook his head slowly. "I admire your inventiveness, Turnbull, but it would not be practicable. I had great difficulty even keeping abreast of the engine. To essay a landing on a moving object would be extremely hazardous."

We both recognized the urgency of finding a solution. For an hour or more we argued our ideas back and forth, but we arrived at nothing satisfactory. In the end, we went to the drawing-room where Amelia was waiting for us, and presented the problem to her.

She thought for a while, then said: "I see no difficulty. We have plenty of grenades, and can therefore afford a few misses. All we should do is hover above our target, although at a somewhat greater height than today. Mr Wells then switches off the attenuation field, and while we fall through the air Edward can lob a grenade at the Martian. By the time the bomb explodes, we should be safely back inside the attenuated dimension, and it will not matter how close we are to the explosion."

I stared at Mr Wells, then at Amelia, considering the implications of such a hair-raising scheme.

"It sounds awfully dangerous," I said in the end.

"We can strap ourselves to the Space Machine," Amelia said. "We need not fall out."

"But even so. . . ."

"Do you have an alternative plan?" she said.

iii

The following morning we made our preparations, and were ready to set out at an early hour.

I must confess to considerable trepidation at the whole enterprise, and I think Mr Wells shared some of my misgivings. Only Amelia seemed confident of the plan, to the extent that she offered to take on the task of aiming the hand-grenades herself. Naturally, I would hear nothing of this, but she remained the only one of the three of us who exuded optimism and confidence that morning. Indeed, she had been up since first light and made us all sandwiches, so that we need not feel constrained to return to the house for lunch. Additionally, she had fixed some straps—which she had made from leather trouser-belts—across the bedstead's cushions to hold us in place.

Just as we were about to leave, Amelia walked abruptly from the laboratory, and Mr Wells and I stared after her. She returned in a few moments, this time carrying a large suitcase.

I looked at it with interest, not recognizing it at first for what it was.

Amelia set it down on the floor, and opened the lid. Inside, wrapped carefully in tissue-paper, were the three pairs of goggles I had brought with me the day I came to see Sir William!

She passed one pair to me, smiling a little. Mr Wells took his at once.

"Capital notion, Miss Fitzgibbon," he said. "Our eyes will need protection if we are to fall through the air."

Amelia put hers on before we left, and I helped her with the clasp, making sure that it did not get caught in her hair. She settled the goggles on her brow.

"Now we are better equipped for our outing," she said, and went towards the Space Machine.

I followed, holding my goggles in my hand, and trying not to dwell on my memories.

iv

We were in for a day of remarkably good hunting. Within a few minutes of sailing out over the Thames, Amelia let forth a cry, and pointed to the west. There, walking slowly through the streets of Twickenham, was a Martian battle-machine. It had its metal arms dangling, and it was moving from house to house, evidently seeking human survivors. By the emptiness of the mesh net that hung behind the platform we judged that its pickings had been poor. It seemed incredible to us that there should still be any survivors at all in these ravaged towns, although our own survival was a clue to the fact that several people must still be clinging to life in the cellars and basements of the houses.

We circled warily around the evil machine, once again experiencing that unease we had felt the day before.

"Take the Space Machine higher, if you will," Amelia said to Mr Wells. "We must judge our approach carefully."

I took a hand-grenade, and held it in readiness. The battle-machine had paused momentarily, reaching through the upper window of a house with one of its long, articulate arms.

Mr Wells brought the Space Machine to a halt, some fifty feet above the platform.

Amelia pulled her goggles down over her eyes, and advised us to do the same. Mr Wells and I fixed our goggles in place, and checked the position of the Martian. It was quite motionless, but for the reaching of its metal arms.

"I'm ready, sir," I said, and slid the pin from the striking lever.

"Very well," said Mr Wells. "I am turning off the attenuation . . . *now!*"

As he spoke we all experienced an unpleasant lurching sensation, our stomachs seemed to turn a somersault, and the air rushed past us. At the behest of gravity we plunged towards the Martian machine. In the same instant I hurled the grenade desperately down at the Martian.

"Bombs away!" I shouted.

Then there was a second lurch, and our fall was arrested. Mr Wells manipulated his levers, and we soared away to one side in the dead silence of that weird dimension.

Looking back at the Martian we waited for the explosion . . . and seconds later it came. My aim had been accurate, and a ball of smoke and fire blossomed silently on the roof of the battle-machine.

The monster-creature inside the platform, taken by surprise, reacted with astonishing alacrity. The tower leaped back from the house, and in the same moment we saw the barrel of the heat-cannon snapping into position. The cowl of the platform swung round as the monster sought its attacker. As the smoke of the grenade drifted away we saw that the explosion had blown a jagged hole in the roof, and the engine inside must have been damaged. The battle-machine's movements were not as smooth or as fast as some we had seen, and a dense green smoke was pouring from within.

The heat-beam flared into action, swinging erratically in all directions. The battle-machine took three steps forward, hesitated, then staggered back again. The heat-beam flashed across several of the near-by houses, causing the roofs to burst into flame.

Then, in a ball of brilliant-green fire, the whole hideous platform exploded. Our bomb had ruptured the furnace inside.

To us, sitting inside the silence and safety of attenuation, the destruction of the Martian was a soundless, mysterious event. We saw the fragments of the destructive engine flying in all directions, saw one of the huge legs cartwheeling away, saw the bulk of the shattered platform fall in a hundred pieces across the rooftops of Twickenham.

Curiously enough, I was not elated by this sight, and this sentiment was shared by the other two. Amelia stared quietly across at the twisted metal that once had been an engine of war, and Mr Wells merely said: "I see another."

Towards the south, striding in the direction of Molesey, was a second battle-machine.

Mr Wells swung his levers, and soon we were speeding towards our next target.

v

By midday we had accounted for a total of four Martians: three of these were in their tripods, and one was in the control cabin of one of the legged vehicles. Each attack was conducted without danger to ourselves, and each time the chosen monster had been taken by surprise. Our activities were not going unnoticed, however, for the legged vehicle had been speeding towards the destroyed tripod in Twickenham when we spotted it. We realized from this that the Martians must have had some kind of intricate signalling system between themselves—Mr Wells hypothesized that it was a telepathic communication, although Amelia and I, having seen the sophisticated science on Mars, suspected that it would be a technical device—for our vengeful activities seemed to have provoked a good deal of movement on the Martians' behalf. As we flew to and fro across the valley, we saw several tripods approaching from the direction of London, and we knew that we would not run short of targets that day.

With the killing of the fourth Martian, though, Amelia suggested we rest and eat the sandwiches we had brought. As she said this we were still hovering about the battle-machine we had just attacked.

The killing of this monster had been an odd affair. We had found the battle-machine standing alone on the edge of Richmond Park, facing towards the south-west. Its three legs had been drawn together, and its metal arms were furled, and at first we suspected that the machine was unoccupied. Moving in for the kill, though, we had passed in front of the multi-faceted ports and for a moment we had glimpsed those saucer-eyes staring balefully out across Kingston.

We had taken our time with this attack, and with my increasing experience I was able to lob the grenade into the platform with great accuracy. When the bomb went off it had exploded inside the cabin occupied by the monster, blasting open several metal plates and presumably destroying the monster outright, but the furnace itself had not been ruptured. The tower still stood, leaning slightly to one side and with green smoke pouring from within, but substantially intact.

Mr Wells took the Space Machine a decent distance away from the battle-machine, and settled it near the ground. By consensus we agreed to stay inside the attenuation, for the green smoke was making us nervous that the furnace might yet explode of its own accord.

So, overshadowed by the damaged Titan, we quickly ate what must have been one of the strangest picnic lunches ever taken in the rolling countryside of the Park.

We were about to set off again when Mr Wells drew our attention to the fact that another battle-machine had appeared. This was hurrying towards us, evidently coming to investigate the work we had done on its colleague.

We were safe enough, but agreed to take the Space Machine into the air, and so be ready for a quick foray.

Our confidence was increasing; with four kills behind us we were establishing a deadly routine. Now, as we rose above the Park, and saw the approaching battle-machine, we could not help but see that its heat-cannon was raised and its articulate arms were poised to strike. Clearly its monstrous driver knew that someone or something had attacked successfully, and was determined to defend itself.

We stayed at a safe distance, and watched as the newcomer went to the tower and closely inspected the damage.

I said: "Mr Wells, shall we bomb it now?"

Mr Wells stayed silent, his brow furrowed over the top of his goggles.

"The creature is very alert," he said. "We cannot risk a chance shot from the heat-cannon."

"Then let us seek another target," I said.

Nevertheless, we stayed on watch for several minutes, hoping the Martian would relax its guard long enough to allow us to attack. However, even as the creature inside carried out a cautious examination of the damage, the heat-cannon turned menacingly above the roof and the tentacular metal arms flexed nervously.

With some reluctance we turned away at last, and headed back towards the west. As we flew, Amelia and I cast several backward glances, still wary of what the second Martian would do. Thus it was that we saw, when we were less than half a mile away, that our grenade had, after all, weakened the casing of the furnace. We saw an immense, billowing explosion of green ... and the second battle-machine staggered backwards and crashed in a tangle of metal to the floor of the Park.

That was how, by a stroke of good fortune, we slaughtered our fifth Martian monster.

vi

Considerably cheered by this accidental success we continued our quest, although it was now with a bravura tempered by caution. As Mr Wells pointed out, it was not the Martian machines we had to destroy, but the monster-creatures themselves. A battle-machine was agile and well-armed, and although its destruction certainly killed its driver, the legged ground vehicles were easier targets because the driver was not enclosed above.

So it was that we agreed to concentrate on the smaller vehicles.

That afternoon was one of almost unqualified success. Only once did we fail to kill a Martian with our first strike and that was when I, in my haste, neglected to pull the pin from the grenade. However, on our second pass the monster was effectively and spectacularly destroyed.

When we returned to Reynolds House in the evening, we had accounted for a total of eleven of the Martian brutes. This, if our estimate that each projectile carried five monsters was correct, accounted for more than one-fifth of their total army!

It was with considerable optimism that we retired to bed that night.

The following day we loaded our Space Machine with more grenades, and set off again.

To our consternation we discovered that the Martians had learned by our ventures of the day before. Now no legged ground vehicle moved unless it was accompanied by a battle-machine, but so assured of our impregnability were we that we resolved that this presented us with two targets instead of one!

Accordingly, we prepared our attack with great precision, swooped down from above, and were rewarded with the sight of the battle-machine being blown to smithereens! From there, it was but a simple task to chase and destroy the legged ground vehicle.

Later that day we disposed of two more in the same way, but that was our total score for the day. (One legged vehicle was allowed to pass unharmed, for it was carrying a score or more of human captives.) Four was not as healthy a tally as eleven, but even so we considered we had done well, and so once more retired in a state of elation.

The next day was one with no success at all, for we saw no Martians about. We ranged, in our search, even as far as the fire-blackened heath at Woking, but here simply found the pit and its projectile empty both of Martians and their devices.

At the sight of the ruined town on the hill, Amelia and I noticed that Mr Wells grew wistful, and we recalled how he had been so abruptly separated from his wife.

"Sir, would you like us to fly to Leatherhead?" I said.

He shook his head forcefully. "I wish I could allow myself the indulgence, but our business is with the Martians. My wife will be well; it is obvious that the invaders moved to the north-east from here. There will be time enough for reunion."

I admired the resolution in his voice, but later that evening Amelia told me that she had noticed a tear running down Mr Wells's cheek. Perhaps, she said, Mr Wells suspected that his wife had already been killed, and that he was not yet ready to face up to this.

For this reason, as well as for our lack of success, we were in no great spirits that night, and so we retired early.

The next day we were luckier: two Martians succumbed to our grenades. This was the odd fact though: both the battle-machines stood, like the one we had found near Kingston, alone and still, the three legs drawn together. There was no attempt at self-defence; one stood with its heat-cannon pointing stiffly towards the sky, the other had not even raised its. Of course, as we were attacking battle-machines we swooped with great care, but we all agreed that our kills were suspiciously easy.

Then came another day with no more Martians seen at all, and on that evening Mr Wells pronounced a verdict.

"We must," he said, "turn our attention at last to London. We have so far been snipers against the straggling flanks of a mighty army. Now we must confront the concentrated strength of that army, and fight it to the death."

Brave words indeed, but ones which did not reflect the suspicion which, I afterwards discovered, had been growing in us all for the last three days.

Chapter Twenty-Four
OF SCIENCE AND CONSCIENCE

i

The day following Mr Wells's stern pronouncement, we stowed the remainder of our hand-grenades aboard the Space Machine, and set off at a moderate speed towards London. We kept our eyes open for a sign of the battle-machines, but there was none about.

We flew first over Richmond town, and saw the dark residue of the black smoke that had suffocated its streets. Only by the river, where the red weed grew in mountainous tangling clumps, was there relief from the sight of the black, sooty powder that covered everything. North of Richmond was Kew Gardens, and here, although the Pagoda still stood, most of the priceless plantations of tropical plants had succumbed to the vile weed.

We headed more directly towards London then, flying over Mortlake. Not far from the brewery, in the centre of an estate of modern villas, one of the projectiles had landed, and here it had caused untold damage with the force of its explosive landing. I saw that Mr Wells was regarding the scene thoughtfully, so I suggested to him that we might fly a little closer. Accordingly he brought the Space Machine down in a gentle approach, and for a few minutes we hovered above the terrible desolation.

In the centre of the pit was, of course, the empty shell of the projectile. What was much more interesting was the evidence that, for some time at least, this place had been a centre of the Martians' activity. There were no battle-machines in sight, but standing beside the gaping mouth of the projectile were two of the legged ground vehicles, and sprawled untidily behind them was one of the spiderlike handling-machines. Its many metal tentacles were folded, and the normal brilliant sheen of the polished surfaces had started to corrode in the oxygen-rich air.

I was all for landing the Space Machine and exploring on foot, so quiet was the scene, but neither Amelia nor Mr Wells considered it safe. Instead, we allowed the Machine to drift slowly about the pit, while we sat in silence. We were daunted and impressed by what we saw: the pit itself had been re-fashioned, so that the earth thrown up by the impact had been built into high ramparts, and the floor had been levelled to facilitate the machines' movements. One end of the pit had been reworked to provide a sloping ramp for the ground vehicles.

Suddenly, Amelia gasped, and covered her mouth with her hand.

"Oh, Edward. . . ." she said, and turned her face away.

I saw what she had noticed. Dwarfed by the looming bulk of the projectile, and nestling in its shadow, was one of the killing cubicles. Lying all about, some half-buried, were the bodies of human beings. Mr Wells had seen the shocking sight in the same instant, and without further ado he sent the Space Machine soaring away from that place of hell . . . but not before we had realized that lying in the shadow of the projectile were perhaps a hundred or more of the corpses.

We flew on, heading in an easterly direction, and in almost no time we were over the grey, mean streets of Wandsworth. Mr Wells slowed our passage, and set the Machine to hover.

He shook his head.

"I had no idea of the scale of their murders," he said.

"We had allowed ourselves to neglect the fact," I said. "Each monster requires the blood of a human being every day. The longer the Martians are allowed to stay alive, the longer that slaughter will continue."

Amelia said nothing, clutching my hand.

"We cannot delay," said Mr Wells. "We must continue bombing until every one is dead."

"But where are the Martians?" I said. "I assumed London would be teeming with them."

We looked in every direction, but apart from isolated pillars of smoke, where buildings yet burned, there was not a single sign of the invaders.

"We must search them out," said Mr Wells. "However long it takes."

"Are they still in London?" said Amelia. "How do we know that they have not finished their work here, and are not even now destroying other cities?"

Neither I nor Mr Wells knew the answer to that.

"All we can do," I said, "is to search for them and kill them. If London has been abandoned by them, we will have to go in pursuit. I see no alternative."

Mr Wells had been staring down disparagingly at the streets of Wandsworth; that most ugly of London suburbs had, unaccountably, been spared by the Martians, although like everywhere else it was deserted. He moved the controlling levers decisively, and set our course again for the heart of London.

ii

Of all the Thames bridges we saw, Westminster was the one least overgrown with the red weed, and so Mr Wells took us down and we landed in the centre of the roadway. No Martian could approach us without walking out across the bridge, and that would give us enough warning so that we could start the Space Machine and escape.

For the last hour we had flown over the southern suburbs of the city. The extent of the desolation was almost beyond words. Where the Martians had not attacked with their heat-beams they had smothered with their black smoke, and where neither had been brought to bear the red weed had sprung willingly from the river to choke and tangle.

We had seen nobody at all; the only movement had been that of a hungry dog, hopping with one leg broken through the streets of Lambeth.

Much debris floated in the river, and we saw many small boats overturned. In the Pool of London we had seen a score of corpses, caught by some freak of the tide, bobbing whitely by the entrance to Surrey Docks.

Then we had set our course by the landmarks we knew, and come to Westminster Bridge. We had seen the Tower of London, with its stout walls unscathed by the Martians, but its green swards had become a jungle of Martian weed. Tower Bridge too, its roadway left open, had long strands of weed cobwebbing its graceful lines. Then we had seen the high dome of St Paul's, and noticed how it stood undamaged above the lower buildings of the City; our mood changed as we passed beyond it and saw that on its western side a gaping hole had been made.

So at last we landed on Westminster Bridge, well depressed by what we had seen. Mr Wells turned off the attenuation, and at once we breathed the air of London, and heard its sounds.

We smelt. . . .

We smelt the residue of smoke; the bitter, metallic tang of the weed; the sweetness of putrefaction; the cool salty airs of the river; the heady odour of the macadamed roadway, simmering in the summer's sunshine.

We heard. . . .

A great silence overwhelmed London. There was the flow of the river below the bridge, and an occasional creak from the weed which still grew prolifically by the parapet. But there was no clatter of hooves, no grind of wheels, no cries or calls of people, nor sound of footfall.

Directly before us stood the Palace of Westminster, topped by the tower of Big Ben, unharmed. The clock had stopped at seventeen minutes past two.

We pushed back our goggles, and stepped down from the Space Machine. I went with Amelia to stand by the side of the bridge, staring up the river. Mr Wells walked off alone, looking in a brooding fashion at the mountainous piles of weed that had submerged the Victoria Embankment. He had been silent and thoughtful as we toured the deathful city, and now as he stood by himself, staring down at the sluggishly flowing river, I saw that his shoulders were slumped and his expression was pensive.

Amelia too was staring at our friend, but then she slipped her hand into mine and for a moment rested her cheek against my shoulder.

"Edward, this is terrible! I had no idea that things were so bad."

I stared gloomily at the view, trying to find something about it that would indicate some optimistic development, but the emptiness and stillness were total. I had never before seen the skies above London so free of soot, but that was hardly recompense for this utter destruction of the greatest city in the world.

"Soon everywhere will be like this," Amelia said. "We were wrong to think we could tackle the Martians, even though we have killed a few. What I find hardest to accept is that all this is our doing, Edward. We brought this menace to the world."

"No," I said instantly. "We are not to blame."

I felt her stiffen. "We can't absolve ourselves of this."

I said: "The Martians would have invaded Earth whether we took a part or not. We saw their preparations. If there is any consolation to be found, then it is that only ten projectiles made it to Earth. Your revolution prevented the monsters from carrying out their plans to the full. What we see is bad enough, but think how much worse it might have been."

"I suppose so."

She fell silent for a few seconds, but then went on: "Edward, we must return to Mars. While there is any chance that the monsters rule that world, Earthmen can never relax their guard. We have the Space Machine to take us, for if one can be built so hastily in the urgent circumstances in which we worked, another more powerful Machine can be built, one that would carry a thousand armed men. I promised the people of Mars that I would return, and now we must."

I listened to her words carefully, and realized that the passions that had driven her on Mars had been replaced by wisdom and understanding.

"We will go back to Mars one day," I said. "There is no alternative."

We had both forgotten Mr Wells's presence while we spoke,

but now he turned from his position and walked slowly back towards us. I saw that in the few minutes he had been by himself a fundamental change had come over his bearing. The weight of defeat had been removed from his shoulders, and his eyes were gleaming once more.

"You two look most uncommonly miserable!" he cried. "There is no cause for that. Our work is over. The Martians have not left ... they are still in London, and the battle is won!"

iii

Amelia and I stared uncomprehendingly at Mr Wells after he had made this unexpected statement. He moved towards the Space Machine, and placing one foot on the iron frame he turned to face us, clasping his jacket lapels in his fists. He cleared his throat.

"This has been a war of worlds," said Mr Wells, speaking calmly and in a clear, ringing voice. "Where we have been mistaken is to treat it as a war of intelligences. We have seen the invaders' monstrous appearance, but persuaded by their qualities of cunning, valour and intelligence have thought of them as men. So we have fought them as if they were men, and we have not done well. Our Army was overrun, and our houses were burnt and crushed. However, the Martians' domain on Earth is a small one. I dare say when the recovery is made we shall discover that no more than a few hundred square miles of territory have been conquered. Even so, small as has been the battleground, this has been a war between worlds, and when the Martians came to Earth so rudely they did not realize what they were taking on."

"Sir," I said, "if you are speaking of allies, we have seen none. No armies have come to our assistance, unless they too were instantly overcome."

Mr Wells gestured impatiently. "I am not speaking of armies, Turnbull, although they will come in good time, as will the grain-ships and the goods-trains. No, our true allies are all about us, invisible, just as we in our Machine were invisible!"

I glanced upwards reflexively, almost expecting a second Space Machine to appear from the sky.

"Look at the weeds, Turnbull!" Mr Wells pointed to the stems that grew a few feet from where we stood. "See how the leaves are blighted? See how the stems are splitting even as they grow? While mankind has been concerned with the terrible intelligence of the monsters, these plants have been waging their own battles. Our soil will not feed them with the minerals they require, and our bees will not pollinate their flowers. These weeds are dying, Turnbull. In the same way, the Martian monsters will die even if they have not done so already. The Martian effort is at an end, because intelligence is no match for nature. As the humans on Mars tampered with nature to make the monsters, and thereby provoked Nemesis, so the monsters sought to tamper with life on Earth, and they too have destroyed themselves."

"Then where are the monsters now?" said Amelia.

"We shall find them soon enough," Mr Wells said, "but that will come in time. Our problem is no longer how to confront this menace, but how to enjoy the spoils of victory. We have the products of the Martian intelligence all about us, and these will be eagerly taken by our scientists. I suspect that the peaceful days of the past will never entirely return, for these battle-machines and walking vehicles are likely to bring fundamental changes to the way of life of everyone in the world. We stand in the early years of a new century, and it is one which will see many changes. At the heart of those changes will be a new battle: one between Science and Conscience. This is the battle the Martians lost, and it is one we must now fight!"

iv

Mr Wells lapsed into silence, his breathing heavy, and Amelia and I stood nervously before him.

At length he moved from his position, and lowered his fists. He cleared his throat again.

"I think this is no time for speech-making," he said, apparently disconcerted at the way his eloquence had silenced us. "To see this through, we must find the Martians. Later, I will contact my publisher and see if he would be interested in an edition of my thoughts on this topic."

I looked around at the silent city. "You cannot believe, sir, that after this the life of London will return to normal?"

"Not to normal, Turnbull. This war is not an ending, but a beginning! The people who fled will return; our institutions will re-establish themselves. Even the fabric of the city is, for the most part, intact, and can be quickly rebuilt. The work of rebuilding will not end with structural repairs, for the Martian intrusion has itself served to heighten our own intelligence. As I have said, that presents its own dangers, but we will deal with those as the need arises."

Amelia had been staring across the rooftops throughout our exchange, and now she pointed towards the north-west.

"Look, Edward, Mr Wells! I think there are some birds there!"

We looked in the direction she was indicating, and saw a flight of large birds, black against the brilliant sky, whirling and diving. They seemed to be a long way away.

"Let us investigate this," said Mr Wells, adjusting the goggles over his eyes once more.

We went back to the Space Machine, and just as we were about to step aboard we heard an intrusive sound. It was one so familiar to us that we all reacted in the same moment: it was the braying call of a Martian, its siren voice echoing from the faces of the buildings that fronted the river. But this was no war-cry, nor call of the hunt. Instead it was coloured by pain and fear, an alien lament across a broken city.

The call was two notes, one following the other, endlessly repeated: "Ulla, ulla, ulla, ulla. . . ."

v

We saw the first battle-machine in Regent's Park, standing alone. I reached immediately for a hand-grenade, but Mr Wells restrained me.

"No need for that, Turnbull," he said.

He brought the Space Machine in close to the platform, and we saw the cluster of crows that surrounded it. The birds had found a way into the platform, and now they pecked and snatched at the flesh of the Martian within.

Its eyes gazed blankly at us through one of the ports at the front. The gaze was as baleful as ever, but where once it had been cold and malicious, now it was the fixed glare of death.

There was a second battle-machine at the foot of Primrose Hill, and here the birds had finished their work. Splashings of dried blood and discarded flesh lay on the grass a hundred feet beneath the platform.

So we came to the great pit that the Martians had built at the top of Primrose Hill. This, the largest of all, had become the centre of their operations against London. The earthworks covered the entire crest of the Hill, and ran down the far side. At the heart of them lay the projectile that had first landed here, but the fact that the pit had been subsequently enlarged and fortified was everywhere evident.

Here was the Martians' arsenal. Here had been brought their battle-machines, and the spiderlike handling-machines. And here, scattered all about, were the bodies of the dead Martians. Some were sprawled in the mouth of the projectile, some simply lay on the ground. Others, in a last valiant effort to confront the invisible foe, were inside the many battle-machines that stood all about.

Mr Wells landed the Space Machine a short distance away from the pit, and turned off the attenuation. He had landed up-wind of the pit, so we were spared the worst effects of the terrible stench that emanated from the creatures.

With the attenuation off we could once more hear the cry of the dying Martian. It came from one of the battle-machines standing beside the pit. The cry was faltering now, and very weak. We saw that the crows were in attendance, and even as we stepped out of the Space Machine the last call of pain was stilled.

"Mr Wells," I said. "It is just as you were saying. The Martians seemed to have been afflicted with some disease, from drinking the red blood of Englishmen!"

I realized that Mr Wells was paying no attention either to me or Amelia, and that he was staring out across London, seeing the immense stillness of the city with tear-filled eyes. We stood beside him, overwhelmed by the sight of the abandoned city, and still nervous of the alien towers that stood around us.

Mr Wells mopped his eyes with his kerchief, then wandered away from us towards the Martian whose call we had heard.

Amelia and I stood by our Space Machine, and watched him as he carefully skirted the rim of the pit, then stood beneath the battle-machine, staring up at the glittering engine above. I saw him fumble in a pocket, and produce the leather-bound notebook he had been using in the laboratory. He wrote something inside this, then returned it to his pocket.

He was by the battle-machine for several minutes, but at last he returned to us. He seemed to have recovered from his moment of emotion, and walked briskly and directly towards us.

"There is something I have never said to you before," he said, addressing us both. "I believe you saved my life, the day you found me by the river with the curate. I have never thanked you enough."

I said: "You built the Space Machine, Mr Wells. Nothing that we have accomplished would have been possible without that."

He dismissed this remark with a wave of his hand.

"Miss Fitzgibbon," he said. "Will you excuse me if I leave on my own?"

"You are not going, Mr Wells?"

"I have much to do. We will meet again, never fear. I shall call on you at Richmond at the earliest opportunity."

"But sir," I said. "Where are you going?"

"I think I must find my way to Leatherhead, Mr Turnbull. I was on a journey to find my wife when you met me, and now I must complete that journey. Whether she is dead or alive is something that is only my concern."

"But we could take you to Leatherhead in the Space Machine," said Amelia.

"There will be no need for that. I can find my way."

He extended his hand to me, and I took it uncertainly. Mr Wells's grip was firm, but I did not understand why he should leave us so unexpectedly. When he released my hand he turned to Amelia, and she embraced him warmly.

He nodded to me, then turned away and walked down the side of the Hill.

Somewhere behind us there came a sudden sound: it was a high-pitched shrieking, not at all unlike the Martians' sirens. I jumped in alarm, and looked all about me . . . but there was no movement from any of the Martian devices. Amelia, standing beside me, had also reacted to the sound, but her attention was taken up with Mr Wells's actions.

The gentleman in question had gone no more than a few yards, and, disregarding the shriek, was looking through the notebook. I saw him take two or three of the pages, then rip them out. He screwed them up in his hand, and tossed them amongst the debris of the Martians' presence. He glanced back at us, and saw we were both watching him.

After a moment he climbed back to where we stood.

"There's just one other thing, Turnbull," he said. "I have treated the account of your adventures on Mars with great seriousness, improbable as your story sometimes seemed."

"But Mr Wells—"

He raised his hand to silence me. "It would not be right to dismiss your account as total fabrication, but you would be hard put to substantiate what you told me."

I was astounded to hear my friend say such things! His implication was no less than that Amelia and I were not telling the truth! I stepped forward angrily . . . but then I felt a gentle touch on my arm.

I looked at Amelia, and saw that she was smiling.

"Edward, there is no need for this," she said.

I saw that Mr Wells was smiling too, and that there was something of a gleam in his eye.

"We all have our tales to tell, Mr Turnbull," he said. "Good day to you."

With that, he turned away and strode determinedly down the Hill, replacing the notebook in his breast-pocket.

"Mr Wells is behaving very strangely," I said. "He has come with us to this cataclysm, when suddenly he abandons us just when we most need him. Now he is casting doubt on—"

I was interrupted by a repetition of the shrieking sound we had heard a minute or so earlier. It was much closer now, and both Amelia and I realized simultaneously what it was.

We turned and stared down the Hill, towards the north-eastern side, where the railway-line runs towards Euston. A moment later we saw the train moving slowly over the rusting lines, throwing up huge white clouds of steam. The driver blew the whistle for the third time, and the shriek reverberated around the whole city below. As if in answer there came a second sound. A bell began to toll in a church by St John's Wood. Startled, the crows left their macabre pickings and flapped noisily into the sky.

Amelia and I leapt up and down at the crest of Primrose Hill, waving our kerchiefs to the passengers. As the train moved slowly out of sight, I took Amelia into my arms. I kissed her passionately, and, with a joyous sense of reawakening hope, we sat down on the bedstead to wait for the first people to arrive.

THE END

A DREAM OF WESSEX

To Martin Walker

"May you live through interesting times."

Ancient Chinese curse

□□□□□□ The Tartan Army had planted a bomb at Heathrow,
    I   and Julia Stretton, who had gone the long way round
         past the airport to avoid the usual congestion on the
         approach-roads to the M3, had been delayed for two
hours by police and army checkpoints. By the time she joined
the motorway further down she was so late that she was able
to put thoughts of Paul Mason out of her mind, and concentrate
on her driving. She drove quickly for an hour, breaking the speed-
limit all the way and not particularly concerned should one of
the police helicopters spot her.

She left the motorway near Basingstoke, and drove steadily
down the main road towards Salisbury. The plain was grey and
misty, with low clouds softening the lines of the higher mounds.
It had been a cool, wet summer in Britain, or so everyone told
her, and now in July there had been reports of snow-flurries
along the Yorkshire coast, and flooding in parts of Cornwall. It
all seemed remote from her own life, and she had registered only
mild surprise when on complaining of the cold a few days earlier
she had been reminded of the time of year.

A few miles beyond Salisbury, on the road to Blandford Forum,
Julia stopped at a roadside café for a cup of coffee, and as she
sat at the plastic-topped table she had time at last for reflection.

It had been the surprise of seeing Paul Mason that had probably upset her more than anything else; that, and the way it had
happened, and the place.

Wessex House in High Holborn was a dark, gloomy place at
weekends, and she had been there only because she had been
instructed to. One of the trustees of the Wessex Foundation, a
dry, acerbic lawyer named Bonner, had called her in to see him
before she returned to Dorchester from leave. The urgent sum-
mons had turned out to be about a minor, irritating matter, and
when she left his office in a mood of suppressed anger, and was
walking down to the car-park, she met Paul Mason.

Paul at Wessex House: it was like the breach of a sanctuary.
Paul an intruder from her past life; Paul who had almost destroyed her once; Paul whom she had left behind her six years
before.

Sitting in the roadside café, Julia stirred her coffee with the
plastic spoon, slopping some of the pale brown liquid into the
saucer. She was still angry. She had never wanted to see Paul
again, and she was reacting as if he had deliberately followed and

A*

waylaid her. He had sounded as surprised to see her as she was to see him, and if he had faked it he was faking well. "Julia! What are you doing here! You look well." Well enough, Paul. He was still the same Paul, hard-featured but plausible, more debonair now, perhaps, than the egocentric student he had been when she fell for him during their last year at Durham. They'd lived together in London after that, while Paul built his career and she squandered three years of higher education in a succession of secretarial jobs. Then at last the break-up, and the freedom from him, and the lingering, paradoxical dependence on him she'd felt. All in the past, until yesterday.

She glanced at her wristwatch; she was still late, and all the hurrying on the road had made up no time. She had been in touch with Dr Eliot at Maiden Castle before the weekend, and she had told him she would be in Dorchester by lunchtime. But it was already past two-thirty. Julia wondered if she ought to telephone again, and warn Eliot and his staff, but she looked around the interior of the café and couldn't see a pay-phone. It didn't matter; if she was delaying them, they would have to wait. Someone would ring Wessex House, and find out she was on her way.

Such indifference to the administration of the Wessex project was not like her. She had Paul to thank for that. She was still marvelling to herself at the way he had the ability to invade her life. He'd always done it, of course; while they were living together he had treated her as he would treat one of his arms, as an unquestioning, uninteresting, but useful part of himself.

But now, six years after she had last seen him, she was furious with herself for letting him do it again.

It was this anger at herself that had started the row yesterday. She stared blankly at the dirty table-top, seeing Paul's face again, his eyes narrowed with cold indifference to her independence; she could hear again his calm but provocative words, subtly insinuating her reliance on him. Playing the truth game she had called it in the old days, the destructive days of that last lacerating year with him. He had a way of playing on secrets she had once confided to him, then turning them against her to expose her weaknesses and to get his own way. Yesterday he'd done it again, and the old truths still held; the old secrets still betrayed her. He didn't get it all his own way, though: the inevitable sexual pass had been made, and she passed it straight back, as cold with her body as he was with his eyes. It was her only moment of triumph, and it was one that made her feel sordid; another strike for Paul.

The coffee, like the recollection, left a bitter taste in the mouth. She was still thirsty, but decided against having a second cup. She went to the loo, then returned to the car.

It had started to rain while she was in the café, so Julia ran the engine and turned on the heater. The weekend encounter with Paul was still foremost in her mind, and some rebellious quirk made her disinclined to drive on, the irritation transferred illogically from Paul to her job. She sat and watched the rain run bright channels down the windscreen.

She still hadn't found out what Paul had been doing at Wessex House at all, let alone on a Sunday. The only explanation could be that he had taken a job there, was working for the trustees. The thought induced a quiet panic in her; when she had started to work for the Foundation four years ago, she hadn't been able to shake off the notion that it was a refuge from Paul, and even today, deeply involved in her work as she was, she couldn't rid herself of this residual motive. But Paul had found her there, by accident or design. She could ask Dr Eliot if he knew anything about it . . . he needn't be told why she wanted to know.

It was a relief to return to Dorchester, because Paul, even if he was working for the Foundation, could not follow her. No one could follow, and like a genuine sanctuary it was impregnable and timeless.

She drove on then, still annoyed with herself for letting Paul disrupt her life again.

Three miles before she reached the town of Blandford Forum, Julia was waved down by an army checkpoint, and she drew in behind a line of three other cars. Passing through these checkpoints was normally a matter of routine – she carried a government pass, and her car was listed as a regular user of this road – but even so she was detained for ten minutes.

This remote area of Dorset seemed an unlikely place for acts of terrorism to happen, even though there were army-bases all over Salisbury Plain, and Blandford Camp itself was only half a mile fom here. Julia stood in the rain, leaning against the side of the car under the dripping trees, realizing that guerrilla violence was now a usual, almost expected, part of everyday life in the big cities, but that the countryside continued to feel immune from the troubles. However many targets there were around

3

here, a bomb explosion in Dorset would be an extraordinary event.

She felt cold and restless. Two soldiers came to inspect her documents and car, and they searched the passenger-compartment and boot. An officer watched them, watched her. Julia thought how young they all seemed.

Later, when she and her car had been cleared, and she was driving on towards Dorchester, she thought about David Harkman. He was believed by some of the Wessex participants to be a soldier now, but it was just a theory, as good as any other. No one knew where he was, nor what he was doing, and in the weeks ahead it would be Julia's responsibility to find him. During her week's leave she had spent some time in London talking to Harkman's former wife, hoping to gain some extra insight into his personality; it had been a dispiriting meeting, though, with his ex-wife still suppressing resentments, seven years after their divorce.

The character profile was her only hope of finding him. A lecturer in social history, David Harkman had been at the London School of Economics before joining the Wessex project. His colleagues at the L.S.E. had spoken of him as an assertive man, stable and authoritative, but not ambitious. Julia would agree with the judgment of assertiveness; during the time the Wessex project was being set up, Harkman had often been stubborn, pressing his own ideas and opinions in the face of others. She had not much liked him, and now she found it ironical – after her disastrous meeting with Paul – that she should be the one chosen to look for him. She was escaping from one man she detested, to seek another she did not care for.

Even so, she was not discontented. She was glad to be getting back to work.

She drove through Blandford Forum and took the Dorchester road. As soon as the car had breasted the first rise after the river the rain stopped. Looking ahead as she drove, she saw the sky was brighter, but low clouds moved quickly from the south-west. It was Dorset weather: windy, wet, changeable.

She was tired from the long journey, and not in the best condition to start work. Even more unsuited, perhaps, was her state of mind; she needed to be calm and single-minded and receptive, and instead she was fretting about Paul. As she drove quickly through Dorchester, and took the road towards the south, Julia wondered again about what he wanted. She sensed an urge in

4

him to destroy – for that, after all, was what he had done to her ever since she had known him – and she wished she knew more about what was going on. Why hadn't she asked him while she had the chance?

The gate to the car-park of Maiden Castle was closed, and she blew the horn until Mr Wentworth appeared. He came out of his wooden hut, smiling when he recognized the car.

When she had driven through the gate, and parked the car, she climbed out and waited for him as he walked towards her.

"Only a week off this time, Miss Stretton?" he said.

"It was all I needed," she said. "Look, Mr Wentworth, I didn't have time to go to Bincombe House. Do you think you could have these delivered to my room?"

She gave him her suitcase of clothes, and a holdall containing several books. This had been her fourth period of leave since the project began, and as she found on the other three occasions, the return to London had destroyed her concentration. She intended spending her next leave in Dorset; Bincombe House was large and comfortable, and she had a room of her own there. At Bincombe one could always see other members of the project, and so help to maintain a continuity of purpose between spells inside the projector.

"Will the car be O.K. here?" She glanced over the long line of cars, parked in three ranks, close to each other. Several of them were dirty; one of Mr Wentworth's tasks was to wash the cars from time to time, but he only did it under protest.

"You leave it there, Miss. I'll get it out of the way if someone wants to move."

She gave him the ignition-key, and he took a paper tag from his pocket and tied it to it. Julia leaned over, and looked towards the far end of the car-park. David Harkman's yellow Rover 2000 was still there, as it had been for two years, unclaimed by its owner.

"Has anyone been asking for me?" Julia said.

"Well, Dr Trowbridge rang down earlier."

"Yes?"

"He said to send you to see Dr Eliot as soon as you arrived."

She turned away from him, casting her eyes towards the ground. Julia had a minor superstition, that persisted from childhood, that if she looked at anyone thinking that it was the last time she would see him – and thus hold a mental photograph – then it would come to be so. It was always there, as she went

5

back to the Castle, this feeling of finality, the danger of never returning. As she started to climb the grassy slope of the lowest and nearest rampart of the Castle, Julia looked back in Mr Wentworth's general direction, trying to see him with her peripheral vision, so that she would have no clear memory of how he appeared on her last sight of him. This sideways look that Julia gave people as she left them was something of which she was acutely conscious. Paul used to call it her shifty look, but he was the last person she would ever have tried to explain it to.

She came to the top of the first of the earth ramparts that surrounded the ancient hill-fort. On this northerly side of Maiden Castle there were three of these, each one higher and steeper than the one before it, and there was no other way in to the Castle than to climb each one. A well-worn path took the easiest route and she followed this, her hair blowing across her face in the stiff wind. She was cold now, her thin city clothes pressed against her body, her skirt whipping in the wind. As she walked down into the lee of the second earth ridge the wind let her alone, and she swept back her hair and laughed. The Castle often engendered an elemental unconcern in those who found it, whether they were casual visitors – who were still allowed access to certain parts – or the staff of the Wessex project. The Castle was ancient and solid, and permanent; its grass-covered shoulders had shrugged off decay for five thousand years, and it would still be here in five thousand years' time. Julia felt this sense of abandonment whenever she arrived at the Castle from London, and today was no different. By the time she had reached the top of the second ridge she was running, gasping in the cold wind, and she left the path and skipped over the tufty grass.

From here she could see down into the dip between the second and third ramparts, where the entrance to the underground workings lay. No one could be seen there. Although Mr Wentworth had probably telephoned the word of her arrival to Trowbridge or Eliot, she had a few minutes to spare.

She put down her briefcase and looked about. The sky, the wind, the grass. Two or three seagulls, soaring above her in the wind-waves thrown up by the humps of the Castle; they were a long way from the sea, but gulls were common inland birds these days.

The city of Dorchester lay below her and to the left, spreading out untidily across the side of its hill. She could see the wireless-telegraphy station on the heath behind it, and traffic moving on the roads around the town. A train stood at a signal just outside the station. Beyond, the soft rolling Dorset hills around Cerne Abbas and Charminster and Tolpuddle. She stared at the view for some time, drawn to it by the images and memories she had of another time, another summer. . . .

It was not far to the view across to the east, so Julia picked up her briefcase and strode out along the edge of the ridge, looking ahead. Soon she reached the place where the ramparts circled round to the south, and from here the view across the Frome Valley was uninterrupted. It was flat and windswept, the river meandering across its floor, flowing slowly towards the mud-flats of Wareham, and Poole Harbour beyond. This was Hardy country, Egdon Heath and Anglebury, Casterbridge and Bud-mouth . . . she hadn't read the books since school. From this position it was difficult to see why so many people liked the Dorset scenery, because it seemed grey and flat and dull. Only to her right was there a green rise of land; the downs leading to the Purbeck Hills beyond, far to the east, hiding the sea.

Time was pressing; she had taken too long already. The wind had chilled her. Clouds, looming up in the south-west, threatened another shower.

Julia walked back, scrambling down into the lee of the third ridge, looking for the entrance to the workings.

□□□□□□ In the third century BC, the inhabitants of Maiden
2   Castle had fortified their hilltop home by the building of wood and earth ramparts that entirely circled the two knolls on which the settlement had been made. Never a castle in the commonly understood sense, the ramparts had enclosed farming-land and a village, to which most of the inhabitants of ancient Wessex fled whenever hostile tribes in-vaded the region. In the twentieth century, by which time the earth walls had weathered to rounded, grassy slopes, such de-fences seemed inadequate, for they could be penetrated in a few minutes by even the most unambitious walker, but in pre-Roman Britain the ramparts and their closely defended gates were pre-caution enough against sling-shots and spears.

The site had been thoroughly excavated during the 1930s. Remains similar to those found in hill-forts all over southern

7

England had been discovered, and the more interesting fragments placed on display in the Dorchester Museum. There had been a massacre of the villagers by Vespasian's legions in AD 43, and the most singular discovery in Maiden Castle was that of a primitive mass burial-ground, containing thousands of human bodies.

The archaeological workings had been covered before the Second World War, and from then until the early 1980s Maiden Castle had reverted to a former rôle: agricultural and pastoral land, walked over by casual visitor and sheep.

Maiden Castle had been selected as the site for the Wessex project for various reasons. It was partly because of its proximity to Dorchester, and road and rail connections to London, partly because of its height of 132 metres above sea-level, partly because of its commanding view across the Frome Valley, but especially because the Castle, of all the man-made constructions in the region, was the one most assured of permanence.

Julia Stretton had not visited the Castle while the underground laboratories were being tunnelled and equipped, and she had only a dim childhood memory of visiting the place with her parents, but she assumed that after the construction crews had left, and the surface had been tidied up, the outward appearance of the Castle had not been much changed. The car-park had been enlarged, and there was the entrance to the laboratories, but as far as possible the outside was untouched. The Duchy of Cornwall, the owners of the Castle, had insisted on that.

In the entrance to the laboratory – the only part open to the public – several glass cases held a selection of fragments unearthed during the tunnelling. The ancient Wessexmen buried tributes with their dead, and many cups and trinkets and pots had been found, as well as the inevitable macabre selection of bones. One almost complete skeleton was on show, the neckbones neatly labelled where they had been shattered by a Roman arrow-head. A security-guard sat at a desk beside the case containing the skeleton, and as Julia passed him, holding out her identity-card, he nodded to her.

The elevator used by the medical teams was open, but Julia used the flight of concrete steps that went down around it. At the bottom, she walked along the main corridor, passing the rows of steel, white-painted lockers, and the many numbered doors.

She stopped at one room, knocked, then opened the door. As

8

she had hoped, Marilyn James, one of the physiotherapists on the project, was there.

"Hello, Marilyn. I'm looking for John Eliot."

"He's been looking for you. I think he's in the conference room."

"I'm late. I was stuck in traffic."

"I don't think it matters," Marilyn said. "We were just a bit worried in case there had been an accident. Did you have a good holiday?"

"So-so," Julia said, thinking of Paul, thinking of the bitterness of the night before. "It wasn't long enough to enjoy myself."

It was cold in the tunnel, although it was supposed to be heated. Julia walked on, thinking about Paul again.

The conference room was at the very end of the main corridor, and Julia went straight in. Dr Eliot was here, sitting back in one of the armchairs, and reading a typewritten report. At the far end of the room, where the coffee-machine was, a group of five of the technicians sat at a table playing cards.

"Have I kept you waiting?" she said to Eliot.

"Come and sit down, Julia. Have you eaten today?"

"A slice of toast for breakfast," she said. "And I had a cup of coffee on the way down."

"Nothing more? Good."

Since the death of Carl Ridpath eighteen months before, John Eliot had been in charge of all projector functions at the Castle. He and Ridpath had worked in associated fields of neurhypnological research for several years, and it was partly as a result of a paper about neural conduction Eliot had published some fifteen years before that Ridpath developed his equipment. The fact that the neurhypnological projector bore Ridpath's name gave no indication of the debt he owed Eliot, one which he repeatedly affirmed in his lifetime, and yet it was as the "Ridpath projector" that the equipment was now known, not only by those sections of the media which took an interest in such matters, but by the participants too.

During Ridpath's last illness Eliot had taken over the running of the project as if it had been his all along. Unlike Ridpath, though, who until the appearance of the cancer had enjoyed excellent health, Eliot suffered from a recurrent heart-murmur, and had never himself entered a projection, even for experimental purposes. He sometimes spoke to the participants about this, not enviously, but regretfully.

9

Now as Julia sat down beside him, he handed her a small pile of reports, including the one of her own she had filed a week before.

She settled down to concentrate on them, forcing thoughts of her private life out of her mind. This reading of reports was one of the more irksome duties to which she had to attend, but also one of the most crucial.

After this she asked for, and was granted, some time to herself, and she went to one of the private cubicles to study the file she had been compiling on David Harkman. The conversation with his ex-wife hadn't seemed to yield much at the time, but she went through the notes again, looking for anything that might add insights into his personality, however remotely.

Eliot came to the cubicle.

"This was sent down from Bincombe," he said to her, and gave her an envelope. "It arrived on Saturday."

Julia glanced at the handwriting. "Should I read it now?"

"It's up to you, of course. Do you know who it's from?"

"I don't think so." But there was an old familiarity to it, an unpleasant association. "Leave it here. I'll read it later."

When Eliot had gone, she picked up the envelope and slit it hurriedly. She knew the handwriting: it was Paul Mason's.

Inside was a single sheet of paper, folded in half. She held it without opening it, logic struggling with curiosity.

She knew that concentration on her work was essential in the next hour, and that distraction would only hamper this. To read any kind of personal letter shortly before rejoining the projection was unwise, and one from Paul, who, with such unerring skill, could throw up so much emotional static in her, was especially risky. On the other hand, during yesterday's unpleasant scene with him she had not found out what was his connection with the Wessex project, and she was anxious to know. The letter, obviously written before the weekend, might have the answer.

At last she decided to read it, realizing that if she didn't the continuing curiosity would be as much a distraction as anything the letter might contain. As a compromise with herself, she resolved to practise the rote mnemonics afterwards, like an errant nun imposing twelve Hail Marys on herself.

The letter was short, and, to anyone not herself, apparently harmless. As soon as she had read it Julia put aside her file and went to take a shower.

10

Dear Julia,

I suppose you'll be as surprised to read this as I was to discover that our paths have crossed once more. I've been wondering what you've been up to recently, and how you've been keeping. Well, now I know. I'm hoping to come down to visit Maiden Castle soon, so I hope you can get an evening off to have dinner with me. I'm still very fond of you, and would like to see you again. I'm sure we will have a lot to say to each other.

Paul

Julia soaped herself angrily in the shower. Paul's knack for touching on old wounds was amazing. "Now I know" . . . how much did he know? Why should he want to? Written by anyone else it was a mild platitude; written by Paul it reawakened all the paranoia of old. "I'm sure we will have a lot to say to each other"; he'd written that before the weekend, before they discovered that what they had to say to each other was like the leftovers from a meal gone cold six years before, spiced up with many an afterthought.

And he had always been *fond* of her, like a possessive child is fond of a tormented puppy; he'd never used the word "love", not once. Not even when they were closest. Not even to sign off a letter.

She left the shower, and dried herself, then sat naked on the edge of the wooden chair in the cubicle. She closed her eyes, and determinedly recited the mnemonics to herself, fulfilling the terms of her own compromise. This late in the projection, the mnemonics had lost much of their earlier use, but they still had the function of concentrating the mind.

Ideally, the minds of the participants should be as uncluttered with personal thoughts as was humanly possible. Personal identity continued, of course, on an unconscious level, but the maximum projective effect was achieved when the conscious mind was directed along the chosen course. In this case, Julia's main function was to establish contact with David Harkman, and the better she concentrated on that now the better the chance later of making that contact.

She glanced over her file on Harkman once again, then put on the simple surgical gown that had been left in the cubicle for her use. She folded up the rest of her clothes, and scribbled a note asking one of the staff to take them up to her room at Bincombe House.

Dr Eliot was waiting for her in the conference room.

"Don't forget to sign the release," he said, pushing a printed form across to her. Julia signed it without reading it, knowing it was the standard permission form, allowing Eliot to hypnotize her and place her body inside the Ridpath.

"I'd like to see Harkman," she said.

"We thought so. He's ready."

She followed Eliot into the large, brightly lit room that the participants called, with conscious irony, the mortuary. It was more properly known as the projection hall, for it was here that the thirty-nine cabinets of the Ridpath projector were placed. In spite of the many electric lights beamed down on to the cabinets – necessary illumination for the constant medical attention the participants required – the hall was always cold, because it was air-conditioned by a refrigerant system, so that the effect of working by the cabinets was akin to sunbathing in an Arctic breeze. As Dr Eliot and one of the technicians slid Harkman's body out on the drawer of the cabinet, Julia wrapped her arms about her body, shivering.

Harkman lay as if dead. His body had been placed full-length along the surface of the drawer, with his head inwards. He was lying face-up, with his head and shoulders resting on the moulded supports so that his neck and spine made contact with the neural sensors implanted in the drawer. Seeing this, Julia felt a twinge of sympathetic pain in her own back, knowing the burning sensation she felt whenever she was taken from the projector.

Harkman had been inside the machine for almost two years without a break, and in that time his body had grown soft and flabby, in spite of the constant physiotherapy he received. His face was pale and waxen, as if embalmed, and his hair had grown long.

Julia stared impassively, watching his facial muscles twitch occasionally, and his hands, folded across his chest, tremble as if about to grasp at something. Beneath his lids, his eyes flickered like those of a man dreaming.

He *was* dreaming in a sense: a dream that had lasted nearly two years so far, a dream of a distant time and a strange society.

Dr Trowbridge, who was Eliot's chief assistant, came over to them from where he had been working at the far end of the hall.

"Is there anything wrong, Dr Eliot?"

"No . . . Miss Stretton is familiarizing herself with Harkman's appearance."

12

Trowbridge looked down at the face of the man in the drawer. "Would photographs not give a more accurate impression? Harkman has put on so much weight."

Julia said, still staring at the unconscious man: "I suppose he could have wilfully changed his appearance."

"Have any of the others?" Eliot said.

"Not as far as I know."

"It's not consistent with his profile," Eliot said. "Everything we know about him underlines an inherent stability. There are no lapses. Harkman's personality is ideal for projection."

"Perhaps too ideal," Julia said, remembering his forceful arguments. She looked intently at the pale face, trying to imprint it on her memory, at the same time remembering how he had talked and acted before the projection began. This body was too like a dummy to imagine it alive and thinking. She said: "I wonder if he was repressing some resentment against the others? Perhaps he felt we were somehow intruding, and on projecting he willed himself away from the rest of us."

"It still isn't likely," Eliot said. "There's nothing in his pre-projection notes to indicate that. It has to be a case of unconscious programming. We've had several minor cases of that."

"And one major one, perhaps," Julia said. She nodded to Trowbridge and the technician. "You can put him back. I think I'm ready."

They slid the drawer, and it closed with a sound of heavy, cushioned metal.

Eliot said to Trowbridge: "I think we should cut back on his intra-venous feeding. I'll talk to you later."

He took Julia's arm, and they went back through the side-tunnel to his surgery. As she followed him into the room, and he closed the door behind her, Julia thought momentarily of Paul. She remembered the row, and his letter, but she thought of them as unpleasant incidents in her experience, not as intrusions into her life. She felt a certain satisfaction that she had the strength at last to file him away into a cubby-hole of her conscious mind.

She went to sit in the deep chair in front of Eliot's littered desk, ready to accept his will.

Later, as she listened to Eliot speak to her of the Wessex projection, she wanted to look away, to see him with her peripheral vision, but she was unable to. Sitting before her, Eliot spoke calmly, repetitively, quietly, and soon she fell into a trance.

☐☐☐☐☐☐ It was late afternoon in Dorchester, and the open-air
cafés along Marine Boulevard were enjoying a busy
trade as the tourists returned from the beaches. Inside
the harbour, the whole extent of which could be seen
by the people strolling along the Boulevard, the private yachts
were marooned on the pebbles and mud of low tide, held upright
by ropes and pontoons. A few men and women from the hired
crews were on some of the boats, but most of the owners and
their guests were ashore. When the tide was in, the private section of the harbour was a bustle of yachts coming and going,
with visitors sitting on the decks enjoying the view and the sunshine, but for the moment those visitors still aboard their boats
were concealed from public gaze beneath their gaily coloured
canopies and festoons.

Outside the harbour, a small fleet of fishing boats was waiting
for the tide.

Along the walls and quays that surrounded the harbour, and
for the length of Marine Boulevard, hundreds of people milled
about with an air of pleasurable languor. Beggar-musicians moved
amongst them, collecting-bags swinging from the necks of their
guitars, and along the part of the Boulevard overlooking the
harbour were the licensed stalls and entertainers, the book and
magazine stands, Sekker's Bar, and the store where tide-skimmers could be bought or hired and where the fashionable were
always to be seen. It was in this part of town, at this time of
day, that the visitors gathered.

The building of the English Regional Commission was situated
in one of the sidestreets leading into Marine Boulevard, and it
was from this that Donald Mander and Frederick Cro emerged.
They walked slowly through the crowd towards the harbour,
Cro still wearing his jacket, but Mander carrying his over his
arm.

They walked as far as the end of the quay, where they stopped
to buy two *citrons pressés* at the soft-drinks bar.

From this position it became possible to see under the canopy
of one of the yachts, and there, otherwise invisible from the
harbour walls, were two young men and a woman. Although the
men were dressed in beach-shorts and shirts, the young woman
was naked. She sat quietly in a canvas chair, flipping through a
magazine.

The Commission men both noticed her at the same time, but
neither of them remarked on her. They were habitually guarded

14

in what they said to each other, and by nature discreet with their reactions. Both men were bachelors in their fifties, and although they had worked in adjacent offices at the Regional Commission for more than twenty years they were still not on first-name terms.

When they had finished their drinks they walked slowly back down the quay.

Mander pointed towards the waiting fishing boats, most of which were grouped together in the deeper water about fifty metres from the harbour entrance. Several of the boats were lying low in the water, while their crews sat lazily in the warm sunlight on deck.

"There's been a good catch," Mander said.

Cro nodded, and Mander smiled to himself. He knew that the other man detested sea-food, and rarely ate in the local restaurants. One of the few facts Mander knew about Cro was that he lived on parcels of provisions, sent over by his parents, who were still alive and lived in relative affluence on the English mainland.

On the far side of the harbour, where the commercial work of the port was done, a steam crane emitted a loud hissing noise accompanied by a white jet of vapour. In a moment it trundled slowly along its rails to the regular berth of the hydrofoil service from the mainland. The boat was late this evening, and the carts of several tradesmen from the town stood waiting by.

Beyond, the bay was calm and blue.

The two men left the quay and walked into the crowd on Marine Boulevard, heading for Sekker's Bar. They looked out of place in this leisurely part of town, more for their watchful manner than their clothes. The tourists stared as they sauntered in the warm air, caring only to notice and be noticed; Mander and Cro, though, glanced uneasily about them, minor public servants constantly on watch for minor details.

As they came near to the multi-coloured umbrellas over the tables of Sekker's Bar, Cro pointed towards one of the stalls of merchandise.

"The people from Maiden Castle," he said. "They're still here. I thought you were going to check their licence."

"I did. There's nothing irregular."

"Then it must be revoked. How did they get hold of one?"

"In the usual way," Mander said. "It was bought in the office."

"We could find an ideological objection. . . ."

15

Mander shook his head, but not so the other would see. "It's never as easy as that."

The stall Cro had indicated would have seemed innocuous enough to eyes less instantly hostile. It was no larger than any of the others, and constructed along the same lines. Even the goods on offer were similar, at first sight, to those peddled from stalls all along the Boulevard. The wooden surface of the counter had been covered with a green woollen cloth, and spread out across this was a selection of hand-crafted goods: wooden bowls and candlesticks, ornamented chess-sets, brooches and armbands set with polished semi-precious stones, unglazed pottery; each item seemed well made and substantial, but with an appealing roughness to the finish that served only to emphasize the essential craft.

In this way the goods differed from those offered at the other stalls, for they sold inexpensive but uniform wares, mass-produced in cooperatives on the mainland. This individual quality was not lost on the tourists, for the stall was attracting more customers than most of the others.

Cro glanced disparagingly at the goods, and at the people selling them.

There were two women and a man behind the simple counter. One of the women sat upright on a stool at the back, but she was at ease and with her eyes closed. She wore the clothes that the Commission men had immediately recognized, the plain, dull-brown hand woven garments that were worn by the entire community at Maiden Castle. The man and the other woman were both younger, although the man – who was thin and pale, and had prematurely balding hair – was moving slowly, as if tired.

Mander and Cro lingered by the stall for a few moments, and although the young woman serving noticed their approach she gave no sign of recognition. Mander, who had often remarked to himself on her pretty face and attractive figure, was hoping she might look his way again so that he could give her a secret reassuring smile, but she seemed determined to ignore them.

At last they walked on, and went up the steps to the patio of Sekker's Bar.

As they sat down at a vacant table, a distant explosion sounded across the bay, echoing from Purbeck Island in the south. This was the cannon mounted above Blandford Passage, which was fired twice a day to warn shipping and swimmers of

16

the flood tide. At this hour of the day few people would be swimming, and apart from the fishing boats outside the harbour there were only one or two private yachts in sight. As usual, many people moved to the sea wall at the sound of the cannon, for a first sight of the tidal bore, but it would not be visible for several more minutes.

Cro said: "How much do you know about the new man?"

"Harkman? As much as you."

"I thought he'd been appointed to your department."

Mander shook his head, but vaguely; an evasion, not a denial. "He's working on some kind of research."

"Is he English?"

"No, British. His mother defected from Scotland." Mander looked across the Boulevard, and out to sea. "I gather he's visited the States."

Cro nodded as if he knew this already, but said: "West or East?"

"Both, so far as I know. Look, I think that must be Nadja Morovin."

A man and a young woman were strolling past Sekker's, arm in arm. The woman whom Mander had indicated, wore a wide-brimmed hat low over her face, but her sleeves were rolled up and her skirt was short, provocatively revealing the pallor of her plump limbs. The glamorous couple were affecting not to notice the fact that she was instantly recognizable, and as they walked slowly through the crowd they seemed not to realize that the people approaching them were stepping unobtrusively to one side. Behind them, people stared openly, and a short way away a young man – apparently a tourist from the States – was taking one photograph after another, using a powerful telephoto lens.

A few moments later, Mander and Cro lost sight of them as they went into the tide-skimmer shop.

"Isn't that the hydrofoil?" Mander said.

Cro looked out to sea again, then stood up for a better view, even though the patio at Sekker's gave one of the best panoramas in town. Several hundred people were now standing by the sea wall, waiting to see the tidal bore as it burst through Blandford Passage. From this distance, more than thirty kilometres, only the white crest of the wave could be seen with the naked eye, but recent tides had been high and the telescope renters along the front had been illegally increasing their prices.

Mander was pointing to the south of the Passage. From that direction, skimming along past Lawrence Island, came the hydrofoil. On the deepening blue of the presently calm waters of the bay it was the only sign of movement.

"The tide will be through any minute now," Cro said. "Do you suppose the pilot realizes?"

"He'll know," Mander said.

A few seconds later, the people who had hired telescopes bent to their instruments, and the tidal wave appeared. Several of the tourists pointed seawards, pointing excitedly, and children were held aloft on the shoulders of their parents.

The waiter arrived to take their order, and Cro sat down.

"Is this . . . Mr Harkman on the hydrofoil?" he said, when two beers had been brought.

"I can't think why else it should be late," Mander said, watching the other man for his reaction.

"I heard he wasn't rated above Regional Adviser. Would the boat be held for you or me?"

"It would depend on the circumstances."

Well pleased with Cro's reaction, Mander sipped his beer. Earlier in the day he had heard that the low-water berth at Poundbury was going to be busy all day, obliging the hydrofoil to wait for the tide. He assumed Cro hadn't heard this, but decided against mentioning it because he liked Cro to have a few mysteries.

Cro took a mouthful of beer. He wiped his lips with his handkerchief, then stood up again.

Out in the bay the hydrofoil had slowed down, so that its hull had entered the water again. The boat had turned to face the flooding tide, and as Cro stepped down from Sekker's patio and crossed the Boulevard to the sea wall the first turbulence reached it. The boat yawed and pitched dramatically, but as soon as the first large waves were past it turned again towards Dorchester, and accelerated through the choppy water in the wake of the bore.

Still seated at the table, Mander looked at Cro with irritation. The arrival of any high-level appointee brought inevitable conflicts within the office, as the hierarchy unwillingly accommodated the newcomer, but Harkman's appointment to Dorchester threatened the recent smooth state of office politics as surely as the twice-daily tides disrupted the calm waters of the bay.

It was the vagueness of Harkman's position at the Regional

Commission that was the main problem. Mander had been told that Harkman was to be given access to whatever files or records he requested, and that Commissioner Borovitin's authorization would be channelled through his own office. As Mander's area of responsibility was Administration, this made sense, but he was still unsure of the nature of Harkman's intended research. Cro was displaying an unnatural amount of interest in the new man, so Mander suspected that he knew more than he was letting on. His questioning of Mander was probably less for his own information than to try to discover how much Mander knew.

Cro, a master at office manœuvring, would be delighted to have someone working in his own department who had relative freedom of movement, as he would be certain to find some way of benefiting from it.

"Do you want another beer?" Mander said, when the other man returned to the table.

Cro looked at his wristwatch. "I think we've time. The boat won't be in for another ten minutes."

Mander took this as an acceptance, and summoned the waiter.

In the bay, the flooding tidal wave from the north spread in a flattening semi-circle, the first turbulence subsiding. The rising tide still poured through Blandford Passage, and would continue to do so for another hour, but the initial violence of its arrival was past. In Dorchester Harbour the water-level, which all afternoon had risen only a metre or two, now came up quickly. The grounded pleasure-yachts lifted steadily, their hulls colliding gently with the supporting pontoons, and outside the harbour the waiting fishing boats started their engines and circled round, entering port one by one. By the time the last had tied up beside the fish-sheds the hydrofoil had arrived, and was nosing slowly towards its own berth. In the tourist part of the harbour not much had changed, except that those who idled on the decks were now in full view of those who strolled around the harbour; the commercial side of the port, by contrast, was bustling and noisy. Several of the boats had started to unload their cargoes of fish, and the tradesmen's carts and drays had moved forward to pick up the supplies brought from the mainland by the hydrofoil.

The horse-drawn Post Office van clattered through the crowds in Marine Boulevard, and turned down the ramp towards the hydrofoil berth.

Then Cro played a high card; perhaps it was a trump.

"I hear the man's an historian," he said. "Would that be so?"

"Possibly."

Cro's most recent bureaucratic acquisition was supervision of the Commission's archives; it had been his triumph of the year before. If Harkman was an historian, he would certainly be working with Cro as a consequence.

As Mander finished his beer and stood up, he could already imagine the petty power-struggles of the weeks ahead.

He and Cro walked slowly across the Boulevard, and went towards the commercial side of the port.

By the time the first two passengers – an elderly couple from the States – had stepped ashore from the hydrofoil, Mander and Cro were waiting beside the fish-sheds, with a clear view of the landing stage.

More tourists stepped down from the boat, helped ashore by the cabin stewards. Mander looked at each of them as they appeared, wondering what Harkman would look like. He was impressed in spite of himself, and irritated because of himself, by Cro's political advantage.

A figure dressed in a plain brown garment walked slowly past the two Commission men; it was the girl who had been serving at the craft stall, the girl from Maiden Castle. She stood a short distance in front of Cro and Mander, facing towards the hydrofoil.

Mander was distracted by her presence, as he always was when he happened to see her at the stall. From where he was waiting he could see her face in quarter-profile, and he could understand simultaneously why people like Cro thought of her and her community as a vague threat to the ordered existence of Soviet Wessex, and also why Cro and the others were wrong. At first glance the young woman seemed degenerate and wanton, giving off an aura of anarchy and irresponsibility: she had long, tousled hair, her dress was loose and immodest, and her legs and feet, clad in thin rope sandals, were dusty. But she also stood with poise and a certain elegance, her features were regular, and her eyes held a deep intelligence. In the same way, the other people from the Castle, who were occasionally seen about the town, behaved with a dignity and unobtrusiveness inconsistent with their primitive appearance, and the goods they sold were well made and distinctive.

Cro suddenly pointed towards someone who had just stepped down from the boat: "That's our man. That's Harkman."

"Are you sure?" Mander said, narrowing his eyes, but he knew

Cro was right. The man was quite unlike anyone else on the quay. All the other passengers on the hydrofoil were obviously tourists or tradesmen; the former looked around uncertainly, seeking transport into town or help with their baggage, the latter immediately blended with the bustle around them.

Harkman, though, stood at the edge of the quay and looked appraisingly across the harbour towards the town. He seemed genuinely interested in what he saw, shading his eyes with his hand. Then he turned, looking away from the harbour towards the south, where Maiden Castle stood on its promontory overlooking the bay. To Mander he appeared to be about forty years old, dark-haired and lean; his bearing was relaxed and athletic, not at all that of the bookish historian Mander had imagined from what little he had heard about the man. Unlike the tourists, Harkman was unencumbered with luggage, but had with him just a small bag which was slung casually across his shoulders.

"He's not as young as I thought," Cro said, eventually. "The photo on file must be an old one."

"Which photo?" Mander said, but Cro made no answer.

The girl from Maiden Castle was watching Harkman too. She was standing quite close to him, making no effort to disguise her interest. When he turned to walk along the quay towards the town he passed her and they glanced at each other momentarily. She moved away to where the dock labourers were unloading crates of beer from the hold of the ship, and sat down on a stone bollard, staring out into the bay.

As Harkman passed the two Commission men he seemed to recognize them as colleagues, for he nodded to them briefly, but made no move to introduce himself.

Cro and Mander waited on the quay for a few minutes, by which time Harkman had vanished into the crowd in Marine Boulevard. On the minaret of the mosque that had been built for the visitors, the muezzin was calling the devout to prayer.

□□□□□□ David Harkman breakfasted alone in the refectory of
4 the Commission hostel. He assumed that the other people he saw were also employees of the Commission, but he made no attempt to introduce himself, and instead suffered their curious stares with an indifference affected out of self-defence. Friends in London had warned him of the

21

protocol of the Regional Commissions, and that there would be a well-established order of precedence by which he would be introduced to his new colleagues. He had no intention of upsetting the balance of territorial claims within the office; his years at the Bureau of English Culture had made him wise in the ways of civil servants.

He cut short his uneasiness, and the curiosity of the others, by finishing his breakfast quickly, and with noncommittal nods to all in sight he left the hostel building and went for an exploratory stroll around the town.

It was a relief to be in Dorchester at last, after two years of waiting for the appointment to come through. Sometimes he had thought that Wessex Island was a part of the world as unreachable from London as the Presidential Palace in Riyadh. It wasn't that his security-rating was less than impeccable; he had, after all, been given the temporary posting to Baltimore in the Western Emirate States, and had advised the Cultural Attaché in Rome for one very unexpected week a few years ago. Much more likely was the inevitable grinding slowness of the Party administrative machine.

Not that Wessex was a place to which Party employees were freely transferred. With its mosques and casinos, and the thousands of idle-rich tourists from all over the States, Wessex Island was an area of some ideological embarrassment to the Party theorists.

Dorchester itself was the focus of this embarrassment for not only was it the nearest large town to the English mainland, but it was also the place to which most of the tourists came.

Only the fact that Wessex was physically distinct from the mainland made it acceptable to the Party; so long as travel was restricted in England, and permits to visit the international tourist zones of the island were granted only to foreign nationals and selected Party workers, the local inhabitants couldn't very well proclaim the evils of capitalism to the English populace at large. Or so the Party sophistry went; Harkman, like most people with a gram of intelligence or information, realized that the flood of Emirate dollars was a major contribution to the Westminster budget.

It was actually a concern for, and an interest in, the local population that had ostensibly brought Harkman to Wessex.

Ever since the catastrophic earthquakes and land subsidence

22

of the previous century, what had formerly been south-west England had been separated from the mainland by the narrow but deep channel that was known as Blandford Passage. Wessexmen had been left to fend for themselves for many decades, until the Westminster government had realized the potential of the island as a tourist resort, since when it had been administered and developed and taxed in the same way as the other regions of England.

Harkman's interest, as a social historian, was in what had happened in Wessex during the years of isolation. There were still people alive on the island who remembered those days, and there were records scattered about – mainly in Dorchester, Plymouth and Truro – relating to conditions at the time, and Harkman intended to compile an exhaustive and definitive documentary account. It would probably take him many years, and he was prepared to treat it as his life's work.

This was his ostensible reason for the move to Dorchester, and it was the one which had obtained him his permission. But in his heart he knew that it was not the sole motive.

There was Wessex itself. From the day that he had conceived of the project, Harkman had felt that there was some indefinable insufficiency in his life. It wasn't just that his work at the Bureau of English Culture was unsatisfying – although in many respects it was – nor that he felt a sense of inadequacy about his life in London; more directly, it was an instinctive knowledge that Wessex was a spiritual and emotional home.

It had started with something he'd read about the community at Maiden Castle; it had interested him, and in trying to discover more about it he had sensed a growing involvement with the Castle and the island on which it stood. He simply hadn't understood it, and the need to understand had compelled him with more force than anything the intellectual challenge of his social research could muster.

So as he had arrived in Dorchester the previous evening, he had not only seen that day as the first on which his life's work began, but also as the last on which he had awakened with the feeling of separation from a place that had dominated his thoughts and actions for two years.

Then too, almost incidentally, there was the fact of the tidal bore through Blandford Passage.

Many years before, as a young man, he had had the chance to sample the terrors and excitements of wave-riding. He had had

23

only three weeks in which to learn the elemental violence of the tidal wave, but it was a violence which, once experienced, always enthralled one.

Wave-riding was undeniably a young man's sport – and one for the rich – but over the years Harkman had kept himself in physical trim, and he'd been saving his wages all his life. He had the opportunity, the money and the will to ride the Blandford wave again, and he was determined that he wouldn't waste them.

It was a fine, bright morning in Dorchester, and Harkman relished the lightness and cleanness of the air, the decadence of the architecture, the narrowness of the streets. It was a town with a sunny hangover; the night-clubs and bars of Dorchester catered to the tastes of the visitors late into the night, and the shutters and louvred doors of the villas and apartment-blocks were closed against the freshness of the morning. Even so, there were many holidaymakers already about, strolling through the streets to do a little concessionary shopping before departing to one of the beaches outside town.

Impossible to believe that London was less than two hundred kilometres away!

When he reached the street where the Commission building was situated, Harkman made an instant decision and walked on past. He had an appointment to see Commissioner Borovitin, but there were still a few minutes in hand. He remembered having seen a skimmer-shop by the harbour when he landed the previous evening, and thought he would visit it.

He walked out of the narrow sidestreets into the bright sunlight of the Boulevard, and went down to the harbour. Here many yachts were moving in and out, for the tide was falling and in an hour or two it would be unnavigable. Harkman walked past the cafés and stalls on the Boulevard to the skimmer-shop, where, in a brightly coloured display, the various pieces of equipment needed for the sport were laid out.

Harkman looked first at the tide-skimmers themselves, of which several dozen were stacked under the awning outside the shop. These came in a variety of sizes and designs, and with a surprisingly wide range in prices. Harkman lifted one away from the stack, weighed it in his hands. He had forgotten how heavy a skimmer was, even unloaded! It seemed strong enough, and the painted finish was superb: bright flashes of red and yellow against a white background, polished to a high-gloss surface . . . but there

24

was something wrong with the balance, an instinctive feeling he had, something not quite perfect.

He leaned it back against the pile, selected another.

In a moment he walked into the interior of the shop, and looked around. There were several posters attached to one wall, depicting various incidents from the sport. One in particular attracted Harkman's attention: thirty or forty wave-riders standing on their boards in the calm of Blandford Passage, while the tidal wave roared towards them from behind, fifty metres or more in height. It was a superb photograph, catching in its frozen instant the very essence of the sport: the sheer violence of the tide-race, the elemental quality of man against the forces of nature.

Most of the stock was very high-priced: wet-suits were offered for just under ten thousand dollars, breathing-apparatus started at around fifteen thousand. Even the various books and instruction-manuals seemed to be priced above what one would expect to pay in London.

There were some assistants standing around in the shop – three young men with fashionably pale skin, and dressed in sweatshirts and loose, baggy shorts – but none of them seemed anxious for his custom, being involved in a conversation on the other side of the store. Harkman went outside again, and looked once more at the skimmers on sale.

The ideal craft had a combination of strength, balance and speed; the lower planes should be polished, the upper should be rough-grained enough for the rider's feet to gain a firm grip even when the skimmer was waterlogged. The engine-housing had to be flat and streamlined, the tanks distributed so that as the fuel was used up the balance of the craft was not disturbed. The whole craft, fully fuelled and with the engine installed, should be light enough for a strong man to carry, yet heavy enough to provide stability when the same man was standing on it in rough water. There was no perfect or standard tide-skimmer; the rider's demands of the best craft were as personal as the choice of a spouse.

Harkman sampled several more skimmers, taking them from the stack and balancing them as best he could in his hands. He looked in through the shop doorway, but the assistants continued to show no interest in him. He wished he could take one or two selected craft out on the water, to see how they handled.

He glanced at his wristwatch, and saw that he ought to return to the Commission. He took down one more tide-skimmer and held it in both hands above his head, but now each one felt like the one before it.

"Do you want to buy a skimmer?"

Harkman turned, thinking that one of the assistants had at last come forward, but the speaker was a young woman, standing in the shadow of the awning.

"I've been watching you," she said. "You don't look like the usual sort of buyer. Our skimmers are much cheaper."

Harkman went across to her, and recognized her as the attractive but rather dishevelled girl he'd seen on the quay the evening before.

"You sell skimmers too?" he said.

"We make them. They're hand-made, and can be finished exactly as you want them."

"The problem is I don't really know what I want. It's been a long time since I did any wave-riding."

"Then try a few. We've got a lot of samples."

"Are they here?"

At that moment, two of the assistants came through the doorway of the shop and walked quickly across to them.

"You!" shouted one of them, jabbing the girl roughly on her shoulder. "Get the hell out of here! We've told you before."

She stepped back into the sunlight, and Harkman turned to face the man.

"We were just talk . . ."

"We know what she wants. Can we help you, sir?"

Harkman said: "No."

He turned his back on the two men, and followed the girl. She was smiling.

"Did he hurt you?" he said.

"I'm used to it. What about our skimmers? Are you interested?"

"I'd like to see some, but I'm late for an appointment. Will you be here tomorrow?"

"I could be. That's our stall there." She pointed to the craft-stall, overlooking the harbour. "But we don't sell skimmers in the town, because we're not licensed for them. Why don't you come up to the Castle? You could see everything we have there."

"You mean Maiden Castle?" Harkman said, and looked at once across the bay towards the green mound on the promontory.

"Yes." She was a pretty girl, about twenty-seven years old,

26

Harkman supposed. He looked at her plain, unflattering smock, her tangled hair, her grimy legs and feet.

"I'll go to the Castle tomorrow," he said. "How will I find you?"

"Ask any of the others. I'm Julia."

"Do you want my name?"

"I'll remember you," she said, staring down at the boats in the harbour.

"I'm David Harkman," he said, but she seemed not to be listening. She walked away from him, not looking back, and Harkman felt she had lost interest.

Then she said: "I'll wait until you arrive," but still she did not look back at him.

A large yacht had just berthed in the harbour, and a crowd was gathering by her stall.

□□□□□□ The Commissioner in Dorchester was a man named

5 Peter Borovitin. Russian name but English blood, back through three generations. Before leaving London, Harkman had found out what he could about the man, but it wasn't much. His reading of what he had learned was that Borovitin had risen in the Regional Service more on the strength of his family name than for any individual qualities within the Party. It suited the Soviet to administer the regions with native-born Englishmen, but Harkman had heard that at least a half of the Commissioners presently in service were Slav either in name or ancestry.

By repute, Borovitin was a good Commissioner, administering the Dorchester area of Wessex fairly and competently, if unimaginatively.

The interview in Borovitin's office – a sunny but bare room on the top floor of the Commission building, with a huge photograph of the Supreme President glaring down from the wall – was a brief one. Either Borovitin disliked Harkman, or he was not interested in him, but he seemed anxious to be finished.

After he had read Harkman's letter of introduction from the head of the Bureau, Borovitin stared heavily at him for at least a minute.

At last he said: "What kind of research are you intending to do, Mr Harkman?"

"At first I want to do a lot of reading. Newspapers, local-government files, and so on. This will give me an insight into the way the island is run. Later I want to talk to local people. It will involve a certain amount of travelling." Borovitin was still staring at him, so Harkman added: "Is there likely to be any restriction on my movements, sir?"

"Not if you get my authorization first. Where are you going?"

Harkman knew if his project was to be done at all realistically, he would eventually have to visit every part of Wessex, but he also knew that unless he kept his early expectations modest he would find his movements strictly watched or controlled by the régime.

"I shall be staying in Dorchester for a few months at least," he said. "Perhaps next year I will need to visit Plymouth."

Borovitin nodded, and Harkman felt that his approach had been correct. But then Borovitin said: "I don't know what you expect to find in Dorchester."

"There are the Commission archives, sir. Those will be a major source for my work. And I'd like to visit Maiden Castle."

"Why?"

The response came so quickly that Harkman was taken off-guard.

He said: "Is there any reason why I should not, sir?"

"No." Borovitin was glancing over the introductory letter again, as if the first time he read it he had missed something of relevance. "I don't see why you need to go there."

"It's historically of importance and interest." Borovitin was staring at him again; suspicion or disinterest? Harkman went on: "With the greatest respect, sir, I dare say that you have not worked in sociology. In the ancient past, Maiden Castle was a more important place than Dorchester. I believe that during the years Wessex was isolated from the rest of England Maiden Castle would have reverted to a rôle of great strategic and sociological importance."

"You don't need my authorization to go there," Borovitin said flatly.

This time Harkman stared back, aware that the Commissioner was not as disconcerted as he was by long silences. The reason he had offered for wanting to go to the Castle had been impromptu, but he felt he had produced an authentic-sounding reply. The fact was that he had to visit the Castle to fulfil some deeper, unspecified need, and he had no explanation for that.

And there was another reason now: to see the girl, to buy a tide-skimmer.

"About the archives, sir," he said in the end, no longer ill at ease under the Commissioner's bland scrutiny, but anxious to bring the interview to an end. "Could I have your authority to inspect the Commission records?"

"You'll have to file a formal application. See Mander."

"But I understood that the archives were under the jurisdiction of a Mr Cro. It was he who wrote to confirm my appointment."

"All administrative functions are channelled through Mr Mander."

A few minutes later, Harkman found the office that had been allocated to him for his use. Although it was quite large, and the previous occupant had cleared it out thoroughly, Harkman disliked the room immediately. It had only one window, and although it could be opened it was set high in the wall and only by standing on a chair could he see out. The effect of it was, as Harkman reflected as he tried it for the first time, that he could sit all day under the sterile glare of fluorescent strip-lights, and smell the fragrance of flowers, hear the buzzing of insects, and listen to the sounds of the holidaymakers walking in the narrow sunlit street outside.

Donald Mander came to see him, and Harkman's first impressions of the man were favourable. He was a florid-faced middle-aged man, with just a few wisps of hair feathering his pink, shiny head. He laughed a lot – although Harkman guessed it was intended to put him at his ease – and had what appeared to be a noncommittal and cynical way of describing the office routines and personnel.

"Commissioner Borovitin tells me I must file an application for use of the archives through you."

"That's right, yes."

"Then could you take it that I have applied? I'd like to start as soon as possible."

"You'll need a form, Harkman. I'll look one out for you, and send it down."

Mander had brought a chair with him from the next office, and the swivel-joint was creaking as he changed his position.

"Couldn't I just have a note typed out?" Harkman said.

"It has to be on the proper form," Mander said, and laughed. Harkman thought that anyone who found that idea funny must have been working too long in one place.

He said: "I gather Mr Cro is in charge of the archives."

"I'll introduce you to him later. Yes, the archives are his responsibility."

From the mosque across the street, the muezzin called over the rooftops. The eerie, rising voice reminded Harkman of his short visit to the embassy in the Western States. It was the Muslim culture in North America that he had found the strangest of all strange things he had noticed in the trip. Five times daily the nation prostrated itself and prayed towards the east. It was as if the once independent America had to pay daily homage to a greater power than Allah, the power of oil-dollars, the power that had eventually absorbed a culture. This mosque in Dorchester, like the others in the main tourist centres of Wessex, was only a gesture to that power, but a reminder to the English, to the Wessexmen, of the alternatives to socialism.

"Perhaps I could meet Mr Cro?" Harkman said, wishing there was an alternative to this.

Mander swivelled in his chair again. "Of course. And I'll show you round the building at the same time."

The day passed slowly, and at the end of it Harkman was tired and irritable. The only positive thing he had to show for his day's efforts was that Cro had lent him a part of the index to the archives. As it was barely more than a list of numbers, it wasn't much better than nothing.

After leaving the Commission in the evening, and having declined an invitation to drinks with Mander and some of his colleagues, Harkman went for a long, solitary stroll around the town.

It was curious that the relaxed mood of the resort did not penetrate to the Commission offices. It was like one of the smaller administrative government offices in London that he had sometimes come up against; one was constantly reminded of form and manner and priorities, as if the Supreme President of the Soviet was expected at any moment.

Only in the front office, where there were public counters, was there any hint that Dorchester was the most fashionable resort in the country; here the large windows looked out across a tree-filled square, where there were two cafés and where several painters were at work. In the mornings the sun shone in, and all day there would be queues in the two carefully separated areas. In one, English nationals – Party employees, local residents and immigrant workers – came in and out to collect items of mail, to register for State employment funds, to buy licences for trade, and to submit to various other demands on their time and attention; at the other desk, States tourists could apply for visas to visit the English mainland, and their colourful clothes and relaxed manner made a noticeable contrast.

Harkman stood behind the counters for several minutes to watch this ordinary business of the Commission, but instead he had been distracted by the pervasive mood of leisure beyond the plate glass windows.

He walked out of the centre of town and went towards Poundbury Camp to the north, and stood for a long time watching the little yachts from Charminster across the inlet. Charminster, unlike its larger and more cosmopolitan neighbour, catered with its State-controlled hotels and villas for English families, who travelled to Wessex by a route that took them to the north coast of the island and passed nowhere near Dorchester.

Glancing back towards Dorchester, Harkman thought of the pictures he had seen of the town that had once stood on the same site. All the buildings of Old Dorchester had gone, and all their ancient associations with them. Those that had not been shaken down in the earthquakes had been flooded in the subsidence. The new Dorchester was a successful compromise between strength and amenity, between function and aesthetic. Although no tremors had been felt in the region for more than forty years the law required every building to be capable of withstanding an earth shock of 6 on the Richter Scale; equally, every new building had to blend with the planners' conception of a holiday centre. Accordingly, the reinforced steel and concrete shells of the buildings were faced with plaster and stucco and whitewash; the balconies and terraces overlooking the sea were integral parts of the tensioned skeletons, and yet were decorated with wrought-iron filigrees, and pinewood panels, and trailing abundant greenery; the windows were laminated, the roofs were prefabricated in one piece to appear as if tiled, and the streets, although charmingly narrow and cobbled, were straight enough and wide enough to allow emergency service vehicles access to any part of the town.

Even the mosque, whose dome and minarets dominated the town, would suffer only surface cracks should an earthquake strike.

In the distance, the Blandford cannon boomed, and Harkman sat down on the dry grass to wait for the tide to flood into the

31

inlet. Here the water was always deeper than by Dorchester Harbour, and when the effect of the wave arrived twenty minutes later it was no more than about half a metre high. The little yachts were able to ride it out without difficulty, and across the water Harkman could hear the shrill, excited cries of children.

This was, in fact, not the wave at all, but the first ripple caused by the monstrous arrival of the main wave at Blandford Passage. But it was enough to remind Harkman of his intention to buy a skimmer the next day, and as more and more waves swept slowly down the inlet as the tide rose he was wondering if by the following evening he would have the nerve to make his first attempt at the Blandford wave.

That night, though, as he lay in his room at the Commission hostel, Harkman's thoughts were of Maiden Castle, and of a pretty dishevelled girl with evasive eyes.

□□□□□□ Julia was woken by Greg's hands moving over her body.
  6   She lay with her back towards him, feeling him press himself against her. It was always like this in the mornings: Greg woke first, aroused, and before she was barely conscious he would want to make love. Each night, as sleep came on her, she would dread the morning, knowing the inevitability of his demands.

Still dreamy with sleep she tried to slip back, as if this alone would push him away from her.

Greg reached over her, put a hand under her cheek and turned her face towards his. He kissed her, and she felt his hot breath and moist lips on her mouth, his beard rasping on her cheek. She was limp, unresponding; she could not even make her eyes open.

"Julia . . . kiss me," he said hoarsely, but his mouth was against her ear now, and the words were a gassy, hissing intrusion. He thrust his hand through her legs from behind, and clutched at her sex. She turned towards him then, forcing him to take his hand away, and he put both his arms around her, kissing her voraciously. She stayed unresisting, and in a moment he pushed his way into her. She was dry and unaroused, and the gasp she gave he mistook for passion, and his movements became urgent and possessive. Through long habit she moved with him, but she felt nothing, only discomfort.

The pleasure of it was his alone; she could not remember the last time she had enjoyed sex with him.

By the time he had reached his panting, noisy climax she was fully awake, and she lay under his weight feeling tense and very aware of her own sexuality. She could feel him inside her, shrinking wetly, and she contracted her muscles against him, reaching for sensation . . . but Greg, not noticing, pulled himself away from her without a word and lay beside her on his face, breathing deeply.

Every day it was the same! She responded to him, but too late, and when she was ready he was finished. She reached down and felt herself damp and warm, and the pressure of her hand brought an involuntary contraction of the muscles.

She looked at Greg beside her; he was not asleep, but his desire was exhausted. She would not stir him, would not try to. Greg made love his own way.

Julia waited for a few minutes longer, but Greg did not move again, so she slid out from beneath the rough sheet and walked across to the door of the hut. As she opened it, bright sunlight dazzled her.

She found a towel, wrapped it around the lower half of her body, then walked the short distance to the communal showers. The water was lukewarm and salt, but it refreshed her and flushed away the last remnants of her unfulfilled desire. By the time she returned, Greg had left the hut. She glanced around the dirty, untidy interior, wishing she had more will to clean the place up.

When she had had some food she went in search of Tom Benedict, who was one of the older members of the Castle community. She found him by one of the kilns, raking out the cinders from the fire-tray.

"Can I speak to you, Tom?"

He turned to look at her, and she saw that his eyes were red and watery, and that he held the rake in both hands, hunching a shoulder awkwardly. He let the rake go, and reached out a hand towards her.

"Julia. Help me up, will you?"

"Are you ill, Tom?"

She took his hand, and felt the large, bony knuckles bulging through his papery skin. His fingers were callused and dirty.

"I'm fine, Julia. I slept badly, that's all."

He was standing now, but he did not release her hand. She

led him to the bench beside the kiln and they sat down. He was wheezing.

Julia had been busy at the stall for the last two or three weeks, because the influx of tourists was at its peak, and she had not seen much of Tom, except late in the evenings. Of all the people at the Castle, she probably knew more about Tom than anyone else because he had befriended her soon after his arrival. In the couple of years he had been at the Castle he had grown steadily more withdrawn, but she knew that he came from the mainland, that he had been happily married for many years, that he had a daughter who worked in Nottingham. There were two grandchildren, too. He had never directly explained why he had joined the Castle community, but from various things he said Julia understood that after the death of his wife he had had to live with his daughter, but had not got along well with her husband. Being older than most of the others at the Castle he had taken a long time to settle down, but he was now accepted by everyone. Several members of the community, Julia in particular, looked to him for guidance or advice.

"You shouldn't be working," Julia said. "What's happened to your arm?"

"I must have slept in a draught." His weak eyes were looking into his lap as he said this.

"It's been hurting for some time, hasn't it?"

"Just a day or two."

"Have you seen Allen?" He was the community doctor, but he was a remote and difficult man.

"I saw him."

"No you didn't, Tom. I know you too well."

"I'll see him today."

"You ought to go into Dorchester. Go to the hospital."

Julia stayed with Tom for half an hour, trying to persuade him to have medical treatment. It seemed to her that he was more frightened than obstinate, and Julia decided to speak to Allen herself, if Tom wouldn't do it.

Her problem, though, had been put out of her mind. She had approached Tom with the half-formed resolution to try to talk to him about Greg, about the misery of a loveless, passionless partner, and the stirrings of her body. She could not speak directly of these, of course, but even to talk about unspecified discontents would have been good enough.

Later, she went to the eastern end of the village to help out for a while with the children. Being on this edge of the village, and near the ramparts, the schoolhouse overlooked the sea. The community included about thirty children, and whenever Julia wasn't at the stall in Dorchester she went to help at the school.

Education at Maiden Castle only had the appearance of being casual; the classes were held in the open air whenever the weather allowed, and the attire of both teachers and pupils was informal, but ever since the Commission had sent inspectors to the Castle three years earlier, the content of the lessons had adhered to State doctrine. Children were educated at the Castle until the age of ten; after that they had to attend the State school in Dorchester.

Julia's assistance was generally confined to recreational activities, and on this particular morning she was given charge of a bunch of nine year olds, and organized them into two teams for football. Before long, she had become an active participant in the game, kicking the ball wildly whenever it was in reach, much to the amusement of the more ambitious children. Football was taken very seriously at Maiden Castle, and Julia's ineptitude revealed itself several times when puffing toddlers whisked the ball away from her just as she was about to kick it.

After an hour of this she noticed that the impromptu match had a spectator: a man, standing alone, watching her.

She left the game at once, and went over to him. He was standing as she had seen him when he arrived on the hydrofoil: at ease and watchful, his jacket over his shoulder. He was grinning as she trotted towards him, and his frank look made her uncharacteristically self-conscious about her appearance. She was hot and untidy from running around, and wished she could brush her hair.

"I can wait," he said. "I was enjoying watching you."

"No, I was only helping. You've come about the tide-skimmer."

"I didn't think you'd remember."

She had wanted to forget. As soon as she'd spoken to him at the skimmer-shop she had regretted it; Greg was possessive in ways other than sexual, and as soon as she had looked at this man she had recognized a response in herself, and a response in him.

"You're . . . David Harkman," she said, hesitant with the name as if its use would convey some deeper significance to him, similar to the one it held for her.

"Yes. And you're Julia."

He looked very cool. There was always a breeze on top of Maiden Castle however hot the sun, but she felt red-faced and sweaty in his company. She swept back the hair from her face.

"Did you come over in a boat?" she said.

"No, I walked around the shore. I wanted to take time from the office."

"You work for the Commission."

"I work in the building, but I'm not really on the staff."

She was watching his face, sensing some recognition, a familiarity. There was no way they could have met before, no possibility of contact. And yet, the evening on the quay when he had arrived, yesterday by the skimmer-shop, now today. . . . A nagging recognition of him. Even his name was no surprise. Harkman, Harkman . . . it was a part of her.

Trying to put the uncertainty aside, she said: "Would you like to see some skimmers?"

"I'd like to try one or two, if that's possible."

She glanced at his clothes. "Is that how you normally dress for wave-riding?"

He laughed as he followed her along the edge of the sports field. "I've brought a swimming costume."

"We don't normally bother with those here."

"So I see."

During the summer months the people at the Castle normally wore very few clothes. Most of the children went entirely naked, and several adults too. In the workshops, clothes were worn for protection, but those who worked in the fields generally only wore a single garment, Julia wore her brown smock by habit, but only because she liked to have pockets. Walking next to David Harkman, she was aware of his machine-made clothes, the pressed trousers and polished shoes, the pale blue shirt. He looked unusual in the Castle surroundings, but the people they passed barely afforded him a glance.

They were walking towards the southern side of the Castle, where the encircling ramparts were laid in a more complex pattern than elsewhere. Julia led the way down into the first dip. They walked along the bottom of this for a short distance until they came to a break in the next wall. Here the ancient Wessexmen had had one of their gates, and it made walking through to the next dip a simple matter.

They came eventually to a recent construction: a large wooden building. It was open at the front, and looked down through another gap in the ramparts to an inlet of the bay below.

Julia walked inside, and at once they were assailed by the unique smells of the workshop: the heady, acidic cellulose paint, the fragrance of sawdust, of wood-glue. The paint-shop was in a separate part of the building, screened from the drifting, settling sawdust, but the paint smell was everywhere.

"Is Greg here?" Julia shouted to the group of men and women busy in the workshop, cutting and planing wood, sawing, sanding, hammering.

"In the paint-shop."

At that moment Greg came out of the curtained area, wearing a white mask over his nose and mouth. When he saw Julia with Harkman he pulled the mask down, nodded to Harkman.

"Greg, this is David Harkman. He'd like to see some skimmers."

"What sort of thing are you looking for, Harkman?"

"I don't know. I'd like to try a few."

"Heavy? Light? What size engine?"

"I'm not sure. It's a long time since I did any wave-riding. What do you think?"

Greg looked him up and down. "What do you weigh? About eighty kilos?"

"About that."

"You'll need quite a large craft. If you're just getting back into riding, though, I wouldn't go for one with a big engine."

"Have you got anything that might be right?"

"Let's have a look."

Greg walked out of the workshop, and towards a smaller building at its side. Julia and Harkman followed. There were about two dozen completed craft in the shed, stacked one on top of the other.

"None of these has motors," Greg said. "But if you pick one out, I can get one fitted."

For the next few minutes, Harkman and Greg took several of the skimmers from the stack, and carried them outside. Greg's advice was curt, and had a patronizing undertone that Julia had rarely heard in him. For all his unsatisfactory sexual demands, Greg was usually a generous and quiet man, and the only explanation was that he had detected something of her own awareness of Harkman's presence.

She watched as Harkman chose five of the skimmers. As he

37

lifted each one to feel its balance she noticed that Greg was watching critically. He seemed ready to assume that Harkman was a complete novice.

"How much do you charge for one of these?"

Greg started to say: "It depends . . .", but Julia interrupted.

"Find one you like first," she said. "They're all different prices."

"Can I try these two?" Harkman said, indicating his choices.

"I'll get some motors," Greg said, and walked back to the workshop. It took about half an hour for him and another man to install the engines, and explain the controls. The craft were carried down to a tiny beach beside the Castle ramparts.

As Harkman laid them out on the sand, Julia took Greg to one side.

"I can deal with him now," she said.

"I think I'll stay around," Greg said.

"He's my customer. I brought him up here."

"Just a customer, is he? I don't like the way he was looking at you."

"Greg, he's a Commission man. I want this sale for myself."

The young man looked critically again at Harkman, and Julia saw in his eyes the same possessive expression she saw when his jealousies were aroused. She hadn't been aware that Harkman had been looking at her in any certain way, and the information pleased her.

"Get the best price you can, then. If he's from the Commission he can afford the same prices as the government shop."

"I run the stall, Greg. I know how to make a sale." The young man still showed no sign of returning to the workshop. She added: "I'll talk to you later."

Greg hesitated a few moments longer, then, with one more wary look at Harkman, he clambered up the slope of the nearest rampart, and shortly was out of sight.

□□□□□□ David Harkman leaned forward to take the balance,
  opened the skimmer's throttle, and felt the surge of
7 acceleration beneath his feet. He throttled back at once,
  alarmed at the instant response of the engine. He
guided the craft towards the shallow end of the inlet, and executed a wide, gentle turn. Facing towards the sea, he accelerated

again, this time allowing the engine to take the craft as fast as it would go. The inlet, sheltered on one side by the bulk of the Castle and by a forested hill on the other, was as smooth as glass. The only thing that would tip him off the skimmer was his own inexperience.

As he passed the little beach where he had launched the skimmer, he looked for Julia to wave to her, but there was no sign of her. He reached the neck of the inlet and turned again, this time trying the standard skimmer-turn: flipping the board with his weight, turning it through a hundred and eighty degrees in not much more than its own length.

He started back with renewed confidence, and then he saw Julia. She was swimming, and he saw her arm wave from the water.

He liked the way the craft handled, and so he took it up and down the narrow creek three more times, acquiring confidence and regaining old skills each time. At last he took the skimmer to where Julia was swimming, and he slowed it, letting the engine idle.

She swam over to him. Her hair swept wetly back from her face, clinging to her head like the coat of an animal. As she rested her hands on the edge of the skimmer, he saw she was naked.

"You're as pale as the tourists!" she said, laughing, and splashed water up at his legs.

"I've been working in offices all my life," he said, trying to keep his balance because she was deliberately wobbling him.

"Come and have a swim."

"No, I want to try the other board."

"I'll tip you in!"

He gunned the engine and swung away. When he was a short distance from her he turned and headed straight back, pulling up short a couple of metres away and sending a sheet of water spraying over her. Julia went under, and came up spitting water.

Laughing, Harkman accelerated away down the creek.

Julia was still swimming five minutes later, so he went back to the beach and dragged the second skimmer down to the water. It didn't take him more than one ride down the inlet to discover that this one, compared to the first, seemed slower and heavier.

He saw Julia standing in the shallows, up to her waist in the water, so he took the craft over to her.

"I'm going to take the first one," he said, standing on the board and looking down at her. "How much?"

She grinned sweetly at him, then tipped the skimmer with

both hands. Harkman swung his arms wildly, and toppled backwards into the water. As soon as he had recovered his sense of direction he lunged at Julia, splashing water, trying to give her a second ducking . . . but she was wading out.

"Don't you want to swim?" he said, standing up with his hands on his hips.

"I've had enough. I was getting cold. I'll wait here."

She picked up her discarded smock and began dabbing the water from her body with it. Harkman turned round and dived, and swam out to the deeper, greener water of the inlet, thinking it would have been a more interesting swim to be splashing around with a naked girl. He floated on his back, and saw that Julia had put her smock on the sand, and was lying down beside it, waiting for him.

Five minutes later he walked up the beach, and Julia tossed him her smock. "Here . . . you can dry yourself with this."

He wiped his face and neck, and sat down beside her. "I think I'll dry out in the sun."

He lay back on the sand, aware of her nearness to him, aware of her nakedness.

"They're good skimmers," he said, trying to keep his mind on other matters. Nudity was a commonplace in this part of Wessex; there was no invitation implied in her casual behaviour.

"I suppose so," Julia said.

"Who designs them?"

"A couple of the men in the workshop."

He wondered if she was aware of the tension he was feeling. They were talking in an off-hand, disinterested way, as if unwilling to confront each other with more direct statements. Or was it only he who felt it? She was lying back, supporting her weight on her elbows, and staring out across the inlet. Trying not to be too obvious about it, Harkman appraised her body, admired the neatness of her figure. Her skin was tanned all over to a mellow brown.

In an effort to persuade himself that he was not alone, Harkman wondered why Julia delayed here at the beach with him. If it was just a question of selling him the skimmer, the deal would be concluded now.

His clothes were piled near by, and he fumbled through the pockets of his jacket and found his cigarettes.

"Do you smoke?" he said.

"No thanks."

He leaned back and inhaled smoke. The Castle heaped behind them, seeming to glow in the heat of the sun, radiating an ancient heat, an inner life. Was it just this that was affecting him? He had responded at last to the compulsion that had afflicted him in London, and he had visited the Castle. Yet it had been nothing, just as now, as he lay under the slope of its ramparts, it was nothing.

Julia was restless, and stared back up the rampart several times.

"Was that your boyfriend?" Harkman said in the end, breaking a silence that had endured for several minutes. "The one in the paint-shop?"

"Greg? He's no one special."

"I thought you were waiting for him to come back."

"No . . . it's just. . . ." She sat up, and turned round to face him. "I shouldn't be here with you."

"Do you want to put on your dress again?"

"It's not that. If Greg . . . or anybody came back, they'd wonder why I was still sitting here."

"Well? Why are you?"

"I don't know."

"Shall we close the deal?" Harkman said. "I've brought the money with me."

"No." She put a hand on his. "Please don't. Stay and talk to me."

And there it was: for Harkman, a confirmation of his own feeling. Nothing specific, nothing he could put into words. No reasons, but a need to stay with her, a need to talk and make some kind of contact.

He said: "When I arrived in Dorchester two days ago, I felt I recognized you. Do you know what I mean?"

She nodded. "I knew your name. David Harkman . . . it was as if it was written in large letters all over you."

"Was it?" he said, smiling.

"No . . . but I knew it. Have we met before?"

"I don't think so. I've never been to Wessex in my life."

"I've only been here for about three years." She spoke then of her past, as if to set out a sequence of events where their lives might have intersected. Harkman listened, but he knew that there was nowhere they could have seen each other: she had been brought up on a cooperative farm near Hereford, and lived there until three years ago. She'd never been to London, never even travelled further east than Malvern, where she had been to school.

Harkman thought of his own life, but didn't speak of it. He felt his age, realizing that he must be nearly fifteen years older than her . . . and that those fifteen years would take longer to tell than the story of her own whole life. And yet, in terms of events nothing much had happened: education, career, marriage, career, divorce, career . . . offices, government departments, reports written and published. Not much for more than forty years of life, but more than he wanted to describe to her.

"Then what is it?" she said. "Why do I know you?"

"You really do feel it."

She was looking at him directly, almost earnestly, and he remembered the evasiveness of those same eyes when they had been talking outside the shop.

"I'm glad you said something," Julia said. "I thought it was only me."

"I'll say it plainly: I'm attracted to you."

A large fly buzzed around Julia's face, and she flicked a hand at it. Undeterred, it landed on her leg and walked up her thigh in quick, staccato movements. She knocked it away.

She said: "I thought for a time that I. . . . It's difficult to say. Yesterday at the shop. Well, I thought it was one of those sexual things. You know, when you can't control it."

"You're very attractive, Julia."

"But it's not that, is it? Not just that."

"I'm tempted to say yes," he said. "I wish it was only that, because it would be simpler. It's there for me . . . but that's not all."

"I'd like my dress, please."

He passed it to her without a word, and watched as she pulled it over her head. She stood up to shake it down over her legs, then sat beside him again.

"Did you get dressed because we were talking about sex?" he said.

"Yes."

"Then I think we understand one another." He had a sudden urge to touch her, and he reached out to take her hand, but she moved it away from him. He went on: "I feel that we somehow possess each other, Julia. That we are linked in some way, and that it was inevitable we would meet. Do you know what I mean?"

"I think so."

"I'd like a direct answer."

She said: "I'm not sure I can give you one."

Harkman flicked away the end of his cigarette, and it cart-wheeled into the water and hissed. He lit another immediately.

"Am I offending you by talking about this?"

"No, but it's very difficult. I know what you mean, because I feel it too. As soon as I saw you I felt it."

Harkman said: "Julia, two years ago I was working at my office in London, when I suddenly felt a tremendous necessity to live and work here in Wessex. It obsessed me, I couldn't stop thinking about it. Eventually I applied for a transfer to Dorchester . . . and although it took two years for the permit to come through, I got here in the end. Now I'm here, and I still don't know why. It feels to me now, as I talk to you, that it was to meet you, or someone like you. But I know rationally that that's nonsense."

He paused, remembering how he had fretted in London, waiting for the appointment to be confirmed.

"Go on."

"That's about it. Except that now I've met you, it feels as if my reason for coming here was just a pretext."

Julia said, unexpectedly: "I think I understand. When I came to Maiden Castle for the first time, everything that had happened before seemed unreal."

Harkman looked at her in surprise. "Are you making that up?"

"No. I can remember my father and mother, and I can remember the farm, and schooldays . . . and all that. But at the same time I can hardly remember what it was really like."

"Do you ever see your parents?"

"Sometimes. I think I saw them . . . recently. I'm not sure."

"And you'd never go back to the farm?"

She shook her head. "It would be impossible."

"Do you know why?"

"Because I'm committed to the Castle." She was looking away from him. "No, it isn't just that. My place is here. I can't say why."

"My place is with you," Harkman said. "I don't know why, either. I'll never leave Wessex."

"What do you want, David?"

"I want you, Julia . . . and I want to know *why*."

Looking directly at him, she said: "If you had to settle for one, which would it be?"

43

And she looked away, just as she had done outside the skimmer-shop.

There was a noise above them, and Harkman turned. Greg had appeared at the top of the nearest rampart, and was walking down towards them. Julia had seen him too.

Harkman said: "Will you come to my room tonight? In Dorchester."

"No, I can't. It's impossible."

"Tomorrow, then."

She shook her head, watching Greg come towards them, but said: "I don't know where it is."

She stood up, straightening her smock with guilty movements of her hands.

"The Commission hostel. Room 14."

Greg scrambled down on to the sand, and walked towards them. Harkman turned to face him.

"I'd like this one," he said.

Greg said: "Two thousand dollars. Seven thousand extra for the engine."

"Greg, that's not the usual price," Julia said.

Harkman looked at her, and, conscious of the double meaning, said: "Well?"

Julia brushed the sand from her smock, keeping her face averted. "We normally charge six thousand for the whole unit."

Greg showed no response.

"That seems a fair price." Harkman bent down and picked up his jacket.

"I'll deliver it myself," Julia said. "Tomorrow evening."

As Harkman counted the money into Greg's hand, Julia was standing by the edge of the waves, staring out across the narrow inlet.

□□□□□□ By mid-afternoon, Tom Benedict was plainly very ill,
8   and Julia's intrigued day-dreams about David Harkman
          were interrupted as she arranged for Tom to be taken
          to the infirmary in the Castle village. Hannah and
Mark, who ran the stall in Dorchester with her, were expecting
her there for the evening trade, and she had to take time to
send someone down with a message.

When she returned to the infirmary, Allen had already visited

Tom, and the old man was laid out as comfortably as possible in the cool, white-painted ward. He recognized Julia when she arrived, but soon afterwards fell asleep.

The Castle infirmary was run on an entirely voluntary basis, and had no proper medical facilities. It was simply a long, low hut, which was kept clean and ventilated, and contained sixteen beds where people suffering from minor ailments could be looked after. A few medical supplies were kept in a small room at one end, but any serious disease had to be treated in the Dorchester hospital.

Julia sought out one of the women who served occasional duties as a nurse.

"Where's Allen?" she said. "What's he doing for Tom?"

"He said he needed rest. He's sent away to Dorchester, and someone's coming up this evening."

"This evening! That might be too late. Did he say what was wrong?"

"No, Julia. Tom's old . . . it could be anything."

Exasperated, Julia returned to the bedside and took Tom's tight-skinned hand in hers. The fingers were cold and stiff, and for a moment she thought he must have died while she was away from the bed. Then she saw a very slow, very shallow movement of his chest. She slipped his hand beneath the blanket and continued to hold it, trying to warm him.

It felt cold in the ward, because the windows were open and although there was only a slight breeze the sun never seemed to warm the infirmary. Julia swept back the thin white hair from the old man's brow, and felt that the skin there was also cool, not perspiring.

Julia felt closer to Tom than she could ever say; closer than she felt to her parents, closer than she felt to Greg . . . and yet it was neither a blood relationship nor a sexual one. There was an affinity there, an unspoken understanding.

There were approximately two hundred people in the Castle community, children included, but of these only a handful had any influence on her life or thoughts. She thought of the rest as pale shadows, lacking in personality, following where others led.

Allen, the doctor, was one such. He was unquestionably qualified for medical practice, and in the treatment of minor ailments and in diagnosing diseases he was excellent. But he seemed never to act; anything that could not be treated with available medicines was referred immediately to the hospital in Dorchester.

45

Perhaps it was right that this should be so . . . but Allen's personality was negative, unforthcoming.

Greg was another. In spite of the fact that she had slept with him for months, and in spite of there having been a certain amount of mutual interest at the start, Julia had never really grown to know the young man. He was, to her, always the distant, efficient craftsman who worked in the skimmer workshop, or the inconsiderate, selfish and loveless man who used her body. In the Castle community Greg seemed to be one of the more popular people – and when Julia was not suffering his physical attentions she found him amusing and pleasant company – but he too had this paleness to his character that was a constant frustration to her. Sometimes, when she was alone with him, Julia wanted to shout at him or scream at him or wave her arms . . . anything to elicit some kind of positive response.

There were the others, though, and they were here at the Castle, and in Dorchester and the surrounding countryside.

There was Nathan Williams, who played a great part in organizing and shaping the community; some said he had been at the Castle when the community was first formed. There was a woman named Mary, who was one of the potters. There was Rod, who worked on the fishing smack owned by the Castle. There was Alicia, one of the teachers. There was Tom Benedict.

Sometimes, while she was working on the stall in Dorchester, Julia would see local people passing the harbour . . . and she would detect that with them, too, there was this certain affinity.

For a long time she had felt it was a talent, an uncontrollable clairvoyance. She had wondered if she had powers of telepathy, or something similar, but there were never any other kinds of manifestation. Just an empathic understanding, a recognition.

Ignoring it, as she had tried to do for some time, it became less important, but meeting David Harkman had reminded her that it was a real and inexplicable fact of her life. Although with David there was another thing, a sexual charge, a physical desire, an emotional tension.

"Is that you, Julia?"

Tom spoke very weakly. His eyes hadn't opened. She squeezed his hand gently, under the blanket.

"I'm here, Tom. Don't worry. There's a doctor coming from Dorchester."

"Don't let go. . . ."

She looked around. She and Tom were alone in the infirmary;

summer was a healthy time for the villagers. But she wished there were someone with them, a trained nurse . . . or Allen.

Through one of the windows she could see children running around, playing and calling to each other with shrill voices. School had finished for the day, evening would soon be here.

She never detected the affinity with any of the children, although she liked them, and the teachers at the school were always glad of her help. She saw the children as a milling, diminutive presence: noisy, quick-moving, demanding of time and energy. But as David Harkman had said of his career, and as she felt about her own past, the children were a fact, not something she had any feeling about.

One of the women in the village had given birth a few weeks before, and Julia had seen the mother and child soon afterwards. It had been like a classic portrait of healthy motherhood: the woman sitting up in bed in the infirmary, her hair tangled, a cardigan pinned around her shoulders. The child cried in her arms, pink and damp and very small. The mother's eyes were bright and tired, the bedclothes had been straightened over her. Nothing had gone wrong, no worries: mother and child doing well. Julia had never known a crisis for any of the village people; there were 'flu epidemics, and the children passed measles and mumps to one another . . . but she had never known anyone fall and break a leg, nor was there ever a pregnancy that went wrong, nor did anyone ever die violently. There was a graveyard at the western end of the Castle compound, but the few deaths that occurred happened quietly, unobtrusively.

It was a sheltered, undangerous place; the harsher realities of life seemed as if they were postponed.

Then, as if contradicting the thought, Tom groaned, and his head turned restlessly.

Tom was different, though, Tom recognized the affinity. He had always been at the front of the stage for her; a leading player, not a member of the chorus. This analogy had often occurred to her as if it would solve the puzzle, but all it ever did was underline the feeling.

Until she had spoken of it with David Harkman, she had never directly acknowledged the feeling to anyone else. Not to Nathan, or Mary . . . not even to Tom. But David Harkman had spoken of it himself, had pointed directly to it.

We are different, you and I, he had said. We are different, because we are the same.

47

The nursing woman appeared at the entrance to the ward, leading a small child by the hand. She walked slowly towards the bed and Julia turned anxiously towards her, but not releasing Tom's hand.

"Is the doctor coming?" she said.

"I told you, dear, he's on his way. They're probably busy in Dorchester, what with all the foreigners coming in."

"Then will you try to find Allen?" Julia said. "Tom's very ill. I don't know what to do."

The woman reached past her, and touched the palm of her hand to the old man's brow.

"He's not feverish. He's just sleeping."

"Look, please find Allen! I'm very worried."

"I'll see where he is."

The woman's child had been raising himself up and down on the end of the bed, falling across his stomach and laughing, uncaring that Tom's legs, which were directly under him, might be hurting. The woman took the child's hand again, and walked slowly towards the door. Julia wanted to urge her again to hurry, sensing somehow that things had reached a critical stage for Tom. His head was still moving slowly from side to side, and his eyes were open, but unseeing.

"Do you think he'd like some food?" The woman had paused by the door, looking back at her.

Julia turned towards her again. "No. Get Allen . . . and please, for Tom's benefit, find him as soon – "

As she spoke, Julia felt Tom's hand move away from her own. Still facing the woman by the door, she reached further under the blanket, groping for him. She turned back to the bed, fearing the worst . . . but totally unprepared for what she saw.

The bed was empty.

The blanket was still crumpled over where he had lain, and the sheet beneath it bore a trace of the residual warmth of his old body, but Tom had vanished.

Julia gasped aloud and stood back, scraping her chair noisily. "Tom! For God's sake, Tom!"

The nursing woman was watching her from the door. "What's going on?"

"He's gone!"

Disbelieving, Julia threw back the blanket, as if the old man had somehow wriggled down under the bedclothes like a child playfully hiding. The blanket fell over the metal bed-end, humped

48

on to the floor. The lower sheet still bore the impression of Tom's body.

"What are you doing in here, Julia? You know no one's here – "

Julia scrambled on to the bed, kneeling on it, leaning over to the far side, in the desperate inspired hope that Tom had fallen from the bed, that he was still there . . . but the floor was bare.

The woman had left the child by the door, and was striding towards her. As she reached the bed she seized Julia's arm, and pulled her round.

"If you were the one who had to make these beds. . . ."

"Tom has vanished! He was here! I was holding his hand!"

"What are you talking about? There's no one here."

Julia felt like screaming at the woman. She pointed in silent agony at the bed, its emptiness self-evident proof of what she was saying.

The woman pulled officiously at the blanket Julia had thrown back. "These beds have to be kept ready. What are you doing here? Are you ill?"

The woman's words were meaningless. Julia moved back from the bed and stood before her, still trying to express the impossibility of what had happened.

"Tom! Tom Benedict! You saw him . . . he was here."

The woman was scuffing her hand across the lower sheet, smoothing it out, as if erasing the last evidence of Tom's presence. In one last desperate attempt, Julia foolishly snatched away the pillow, as if Tom's frail body could somehow be concealed beneath it. The woman took it away from her, fluffed it with her hands and replaced it.

Julia stepped back, watching the nursing woman remake the bed. The child stood by the door, kicking the frame idly. The rest of the ward was bare, empty, quiet. It was beyond all reason: Tom could not slip away from her, vanish from the face of the earth!

Still uncomprehending, Julia turned again to the woman. "Please! You saw Tom in this bed. He was dying! You felt his brow. You said he had no fever, and you were going to find Allen."

At the mention of the doctor's name the woman looked at her. "Allen? He's in Dorchester, I think. I haven't seen him all day."

"But you did see Tom Benedict here?"

The woman shook her head slowly. "Tom . . . Benedict? Who's that?"

"You know! Tom! Everyone knew him!"

The woman tucked the blanket under the mattress, smoothed it over with her hand, and then straightened.

"I'm sorry, Julia. I don't know what you're talking about. I find you all by yourself in here, wrecking the bed. What do you expect me to think? Are you saying someone's ill?"

Julia took a breath to say it all again, but suddenly realized that the woman genuinely had no idea what she was saying. The ward had an aseptic, unused feel to it: no one in the community had been ill for weeks.

"I'm sorry . . . I don't know what came over me."

She walked slowly from the ward, past the child, and out into the sunlight. Children still played, a ball was being kicked around. One of the children ran from the crowd, crying. Two others followed, then went back to the game. In the distance, Julia could see the people working in the fields.

She waited outside the infirmary until the woman came out. She closed the door, looked curiously at Julia, then walked off towards the village.

Julia stayed by the infirmary, still unable to comprehend what had happened, still unwilling to leave the scene, as if by staying Tom would somehow return . . . the old grin on his face, confessing to a hoax.

She sat down on the grass, oblivious of all around her, and suddenly started to cry.

A little later she walked around the infirmary building, trying to see if there was some way Tom could have left the building without her noticing. There were two other doors, but they were both locked.

In the evening she spoke to Nathan Williams. "Have you seen Tom?"

"Tom? Tom who?"

"Benedict. Tom Benedict."

"Never heard of him."

No one knew him. Later she found Allen, spoke to him.

"Did you treat Tom today?"

"I've been in Dorchester, Julia. Is he still ill? Who is it?"

"Tom. . . ."

Then she found that she couldn't remember his surname. She ate a meal with a group of the others, trying to think of it . . .

but by the time the meal was finished she could not even remember his first name.

She felt a sense of great loss, and an overwhelming sadness, and a sure knowledge that someone she had loved was no longer there.

Someone had died that day, or left the community. She wasn't sure which. Nor who it had been. It was very uncertain. Was it a man or woman . . . ?

By the time she lay down beside Greg that night, the feeling had become one of general sadness, not localized to any particular event or person.

She slept well, and when in the morning she was woken by Greg's insistent sexual advances she had no memory of what had happened the previous evening. Her sadness had gone, and as she lay with Greg thrusting himself into her she was thinking instead of David Harkman, and her intention to visit him in the evening. The intrigue and excitement were still there, and, because she was thinking of David, Greg's lovemaking for once did not leave her unsatisfied.

□□□□□□ Before Greg left the hut to go to the workshop, Julia
9   told him she was going to spend the day at the stall in Dorchester, and return in the late afternoon to collect the skimmer for David Harkman.

"Why don't you take it with you now?"

"The boat's going to be fully loaded," she said. "I've got to come back to the Castle this afternoon anyway. I can make a special journey."

Greg looked at her suspiciously, and for a moment Julia thought he was going to say that he would deliver the skimmer to Harkman himself. She was prepared for that: although she had made up her mind about David Harkman, a residual doubt about the possible consequences would be appeased by the decision being made for her. Instead, Greg said nothing, and soon afterwards he went to the workshop.

When she was alone, Julia washed hurriedly, then went to find Mark and Hannah. Mark had already left for the town on foot, and Hannah was preparing the boat in which the Castle's wares were carried across to the town. It was a small dinghy, fitted with an old-fashioned petrol engine. It was the only motorized boat the Castle possessed – indeed, it was the only motorized vehicle of any kind – and it was moored overnight on a stretch of sand beneath the north-eastern ramparts of the Castle.

"I'll need the boat this evening, Hannah. I'll be returning to the Castle in the afternoon. Can you and Mark walk back this evening?"

Hannah was a quiet woman approaching middle age, and she nodded briefly.

Julia said: "I'll walk over to Dorchester this morning. I've got a few things to do here first."

Hannah nodded again, seeming to stare past her. Julia had found her a difficult person to get on with from the start, and the two women still hardly knew each other. Sometimes, two or three days would pass at the stall without their speaking to each other. It seemed not to matter.

Julia helped her launch the boat, and pushed it out into deeper water before Hannah started the engine.

She watched from the beach as the little boat chugged away, and then she walked back along the shore, beneath the northern ramparts. The skirt of her smock had got wet when she waded out into the sea, and so she took it off and laid it in the sunshine for a few minutes.

The warmth of the sun on her body reminded her of the day before, as she had lain on the sandy beach of the inlet, watching David Harkman swimming, and feeling the piquancy of sexual anticipation. That anticipation was still there. The prospect of the evening made her feel like she had when she was sixteen, when everything had been full of mystery and dangerous promise, when every young man on the farming cooperative had begun to look at her with new interest, and when she had started to explore the possibilities of that interest.

Those early experiences now felt remote and unreal; perhaps they had been changed in hindsight by the long months of sexual monotony with Greg, or perhaps the only real charge they had ever held was that of novelty.

Thinking of David Harkman, thinking of the intangible magnetism that drew them together, Julia felt an anticipatory moistness in her mouth, a tightness in her stomach: physical excitement, emotional arousal.

After a few minutes of such idle but pleasurable thoughts, Julia sat up and felt the skirt of her smock. It was still damp, but she felt like walking and so she pulled it on again.

She climbed the first rampart and stood for a while to stare out across the blue bay. The tide was high but ebbing, and dozens of pleasure craft were sailing on the calm water. There was a slight haze in the air, and the hills around Blandford Passage were invisible from the Castle. Sometimes Julia envied the rich tourists, for they could buy and enjoy this beautiful place and stay shielded from the less glamorous quotidian concerns of the local people. No one in this part of Wessex actually lived in poverty, but the villas and apartments and hotels that the visitors saw were a world away from local housing standards. The winter months in Wessex were hard for everybody, and when the tidal bore broke through the Passage in its midwinter fury it was as a reminder of the elemental forces that had shaped this region, not as a tourist attraction for the rich and idle.

The fact that Maiden Castle derived a substantial part of its income from supplying equipment for that attraction held a double irony for Julia. The first was implicit – for the Castle community could not survive without the sales of its skimmers – and the second was that it had brought David Harkman to her, and she thought of him as neither rich nor idle.

She turned and headed inland, walking along the crest of the first rampart. After a while she ran down the slope, and took a path that meandered over the meadows between the Castle and Dorchester, leading nowhere in particular but heading away from the sea. There was a favourite place of hers along here, a quiet hollow, a secret sanctuary.

The sea, however calm or windless, always scented the air at its shore; once inland, Julia felt its presence slipping away behind her, and the air seemed warmer, stiller, more dusty and laden with life. Insects flew and hummed, grass rustled, plants grew green and moist, and underfoot the soil was softer, browner. Julia walked slowly, feeling free and without worries.

She came at last to the place she was looking for: a mound of higher ground, overgrown with bracken. This was some distance from the Castle, although from one side of the low mound a part of the Castle could be seen through a break in the trees around the tiny hamlet of Clandon. Julia walked up the slope, pushing a way through the pathless bracken which grew, in places, as high as her shoulders. The ground was mossy, alive with all manner of tiny animals and insects. On the far side of the rise there was a natural break in the vegetation: the ground was stonier here, and the bracken grew less thickly.

Julia sat down, hugging her arms around her knees, and stared towards the south. She had never seen anyone from the Castle here. It was the one place she could come to and know she would be alone.

She sat and dreamed for about an hour, enjoying the warmth, relishing the solitude. Later, she turned and walked back through the bracken, intending to take as long as possible to reach Dorchester, and then spend the rest of the day at the stall before taking the boat back to the Castle.

Unexpectedly, there came a sudden glint of dazzling light in her eyes, and she blinked and turned her head, as if trying to flick away a piece of grit. She looked around, trying to see the source of the light: it had come from her right, through the bracken.

She moved to one side, trying to peer across the thickly growing vegetation. There was nothing there, no movement, no sign of anything.

She walked on, but moving towards the right, as if to investigate it.

As she pushed aside a large growth of bracken she saw a gleam of white light travelling quickly and erratically across the stalks and leaves towards her. In an instant it found her, and again the brilliance of reflected sunlight dazzled her. She ducked away, and at once saw the source of the light: there was a young man crouching in the bracken about twenty metres away from her, holding a piece of glass in his hand.

He stood up as soon as he realized she had seen him.

"What are you doing?" she called to him, holding up her hand in case he played the light on her again.

"Watching you, m'dear." A local accent and intonation, but her doubts were raised immediately by something she sensed in the voice, as if it were an assumed accent.

He was stepping towards her, brushing aside the bracken with his hands. She saw that he was dark-haired and good-looking, and with an easy walk and physique, but the smile on his face was vaguely sinister. She sensed danger, but then saw that he was dressed in a smock similar to her own, which meant that he was from the Castle. But she didn't know his face.

"Who are you?"

"Never mind who I am," he said, and again there was a trace of the old Wessex lilt. "I know you're Julia. That right?"

She nodded before she could stop herself. "Are you from the Castle?"

"You could say that."

"I've never seen you before."

"I only just arrived, after a manner of speaking."

He was standing before her now, not threatening her in any way but apparently amused at the sight of her. He was holding a mirror in his right hand, a small circle of polished and silvered glass, quite ordinary. He was playing with it as he stood there, turning it from side to side at shoulder height, and Julia glimpsed whirling reflections of bracken and sky and herself.

"What do you want?"

"Surely you know that, m'dear."

Once again there was no suggestion of threat, but he seemed surprised that she did not know.

"I'm going back to the Castle," she said, trying to move past him.

"So am I. We'll walk together."

As he said this he stepped to one side, and the sun fell across his face. Once more the mirror caught the sun, and he flashed it at her so that the light went into her eyes.

She turned her face away. "Don't do that, please!"

"Look into it, Julia."

He held it towards her at eye-level. She wouldn't look at first, not wanting to be dazzled again, but this time he was holding it so that she could see a reflection of herself. His hand was steady, but the mirror was angled down very slightly so that she saw a reflection of her own chin and neck. Automatically, she stooped a little so that she could look into her own eyes.

"Hold still, Julia."

She hardly heard what he said, because as she looked at her own eyes it was as if she was staring into a deep cavern. It frightened her and fascinated her, because the more obsessively she looked the deeper became the gaze of her own reflection.

She stepped back involuntarily, and blinked.

"Did you see yourself, Julia?"

"Please . . . I don't understand. What are you doing?"

He was still holding the mirror out to her, but she had moved away so that she was no longer transfixed by her own gaze. Then, in the mirror, she saw a second reflection. There was some- one behind —

She turned, gasping aloud. Another man had come up behind

her, silently through the bracken. He too was holding a mirror towards her, trying to make her see her own reflection.

Some dim awareness, a distant memory. . . .

"No!" she said. "Please!"

The first man was twirling his mirror again, catching the sun, making the brilliant rays flash about her head, whisk across her face.

She closed her eyes, trying to avoid the light, trying to rid herself of the terror that was in her.

The second man said: "Julia, look into the mirror."

He was standing beside the first man now, and they both had their mirrors held before her face. Although she was backing away, stumbling through the bracken, they were always in front of her, and soon it was inevitable that she –

Her gaze became locked with that of her reflected self. The same fright and fascination were there, drawing her in, holding her in the limbo of the illusory mirrored world. She became two-dimensional, spread across the plane between glass and silver. She felt a last, terrible compulsion to run, to hide, but it was too late and she was held in the mirror.

Later, she found herself walking back along the path she had followed, one man in front of her, the other behind. Her trance excluded all awareness of the things around her, except for the sight of the back of the man ahead, the sound of the man behind.

They came to Maiden Castle, and she walked with them up the slopes of the ramparts. They went over the first earthwork, then the second, then along the trough between second and third. There were a few people about, but Julia paid no attention to them, and they did not notice her.

At last they came to an artificial construction in the trough: a low, concrete building. It was open on one side, and they walked in. There was nothing here: rubble littered the floor, and the walls and ceiling were cracked. Daylight showed in many places. On the far side there was a flight of steps, leading down, and the first man led the way. They walked slowly and carefully, stepping over small heaps of broken plaster and concrete. The air was chill, and smelled of clay. At the bottom of the stairs it was dark, because an electric light-bulb attached to the wall had broken, but ahead was a long corridor, a tunnel, leading under the village of Maiden Castle, and this was well-lit.

They walked along the tunnel, and Julia saw that the floor was untidy with scraps of paper, broken glass, pools of water.

Circular mirrors, lying as if discarded, winked up at her as she passed.

"In here, Julia."

They walked into a long, low hall, chill and almost completely dark. Only one light-bulb burned, radiating a pool of light into a bright circle in the centre of the floor.

She felt numbness and fear, compounded by the sense of unwilling compliance with the men's will. The warmth of the sun, the breezes and brightness of the bay, the people in her life . . . they were already long behind her, almost forgotten.

Along the length of one wall, barely visible in the gloom, there was a row of metal cabinets, grey-painted, dull-sheened. The second man, the one who walked behind, went across to these and walked along until he had found the one he was looking for. He put his hands on a steel handle, and pulled . . . and a long shallow drawer appeared.

Julia walked towards it without being told.

The younger man, the dark-haired one with the Wessex voice, stood beside her.

"Don't you be frightened, Julia."

She saw in him the affinity, the sense of recognition.

"What do you want me to do?"

"Take off your dress. Lie on the drawer."

Talking had weakened the trance. She looked away from him, feeling a return of her sense of identity.

"No," she said, but her voice was uncertain, trembling.

Watching her, he raised the little mirror again, and she shrank back from it, not wanting to see her own face. She felt the cold edge of the metal drawer against her hip.

"Take off your dress, Julia."

"No, I won't."

"I'll hold her down, Steve. You get it off."

Before she could resist, Julia was pushed back against the drawer, and one of the men seized her from behind, his arm holding tightly across her shoulders. The other man snatched at the laces at the front, opening the dress, pulling it down. She struggled at first, but she was still under the partial influence of the mirror and in a few seconds she was naked.

"O.K., that's it."

They turned her and pushed her down along the length of the drawer. The metal was cold against her flesh, and she resisted again . . . but they were too strong and too determined. She felt their hands on her body, pulling her and holding her arms and legs. Her head was pushed down into a contoured support, and she felt a sharp pricking in her neck and back.

At once, she felt she had been paralysed.

The men released her, and together they pushed the drawer. Julia slid backwards, into darkness.

As the drawer closed a brilliant light came on, and Julia saw that on the roof of the tiny cubicle, just above her, there was a round mirror, about half a metre in diameter. She saw in it a reflection of her naked body, supine on the drawer. For a moment of disorientation she felt as if she were standing before a mirror, staring at herself . . . but then she saw the reflection of her own eyes, and the mirror held her absolutely, and she surrendered to it.

For a moment, the light inside the cabinet seemed to brighten, but then it dimmed rapidly.

□□□□□□ Julia's return was instantaneous. As the lights inside
10   the cabinet were extinguished, a bell began to ring and she felt the drawer sliding outwards again, of its own volition. Moments later, there was a cold draught blowing over her, and a woman spoke loudly.

"Dr Trowbridge! It's Miss Stretton."

"Sedative please, nurse."

Julia tried to open her eyes, but before she could do so she felt something damp and cold inside her elbow, and a needle pricked into her. She parted her eyelids weakly, and with filmy eyes saw Dr Trowbridge looking down at her.

"Don't try to say anything, Julia. It's all right. You're safe."

She was lifted away from the drawer, and someone bathed her neck and shoulders with a liquid that stung, and smelt of iodine. Soon afterwards she was lifted on to a stretcher on a trolley, and tucked in beneath some blankets.

The trolley was pushed down a long corridor, fluorescent strips sliding down her vision like thin vertical windows to a brighter world; she thought for a moment that she was rising, as if in an elevator, but it was just the steady rolling of the trolley. Her perception was easily upset; for a time she closed her eyes and at once could imagine that the trolley was being pushed in the other direction, feet first, just as she had sometimes done as a child on train-journeys, as they hurtled through tunnels. As she opened her eyes, and saw the ceiling sliding above her, the alienating effect was the same; it was a jolt to return to reality.

She was about to try it again when the trolley halted. Metal gates were opened, and she was trundled into the compartment of a real elevator; it rose jerkily, a distant humming deep below, but she could not see the walls of the shaft, so she tried no experiments with perception.

At the top she was wheeled into the open air, and she felt cold wind and the spray of rain on her cheeks. A Land Rover was standing by, its engine running, and the two men who had been pushing her slid the trolley into the compartment at the back. Inside it was clean and warm, and rain drummed on the steel roof. The doors closed, and the vehicle pulled away. Through a window in the wall above her, Julia could see one of the shoulders of the Maiden Castle ramparts sliding by. The driver went slowly, taking the smoothest route.

There was a girl sitting with her in the back of the Land Rover, and she was smiling at her.

"Welcome back."

"Ma – Marilyn." It was difficult to talk, because the drug was taking effect, and the blankets lay heavily across her chin.

"Don't talk, Julia. We're going to Bincombe House."

She remembered then, her first real memory. Bincombe. The old country house used by the staff of the Wessex project. The familiarity of the memory made her want to cry. Marilyn reached over and clasped her hand.

The Land Rover lurched for the last time as it reached the car-park, and accelerated smoothly, crunching across the loose gravel. Julia wished she could sit up and see outside. Rain ran jerkily and diagonally down the window above her face, and as the Land Rover turned on to a paved road the metal bodywork of the vehicle began humming and droning in tune with the tyres.

She felt she was still in Wessex. The last events had happened only minutes before: the two young men with their mirrors, scaring her and wrenching her away from her life and her plans. She recognized them now: Andy and Steve, the two they knew as the retrievers, the ones who entered the projection to bring the participants back to reality . . . but inside the projection it was always the same, the lack of readiness, the sense of intrusion.

Marilyn, sitting across the compartment from her, continued to hold her hand, but was having to brace herself against the movements of the vehicle.

"It won't be long," she said. "We're nearly there."

How long it took made no difference to Julia. It was always a relief to be back, the same shuddery instinctive relief one felt when reaching home after walking alone late at night. An irrational fear, a welcoming of the safety of the familiar. She knew she was back, knew she was herself again. This was the fifth time she had returned from Wessex, and this never changed. She embraced her memories as if they were long-forgotten friends.

The Land Rover slowed and turned, and Julia heard its wheels splashing through deep puddles. In a moment it halted, and the engine was turned off. She heard the driver's door open and close, boots scraped on grit, and the main doors at the back were opened. The driver called to someone and a second man appeared, presumably from within the house. Outside, wind and rain on her face again, the blankets lifting to allow a cold draught to blow on her, and then she was on a second trolley, wheeling down a corridor laid with soft, rubbery tiles. There was a good smell in the house: food and people and paintwork. Somewhere a telephone was ringing, and from behind a closed door she heard a radio playing. Two girls passed the trolley, smiling down at her, and she saw that they were wearing ordinary clothes, jeans, woollen sweaters.

Julia's arms were folded across her stomach, and she raised them clear of the blanket. She lifted them and held them over her head, as if stretching after a long sleep, and luxuriated in the use of her muscles again. She let them drop immediately: she was weak and stiff, mentally exhausted.

They wheeled her into her room – the same old bed, the large window overlooking the grounds – and brought the trolley alongside the bed.

Marilyn had been following, and she came and stood beside her.

"I'll tell Dr Eliot you're here," she said, and Julia nodded wearily.

She was lifted from the trolley to the bed, and the sheets were pulled over her. As Marilyn and the two attendants left the room, Julia breathed out loudly, a sigh, a great gasp of pleasure, and she lay against the soft pillow and closed her eyes. Whether or not Dr Eliot came to see her Julia did not know, because within a few seconds she had fallen into a deep and natural sleep.

She awoke to daylight, and the feel of her hair lying across her face. She moved instinctively to brush it aside, and at once a nurse, who had been waiting in an armchair on the other side of the room, crossed to the bed and leaned over her.

"Are you awake, Miss Stretton?" she said softly.

"Mmm." Julia turned without opening her eyes, stretched, pulled the sheet around her shoulders again.

"Would you like a cup of tea?"

"Mmm." She was still waking, still in the half-world between awareness and dreams. She heard the nurse speaking into a telephone, heard the clatter of the receiver as it was replaced. She wanted to sleep for ever.

"The doctor will come as soon as you've had your tea."

She wasn't going to be allowed to drift back.

"Breakfast," Julia said, and struggled up on the pillow. She looked blearily at the nurse. "Can I have breakfast?"

"What would you like?"

"Something cooked. Bacon . . . lots of bacon. And eggs. And I'd like coffee, not tea."

"You mustn't overdo things," the nurse said.

"I'm not ill, I'm hungry. I haven't eaten for . . . how long was it this time?"

"Three weeks."

"That's how hungry I am."

Only three weeks. They had brought her back so soon! She had never before been in the projection for less than two months, and it was usually much longer. She should have been left alone, because there was always so much to accomplish. David Harkman . . . she remembered then that her retrieval had prevented her from seeing him in the evening, and in spite of the fact that her rational mind was in control, she felt again the sensations of curiosity and excitement that had so distracted her alter ego.

Although there was now, in addition, a sense of frustration.

The nurse had continued to look disapproving at Julia's request for breakfast, but nevertheless she had gone back to the telephone and was speaking to the kitchen.

Julia sat up in the bed, and arranged the pillow behind her. Many of her belongings were on the bedside table, and she picked up her hairbrush. It was impossible to wash the participants' hair while they were in the projection, and hers was always greasy and tangled after retrieval. She brushed it, hearing and feeling it crackle. It made her scalp feel good and fresh. She found a mirror and comb, and tidied herself up.

She looked calmly into the circular mirror, and saw the steady gaze of her own eyes. She stuck out her tongue; it was white and dry. Her pores were dirty; she would have a bath as soon as she got out of bed.

It felt good to be real again!

After she had eaten her breakfast, Dr Trowbridge came to see her. He examined her briefly, then got her to stand up and walk about the room.

"Any stiffness?"

"A little bit. Nothing unusual."

"Is there any discomfort in the spine?"

"Some. I shouldn't care to carry anything heavy."

He nodded. "You can have a massage if you want it, but don't over-exert yourself for a day or two. Plenty of light exercise and fresh air would be good for you."

Julia still felt that medical aftercare was over-solicitous on the project, but from the participants' point of view things had improved since the early days. On her first return, Julia had had to endure several days of tests and X-rays.

There was a bathroom attached to her room, and after Dr Trowbridge had left Julia took a leisurely bath. The sore patch on the back of her neck was sensitive to hot water, but she had a long, pleasurable wallow, and afterwards she dried her hair and put on a favourite dress. She looked through the window at the weather; it was not raining today, but a strong wind blew. She wondered idly about the date. The nurse said she had been gone for three weeks, so it must now be near the middle of August.

"Do you need me any more, Miss Stretton?" It was the nurse, looking round the door from outside.

"I don't think so. Dr Trowbridge has seen me."

"Would you like me to arrange a massage for you?"

"Not at the moment. Perhaps this evening. By the way, what's the time?"

"About ten-fifteen."

After the nurse had left, Julia found her wristwatch, set it to the time and shook it to make it work. It was always disorienting after a return. When she came to the house yesterday it must have been during the afternoon. How long had she slept? Sixteen hours? She felt refreshed for it, however long it had been.

A little while later, as Julia was sitting at the dressing-table making up her face, Marilyn came to the room.

"Are you feeling better, Julia?"

"Yes, fine."

"You looked really ill yesterday. It was the first time I'd seen you come out of the mortuary."

"I was just very tired. And drugged."

Julia had seen participants immediately after they returned, and she was sufficiently vain to hope that no one she knew well would ever see her in that state. Looking into the dressing-table mirror, she judged that the damage had been repaired.

Marilyn said: "There's a meeting this morning. At eleven. They want you to go."

"Yes, of course. Listen, Marilyn, do you know why I was retrieved so soon? The nurse said it was only three weeks."

"Didn't Dr Eliot tell you?"

"I haven't seen him. Dr Trowbridge came."

Marilyn said: "It was because of Tom Benedict."

Julia frowned, not understanding. Then she remembered: she hadn't thought of Tom since —

"What's happened to Tom?"

"He died, Julia. In the projector. He had a stroke, and it wasn't discovered until too late."

Julia stared at her in genuine shock. The double memories created by the projector always confused and alarmed her after a return, because of the way realities seemed to overlap . . . but this time it was as if she had to suffer the experience twice. She remembered Tom lying in the Castle infirmary and holding her hand, and she remembered that afterwards she had forgotten about him, his identity slipping from the grasp of her memory as surely as his hand had slipped from hers.

Then this: the return to her real life, with the forgetfulness remaining until now.

"But Marilyn . . . I didn't know!"

"There's to be an inquiry. You might have to go."

"I didn't realize. You see, Marilyn, I was there! I was with him when he died!"

"In Wessex?"

"It was the strangest thing." The memory was there in full now. "I was holding his hand, he was ill. There was no doctor, no proper treatment. Then he vanished. He ceased to exist. And no one could remember him!"

She felt tears in her eyes, and she turned away and found a Kleenex.

"Tom was a friend of yours, wasn't he?" Marilyn said.

"A friend of my father's. It was Tom who got me this job. I wouldn't be here if it wasn't for him." She blew her nose, then tucked the crumpled tissue into the sleeve of her dress. "Of course, it makes sense now. I couldn't understand it when he vanished! But it must have been when he died. He simply stopped projecting."

When she was in Wessex she had no way of recognizing it, but whenever she returned she was intrigued by the way her deeper feelings found parallels. Tom Benedict had always been like one of her family; one of her earliest memories was of sitting on his lap when she was four, trying to catch soap-bubbles as he blew them. He and her father had known each other for years, and Tom, who had never married in spite of frequent urgings by his closest friends, often spent his holidays with the family. As she grew older, and made her own friends and left home, Julia had seen less of Tom, but his avuncular interest was always there in the background. Four years ago, while she was still in the two-year vacuum that had followed the break-up with Paul Mason, Tom had recommended her for a job with the Wessex Foundation. He was one of the trustees of the Foundation fund that financed the operation, and with his influence on the other trustees her appointment had gone through after the most cursory of interviews. She felt she had made her own way after that, and worked as hard and contributed as much as anyone else, but she and Tom had always been close. It was inevitable that when they were in the projector, in Wessex, there would be a similar harmony, and so it was. She had only seen Tom once since the beginning – seen him here in the real world, that is – and they had enjoyed their reminiscences of the future.

As he had been in his own life, Tom in Wessex had been wise, jolly, warm. It seemed a pitiless, lonely death, to die inside the projector, but his consciousness had been in Wessex, and he had known she was beside him.

Julia realized she had been silent for some time, and that Marilyn was watching her uncomfortably.

"Has Tom been buried yet?"

"No, the funeral's tomorrow. Will you go?"

"Of course. Have his relatives been told?"

Marilyn nodded. "I believe your parents will be there."

Julia thought about seeing them again; it would be very strange. Her memories of them were partly confused with those of her "parents" in Wessex. Once, during a period of leave, she

64

had telephoned her father and during the conversation she had asked him some question about the farming cooperative. He owned a large and prospering dairy-farm near Hereford, and to say the least he hadn't understood. She had made a weak joke to cover the slip; to explain would have taken far too long. Her parents had only the vaguest notion of what her work entailed.

It was a quarter to eleven.

Marilyn said: "I suppose you had better go along to the meeting. I take it you haven't made a report yet?"

"I haven't had a chance."

They went out into the corridor, and Julia said: "By the way, I've found David Harkman. He's working at — "

"At the Regional Commission," Marilyn said. "Don Mander told us."

"Is Don back too?"

"He wants to talk to you about David. He thinks you're up to something."

Julia smiled at her memories.

She called in at the office on her way to the meeting, and picked up the mail that had accumulated over the last three weeks. There were about fifteen letters in all, and she sorted through them quickly. Most had been forwarded on from her flat in London, and most were bills. These she left with one of the secretaries; the Wessex participants all had their affairs looked after for them while they were inside the projector.

As she left the office a door on the opposite side of the corridor opened, and a man stepped out.

He said: "Hello, Julia. I was told I would find you here."

It was Paul Mason. The sight of him was so wholly unexpected that Julia froze in mid-step. She pressed herself back against the wall. Looking at him, seeing his confident, smiling face, Julia wanted to run. She felt a total compulsion to return to Maiden Castle at once, to bury herself in the future for ever.

□□□□□□ Paul said: "Aren't you pleased to see me?"

II   Everything that Julia had done since her return, and everything that she had thought about, was ejected from her mind by the sight of him as totally and efficiently as the memories of her own life were wiped out by the Ridpath projector. She saw Paul, only Paul, and all that he stood for in her past: the destruction of her pride, of her sense of identity, of her self-respect. In the same way that she had been morbidly obsessed with him after she had seen him during her last weekend in London, so he was now someone who by his very existence demanded, and received, her complete attention.

"Are you following me?" she said, and in so saying recognized in her own voice the sound of paranoia.

"What do you mean, Julia?" Was his innocent expression feigned?

"Look, Paul, I told you. We're finished. I don't want anything more to do with you."

"So you keep saying."

"Then what are you doing here?"

He smiled, and it was patronizingly reassuring. "Not to see you, if that's what you think. We happen to work in the same job, that's all."

Before she could stop herself, Julia said: "You're not a member of the project!"

"I work for the trustees."

Julia looked from side to side along the corridor. Marilyn had gone off to beg a lift back to the Castle, and was probably already out of the house. There was no one else in sight, but several doors along the corridor were open.

"We can't talk here," Julia said. "Someone will hear us."

"You haven't got anything to hide, have you?"

Julia pushed past him and went into the room he had been in. It was an office, and the desk was cluttered with papers. She recognized what the papers were the instant she saw them: some of the many reports filed by members of the projection during their periods of return from Wessex. These reports were the raw material of the projection, from which the periodic findings presented to the trustees were compiled. To Julia, the fact that someone like Paul Mason could have access to them was the grossest imaginable breach of privacy.

Paul was standing by the door.

"If you want to talk to me," Julia said, "come in here."

"You seem to be the one who wants to talk," Paul said, but he came into the room and closed the door.

"Is this your room?" Julia said.

"It is for the moment. There's another room coming free this week, and I'll be moving into that."

66

He meant Tom Benedict's room. Julia knew without having to be told.

With the door closed, Paul's manner changed. In the corridor he had had an air of amused formality, presumably because other people might have passed, but now that they were alone together Julia saw a more familiar Paul, one she recognized from the old days. In a particular sense this sudden change was a relief to her, for it confirmed her prejudices about him; there was always a doubt, when she was not with him, that she had imagined his destructive instincts.

Paul had walked round the desk, and was sitting behind it. He gave her a knowing look, then picked up two or three of the reports and held them for her to see.

"I'm interested in your dreamworld," he said. "It sounds pleasantly comforting."

"Comforting?" she said. "What do you mean?"

"It's just the sort of escape from reality you specialize in."

Paul was never content with an intrusion into privacy; he always had to pass comment sooner or later.

"Look, Paul, it's a real world."

"But it is a fantasy, isn't it? You mould it to your own desires."

"It's a scientific project."

"It was intended to be. I've read your reports . . . it's quite an idyllic little place you've worked out for yourself."

Julia, simultaneously angry and embarrassed, felt again the urge to run from him, but she knew that this time she would have to face up to him. The charge that the project members were indulging themselves in a wish-fulfilment fantasy was one that had been made several times by the board of trustees. It was inevitable when the nature of the project was understood. Of necessity, any projection would reflect the unconscious desires of the participants, and thus become a congenial environment to them. For all that, though, the scientific nature of the work was paramount.

But for Paul to make this charge, and to make it to *her*, pitched it on an altogether different level.

"You know nothing about Wessex," she said.

"I've read the reports. And I know you, Julia. Isn't it right up your street? Remember all those movies you used to see?"

"I don't know what you mean!" Julia said, but Paul smiled at her in a sly way, and she knew exactly what he meant.

There had been a time, about nine months before she left him, when she had felt she could go on no longer. She had been in one of her many secretarial jobs, bored and miserable, and in the evenings when she went back to the flat Paul was there to remind her of her failings and her faults, and the contempt he felt for her was only too clear. One evening, unable to face him, she'd rung him up and told him she had to work overtime . . . and went to the cinema instead. The two or three hours of relief had been sweet indeed, and the following evening she did the same. Over a period of three weeks she went alone to a cinema more often than she went home. And of course Paul had eventually found out. Trying to explain herself, trying to communicate her desperation, Julia had told him why, exactly why, but instead of sympathy she received only more contempt. From that day, "going to the movies" had become another phrase in Paul's unique vocabulary of destructive criticism, a metaphor for her inadequacy to face up to the real world.

Paul never forgot; the vocabulary was still intact, and it spoke across the years she had been free of him.

"You've always run away," Paul said. "You even ran away from me."

"It was all you deserved."

"You used to say I was the most important person in your life. Remember?"

"I thought it for about a week."

The first week. Those first deadly days when she had trusted and admired and loved him, or so she thought. The days when she had confided in him and talked frankly about herself, and at the same time was unknowingly sowing the seeds which would grow into the poisonous plants that he would be forever reaping.

"You can't run away again. You made the mistake once . . . but you know how you depend on me."

Anger prevailed. "My God, I don't need you! I've finished with you as completely as it's possible to be free of anyone. If I never see you again, I won't give a damn!"

"I seem to have heard that somewhere before."

"This time it's final. I've got my own life."

"Ah, yes. Your little escapist fantasy. How I admire you."

Julia turned away from him, and went to the door, the fury trembling in her.

"Still running, Julia?"

As she turned the handle, she paused. Looking back at Paul she saw that he was at ease, and smiling. He'd always enjoyed peeling back the skin to expose her sensitive nerves, then picking at them with his fingernails.

"I don't need to run from you any more. You're nothing to me."

"So I see. Then we'll test that in the projection."

"What do you mean?"

"We'll see how your unconscious reacts to mine."

She stared at him with a new horror. "You're not going into the projection!"

"No, no, of course not. How could I have ever thought you would allow me to upset your life."

Of all the various weapons at his disposal, sarcasm was the one most blunted by over-use.

Julia said: "Paul, so help me I'll do everything in my power to make sure you go nowhere near the projector."

He laughed as if to diminish the power she invoked. "I suppose the trustees have no say in the matter. I'm answerable to them, not to you."

"I'm a full participant. If I don't want you to join, I can stop you."

"Against the majority vote of the others, naturally."

There was a way . . . she knew there was a way.

"I can stop you, Paul," she said again.

In the early days a tacit agreement had been reached by all the participants. The nature of the projection was so delicately determined by the unconscious minds of the participants that its balance could be upset by the reactions of one personality to another. From the start they had all agreed: no relationships outside the projection. No affairs, no forming of liaisons, no cliques. Personal animus would be resolved one way or another before the projection began, or one or both of the parties would resign. With the same delicacy as they had created the nuances of the projected world, the participants had achieved this somehow. They stayed of accord, they stayed of a mind . . . but outside the projection they lived their own lives, and met only to discuss the work.

Paul was waiting, smiling at her.

"There's a rule we abide by," she said. "I have only to tell the others what you are to me, and you'll be out."

"So you would tell them you still fancy me?"

69

"No, you bastard. I'll tell them how much I loathe you. I'll tell them what you've done to me in the past, and I'll tell them what's happened today. I'll tell them anything . . . just to keep you out of Wessex."

Paul's smile had vanished, but his eyes held the same expression they had held all along: a narrow, calculating look.

"I suppose that knife could be made to cut two ways," he said.

"How?"

"It could be used on you as much as me." He stood up quickly, alarming her, and she stepped back. Her hand was still on the door-knob, but she hadn't the strength to turn it. "I've worked for a long time for an opportunity like this. I'm in this because it's my chance, and I'm going to take it. Nothing's going to get in my way, certainly not some frigid little bitch who's spent half her life blaming others for her own weakness. You can find somewhere else to hide. If it's between you and me, then it's going to be me."

Julia said, summoning her last reserves of strength, knowing she could stand no more of this: "I'm already established. You won't be allowed in."

"Then we'll put it to the test. See what the others think. Who's going to tell them? You or me?"

Julia shook her head miserably.

Paul said: "And while we're talking about that, shall we also mention your friendship with Benedict? Shall we tell them how you got your job?"

"No, Paul!"

"So we know what to tell the others. That's fine by me."

Julia felt she was going to faint. In the last ten minutes every single one of her deepest and most intimate nightmares had come to pass. She had known Paul was ruthless, she had known he was ambitious; she knew everything and more about the chemistry of destruction that worked between them, but she had never realized that the three could combine to such spectacularly explosive effect. She let out an uncontrollable low moan of misery and despair, and turned away. Paul, sitting down behind his desk, was grinning again.

As she let herself out of the office, she heard him rustling through the personal reports that lay on his desk.

□□□□□□ Although it was after one o'clock in the morning, the

I2 cafés and night-clubs of Dorchester were full, and the streets were thronged with people. It was a warm, stuffy night, a storm threatening. Music and voices competed on the patios of the cafés, and the open doors of the bars and night-clubs released a hot, aromatic radiance: music, body-heat, tobacco-smoke, glowing lights, like the open gates of a boilerhouse. People danced and sang and shouted, their faces shining, their thin clothes sticking to their bodies.

Only the sound of the sea, breaking against the concrete seawall, gave a cooling presence, a reminder of the wind.

Coloured lights were strung along the trees in Marine Boulevard, and these, with the golden, hissing glow of the gas-lamps against the sides of the buildings, cast an attractive multi-hued radiance over the passers-by.

David Harkman walked slowly down the Boulevard towards the harbour, his right arm resting lightly on Julia's shoulders. She held herself close to him, and her head rested against his chest; the nearness was a shadow of their earlier intimacy.

She seemed small against him, for his arm could pass right around her back. He felt very tender towards her, because she had been with him all evening, from the moment she knocked on the door of his hostel room. Their evening had been simple: they had gone to the harbour to move his new skimmer to the mooring he had rented earlier in the day, and after that they had eaten a meal at Sekker's Bar. From there they had returned to his room for the rest of the evening. They had been awkward with each other at first, neither of them wanting to talk about the strange link they both felt, but afterwards this mutual understanding had been acknowledged in an unspoken, physical way. Their lovemaking had been affectionate and passionate, exhausting them both.

Even so, as they walked in the humid night Harkman felt that the bond was weaker. It was not just that they had consummated the sexual desire, nor that mysteries had been dispelled. He had felt it as soon as she arrived: the intangible bond between them had been untied.

As they strolled along the Boulevard, Harkman realized that already the memory of their lovemaking had the same quality to it as those memories of his life before he had applied for the Dorchester posting. He remembered the fact of what they had done together, but the memory of it was remote.

Even as he thought this, Harkman knew that it was neither fair nor right. He had *felt* and *experienced*, had lived the moments.

He suspected and feared that it was a shortcoming in himself, an inability to feel, and he tried unsuccessfully to put it from his mind.

Julia was warm under his arm, and he could detect her heart beating against the side of his body. It was a clinical observation, like a test of reality.

When they reached the harbour, they went down the concrete steps together, and he helped Julia into her boat. They kissed briefly, but with passion.

"Will you come again?"

"If you'd like me to," she said.

"You know I would. But only if you want to."

"I'll come . . . tomorrow, I think." She was standing unsteadily in the boat, holding his hands as he balanced on the edge of the steps. She said: "David . . . I do want to see you again."

They kissed once more, then at last Julia settled herself at the back of the boat, started the engine and in a moment had steered away across the harbour. The water was black and calm, and the coloured lights hanging on the far side reflected back from the surface in perfect symmetry with themselves. As her boat churned up the water, the wake sent the colours flashing and colliding.

Harkman stood on the harbour wall at the top of the steps until he could hear the engine no more, then walked back through the town.

It was odd how memory seemed to detach itself from experience; already, the sight of Julia's boat heading out across the black, multi-coloured water seemed distant from himself. It was as if there were a false experience in memory, one given to him. It seemed that he had been walking alone through the Boulevard all evening and into the night, with entirely spurious memories appearing in sequence to supply the false experience.

Memory was created *by* events, surely?

It could not be the other way around.

He had said nothing of this dilemma to Julia, although he had been aware of reality reshaping itself behind him all evening.

The meal at Sekker's: a remarkably good sea-food casserole, with wine from the north of France, it had been the most delicious meal Harkman had had since his arrival. Julia said she had never eaten at Sekker's before. Small incidents were memorable:

72

the waiter who had given Julia a rose; the four musicians who had deafened everyone on the patio until being asked to leave by the head waiter; the uproarious party at the next table, with six States Americans dressed in Arab robes and singing campus chants. The meal had *happened*; his stomach could still feel its weight.

And yet, even as they left Sekker's, Harkman had had a nagging sense that the memory of it was false.

With Julia, too: as they'd made love Harkman had a sudden insight that her arrival in his bed was spontaneous, that she had always been there, and that the events leading up to the moment were there only in implanted memory.

Afterwards, the sex itself became a memory, the drained, relaxed hour that followed being in its turn the only reality.

And now, as he walked back towards the Commission hostel, Harkman thought of the whispered departure from the harbour, and the boat crossing the smooth black water, as events created by memory.

It was as if Julia had not been there, that she did not exist except as some palpable extension of his own imagination, which, like a childhood ghoul, had substance only as long as he concentrated on it.

He reached the hostel and made his way up to his room, careful not to meet any of his colleagues from the Commission. They all appeared to be in bed, for the building was silent.

He washed and undressed, and pulled back the crumpled covers of the bed. There, on the lower sheet, was a small damp patch of deeply intimate memory. Harkman stared at it thoughtfully, knowing that it was as real to him as all his other recollections of the evening; as real . . . and as remote from memory.

As he lay naked in the bed, waiting for sleep, the patch of damp was against his back, cold and sticky.

□□□□□□ Donald Mander was on the telephone to Wessex House
13 in London. He had been brought back from Wessex a day before Julia Stretton and the others, and any signs of residual strain had passed. He felt rested and well, although the news of Tom Benedict's death had had a sobering effect on him. At fifty-four he was now the oldest member of the projection.

". . . the inquiry will be held the day after tomorrow," he was saying to Gerald Bonner, the trustees' legal adviser. "Yes, after the funeral."

Bonner was concerned about the possibility of adverse publicity following Tom's death. Although the Wessex project was not secret, after the initial interest shown at the inception of the projection, the media had turned its fickle ear to other matters and for most of the two years' life of the projection the work had gone on with what had become jealously guarded privacy and concentration.

". . . no, there's no need for a post-mortem, apparently. Tom was technically under medical supervision. Yes, naturally we're being careful. The medical checks will be intensified before anyone goes back into the projection."

He listened to Bonner talking about the possibility of a claim from Benedict's dependants, and how much that might cost.

"He wasn't married," Mander said. "But I'll see if anyone here knows about his family."

Afterwards, Mander rang through to Maiden Castle and spoke to John Eliot, who had requested a meeting of participants this morning.

"We'll be ready to start in a few minutes," he said.

Eliot confirmed that observation of all the participants had been stepped up. The only real cause for alarm was David Harkman; he was now the only participant who had never been brought back. The fact that he had been traced at last meant that it was only a matter of time, but for a human body to be held in suspension for more than two years could have any number of physiological side-effects. The two projection retrievers – Andrew Holder and Steve Carlsen – were in Wessex looking for him at the moment, but whether Harkman's long exposure to the future had weakened the mnemonics and the deep-hypnotic triggers was something nobody knew.

The retrievals were overlaid with elements of chance, and Mander himself couldn't help being amused at the way in which he had been retrieved this time.

Andy and Steve had presented themselves at the Commission, asking for a visa to visit France. The clerk on the desk had noticed the rough-sewn clothes – the unmistakable style of the Maiden Castle community – and had stonewalled them for an hour. The two young men had persisted, until the clerk summoned

74

Mander. Once they were in his office they produced their little mirrors, and he had followed them back to the Castle without any resistance.

It was always a haphazard operation. Neither the participants nor Steve and Andy had any real idea, while they were in their future personae, of why they should meet, and it was a credit to their own initiative and mnemonic training that they ever found the people they were looking for.

Like all the others, Donald Mander always felt an acute sense of frustration in the hours after being brought back. Once one had the perspective of one's real memories it was always so simple to see what could have been done as an alternative. But the future alter ego took over completely; personality and memory were left behind.

It was at the heart of the problem concerning Harkman: inside the projection he was motivated by the memories and personality of his alter ego.

By the time Mander had collected together his various notes, and the report he had typed up the night before, John Eliot had arrived from the Castle, and they met in the hall downstairs.

"Have you seen Paul Mason yet?" Eliot said, as they walked slowly down the corridor to the lounge they used for the meetings.

"I spoke to him briefly last night after I'd seen you. I didn't find out much about him."

"He's got a good degree. Durham University. He did a spell in journalism, but for the last five years he's been in commerce. Technically, he's just what we need to replace Tom. He worked with a property research group, planning capital outlay."

"But do you really think he'll fit in?" Mander said, expressing the one doubt that could never be allayed by Eliot's talk of qualifications and experience. Yesterday evening, he and Eliot had had a long, private argument, Mander voicing what he imagined would be the objection of all the other participants: that no one new could join the projection this late in its existence and not bring drastic changes to its shape.

"Whether he fits in or not, you'll have to prepare yourself for him. The trustees are adamant about his joining. But I don't see any problems. He's a very personable young man, and he's certainly grasped the principle of projection quickly."

"I gather he's coming to this meeting."

"That's right. I thought he should meet one or two of the others." They had reached the door, and Eliot pushed it open. "After you."

Because the projection was weakened by the removal of participants, it was held that at any one time no more than five people should be out of the projector, and with Tom Benedict's death this number had been reduced to four.

At the moment, in addition to Don Mander himself, Colin Willment had been brought back, as he was due for a period of leave. Mary Rickard had been retrieved also, at the request of her family, but she was expected to stay out of the projection for only a few days. In addition, Julia Stretton had been retrieved for further discussions about David Harkman, and the situation arising out of Tom's death.

When Mander and Eliot walked into the lounge, Colin and Mary were waiting for them. Julia had still not arrived.

Mander nodded to them with the slightly wary expression he found himself adopting whenever he met fellow participants outside the projection.

Apart from himself, Mary Rickard was the most senior member present. She was a biochemist from Bristol University, and had been with the projection from its earliest days. A shrewd judge of character, and a forceful theoretician about the nature of the projection, Mary had gained the respect of the others in the early, planning days, but since then, because of her inadvertently secondary rôle in Wessex, her manner had mellowed somewhat. Mary's future alter ego was a member of the Maiden Castle craft community, and neither she nor Mander had any recollection of their ever meeting in Wessex.

Colin Willment was the project's economist, and had been missing, for a time, in the way that Harkman had been missing. He had been traced eventually to the commercial dock at Poundbury, where his alter ego worked as a stevedore.

While they waited for the others to arrive, Mander and Eliot poured themselves coffee from the electric percolator that the staff at Bincombe provided.

Mary Rickard said: "Don, I'd like to go to Tom's funeral. Will that be possible?"

"Yes, of course. I imagine Julia will want to go too."

"Has she been retrieved?" Mary said.

"Yesterday. She should be here. Does anyone know where she is?"

John Eliot said: "Trowbridge examined her this morning. She knows about the meeting . . . she should be here."

As Mander and Eliot found chairs, Julia walked into the room. Mander's first thought was that she was still recovering from the after-effects of retrieval: she looked pale and drawn, and seemed very tense. She said hello to the others, then went to the sideboard to pour herself a cup of coffee. He noticed that her hands were shaking, and that as she spooned sugar into her cup she spilled a lot of it into the saucer.

Watching her, Mander was reminded of the many times he had seen her future persona at the stall in Dorchester. His own alter ego was a mildly lecherous one, and purposely passed the stall during his evening strolls. The first time he had met Julia outside the projection, he had explained to her that his frequent winks and knowing smiles were obviously a symptom of the subliminal recognition that members of the projection often experienced between each other in Wessex.

To the amused embarrassment of his real self, the Wessex Mander's lechery had continued afterwards, and showed no sign of abating. Once she had caught him standing on tiptoe to peep down the front of her dress as she leaned forward . . . and the look she had given him then had not been one of projective recognition.

As Julia sat down, John Eliot said: "I'm afraid we have quite a lot of work to get through this morning, but first we must establish who will be returning to the projection this week. Mary, you have to go up to London?"

Mary nodded; her house had been occupied by squatters, and there was a court-order to apply for. She said: "I'll probably be away for a couple of days."

"The problem is," Eliot said, "that Andy and Steve are likely to be retrieving David Harkman very soon. That will mean another three will be leaving the projection. Julia, I take it you could go back in the next two or three days? And you too, Don?"

They both confirmed this, Julia staring away from them, looking through the window and across the grounds.

"And you, Colin? You're due for leave."

Colin said: "I'll take it if I have to . . . but if I'm needed I'll go back in tomorrow."

"You're all eager to stay. Sometimes I think you're happier in Wessex than you are here."

No one said anything to that, and Mander, glancing round the group, saw something of the bond between them, the bond that tied them inside the projection. This was rarely discussed when they were in these meetings, but speaking in private he had found that his own experience was typical: Wessex had become the ideal retreat, a place where there was no danger, where the whims of the unconscious were satisfied. Life had a hypnotic quality of peace and security, an ordered languor; it was a restful, secure place. Even the climate was good.

Most of the participants came from or presently lived in the cities; at least half came from London. Life today in the cities was far from pleasant. Housing was in increasingly short supply, leading to the almost automatic occupation by squatters of any property left unoccupied for more than a day; exactly what had happened to Mary Rickard, in fact. Also, with the phenomenal cost of any kind of heating or fuel, the recurring food-shortages and consequent black-markets, the daily life of the average city-dweller, according to what remained of the responsible press, was approaching the level of urban savagery. All this compounded with the ever-increasing incidence of violent crime and the terrorist attacks, made anywhere more than twenty miles from a city a place of temporary escape.

Wessex, tourist island in an imagined future, became the ultimate escapist fantasy, a bolt-hole from reality.

Mander knew that none of the participants would admit to this, for it coloured in garish poster-paint a response which was for him, and for those with whom he had discussed it, a delicate watercolour of an experience.

The attraction Wessex held for him was a subtle affair; he knew that his own alter ego was discontented with his job, and had been for many years, and there was a routine dullness to life in the Regional Commission that he had not had to endure since an office-job he had taken during one university vacation thirty-five years ago. Even so, Mander always felt restless when he was out of the projection, hungered for the return.

Eliot said: "There's one other matter of great importance, and that's the effect on the projection of Tom Benedict's tragic death."

Mander glanced at the others and saw that they looked as uncomfortable about it as he felt. On the one hand there was the human tragedy of the death, but on the other the projection would have to go on. The majority of the participants, in other words those presently inside the projection, would have no knowledge of what had happened.

"Tom was very centralist," Colin Willment said. "I was in the projection until yesterday, and I'm not aware of any change that followed."

"I think we all appreciate that," Eliot said. "The real problem is with the trustees. You all know that there have been various suggestions from London that the projection has now outlived its usefulness, and that it must be run down soon. I know that when they heard the news about Tom, the first reaction was that this was as good a reason as any to close it now."

"But was Tom's death directly caused by being inside the projector?" Mary said.

"I don't think so. I shall be giving evidence at the inquiry, and as the senior doctor on the project, my opinion is that it was death from natural causes."

"And you've said this to the trustees?" Mary said.

"Of course. That was their first reaction, as I said. On later consideration, it seemed to them that the projection could continue, but at the same time it would be possible to correct some of what they see as its present shortcomings."

Eliot looked briefly at Mander as he said this. It was a sensitive area to tread, for the participants were fiercely jealous of their creation.

Eliot went on: "You've heard the criticism before . . . the belief held by some of the trustees that in certain ways the projection has become an end in itself."

Looking at Mary Rickard and the others, Mander again saw his own thoughts reflected. It was a charge against which they were more or less defenceless. In the early days the reports the participants had made had reflected the spirit of the projection: that they were discovering a society, and speculating about the way it was run. As time passed, though, and as the participants became more deeply embedded in that society, their reports had gradually become more factual in tone, relating the future society to *itself* rather than to the present. Expressed in a different way, it meant that the participants were treating the projection as a real world, rather than one which was a conscious extrapolation from their own.

But this was inevitable and always had been, although no one had realized it at the time. Because Wessex was created in part

79

by the unconscious, it became real for the period of the projection.

The trustees, who had budget considerations always in mind, had not been getting the results they were seeking.

It was a daring and imaginative conception: to postulate a future society so far ahead of the present day that the contemporary concerns and problems of the world would have been solved, one way or another. There would be no famine, because the projection created a world with plenty of food. There would be no threat of worldwide war, because the projection imagined a stable world political situation. The population explosion would be contained, because the projection decided that would be so. The use of technology and fossil fuels would have stabilized, because the projection created a world where this was achieved.

The projection itself created the ends; the participants, by moving within that society, would discover the means by which they had been achieved . . . and this was the purpose of the projection.

Two years since the projection began, the processes of the solutions were still not understood. Wessex in the early years of the twenty-second century, and the place it occupied in the world as a whole, was imagined and understood in the finest detail, but only the barest hints of how the stability had been achieved were capable of being passed back to the Foundation that funded the research.

"Some of you will be aware," Eliot said, "that the trustees have employed a Mr Paul Mason to replace Tom Benedict. I gather that Mr Mason was appointed two or three months ago, to assist the trustees in assessing the worth of the project's findings, but after the news of Tom's death it was suggested that Mason should replace him. They believe that he has the necessary qualities to direct our work more towards obtaining the information they require."

Mander said: "Do the trustees realize the effect a newcomer might have on the projection?"

"You mean in possible changes to the projected society?" Eliot, cast in the unlikely rôle of apologist for the trustees, seemed uneasy. "I believe so. Mason is quite clearly a man of formidable intelligence, and has spent the last few weeks familiarizing himself not only with the original program, but also with the reports that have been filed. I've spent a lot of time with him myself, and his grasp of what we are doing is remarkable. I believe that

80

any changes that might happen as a result of his joining the projection would be slight. No more, in fact, than those caused by Tom's death."

"But Tom's projective part was very much a consensus one," Mary Rickard said.

"How do you know that Mason's is not?" Eliot said. "I'd like you to meet him this morning. He's waiting outside. You can make up your own minds about him."

"And if we do not think him suitable?" Mander said.

"Then, presumably, the trustees would expect the projection to be closed in the next few weeks."

"So we shall have no real choice," Mary said.

"I think you'll find that Mason isn't as much of a threat as you think. He seems committed to the projection."

Again, Mander saw Mary Rickard and Colin Willment catching his eye. He knew their doubts without being told, for they were the same as his own. No one could be "committed" to the projection without entering it. It could not be experienced by sampling the reports, nor understood by reading the program. It had to be lived in to be felt . . . and only then was a commitment formed.

But the projection was an intensely private world; any newcomer, however sympathetic, would be an intruder. Paul Mason would not be welcomed until he had made the world reflect his own personality . . . and no one in the projection would willingly allow him to do that.

Mander said: "I suppose we should meet Mr Mason."

"May I bring him in then?" Eliot looked at the others for their approval. "Good. I'll go and find him."

Eliot left the room, and as soon as the door was closed Mander turned to the others.

"What do we do?" he said.

Colin shrugged. "We're tied. We have to accept him."

Mary Rickard said: "We're being blackmailed. If we accept him, he'll affect the projection. If we reject him, the projection will be closed."

"So what do you think?"

"We'll have to accept him."

"Julia? What about you?"

Throughout the discussion Julia had sat silently in her armchair. She looked pale and fragile, and the coffee she had poured herself was untouched.

"Are you feeling unwell, Julia?" Mary said.

"No . . . I'm all right."

Just then, Eliot came back into the room, and following him was a tall, smartly dressed young man, clearly at his ease.

Mander stood up, walked across to him and extended his hand. "Mr Mason. Good to see you again." He turned towards the others. I'd like you to meet your new colleagues. Mrs. Rickard, Miss Stretton, Mr Willment. . . ."

Paul Mason shook hands with them all, one by one, and Colin Willment rocked the percolator to see if there was any coffee left.

◻◻◻◻◻◻ Julia felt better as soon as Paul came into the room.

So obsessed had she been with the short, fraught con-

14 versation in Paul's office that she barely heard what John Eliot and Don Mander had been saying. Only at the end, when Eliot had been out of the room, had she realized that Mary and Colin had their own reasons for not wanting Paul in the projection.

Then Paul came in, and the unseen threat that had been lurking outside became a visible antagonist, and thus less fearful.

"How do you do, Miss Stretton?" he had said, for all the world as if they were total strangers . . . and the menace he presented became containable. The introduction had been a time when he could have revealed that they knew each other, but he had let the chance slip by, and played a part instead.

He had the trustees behind him; he didn't have to force a confrontation with her to join the projection.

She sat back in her armchair, trying to steady her breathing, and she watched Paul. She had had the strength once to defy him, and she must do it again.

He was sitting forward, listening and talking to Mander and Eliot. He had an intent, interested expression on his face . . . the one he reserved for polite company, when he wanted to make an impression and be liked by those around him. She had not seen the expression for years, but she recognized it instantly. It reminded her of the time –

The recollection was like a physical blow, and she felt herself reddening as if a hand had raked across her face. The memory had been buried in the past, but Paul's presence dug it out as easily as if it had lain on the surface for all that time.

82

It had been soon after she started living with him in London, long before the final rows. Some instinct for self-preservation had surfaced; it was only an instinct, then, because she was too heavily influenced by him to rationalize her miseries, and she believed what he told her about herself. Trying to express her uncertainties she had started a diary, a secret, honest diary, the sort that was never meant to be read, not even by its author. She'd written about herself, about her dreams, about her ambitions, about her sexual fantasies; they all poured out in an ungrammatical, unpunctuated gush of abbreviated words, like a scream from the unconscious. The diary was always locked away, pointedly, punctiliously, but it was Paul's flat and he had keys for everything. A few weeks after she'd begun the diary they had gone to dinner at the house of a magazine-editor Paul was then trying to impress. He'd sat at the dinner-table with this expression on his face, polite interest, an openness to other people's ideas . . . and then, after the editor had related an anecdote, Paul had answered by quoting aloud something she had scribbled in her diary the night before. It had to be deliberate, but it was done so that it sounded in context like something he'd made up himself; he even laughed at himself for saying it, apologized for triviality.

Then he smiled at her, seeming to seek her approval, but saying with his eyes what she was to learn a hundred times over in the months ahead: I possess you and control you. There is nothing of yours I cannot touch or colour. There is nothing of yours you may call your own.

And as Paul listened to the others he sometimes looked towards her, and his eyes were saying the same.

Don Mander at least seemed to have accepted that Paul would join the projection, although it was noticeable to Julia how quiet Colin and Mary were keeping.

Mander was saying: ". . . because the Ridpath operates on the unconscious as well as the conscious mind, our original program had to conform to a realistic consensus view of what this future might actually be like. If there were any deep doubts in the minds of the participants, they had to be allayed before we began."

Julia remembered the early days, when the interminable planning discussions were going on. Sometimes for weeks on end it seemed that an impasse had been reached, that there would be a minority of dissenters to every proposal put forward.

"I'm interested in the notion of communist control," Paul said. "Surely this would have seemed unlikely? Is it really possible that Britain could ever accept state socialism?"

"We felt it was," Eliot said. "Remember, it's not Britain as a whole that's being considered. One important feature is the assumption that Scotland will eventually break away from the union, and keep control of the oil-deposits in the North Sea. We've also assumed a different economic rôle for the oil itself; the natural deposits become state reserves, like gold. The oil left in the ground would be worth more than that taken out and used. Without this kind of commodity asset, England by itself would have no economic strength. It would be ripe for takeover."

"But why the eastern bloc, Dr Eliot?"

There was a reason for everything, Julia thought. In spite of herself and her intense feelings, she was being beguiled by Paul's reasonable manner. He was, after all, only asking the sort of questions anyone might. It occurred to her, for approximately the thousandth time in her life, that it might be only she who ever saw the bad side of Paul, that her prejudice was unfair.

She realized that the coffee she had poured herself had gone cold, so she went to the sideboard and took a fresh cup. Mary glanced at her as she walked back to her chair; both she and Colin were as quiet as Julia. Colin, affecting disinterest, was sprawling back across the sofa.

Julia had always liked this room, with its blackened beams and its huge Portland stone fireplace. Someone famous had lived here during the nineteenth century, and the house was listed as a monument to preserve it for future generations. But Julia had walked across these downs one day – one day in Wessex – and the house had no longer been here. She had been saddened when she realized it after retrieval, and lying in her room at the other end of the house she'd remembered the future when the place was gone. Bincombe House was warm with age, full of glad memories of other centuries. The sort of tensions that Paul created had no place here.

She tried to concentrate on what Eliot and Mander were explaining to Paul, hoping to come to terms with the new situation by involving herself in it more.

Mander was talking about the political shape of the twenty-second century, as conceived in the projection: the Muslim-dominated Emirate States that half the world would comprise, and which would include both Americas, most of Africa, the

Middle East, southern Europe. The communist bloc that made up most of the rest: northern Europe, England, Iceland, Scandinavia, most of Asia including India. A few countries still independent of both: Canada, Scotland, Switzerland, Eire, Australia. No Third World, unless you counted southern Africa, which called itself independent.

Part of the scenario had concentrated on energy resources. Oil would not be refined on such a universal scale: there would be petrol, but only for the very rich, or for reserved uses. Coal and hydro-electrics would still generate electricity, but there would be much more use of local resources: solar energy in the tropics; wood burning; geothermal drilling; wave and tidal power.

Julia had worked with the energy-resources team for a while. There was known to be some oil beneath Dorset, and, to a much more exploitable degree, a deep layer of hot rocks.

Don Mander was telling Paul of the geophysical nature of this speculated future world, and for the first time Julia heard her name mentioned. Paul glanced at her; he was still playing his part, for he nodded politely.

Geothermal drilling had so far only been tried on a small scale, and with limited success. Julia, working with the other people, had reached the conclusion that if the particular deposit of rocks five miles beneath the Frome Valley was exploited for its energy content, then several dangers would appear. The main one of these was that the rocks would cool when water was injected to tap the heat. This would probably result in seismic activity. The Wessex project included a seismologist – Kieran Santesson, who was presently inside the projection – and he had calculated that in an otherwise stable seismic zone, large earthquakes and widespread subsidence could occur. In an early test-run of the Ridpath, results indicated that certain parts of Dorset could sink as much as two hundred and fifty feet, thus effectively cutting off the West Country from the mainland.

This notion, that Wessex could become an island, had appealed to everyone in the project, and it had immediately become a dominant image in the program.

Eliot was saying: ". . . you see, Mason, the conscious shape of the projection can be predetermined. What we cannot control is the unconscious nature of the landscape, nor the rôles played by the alter egos."

This had been Don Mander's province during the planning. Mander, one of the two psychologists on the project, had described the projection as a psychodrama of the mind, and for Julia the term had had sinister undertones, as if a clinical experiment was to take place. She had not been alone in this reaction. Many of the participants had had their doubts from the beginning; there was something almost indecent about the idea of pooling one's unconscious mind with comparative strangers. No one could rape the mind of anyone else, though, for the effect of the Ridpath was to blend the unconscious, to produce a kind of corporate dream.

The unconscious produced its illogicalities, especially in the way it treated the lives of the alter egos. The participants took rôles that reflected not their training or qualifications, but some deeper wish. Mander became a bureaucrat, Mary a potter; Kieran – the seismologist – worked as a chef in one of the waterfront restaurants; Colin Willment was a labourer in the docks. To one extent or another these could be traced to the real lives of the participants: Mary Rickard did pottery for relaxation, Colin often spoke of his frustrations about the purely theoretical nature of his work as an economist, Kieran was known to be an excellent cook.

The landscape, too, reflected the unconscious. It had its idiosyncracies and illogicalities – the climate was either dramatically good or dramatically bad, the days seemed longer, the hills seemed higher and the valleys deeper – but it was still a recognizable version of the true Dorset.

Someone had remarked at the beginning that the collective unconscious would produce archetypal horrors, nightmare images, dreamlike situations. It had been a semi-facetious remark, but many had taken it seriously. Unlike the dream-state, though, the Wessex of the group mind was controllable. There was constant correction stemming from reason, sanity, experience; the conscious mind could override the unconscious. The nightmare fantasies did not appear.

But the dreamlike quality was always there, and they all shared it. The participants had grown used to each other. Wessex had been shaped, and it belonged to those who had shaped it. An outsider trying to interfere with it presented a threat which acted on the deepest levels of identity, memory and mind.

When that outsider was somone like Paul, who, even when Julia disregarded her private feelings, was by his own account self-seeking and ambitious, the unconscious quality of the projection would be inevitably affected.

She was trying to be rational, trying to argue with herself. There was always a chance that if Paul entered the projection the results would not be as bad as she feared. He was intelligent enough, after all, and from his manner he seemed prepared to cooperate, to blend his will with that of the others.

She wondered what had been happening to him in the last six years. There must have been another woman in that time, perhaps several women. He had not mentioned them to her, either today or during her last weekend in London. Perhaps there was someone he was involved with now. Could it be just Julia's own paranoid imaginings that he was still motivated to control and dominate her? Had that scarring, devastating affaire been simply a product of youth, and they had both matured since?

And when the worst happened, what then? When Paul entered the projection, and they were there together in Wessex, was it possible that the old differences would be forgotten, along with their memories of the real world?

It was a possibility. Many of the participants had written about this in the personal sections of their reports. They found that the identity assumed by their alter egos lacked the cares of their real lives.

Thinking of this, Julia remembered Greg. He did not exist in reality; he was not a member of the projection.

Greg was one of the people of Wessex, imagined into being by the group unconscious. To use Don Mander's psychodrama analogy, Greg was one of the thousands of unscripted supporting rôles, the auxiliary egos. Most of these were in the background, like extras in a film . . . but sometimes the participants gave minor speaking parts to these players. Julia's unconscious had written a script for Greg, one that had a direct bearing on some inner need of her own. Greg became a physical lover, an incubus of the mind.

But the unconscious played its tricks: Greg was an unsatisfactory sexual partner.

In her own reports Julia had described the fact of the sexual relationship with Greg, but she had never detailed the way he almost invariably left her unsatisfied. In this, her reports were less than complete, but, realizing that the nature of the relationship with Greg would reveal a very personal and intimate inadequacy, Julia felt justified in omitting this.

It was all directly relevant to Paul Mason.

She had long ago come to the conclusion that Paul's destructive, poisonous attitude to her came from an inner need of his own, a compensation for some physical failing.

If Paul still felt this failing, and he entered the projection, then it was almost certain that he too would find himself in some imagined, unconscious relationship with an auxiliary ego of his own. Perhaps he would learn from this, as she had learned from Greg.

It was a pious hope, but still a hope . . . and when, a few minutes later, the discussion was interrupted by the lunch-bell, Julia felt calmer about the prospects than she had since she met Paul that morning.

□□□□□□ David Harkman had set his alarm-clock for six-thirty
15 in the morning, and in spite of his late night was
awake in seconds. The previous day, knowing that Julia
was going to deliver his new skimmer, he had made
enquiries about the times of the tides. There was usually only
one tidal bore a day which could be ridden, and as the time of
the tides moved forward about half an hour every day the evening flood was now too close to nightfall to be safe. Today's
tidal wave suitable for riders was due to appear at about eight
forty-five in the morning, and Harkman was eager to try his
skill.

He dressed hurriedly, putting on a pair of swimming trunks
beneath his trousers, and left the Commission hostel.

Dorchester had a grey, dismal appearance. The humid weather
of the day before had broken, and a heavy, wetting drizzle drifted
across the town, making the buildings look dank and cheerless.
It was difficult to imagine that Marine Boulevard, in this deaden-
ing early-morning light, could have been the scene of colourful
revelry only a few hours before. The lights were off, the bars and
cafés were shuttered.

There were only a few people about, and most of those, like
himself, were heading for the harbour.

He went first to the skimmer-shop, which adjusted its opening hours to those of the tides. At this time of day the management knew its customers and their needs exactly, and there was
no sign of the careless indifference that Harkman had seen on
his first visit. As he went into the shop an assistant came for-

ward, and within twenty minutes Harkman was equipped with the necessary rubber wet-suit and breathing-apparatus.

At low tide the harbour was unnavigable, and the Child Okeford launch was waiting in the deeper water against the outside of the harbour wall. There were already more than two dozen people sitting on the benches on the forward deck, many of them wearing their shiny black wet-suits, like so many seals clustered on a rock.

The rear part of the boat was filled with the riders' equipment: the skimmers were stacked on special wooden racks, so that one did not rest on another, and there were several piles of clothing, wet-suits and breathing- and flotation-apparatus.

Harkman went down the concrete steps to the two men standing by the rail of the launch, paid his fare and dumped his newly bought gear on the deck.

There were several boys from the town standing around – such occasions inevitably brought them out to watch – and Harkman got two of them to help him remove his skimmer from its mooring, and carry it to a place on one of the racks. After this, he went to the forward deck and waited with the others for the launch to depart.

The drizzle persisted, soaking his clothes and slicking his hair over his forehead. Sitting in the crowd, Harkman reflected that the idea of wearing a wet-suit was not such a bad one after all.

Most of the other riders were men, but there was also a small group of women sitting together. They looked muscular and masculine in the padded rubber suits, and Harkman tried to imagine what Julia's slim body would look like in one. The thought of her immediately reminded him of the unusual sense of false memory he had felt the previous night – indeed, the recollection itself had the same abstract quality that had so disconcerted him – and he looked away from the women, and stared into the harbour at the rows of private yachts, dripping and melancholy at their moorings.

At last the craft nosed slowly away from the harbour wall, seeking the deeper water. The craft was flat-bottomed, but even so it bumped and scraped on the pebbly sea-bed. As soon as they were out of the shallows, the captain lowered the keel, and the engine accelerated the launch towards the east.

Harkman watched the coast as they roared past, seeing the broad flat beaches that during the days attracted so many visitors.

The journey to Blandford Passage took more than half an hour, and it was after eight o'clock when the launch moved slowly into the harbour at Child Okeford. There was a slight delay during disembarkation as Okeford was on mainland England and the visas of the overseas visitors had to be checked.

Here, in Blandford Passage itself, was the narrowest gap between England and Wessex Island. During the seismic disturbances of the previous century, the valley of the River Stour had been transformed from a shallow pass through the North Dorset Downs into a deep, narrow chasm, bounded on each side by crumbling chalk cliffs. To the north lay the wide Somerset Sea, which stretched from the Quantock Hills on Wessex Island to the Mendip Hills in England, and opened out into what had been the Bristol Channel. This triangular sea, whose southerly funnel was the pass over the remains of Blandford Forum, took the effect of the rising tide an hour before the sheltered waters of Dorchester Bay, which opened into the English Channel far to the east. Twice every day, as the level of the Somerset Sea rose, a tidal bore moved towards the south. Between the Quantocks and the Mendips its presence was imperceptible; as it passed the Wessex coastal town of Crewkerne it could be clearly seen as a wave of water some two or three metres high; as it reached Child Okeford, at the head of the narrow Passage, it was rarely less than twenty metres high, and in the seasonal spring tides had been known to reach fifty metres or more.

When the wind blew from the south-east the wave became a deadly rolling breaker, bursting out of the Passage in a spectacular cascade of foaming surf. It was this unique phenomenon that had first attracted visitors to the region, and it was this that had been the cause of the development of tourism on Wessex and the mainland.

Child Okeford, set high on the safety of Hambledon Hill, had become the centre for wave-riders, although it was Dorchester that attracted the visitors, with its night-life and beaches, its casino and mosque.

When Harkman left the launch, and had unloaded his equipment with the help of stewards, he went to the nearby pavilion to change. The wave-riders were obliged to follow many safety regulations, not the least of which was that all riders had to be out of Child Okeford harbour fifteen minutes before the wave arrived. This was so that the boom could be lowered over the harbour entrance, to prevent a potentially catastrophic inflooding of water as the wave passed. In any event, the riders needed to be ready in the centre of the Passage, well before the wave arrived.

Harkman struggled into his new wet-suit, pulling it on over his swimming trunks. The assistant in the shop had measured him for fit, but even so it felt tighter than it should. The Party had introduced new safety measures for riders, and there was more padding inside the suit than in the one he had worn when wave-riding in his youth. When he had finally got it on he went out-side, needing help with the breathing-apparatus. This had to be checked by a steward to ensure it conformed to the regulations, and he was asked if this was to be his first ride; in that case he would have needed to have an approved supervisor following him, at an extra cost of ten thousand dollars.

The skimmer's engine started smoothly, and after a few sec-onds to allow it to warm up, Harkman stepped down on to the broad surface of the craft, balanced himself, then accelerated smoothly across the harbour. As he passed through into the open Passage he saw that there were already some thirty or more riders ahead of him, with others following; it was more crowded than he would have liked, but still manageable.

While riding out he tried a few more practice turns, executing each without the ignominy of a fall. It was one thing to practise in the sheltered water of a creek by Maiden Castle, it was an-other to do it with the Okeford stewards watching from the shore.

He remembered his first fall, while learning to ride a skimmer. The throttle of the engine had remained open, and the little craft had skipped off into the wide stretches of the Somerset Sea on its own. Three days had passed before an army helicopter had spotted and retrieved it.

Another memory: flat and cool in the mind. Had it really happened?

A rider passed him, going in the same direction.

"Thirty metres!" he shouted, but with the noise of the engine, and the helmet of his suit covering his head, Harkman barely heard him.

"What?" he shouted back, but the other rider had gone on. A little later, another rider passed the same information. This time Harkman heard him and, entering into the spirit, shouted it to another when he got the chance. Someone must have had a wave-height estimate from the stewards.

He looked towards the north, but there was as yet no discernible sign of the bore. Harkman remembered from the years before that distances were often deceptive, and that the only reliable guide was to watch the walls of the chasm for the signs of the swell.

His muscles were tense, so in the few minutes he had left he went through the rote of his old training, flexing his arms and legs, trying to make his body as supple as possible. He couldn't help but be tense with expectation; in the past he had suffered many falls on the wave, and he knew too well the violence of the breaker.

The safest position for an uncertain rider was in the centre of the channel, but it was there that most of the riders congregated. Harkman liked freedom of manœuvre, and so he moved to the Wessex side, knowing that if the wave was higher than he could safely ride, the smoothness of the cliffs on that side would keep the surface of the swell relatively stable while he moved back to the centre.

In the distance there was a loud explosion: the cannon fired to warn shipping, but the sound which, by tradition, started the riders jockeying to and fro in anticipation of the wave. Harkman glanced again towards the north, and this time he saw the wave as a dark line across the smooth sea. It was already nearer and higher than he had expected. He turned the skimmer round in one last practice flip, still not entirely at ease with the new equipment, but knowing that at this late stage there was no avoiding the wave.

Moments later there came the sound of breaking water, and Harkman saw the swell creaming against the base of the cliff.

He opened the throttle and moved sideways, away from the cliff and towards the centre of the channel; after a few metres he flipped round, went back again. Then he felt the swell lifting him, so he accelerated forward and across the wave, staying in front of it but feeling the board tipping up from behind. The wave was rising quickly, as it raced into the constricted width of the Passage.

After a few seconds Harkman saw that he was moving perilously close to other riders, and so he did a standard reversal flip, turning in the skimmer's own length and moving back the other way. He was still racing away from the wave, but gradually it was catching up with him so that he was riding on its forward face.

92

For the moment the wave was unbroken, except where it rushed against the wall of the cliff, and here it roared and rebounded in white fury. Harkman flipped the board again, moving back towards the centre, and as he did so he found he was looking directly across the breadth of the wave, a terrifying mound of rising water, rushing through the Passage. Many of the riders at the centre had reached the crest too soon, and were leaning forward on their skimmers, racing their engines to keep abreast of the speed of the wave. Many fell or slipped back, were lost to sight behind the ever-rising wave.

Harkman was about halfway up the wave now, still racing forwards to avoid the crest, but zig-zagging broadly to time it as accurately as possible.

He flipped back, away from the other riders, but found at once that the wave had taken him much further into the Passage than he had thought, and that the cliff wall was only a few metres from him. Badly shocked, he flipped again, and with a quick movement of his hand turned on his air-supply.

The mouth of the Passage was ahead: a rocky, jagged pass into the open waters of the bay. It was less than a hundred metres away. Now was the time to reach the crest!

He throttled the engine back, and allowed the skimmer to ride diagonally up the wave. The gradient was steep, and already in places white spume was blowing up from the crest. Harkman was unpractised: he reached the crest too soon, before the wave had started to curl, and for an instant he slipped behind. He gunned the engine to its maximum, and regained the crest.

The wave had reached the mouth of the Passage, and it curled.

Harkman saw for an instant the spectacle that only riders of the wave ever saw: the calm stretch of the bay, grey under the cloudy sky, reaching from Dorchester in the west to the distant hills of Bournemouth in the east; the island of Purbeck was a black mound ahead.

As the wave curled the crest thinned and shot Harkman forward. He slid forward and down, falling through to the shimmering slope of rising water beneath. The practised wave-rider would anticipate, would try to land on the slope, and accelerate down the wave to safety before it crashed on top of him. But Harkman was taken unawares, and the skimmer landed tail-first. For an instant he thought he had recovered balance, but the skimmer was turning to one side . . . and the dark tunnel of the immense pipeline wave was closing above him.

He closed his eyes, and forced his limbs to relax.

He was thrown from the board with a violence that almost knocked him senseless, and then he was in a black bedlam of noise and pressure and gigantic currents, tearing him up, down, sideways.

The wave was collapsing, bursting into Dorchester Bay in a swathe of white foam that stretched for more than a kilometre. Harkman, inside the turmoil of raging water, plunged by the weight of the wave to the depths of the bay, was crushed and turned and wrenched. He made himself breathe steadily through his mask, tried not to resist the pressures on his body, knowing that the violence would subside in the end.

And at last it did, and Harkman surfaced, his head surrounded by the brilliant yellow of the flotation bags that he inflated from his air-supply the instant he saw the sky.

Half an hour later, the stewards' launch from Winterbourne found him, and he was plucked out of the water. Only seven other riders had made it as far as the bay, and as the launch ploughed back through the now navigable tidal flood towards Child Okeford, Harkman learned from the regular riders that the wave had been satisfactory, but not as big as usual.

Harkman was shivering, but it was not from cold, for the clouds had cleared at last and the sun was shining hotly.

As soon as he got back to Dorchester, he went to see Julia at the stall, and they arranged to meet again in the evening. He was so exhilarated by his ride that it was impossible to work, and spent the day in his office restlessly.

During the afternoon he heard that his skimmer had been recovered undamaged from the bay, and that there was a salvage fee to pay.

□□□□□□ Marilyn had come back from the Castle for lunch, and
16 Julia shared a table with her. She was glad of the break from the emotional stresses of the hour before. She saw Paul sharing a table with Eliot and Mander at the far end of the room, and Paul had his back towards her. It was as if someone had turned an electric fire away from her, so that the radiance was directed elsewhere.

The dining-room was in the old part of Bincombe House, and it was a high, stately room with small leaded windows. Relics of the past were attached to the walls: crossed pikestaffs, old shields, axes. In two glass cases were assortments of coins and pottery taken from archaeological digs in the grounds, and half of one wall was covered by an ancient brocade, protected by transparent plastic sheeting.

Marilyn filled her in on the gossip and news that had accumulated while she had been inside the projector. The gossip didn't interest Julia much – living with two separate identities of her own provided her with enough involvements without wondering about the private lives of others – but she always asked about it, because Marilyn was funny when she gossiped.

The news was more involving, and more depressing. Ever since the British troops had withdrawn from Northern Ireland, the Loyalist extremists had thrown in their lot with para-military Scottish independence groups, and for the last two years an intense urban bombing campaign had been conducted in English cities. For two of the three weeks Julia had been inside the projection there had been a lull, but on the day the Scottish Assembly had been surrounded by British troops – to protect the elected representatives, according to Westminster – two major bus-bombs had been set off, one in London, one in Bristol. At the same time, a bomb had exploded inside a rush-hour London Underground train. The casualties had been frightful. Public transport in every English city had come to a standstill as a result. There was other news too: another war in the Middle East, a dollar crisis, a royal pregnancy.

Julia listened with a feeling of growing detachment; the projection did that for her, and she knew that the others felt it too. Although they were sometimes accused of running away from the real world, the fact was that once they had lived in Wessex the participants became distanced from real life, and there was no need to hide from something insubstantial.

In another sense, though, Julia welcomed Marilyn's talk about matters outside, because it took her mind off Paul. She was feeling stronger about that, and as Marilyn chatted on Paul's malign presence faded.

After lunch they reassembled in the lounge, and they were helping themselves to more coffee when John Eliot was called away to the telephone. While they waited, Paul offered her a cigarette, and she refused it. Others were present; still no sign passed between them that they were anything other than recent acquaintances.

When Eliot came back he seemed preoccupied, and poured himself a coffee from the sideboard without saying anything.

Then, as he sat down, he said: "That was Trowbridge at the Castle. Andy and Steve have just come back from Wessex."

"Did they locate Harkman?" Don Mander said.

"Apparently, yes. But they couldn't retrieve him."

"Did something go wrong?"

"I've only had a partial account, because they're still recovering. But from what I gather, Harkman didn't respond to the mirrors."

"But that's impossible," Mander said. "Are they sure?"

"It's what they said."

The little circular mirrors that Andy and Steve used were the only known way of retrieving anyone from Wessex. It was a system Ridpath and Eliot had worked out between them: because of the loss of real identity within the projection, the participants would need an independent post-hypnotic trigger to make them abandon the unconscious world. They had decided on the use of mirrors. Nowhere in Wessex – and, for all they knew, nowhere in the whole imagined future world – was there another circular mirror. Square mirrors, rectangular mirrors, oval mirrors . . . but none circular. The only ones in existence were at Maiden Castle.

"Do you think it's possible that Harkman has become resistant?" Mander said.

"That's what it seems," Eliot said. "Apparently, Steve found him at the stall in Dorchester. He tried to sell him a mirror, but when he held it out Harkman simply said 'no thanks', and Steve left it at that. I gather you were there too, Julia."

That took her by surprise. "You mean at the stall?"

"Steve said you took the mirror from him, and threw it away. Then there was an argument, about the sort of goods that the stall should sell."

Julia smiled; her alter ego had firm ideas about that sort of thing.

"When was this?" Mander said.

"This morning."

When the participants had first discovered that their alter egos lived on in Wessex *after* retrieval there had been considerable confusion, especially in the minds of those people still projecting. How could the future identity continue to have substance without the projected personality? The answer was that during the period of return, the alter ego existed in the unconscious minds of the others; it became an auxiliary ego for the duration, projected by those who were in closest contact in the future world.

While the participant was outside the projector, it was of course impossible to discover what the alter ego was doing, but on rejoining the projection there would be full memories of the interim period.

Julia was aware that when she went back to Wessex she would know exactly what the imagined Julia had done in the meantime; she would know because it would seem to be a part of her experience.

On the evening of the day she had been retrieved she had been intending to meet David Harkman in Dorchester. She wondered if they had met as planned.

In the same way that she had a double, and sometimes contradictory, image of herself and her own future persona, so Julia had conflicting feelings about David Harkman. As she was here, living her real life in the real world, Harkman was just another member of the projection, if one in an unusual situation. But her memory of Harkman's alter ego was altogether different: warm, intrigued, excited, deeply personal.

If she had been seen in Dorchester with David Harkman it could mean only one thing: that her ego was being projected by him. He was relating closely to her, she had reached his unconscious mind. Just as the participants projected auxiliary egos to satisfy some unconscious longing, so Harkman was projecting an image of her in her absence.

This realization stirred a profound response in Julia; as Wessex had become an unconscious refuge for all the participants, so David Harkman had become a personal one for her. She felt again the call of the future, but this time it was one emanating from a particular source.

Her reports already omitted the personal dissatisfactions of her life with Greg; there was no reason why she should report the satisfactions she felt with someone else. It would be something no one need ever discover, an area of her life she could exclude from everyone.

She noticed that Paul was staring at her across the room, and she looked straight back at him. David Harkman had become a source of strength; he was one thing that Paul could never tamper with!

Lost in her own thoughts, Julia was paying little attention to what was going on around her. The purpose of a meeting like this was usually for the various participants to talk about their latest experiences in Wessex. Although written reports were always filed, verbal exchanges were considered to be of equal importance for being informal. A process known as conscious assimilation was supposed to take place: unexplained gaps in the projected world's structure, as seen from one person's point of view, could sometimes be filled by another's observations.

Colin Willment was speaking at the moment, describing the last few weeks in Wessex. Normally, Julia would listen to the others' reports with interest, but today her mind was elsewhere.

It was still Paul who was distracting her. It frightened her to think that he might have more emotional trapdoors to open under her, but she was calmer now, better able to cope.

For the moment there was equilibrium. Paul was to join the projection, and she had inner strengths to draw on.

Colin finished his verbal report in a few minutes, and Mary Rickard followed. Julia knew her turn would come, and so she thought more directly about what she would say. She wanted nothing inadvertent to slip out, especially about David, nothing that would give Paul any more information about her part in the projection than he already had.

Part of the difficulty was that Don, Mary and Colin were present. How much should be stated, how much remain private?

Julia wondered if her interest in David's alter ego was already known to them. Matters of this sort trickled through into the consciousness. She knew, for instance, that Colin Willment was "married" in Wessex, just as he was married in reality. She knew also, although she had never been told, that his projected wife was quite different from his real wife.

It was something she understood on an instinctive level, and one she felt honour-bound not to explore further.

So although the other participants would already have an inkling that something was developing between her and Harkman, Julia saw no reason to talk about it. If it was being assimilated on an unconscious level, why accelerate the process by drawing attention to it now?

She waited while Mary talked, not listening to her but organizing her thoughts and memories. Paul was still watching.

Then John Eliot said: "Julia, since we're interested in David Harkman at the moment, and you were trying to locate him, perhaps you could report next."

She hadn't realized that Mary had finished. She sat forward in her chair, trying to look as if she had been following what she had said.

"Miss Stretton," Eliot said to Paul, "is the geologist in the team."

"Yes, I know," Paul said. "We're old friends."

It came so unexpectedly, and was said in such an off-hand manner, that for a moment or two Julia hardly realized that Paul had thrown the hand-grenade whose pin he had removed that morning. But she had had time to recover from that surprise, and as the bomb landed she was able to pick it up and toss it back.

"Well, hardly old friends," she said, and affected a light laugh. "It seems we were at university together. Quite a coincidence really."

Mary, sitting next to Julia, said unexpectedly: "Mr Mason, you know there's a rule we have in the project? We discourage relationships outside the projection."

"Mary, you're embarrassing Julia," Don Mander said.

"Not at all," Julia said, suddenly aware that Mary at least had revealed where her loyalties lay. "We're almost strangers to each other. I didn't recognize Mr Mason until he introduced himself."

Eliot, who had been looking from Paul to Julia, seemed relieved by the casual tone of her answer.

"Go on, Julia . . . tell us about David Harkman."

"There's not much to tell." She was trying to avoid thinking of the consequences of what had just happened. Paul had tried to carry out his threat, and it had failed. Would he try again? What would he do next?

"I think I'd been in the projection a fortnight before Harkman appeared," she said, talking, making words. "You know that the stall is on the harbour, and one evening . . ."

She was talking too quickly, trying to get her story out. The censor she had invoked stayed in place, but she was embellishing her report with too many irrelevant details. She didn't want to seem as if thrown off-balance by Paul, or anyone, and it was a relief to speak of the thing she knew best. By the time she had been talking for about five minutes she was more in control of herself, and kept her story factual and to the point. She described meeting Harkman outside the skimmer-shop, and the next day when he visited the Castle. She described where Harkman was known to be living and working, where the retrievers would have their best chance of finding him. After this, she talked about Tom Benedict, and what had happened to him.

If the others were aware of the tension she felt they did not show it. They listened with interest, asking occasional questions.

But Paul was silent, sitting opposite her. He was leaning back in his chair, with his legs crossed, and all the time she was talking his hard eyes never once turned away from her.

□□□□□□ The meeting lasted all day. In the evening, as they
17 walked along the corridor to the dining-room, Paul fell
in beside her. John Eliot and Mander were a few yards
ahead of them; Mary and Colin walked a few paces
behind.

Paul said: "I want a word with you."

She stared ahead, trying not to acknowledge him.

Each table was set for four, and Julia headed for the one she had used at lunchtime. Paul followed, and sat at the same table.

John Eliot saw this, and came over to them.

"I expect you two have a lot in common," he said, smiling at Julia.

"Old college days," Paul said. "Which year did you take your finals, Miss Stretton?"

As Eliot went over to sit at another table with Mander, Julia said softly: "You can drop the pretence, Paul. I'm going to tell them."

"What? Everything? You wouldn't dare."

"Everything they need to know. I'm not the only one who doesn't want you here."

"Tell them whatever you like. Suits me. Are you going to tell them about the money?"

"What money?" Julia said at once.

"The fifty quid you owe me."

"I don't know what you mean." A movement by the door caught her eye, and she turned away from him, her face reddening. It was Marilyn, and Julia waved to her to come to the table.

Julia went through the motions of introducing her to Paul, but inside she felt a deep, familiar dread. She knew which fifty pounds Paul meant, but it didn't matter. Not now.

Paul said to Marilyn: "You've just saved Julia from an old debt. She owes me fifty pounds."

100

Marilyn laughed. "I thought you two had only just met!"

"He's joking," Julia said, and forced a laugh of her own.

One day they'd had a row. Why it was that day and that row didn't matter . . . it was just one of dozens. Paul had won an office sweep, and he had come in from work brandishing the winnings. He was talking big in those days, wanted to set up on his own. Julia – it felt like a different Julia now – had spent the day job-hunting, was tired and bitter. An argument had started, the row developed. At the end, Julia had snatched the money from where he'd put it, stormed out of the flat. Stupidly, stupidly, she lost her purse, and with it went the money and her door-key. Afterwards, he would only let her in after she wept and knelt outside the door, and he'd pushed her on the bed and possessed her violently. There was a parting shot, there always was with Paul: the worst fifty quid's worth he'd had. That week.

Later he told the story for laughs, changing the facts to suit his own vanity. He always told the story in her presence, always got his laugh. After that, whenever money was mentioned, any money, he always somehow equated it with sex.

The surface of the dining-table was deep-grained, dark-polished wood, and Julia stared at the rush place-mat in front of her, shifting it with her fingers and making the cutlery tinkle. Paul was talking in a friendly way to Marilyn, the fifty pounds wasn't being mentioned.

She had never paid it back, never got round to it. She was always broke in the old days, and since then, since leaving Paul, she had put it out of her mind. She could pay it back now, pay it back twenty times and hardly miss it . . . but that wasn't the point. If she offered it to him he would refuse it; if she didn't he would never let her forget. But of course it wasn't the money itself. It had become a symbolic debt, the repayment that was due for walking out on him.

But then, as had happened during the afternoon, Julia felt her spirits rallying.

The debt was one she did not acknowledge; the money was irrelevant, and if she had ever done one thing in her life she never regretted it was leaving Paul.

While the first course was being served, Julia noticed Paul eyeing Marilyn's body. She was a bigger, more bosomy, girl than Julia, and this evening she was wearing a skinny-thin sweater without a bra. Paul would like that, Paul had a thing about breasts. Even in that he had tried to make her feel inadequate;

he used to point out other girls to her, and complain that she was too thin and round-shouldered.

Her spirits were still high: it suddenly occurred to her that the only remaining vulnerabilities were petty and unimportant. A small sum of money, her bust-measurement: were these *all* that Paul could threaten her with?

Her sardonic amusement must have revealed itself on her face, because Marilyn suddenly looked away from Paul and grinned at her.

"Do you feel like going out for a drink this evening?" she said to her.

Julia shook her head. "No . . . I'd better stay in. I've got to write my report tonight."

Paul said nothing, but Julia saw him looking towards her. He was wearing a broad, false smile, and he winked lewdly at her. Marilyn, looking round for some butter, didn't see. It seemed to be a pointless thing to do.

Julia said very little during the meal, and as soon as she had had her dessert she excused herself from the table.

She went across to John Eliot, who was still eating.

"Dr Eliot, I'd like to rejoin the projection as soon as possible. Can it be tomorrow evening?"

"You'll be going to Tom's funeral?"

"Of course."

"I'm not sure. You've only just been retrieved. We really should leave it for three days."

"What's the hurry, Julia?" Don Mander said.

"No hurry. I feel I'm wasting time here, and the projection is weak at the moment. Even Andy and Steve are out."

Eliot said: "We'll need a written report from you, and – "

"I'm going to my room to do it now. Look, I'm perfectly fit. I've got a feeling I'm the only person who can get David Harkman back, and I want to try. We've wasted all day talking, and the one thing we should be worrying about is David. How can he have developed resistance to the mirrors?"

"We were just discussing that. Don thinks that Steve must have made a mistake."

"Then that's what we've got to find out," Julia said. "When will he and Andy be ready for another try?"

"In two or three days."

"I want to be in Wessex before then. You made him my responsibility."

She turned away from their table before they could answer. Paul and Marilyn were at their table, and she walked past them quickly. She saw Marilyn turn, but she didn't look back.

Her room had been cleaned during the day, and the mess she had made in the bathroom had been tidied up. It was cold, so she lit the gas-fire then sat on the floor in front of it, staring at the orange-glowing radiants. Her nails had grown while she was inside the projector, and so she found her scissors and file and began reshaping them, deliberately not thinking about the day.

When the room had warmed she cleared a space on the table, then set up her portable typewriter and a light.

She worked for two hours, trying to present an objective account of all she had seen and done in Wessex. The verbal accounts were useful, but their effectiveness was limited to those people who heard them. The written reports were the only way of communicating with the other participants.

And that reminded her that she had her own reading to do: several reports would have accumulated in the last three weeks. She would have to go over to Salisbury in the morning for the funeral, and she would see if she could travel in Marilyn's car, and read them on the way.

In her report she described David Harkman's projected appearance in detail; they knew where he was for the moment, but there was never any certainty they wouldn't lose him again. The description was important. She remembered the pallid, waxen David Harkman she had seen in the mortuary before she went to Wessex last time, and the difference she had seen in the man she met. Pale, yes, but from working in offices, not from the weird half-life of the projector. She thought of the slim, muscular body riding the skimmer, and the easy, athletic walk across the quay.

She also described the disappearance of Tom Benedict in as much detail as she could recall; this was difficult, because the amnesia she had suffered directly afterwards had made the incident vague. She remembered his hand holding hers under the sheet, she remembered the cool white ward, and the officious woman with the child.

There were the same omissions in this written report as she had made in the afternoon. Feelings, mostly, and hopes. She wrote about the affinity she had detected with David Harkman, and with Tom Benedict, the sense of recognition when Andy had held the mirror before her eyes . . . but this was well known to them

103

all. What she omitted were the things that mattered to her, that were as private to her as the whole projection was to them all. Moments like those few seconds on the quayside when she had seen David Harkman walking towards her, and she'd caught her breath and felt her nipples hardening under the coarse fabric of her dress. Or down at the creek when she had agreed to go to David's room, with Greg a short distance away . . . and she had *seen* Greg falter in his stride, she had *made* Greg look away until she could agree.

To write of Wessex was to be reminded of it, even if for her it was only a partial account. It was always like this. In the hours following a return, one's real life intersected with the projection, and memories became confused.

Wessex became an obsession, a waking dream, a constant yearning.

It had given her the first real function in life, and Wessex had become her first reality.

All that went before Wessex seemed like a half-hearted rehearsal for an improvised play. Wessex was the play, and it dominated her personality as a strong character will dominate a good actor.

Only Paul, and all that he stood for, had as powerful an influence on her. And that had been a destructive, selfish influence; it was right that she should put it behind her.

Wessex was real, and it seduced her, in the same way that Paul had once seduced her. It grew around her, adapting to her personality. It was an unconscious wish come true, an extension of her own identity that totally embraced her; the perfect lover.

She stared at the sheet of typewritten paper, thinking how the words only described the surface-qualities of the experience. It was true what John Eliot had said that morning; the reports were no longer observations of anything functional to the project. Now the true experiences were held back, recycled through the unconscious to the further enrichment of the projection.

Like a genuine and deeply felt relationship, the fundamental truths need never be stated.

Julia decided she had finished her report, so she turned the last sheet out of the typewriter and separated it from the carbon-copy. She read it through, making a few small corrections, then laid it aside.

It was still fairly early in the evening, and she wondered for a moment if she should look for the others. They had probably gone into Dorchester for a drink. But Paul would be with them, and anyway the months inside the projection had taken away her taste for alcohol and cigarettes.

She tidied the desk, then went into the bathroom and undressed and washed. Afterwards, wearing her dressing-gown, she sat again on the mat in front of the gas-fire and stared blankly into the flames. She wished she had a pack of cards; she felt like a game of patience.

Then the door opened and closed, and Paul was there.

□□□□□□ Julia said: "Paul, go away."

18 He walked across the room, sat down in the armchair. "I thought I'd drop in to say goodnight. We haven't had much chance to talk today."

"I've nothing to say to you. I told you this morning: I've finished with you for good. I'm happy now."

"So you say. That isn't what John Eliot says about you."

A trout snaps at bait without knowing what it is; Julia recognized it, couldn't resist it. "What do you mean?"

"He thinks you're over-tired. Been projecting too long. He wants you to take long leave."

"Paul, you're lying." She closed her eyes, turned her face away. "For God's sake, get out!"

She heard him tap a cigarette against the side of a packet, then a match struck. When she looked back at him he was holding the match vertically so that the flame burned high. He blew it out with a long funnel of smoke, then flicked the match with his nail so that the black end flew away. He always did that, and she wondered how many thousands of times he had done it in the six years she hadn't seen him.

"Do you have an ash-tray?" he said, curling the match in his fingers.

"I don't smoke."

He dropped the match on the carpet. "Such will-power. You used to smoke more than me."

"Paul, I don't know what you're doing in here, nor what you want, but it isn't going to work. I don't want you here, I don't want you in the project, I never want to see you again!"

"The same old paranoia," he said. "I'm handy to have around, aren't I? Without me you'd have no one to blame for your short-comings."

She moved so that she turned her back towards him. Where were the inner strengths she had found during the day? Had they been a delusion?

"If you don't get out of here in the next five seconds, I'm going to call the others."

"Supposing they could hear you," he said. "And what would happen then? We have our showdown? O.K., if that's what you want. We'll tell them that we are, after all, old and intimate friends, and that you're having doubts about the work. I'll say that I agree you're over-tired, and after all didn't I live with you long enough to know you better than I know myself? You look pale and haggard, Julia. Perhaps you should have a holiday?"

"So you do want me out of the project!"

"Only if you force me."

She said nothing, staring at the carpet.

"Turn round so I can see you, Julia."

"Why?"

"I can always tell what you're thinking when I see your face."

She didn't move, and in a moment heard him leave his chair. She braced herself against his touch, but he walked past her, flicking ash towards the gas-fire as he did so. He sat on the bed, facing her.

"Why do you want to get into the project so badly?" she said.

"I told you: it's the finest opportunity of my career."

"You self-seeking bastard!"

"And you're in it for totally unselfish reasons, I suppose?"

"I'm involved because I believe in it."

"Then for once we agree," Paul said. "There's only one Ridpath projector, and I want to use it."

"I, I, I. Never mind the others."

"I'm needed because I've got something that none of you have. An objective and intelligent viewpoint."

She glared up at him. "Are you trying to say — ?"

"The word was objective. I was hired by the trustees because the projection is subjective and indulgent. They're paying for results, and that means new ideas."

"Which you have, presumably."

"I have one idea."

"What is it?"

Paul had his calculating grin again. "If I told you it would become your idea, wouldn't it? Let's just say that your little world has one omission so obvious I'm surprised no one thought of it before. I intend to rectify it."

"You're going to change the projection!"

"Not at all. I know how dear it is to you. After all, we mustn't *ever* change the projection."

"Paul, you're interfering in something you don't understand!"

"I understand only too well." Paul's voice had changed from false reasonableness to genuine harshness. "It's a fantasy-world for emotionally immature academics. All this talk of psychodrama! What we're talking about is failure, inadequacy! Look at you, you little slut. Incapable of enjoying sex in real life, you have to dream up some half-wit mechanic to screw you every night."

"You've been reading my reports!"

"I'm not obsessed with you. I've read them all. Not just yours."

She felt a surge of hysterical rage, and she scrambled to her feet, reaching out for him. She raised her hand to hit him, but he caught it and twisted her wrist painfully. She tore herself away, kicked out at him, then threw herself face-down across the armchair and began to sob.

Paul waited. He finished his cigarette, ground it out in the grate, then lit another.

"I'd like to meet this guy you've conjured up. I can see him now. Well-hung, and as stupid as – "

"Paul, *shut up*!" Sobbing, she tried to cover her ears. "Go away!"

"And of course he fucks you better than I ever could. I'll bet he's everything you said I wasn't."

She closed her mind to the voice, the intrusive, damaging presence. He always talked dirty to anger her, because he knew she couldn't stand it.

He had made her think of Greg, and after this the young man in Wessex, whom everybody liked, whose only fault was that he didn't know how to satisfy her, seemed safe and gentle and reassuring.

She began to calm down, and realized that Paul had stopped talking. She lay where she was, sprawled across the floor with

107

her head and chest in the seat of the armchair, breathing deeply to steady herself, trying to restore order to the chaos of her emotions.

The projection used mental techniques; the mnemonics trained the mind, taught discipline and self-control. The experience of the projection itself had a similar effect: it taught one the power of the unconscious mind, the way to use the conscious.

She thought: it's Greg! Paul cannot come to terms with the fact that my unconscious has created Greg!

But not David Harkman . . . no mention of David. He doesn't know, because no one knows.

David was the strength with which she could resist him.

Once in her life she had defied Paul by leaving him, and suddenly she realized that she had, quite unwittingly, done it again. His ego could not accept the notion that her Wessex lover might be better in bed than he was.

She raised her face from the cushion, and wiped her eyes on her sleeve. As she turned back to face Paul she discovered that as she had sprawled into the chair her shortie dressing-gown had ridden up, exposing her.

Paul, sitting on the bed, watched as she tried to cover herself. "I've seen it all before, Julia."

"You can say what you like. I don't care what you look at, I don't care what you think happens in Wessex, and I don't even care if you go there and see for yourself. I just want you to get out of my room, otherwise I'll bring everyone in the house here."

She said the words calmly and factually, for once expressing her true and total feelings.

Paul stared silently for a moment, and then stood up. As he did so, Julia realized that his watching of her exposed body had been more callous than she could have imagined, for as he turned she saw that he was noticeably aroused.

He took off the jacket of his suit, and hung it on the hook on the door.

"Don't get any ideas, Paul."

"I came to say goodnight, remember? You know what that means. We were always good together."

"Paul, I'll scream if you come near me!"

But she didn't scream, even then. A paralysis held her, the old familiar paralysis. Paul stepped quickly to her, and put his hand across her mouth, pressing his thumb and fingers into her cheeks.

It was the first time he had deliberately touched her, and as if this released a long-coiled spring, she struggled violently to escape. His hand swiped against the side of her head, half stunning her. He moved behind her, still pressing his hand across her mouth, pulling her head back.

"You like me rough, you little bitch. Well, you're going to enjoy this more than ever. . . ."

With his free hand he reached down and tore at the front of her gown. One button tore away, the other pulled the fabric with it, hanging on threads. The gown fell open and his hand snatched at her breast, twisting and pulling at the nipple. She tried to gasp, but he was choking her. He released her mouth for an instant, but before she could draw breath he had clamped his arm across her throat, making her gag. She could feel him pressing himself against her back, could feel the hardness of his arousal pushing into her buttocks.

She tried to scream, had no breath. She was clawing at his arm with her hands, kicking backwards . . . *anything* to get him to release her!

He was fumbling with his trousers now, and she knew that this was the only moment when she had a chance of freedom. With all her strength she forced her body down, leaning forwards. His arm pulled back, throttling her. She straightened, but then, using her last resource of strength, forced herself forward again.

His arm weakened, and she stumbled away.

She turned to face him, one half of her gown torn from her body, hanging down. Paul stood before her, his penis jutting from the front of his trousers.

"Don't move!" she said, and her bruised throat made her cough painfully. "Not one inch nearer!"

Paul, red in the face and breathing heavily, took a step towards her.

Julia saw the nail-scissors on the floor by the gas-fire, and snatched them up.

Holding one of the tiny blades out like a knife, Julia said: "Paul, I'll kill you." He took another step, and she said: "I mean it!"

"You like me rough," he said for the second time, but now it was without menace, almost pleadingly.

"Get out." She was more terrified than she had ever been in her life.

They stared in glaring silence, like two animals cornered by each other, but then Paul relaxed.

He reached down into the front of his trousers, straightened himself up, zipped the fly. He walked slowly to the door, took down his jacket.

Julia watched his every movement.

When he had put on his jacket he swept back the hair from his face, and opened the door.

"I'm sorry, Miss Stretton," he said loudly, into the corridor. "I thought you were playing hard to get."

As the door slammed behind him, Julia dropped the scissors, and fell across the bed and sobbed uncontrollably.

Half an hour later, she went to the door, turned the lock, then went to have a bath. She had a purple bruise across her throat, and there were scratches on her cheek where his fingernails had raked her. Her right breast was swollen and sore. She felt soiled, dirtied.

But later, as she lay awake in the dark, trying for sleep, she realized that Paul could not threaten her again. She could match him psychologically. She *knew* him now as she had never known him before, and she could contain the knowledge.

And she felt, without fear, that Paul had the same knowledge of her.

□□□□□□ While they were driving back from the funeral in
19 Salisbury, Julia read the other reports as she had planned. Her heart and mind weren't in them though, and she skimmed them, hoping to glean the necessary information with her eyes alone. Funerals always dispirited her, and the windswept grounds of the crematorium, with the processions of hearses leaving and arriving every few minutes, had seemed like the setting for a continuous, organized tragedy, staged scrupulously and tastefully.

Afterwards there had been the other ordeal: the nice cup of tea with her parents. Her father looked awkward and large in his dark suit, and her mother, tearful during the service, transferred her grief for Tom to nagging concern for Julia. "You don't look as if you get any fresh air, dear," and "I hope they're feeding you well", and "Do you ever hear from that nice boy you used to see in London?" I'm very busy, Mum, and I'm happy,

110

and yet isn't it sad about Tom, and I get all the fresh air I want, and I think we ought to be getting back pretty soon. . . .

Marilyn had gone with her to the tea-shop, and pretended not to listen to the conversation.

There had been no sign of Paul in the morning, but she did not even feel relief. If she had any feelings left about Paul, they were fatalistic ones. He might yet try to take revenge, but she was ready for anything. She was prepared to take the silk scarf from her throat, to show what it presently concealed, and bare her bruised breast if it would be enough to convince the others that it was Paul who was a threat to the projection, not her.

Marilyn had sensed that something climactic had happened the previous evening, but Julia had sidestepped her questions. When the participants returned from Wessex they were often in an upset state for hours afterwards, and Marilyn had grown accustomed to it. Although she was not directly involved with the projection, Marilyn had grown to know the participants, and had sometimes remarked to Julia on the way it was changing them.

"How has it changed me?" Julia had once asked her.

"For the better," was the answer, but it was a laughing one and Marilyn had said no more.

As they drove out of Dorchester, and crossed the Frome Valley towards Maiden Castle and Bincombe House beyond, Julia looked at the bleak, wind-blown scenery, trying to see it with her Wessex eyes, to see the calm, blue bay, dotted with boats. The southern side of Dorchester was ugly, with the post-war council houses of Victoria Park lining the hills. There was no sign of their existence in Wessex, evidence of the participants' unconscious consensus of distaste.

The main road passed Maiden Castle, which loomed up on its hill to their right. Glancing at it, Julia said: "Marilyn, do you know any reason why I shouldn't go back into the projection to-day?"

"You know it isn't anything to do with me."

"Yes, but I wondered if you'd heard anything."

"About you?"

"Not specially," Julia said. "But I returned only the day before yesterday, and someone was saying that after Tom's death the periods outside the projector should be longer."

"The only thing I've heard is that the medical examinations are going to be more rigorous."

"I'd heard that too."

Before they had left for Salisbury in the morning, Don Mander had called a brief meeting. It was urgent that at least two people should rejoin the projection, as there was now a total of seven participants out, although Steve and Andy were not counted as full projecting members. Colin Willment had gone on to London after the funeral, although it was likely he would be back in a day or two. Don Mander himself was undecided whether or not to take leave. Mary and Julia had offered themselves for an immediate return, although Mary needed at least one day to herself in London.

Of Paul Mason, nothing had been said.

When they reached Bincombe House, Julia went to her room and began to go through her clothes, wondering if she would need them in the next few days. There were a few that needed laundering, and she put them aside for the staff to deal with. She now had more clothes here than she had at her flat in London, but she never needed more than a few. She had brought most of them down with her the last time she came from London; now she was thinking she might take some of them back.

On the way down to Salisbury she had stopped for a snack with Marilyn, but hadn't eaten since . . . not even tea-cakes or scones in the afternoon, much to her parents' surprise. She was hungry now, and if she was rejoining the projection she should stay that way. She wanted to see John Eliot or Mander, and see what they wanted her to do. In spite of her new equanimity about Paul, his barb about her needing long leave still clung to her.

She went downstairs, but there was no one about. She stood indecisively by the fireplace in the lounge for ten minutes, wondering where Paul had been during the day. Marilyn had told her on the way back from the funeral that he was staying at the Antelope Hotel in Dorchester, so that accounted for why she hadn't seen him in Bincombe during the morning, but she had fully expected him to be there when they got back.

Upstairs, she found Mary Rickard packing a suitcase.

"I hope your house is going to be all right," Julia said. "What are you going to do about it?"

"I'll have to take out a court-order tomorrow, then give power of attorney to my ex-husband. It should be quite straight-forward, because the house used to be in his name anyway."

112

"When do you hope to be back here?"

"The day after tomorrow," Mary said. "I wasn't expecting to see you . . . I thought you were back in Wessex."

"I'm still waiting to hear from John Eliot."

"From what I know, he's waiting for you. He told me you were rejoining immediately after the funeral."

"So I'm going back!"

Julia felt a pleasant sense of relief, and also a thrill of excitement. Wessex was still there for her.

"Mary, what do you think of Paul Mason?"

"He seems a pleasant young man."

As she said this, Mary was folding a skirt and she did not look at Julia.

"Come on Mary. I'd like to know."

"He's a friend of yours, isn't he?"

"Did he tell you that?"

"No . . . but you said you were at university together."

"We were there at the same time," Julia said. "I remember him vaguely."

"So you say, dear. It doesn't matter to me. I noticed the way he was watching you."

For a moment Julia was tempted to tell her what had happened last night, but she had long been in the habit of not confiding in other members of the projection – consciously, at least – and she knew Mary less well than most.

"I did go out with him once or twice."

"I said it doesn't matter. In spite of what I said today, I was never one who believed we should treat each other as if we weren't human. Anyway, I happen to know that before the projection began there was at least one affaire going on. It doesn't seem to have made much difference.

Julia said, with interest: "Who was it between?"

"A man and a woman," Mary said, with a smile. "It was finished without blood or tears, as far as I know. So if you once had something going with Paul Mason, and you don't want to talk about it, then that's your business."

"You still haven't told me what you think of him."

Mary closed the suitcase lid, and sat down on the edge of her bed. She had large, soft features, kind eyes.

"I'll tell you, Julia, because that does matter to me. I think he's a dangerous and self-centred man. I think he will harm the projection, and there's nothing we can do about it."

She was speaking quietly, calmly. Mary rarely exaggerated: her reports were always exemplary of precise observation, telling images.

Julia said: "Do you know anything about him?"

"Nothing I can't see with my own eyes. And nothing I can't work out for myself. The trustees have hired him because he's just the kind of sharp young man they think the projection needs. But they don't realize what a malevolent ambition could do."

"I thought Don Mander and John Eliot liked him."

"Eliot likes him, Don doesn't. It doesn't matter what the participants think, anyway. The trustees want their money's worth, and they think a slick young operator with a background in gutter journalism and property speculation will get that for them. I suppose it's our own fault, ultimately. The trustees have always been out of touch with the projection. Julia, Wessex is *real* for me. I don't want it changed."

Julia remembered Paul in her room; the calculating grin before he tried to rape her.

"Mary, last night . . . I spoke to Paul Mason. He was talking about what he was going to do with the projection."

"What did he say?"

"Nothing specific. But he dropped a large hint, said there was an obvious omission in the projection."

"I heard him talking to John Eliot," Mary said. "He was asking how the projection equipment was used in Wessex. Eliot said it was used to retrieve the participants, and Paul asked him if it could be used for anything else. Do you suppose this is the same thing?"

"It might be. What did Eliot say?"

"He said, of course, that it couldn't. That's all I heard."

Julia said: "He's up to something. Mary, what's it going to be?"

"We'll find out eventually. But we have a consolation."

"What's that?"

"We know the projection better than he does. It's ours, and we can keep it ours. There are thirty-eight of us, Julia, and only one of him. No one can change the projection alone . . . Wessex is too deeply embedded now."

Julia thought of Paul, the ambitious graduate who claimed that no job was too big for him and his talents, and had been

114

right. Paul the career-climber, the rat-race smoothie. She knew Paul would have the will.

Mary said: "If we succumb to Paul he'll do what he wants. Our only hope is to be united with ourselves."

"But only four of us know about Paul! And Colin's on leave, and you're going back to London."

"I've already talked to Colin. He feels the same as us. He's entitled to his leave, but he'll be coming back as soon as he can. Maybe in a day or two. I'll be back in two days' time. As for the others . . . they'll have to be told as they're retrieved. Although if Paul makes changes, they'll see what's happening for themselves while they're in Wessex."

Mary stood up, and took her coat down from the door.

"I want to catch the last train," she said. "And I'll have to ring for a taxi."

Julia watched as Mary checked that the suitcase was firmly closed, then glanced about the room to make sure she hadn't forgotten anything. Julia followed her out of the room, and they went downstairs together. Don Mander was waiting for them in the hall.

Julia caught Mary's arm as they turned on the stairs, holding her back before Don saw them. She had suddenly realized that after Mary left she and Don would be the only two active participants at Bincombe. The thought frightened her, and made her understand how Mary had become an unexpected ally against Paul. Don Mander she didn't trust; he seemed altogether too ready to accept the trustees' appointment of Paul.

"Mary," she said softly, "can't we do something to stop Paul?"

"I think not, dear. He joined the projection this afternoon."

"Then it's too late."

"To do anything here, yes. But we'll be in Wessex."

Julia followed her down to the hall, and waited with Mary until the taxi arrived from Dorchester. When the car had driven away, Julia went up to her room, tidied her things, put away her clothes. She was thirsty, so she drank a little water from the toothbrush glass in the bathroom, then went downstairs again and talked to Don Mander. She was to return to Wessex that evening; there was no special brief for her, except to keep in contact with David Harkman; John Eliot and his staff were waiting for her at Maiden Castle.

Later, as Julia refreshed the mnemonics in her mind, she was

115

thinking of David, remembering how, when oppressed by Paul, the thought of him had strengthened her.

Once Wessex itself had been the unacknowledged refuge from Paul; now there was only David, and Paul did not know.

□□□□□□ It was suffocatingly warm in David Harkman's office,
20 and he sat with his jacket off and his tie undone. Even though the window was wide open, there was no draught to speak of, and the sounds of the tourists walking in the cobbled street outside were a continual distraction. He was reading through the Minutes of the Culture and Arts Committee, the body in the Commission theoretically responsible for subsidies to local drama workshops, art-galleries, playwrights, libraries and musical societies. Very little money was ever approved for direct sponsorship of the arts, because most of the Committee's allocation seemed to be spent on administrative expenses. It made depressing reading, and the page of Harkman's notebook, on which he had started to jot down observations, was still almost blank.

He picked up the internal telephone, and dialled a number.

"Is that Mr Mander?"

"Speaking."

"David Harkman. Has the Commissioner had a chance to approve my application?"

"Mr Borovitin has been engaged all day, Harkman. Will you try again in the morning?"

"I've been waiting for two days already. I can't start work until I have access to the archives."

"Call me again tomorrow."

Harkman had grown accustomed to the bureaucratic delays of Westminster, and had learned how to take short cuts when it was necessary, but he had not expected to come up against similar habitual obstructiveness here. Civil servants were probably the same all over the world, but the departmental mind was dissonant with the idyllic atmosphere of Dorchester.

Harkman closed the Culture and Arts file, and leaned back in his chair, staring irritably at the opposite wall. He was blocked in every way. The work he was paid to do couldn't be started properly, Julia was busy during the days, and even wave-riding

116

was excluded from him. High tide came just too late now, at a time when he was supposed to be at his desk. The exhilaration of his ride of the day before was still in him, but his next day off wasn't for another week, and it would be only towards the end of the week following that the wave would arrive late enough in the afternoon for him to take the time off.

It was at moments like this, when his external drives were temporarily thwarted, that Harkman felt his inner compulsion the strongest. It was what he had talked to Julia about, that morning at the Castle: the unaccountable urge to be in Wessex, to live and work in Dorchester. But it was not only Dorchester and Wessex, because he was here and the urge had been satisfied.

Maiden Castle was the focus. He was obsessed and dominated by it. He could not walk the streets of the town without looking frequently to the south-west, he could not conceive of Dorchester without the Castle beside it, he could not feel at ease unless he knew in which direction it lay from where he was. Just as the States tourists prostrated themselves five times daily towards Mecca, so Harkman paid frequent instinctive homage to the low, rounded hill-fort overlooking the bay.

Dwelling again on these matters renewed his frustration at the bureaucratic delay. As the days passed, Harkman realized that his own work would have to be set aside until he had investigated whatever records there were about Maiden Castle and its community.

On an impulse, Harkman hurried out of his office, determined to go directly to the Castle, as if this alone would dispel the compulsion, but before he was halfway along the corridor that led to the front office he had changed his mind. He had already been to the Castle, and it had not satisfied the urge.

He walked on, with less resolution than before. He passed through the front office and saw the usual line of States tourists, waiting patiently to apply for English visas.

As soon as he entered Marine Boulevard, Harkman looked towards the south-west, like the needle of a compass swinging towards the north. He could see the Castle across the bay: the day was sunny and humid, but in the sky beyond the Castle dark clouds were lowering. A weird light seemed to surround the hilltop, a glowing golden green, sunlight on storm; Harkman could almost detect the thermal of rising heat, like the hypnotic power of the Castle had over him, an invisible but detectable radiation, mystical and elemental.

A high tide in the morning made it impossible for him to ride the Blandford wave, but it meant that the harbour was open all during the rest of the day, and when Harkman reached the stall he found it crowded with visitors.

He managed to catch Julia's attention.

"Can you get away?" he said.

"Not until later. We're too busy."

As she spoke, an argument broke out between two of the customers over which of them had picked up a fragile crystal vase first. The two men squabbled in a fast North American dialect, rich in Arabic words, incomprehensible to the English.

"Five o'clock?" Harkman said.

"All right. If this has quietened down."

She turned away from him, and took the vase gently from the man who was clutching it. Harkman watched as she deftly intervened in the argument, clearly favouring one of the two, yet appeasing the other with a combination of flattery and the production of a slightly more expensive piece of merchandise. She spoke in English, and this itself had a calming effect. Harkman waited until both sales had been made, and then he walked away through the crowd of strolling tourists and went to the far end of the quay, overlooking the entrance to the harbour. He sat down on the paving-stones, feeling the sun's warmth through the fabric of his suit, a reminder of the long timeless summer, and his incongruous preoccupations in this tourist centre.

Many private cruisers were taking advantage of the tide, and the harbour remained busy until well after five. Harkman waited until half-past before walking back to the stall.

Julia looked tired, but she seemed pleased to see him, and as soon as she had spoken to the other two people behind the stall she left with him.

"What would you like to do?" he said, as they walked up the hill away from the shore, and towards the wild heaths that spread for miles around the town.

"Be with you," she said. "Alone."

What they had together was still a novelty, and no habits had formed. They walked quickly, although the air was hot and humid, until they found a sheltered dell away from the path, and there they made love. The newness, the freshness of what they had gave them the excitement of recent encounter, the sense of mutual conquest.

Harkman felt relaxed and tender, and when Julia had pulled

on her loose-fitting dress again he hugged her against him, and they lay back in the long grass together.

"Julia, I love you."

Her face was turned towards him, and she stretched up to kiss his neck beneath his ear.

"I love you too, David."

Last night they had said the same words again and again, a dozen times in an hour, and each time it had seemed fresh and original, the feeling belied by the inadequacy of the words. This evening it was as if they said them for the first time.

Because he had spent much of the afternoon pondering on the intangible compulsion of the Castle, Harkman had allowed himself to overlook the feeling of displaced memory that Julia aroused in him. He had felt it again as they met, and he felt it now as she lay in his arms. If he held her tightly he could diminish it, but nothing could dispel it entirely.

It was not that Julia gave only a part of herself to him, nor that she was distant or unaffectionate, because the first tendernesses came from her, the first loving kisses. She was in every way as dependent on him as he was on her, and in the manner of responses or of gestures, or of physical commitment, she satisfied him utterly.

He possessed Julia in every conceivable way bar their permanently living together, but he did not *experience* her. He remembered her into existence.

The thundercloud Harkman had seen earlier was blacker than before, but seemed no closer. A breeze had sprung up from the sea, and as it moved through the long grass it made a soothing, sweeping sound, at variance with the calm which tradition laid before the storm. They had heard the rumbling of thunder all afternoon, but the storm did not seem likely to strike for an hour or more.

Harkman, holding Julia, felt the stillness of fulfilment, felt the breeze of disconcerting compulsions, awaited the onset of what was to come.

She moved in his arms, and turned to lie on her back beside him, her head resting on his arm. She stared up at the sky. If the storm did not break beforehand there were about two hours until sunset, the time when they both knew she would return to Maiden Castle.

This temporary, borrowed aspect of their affaire had begun to have a corroding effect on Harkman.

He said, in a while: "Julia, I want you to leave the Castle. Come and live with me in Dorchester. We can find somewhere – "

"No. It's impossible!"

The readiness, and finality, of her answer came as a shock to him.

"What do you mean?" he said.

"I can't leave the community."

"Is it more important?"

She turned to face him and laid her hand on his chest, stroking him. Her touch suddenly felt alien, unwelcome.

"Don't let's argue about it," she said.

"Argue? It's too important for an argument! Do you love me?"

"Of course."

"Then there's no question. Julia, I love you so much I couldn't – "

"David, it's no good. I simply can't leave the Castle now."

"Now? But later?"

"I don't think so," she said.

There was one matter that Harkman had never raised with her, preferring to imagine the best than know the worst, but there could be no more avoiding it. He had to know.

"There's someone else," he said. "Another man."

She said, very quietly: "Of course."

"Then who – ?"

"But it isn't that, David. I'd leave him for you. Surely you know that?"

"Who is it?"

"You haven't met him. His name wouldn't mean anything to you." She sat up and faced him, looking down seriously at him. The breeze played with her hair, and behind her the storm-cloud loomed. "Don't question me about him. If it was just that I'd leave today."

Harkman, still burned by the fires of possessiveness and jealousy, barely heard this.

He said: "But I have met him. The man with the beard . . . at the workshop. Greg, wasn't it?"

She laughed dismissively, but there was strain in the sound. "It's not Greg. I told you, you haven't met him."

"He was acting very strangely that day."

She shook her head firmly. "Greg's always like that. It was

because you were from the Commission. He wanted to make you pay more."

"Then who is it?"

"Someone else. You haven't met him, probably never will. It doesn't matter who he is."

"It does to me."

It occurred to him then that Julia might be lying. There had been that unmistakable expression on Greg's face, that morning at the Castle, the expression which seemed to plant territorial fences around Julia whenever he looked at her.

"David, please don't go on asking about it. I love you, surely you know that?"

"Then come and live with me."

"I can't."

Again, the finality.

"Give me one reason, apart from this other man, why you will not."

She said nothing for a long time, so long in fact that Harkman thought she was going to avoid the question by maintaining the silence. But at last she said: "I can't leave the Castle because I live and work there."

"You work in Dorchester."

She said: "I'm not going back to the stall again. I've finished there."

"You haven't told me this before."

"You haven't given me a chance. I was going to tell you later. From tomorrow I shall be at the Castle all the time."

"Then I could live with you there?"

"No, David. . . ."

"So we come back to this other man, whose name you won't tell me."

"I suppose so," she said.

Harkman felt disappointed, angry, hurt. For a moment he thought he had seen a way round the problem, but it returned to source.

"What is it? Are you in love with him?"

Her eyes widened, not in affected innocence but in a surprise that seemed genuine. "Oh no, David. I love *you*."

"You live with him . . . is it because of the sex?"

"It used to be. Not now. He repels me. *Really*. That side of it is finished, but I need more time to work it out. I've only known you for five days. . . ."

He had to allow her that. What they had was profound, but it was certainly recent. For him there was a feeling of rightness about it that rose above the conventions, and in that moment of hope he had thought there was a way: he had been prepared to leave his work to live with her, to become one of the community at the Castle. The idea still appealed to him, because of its simplicity, but he knew too that if it came to a decision — here, on this heath, in this instant — he'd want more time to think about it.

Wasn't Julia only asking the same?

But the vagueness of her relationship with the other man, or at least the vagueness of how she presented it to him, was as potentially hurtful to him as the pain a hidden weapon could inflict. He was nervous of it, watchful for it, uncertain of how it might be used against him.

"Will you try to work it out, Julia? Can you?"

"I think so. Give me time."

"Tell me you love me."

"I do, I do," she said, and leant forward to kiss him on the lips, but as soon as the kiss was finished she drew away again.

"David, it's not just this other man. If I told you the rest, would it be between us alone? Completely confidential?"

"You know it would."

"I mean the Commission. You know there are several people there who are set against the Castle, and because you work at the Commission, I'm . . . well, unsure — "

"I'm only attached to the place because of the archives," he said at once. "I'm not a civil servant, and I confide in no one there."

She was staring at him very closely, and he felt uneasy under the intensity of her gaze.

"We're doing something at the Castle that no one at the Commission knows about. It's not illegal . . . but if Commissioner Borovitin or one of his deputies found out there'd be so much interference that the work would become impossible."

"Then it must be illegal."

"No . . . secret. There's a distinction."

"It wouldn't seem much of a difference to Borovitin."

"That's it precisely." She was sitting away from him now. Her legs were crossed, but she leaned forward towards him earnestly. "All that you saw at the Castle the other day, the craftwork, the skimmers, they're cover for something else. Most

122

of the people at the Castle are scientists and academics, drawn from all parts of England. They have a common ideal, and the Castle is the only place they can pursue it."

"Don't they have ideals in universities any more?"

"The universities are State-controlled. The only research that's possible is under the management of politicians and bureaucrats. What we're interested in is social and economic research, free of political pressure. The facilities for that exist at the Castle, and that is why the community was established."

"You said 'we'," Harkman said.

"I'm one of them. Our real work at the Castle is just about to start, and I'm going to be heavily involved in a few days' time. When it's finished, things will be different."

He did not see why this should prevent him from living with her at the Castle, but then he did. There was always the other man. He stared back at her in silence, feeling that something he valued above all else had been taken away from him.

Apparently thinking that what she said was insufficient to convince him, Julia leaned forward again, placed her hand on his wrist.

"It's utterly serious, David. I'm not asking much of you, except patience. The results of this project could ultimately affect everyone in England, and I have to commit myself to that. You should understand: you have your own work."

"It doesn't come between you and me."

"It does so long as you're attached to the Commission."

Harkman said: "What is this project at the Castle?"

"Obviously I can't tell you. It's . . . a little like your work, except that your research is with the past."

"And yours is with the future." He meant it ironically, but she reacted at once by taking away her hand and staring into her lap.

"It's a new kind of sociological research," she said. "A different way of seeing the present." She turned her head, glanced back at the storm-cloud in the distance. "I've probably said too much. But do you understand how important it is?"

He looked back at her, trying to betray nothing. "I understand that I won't see you. That you live with someone else. That your work is more important to you than I am. That all this has happened in the last few minutes."

"There's something else, David. Stronger than any of those."

"What's that?"

"I love you. I wouldn't say it if I didn't mean it. I love you more than anyone I have ever known."

He shook his head, and said nothing.

Julia drew away, and stood up. She looked about her: the grass of the heath waved in the breeze.

"What is it?" David sat up, propping himself on an elbow. "Is someone there?"

"Please wait . . . just for a minute."

Before he could answer she moved away from him, walking quickly up the slope of the little hollow where they had been lying, and went across the heath towards the west. The great cumulonimbus which straddled the horizon, blue-black at its base, a soaring white anvil at its peak, seemed about to obscure the sun, for it spread laterally and hugely towards it. Julia walked in front of the sun, and for a moment he was dazzled by it. He saw her pause, raise her hands to her face, lower her head.

He thought she was crying, but nothing in her mood had warned of that . . . and as he watched he saw that she was motionless, as if meditating or waiting. Then she raised her head and looked towards the south, to where the mound of Maiden Castle breasted its hill.

She seemed to be waiting, and so he waited with her, aware above all else of the juxtaposition of the three: the Castle and Julia and himself. There was some incontestable link between them, and yet it was something that also threatened to divide them. In those moments, while Julia stood on the grassy edge of the hollow, profiled against the turbulent sky, Harkman tried to understand everything that had been said in the last few minutes. Unexpectedly, the explanation came from the enigma that had dogged him since the first night.

What he had heard from her had not actually been said: he had *remembered* it into his experience.

The only reality was the girl in the sun, black and wary against the sky. The sensation was more marked now than Harkman had ever known it. It was all illusory, remembered by him, remembered for him; not real.

Had they talked of love, of another man, of a scientific project?

He knew they had and he knew they hadn't. The contradiction was ultimate. Reality began at this instant, at every instant, and the past became false.

Then Julia turned towards him, hurrying back, skipping in the grass.

"David!" she called. "David, I'm here!"

He stood up as she ran towards him, because he recognized something in her at last, something he had been seeking. She rushed towards him, and went into his arms, kissing him, holding him.

"David," she said breathlessly, kissing his face. "Oh I love you!"

He looked into her eyes, and it was there. The intangible; the life; the reality.

Harkman felt her in his arms and in his heart. The sensation that memory created her was gone. Julia was there, and she was real, and total. She had returned to him.

But as he embraced her, the darkening shoulders of Maiden Castle stood behind her, calling her back.

☐☐☐☐☐☐ They hurried, because the sun had gone in behind the
21 encroaching cloud, and the storm was almost upon them.
No rain had yet fallen, but the breeze had died and the
countryside lay humid and silent in anticipation.

The path divided by the stretch of shore known locally as Victoria Beach, and as she and David embraced Julia noticed that the sand was still crowded with tourists, apparently unheeding of the imminent downpour. Foreign tourists never seemed to learn the vagaries of English weather, and she knew that in a few minutes they would all be scurrying for cover, exclaiming about the unannounced storm. After she had left David, and was walking back to the Castle, she allowed more charitably that they were probably waiting until the last possible moment before returning to town; sea-bathing was impossible almost everywhere else in the world, because of industrial pollution, and one of the undeniable attractions of Wessex was its clean sea.

She was trying not to think of what had passed between her and David, because she had presented the truth to him and he had found it unpalatable. Looking at the visitors on the beach, as she walked quickly towards the Castle, she felt a deep and vague sadness about David, and she wished her function here was as simple as that of the tourists.

It had always been like this, though. She should not have allowed herself the luxury of David Harkman. There had always been the monotony of the detailed preparations at the Castle, the need for concentration and absorption in her work.

(Then: a ghost. Another summer, another life. David at the stall, then arriving at the Castle one morning, trying out the skimmers as she lazed on the beach of the inlet. Five days ago . . . or never? When had she ever had the time to spend like that?)

She had reached the first of the Castle's ramparts as this spectral memory struck her, and she paused reflexively. Like the recollection of a dream it had momentary conviction, but unlike the breaking of a dream the memory remained in her mind for her to explore.

There was a duality: on the one hand a complete certainty that for the last few months, all through the long summer, she and the others had been absorbed in their preparations in the tunnels beneath the Castle; on the other, a faint but quite distinct memory of a different kind of summer, the stall, the harbour, the crowds of tourists . . . and Greg.

David had talked of Greg, thinking that he and she were lovers, but she denied it. Of course she denied it: Greg was nothing to her.

The fainter memory placed Greg beside her, possessing her.

There was a brilliant flash of lightning, and Julia turned sharply, expecting the crack of thunder to come on cue, a momentous natural event to celebrate a momentous realization . . . but thunder did not sound.

She glanced up the wall of the rampart, seeing the cloud massing above. It was almost on top of her, and the nearness to it had changed the colour from its earlier blue-black to a sickly yellowish grey. She looked towards the west, from where the storm was approaching, and saw that already the landscape had disappeared in a grey mist; the rain was almost upon her.

She hurried on, going up the path across the side of the first rampart, following its curving, dipping course towards the second. She was running, suddenly frightened of the might of the storm.

She had intended to go to the house she shared with Paul, but that was too far away on the other side of the village. Her fear of the storm became panicky, a terror of being struck by lightning in the open spaces at the top of the Castle, so she left

126

the path and ran down the slope towards the entrance to the underground passages. Several people from the village were crowded into the doorway, looking apprehensively at the sky.

Thunder rolled and rumbled, and the rain started: heavy drops hissing down on to the sun-baked earth. Within seconds the rain had become a deluge, water and ice combined, sluicing down in a vicious torrent. The hailstones stung her shoulders and neck and legs, scattered on the ground before her as she ran with the wind. Her hair and dress had plastered wetly to her body in the first few moments of the downpour.

She reached the shelter at last, panting and frightened. She expected, without thinking, that the crowd of people would step back to let her in, but they seemed not to have noticed her, and she stood in front of them in the driving rain. Lightning flashed again, and thunder cracked immediately afterwards. She pushed against the people, forcing them to move back, and at last she was out of the worst of the rain.

The people clustering in the entrance to the shelter continued to pay no attention to her, even though she was pressed against at least three of them. She knew none of them, except by sight: they were mostly farmers, or artisans from the craft workshops. None of them was involved with the real work of the community.

Angrily, she pressed against them, forcing a passage, and they moved reluctantly aside, complaining to each other – but not directly at her – about her persistence.

When she broke free of the press of bodies she was well inside the bare, unlit construction, standing under the cracked concrete roof. For the first time she noticed that Greg had been among the people blocking the entrance, but he had not acknowledged her. He, like the others, was peering out at the spectacular weather from the safety of the shelter.

Outside, there was another brilliant white flash of lightning, accompanied by a deafening crash of thunder.

Julia turned away, and walked across the rubble-littered floor towards the narrow staircase at the back. She pinched the damp fabric between thumb and forefinger of each hand, and lifted it away from her thighs, then went quickly down the stairs. The tunnels and cells of the laboratories were about fifteen metres below the surface, and before she had reached the bottom of the stairs the storm had become inaudible. Here, in the depths of Maiden Castle, they could not be touched by the elements.

John Eliot's room was empty, as she had expected, so she went on down to the end of the corridor and entered the conference room.

This was the only place in the whole underground system that was heated, and by common consent it had become the centre of all the preparatory activity. Here, in contrast with the other rooms, they had made a more than minimal effort to furnish it comfortably, bringing down from the village many chairs and tables. Several of the Castle's better craft products had been placed ornamentally on view, and many hundreds of books were stacked on shelves along one of the walls.

About fifteen of the chosen participants were in the conference room, as well as Dr Eliot and some of his staff. Marilyn was there, and as soon as she saw Julia she waved to her. She was sitting at the large table at the far end of the room, listening in to one of the interminable policy-discussions.

John Eliot noticed her, left the discussion and came over to her.

"Where have you been?" he said. "We were waiting for you."

"I was caught in the storm," she said, realizing that Eliot probably had no knowledge of the weather. Neither he nor any of the staff ever seemed to leave the underground passages.

"So I noticed," Eliot said, glancing at her rain-soaked dress. "Do you want to change?"

"I'll do it later. It's still raining out. I can keep warm here."

"There's more reading for you. Will you do it on your own, or are you going to join the discussion?"

"What's it about this evening?" Julia said.

"The election of a new member. At the moment opinion seems to be split."

"Who is it to be?"

"A man called Donald Mander. He's a Commission official. He'd make an excellent administrator."

"Someone from the Commission?" Julia said, frowning. "That's an unusual step."

"So some of us think. Others think it would be worth the risk."

She stared at Eliot blankly, thinking of David. If they could seriously consider a government official for the project then they could hardly object to David. Her negative answer to David's simple, understandable request had hurt him bitterly . . . but then she had not seen a way. But now, perhaps she could suggest . . .

No, there was Paul. Always Paul.

"Is Paul here?"

"He's in the mortuary at the moment," Eliot said. "He'll be back later."

"What does Paul think about Mander?"

"He's for him."

"So am I," Julia said.

"Do you know him?"

"I've seen him about Dorchester. I don't know much about him, but he used to smile at me when I was at the stall."

"I didn't know you were vain, Julia."

"I'm not. I've a feeling about Mander. That's been enough for the rest of us, hasn't it?"

Eliot nodded, but vaguely. Julia and the others had tried to explain about the intangible sense of recognition, but Eliot claimed he never experienced it. It had now become the fundamental criterion by which people were invited to join the project. Julia herself knew the intangible well enough, because it was the same with David.

The same, but *different* with David.

"Are you going to speak up in Mander's favour?" Eliot said, looking towards the table, where the arguments had continued as they had been speaking.

"No need. He'll be accepted in the end. You can put me down for an 'aye', if you like. Where's the reading I have to do?"

Julia looked around for somewhere to sit, while Eliot went to the shelves to find a book. In the warm air of the conference room her wet clothes did not feel too uncomfortable. She found a chair near one of the heaters, thinking that she could steam quietly by herself until dry. She tossed back her hair, wondering if she could borrow a brush or a comb from Marilyn.

She looked to see who was already here. She recognized Rod, Nathan, Alicia and Clark from the Castle community; she knew each of these well, as they had been in Wessex for many months. There were several other people at the table, people she recognized from other conferences, to whom she had been introduced but whose names she had since forgotten. They were all from Dorchester or its environs. One man worked on a farm near Cerne Abbas; two of the women came from villages on the southern shore of the bay. All had social or academic qualifications, all were living double lives to facilitate their work here. It was a strange contrivance, and she was glad that because she was already a member of the Castle community she did not have to resort to elaborate deceptions to come here.

Eliot returned with the book, opening it at the pages he had selected.

"This is the passage to read," he said.

The book was an old work, describing the geological substrata of the Wessex region before the seismic upheavals of the previous century. The idea, Eliot explained, was to work out a theory by which the present land subsidence could be seen as but a temporary phase in geophysical evolution, so that a return to something like the former circumstances could be envisaged.

Julia took the book with mixed feelings: geology was her subject, so there would be no difficulty with technical language – which made her work harder in other faculties – but at the same time it meant she would have to cover old ground, in an almost literal sense. What had thrilled her during her studies had been the *present* geological structure of this region, one which on a geological scale had been shaped only yesterday.

Old theories, old facts, had to be learned; the present had to be unlearned.

Nevertheless, in spite of these misgivings, she soon became interested in the book, and was still reading half an hour later when Paul Mason walked into the room.

Everyone noticed his arrival; he was that sort of man. As the director of this project he commanded immediate respect and attention. All the work, all the eventual functions of the project, were his. He had worked for several years to bring these people together; he was an idealist with an achieved ideal, and he inspired the others.

As he walked across the room he saw Julia, and gave her one of his secret smiles, the sort he reserved for her alone. She responded automatically, feeling, as she always did, the instinctive and selfish pride of ownership.

She shared Paul with no one; she was his woman.

That look he gave her spoke of the things no one here could ever intrude into: the secret life, the private man. Only she was allowed this insight into the other Paul, and it was allowed because of their intimate understanding of each other.

Deep inside her, a spectral memory flared like a match-flame in a darkened cellar . . . and a spectral version of herself recoiled in horror.

As Paul sat down at the table with the others, Julia stared with unfocused eyes at the floor, her spectral identity struggling for release. She thought of David, she thought of his love, she thought of hers.

Soon, she began to tremble.

□□□□□□ The heavy thunderstorm had brought a break in the
22   weather, and six days later it was cool, windy and
squally in Dorchester. David Harkman's frustration
continued; he had not seen Julia since the afternoon on the heath, and discreet enquiries, mainly of the two Castle people working behind the stall, got him nowhere. They appeared to know nothing of her, and were surprised that he should be interested.

He was still being blocked by Mander's apparent reluctance to let him at the archives, and on the fourth day he had left the Commission in a rage and travelled up to Child Okeford to ride the Blandford wave. This too had left him unsatisfied; the tide was unseasonally low, and the wave had been crowded with inept amateurs. Swerving to avoid a group of riders, Harkman had slipped behind the crest of the wave, making the whole expedition futile and irritating.

Futility and irritation were two feelings he was well acquainted with, and Harkman had little doubt whence they grew.

It was a cruel irony that within a few minutes of Julia's apparent return to him – his knowledge that the intangible was there again – she had left him. And in spite of what she told him, Harkman remained convinced that she had left him for some other man.

His response was human and straightforward: he suffered an abiding and wounding jealousy.

On the sixth morning he enquired again about the matter of the archives, and once more Mander told him that Commissioner Borovitin was "considering" his request. Harkman, enraged again, left the Commission offices and for want of anything better to do strolled along the sea-front, watching the holiday-makers with a mixture of boredom and envy. He walked the length of the Boulevard, past the skimmer-shop and all the stalls, past Sekker's Bar, and along the road that led to Victoria Beach.

Two peddlers approached him, holding out some of their wares. At first he didn't see what they were offering, noticing instead that they were wearing Castle clothes.

"Will you look at a mirror, sir?" said one of the two, and held a little circular piece of glass before his eyes.

Harkman saw a crazy, flashing reflection of himself, but then he pushed past them and walked on. The mirror was a cheap bauble, a common ornament. It was the second time peddlers had tried to sell him one.

Victoria Beach was as crowded as usual, in spite of the cool weather. Many of the visitors lay on the sand, presenting their naked bodies to the cloudy sky, apparently relishing this opportunity for fashionable exhibitionism without the risk of unfashionable suntan. Harkman paused for a few minutes, staring down at them. People always seemed to behave the same on a beach, discarding normal behaviour with their clothes.

Beyond the beach, set on its hill, was Maiden Castle: symbol and embodiment of his discontents.

Julia was there, but his jealousy was defensive, and he dared not seek her out.

Standing by the rail overlooking the beach, Harkman felt again the primal instinct that drew him to the Castle. It represented the permanence of time, an inexplicable link with the past.

It came from the past, the real past, the historical past.

Maiden Castle had been there on its hilltop as Dorchester was being rebuilt after the earthquakes. It had been there as the earth had shaken and subsided, and as the sea crept towards it, submerging the valleys around. It had stood on its hill indifferent to the nations and races of the world, as they argued and warred about territory and money, maize and oil and copper, ideology and torture, political influence and frenetic arms-race. It had been there as the first steam-train followed its bright new iron tracks towards Weymouth in the south, and it had been there as kings struggled with parliaments, and as feudal lords and seigneurs raised private armies to extend their lands. The Romans had sacked it, the ancient Britons had raised it. Time was deposited about Maiden Castle like layers of sedimentary rock, and Harkman could excavate it with his imagination.

It distracted him because it was the focus of his interest in Wessex.

He had not come to find Julia, although he had found her, and he had not come to ride the Blandford wave, although he had done so and would again. The Castle was central to everything: a sense of past, of continuity, of permanence.

If he walked along Victoria Beach from here he would be at the Castle in ten minutes. Harkman tested his courage against his jealousies, and his courage failed. He glanced once more at the glowing green mound, then turned back and walked quickly into Dorchester.

He had been at his desk for no more than ten minutes when the internal telephone rang.

"Mr Harkman? This is Cro, of Information. I understand that the Commissioner has authorized you to examine our archives."

"I thought Mander was in charge of those."

"Mr Mander is taking a few days' leave of absence. Before he went I took it upon myself to make sure you received your clearance. Do you wish to use the archives today?"

"Yes, of course. I'll come now."

He went first to Cro's office, then followed the portly little man to the elevator.

The archives were kept in the basement of the building: a huge storehouse behind a fireproof wall, filled with metal racks that covered all four walls and made artificial aisles across the width of the room. On these shelves were stacked the records: cardboard-boxfuls of papers, books, pamphlets, bound folders, licences, records of births and deaths, notes of court-proceedings, file upon file of memoranda from Westminster and the other provincial Commissions, statutes, minutes of meetings, newspapers, government posters, police-records . . . all the dusty memorabilia of service to and administration of the State, and a mouldering testament to the pedantic mind of the bureaucrat, which will never allow anything to be thrown away.

"I'll have to lock you in, Harkman," Cro said.

"That's all right." Harkman looked at his watch: it was just after two. "Come down for me at five, unless I telephone beforehand. And I'll probably want to spend all day tomorrow here."

Cro pointed to a browned, faded sign above the door. "You can't smoke in here."

"I wasn't intending to."

"You'd better give me your cigarettes, in case."

Harkman stared at Cro aggressively, fighting to keep his temper. He had had only occasional contact with this man, but he felt he knew and understood him, or his type. Because of Harkman's status as an attached academic, Cro was administratively his junior, but the archives were his domain. To avoid a needless scene, Harkman handed over his cigarettes, aware that he was scowling like a schoolboy caught smoking behind the gym.

He forced a grin. "I suppose I might have been tempted."

"I'll keep them for you," Cro said, and put them on a shelf outside the room. He closed and locked the door, then nodded to Harkman through the heavy glass window, and walked away. Harkman stared thoughtfully through the window at his cigarettes, knowing that if Cro had taken them with him he would have forgotten them. Now he wanted a smoke.

He turned away, intent on getting on with what he had come down here for.

Until now, the only aspect of the archives he had had access to was a part of the index, so he already had a partial understanding of the filing-system, and the numbered codes used to identify different classifications.

He walked up and down the aisles, looking at the boxes and folders. The newer additions to the collection stood out from the others, for their labels were as yet clean, unyellowed by age. Harkman tried to read the words inscribed on the spines of various folders, lifted the dusty lids of boxes to peer inside. The air in the vault was dry and stale, and even just walking raised clouds of fine dust, making his eyes water and his nose itch.

He worked aimlessly for half an hour, not only unsure of where to look, but uncertain of what it was he was seeking. The rows of dirty folders confused him; the order in which they were stacked appeared to be random, with the court-records for one year placed with seeming purpose next to the register of marriages for another, twenty-three years before.

He returned to the index, and chose a few entries at random, trying to work out the system. After some false starts he managed to trace a chosen item: *Housing Committee, Minutes of Meetings, 2117–2119.* He had no interest in the proceedings of a committee sitting some twenty years before, but finding it had helped him understand the system.

Now with more than an inkling of how to go about his search,

Harkman settled down at one of the desks with the index in front of him. He had already abstracted a list of certain records he wanted to examine, and he took out his notebook and checked off two or three items of special interest. By a quarter past three he had a list of some forty entries that might contain what he was looking for, and he went in search of them. He couldn't find them all, but he soon had at his desk a land-registry that covered the whole of the twenty-first century, news-paper files, Commission year-books for the last three decades, minutes of Party meetings and congresses, a popular history of the twentieth century, several guide-books to Maiden Castle, and copies of various memoranda sent between Westminster and the Resources Attaché's office in the last two years.

In this last folder he discovered the first reference to Maiden Castle.

A query had been raised in the Regional Office in London about the power-consumption of the Castle community; the answer, amid much elaborate qualification, said that the community had access to mains electrical supply, but that its consumption was negligible provided certain unidentified equipment was not in use.

Later, Harkman discovered more correspondence in the same folder, this time concerned with a query about the possible scrap- or salvage-value of the research equipment; the Commission's answer – signed by D. Mander – took the form of a letter attached to a printed circular. The circular was a Party directive concerning self-sufficient craft cooperatives, and the desirability of minimal government interference; the typewritten note merely added that the present condition of the Ridpath apparatus was not known, and was assumed to be worthless.

The proper name of the equipment held no significance for Harkman.

In the land-registry of the previous century, Harkman discovered extracts of the deeds by which title to the land on which Maiden Castle stood was transferred formally from the Duchy of Cornwall to the Soviet Land and Agriculture Board. This was in the year 2021. The transfer was one of several hundred, in which all land not nominally State-controlled was handed over to Westminster.

There followed a fruitless search, where he found several documents relating to Maiden Castle, or referring to it, but they were normal bureaucratic fodder: population estimates, land-surveys, health reports, an advisory document on education, the findings of a team of sanitary inspectors.

Harkman had not looked at the newspaper file since locating it, thinking of it as a last resort, but on searching through he discovered that in the early years at least of the Commission's administration, there had been diligent attempts to collect items of local interest. There were all sorts of cuttings here: details of a road-building project (since abandoned), the reconstruction of Dorchester after the earthquakes, the first ideas publicly discussed for the development of Dorchester as a tourist centre.

Then, stuffed into a pocket at the back of the file, Harkman found several other clippings from a much earlier period. He pulled them out and unfolded them carefully; they were brown with age, and as dry as the dust that lay on them.

The first one had a lurid headline, set in an old-fashioned typeface: A JOURNEY TO THE FUTURE! Underneath, written in short paragraphs and sensational English, was a report on the formation of what the newspaper called "an electronic think-tank", whose members would "step into the future" and "contact our descendants", all with the aim of "solving the burning problems of today".

There were several more of a similar ilk, each one concentrating, presumably for the benefit of a semi-literate audience, on such ideas as time-travel, exploration of the future, visiting the ends of time, and so forth. These were in cuttings dated from the beginning of 1983 until the summer of 1985. Maiden Castle ("shrouded in antiquity") was mentioned several times, and the name of Dr Carl Ridpath (variously a "boffin", "inventor" or "genius") featured prominently.

Harkman read them in chronological order, learning more from each one, and recognizing also which elements of the reporting could be discounted as sensationalism or speculation.

As he finished the last cutting, Harkman felt that he had found what he had been seeking. At some time in the late twentieth century – presumably in 1985 – a scientific research foundation had developed a means whereby the future could be investigated. It was not a form of travel through time, in the sense the newspapers used it, but a controlled, conscious extrapolation, visualized and given shape by Dr Ridpath's projection equipment. The work would be carried out in a special laboratory constructed beneath Maiden Castle.

Clearly this was the apparatus that was mentioned in the Commission files!

Harkman was suddenly struck with an intriguing notion, and he turned back through the cuttings. There was common consent in the reports on one matter: that the chosen period for the projected "future" would be exactly one hundred and fifty years.

In other words, they were envisaging the year 2135 . . . just two years ago!

Harkman wondered wryly what they had made of what they found.

He stared at the aged newsprint for several minutes, realizing that these ancient pieces of paper were themselves a link with that optimistic past, a time when man and his technology had not stagnated, when they could still look forward. Just as Maiden Castle itself had been built for defence against the enemies of the day, and had survived to withstand the decay of time, so these words, hastily written and hastily printed, had outlived their makers.

The men were dust, but the words and ideas lived on.

Harkman shuffled the cuttings into a pile, then slid them back into their pocket in the folder. He felt a slight obstruction, so he pulled them out again and peered inside.

At the very back, concertinaed by the pressure of the others, was one more cutting. Harkman reached inside, and pulled it out carefully.

He smoothed it with his hand, pressing it out on the desk-top.

It was printed in a different style from the others, with a more sober presentation: from the printing at the top he learned that it was taken from *The Times*, 4th August 1985.

The headline was: MAIDEN CASTLE – AN EXPENSIVE DREAM?

Harkman read through the piece quickly.

Today, in an Ancient British hill-fort near Dorchester, a group
of intellectuals, economists, sociologists and scientists will
pool their conscious minds in an attempt to see into the
future of Britain and, indeed, the world. Questions have been
asked in Parliament, and much comment has been heard
from informed sources, about the expense involved in what
to some is no more than an indulgent fantasy of some of the
best brains in Britain. Would the money not be better spent,

say the critics, on more positive and social research –
indeed, the very kinds of research that in many cases the
participants have abandoned in order to take part?

In fact, although the Wessex Foundation is partly subsidized
by the Government – through the Science Research Council –
most of the funds have been raised from private and
industrial sources.

There followed a paragraph discussing the financing of the
project. Harkman glanced over this, then read on.

Much has been heard about the 'time-travelling' ability the
participants will develop when their minds are electronically
pooled, but this is strenuously denied.

Speaking at yesterday's press-conference in Dorchester,
Dr Nathan Williams of Keele University said, "We are
imagining a future world, which is made palpable to us by
the Ridpath projector. Our bodies will be inside the projector
itself, and will not leave it. Even our minds, which will
seem to experience the projected world, will in fact stay
within the program dictated by the equipment."

For the Trustees of the Wessex Foundation, Mr Thomas
Benedict, who is himself to take part in the experiment,
added, "In terms of what we hope to achieve, we believe that
what we shall learn from the world of 2135 will amply
repay every penny of what has been invested here."

There is a total of thirty-nine participants in the project,
and together their qualifications present a formidable array of
talent. Many have taken indefinite leave of absence from
their university posts to contribute to the Ridpath projection,
and several more have left brilliant industrial careers for
a chance to deploy their speciality in this experiment.

Dr Carl Ridpath, who developed his mental visualization
and projection equipment at the University of London,
was unable to attend yesterday's press-conference. Speaking
from a West London clinic, where he is recovering from an
operation, he said, "This is the fulfilment of a dream."

Alongside the article were eight photographs of some of the
participants, tiny faces staring out at Harkman across the years.
One was of Ridpath, a small, intense expression; another was of
Dr Williams, a middle-aged, balding man with a square, intelligent face.

138

At the very bottom of the double column of photographs were two at which Harkman stared uncomprehendingly.

The first face was his own. Underneath, the caption said: *Mr David Harkman, 41, Reader in Social History, London School of Economics.*

The second photograph was of a pretty, dark-haired girl: *Miss Julia Stretton, 27, Geologist (Durham University). Miss Stretton is the youngest of the participants.*

Harkman's first reaction to this was disbelief, and he closed his eyes and turned away his face, as if this would remove some incredible sight. Then he stared again at the pictures, and glanced through the article, his heart speeding up as his nervous response stimulated the adrenal gland. The girl's photograph was unmistakably Julia; the man given his name was undoubtedly himself.

Harkman felt something akin to a jolt of electricity pass through his mind, like a short-circuit in the synapses, and his head jerked back involuntarily; reality blurred.

He tried to be calm, tried to understand.

According to the newspaper, a hundred and fifty years ago – a hundred and fifty-two, to be precise – a man called David Harkman had joined this mind-projection experiment. The chosen year was 2135. *(How could they imagine it? On what did they base their information?)*

Julia, or a girl with her name and appearance, had also joined the project.

And yet he, the real David Harkman, lived here in the year 2137. Julia lived here.

He had been born in 2094 *(he was 43, like his alter ego would be!)* . . . he had been born in 2094, had been educated at Bracknell State School, had studied at the London Collegiate, had graduated in Social History, had married . . . this was what he knew!

The year, the world, the people . . . they were all around him. He was *of* this world, this real, uncomfortable and dangerous world.

Was this the sort of world these twentieth-century academics could visualize?

Harkman shook his head, disbelieving. No one could grapple with the innumerable subtleties of an entire social order.

(1985: before the destruction of the British union, during the last years of the monarchy, before the collectivization of industry

and agriculture, before the absorption into the Soviet bloc. No one who was alive then could have foreseen this society!)

Extrapolation, in the social sense, meant the opposite of history. It implied the ability to draw inferences about the future from observations of the present. Harkman did not doubt the ability of these academics to speculate intelligently, but he knew as a certainty that any speculation about *his* world would be wrong. The history of the last century and a half, with all its complexities, was known to him almost as thoroughly as he knew the story of his own life.

History was the critical order that the present imposed on the past; it could not be created forwards!

This sudden urge to dispute the principles of the theory was his intellect's way of evading the true emotional shock.

Who was this David Harkman?

He stared with renewed amazement at the photograph in the cutting, then reached into the back pocket of his trousers and found his Commission identity-card. He laid it next to the photograph, still disbelieving.

The newspaper picture looked stiff and unnatural, as if it had been taken in a cold studio, and he seemed older than he looked in the identity-photograph. His face was fuller now, his hair was longer and he had greater poise.

Nevertheless, the two photographs were indisputably of the same man.

And he had only to look at the ancient photograph of the girl called Julia Stretton to know that it was her.

Confronted with the impossible, Harkman found that he could not cope. His first impulse was to stand up and walk away from the desk, but he had gone no further than the nearest rack of old folders before he returned. He stumbled as he sat down, nearly fell off his chair.

His hands were shaking, and he could feel his shirt clinging damply to his back.

For a few minutes he sat quite still, holding the edge of the desk in each hand.

At last he looked again at the text of the newspaper cutting, and reread the quoted words of Dr Williams: ". . . our minds, which will seem to experience the projected world, will in fact stay within the program. . . ."

For a moment Harkman felt that in these words lay the clue: there had been a mistake, something had gone wrong. All that

140

apparent sensationalism in the other newspapers was, after all, right: *he had travelled in time!*

It seemed to be the only solution to the dilemma, and irrational and incomprehensible as it was it would explain . . .

The notion took hold for a few seconds, then slackened its grip, fell away.

It could *not* be so: he had no memory of the twentieth century, nor of any time before his own life. Forty-three years, perhaps thirty-eight of them remembered with any clarity. No more. An ordinary life.

He looked again at Williams's words: ". . . our minds will seem to experience . . ."

It was possible, just marginally possible, that this was the central statement.

In effect, everything he saw, everything about him, what he ate, what he read, what he remembered . . . was a mental illusion.

Again, he kicked back his chair and walked in torment from the desk and along the nearest aisle.

He paced agitatedly to and fro.

All *this* was reality. He could touch it, smell it. He breathed the musty air of the vault, sweated in the unventilated room, kicked up clouds of ancient dust: this was the world of external reality, and it was necessarily so. As he strode past the seemingly endless rows of files and books, each of which contained its own fragments of remembered past, he concentrated on what he himself conceived as reality.

Was there an inner reality of the mind which was more plausible than that of external sensations? Did the fact that he could touch something mean that it was as a consequence real? Could it not also be that the mind itself was able to *create*, to the last detail, every sensual experience? That he dreamed of this dust, that he hallucinated this heat?

He halted in his fretful pacing, closed his eyes. He willed the vault to vanish . . . let it be gone!

He waited, but the dust he had kicked up was irritating his nose, and he spluttered a great and messy sneeze . . . and the vault was still there.

Wiping his eyes and nose, Harkman walked back to the desk.

There was something else in the cutting, something that had left a barb that snagged at his memory.

He scanned the faded newsprint once again, but couldn't see

it. Then he noticed the date. It was printed at the top: 4th August 1985.

There was something incontestable about a date, an impartiality, a known and labelled event shared by all.

The newspaper had described the initiation of the project as taking place "today" . . . presumably the same date. In which case the projected future would have begun on 4th August 2135.

Where had he been on that day? What had he been doing?

He knew the general answer at once: for the last few years he had been in London, working at the Bureau. That would seem to be rejection enough of any but a coincidental link with this twentieth-century experiment, because his roots extended beyond or before the incident date. But he was still not satisfied.

Why was August 2135 a significant month to him?

Then he had it: that was the month he had applied to the Bureau for transfer to Dorchester. He remembered because his birthday was 7th August, and he had filed the application with a feeling of resolution and changed direction, a present to himself. It had felt then like the fulfilment of a long-felt need, but he knew that the decision had been a relatively sudden one. He had become obsessed with the idea three days before, when he had had the realization that until he was able to live and work in Wessex he would never be content.

Three days before! That would be 4th August!

His incomprehensible urge to go to Maiden Castle, feebly rationalized, had started on the very day the project began.

The significance of it was awful, but for the life of him Harkman couldn't see why. His memories before that date were his hold on reality; so long as they extended before then he knew that his identity was safe.

The memories were there: education, career, marriage, career . . .

Talking to Julia a few days ago he had had the same static memories. The events stood out like check-marks on a list.

They had happened, and they had not happened. In precisely the same way that Julia had seemed for a time to be an illusion, so Harkman realized that his life until 4th August 2135 had been remembered into existence.

And the newspaper photographs lay on the desk before him, and they told him who he was and where he had come from.

An hour and a half later the door to the vault was opened from the other side, and Cro arrived to let him out.

Harkman barely noticed. He picked up the cutting and slipped it into his pocket, and followed the man to street level. As Cro went on up the stairs, Harkman walked out into the street. The buildings of the town seemed insubstantial, shifting, shadowy.

He walked down to the sea-front. While he had been inside the vault the wind and rain had increased, gusting in from the heaths behind the town. The smoke from the oil-refinery poured over the town, dark and depressing and greasy. There were very few people about and the trees along the front were dulled and dirty.

The tide was going out, and for a moment Harkman had an hallucinatory image of some bottomless drain far out at sea, into which the water was emptying, drawing back from the shore and leaving the bay sodden and bare, the muddy remains of the twentieth century scattered like shipwrecks across the land.

□□□□□□ After introducing him to everyone present, and out-
23 lining the nature of the project, Paul Mason took Mander to see the Ridpath projection equipment. Mander, still bemused by the speed with which not only had he been accepted by the others, but also with which he himself had adapted to the project, followed the young director down a side-tunnel into a long, low-ceilinged hall, lit dimly by two electric bulbs.

"We call this the mortuary, Don," Mason said, and turned on more lights to illuminate the equipment.

Mander winced mentally at the first-name familiarity; more than a quarter of a century in public service had made him un-used to anything more personal than initials.

Spotlights were grouped in clusters at both ends of the long room, and as they came on Mander looked without too great an interest at what appeared to be a row of large filing-cabinets set against one wall. Mason, and some of the others, were in-terested in the mechanical process by which the futurological projection would be achieved, but for Mander it was the psycho-logical implications that were fascinating. His years in the Regional Service had left his early training behind, and all that he retained was an instinctive understanding of human mental processes – which, in his moments of greatest self-awareness,

143

he knew he used best in interdepartmental politicking – and a rudimentary and probably out-dated vocabulary of psychologists' jargon.

He had joined the Regional Service in the naïve belief that trained psychologists had a useful rôle to play in the sometimes delicate administration of State affairs; that, at least, had been the policy of the Regional Office in Westminster when he had taken the appointment, but successive changes of Party leadership – both in England and in Russia – and subtle reshadings of ideological colouring had progressively eroded any useful function he might once have had. Now, twenty-seven years later, routine promotions had provided him with a stable income and a position of authority, and the rather ambitious twenty-seven year old industrial psychologist had developed into a reliable fifty-four year old administrator.

Paul Mason went to the nearest of the drawers and pulled it open, pressing one hand against the body of the machine for leverage. After initial resistance, the mechanism slid open smoothly enough, as if the roller-bearings of the drawer had stayed free over the years of disuse.

"It's inoperative at the moment," Mason said. "You can try it if you like."

"You mean I should climb on?"

"Well, we normally refer to it as climbing in." Mason smiled at his own pedantry, and Mander felt again the instinctive liking he had had for the young man from the moment they met. The popularity Mason enjoyed was total; it was as if everyone involved in the project had become captivated by the young man's good looks and personality. "Nothing can happen to you until the power is switched on," Mason went on, and to demonstrate he laid his hand across the bright metal points of the neural contacts.

Mander said: "If I were to climb in, what would happen to me?"

"Nothing at the moment. You don't suffer from claustrophobia do you, Don?"

"Not at all."

Mander shook his head at once, anxious to make it clear that not even a minor neurosis existed to prevent him from joining the team. In the short time he had been at the Castle he had developed a strong wish to be accepted.

Until that man – what was his name, Nathan Williams? –

had called on him at his office, Mander had had no notion that there was anything at all going on at the Castle. Now some inner voice urged him to join the others, become as one with them.

"You see," Paul Mason was saying, "the inside of each projection unit is cramped, and although the person inside will be unconscious, some people might find the idea disturbing."

"Let me try it," Mander said, sensing a trace of doubt in Mason's voice. He was anxious to prove his worth in the eyes of the project director.

There was also the matter of his age; during the introductions someone had pointedly asked him about this, and although the reactions had been civil he had been left with the impression that some might think him too old.

Willingness to show interest, keenness to participate, these were the qualities he was hoping to communicate.

Mason helped him to lie down on the drawer, and showed him how to rest his shoulders in the supports. Mander felt the neural contacts pressing against him, blunted by the fabric of his clothes.

"It will be uncomfortable," Mason said, "but don't struggle if you get an attack of claustrophobia. I'll pull you out again after a few seconds. Now, are you ready?"

"Yes."

"There's no air circulating inside. That's because the fans are off. And it will be dark."

Mason put his weight against the drawer, and Mander felt himself sliding. He passed into the darkness of the interior, and moments later the drawer halted against spring-loaded clamps. He raised his head instinctively, to try to look around, but at once his forehead struck something smooth and cold and hard directly above him. He felt with his hands, moving them out from his body, but they hit the metal sides of the drawer and he realized that with only a few millimetres leeway he was all but confined. It was cold and airless inside the machine. He had not lied about the claustrophobia, but when he had been inside for several seconds it occurred to him that he had only Mason's word to trust, and that if he chose to leave him here he would be trapped.

To his relief, before he was put to further test, he felt the drawer move, and grey light shone in around the end of the drawer by his feet. He looked to each side of him and saw a wire-mesh grid, some metal tubes extending the length of the tiny cubicle, grey paintwork slightly tarnished.

Looking up he saw, fleetingly, a reflection of his own face . . . but then the drawer was pulled right out and he was staring up at Paul Mason. He felt foolish lying there, like a body on a slab awaiting dissection, and he remembered the wry nickname given to this place.

"Well? Do you feel up to it?"

Mason helped him down from the drawer, and as his feet touched the ground a slight dizziness came over him. He concealed it by turning round, banging a hand expressively against the cool metal. "It's an odd experience."

"You're with us then?"

"Of course."

His dizziness had been caused by something quite other than the containment in the dark. There had been that glimpsed reflection of his own face . . . an instant of self-recognition, a face in a circular mirror.

Mason slid the drawer back into place, and the line of grey-painted cabinets became uniform again. There was a cool surgical efficiency to this machine, lying unused beneath the Castle for a century and a half; a legacy from a richer age.

They walked slowly down the row of cabinets, Mason occasionally reaching out to brush his fingers lightly against the metal handles of the drawers.

"How many are there in all?" Mander said.

"Thirty-nine. This gives us an effective limit to the number of people involved."

"Do you have a full complement yet?"

"Thirty-six so far. Thirty-eight, including you and me."

Mander was on the point of remarking on the obvious, that there was still one more person to find, when he detected the subtle emphasis on the thirty-six confirmed participants. He was still not quite accepted.

He brooded on this as they reached the end of the long line of cabinets, and turned back.

"Paul . . . are you not concerned that I work for the Commission? Someone in the conference room said — "

"It makes no difference. I'm for you."

"Your decision alone?"

"No, there was a vote. If you wish to take part in this, you may. Do you have any reservations?"

146

"Not at all."

"Then what were you thinking?" Mason said.

Mander looked guardedly at the other man, but his gaze was met with a frankness that disarmed him.

"The dissident nature of this project," he said. "I know Party policy about research projects as well as anyone. I have only to go back to Dorchester and telegraph to Westminster a list of the names of all the people I've met today, and within a couple of hours you'll all be under arrest."

"But you wouldn't do that, would you, Don?"

Said by anyone else there would have been an undertone of threat in the words, but because it was Mason saying them it became a straightforward question. It was one to which Mander had a straightforward answer.

"No, I wouldn't. But I wondered if you were aware of the possibility."

"It was discussed."

"And . . . ?"

"I've told you. You have been accepted, without reservation."

They left the mortuary, and Paul Mason switched off all the lights but for the two embedded in the concrete ceiling. They walked back towards the conference room.

Mander was thinking: I am accepted, as I have accepted them.

Now that he had made a break with his life at the Commission it felt an absolutely right thing to have done. He recognized the people here. Even the strangers, the people he was told had come from other parts of the country, behaved in a friendly, familiar way towards him, as if he was already a colleague. Then there were the others: the people he had often seen around Dorchester, whose names he did not know but whose faces were known to him. The girl on the stall, for instance; he had spoken to her for the first time and learned her name: Julia Stretton. Inexplicably, she seemed to be one of those most in favour of his inclusion in the project, and while some of the others had been questioning him about his career at the Commission, she had sometimes offered a spontaneous defence on his behalf.

These early reservations aside, Mander had been astonished by the evident rapport within the group. He could feel it growing in himself, paralleled by an excitement at the possibilities of the project. During his long career with the Party, Mander

147

had sometimes been complacent about its achievements, but when he was younger he had often been critical of the means by which it achieved its ends. Those discontents had never really been removed, but as he grew older he realized that the worst result of the Soviet régime was the fact that English culture and society had stagnated. The country was ready for a social revolution of the same scale as the political revolution that had taken place at the end of the twentieth century. The problems of that troubled period were as far in the past as the years themselves, but no society was ideal. A glimpse into the future might suggest a course to be taken.

"We're still one member short, Don. Do you have any idea of someone we might approach?"

"Couldn't you use your usual procedure?"

"Oh yes. That's why I'm asking you. Selection is based on the recommendation of other participants."

Mander shook his head. "I don't think I'd know anyone suitable."

They had reached the end of the side-tunnel, and were standing at the corner. A damp draught sprang from somewhere, curling around Mander's legs. A few metres away the door to the conference room was open, and light and voices spilled out.

"You understand that I'd like the project to start as soon as possible. Later today, I think."

"So soon?" Mander said. "But proposing someone for work as important as this. . . . Would it be only at my suggestion?"

"The group will decide. That's how it is always done. Offer a few names. We'll know as soon as we hear the right one."

"May I ask how?"

"In the same way that we recognized your name as soon as it was put forward."

"I really don't know many people in Dorchester," Mander said.

His solitary private life, which for years he had seen as a psychological bulwark against the strains of his daily work, suddenly seemed a social disadvantage. As he and Paul Mason walked into the conference room, Mander was thinking over his few acquaintances and trying to visualize them here. As soon as each name came to mind, he automatically discarded it.

An open forum session was in progress, a relaxed meeting of all the chosen participants, in which their ideas about the future world were expressed and discussed and eventually pooled.

Mander and Paul Mason found two spare chairs, and joined in . . . and at once Mander detected a shift in the emphasis of the discussion. Instead of speaking across the room, people turned towards Paul, and it was he who led and shaped. Seen here, in the company of the others, Paul Mason was the obvious leader. The respect they had for him was transparent: he had only to start speaking to bring silence to the others, and if he made a suggestion it found ready approval. In spite of this, Paul did not abuse his position, seeming open to ideas, receptive to the suggestions of others. In all, he conducted the discussion with good sense and humour, and Mander found himself admiring his intellect and warming to his personality.

Only one person showed the least resistance to the group's natural leader, and that was the girl from the stall, Julia. She happened to be sitting opposite Mander, and on the occasions when she spoke he was aware that she was looking in his own direction. Because she was moving against the psychological current of the meeting he began to wonder why. At first he suspected that some conflict existed between her and Paul, but there was nothing of this sort apparent in what she was saying. Later, he observed a momentary look on Paul's face when speaking to her, and he guessed that something more than a working relationship was going on. That might account for it.

Once, when Mander himself put forward an idea for discussion, it was Julia who responded first, seeming eager to agree with him. He found this pleasant, though oddly puzzling. A few minutes afterwards he made a second suggestion to test her response, and again she spoke first.

There came a break for coffee, and during this Mander noticed that Paul took Julia aside and spoke to her at some length. She smiled and nodded and seemed to be agreeing with him, but Mander noticed that the knuckles of her hand showed white with stress.

Mander used the break to talk informally to as many other people as possible.

One man he was most interested to meet was a former research chemist from York Collegiate, who was presently masquerading as a fisherman in the nearby village of Broadmayne. The man's name had come to Mander's notice at the Commission, because his frequent absences from his cottage had aroused the suspicions of a neighbour that he was selling fish for private gain. In fact, some quirk of absent-mindedness had made Mander overlook the complaint, and the papers lay unread in a wire basket on his desk.

When Paul Mason returned to his chair it was clear that the break had finished, and everyone else sat down again.

"Before we can proceed further," he said, "we must select the last member of our team. Does anyone have any suggestions?"

Mander felt the weight of responsibility on him, but he decided to listen to the others. There was a general discussion of the type of personality deemed suitable for the work, but no names were proposed.

Paul looked in his direction.

"How about you, Don? Any ideas?"

"I told you, Paul. I don't seem to know many people around here."

No one said anything, but Paul continued to stare at him.

Then Julia said: "Somebody at the Commission, perhaps. . . ?"

Mander shook his head at once. There was no one there.

Again Julia spoke. She said: "Don, I'm sure you can think of someone."

Paul glanced at her sharply as she said this, and Mander noticed that her hands were clenched tightly across her lap. Once again he was sure that she was suppressing some deeper tension.

"Well, I don't know," he said. He thought of Commissioner Borovitin, of Cro, of one of the clerks in the front office he sometimes lunched with. "There's only . . ."

"Who, Don?"

"An historian from London, doing some research here. David Harkman."

Someone said: "He's the one!"

It was as if a draught of cool fresh air had swept into the stuffy room. Julia laughed, as if with relief, and Mander felt for the first time a true sense of empathy with her, with everyone on the project. David Harkman was right, he was the missing participant. With him, the project would be complete.

People were talking across the room, and several got up from their chairs.

Only Paul Mason was unmoving, looking silently across the room, first at him, then at Julia. Mander stared back at Mason, and noticed a wildness in his eyes, a fanaticism, that had not been there before.

150

24 □□□□□□ The memory of Paul's angry face haunted Julia as she hurried down the last of the Castle's ramparts, bending her head against the rain. Paul, smiling reasonably; Paul, suggesting that Don Mander should go to find Harkman; Paul, standing by the door of the conference room as if to hold it open for her, while actually trying to block her way without the others seeing.

She had defied him, though, and she had done it with silence. "Why not let Don go, Julia?" No answer, Paul. "How will you recognize him, Julia?" No answer, Paul. She alone in that room had detected the undercurrents of his apparently pleasant manner: for the first time in the three years he had lived with her at the Castle, Paul suspected her of something.

No answer to that, Paul, because this time, the first time, there was cause.

The others were hypnotized by Paul, just as she had been hypnotized by him when he arrived at the Castle . . . but all that had changed for her since David.

She ran through the long grass, wetting her feet and legs, and came to the concrete sea-wall that enclosed the shore at this point. Julia could feel Paul's influence fading, to be replaced by a joyful anticipation of David.

After the confined and damp surroundings of the tunnels, the open air smelled fresh and clear, but it was only relative. In spite of the wind and rain, there was the usual dirty haze in the air, muting the landscape with a mottled grey film and saddening the grass and trees.

She had borrowed a raincoat from Marilyn, and as she walked along the puddled, rust-streaked concrete wall, Julia thrust her hands deep inside the pockets, trying to keep warm and dry.

The tide was going out. As the sea receded it left its usual scum at high-water mark: a black smear of oil-spillage, driftwood, plastic containers, the bodies of sea-birds and fish. There was always a smell of acidic chemicals during an ebb-tide, as if the sea, on drawing back, laid bare the new noxious compounds and poisons it had itself created by reacting with the mud and grit of the filthy beach.

Ahead, through the veils of dismal rain, Julia could see the source of much of the bay's pollution: the unloved town of Dorchester: oil-town, spoil-town, used and usurer.

At Victoria Beach the pipelines came ashore, four dead metal worms crawling out of the sea, and where they crossed the sea-wall there was a military guard-post. Julia passed through unchallenged, and she glanced down at the black welded pipes, which, where they rose from the sea, created an artificial breakwater, making the waves sluice greasily along the channels between them. There were only two sentries in sight: one standing on the parapet of the sea-wall, his rifle slung over his shoulder, the other waiting by the doorway of the guard-post. Both soldiers were staring out into the bay, watching the constant traffic of lighters and diving-ships and helicopters, swarming like jungle vermin through the flooded forest of drilling-rigs and platforms.

Inland from the sea-wall, the four parallel pipelines turned together towards the refinery that dominated the landscape behind Dorchester: a bizarre agglomeration of rust-red and silver, towers and gantries and cables, lights and flames and fumes, white-painted storage tanks standing in lines across the countryside, modern tumuli rich in fossil deposits.

Julia, thinking of David, remembered the lovemaking on the heath.

She was following the long curve of Victoria Beach, seeing the grey ribbon of the sea-wall turning towards Dorchester on its bayside hill. The wind came across the heath, drenching her with drizzle. She was out of breath from hurrying, drawn towards the town because of David, repelled by it because of what it was. Leaving the Castle was like escaping from some dungeon; not the twilight incarceration of the tunnels, but the uncanny psychological embrace Paul put around her. When she was with him he managed somehow to exclude David from her life, as if he knew . . . but not until a few minutes ago, when Mander had uttered his name, had Paul ever had the least intimation of David's existence.

Now, almost as if it were against Paul's will, but with the empathic support of the others, David could join the project.

She started to run, her feet splashing in the puddles that cratered the causeway at the top of the wall.

Then: "Julia!"

The wind took the words, but she recognized David's voice at once. He was close but she couldn't see him, and something made her look out to sea, towards the skeletal rigs black against the drizzly sea, orange fireflies of burning waste-gases jetting from their heights.

"Julia, down here!"

She turned at once, laughing, and saw David running towards her on the land side of the sea-wall. She called his name, feeling again a sensation she had had at the Castle when she heard Don Mander speak his name: it did not contain the man, nor any words the love.

He reached the bottom of the wall below her, looking from side to side for a way up to her. On the seaward side the wall had been smoothly angled, with a concave lip to turn back storm-waves, but on the other side the builders had left it rough and perpendicular. In certain places concrete steps, like those built against harbour walls, had been placed against the face, but none were anywhere near.

"Along there!" she called, pointing back towards the Castle, knowing that where the oil pipelines went through the wall there were several places where access to the top could be gained.

He ran at once, and she ran too, keeping abreast of him and looking down.

He reached the bottom of the first flight of steps, and took them two at a time. Panting and laughing she went into his arms, and they kissed as if it had been six years, and not six days, since they had seen each other. She felt his lips, cold and wet from the rain, against her face and neck, and his hair, when she put her hand against it, was dewed and crisp.

"What are you doing out here?" he said, drawing back from her. "I thought you'd be at the Castle."

"I'm looking for you," she said, and tightened her hold on him, pulling him down so that their faces nestled side by side. She kissed his ear, felt the wetness of his hair against her forehead. "Come to the Castle, David. It's all changed now. They want you there."

He said nothing.

"David? I told you: it's what you were asking for."

He moved back from her and stood by the edge of the sea-wall, looking across the miserable, rain-swept country towards the refinery.

"I don't want that," he said. "Not any more. And I don't want you there."

She stared at him uncomprehendingly, then took his hand. "It's *right*, David. It's right that you should be there. Paul, Don Mander . . . all the others. They need you. I've come to find you."

"Just because the others want me?" he said, glancing at her.

"No. I came . . . because I can't stop thinking about you, and you wanted to live with me at the Castle."

"Or the alternative. Live with me away from the Castle. In Dorchester, anywhere. Not there."

"David, I have to go back."

She said it quietly, scared of the same impasse they had reached the last time they were together. She could face up to Paul if David was with her . . . he mustn't let the fear of that prevent him from going.

Another squall of rain swept across the wall, and they both turned their backs to it. David was wearing his office clothes, and they were soaked through. He looked so cold and depressed; she went to his side, put an arm around him.

"David . . . let's go back to the Castle. Just to get out of the rain. We can talk there."

"No, we'll talk here. I don't want to go to the Castle."

"You were going there just now."

"To find you and take you away." He pointed down at the base of the wall on the land side. "Let's get out of the wind, Julia. For a few minutes."

The rain had laid a sheen of wet over his face, and she could see the darkening of his collar against his neck. "All right."

She followed him down the concrete steps, and as soon as they were below the level of the wall the sound of the sea lessened. At the bottom they sheltered under the steps.

David said: "Tell me what's been happening at the Castle."

"You mean the work we're doing?"

"Yes."

She felt she was trapped. And yet . . . she didn't mind that with David.

"There's a man called Paul Mason. He's in charge of the project, and he's — "

"I know. You don't have to tell me. He's the one you live with."

She took both his hands in hers. "David, I promise you, I haven't slept with Paul since I met you."

"But you still live with him."

"I have to . . . I can't change it just like that. As soon as the work is over, I'll move out. It has to wait until then."

"You'd better tell me about the work, in that case."

"We've got a total of thirty-eight people there. In the next few days we're going to use some equipment that's at the

Castle to create an imaginary future. I don't know how the machine works; Paul handles all that. I can't really explain, but all the people there have a sort of, well, a special understanding. I'm not putting it very well. Everyone's in accord . . . it's like empathy."

Harkman had been watching her as she spoke. "Julia, these people. What are their names?"

"You wouldn't know them."

"I might. You mentioned Don Mander just now. Is he one of them?"

"Yes. He's the only one you'll know."

"Is Nathan Williams there?"

Julia, taken off-guard, said: "How do you know Nathan?"

"I came across the name. Tell me some of the others."

She gave him a few names, sometimes having difficulty remembering surnames. He recognized only one: Mary Rickard's.

"Mary Rickard. The biochemist, from Bristol?"

"That's right. But how — ?"

"What about Thomas Benedict? Or Carl Ridpath?"

Neither name meant anything to her, although the first had a hauntingly familiar ring to it. Harkman seemed puzzled, but pressed her no further. He said: "We can't go to the Castle, Julia."

"Why not?"

"Because I'm scared of what might happen there." There was a strange look in his eyes, and he was standing over her in the confined space, blocking her. She felt a tremor of alarm. "Listen, Julia . . . do you know where we are from? Do you know how we got here?"

"Of course I do!"

"I don't mean your background . . . something else. Wessex, Dorchester, the Castle! I thought I knew where I was, where I was from. But not now." He was speaking quickly, and his meaning was lost on her. "Do you remember? When we last met . . . what did we do?"

"We went on the heath and talked."

"Yes, and we made love. There was a storm coming, but while we were there it was warm and dry. Do you remember that?"

"Yes, David."

"And so do I. I remember loving you out there, on the heath." He pointed suddenly. "Just there, where the refinery is!"

She saw the silver-painted towers, and the fumes and the tanks.

"We were nowhere near the refinery!"

"Do you remember seeing it?"

For the last six days Julia's memory of the lovemaking on the heath had been all that she had to help her resist Paul.

"It was there, David . . . but somewhere behind us."

"Are you sure?"

"I think so. . . ."

The refinery was there, it had always been there.

"And I think so too. I'm not sure, though. I know that the refinery has been here for years, that when Dorchester was rebuilt it was as an oil-port, and that the economy of Wessex depends on the wells here. But do you remember the tourists?"

"What? Here in Dorchester?" She laughed.

David said: "I was amused too, when I remembered them."

"There have been one or two," she said. "They visit all parts of Britain."

"Britain?" David said. "Or England?"

She shook her head. "Don't! Please don't!"

"Then listen, Julia, try to understand. You say you are working on some kind of experiment to project a future world, so you must see the consequences of that. If it is to work, if it is to have the least degree of consistency, then it must be a whole world, a *real-seeming* world, one with people you don't know and events you don't understand. And if you are to move in that world, *you too* must be a part of it, with a whole new identity and probably no memory of your existence here."

"How do you know all this?" she said.

"It's true then?"

"Paul says that will happen to us. But it will be only temporary, for as long as the projection lasts."

"However long that is to be," David said. "Julia, this afternoon I came across some newspaper files. In those I read that the equipment at the Castle, the very same equipment, was used once before. During the twentieth century. A group of scientists, thirty-nine people, with names like Nathan Williams and Mary Rickard and David Harkman and Julia Stretton, started a projection of *their* future. The world they projected was this world . . . today, here!"

Julia felt as if she was about to laugh again, but the intensity of his expression was enough to subdue her.

"Do you see, Julia? You and I were in that projection . . . you and I are figments of our own imagination!"

And then he moved unexpectedly, reaching into a back pocket. He pulled out a limp piece of yellowed paper.

"This is what I found. It's genuine, I'm sure it's genuine."

She took the paper from him, and saw that there were eight photographs printed at one side. She looked at the bottom, saw herself and David. Saw the others. . . .

She read the text. One of the names stood out for her.

"Tom," she said. "It mentions Tom Benedict. . . ."

"Do you know him?"

"No, Tom's dead . . . I think. . . . He. . . ."

Suddenly she couldn't remember, and simultaneously she could. There was no photograph of him, but the name was somehow enough. A trustee . . . a Wessex Foundation . . . it was all buried, laid within her unconscious mind.

"I can't understand," she said. "I know most of these people. They're at the Castle now, waiting for me."

"All of them?" David said.

"Not Dr Ridpath. I don't know him. But the others . . . look, here's Nathan, and Mary. But it doesn't mention Paul. That's odd, because he's the director. . . ."

Thoughts started and died in the same instant; reactions were immediately supplanted by contradictory instincts. This was her, but it could not be her. It spoke of Tom, but she knew no one of that name. Paul was not mentioned, but how could any report omit him? These people were alive *now*, not a hundred and fifty years ago. . . .

David said: "Does anyone at the Castle know of this?"

"No one's mentioned it."

"Then like you and me they have no memory of it."

She turned on that. "But I've known some of them for years! They were all born here. I was, you were!"

As she said this an automatic memory came of her mother and father: like a photograph, wordless, motionless. They were there, somewhere in the limbo of her past.

The limbo of her past: it was a phrase she sometimes used lightly, to dismiss her upbringing, to dissociate herself from her background. But did it contain a deeper truth?

"Don't you see what this means for you and me, Julia? We don't belong here, although we think we do. But it's all we know! There's no way back."

Julia, still struggling for a hold on her own reality, shook her head.

"All I know is that I'm bound to the others. Just as you are."

"Not me."

"If you were at the Castle you'd feel it."

"That's why I want you away from there. Julia, I'm in love with *you* . . . you're here and so am I, and I want nothing changed. Don't you see that? It's enough for me. Reality is what I have and hold, and that's you. We can make a life here."

She moved towards him, and he put his arms around her.

"I don't know, David," she said, and they kissed. She wanted to relax, to surrender, but there was too much tension, and after a few moments they drew back from each other.

"I'm all mixed up," he said. "What are we going to do?"

"If you believe this piece of paper," Julia said, "why can't we go back to the Castle?"

"Because I'm frightened of it. Ever since I've been in Dorchester, I've been drawn to the Castle . . . it's been haunting me. I didn't know why, and then I read that. I wanted things to be understood more clearly, and although I think the paper is genuine it confuses me. I understand it, but I can't face up to what it implies."

"So you want to run?"

"With you, yes."

"Why, David?"

"Because I see no alternative."

She was still holding the newspaper cutting, and it was trembling in her fingers. Rain was dripping from the steps above, and two large drops were spreading through the flimsy paper, like oil in cotton.

"Don't you think we should show this to the others?" she said.

He shook his head, and took the paper away from her. He crumpled it with his fingers, and tossed it on the rain-soaked ground.

"That's my answer," he said. "There's no alternative."

Julia stared at the little piece of screwed-up paper on the ground. It was already soaking up the rain. She bent down and picked it up again, stuffing it into the pocket of her coat. David made no attempt to stop her. She stepped away from him, and walked out from under the shelter of the concrete stairs and into the drifting rain.

158

When she left the Castle she thought she had resolved the dilemma. She wanted to be with David more than anything else in her life, and whereas for a time she had seen Paul as someone who would have prevented that, she now knew that if David was with her Paul could be resisted.

It had all seemed so simple, yet David, with his scrap of newsprint, wanted only to run away. That would be denying everything she felt within her, and would resolve nothing.

She looked back at him, standing with his shoulders hunched and his hands in his pockets, sheltering under the concrete steps, watching and waiting. She turned away.

The newsprint cutting was in her pocket, and she took it out and straightened it. A tear had appeared across it, and it was wet and dirty.

Shielding it from the rain with her body, she read it through. Then she read it again, and then a third time. She tried to ignore the fact that a photograph of herself was staring out at her.

It evoked no memories. Try as she might, for her the cutting was no more than an artefact of the past. But the names couldn't be avoided . . . and there was one in particular.

Thomas Benedict. It was a name from a forgotten past, long forsaken. It reminded her of a hot summer, of laughter, of kindness. It was a memory of the undermind, unattainable by the conscious.

She discarded reason – which disallowed knowledge of Tom Benedict – and responded to the irrational. Soon, there were more memories.

There was a tranquil past; another summer she had known. A time of warm blue weather, of crowds of tourists milling through Dorchester, of a loving idyll with David. There was an inlet by the Castle, where David swept to and fro on a skimmer, and where she lay naked in the sun. There was a stall by the harbour, and the heat would rise from the pavement and expensive yachts would moor at the jetty, and foreigners in strange and colourful clothes would haggle with her over prices.

Thomas, Tom, was there in none of these memories. but he was everywhere.

Then, as if her conscious mind was reasserting itself, she looked again at the words on the newspaper cutting, and she saw the date at the top.

In 1985 a man called Nathan Williams had said: ". . . our minds will seem to experience the projected world. . . ."

Wasn't this precisely what she and the others were planning to do at the Castle?

They were seeking to examine a future . . . a better world. Their model for it, a fact asserted again and again by all the participants, was the Britain of the late twentieth century.

They looked to a time, one hundred and fifty years in the future, when Britain had *again* become a constitutional monarchy, when Britain *again* was a unified state, when the world was *again* a keenly competitive place, when the balance of power was *again* between Soviet Russia and the U.S.A., when there were *again* the seemingly insurmountable problems that gave life a challenge and purpose, when technology and science *again* had a vital rôle to play in the world's development. . . .

Was this to be a future modelled on a period of the past, and so very similar to it?

Or was it to be the past itself, the *actual* past on which they were basing their scenario?

David had said: ". . . it must be a whole world, a real-seeming world. . . ."

He had been talking about Paul Mason's project at the Castle, but it applied to their world of Wessex too. This life was real . . . and a hundred and fifty years ago a twentieth-century experiment had set out to create a real-seeming world.

David believed that her life, like his own, was a product of this semblance of reality. And so were the lives of the other participants; they were all of the twentieth century.

If so. . . .

Then she saw it: Paul's project at the Castle would not take them to an imagined future. It was a homing urge. To enter his projection would take them to the past, to the year from which they started!

She walked back to David, knowing that whatever he now said or did, she would go back to the Castle.

She handed back the rain-sodden slip of paper. "David, we – "

"I know what you've decided," he said. "I think I have too. I don't want to stay here, there's nowhere to go."

As David returned the piece of paper to his pocket, she said: "Do you think you can face up to the implications of that?"

"I still don't know," he said.

□□□□□□ As they reached the top of the second earth rampart,
25 and Julia pointed out the entrance to the underground
workings, David Harkman looked across at the plateau
that was the top of the hill-fort. He had expected to
see some kind of habitation here – houses that the participants
used, perhaps – but the grass grew long and was untrampled.
There were no houses, no tracks, no people. The clouds, scud-
ding in from the west, low and leaden, seemed no higher than
an arm's length above them.

He looked towards the east, across the bay with its clustered
drilling-rigs and wells. It looked dark and cold, fouled by man
and his endeavours.

"I wanted to swim there once," he said, and Julia looked at
him in surprise. "There used to be a sport here, sometime in
the past, I think. People would ride on motorized boards, and
try to stay on top of the Blandford wave. When I came down
here I was interested in trying it."

"I've never heard of it," Julia said. "And the wave is just a
large rip-tide. You couldn't ride on it."

"I'd like to have seen it, though."

"Come on, let's get inside," she said.

He followed her down the slope, trying to rid himself of a
dreamlike memory: the swell of the wave beneath the board,
the high-pitched whine of the engine, the white thunder of the
collapsing breaker . . . but it had an elusive quality to it; at
once remembered, but not in his experience.

The long grass brushed wetly around his trouser legs as he
followed Julia, and he shivered. He had been out in the rain
for more than an hour, and he was wet through. This open
wind-swept place seemed to offer no promise of warmth or dry-
ness.

There was no door to the concrete construction. It stood open,
and the wind funnelled in. Pools of dirty water spread over the
floor, and much mud and rubble lay about. Julia led the way
down a flight of steps.

Walking through the rain, she had tried to explain why she
was so adamant about returning to the Castle. She talked of
a way back to the twentieth century . . . but neither of them
had any emotional link with that past. They were both of Wessex.

Harkman had his own reason, though, and it had been the one
that persuaded him there was no hope in trying to escape.

Maiden Castle still exerted its power over him. As long as he lived he would feel its compulsion.

Now he was in the very place that summoned him. Here was the focus of the invisible, radiating source that beckoned him. And, like a reaction to the body of a much-coveted woman suddenly bared before him, he felt a simultaneous sense of fulfilment of long-held desire, and a vague disappointment now that the mystery was removed. The tunnel at the bottom of the stairs was cool, and ill-lit. There were doors on each side, all of them closed and apparently locked. There was litter on the floor: discarded pieces of paper, a few bottles, fragments of broken mirrors, a pair of shoes. The walls were clad in concrete, but there was a pervasive smell of soil or clay.

"You've been down here for the last six days?" he said.

"It's better in the conference room," Julia said.

"The whole place is damp."

"We don't come here for our health." They had reached a door by the end of the corridor, and Julia held him back. "David . . . you're going to meet the others. Are you going to show them the newspaper cutting?"

"What do you think? Should we?"

"I'm not sure. I'm convinced that this is the way back to the twentieth century, and if I'm right and it's where we came from, then we'll understand when we arrive. Do you think anyone will be expecting us there?"

"I can't answer that."

He made a move on, but Julia caught his arm again.

"You're going to meet Paul in a moment," she said. "You're not going to make a scene, are you?"

"Is there any reason why I should?"

"No," she said, and kissed him on the cheek. "You know what I said, and you know what I want." Still holding his arm, but gently now, she opened the door behind him. "This is the conference room."

Harkman walked in, looking around, expecting to find it full of people . . . but it was empty. The lights were on, and it was warm and slightly stuffy. Many books and printed papers were scattered over the tables, and used cups and saucers had been left on the floor next to the chairs. Someone had left a jacket hanging from a hook on the door.

Harkman said, wryly: "Do you suppose they heard we were coming?"

Julia looked around the room again, as if searching would find.

"I only left two hours ago," she said. "They must still be here."

"In one of the other rooms?"

"They're never used. They must have all gone to the projection hall."

He followed her down a side-tunnel towards a doorway, through which bright light was pouring, and as they went into the hall beyond Harkman felt the heat from the lamps glaring down on him. Holding out his hand to shield his eyes, Harkman looked around the room, but it was several seconds before he noticed that someone was waiting: at the far end of the hall, standing beneath one of the clusters of lights, was a man.

He said nothing to them, but watched as they walked in.

On Harkman's left, running for the length of the hall, was a bank of large drawers, painted grey. In the centre of the room, and, for some reason, at the place where the beams of several lights converged, was a large pile of discarded clothing. Harkman thought, whimsically, that it looked like the scene of an orgy that had been interrupted by a police-raid.

"Is that you, Paul?" Julia said, narrowing her eyes against the glare of the lights.

The figure made no movement or sound for nearly half a minute – during which time Harkman stepped forward, to be restrained by Julia's hand on his arm – but then at last he came slowly forward.

"They've all gone," he said. "The project has started."

"Already?" Julia said, in evident surprise. "But you were going to wait – "

"I had all the people I needed. No point delaying."

Julia glanced up at Harkman, and he saw a strange fear in her expression.

She said: "Paul, I've found David Harkman. You remember, Don Mander proposed him?"

"David Harkman, is it?"

"David, this is Paul Mason, the director of our project."

"Mason?" Harkman extended a hand, but Mason ignored him and looked at Julia.

"So this is the David Harkman that's so valuable to my project? Well, it's no good, we've started and it's too late for anyone else." He turned away, and went to stand beside the cabinets.

He reached back with both hands, and pressed his palms against the smooth metal. "I don't know you, Harkman. Where are you from? What do you want here?"

Harkman, irritated by the man's manner – which lay somewhere between psychic disorder and plain rudeness – felt the temptation to give a sharp answer, but he saw Julia flash a warning look at him, and he remembered her request not to make a scene.

He said: "I've been working at the Regional Commission, Mason. I was sent there from the Bureau of English – "

"I don't trust the Commission, Harkman. Nor anyone in it. What do you want here?"

"Paul, he was approved by the others."

"The others have gone. You and I are the only two left. I want to know what this Commission man wants here."

"We want *him*, Paul!"

"So you say. I select the participants for the project, not you."

Julia looked at Harkman again, this time with an expression of puzzled despair, then went forward to Mason. He turned away from her at once and walked down the line of metal cabinets, running a hand obsessively along the metal surfaces.

With all that had happened during the day, Harkman had had no preconception of what he might find at the Castle . . . but this, with Mason apparently distracted beyond sense, was something he had no way of knowing how to deal with.

"Julia, is he sick?" he said quietly.

"I've never seen him like this before," she said. "When I left he was angry . . . but I hadn't expected this. And where is everyone else?"

Harkman said: "What shall we do?"

Julia was silent, staring down the long room at Paul's strangely neurotic figure. He was standing once again under the cluster of lights, his hands pressed against the nearest cabinet.

Looking at him, Harkman could see why Julia had once been attracted to him. He was probably about the same age as she was, and was possessed of undoubted good looks, in a dark-haired, clean-cut way, but there was an ugliness to his mouth and a narrowness to his eyes that made Harkman dislike him. The fact that his dislike was evidently reciprocated came as no surprise: this, after all, was the other man in Julia's life, and such confrontations were supposed to be charged with suppressed feelings.

"Do you know how this machinery works?" Harkman said to Julia.

"Yes . . . Paul was explaining yesterday."

"He seems incapable of explaining anything at the moment. What happens?"

"Each participant has a drawer to himself. Mine is that one." She pointed towards the drawer about eighth or ninth from the nearer end, and Harkman realized that this was one of the three that were still not fully closed.

"How do you know that one is yours?" Harkman said. "They all look the same."

"Because . . . I'm not sure." Julia looked at the other two, shook her head. "I *know* it's mine, because it feels like mine. I can't say why."

"But why is one different from another?"

"It's to do with neural and cerebral patterns. Dr Eliot – "
She broke off suddenly, and looked at Harkman in alarm.

"What is it?" he said.

"Dr Eliot should be here! And Marilyn. And the rest of the staff. Paul was emphatic about this . . . the project musn't be started without medical supervision."

"Then where are they?"

Julia called up the room: "Paul, where's Dr Eliot?"

Paul said something inaudible, but did not turn to face them.

Harkman said: "Go on, Julia. What happens to the participants?"

"We have to lie down in the drawer, and when it's closed lights will come on inside. That will trigger some kind of cerebral response which will link our minds to the projector. There are electrodes inside."

They went to the drawer Julia had said was her own, and pulled it open. At the sound of the metal runners, Paul turned round to face them.

"What are you doing?" he called. "My experiment is in progress. I don't want it interfered with."

Harkman said: "Take no notice of him, Julia. Go on."

She pointed out the padded rests for head and shoulders, and between them an array of short, pointed electrodes.

"We have to lie so those press against the skin," she said. "I've already tried it. They prick the skin, but otherwise don't hurt."

165

Harkman glanced at the pile of clothes in the centre of the floor. "And we undress for this?"

"Of course."

Harkman stared at the drawer with uncertain feelings; the bright lights and Mason's mad words; Julia's earnestness. But he was being infected by it; he was at the centre of his obsession. There was a drawer in this cabinet for him, and he knew which one it was. Like Julia, he didn't know *how* he recognized it . . . but he knew which of the two remaining drawers was his.

Paul Mason was still standing under the battery of lights, watching them.

"I've killed the others!" he shouted. "I'll kill you too. Keep away, Julia . . . you know what will happen to you!"

"Does he mean that?" Harkman said.

Julia, who was clearly disorientated by Paul's irrational behaviour, said: "I don't know. Help me with this."

She laid her hands on the drawer next to hers, and together they pulled it open. Lying inside was the unconscious body of a naked young man, and so still was he that for a moment Harkman thought he was indeed dead. Julia bent over his face and put her cheek beneath the young man's nostrils. She placed her hand on his heart.

"He's still breathing," she said.

"Then what did Mason mean about killing everyone?"

"David, I don't know. We have to ignore him. I don't understand what's gone wrong with him . . . he was perfectly all right this afternoon."

But Mason wasn't to be ignored, for he started coming slowly towards them, pressing his back against the bank of drawers. He was mouthing words, but incoherently.

"Why is he unconscious?" Harkman said, looking at the young man on the drawer.

"Because he's projecting, I think. I'm not even certain of that."

Harkman realized with sudden surprise that he recognized the young man. He was the peddler with the mirrors, the one he had sometimes seen about the streets of Dorchester.

"Who is this?" he said.

"His name's Steve. I don't know much about him."

They pushed the drawer closed again.

"What shall we do, Julia? Are we going to go through with it?"

She looked back at Paul, who was still working his way towards them, muttering to himself.

"I'm frightened, David. Nothing makes sense any more . . . we've only that old newspaper cutting to believe."

"Do you believe it?"

"I have to. And so do you. Everything else is insane."

"Julia, I'll kill you if you get into the machine." Mason was beside them now, staring at them with wild eyes. "I planned all this . . . it has to be you and me alone together. That's what we agreed!"

Harkman said: "Get undressed, Julia. I'll keep Mason away from you."

He stepped to the side, standing between her and Mason. Instantly, Mason leaped at him. He threw an arm around Harkman's neck from behind, and tugged his head back. With his other hand he clawed at his eyes. Julia screamed.

Harkman, taken by surprise, felt himself dragged back. The hand closed over his face, groping fiercely across his nose and eyes; a finger went into his nostril and started pulling. In an instinctive fear, Harkman snatched his head to one side and slammed an elbow backwards into Mason's stomach. At once the grip around his neck loosened. Harkman turned, and with an awkward untrained blow, hit Mason sideways across the temple. The other man staggered back, and fell weakly against the bank of drawers.

"David, are you all right?"

"I'm O.K.," he said, but his heart was racing and he was out of breath. "Please, Julia . . . get into the machine. It's all we can do now."

"I can't go by myself. I'm terrified of what will happen."

"I'll be with you. I promise. I'll follow you."

Behind them, Mason suddenly let out a howl of rage, and tried to get to his feet again. Harkman turned to face him, clenching his fists. He was no fighter, and Mason's insane behaviour was scaring him. As Mason levered himself up, Harkman kicked out at the man's legs, making him fall again.

"Do it, Julia! I'll keep Mason off you."

She hesitated a moment longer, then undid the buttons of the raincoat. Her arm got caught in the sleeve as she pulled it off, and Harkman helped her. She was watching Paul, and her fingers fumbled with her dress.

"*Julia!*" Mason cried. "*Don't go!*"

"Paul, it's what we planned."

"You'll die, Julia! You'll be killed!"

"Don't talk to him," Harkman said. "It makes him worse. Stay calm, and let me handle him."

They managed to get the dress off her at last. She swept back her hair, which was still damp and tangled from the rain, and reached up to kiss Harkman briefly.

"Come straight away," she said. "Do you know which is your drawer?"

"That one, I think." He was pointing towards the one he had recognized as his. It was just beyond where Paul Mason still huddled on the floor.

Julia said: "David, this is right! We both feel it."

"What do I do, though?"

"You can pull yourself in," she said. "There's a handle inside. And a large mirror above you . . . look into it."

Mason was trying to get up, but he seemed dazed and his movements were uncoordinated. Harkman glanced down at him, wondering whether to knock him over again.

"Get into the drawer, Julia. I'll help you."

He made sure the drawer was pulled right out, then Julia sat on the metal surface and lay back. She shifted her head and shoulders a few times, apparently trying to settle herself comfortably, and pushed her hair out of the way so that it did not interfere with any of the electrodes.

"I'm ready, David."

He bent over her and kissed her lightly on the lips.

"I love you, Julia. Are you frightened?"

She smiled up at him. "Not now. This is what we have to do."

"I'm not frightened either. Are you ready?"

On the floor a short distance away, Paul Mason groaned.

"Yes, I'm ready."

David pressed against the drawer, and felt it slide smoothly into the body of the machine. He looked down at her, hoping to catch her expression, but she had turned her eyes away from him, was looking to the side.

The drawer closed. In the last instant Harkman saw a bright light turn on inside the cabinet, and as the drawer settled into place he saw the brilliance outlined squarely.

Mason was on his feet, and he had moved away from the cabinets.

"Where's Julia, Harkman?"

He tried to ignore the man, stepping round him, but Mason side-stepped to block his way.

"You're not interfering any more, Harkman. Who the hell are you, anyway? Where's Julia? What have you done with her?"

"Get out of the way, Mason."

"You're not getting into the machine. I'll kill you."

"You can't stop me."

They stood facing each other, and Harkman's heart started to race again. Mason was crouching, as if ready to leap on him. Then Mason looked away, and stared towards Julia's drawer. The brilliant internal light was fading, and as both men watched it dimmed and went out.

Mason turned towards the cabinets, and Harkman took a step forward.

□□□□□□ There was a bell ringing in darkness, then a jerking,
26   sliding motion, and light shone in her eyes. People
      were moving about, and it was hot.

"It's Miss Stretton!" somebody said, and another voice shouted above the clatter of metal and hubbub of voices: "Nurse! Bring a sedative!"

Julia opened her eyes, and her first impression was the customary one: that the drawer of the Ridpath projector had opened the instant it was closed, and that she was still in Wessex . . . but there were too many people about, and there was no Paul, no David.

A man in a white coat was standing over her, his head turned away and his arm reaching out impatiently towards someone hurrying across to him. He held Julia's wrist in his other hand, his fingers on her pulse. The nurse put a hypodermic needle into the doctor's outstretched hand, and bent over to swab the inside of her elbow.

Julia wriggled, trying to move herself away. Pain shot down her back.

"No!" she said, and her voice felt as if it was breaking through lips swollen with sores; her nasal passage was dry, her throat was hurting. "No . . . please, no sedative."

"Hold her still, nurse."

"No!" Julia said again, and with all the strength she could

169

find she managed to wrench her arm away, and fold it defensively across her stomach. "I'm all right . . . please don't sedate me."

The doctor, whom Julia recognized as Trowbridge, took hold of her wrist again as if he were about to pull her arm forcibly away, but then he looked closely into her eyes.

"Do you know your name?" he said.

"Of course . . . it's Julia Stretton."

"Do you remember where you've been?"

"Inside the Wessex projection."

"All right, lie still." He released her wrist, and passed the hypodermic back to the nurse. "Find Dr Eliot," he said to the nurse, "and tell him Miss Stretton has apparent recall."

The nurse hurried away.

"Can you move your head, Julia? Try it very slowly."

She made to raise her head from its support, but as soon as she did a sharp pain snatched at her neck.

"The electrodes are still in contact," Dr Trowbridge said, "I'll ease you away."

He leaned over her and took both her shoulders in his hands. Moving her a fraction of an inch at a time he raised one of her shoulder-blades, and so lifted her away from the electrodes on that side. By the time he had done this Dr Eliot had arrived, and together the two men lifted her painfully away from the needles. Soon, she was sitting up in the drawer, her head down between her knees, while one of the doctors dabbed the inflamed area of her neck and spine with a soothing ointment. Somebody put a blanket over her, and she hugged it around her.

As awareness grew in her, and she realized what had been happening, Julia felt a conflict of intense emotions: anger and confusion, mixed with the pain. Her fury was directed at Paul; how he had interfered with the projection, how he had distorted the world of Wessex, how he had so effectively intruded and destroyed. Confusion, because the projection hall was crowded with people, most of them medical staff. Peering up between her knees she saw somebody being wheeled way on a trolley, with two orderlies holding oxygen equipment alongside. Another person was being carried away on a stretcher, and while Julia's neck was still being treated she heard Dr Eliot's name called, and he walked quickly away.

But above all this, through her suppressed rage, Julia held a memory of David. In spite of everything, Paul and his insane distortions, and all the changes in Wessex he had wrought, David was the same.

"David? Is David out?" she said.

"David Harkman? He's not here at the moment." Dr Trowbridge pushed her head down between her knees again. "Keep still."

"I've got to talk to someone," she said. "Please. . . ."

"You can speak to Dr Eliot. In a moment."

"But at least tell me what's happening here."

"There's a full-scale emergency. Something must have happened to the projection, because everyone's returning at once."

Dr Trowbridge's name was called, and he left Julia with the lint lying loosely on her neck.

Under his strict injunction not to move, Julia was unable to watch what was happening, but she listened to him speaking to two of the nurses a short distance away. She heard her name mentioned several times, and "no apparent traumata", and "we haven't tested her motor functions, but they seem normal", and "as soon as Dr Eliot is free he'll have to speak to her."

A nurse finished cleaning and dressing her neck, and while this was going on Julia tried again to look to either side of her. She was still sitting up on the surface of the drawer, and her view was obstructed by the many people moving around her, but it seemed to her that most of the drawers were open. She was trying to discover whether David's had been opened yet, but it was too difficult to see.

The nurse fixed the lint in place with some sticking-plaster across her shoulder-blades. "That's finished, Miss Stretton. Remove the dressing tomorrow."

"May I get down now?"

The nurse looked across to where Dr Trowbridge was leaning over someone lying on a trolley. "Has the doctor released you yet?"

"No . . . but I feel all right."

"Let me see you move your arms."

Julia flexed her muscles, and turned her wrists, and apart from the customary stiffness after retrieval there seemed no difficulty.

"I'll find you an orderly," the nurse said.

At that moment, Julia saw a small group of people come into the room.

"There's Marilyn," she said. "She'll help me."

Marilyn spotted her before the nurse could beckon, and the girl called out her name and walked quickly across the room to her.

"John Eliot said you were all right!" she said, and kissed Julia on the cheek. "What happened to the projection, Julia? Do you know?"

"Yes, I saw it all."

"You *can* remember it then?"

"Of course I can."

"Julia, something terrible has gone wrong with the others. They're suffering from amnesia."

"But . . . how?" Julia said.

"We don't know. There's been such a rush. Everyone was returning at once. And one after another, none of them has had any memory of who they are, where they've been, what's happening to them now. Most of them are being taken to Dorchester General Hospital, but a few have gone to Bincombe House. And amnesia is the least of the problems. Dr Eliot says he suspects brain-damage in some cases, and Don Mander has had a stroke."

Julia stared up at her in horror. "What on earth has happened?"

"No one knows. You're probably the only one who can tell us."

She looked at Marilyn, thinking of David inside the projector.

"Is David out yet, David Harkman?"

"I don't think so . . . wait a minute, I'll check."

Marilyn went over to Dr Trowbridge and spoke briefly to him.

"No, he's still in the projection," she said when she returned.

"Marilyn, help me down. I've got to speak to John Eliot."

She put an arm round the other girl's neck, and lowered her feet to the floor. She stood up, supporting her weight on Marilyn, but after a few seconds of uncertainty found that she could manage on her own. She leant against the metal wall of the nearest cabinet, clutching the blanket around her.

"Who else is still in the projection, Marilyn?"

"Just one other . . . Paul Mason."

Julia remembered the brightly lit hall, a future analogue of this one. She remembered Paul's mania and his threats . . . and she thought of David alone with Paul, in Wessex.

She shook her head weakly, not knowing whether she wanted

David to stay there with him . . . or return to this. He had now been inside the projection for more than two years; what the physiological effects would be on him when he returned were too horrid to contemplate, and never mind the amnesia Marilyn had spoken of. Brain-damage, strokes . . . did these await him on his return?

She felt an almost uncontrollable urge to climb back on her drawer, to pull herself inside the cabinet . . . to return to the future.

"Are you all right, Julia?"

She opened her eyes, saw Marilyn standing beside her.

"Yes . . . I'm just a little cold."

"Let's see if we can find your clothes."

"A surgical gown will do. I must talk to Eliot."

They walked together through the hall, then had to stand to one side as another trolley was wheeled out. At is passed, Julia tried to see who was on it, but an oxygen-mask was being held over the person's face. Knowing it was one of the participants, a sharer of her private world, Julia felt a sense of close identification. She wanted to know who it was, but she couldn't even see whether it was a man or a woman. She turned away, looked at the wall until the trolley had passed out of sight.

As they reached the main corridor, Eliot appeared from one of the rooms.

"Julia!" he said. "Have you been examined?"

"Yes, I'm all right."

"Thank God for that! You do have total recall?"

"To the last detail," she said, thinking of the grim ironies of those details.

"Come to my office as soon as you've dressed. We must find out what went wrong."

"Paul Mason went wrong," she said, but it was to herself. She and Marilyn went to the cubicle she used for changing in. The clothes she had been wearing were still there, but a feeling of transience that she wished to preserve turned her away from them. A considerable part of herself was still in Wessex, still with David. Until he was back safely she wouldn't feel safe or permanent in the present.

There was a surgical gown folded up in the cupboard, and she put this on.

They went to Eliot's office immediately, because Julia was anxious for news of what had been happening . . . but all Eliot told her was what she had already heard. The participants had been returning for the last two hours; all, except her, had suffered chronic mental or nervous disturbance. She was the last to return so far.

"Of course, this must mean the end of the projection," Eliot said. "I cannot imagine any circumstances under which it could be revived now."

"But what about David?" Julia said at once.

"The projector will have to be kept in operation, of course. At least until he and Mason are retrieved."

"Is there any attempt being made to get them out?"

Eliot shook his head. "I can't allow anyone inside now."

He told her that three of the trustees would be arriving in Dorchester the next day, to take over the supervision of the projector.

Julia, listening to this, was experiencing the uncanny overlap of realities that always followed a retrieval. Nothing had changed: there were still trustees, and there was still a Foundation. Outside the Castle there was the twentieth century and the world she knew, and it awaited her inevitable return.

But this world was no longer hers. She had ceased to be an organic part of the real world from the day she had first entered the projection. She belonged to the future; life could never again be stable except in the Wessex of her mind.

She could never accept that the future had ceased to be, for it was real to her. Wessex was a world of timeless safety, of certain stability, of unconscious harmony.

These were the qualities of the real Wessex, not the nightmare perversion that Paul's malign consciousness had created.

"Julia," Eliot said, "what happened to the program? Why did everyone return?"

"Because of Mason," she said, thinking of Paul, thinking of David. "Because it was what he wanted, what he intended."

Remembering the evening on the heath with David, which was the exact moment when she had rejoined the projection, she began to speak of the changes Mason had made to Wessex, either consciously or unconsciously. Reliving those few days in the future she experienced again, this time with the perspective of whole awareness, the sense of growing confusion that the protean world had evoked in her. The destruction of Dorchester as a tourist resort; the appearance of the refinery and the oil-wells; the pollution and filth; the countless tiny changes in scenery and populace; the disappearance of the village at the Castle, and of most of the auxiliary egos.

All these . . . and the major change. The madness in Mason.

"While I was back before – a week ago – Paul Mason told me that the trustees had authorized him to change the projection. He didn't say how, not directly. But now I've seen it. He set up a *second* projection, using the Ridpath equipment that exists in Wessex. I can't imagine what he hoped – "

"You didn't report this to me or the others," Eliot said. "You had every opportunity."

Julia fingered her throat, felt the swelling that was still there from Paul's attempt to rape her.

"I couldn't . . . not then." She remembered the guilt and confusion Paul had caused in her; the internal conflicts, the long struggle towards self-control and a sense of her own identity. "He was, well . . . blackmailing me. We used to live together, years ago. It lasted two years, and in the end I ran away from him. He's never forgiven me."

"Julia, it was your duty to tell me this. You know the rule about – "

"It wouldn't have made any difference, John. He had the trustees behind him. Anyway, he turned the rule against me when he found out about it. He made me believe that if I revealed this to you, then it would be me and not him who would be excluded, because of his status with the trustees. I couldn't risk that . . . Wessex is too real to me. . . ."

Then she started to cry, reliving the agonies of the dilemma that Paul's reappearance in her life had produced. All that she had feared had come to pass: Paul had once again destroyed everything she possessed.

Eliot waited in embarrassed silence while she cried, and Marilyn comforted her and found her a tissue.

"You see, this is what Paul has done. It was because of me!" Julia held the tissue in her fingers, compressing it and feeling it shape itself wetly into a ball. "He had an unconscious will to change what *I* had in Wessex. He offered some sort of plan to the trustees, but that wasn't his real intention, because he didn't recognize it himself! He's unstable and neurotically inadequate. I've always known it!"

Calming herself, she told Eliot about the project that Paul had constructed in Wessex. The other participants had been drawn in, unable to change his will. Most of them had had no

175

idea that someone new had joined the projection; the sudden presence of a strong personality, obsessed with itself, had over-powered any resistance they might otherwise have put up. So, drawn into his mania, they'd worked with him to create a new projection . . . one that was based on their buried memories of the real world.

"Paul was directing this! Not only consciously, because he cast himself as project director, but at the same time he was unconsciously diverting everyone else towards an obsession with the present. We all went along with him, because his influence was so powerful."

She paused then, remembering the charismatic personality that Paul's projection of himself had possessed. He had seemed so likeable, so genuine, so strong.

The memory was deeply offensive to her, as if someone had importuned her sexually. In those few days of Wessex – in Paul's version of Wessex – she had seen Paul's unconscious image of himself, and it was one that in her real life she had hated him for.

"Julia, you can't believe that one man could bring all this about."

"I saw it, felt it."

Eliot had never fully understood the real subtleties of a pro-jection. No one who had not been to Wessex could. As she tried to describe what she had experienced, she could hear her own words as if objectively, and she knew they sounded paranoiac. Eliot was being gentle, and trying to understand, but he would never know until he had felt it for himself how one person-ality could so insidiously influence another.

"You seem to have resisted him yourself," he said. "Why is it that you alone have retained your memory?"

Julia knew: it was too strong to ignore. "Because of David Harkman."

"You know Harkman is still in the projection?"

"Yes, of course."

"And did he become involved in this second projection?"

"No. . . ." Julia tried to find the way to explain, a way that would be true to herself.

Then she chose a half-truth to express a whole truth: "John, my alter ego has fallen in love with David Harkman."

Half the truth, because her alter ego did love him . . . but so did she.

176

She went on: "In the projection Paul was trying to possess me, but because of David he couldn't reach me. He overloaded the minds of the others, but he couldn't touch me and he couldn't touch David. He was unconsciously trying to close the projection by returning the others, but he always intended that I should stay in Wessex, alone with him. He said something like, 'I planned this for the two of us'. But he didn't really understand about David."

"Why not, Julia?"

"Because I never told him . . . I never told anyone. Paul didn't realize what David had become for me. . . ."

Just then, the telephone on Eliot's desk rang, and he picked up the receiver. "Yes? Ah, Mr Bonner."

Julia remembered the name: the trustees' legal adviser.

Marilyn, who had been sitting quietly to one side through all this, said: "Do you need another tissue, Julia?"

"No thanks." But she realized that tears were still trickling down her cheeks, and she took the second tissue from her.

Marilyn said: "Do you know why all the others have lost their memories?"

"I suppose it was too much for them to cope with."

Even to herself it didn't sound convincing; the human brain wasn't like an electrical appliance that could blow a fuse.

She tried to listen to Eliot, but he had turned away from them and was talking quietly into the telephone, answering questions, listening to Bonner.

The loss of memory was like the loss they all experienced inside the projection: a total severance from their real lives, and an assumption of a new identity. After two years of experience she had come to terms with it, but on her first retrieval Julia had been frightened by the awareness: the memory of the amnesia, so to speak.

Paul's alter ego had warned them of it. One day, as they planned their project, Paul had said: "On emergence in the future" – he had meant the present – "you will lose your present identities and take on new ones."

He had understood that much of the working of the projector, at least. And it was as he had said: the participants had returned without their memories.

But why? They had all returned from the projection before . . . and they had had total recall then. Julia tried to think why this time it should be different.

The young men with their mirrors, the hypnotic triggers.

That was it. Other retrievals were achieved through hypnotic suggestions placed in the present, in the real world. This retrieval had been achieved in an altogether different way. The projector had been fully functional, used as it was in the present. Even the two retrievers had programmed themselves to take part; Julia remembered seeing Steve inside his drawer, projecting with the others.

No mirrors had been used, except those inside the cabinets.

In the world of Wessex, projected from the present, the participants had created a second projection. They *imagined* themselves into the past. They had become projections of themselves!

Julia recoiled away from the idea.

This was the *real* world, was it not? This was not a projection?

She looked at Marilyn sitting a few feet away from her . . . and at Eliot, talking on the telephone. They were of the real world, of the twentieth century . . . they were not figments of the imagination.

But they had been in Wessex for a time, *inside the projection!*

Paul, or one of the others, had imagined them into existence as auxiliary egos! Julia remembered Eliot at the conferences, remembered borrowing a raincoat from Marilyn.

Marilyn said: "Are you feeling all right, Julia?"

She reached out and touched Marilyn's arm. It was solid, real. She jumped, and snatched away her hand.

"What is it, Julia?"

She stood up, and pushed back her chair. Suddenly she wanted to see the outside world, to see the Frome Valley and the inland town of Dorchester, and the white trails of overhead jets, and the railway-line that passed the Castle, and the roads and the traffic. . . .

Was the world as it was? Was it still there?

She ran out of Eliot's office and into the cool, earth-smelling tunnel. At the far end were the iron gates of the elevator: the way to the outside. She ran towards them, fulfilling a terror of the unconscious.

The days inside the projector had weakened her, and she staggered as she ran, and when she reached the elevator gates she leaned against them, gasping for breath.

Her resolution failed as her body had weakened, and she went no further.

The world would be as it was. It would still be there.

It would be real, or *real-seeming*. It made no difference. It would be as it was, or as she expected it to be . . . and it therefore was of no importance.

She leaned against the gates, trying to recover her breath.

Marilyn had left Eliot's office, and was walking down the tunnel towards her. "Julia, what are you doing?"

"It's all right. I'm O.K. now. I just wanted some fresh air . . . but I changed my mind."

"Let's go back and wait in the office."

Still out of breath from her dash down the corridor, Julia looked again at Marilyn. She realized that even if she were to spend the rest of her life in the company of the other girl, and saw and spoke to her every minute of every day, she would never again be convinced of her true existence.

If she turned her back, would Marilyn vanish? Would she reappear as soon as she looked again?

"Is David Harkman out of the projector yet?" she said, trying to make her voice sound normal, unexcited.

"Let's talk to John Eliot again. He'll know."

"All right, Marilyn."

They walked back together towards the office, but as Marilyn opened the door, Julia ran again. She ran down the tunnel, further into the heart of the Castle. She heard Marilyn shout her name, then call urgently to Dr Eliot.

Julia turned the corner, past the conference room, and ran into the projection hall.

Calm and order had been restored, and Julia was brought up short by the quietness and emptiness. The emergency seemed to be over.

Two more trolleys were standing by, and two teams of orderlies were waiting beside them. Oxygen bottles and blankets were ready near by, and drugs had been set out on a tray. Dr Trowbridge was standing near the orderlies.

As she walked in, he turned towards her.

"Have you seen Dr Eliot?" he said.

"Yes," Julia said. "I'm passed as fit."

She was fit because she wanted to be. Imagine herself ill, and she would become ill.

"You should be resting," said Dr Trowbridge.

"I've got to wait here . . . for John Eliot."

Trowbridge turned away, and Julia walked slowly – and with

contrived idleness of purpose – down the length of the row of cabinets. Now that most of the drawers were opened, it looked as if some mammoth burglary had taken place, with the contents of the drawers rifled indiscriminately. Two drawers were still closed, their precious living contents hidden away from the world.

She tried to imagine what the minds of the two men would be making. It was a projected world of two personalities, and one that would reflect an intense conflict that would be expressed in every way, from the unconscious id, to the conscious mind, to the physical body. She remembered Paul's violence as he attacked David, she remembered his madness.

Julia went to the nearer of the two drawers, the one that David was inside. She saw his name, printed in small black capitals on a white card affixed to the front.

Dr Trowbridge had his back turned towards her, and he was talking to two of the orderlies. Julia put her hands on the handle of David's drawer, but immediately she snatched them away.

She wanted to see him again . . . but dreaded doing so.

The emotion that had welled up when she was talking to Eliot flowed again, and she let out an involuntary sob, which she choked back by swallowing. She pretended a cough . . . but Trowbridge, still talking, took no notice.

She took hold of the handle again, but this time pulled it as strongly as she could manage. The drawer resisted for a moment, then it slid smoothly out.

The body of David Harkman lay before her, and on the instant she saw his face Julia cried aloud.

He was still and stiff, as if dead, but his eyes flickered behind closed lids and his chest was moving steadily up and down. His body had been allowed to deteriorate even further than when she had last seen him here: his naked skin was pale, and his flesh was soft and seemed as if it were waterlogged. His hair was long and matted, and his fingernails curled back towards his palms.

She sank down and laid an arm across his chest, loving him, loving him.

Something unspoken told her that he would never return; that his permanent place was the Wessex of the mind; that he had become as one with the world he had helped create.

She was crying because he was there and she was here, and because she wanted only to be with him.

He had been watching her from under the shelter of the sea-wall, waiting while she read the crumbling piece of newsprint. Of course she remembered it now; the newspaper had carried the story the day the projection began, more than two years ago. "It's genuine, I'm sure it's genuine," he had said. She wanted to tell him now that he was right . . . but what did it matter? She no longer knew what was real, no longer cared. David was her only reality, but David was in Wessex.

Julia cried, and wiped her eyes with the soggy tissue she still clutched. She kissed David's unresponsive face, then stood up. She walked to the front of the drawer, put her weight to it, and in a moment it slid slowly and smoothly home. He was safe again.

She walked numbly towards her own drawer, and found it.

The surgical gown was held with three simple laces at the front, and she slipped it off. Then one of the orderlies noticed, and pointed it out to Dr Trowbridge.

"Miss Stretton . . . what are you doing?"

She made no answer, but reached behind her and found a corner of the sticking-plaster across her shoulders. She pulled, wincing at the pain. It wouldn't tear back, so she tugged harder, and at last it came away. As she dropped it to the ground Julia saw that there were spots of blood, mingling with the yellow stain of antiseptic.

Her drawer was beside her, and so she sat down and drew up her legs.

"Julia!" It was Eliot, who had appeared at the entrance to the hall. Marilyn stood beside him. "Julia, get down from there. Trowbridge, get away from that!"

"I'm going back, John!" she shouted.

"I told you, no one is to use the projector again. I've had instructions to close it down, to turn it off."

Trowbridge had crossed the room and was standing a few feet away from her, apparently uncertain of what to do.

"You can't turn it off with people inside," Julia said. "You know that would kill them."

"I've had instructions from the trustees."

Eliot had been walking slowly towards her as he spoke, and Julia knew that where Trowbridge hesitated Eliot would act. She knew what she wanted. She knew more certainly than anything she had ever known in her life.

Wanting it, she stared her defiance at Trowbridge . . . who turned away.

Wanting it, she stared at Eliot . . . and he came to a halt.

From the doorway, Marilyn called: "Do it, Julia! Take care!"

Julia closed her eyes. She lay back on the drawer, settling herself on the supports, and she gasped with pain as the electrodes went into the old sores. She reached behind her, found the handle inside the cabinet. As she pulled, the extra strain caused the electrodes to snag and tear at her flesh . . . but the drawer was moving, taking her into the dry, warm darkness.

The drawer closed and bright internal lights came on, and Julia stared upwards into a circular mirror.

□□□□□□ Julia ran down the main tunnel beneath Maiden Castle,
27 the coarse fabric of her dress chafing against her legs.
Her memories were intact.

For the first time since the projection had begun, Julia had full knowledge of herself and her place. She could remember Paul's mania in the projection hall, and the shouting and fighting; she could remember her return to the world of the 1980s; she could remember running down this tunnel away from Marilyn, with the girl shouting her name.

But this was Wessex, and there was no Marilyn, no Dr Eliot. She reached the end of the tunnel, and no one called after her. She was alone.

The glaring lights of the projection hall shone down the side-tunnel, and she slowed, not knowing what to expect. Were David and Paul still in conflict? Was Paul still cowering in his corner, babbling of death and power?

All was silent as she walked into the long hall. It seemed like only a few moments before that she had walked in the same way into the same room, desperate for a sight of David. And so it was again: shielding her eyes against the brilliant spotlights, Julia looked for David.

The hall was empty. Along the side, the drawers of the cabinets were closed, a uniform wall of finality. When she left Wessex, two drawers had been opened: one for David, one for Paul. Now all the drawers were closed, their secrets contained.

In the centre of the floor, picked out by the lights, was the pile of discarded clothing.

"David?" she said, her voice unsure and sounding tremulous. This was the first noise she had consciously made since walking into the hall, and at once she was alarmed. She had a sudden irrational fear that it would bring Paul out from some hiding-place.

The room was silent, with only the background hum of the projection equipment.

Because she had expected to find the two men here, Julia was disconcerted by their absence. What had happened to them? Because they hadn't appeared in the present, she had assumed they were still in Wessex. Where were they?

But their drawers were closed: could they have returned to the present without her knowing it? But no, her memory was quite clear: neither had appeared. She remembered the two closed drawers, the two trolleys and the orderlies waiting. And she had seen David's body only seconds before she climbed into her own drawer.

Nagging at her, though, was the knowledge that the transfer from present to future, and vice versa, was instantaneous. It *could* have happened . . . Paul and David could have returned at the same moment as she herself rejoined the projection.

How else to explain it?

She walked across to the drawer that she knew was David's, conscious of the way in which she was continuing to retrace the steps of her alter ego in the present. *That* Julia had walked to this drawer looking for a David she had lost, and that Julia had not found him. With the same instinctive dread, she pulled her hands away from the drawer before she could act.

She stepped back, turned away. Alone in a world that was entirely hers, Julia felt the terror of the unknown.

The pile of discarded clothes was next to her, and she looked down at it. Lying on the top was a jacket she recognized at once as David's. Beneath it, neatly folded, were the rest of his clothes.

She touched the jacket, and it was damp from the rain; she lifted it up and pressed it against the side of her face, holding it as if it were the last trace of him.

In total misery she dropped the jacket on the pile, and cried out his name.

Then, very muffled, she heard: "Julia. . . ?"

It was David's voice . . . and without a thought she ran across the hall and took hold again of the drawer-handle. She pulled with all her strength, and at once his naked body slid into view.

That he was conscious and alert was instantly obvious because he moved his head before the drawer was fully extended, and bumped his forehead against the metal edge.

He winced with agony, and his head fell back.

She looked at his healthy body, his ruddy complexion . . . and the expression on his face, pain and pleasure, comically mixed.

She laughed aloud, almost hysterically, relieved beyond words that he was safe.

"Oh, David. . . ."

"Don't laugh! Help me out of here! I thought I was stuck forever!"

She knelt down and put an arm across his chest, pressing the side of her face against his. She was still laughing, but crying too . . . and David put his arms around her, pulling her down against him.

Then he winced in pain again. "These needles . . . pricking me."

She moved back and helped lift him away from the shoulder-supports. He sat forward, in the way she had been made to sit by Dr Trowbridge, and rubbed the back of his neck with his hand. She looked to see, but the needles had barely penetrated the skin, and there was a faint pink rash along the upper part of his spine.

She hugged him for several minutes, thinking only of him, and being with him.

But then she said: "David, what happened? Why didn't you go back to the present?"

"I did as you said . . . but nothing changed. I stared into a reflection of my own face, wondering what the hell was supposed to happen, and how I was going to get out, until I heard you outside."

"But you should have returned instantly. Has the projector been turned off?"

"Not as far as I know. I certainly didn't touch it, even if I knew how."

"Then Paul must have tampered with it."

David shook his head. He swung his legs to the floor, and walked over to retrieve his clothes. He said: "Mason's in the machine."

"Was there a fight?"

"Not after you left. He was still ranting away, but he ignored me completely and was talking about projecting himself into the future, trying to follow you. He went to the cabinets on his own, I waited until he'd filed himself away . . . and then I tried to come after you. But as you see, it didn't work."

"Why not, David?"

"Perhaps I'm immune."

He said it jokingly, but it struck a resonant chord in Julia's memory; her new memory, the one that stretched back to the twentieth century.

The last time she had been out of the projector, during the meeting when Paul was there: Andy and Steve had come back from Wessex, and reported that David had been shown the mirrors but that he'd resisted it somehow.

(And a deeper memory, several layers down, folded back under itself: a morning at the stall in Dorchester; David exhilarated from having ridden the Blandford wave, and trying to talk about it as the tourists gathered around the stall; Steve appearing with a mirror, and trying to show or sell it to David; herself taking the mirror from him, and smashing it on the ground; David unconcerned, wanting to see her later in the day; Steve going away from the stall.)

David had been in Wessex continuously for more than two years; had the deep-hypnotic triggers been lost? Was he as resistant to the mirror inside the projector as he was to the ones carried by the retrievers?

David said: "You must be immune too. You're still here."

"I'm here because I chose to come back. Everything you talked about was true. Look. . . ." She took his trousers from him just as he was about to put them on, and felt in the back pocket. The newspaper cutting was still there. "This, David . . . it's true. When you put me inside the projector I went back to the twentieth century. As soon as I was there I *remembered* all that's true about us. Neither of us is real, but it doesn't matter! We are real to each other. I saw what was happening in the present, and I couldn't stand it. I had to come back."

She was wondering how to begin telling him what she could remember. The trustees; her past life with Paul Mason; the damaged minds of the other participants.

And David's real body: pallid, bloated, uncared for. If he ever went back, tried to assume his real identity, could he survive?

"David, this is the only reality left! What Paul Mason did . . . I can hardly explain. He set up the second projection here, and I thought it was a way home. But what he is projecting is an *imaginary* twentieth century . . . one where that newspaper was printed!"

David laughed nervously, and took the newsprint from her. "First I'm told by this that I don't exist, and now you tell me this doesn't exist!"

"That's right." She remembered the emergency as the participants returned. "Most of the other people have gone mad . . . in that projected world."

"But not you."

"No . . . I had something to believe in, something I knew to be real."

"What was that?"

She shook her head, and smiled at him. "If you don't know, David, I'm not going to tell you."

He had all his clothes on now, and was straightening the collar of his shirt: a concentration on a familiar, mundane task to avoid thinking about the unthinkable.

"David, don't you understand? The newspaper was right about us at one time, but it's wrong now. When we met, our identities were projections from the past. But Paul Mason changed that. His project, this one, is *imagining* the past. Not the one we're from, but one very like it! And Paul's projection is a complete success; I know, because I've been there! It's a two-way projection . . . people in Wessex, who were projected from the past, are projecting the past from which they started. It's been too much for them. They've lost their minds." She ran a hand through her hair, and found that it was still damp from the rain of an hour before. "I think I'm beginning to lose my own!"

She went to the cabinets, and took hold of the handle of the first drawer she came to.

"If Wessex is still a projection, David, this drawer should be empty. The alter ego that was projected would either vanish, or resume its normal life in Wessex, when the mind of the participant withdraws. But do you know what's inside this? Is someone here . . . or is the drawer empty?"

As she had been talking, David had left his shirt-collar alone, and was watching her thoughtfully. The piece of newsprint had slipped from his fingers, and lay on the pile of clothes.

"Julia, I don't think you should open that drawer," he said.

"I've got to!"

She pulled, felt the familiar resistance . . . and a moment later the drawer slid out. Lying inside was the body of Nathan Wil-

186

liams. He was still, but alive. His chest rose and fell steadily, and behind closed eyelids his eyes were moving.

Julia said: "He's projecting, David. His mind is functioning."

She opened a second drawer, a third. Both contained living bodies of people she knew.

Thinking of their destiny, thinking of what had happened to those minds, Julia closed the drawers again. She had seen their projection.

"Have you looked in your own drawer, Julia?"

"No!"

"You should. Is your drawer empty?"

"It must be . . . I'm here!"

"Are you a figment of your own imagination, as I am of mine?"

"David, I don't want to know!"

He had turned her own argument against her in a way she could not face. She stepped back, and further back, until she reached the further wall. Between her and David lay the pile of clothes . . . and she saw, lying beside a damp raincoat, there was a plain, brown dress, identical to the one she was wearing. She looked down at herself. The bottom of the dress, that had not been covered by the coat, was dark and wet from the rain. She remembered the chafing against her legs as she ran down the tunnel.

The dress lying on the pile was also damp.

She alone had visited the projected past, and had not been harmed. She alone had returned to reality. Her memories were whole. She was in Wessex. The future, the present, the now.

David pulled open the drawer she had used, and stared inside. For several seconds he didn't move, but then he said: "I think you had better look, Julia."

"No, David. No!"

She could see, from where she was standing, that there were two white and naked legs stretched out along the drawer. The rest of the body was hidden by David standing over it.

"You're the same as the others, Julia. You lie here and project, and you stand there and are projected."

"Close the drawer, David. *Please!*"

He turned to look at her. He was grinning.

"You're very beautiful naked," he said. "Come and see what I mean."

She couldn't move, couldn't turn her head away. "David, please close that drawer!"

The momentary roguishness on his face had faded, and with a sober expression he put his weight to the drawer and slid it back into place.

"I don't understand, Julia. Are you real? Am I?"

"I can't think about it any more," she said. She felt as if she were about to faint, or to suffer the same loss as the others. "We are as real as we think we are. I only know that I love you. Is that reality?"

"It is for me."

He went across to her and put his arm around her shoulders.

"I'm sorry, Julia," he said. "I shouldn't have done that . . . with the drawer."

"I think you had to. We had to know. It doesn't seem to make any difference."

"What shall we do?" David said. "Can we leave here?"

"Do you want to?"

"I said, *can* we."

"We can do whatever we wish," Julia said. "We are utterly free, for the moment."

"What do you mean by that?"

"When I was in . . . in the present, I heard that the Ridpath projector was going to be turned off."

"It means nothing to me. What effect would that have?"

"Nobody's really sure," Julia said. "Ridpath himself believed that it would kill anyone inside. It's never been tried."

Then a stray thought – comforting? confusing? – hovered for a moment like a flying insect. As she left the present, Eliot had said the trustees had instructed him to close the projection. But that was in the world she believed was being projected from here! Would that have any effect here? Where was the present from which Wessex was being projected? Were they the same . . . or was the system now closed? Did one world project the other, each dependent upon the other for its own continued reality?

David said: "Julia, I think we should leave. I've got everything I ever wanted. We're together . . . that's enough for me."

Julia, distracted by the uncertainty of her thoughts, felt David's hand on hers. She shook her head, as if to throw off the intruding notion, then saw from David's expression that he had taken this as a negative response to what he had just said.

She tightened her fingers around his hand, and said: "I'm sorry. It's what I want too."

188

"Come on, let's go back to Dorchester."

She felt a sudden fear about what might lie outside the Castle, and who might be there, but knowing David was consciously neglecting to think about this, she made the effort too.

"Do you think it's still raining?" she said. "Should I take the coat?"

"Is it yours?"

"No. I borrowed it . . . from Marilyn."

The auxiliary ego Marilyn, the one who had been in the Castle for a time. Marilyn had vanished, but her coat was still here. As she looked at it, Julia remembered that the real Marilyn, the other Marilyn, had a coat just like this.

"You won't need it," David said. "Leave it here."

They walked together towards the doorway, talking about the coat and the possibility of rain. It was like David straightening his collar: a hold on a plainer reality, a need for the prosaic.

As they stepped into the tunnel, Julia pulled herself away from under David's arm, and turned to face back into the projection hall. Something had been worrying her, nagging at her.

"What is it?" David said.

"Paul Mason!" she said. "What happened to him?"

"I told you: he joined the projection with the others."

"But no . . . he didn't. I was there. He didn't return. I'm sure of that . . . they were waiting for him."

"Is he immune too?"

"No. At least, I don't think so." She grasped David's hand, gripping it tightly in sudden fear. "Are you *sure* he's inside the projector?"

"Of course . . . I saw him close himself in."

"When was that?"

"A few minutes after you. Two, three minutes . . . I'm not sure."

"But. . . ." Julia looked at David in despair. "But Paul *didn't* return," she began again. "I'm certain of that. The doctors were waiting. There was just you to return, and Paul."

"Then he's trapped inside, like I was."

David pushed past her, ran back into the hall.

Something inhuman in her made her say: "Don't let him out, David!"

"If he's trapped, I've got to. This is his drawer, isn't it?"

"I think so, yes. . . ." She hardly dared look.

David pulled the drawer, and she saw pale legs stretched in-

189

ertly out, the feet slightly splayed. As the chest, and then the face, came into sight, Julia started to tremble and she leaned against the tunnel wall. The inhuman instinct was still there: a desire for dreadful revenge on Paul for all those years of humiliation, to slam the drawer closed with him inside, to trap him forever inside the cabinet, alive or dead.

David was bending over the body.

"Is he alive?" Julia said, her fist clenched over her mouth.

"He's breathing . . . his eyes are closed."

"Is he projecting?"

"I don't know . . . you'd better look."

She had been unable to look at her own body inside the drawer, and she was unable to look at Paul. It was he who had dominated all her adult life, first by his presence and then by his absence. He had dominated the projection, he had destroyed.

Now there was a primal dread in her: that she would *never* be free of him.

"Close the drawer, David."

"Not until you tell me what's happening to him."

"Are his eyes moving? Flickering . . . under the eyelids?"

"A little, yes."

"Then he's projecting."

David continued to stare at the unconscious body of the man, and seemed uncertain of what to do. Julia waited in the tunnel, but David kept the drawer open.

"Close it, David. Please."

"But if you say he didn't return to . . . to the past, where *is* he projecting to?"

"For God's sake!" She turned from the tunnel wall, ran into the room. She pushed David aside, and put her hands on the front of the drawer. Then she saw Paul's face.

She paused, realizing that he was indeed projecting. She had been impelled by fear: the idea that he might be lying there pretending, waiting to take some new form of retaliation against her. But her paranoia was unfounded: Paul was as deep inside the projection as all the others. He could not escape; there was no way back.

She stared down steadily at him, gaining strength. She knew she would never see him again, never ever. Looking at him thus, directly and unflinchingly, she pushed against the drawer, and it closed.

David was watching her face, perhaps beginning to realize the order of her fear of Paul. She looked back at him, and forced a smile.

"I'm sorry, David . . . I had to do that. I thought he might sit up again, and start threatening us. Like he did before."

David took her hand. "I don't ever want to know what Mason did to you."

"It doesn't matter any more," she said, and she knew that this time she could say it and know it was true.

"Let's get outside," David said. "I've had enough of this place."

They walked out of the projection hall, leaving the lights burning.

Halfway down the main tunnel, Julia said: "He didn't return to the present. He really didn't."

"Then where is he?"

"In the future? All by himself?"

Paul alone believed in a second projection; Paul alone failed to realize, on an unconscious level, that the future he was planning was actually the past; Paul alone believed in the future as a reality.

As they reached the bottom of the lift-shaft and began to climb the stairs, Julia wondered what any world of Paul's making would be like; one which he alone imagined, and in which he alone exercised unconscious will. Would he take an image of her along with him, an auxiliary ego of his own? Or would he make the world itself auxiliary to his own ego? Would anyone exist in that world who would resist him, who wasn't subservient to his will, who wasn't the butt of his malice and destructive criticism?

Julia felt she had lived once before in that kind of world, and knew it well. But that was in the past.

□□□□□□ The rain had stopped, but the wind was chill. When
28 they reached the top of the earth rampart, Julia and
David paused to look down across the bay towards
Dorchester. It was a heavy, clouded night, and the
town itself was mostly in darkness. Only the harbour was
brightly lit; white arc-lamps flooded the port with brilliance,
because it was never still. Throughout the nights the endless

business of the oil-rigs was conducted, with supply-ships and lighters moving to and fro across the bay.

Behind the town, spreading untidily across the heaths, the refinery was at work, throwing up a pall of smoke that glowed orange from the floodlamps beneath it. Connecting the refinery to the sea, the pipelines crawled in parallel lines, their path floodlit for security. Out in the bay, the dozens of drilling-rigs could be seen, standing squarely in the sea as far as the horizon; lights flared whitely and randomly on the superstructure of the platforms, lights for working by, lights for navigation. Seen from the Castle, the rigs looked like a stationary armada, lying-to offshore, waiting for the tide before sailing in to invade.

Beyond all this, beyond the bay and the town, the Wessex hills lay black against the night horizon.

"Let's wait," David said, and he sat down on the wet grass. Julia sat beside him, oblivious of the cold and wet. She snuggled under his arm, drew warmth from his body.

Time passed, and they did not move. The ground seemed less cold after a while, as if it were they who were warming it. Julia, reaching round with her hand, found that the grass had dried.

"I'm not cold now," she said.

"Neither am I. I think the wind has dropped."

It had slackened to a gentle breeze, one that barely touched them, one that was warm from the day.

"Where shall we live, Julia?"

"I suppose it will have to be Dorchester," she said. "It's the only place I know."

"We're completely alone now?"

"Yes, I think so."

Some time later, David pointed out that the orange flame above the refinery, the torch of burning waste-gas, was dying down. Soon it went out, and around it a cluster of floodlamps were also extinguished. For a long while there seemed to be no reaction within the refinery, and normal work went on.

"Look at the pipeline, David!"

The floodlamps above the four great pipelines were going out, one after another, those nearest to the refinery dying first. To David and Julia it appeared that the pipelines were slowly shrinking away from the refinery, drawing back into the sea whence they had come. As the last of the pipeline flood-lamps was extinguished they saw that in the bay the rigs were turning off their lights, systematically and without haste. Soon only one rig was visible: the large supply-platform in the centre of the bay.

Piece by piece the refinery was vanishing into the dark of the night; lights and flares went out, and with them disappeared the tanks and pipes and gantries. In the town, the arc-lamps of the harbour dimmed quickly. The supply-platform was soon the only light showing; it too vanished in time.

Overhead, the clouds were clearing, and the stars came out. Dorchester, dark and silent, remained on its hill. Its streets and buildings were unlit, the harbour was still.

For a long time nothing more happened, and Julia, still held in David's arms, began to doze. It was warm and comfortable on the rampart of the Castle, as if its glowing life was radiating from within. There was a smell of flowers in the air, a heady, summery smell, anticipating day.

Suddenly, far away, there was a loud explosion, and the sound of it echoed to and fro across the bay, from Purbeck Island to the Wessex Hills, seeming to zig-zag across the funnel-shaped bay.

Julia, stirred by the noise said: "What was that?"

"The cannon at Blandford. The tidal bore is coming through."

It was too far away, and the night was too dark, for them to see the wave, but they both had the same feeling about it: that the incoming tide was refreshing and renewing the waters of the bay, flooding in from the north with the weight of the ocean behind it, cold and clean and alive.

Coloured lights flicked on in Dorchester, the lights that were strung in the trees along the front. They reflected in the sea, which was calm and still, as yet undisturbed by the flooding tide.

Street-lamps came on in Dorchester; windows and doorways became squares of golden light. The harbour moved again: yachts and cruisers, bobbing at their moorings. Across the silence of the bay Julia and David heard music and voices. A group of people were laughing, and as the lights above Sekker's Bar came on, they could just see that the tables on the patio had been cleared away, and that a large crowd was dancing and jostling in the warm night air.

They both slept after this, secure on the Castle rampart, holding each other.

They woke about an hour after dawn, when the sun was still

low over the English hills: a brilliance of yellow in a clean, azure sky.

Holding hands, Julia and David went down into Dorchester, and walking along Victoria Beach, where the white sand was showing again as the new tide receded, they heard the muezzin calling from the mosque.

Later, as they walked along Marine Boulevard, looking at the cafés and stalls shuttered for the night, they saw the fishing boats coming across the empty bay towards the harbour, heavy with their catch.

□□□□□□ There was a sharp wind from the south-east and the
29 waters of Blandford Passage had a deep swell, with white foam rippling back from the southerly mouth of the channel. Protected from the elements by his wet-suit, David Harkman could not feel the wind, although as he left the harbour at Child Okeford and steered his skimmer into the centre of the Passage he was almost upset from his board several times by the swell.

Wave-riding conditions were perfect. It was now too late in the season for all but diehard riders, although the recent spell of fine autumnal weather had brought tourists back to Dorchester in sufficient numbers to persuade the cafés and bars to reopen, and for the last three days Harkman had had to share the wave with no more than about a dozen other riders. The consequent absence of jostling for position on the wave-crest, together with the south-easterly wind and the spring tides, meant that he had had four excellent rides in the last week alone.

He still sought the perfect wave, though . . . one that would set the seal on the season. Now that he was able to wave-ride more frequently, he had become known to many of the regulars in Child Okeford, and heard much of their lore. There was always the quest for perfection: a combination of height, speed, daring, timing.

For David Harkman it would be enough to execute a ride for the whole length of the Passage, and not be caught by the curling wave as it broke into the bay. He had still to achieve this; either he fell behind at the last moment, or he was trapped by the thundering pipeline as it rolled on top of him. The fact that he was regularly riding waves of a height and speed that would daunt anyone less experienced was of no consequence to him. Whether the wave was thirty metres high or, as had been the case for the last week, nearer twice that, he needed for his own satisfaction a wave-ride which he completed.

The height of the wave was, nonetheless, a major consideration. The stewards had been talking recently of prohibiting further rides until the waves became weaker; several riders had been injured in the last few days. In the clubhouse at Child Okeford, older hands were saying that the only waves bigger than these were the winter storm-waves, and no one had been known to ride one of those and survive.

With the regular practice Harkman's proficiency had naturally increased, but as he was waiting for the firing of the cannon he moved to and fro across the Passage, trying to gauge the strength of the swell, getting used to the pressure of the wind.

The wind was an enemy while he climbed the wave; an ally once he reached the crest.

At last the cannon fired, and Harkman and the other riders looked northwards to the Somerset Sea, estimating the distance of the wave. It had been in sight for some minutes; the spring-tides gained body further out in the Sea, and when Harkman looked he saw the advancing swell like a huge cylindrical drum, rolling towards him half-submerged.

He closed his face-mask, turned on the oxygen.

There was time for one more straight run against the swell, and a flip-reversal from the top of one wave to another . . . and then he felt the rising push of the tidal bore. As usual, Harkman had placed himself on the Wessex side of the Passage, and further down towards the mouth than most of the other riders, and by the time he was accelerating before the wave most of the others were at least halfway up.

On a wave as large as this, the engine had to be at full throttle for the whole ride. Harkman drove down and to the side, flipped back and accelerated again, tacking and sheering away from the crest . . . but each time he turned, each time he looked for the crest, it was nearer. The wave was piling height on volume, and the immense speed at which it was bulking towards the gap meant that each turn of his skimmer took him ten or twenty metres higher up the wave: height that had to be lost again if he was not to reach the crest too soon.

Several riders had fallen already, pitched from their skimmers by the ragged swell. Once a rider fell he had almost no chance of regaining the wave, for even if he could mount his skimmer again quickly enough, his engine would certainly lack the power to take him up the reverse side to the crest.

They were now less than a hundred metres from the mouth of the Passage, and Harkman was in the water most broken by the wind. Every swell, every line of foam, was an obstacle to surmount. Each time he flipped the skimmer, and it leapt across the trough from one swell to the next, he could feel the wind beneath the board, lifting and blowing him.

He was judging it exactly right; with less than fifty metres to go to the mouth of the Passage he was almost at the crest of the wave, and he throttled back the engine and let the wave lift him towards its sharpening peak.

As he reached the crest the wave was starting to curl, and he accelerated again, keeping abreast of it. He was heading directly into the wind, feeling the nose of the skimmer being lifted as the wave itself was being held back from breaking.

They passed the mouth of the Passage, and the wave, curling, frothing, continued to rise.

Harkman pushed forward, out to the very edge.

He threw his weight forward, slicing the skimmer down and sideways, diving it through the thinning foam; a moment of grey-green confusion, the suck of water about his head . . . and then he was falling through the air.

Beneath him, the rising inner wall of the wave was almost vertical, and Harkman shifted his weight, bringing the nose of the craft down against the wind, trying to match the gradient.

Above him, the wave was breaking at last: slowly, it seemed, and with great and terrible majesty.

A freak gust of wind came from the side, raising the skimmer's nose, overbalancing him. Harkman, inside the wave's pipeline, windmilled his arms, felt his foothold on the board loosen. . . .

. . . But then silence fell.

The howling vortices of the wind, the persistent whine of the engine, the thunderous roar of the wave . . . they all died away.

Harkman, falling back from the board, was in the air.

He was frozen in flight, naked and alone in a sky. His arms and legs were free, he could turn his head.

Slowly, slowly, he swam around, twisting his abdomen, trying to face down.

Beneath him, the wave, the cliffs and the sea had vanished.

196

He was floating above countryside: a gentle, green, undulating landscape, with meadows and cottages and hedgerows. There was a road down there, and he could see a line of traffic moving along it, the sunshine glinting up from the metal bodywork. Behind him, where Blandford Passage had been, a little town lay in the valley between two hills yellow in the autumnal haze. He could smell woodsmoke, and petrol-fumes, and mown grass.

He felt he was about to fall, and he thrashed his arms and legs as if this would save him . . . but he only turned laterally until he was facing towards the south. Hovering in this alien air, he looked across the Frome Valley towards the Purbeck Hills, and beyond these to the glistening sea, silver and sunlit.

He closed his eyes, forcing the sight away from him . . . but when he opened them again nothing had changed.

Looking towards the ground, Harkman felt for the first time the vertiginous effect of his height, and as if this had released something which until then had suspended him, he began to fall. The air roared in his ears, and he felt the pressure of wind on his arms, legs and stomach. The ground seemed to rise up to strike him, and in real fright he clawed at the air with his hands, as if grasping for a rope or a net.

At once his motion ceased, and he was suspended again in the air, although noticeably lower than before. Now he could hear the traffic on the road; a motorbike was overtaking an articulated lorry, and the sound of its exhaust hammered at him.

Harkman wished himself higher . . . and at once he felt the pressure of the wind on his back, and he soared upwards. When he had attained his former height, he made himself turn around again . . . and he stared across at the quiet countryside, with its wooded hills and its verdant fields and pastures.

What he saw had no meaning for him: it was the product of some unconscious wish that he could not control.

It was something that had excluded him, something that he had in turn rejected.

Because it was from the unconscious past, unremembered, it was at once wholly intimate and voluntarily relinquished. It was the landscape of his dreams, a world that was not real, could not ever become real.

As once before, when he had unconsciously rejected this phantasm from his life, Harkman exercised a conscious option, and expelled the dream.

He looked down at his body: the shiny wet-suit appeared, and was clinging to him, the drops of salt-spray scintillating in the bright sunlight. There was a tightness across his chest, and a weight on his back. Something black and soft and padded wrapped itself around his head, and his vision dimmed as the visor of the helmet fell across his eyes.

Oxygen from the cylinder on his back began to hiss, and he breathed deeply.

He turned himself in the air until he was upright, and he felt for and found the roughened upper surface of the tide-skimmer. The throttle control wrapped itself around his right foot.

He made a few corrections of attitude: leaning forward and tipping the nose of the craft downwards.

The wind started to blow, and the streamlined shape of the skimmer responded, planing in the currents. Harkman kept control, shifting his weight and balance to maintain the craft on an even keel.

A penumbral darkness fell as the Blandford wave curled again over his head; below, the almost vertical rising wall of the wave was a multifaceted frozen mirror of sunlight.

The wave began to move above him, starting and stopping, like the frames of a film inching through a projector. Harkman, truly afraid of the wave's elemental violence, halted the motion, still seeking to balance the skimmer in the cross-current of wind.

He began to fall, and he lost control of the wave. The nose of the skimmer was pushed up by the wind, and with a desperate outbalancing of arms he managed to bring it down again. The skimmer slapped heavily against the water, and at once he gunned the engine, staggering for balance. He glanced up, saw the black pipeline curling down above him . . . and in terror of the wave he raced the skimmer down the slope, down and down and down.

Seconds later, the wave crashed behind him, and foam and spray deluged him, reaching out to clutch him. He was still upright, still racing the wave, still outdistancing it by a few crucial metres that saved him from being overwhelmed by the crushing, swirling spume. He was in the open waters of Dorchester Bay now, the skimmer leaping in spray from the crest of one swell to the next . . . but still the wave tumbled and crashed and flooded behind him, dwarfing him even in its collapse.

As the wave spread and flattened it lost its forward speed, and soon Harkman had left it behind him. He turned the skimmer towards the west, and headed for Dorchester. In time he was passing the beaches, where a few tourists still sprawled beneath their multi-coloured umbrellas, and Harkman waved meaninglessly to the people, trying to convey the excitement that was in him.

He raced the tide all the way, and when he skimmed smoothly into the shallow waters of the harbour the visitors' yachts were still grounded on the mud.

When evening came that day, he and Julia walked down to Sekker's Bar for a meal of local sea-food, and on the way they paused to look at the goods on sale at the Maiden Castle stall. Mark and Hannah were standing behind the counter as usual, but today there was a new girl serving with them. She looked at David and Julia with curiosity but failed to interest them in buying anything.

As they left the stall, a young peddler dressed in the clothes of Maiden Castle stepped out of the crowd and approached them.

"Would you look at a mirror, sir?" he said, and held out a small circular glass before Harkman's face.

"No, thank you," David Harkman said, and Julia, holding his arm, laughed and pressed herself closer to him. As they went up the steps to the patio of Sekker's Bar, they heard a girl's voice shouting angrily, and a few moments later there was a tinkling of broken glass on the paving-stones.

The British Fantasy Society

http://www.geocities.com/soho/6859/

art by Wayne Burns

There is a group of people who know all the latest publishing news and gossip. They enjoy the very best in fiction. They can read articles by and about their favourite authors and know in advance when those authors' books are being published. These people belong to the British Fantasy Society.

The BFS publishes fantasy and horror fiction, speculative articles, artwork, reviews, interviews, comment and much more. They also organise the annual FantasyCon convention to which publishers, editors, authors and fans flock to hear the announcement of the coveted British Fantasy Awards, voted on by the members.

Membership of the BFS is open to everyone. The annual UK subscription is £20.00 which covers the Newsletter and the magazines. To join, send moneys payable to the BFS together with your name and address to:

**The BFS Secretary,
c/o 2 Harwood Street,
Stockport,
SK4 1JJ**

Overseas memberships, please write or email for current details.
The BFS reserves the right to raise membership fees.
Should the fee change, applicants for membership will be advised.

email: syrinx.2112@btinternet.com

EARTHLIGHT

A SELECTED LIST OF SCIENCE FICTION AND FANTASY TITLES AVAILABLE FROM EARTHLIGHT

THE PRICES SHOWN BELOW WERE CORRECT AT THE TIME OF GOING TO PRESS. HOWEVER EARTHLIGHT RESERVE THE RIGHT TO SHOW NEW RETAIL PRICES ON COVERS WHICH MAY DIFFER FROM THOSE PREVIOUSLY ADVERTISED IN THE TEXT OR ELSEWHERE.

All Earthlight titles are available by post from:

Book Service By Post, P.O. Box 29, Douglas, Isle of Man IM99 1BQ

Credit cards accepted. Please telephone 01624 675137,
fax 01624 670923, Internet http://www.bookpost.co.uk or
e-mail: bookshop@enterprise.net for details.

Free postage and packing in the UK. Overseas customers allow
£1 per book (paperbacks) and £3 per book (hardbacks).